Praise f

"This time, Hilderbrand dusts the New England sand off our feet and whisks us to the Caribbean (where she spends part of each year). Our tour guide is Irene Steele of Iowa City, a widow who goes to St. John with her sons to try to make sense of her husband's death in a helicopter crash. Why does he have a fully furnished house on the island? Why was he away from home so much? One man's double life turns out to be his survivors' good fortune in ways I will not reveal. I will just say that twenty-four hours after I started *Winter in Paradise,* I purchased its sequel." —Elisabeth Egan, *New York Times*

"What do you do once you've become queen of the summer novel and mastered the art of the Christmas novel? You start a new series, of course! The incomparable Elin Hilderbrand brings us to St. John for the first novel in her new Paradise series...Another compulsively readable hit by Hilderbrand."
—Brenda Janowitz, *PopSugar* 28 Best New Books to Curl Up with This Fall

"With great verve, Hilderbrand has done it again with her latest, *Winter in Paradise,* the first book in a planned trilogy. She is witty and engaging, and she keeps her readers intrigued with a memorable set of characters...As always, she delivers a story with much detail, weaving her characters and plotlines expertly...Be prepared to read a fast-paced and entertaining novel for several hours, which will keep you longing for the second in the series." —Vivian Payton, *Bookreporter*

"As she does in her books set on Nantucket, Hilderbrand excels at establishing a setting (the food! the luxury! the sea turtles!) that will inspire wanderlust... Hilderbrand is the queen of the summer blockbuster; her fans will be thrilled that she's taken on winter."
—Susan Maguire, *Booklist*

"This fast-paced novel offers the voices of several different characters, as well as a hefty load of intrigue."
—Nancy Carty Lepri, *New York Journal of Books*

"The prodigious Hilderbrand, author of high-style beach reads set on Nantucket, looks to a new island for her twenty-second novel—St. John in the U.S. Virgin Islands... The setting and characters are rendered in classic Hilderbrand style."
—*Kirkus Reviews*

"Hilderbrand's breezy family drama, the first in a series, plays out against the pristine beaches and sparkling waters of St. John in the Caribbean... Readers will be happy to lose themselves in paradise while getting to know these irresistible new characters."
—*Publishers Weekly*

Winter in Paradise

ALSO BY ELIN HILDERBRAND

The Beach Club

Nantucket Nights

Summer People

The Blue Bistro

The Love Season

Barefoot

A Summer Affair

The Castaways

The Island

Silver Girl

Summerland

Beautiful Day

The Matchmaker

Winter Street

The Rumor

Winter Stroll

Here's to Us

Winter Storms

The Identicals

Winter Solstice

The Perfect Couple

Summer of '69

What Happens in Paradise

28 Summers

Troubles in Paradise

Golden Girl

Winter in Paradise

A Novel

Elin Hilderbrand

Back Bay Books
Little, Brown and Company
New York Boston London

To Matt and Julie Lasota

St. John was a place I used to visit—but then I met you and it became home.

The characters and events in this book are fictitious. Any similarity to real persons, living or dead, is coincidental and not intended by the author.

Back Bay Books / Little, Brown and Company
Hachette Book Group
1290 Avenue of the Americas, New York, NY 10104
littlebrown.com

Originally published in hardcover by Little, Brown and Company, October 2018
First Back Bay paperback edition, September 2019
Boxed-set edition, October 2021

Back Bay Books is an imprint of Little, Brown and Company, a division of Hachette Book Group, Inc. The Back Bay Books name and logo are trademarks of Hachette Book Group, Inc.

The publisher is not responsible for websites (or their content) that are not owned by the publisher.

The Hachette Speakers Bureau provides a wide range of authors for speaking events. To find out more, go to hachettespeakersbureau.com or call (866) 376-6591.

ISBN 978-0-316-43551-2 (hc) / 978-0-316-41989-5 (large print) / 978-0-316-42158-4 (signed ed.) / 978-0-316-42160-7 (B&N Black Friday signed ed.) / 978-0-316-42159-1 (BN.COM signed ed.) / 978-0-316-48895-2 (Can. ed.) / 978-0-316-43553-6 (pb) / 978-0-316-33493-8 (boxed-set edition)
LCCN 2018949533

Printing 2, 2023

LSC-C

Printed in the United States of America

AUTHOR'S NOTE

This is the first novel I've written that isn't set on my home island of Nantucket. Instead, it's set on an island I consider a home away from home, my happy place and my refuge: St. John, USVI. I started going to St. John in the spring of 2012, and I have been back every year since for a five-week stretch to finish up my winter books (every book in the Winter Street series was completed there) and to start my summer novels (I wrote large sections of *Beautiful Day, The Matchmaker, The Rumor, Here's to Us,* and *The Identicals* there). Over the years I got to know some of the islanders, and that's when my love of St. John was cemented. I have always maintained that, ultimately, the places we love are about people.

As many of you know, both the United States Virgin Islands and the British Virgin Islands sustained massive damage during Hurricanes Irma, Jose, and Maria in the fall of 2017. I worried I would not be able to return to St. John in the spring of 2018, but by mid-March, the island was ready for me and I returned, jubilant and grateful.

The island is not the same. There are areas of complete devastation, homes lost, trees that look like badly broken bones. Many of the island businesses, places I really and truly loved, either shut down temporarily or closed for good. During my stay in March and April of 2018, the island's two biggest resorts, the Westin and Caneel Bay, were out of commission. But the spirit of St. John remained. People were upbeat and forward-looking. The island thrummed with the spirit of regeneration. I had a wonderful and magical five weeks, as I always do.

I've set this in January 2019 but as if it's January 2017, before the hurricane. There are shops, restaurants, and hotels mentioned that are no longer in business. I felt that to write this novel effectively, I had to write about the St. John I had known and loved, and not complicate the narrative with details of the storm. The storm may yet surface during this trilogy, but it does not in this book. I would like to acknowledge the loss and the hardship that my beloved island and its people suffered—and I want to laud the entire community for its selflessness, cooperation, and bravery. You are an example to us all. God bless you.

The good news is that St. John is ready for you to come back or visit for the first time. It's still paradise, all the more beautiful because of what it has endured.

Part One

Stateside

IRENE: IOWA CITY

It's the first night of the new year.

Irene Steele has spent the day in a state of focused productivity. From nine to one, she filed away every piece of paperwork relating to the complete moth-to-butterfly renovation of her 1892 Queen Anne–style home on Church Street. From one to two, she ate a thick sandwich, chicken salad on pumpernickel (she has always been naturally slender, luckily, so no New Year's diets for her), and then she took a short nap on the velvet fainting couch in front of the fire in the parlor. From two fifteen to three thirty, she composed an email response to her boss, Joseph Feeney, the publisher of *Heartland Home & Style* magazine, who two days earlier had informed her that she was being "promoted" from editor in chief of the magazine to executive editor, a newly created position that reduces both Irene's hours and responsibilities by half and comes with a 30 percent pay cut.

At a quarter of four, she tried calling her husband, Russ, who was away on business. The phone rang six times and went to voicemail. Irene didn't leave a message. Russ never listened to them, anyway.

She tried Russ again at four thirty and was shuttled *straight* to voicemail. She paused, then hung up. Russ was on his phone night and day. Irene wondered if he was intentionally avoiding her call. He might have been upset about their conversation the day before, but first thing this morning, a lavish bouquet of snow-white calla lilies had been delivered to the door with a note: *Because you love callas and I love you. Xo R.* Irene had been delighted; there was nothing like fresh flowers to brighten a house in winter. She was amazed that Russ had been able to find someone who would deliver on the holiday, but his ingenuity knew no bounds.

At five o'clock, Irene poured herself a generous glass of Kendall-Jackson chardonnay, took a shower, and put on the silk and cashmere color-block sweater and black crepe slim pants from Eileen Fisher that Russ had given her for Christmas. She bundled up in her shearling coat, earmuffs, and calfskin leather gloves to walk the four blocks through Iowa City to meet her best friend, esteemed American history professor Lydia Christensen, at the Pullman Bar & Diner.

The New Year's Day dinner is a tradition going into its seventh year. It started when Lydia got divorced from her philandering husband, Philip, and Russ's travel schedule went from "nearly all the time" to "all the time." The dinner is supposed to be a positive, life-affirming ritual: Irene and Lydia count their many, many blessings—this friendship near the top of the list—and state their aspirations for the twelve months ahead. But Irene and Lydia are only human, and so their conversation sometimes lapses into predictable lamentation. The greatest unfairness in this world, according to Lydia, is that men get sexier and better-looking as they get older and women… don't. They just don't.

"The CIA should hire women in their fifties," Lydia says. "We're invisible."

"Would you ladies like more wine?" Ryan, the server, asks.

"Yes, please!" Irene says with her brightest smile. Is *she* invisible? A week ago, she wouldn't have thought so, but news of her "promotion" makes her think maybe Lydia is right. Joseph Feeney is sliding Irene down the masthead (and hoping she won't notice that's what he's doing) and replacing her with Mavis Key, a thirty-one-year-old dynamo who left a high-powered interior design firm in Manhattan to follow her husband to Cedar Rapids. She came waltzing into the magazine's offices only eight months ago with her shiny, sexy résumé, and all of a sudden, Joseph wants the magazine to be more city-slick and sophisticated. He wants to shift attention and resources from the physical magazine to their online version, and, using Mavis Key's expertise, he wants to create a "social media presence." Irene stands in firm opposition. Teenagers and millennials use social media, but the demographic of *Heartland Home & Style* is women 39–65, which also happens to be Irene's demographic. Those readers want magazines they can *hold,* glossies they can page through and coo over at the dentist's office; they want features that reflect the cozy, bread-and-butter values of the Midwest.

Irene's sudden, unexpected, and unwanted "promotion" makes Irene feel like a fuddy-duddy in Mom jeans. It makes her feel completely irrelevant. She will be invited to meetings, the less important ones, but her opinion will be disregarded. She will review layout and content, but no changes will be made. She will visit people in their offices, take advertisers out to lunch, and chat. She has been reduced to a figurehead, a mascot, a pet.

Irene gazes up at Ryan as he fills their glasses with buttery chardonnay—the Cakebread, a splurge—and wonders what he sees when he looks at them. Does he see two vague, female-shaped outlines, the kind that detectives spray-paint around dead bodies? Or does he see two vibrant, interesting, desirable women of a certain age?

Okay, scratch desirable. Ryan, Irene knows (because she eats at the Pullman Bar & Diner at least once a week while Russ is away), is twenty-five years old, working on his graduate degree in applied mathematics, though he doesn't look like any mathematician Irene has ever imagined. He looks like one of the famous Ryans—Ryan Seacrest, Ryan Gosling. Ryan O'Neal.

Ryan *O'Neal?* Now she really *is* aging herself!

Irene has been known to indulge Lydia when she boards the Woe-Is-Me train, but she decides not to do it this evening. "I don't feel invisible," she says. She leans across the table. "In fact, I've been thinking of running for office."

Lydia shrieks like Irene zapped her on the flank with a cattle prod. "What? What do you mean 'run for office'? You mean *Congress*? Or just, like, the Iowa City School Board?"

Irene had been thinking Congress, though when the word comes out of Lydia's mouth, it sounds absurd. Irene knows *nothing* about politics. Not one thing. But as the (former) editor in chief of *Heartland Home & Style* magazine, she knows a lot about getting things done. On a deadline. And she knows about listening to other people's point of view and dealing with difficult personalities. Oh, does she.

"Maybe not run for office," Irene says. "But I need something else." She doesn't want to go into her demotion-disguised-as-promotion right now; the pain is still too fresh.

"*I* need something else," Lydia says. "I need a single man, straight, between the ages of fifty-five and seventy, over six feet tall, with a six-figure income and a sizable IRA. Oh, and a sense of humor. Oh, and hobbies that include grocery shopping, doing the dishes, and folding laundry."

Irene shakes her head. "A man isn't going to solve your problems, Lydia. Didn't we learn that in our consciousness-raising group decades ago?"

"A man *will* solve my problems, because my problem is that I've got no man," Lydia says. She throws back what's left of her wine. "You wouldn't understand because you have Russ, who dotes on you night and day."

"When he's around," Irene says. She knows her complaints fall on deaf ears. Russ joined the Husband Hall of Fame seven years earlier when he hired a barnstormer plane to circle Iowa City dragging a banner that said: HAPPY 50TH IRENE STEELE. I LOVE YOU! Irene's friends had been awestruck, but Irene found the showiness of the birthday wishes a bit off-putting. She would have been happy with just a card.

"Let's get the check," Lydia says. "Maybe that barista with the beard will be working at the bookstore."

Irene and Lydia split the bill as they do every year with the New Year's dinner, then they stroll down South Dubuque from the Pullman to Prairie Lights bookstore. The temperature tonight is a robust thirteen degrees, but Irene barely notices the cold. She was born and raised right here in eastern Iowa, where the winds come straight down from Manitoba. Russ hates the cold. Russ's father was a navy pilot and so Russ grew up in Jacksonville, San Diego, and Corpus Christi; he saw snow for the first time when he went to college at Northwestern. Privately, Irene considers Russ's aversion to the cold a constitutional inferiority. As wonderful as he is, Irene would never describe him as hearty.

Lydia holds open the door to Prairie Lights and winks at Irene. "I see him," she whispers.

"Don't be shy. Order something complicated and strike up a conversation," Irene says. "It's a new year."

Lydia whips off her hat and shakes out her strawberry-blond hair. She's a pretty woman, Irene thinks, and, with the confidence she's displaying now, not at all invisible. Surely Brandon, the fifty-something barista with the thick spectacles and the leather apron—better suited to welding than to making espresso drinks—would be intrigued by Professor Lydia Christensen? She coauthored the definitive biography of our nation's thirty-first president. Herbert Hoover has gotten a bad rap from history, but most Iowans are kindly disposed toward him because he was born and raised in West Branch.

As Lydia marches to the café, Irene floats over to the new fiction. She loves nothing better than a stack of fresh books on her nightstand. What an enriching way to start the new year. Irene spent her New Year's Eve taking down all of her holiday decorations and packing them neatly away. She left the boxes at the bottom of the attic stairs. Russ is due back late tomorrow night or early Thursday morning, he said, and once he returns, he will be fully at her disposal. He left for a "surprise" business trip two days after Christmas. The man has more surprise business trips than anyone Irene has ever heard of and in this case, he was leaving Irene alone for New Year's. They had quarreled about it the previous afternoon on the phone. Russ had said, "I'm fully devoted to you, Irene, and I strive to see your point of view in every disagreement. But let's recall who encouraged whom to take this job. Let's recall who said she didn't want to be married to a corn syrup salesman for the rest of her life."

Their conversation, repeated for years nearly verbatim, ended there, as it always did. Irene *had* pushed Russ to take the job with Ascension, and with that decision came sacrifice. Russ is away more than he's home, but he does call all the time, and he sends flowers and often leaves her a surprise gift on her pillow when he goes away—jewelry or a pair of snazzy reading glasses, gift cards to the Pullman, a monogrammed makeup case. He is so thoughtful and loving that he makes Irene feel chilly and indifferent by comparison. Also, and not inconsequentially, his new job affords them a very nice lifestyle, luxurious by Iowa standards. They own the Victorian, with its extravagant gardens and in-ground swimming pool on a full-acre lot on Church Street. Irene had been able to renovate the house exactly the way she dreamed of, sparing no expense. It took her nearly six years, proceeding one room at a time.

Now the house is a showpiece. Irene lobbied to have it featured in the magazine, but she encountered resistance from Mavis Key, who thought it would seem like shameless self-promotion to splash pictures of their own editor's home across their pages. *Talk about navel-gazing,* Mavis had said, a comment that hurt Irene. She suspects the real problem is Mavis's aversion to Victorian homes. Like Irene, they are out of fashion.

Mavis Key can buzz right off! Irene thinks. Irene's house is a reflection not only of years of painstaking work but also of her soul. The first floor has twelve-foot ceilings and features arched lancet windows with layered window treatments in velvet and damask. The palette throughout the house is one of rich, dark jewel tones—the formal living room is garnet, the parlor amethyst, and the kitchen has accents of topaz and emerald. There are tapestries and ornate rugs throughout, even in the bathrooms. Irene's favorite part of the house isn't a room per se but rather the grand staircase, which ascends two floors. It's paneled in dark walnut and at the top of the second flight of stairs is an exquisite stained-glass window that faces east. In the morning when the sun comes up, the third-floor landing is spangled with bursts of color. Irene has been known to take her mug of tea to the landing and just meditate on the convergence of man-made and natural beauty.

Irene supervised all of the interior carpentry, the refinishing of the floors, the repairs to the crown molding, the intricate painting—including, in the dining room, a wraparound mural of the landscape of Door County, Wisconsin, where Irene spent summers growing up. Irene also handpicked the antiques, traveling as far away as Minneapolis and Portland, Oregon, to attend estate sales.

Now that the house is finished, there is nothing left to do but enjoy it—and this is where Irene has hit a stumbling block. When she tells Lydia that she needs "something else," she isn't kidding. Russ is away for work at *least* two weeks a month, and their boys are grown up. Baker lives in Houston, where he day-trades stocks and serves as a stay-at-home father to his four-year-old son, Floyd. Baker's wife, Dr. Anna Schaffer, is a cardiothoracic surgeon at Memorial Hermann, which is a very stressful and time-consuming job; she, like Russ, is almost never around. Irene's younger son, Cash, lives in Denver, where he owns and operates two outdoor supply stores.

Neither of the boys comes home much anymore, which saddens Irene, although she knows she should be grateful they're out living their own lives.

There was a moment yesterday around dusk when everyone else in America was getting ready for New Year's Eve festivities—showering, pouring dressing drinks, preparing hors d'oeuvres, pulling little black dresses out of closets—that Irene was hit by a profound loneliness. She had spoken to Russ, they had quarreled, and right after they hung up, Irene considered calling him back, but she refrained. There was nothing less attractive than a needy woman—and besides, Russ was busy.

Irene plucks the new story collection by Curtis Sittenfeld off the shelf; Curtis is a graduate of the Iowa Writers' Workshop, which Irene happens to believe is the best in the country.

She hears Lydia laughing and peers around the stacks to see her friend and Brandon engaged in conversation. Brandon is leaning on his forearms on the counter while the espresso machine shrieks behind him. He hardly seems to notice; he's enraptured.

So much for being invisible! Irene thinks. Lydia is glowing like the northern lights.

Irene feels a twinge of an unfamiliar emotion. It's *longing,* she realizes. She misses Russ. Her husband spent years and years gazing at her with love—and, more often than not, she swatted him away, finding his attention overwrought and embarrassing.

Irene is distracted by a buzzing—her phone in her purse. That, she thinks with relief, will be Russ. But when she pulls out her phone, she sees the number is from area code 305. Irene doesn't recognize it and she guesses it's a telemarketer.

She lets the call go, disappointed and more than a little annoyed at Russ. Where *is* he? She hasn't heard from him since midafternoon the day before; it's not like him to go so long without calling. And where is he this week? Did he even tell her? Did she even ask? Russ's "work emergencies" take him to various bland, warm locations—Sarasota, Vero Beach, Naples. He nearly always comes home with a tan, inspiring envy from their friends who care about such things.

Irene notices the time—nine o'clock already—and realizes she has forgotten to call Milly, Russ's mother. Milly is ninety-seven years old; she lives at the Brown Deer retirement community in Coralville, a few miles away. Milly is in the medical unit now, although she's still cogent most of the time, still spry and witty, still a favorite with residents and staff alike. Irene visits Milly once a week and she calls her every night between seven and eight, but she forgot tonight because of her dinner with Lydia. By now, Milly will be fast asleep.

Not a worry, Irene thinks. She'll stop by to see Milly on her way home from work tomorrow. It'll be a good way to fill up her afternoons now that her hours have been cut. Maybe she'll take Milly to the Wig and Pen. Milly likes the chicken wings, though of course they aren't approved by her nutritionist. But what are they going to do, kill her?

The idea of Millicent Steele being finally done in by an order of zippy, peppery wing dings makes Irene smile as she chooses the Curtis Sittenfeld stories as well as *Where'd You Go, Bernadette,* by Maria Semple, which Irene had pretended to read for her book club half a dozen years earlier. With the house finished, she now has time to go back and catch up. Irene heads over to the register to pay. Meanwhile, Lydia is still at the café, still chatting with Brandon; her macchiato lets off the faintest whisper of steam between them.

Lydia turns when she feels Irene's hand on her back.

"Are you leaving?" Lydia asks. Her cheeks are flushed. "I'll probably stay for a while, enjoy my coffee."

"Oh," Irene says. "Okay, then. Thanks for dinner, it was fun, Happy New Year, call me tomorrow, be safe getting home, all of that." Irene smiles at Brandon, but his eyes are fastened on Lydia like she's the only woman in the world.

Good for her! Irene thinks as she walks home. It's a new year and Lydia is going after what she wants. A man. Brandon the barista.

The wind has picked up. It's bitterly cold and Irene has to head right into the teeth of it to get home. She ducks her head as she hurries down Linn Street, past a group of undergrads coming out of Paglia's Pizza, laughing and horsing around. One of the boys bumps into Irene.

"Sorry, ma'am," he says. "Didn't see you."

Invisible, she thinks.

This thought fades when she turns the corner and sees her house, her stunning castle, all lit up from within.

She'll light a fire in the library, she thinks. Make a cup of herbal tea, hunker down on the sofa with her favorite chenille blanket, crack open one of her new books.

Maybe the "something else" she's seeking isn't running for office, Irene thinks. Maybe it's turning her home into a bed-and-breakfast. It has six bedrooms, all with attached baths. If she kept one as a guest room for family, that still left four rooms she could rent out. Four rooms is manageable, right? Irene has a second cousin named Mitzi Quinn who ran an inn on Nantucket until her husband passed away. Mitzi had loved running the inn, although she did say it wasn't for the faint of heart.

Well, Irene's heart is as indestructible as they come.

What would Russ say if she proposed running an inn? She guesses he'd tell her to do whatever makes her happy.

It would solve the problem of her loneliness—people in the house all the time.

Would anyone want to come to Iowa City? Parents' weekend at the university, she supposes. Graduation. Certain football weekends.

It has definite appeal. She'll think on it.

When Irene opens the front door, she hears the house phone ringing. *That* will definitely be Russ, she thinks. No one calls the house phone anymore.

But when Irene reaches for the phone in the study just off the main hall, she sees it's the same 305 number that showed up on her cell phone. She hesitates for a second, then picks up the receiver.

"Hello?" she says. "Steele residence."

"Hello, may I please speak to Irene Steele?" The voice is female, unfamiliar.

"This is she," Irene says.

"Mrs. Steele, this is Todd Croft's secretary, Marilyn Monroe."

Marilyn Monroe, Todd Croft's oddly named secretary. Yes, Irene has heard about this woman, though she's never met her. Irene has only met Todd Croft, Russ's boss, once before. Todd

Croft and Russ had been acquainted at Northwestern, and thirteen years ago, Russ and Irene had bumped into Todd in the lobby of the Drake Hotel in Chicago. That chance meeting led to a job offer, the one Irene had been so eager for Russ to accept. Now Todd Croft is just a name, invoked by Russ again and again. The man has become synonymous with the unseen force that rules their lives. *Todd needs me in Tampa on Tuesday. Todd has new clients he's courting in Lubbock.* "Todd the God," Irene calls him privately. And yet everything she has—this house, the swimming pool and gazebo, the brand-new Lexus in the garage—is thanks to Todd Croft.

"Happy New Year, Marilyn?" Irene says. There's a hesitation in her voice because Irene can't imagine why Marilyn Monroe—Irene has no choice but to picture this woman as a platinum blonde, buxom, with a beauty mark—would be calling. "Is everything...?"

"Mrs. Steele," Marilyn says. "Something has happened."

"Happened?" Irene says.

"There was an accident," Marilyn says. "I'm afraid your husband is dead."

AYERS: ST. JOHN, USVI

Servers across the country—hell, across the world—regard New Year's Eve with dread, and although Ayers Wilson is no exception, she tries to keep an open mind. It's just another night at La Tapa, the best restaurant in St. John, which is the best of the Virgin Islands—U.S. and British combined—in Ayers's opinion. Tonight, for the holiday, there are two seatings with a fixed menu, priced at eighty-five dollars a head, so in many ways it'll be easier than regular service and the tips should be excellent. Ayers will likely clear four hundred dollars. She has no reason to complain.

Except...Rosie is off tonight because the Invisible Man is in town. This means Ayers is working with Tilda, who is not only young and inexperienced but also a relentless scorekeeper, *and* she has a crush on Skip, the bartender; it's both pathetic and annoying to watch her flirt.

The first seating, miraculously, goes smoothly. Ayers waits on one of the families who came on her snorkeling trip to the British Virgin Islands that morning. The mother looks like a woman plucked from a Rubens painting, voluptuous and redhaired, with milky skin. She had wisely spent most of the day under the boat's canopy while Ayers snorkeled with her two teenagers, pointing out spotted eagle rays and hawksbill turtles. Now the mother tilts her head. She knows she recognizes Ayers, but she can't figure out how.

"I'm Ayers," she says. "I was a crew member on *Treasure Island* today."

"Yes!" the mother says. The father grins—kind of a goofy guy, perfectly harmless—and the kids gape. This happens all the time: people are amazed that Ayers works two jobs and that she might appear in their lives in two different capacities *on the same day.*

Ayers's other tables are couples who want to finish eating so they can get down to the Beach Bar to watch the fireworks. In past years, Ayers has managed to squeak out of work by quarter of twelve. She and Mick would change into bathing suits and swim out to Mick's skiff to watch the fireworks from the placid waters of Frank Bay.

Ayers and Mick broke up in November, right after they returned to St. John from the summer season on Cape Cod. Mick, the longtime manager of the Beach Bar, had hired a girl named Brigid, who had no experience waiting tables.

Why on earth did you hire her, then? Ayers asked, but she figured it out in the next instant.

And sure enough, there followed days of Mick staying late to "train" the new hire, whom he later described to Ayers as "green" and "clueless" and "a deer in the headlights." On the third day of this training, Ayers climbed out of bed and drove down to the Beach Bar. It was two thirty in the morning and the town was deserted; the only vehicle anywhere near the bar was Mick's battered blue Jeep. Ayers tiptoed around the side of the building to see Brigid sitting up on the bar counter and Mick with his head between her legs.

Ayers hasn't been to the Beach Bar once since she and Mick split, and she certainly won't go tonight. She has bumped into Mick—alone, thankfully—once at Island Cork and once, incredibly, out in Coral Bay, at Pickles in Paradise, the place "they" always stopped to get sandwiches (one Sidewinder and one Sister's Garden, which "they" shared so "they" could each have half) before "they" went to the stone beach, Grootpan Bay, where "they" were always alone and hence could swim naked. Ayers had been stung to see Mick at the deli—he was picking up the Sidewinder, which was funny because she was picking up a Sister's Garden—and she could tell by the look on his face that he was stung to see *her.* They probably should have divided the island up—Pickles for her, Sam & Jack's for him—but St. John was small enough as it was.

Ayers has also seen Mick driving his blue Jeep with Brigid in the passenger seat—and worse, with Mick's dog, an AmStaff-pit bull mix, Gordon, standing in Brigid's lap. Gordon used to stand in Ayers's lap, but apparently Gordon was as fickle and easily fooled as his owner.

Tilda taps Ayers on the shoulder and hands her a shot glass of beer, which Ayers accepts gratefully.

"Thanks," Ayers says. "I need about forty of these." They click shot glasses and throw the beer back.

"Yeah, you do," Tilda says. "Because *look.*"

Ayers turns to see Mick and Brigid walking into La Tapa, hand in hand. Clover, the hostess, leads them over to Table 11, in Ayers's section.

"No," Ayers says. "Not happening. No way."

"I'll take them," Tilda says. "You can have Table 2. It's the Hesketts. You're welcome."

"Thank you," Ayers says. The Hesketts own a boutique hotel in Chocolate Hole called St. John Guest Suites; they're lovely people, with excellent taste in wine. It's a good trade, and very kind of Tilda, although a part of Ayers, of course, would like to wait on Mick and Brigid and dump some food—ideally the garlicky paella for two—right into Brigid's lap. She's wearing white.

What is Mick *thinking*? And why isn't he *working*? It's New Year's Eve, he's the manager of the Beach Bar, it will be mayhem down there, even now at a quarter to ten. How did he get the night off? The owners *never* give him holidays or weekends off. And why isn't *Brigid* working? Why did they choose La Tapa for dinner when they both knew Ayers would be here? Are they looking for trouble? Because if they are, they found it. Ayers's nostrils flare and she paws at the ground with one clog like an angry bull.

She steps into the alcove by the restroom, pulls out her phone, and texts Rosie. *Where are you? Please come save me. Mick and Brigid are here at La Tapa for second seating!*

A few seconds later, there's a photographic response—a table set for two with a bottle of Krug champagne in an ice bucket.

In the background is the Caribbean, scattered with pinpricks of light—boats heading over to Jost Van Dyke for the invitation-only Wheeland Brothers concert. It has been rumored that Kenny Chesney might sit in for a song or two.

Ayers studies the picture, trying to get an idea of where the Invisible Man's house is. Looks like somewhere near Cinnamon Bay. Rosie refuses to disclose exactly where the Invisible Man lives or even tell Ayers his name. He's very private, Rosie says. His business is sensitive. He travels a lot. Apparently the house is impossible to find. There are lots of places like that on St. John. Rosie stays with the Invisible Man when he's on-island, but otherwise she and her daughter, Maia, live with Rosie's stepfather, Huck, the fishing captain, who owns a house on Jacob's Ladder. It's a strange arrangement, nearly suspect, and yet Rosie seems content with the way things are. Once, after service, when Ayers and Rosie were drinking upstairs at the Quiet Mon, Rosie confided that the Invisible Man paid for all of Rosie and Maia's living expenses, including Maia's tuition at Gifft Hill School.

Ayers makes it her New Year's resolution to find out more about the Invisible Man—at the very least, to figure out where he lives.

She tucks her phone away and heads out to the floor to studiously ignore Mick and Brigid and to hear which fabulous wine the Hesketts are going to end their year with.

After her shift, Ayers greets the new year with a bottle of Schramsberg sparkling rosé, sitting on the west end of Oppenheimer Beach. Because of the wind, she can actually hear the music floating over from Jost. There's a group of West Indians down the beach, drinking on the porch of the community center. At midnight, they sing "Auld Lang Syne." Ayers texts Rosie. *Happy New Year, my friend. Xo.*

Rosie responds immediately. *Love you, my friend.*

At least Rosie loves her, Ayers thinks. That will have to be enough.

It's ten o'clock the next morning when there's a pounding on Ayers's door. She hears Mick's voice. "Ayers! Wake up! Open up! Ayers!"

She groans. Whatever he wants, she doesn't have time for it. He sounds upset. Maybe he got fired, maybe Brigid broke things off, maybe the new year brought the crystal-clear realization that the biggest mistake he ever made was letting his relationship with Ayers go up in smoke.

Ayers rises from the futon and staggers toward the front door. Her head feels like a broken plate. After the Schramsberg on the beach, there had been some shots of tequila here at home, as well as a forbidden cigarette (she quit two years ago but keeps a pack stashed on top of her refrigerator in case of emergency). She needs a gallon of very cold water and fifty Advil.

She swings open the door. There's Mick, with tears streaming down his face. The sight renders Ayers speechless. Mick is a douche bag. He doesn't cry. Ever.

"What?" she says, though it sounds like more of a croak.

"Rosie," Mick says. "Rosie is dead."

CASH: DENVER

After meeting with his accountant, Glenn, at Machete Tequila + Tacos, it becomes clear that Cash is going to lose not only the Cherry Creek store but the one in Belmar as well. All Cash can think is: *Thank God.*

Now he can go back to being a ski bum.

He hadn't really wanted to go into business in the first place, but he had grown tired of receiving envelopes in the mail from his father, with newspaper clippings meant to be encouraging and helpful about young men "just like you" who had stumbled across a way to turn their life's passions into income-generating ventures. Russ was also keen for Cash to "finish your education," and so sometimes the envelopes included advertisements for online college courses or the myriad offerings for nontraditional students at the University of Iowa. *You could live at home!* Russ wrote, and Cash would picture himself trapped with his parents in the suffocating ornateness of their Victorian house. Because Russ was so rarely home, Cash suspected that Russ's true motivation was to have Cash care for his mother and grandmother, chauffeur them to the Wig and Pen, play Bingo with Milly and the other extreme-elders at Brown Deer. No thank you. When Cash talked to his father on the phone, Russ would end each conversation by gently pointing out that sooner or later, Cash was going to need to think about health insurance, a retirement fund, having an infrastructure in place so he could start a family.

Like your brother.

Russ had never actually uttered this phrase, but Cash heard it as the subtext. Cash wanted to point out to his father that while Baker *used to* work the Chicago futures market, and while he *used to* make a ton of money, he now sits at home in Houston, day-trading in his boxer shorts and smoking more weed than Cash could ever hope to get his hands on in *Colorado,* where weed is *legal.* Baker only has two claims to actual legitimacy: He cares for his four-year-old son, Floyd (although Floyd goes to Montessori school every day from eight thirty to three), and he keeps house for his wife, Dr. Anna Schaffer, who has turned into a legitimate Houston superstar. She's the Olajuwon of the cardiothoracic surgery scene.

Cash lets Glenn, the accountant, pick up the tab for the four Cadillac margaritas and order of guac—fifty-seven bucks—and then the two men walk out to the parking lot together. Cash wonders if he will be able to keep his pickup with the name of the store—Savage Season Outdoor Supply—painted on the side. It's an eye-catching truck, made even more gorgeous with his golden retriever, Winnie, in the back.

He fears the truck will be repossessed, like the stores. The bank is coming in the morning. Right now, he needs to go to both stores and empty the registers. There is two hundred and forty-five dollars in the Cherry Creek store and a hundred and eighteen dollars in the Belmar store. This and Winnie are all Cash has left to his name.

He has a rental apartment on 18th Avenue in City Park West but he hasn't paid his rent for January so he envisions a middle-of-the-night pack up and escape to Breckenridge. Jay, who runs the ski school, will be thrilled to have Cash back. Unlike every other twenty-something kid in the Rocky Mountains, Cash knows how to ski as well as snowboard. This means Cash can teach the trophy-wives-of-tech-moguls who want a hot instructor way more than they want to make turns, and it also means huge tips from the moguls who want their ladies taken care of while they go ski the horseshoe bowl on Peak 8.

It's all going to work out, Cash thinks. Losing the stores is just a bump in the road.

As Cash turns onto Third Street, he puts both of the truck's windows down. Winnie automatically sticks her head out the passenger-side window and Cash sticks his head out the driver's side.

He's free!

No more standing behind the register selling Salomon boots to some Gen Z executive in from Manhattan who says he's heard hiking Mount Falcon is "lit," no more biting his tongue to keep from telling Executive Boy Wonder that he could hike Mount Falcon in the Gucci slides he came in wearing. No more worrying about inventory or deliveries or if Dylan, the kid Cash hired to "manage" the Belmar store, was filching from the register in order to pay his oxy dealer.

He's free!

His father will be *very disappointed.* Russ was Cash's only investor, and all of that money is now gone, with absolutely nothing to show for it; it's as though Cash has blown it all on a very expensive video game. Cash will have to call his father and tell him—before he finds out another way, such as an email from the bank. Any other father would be angry, but what Cash knows will happen is that Russ will tell Cash he's "let down," which is so much worse.

Cash will also have to hear from his brother, Baker. Baker didn't like it when Russ "handed" Cash the stores, and he predicted Cash would fail within two years. *Why doesn't Cash have to work for what he gets, like everyone else?* Baker had thundered when he'd found out what was happening. *He won't appreciate the opportunity he has unless he's earned it himself.* In essence, Cash had rolled his eyes at his older brother and chalked the rant up to jealousy. What he wished he'd confided to Baker was that he didn't *want* the stores. They weren't so much *handed to* him as *foisted upon* him by their overeager father. Now that Baker's prediction has come true—the stores are gone, Cash sunk them, and he feels little, if any, personal loss, because his sense of self wasn't vested—Cash will have to endure the inevitable *I told you so.*

Cash loves his brother, in theory. In practice, he can't stand the guy.

In a rare show of courage—probably fueled by the Cadillac margaritas—Cash picks up his phone and dials his father's number. It's eight thirty here, nine thirty at home, ten thirty on the East Coast. Cash isn't sure where his father is this week, but he hopes the late hour works in his favor. His father likes to have a bourbon or two most nights. He hopes that it's one of those nights, and that Russ's mood is buoyant and he and

Cash can laugh off the train wreck of two stores and a two-hundred-thousand-dollar investment as a valuable learning experience.

The call goes to voicemail. Cash experiences a rush of relief that leaves him dizzy.

A few seconds later, his phone lights up and the relief quickly turns to dread. Then relief again when Cash sees that it's not his father calling back. It's his mother.

His mother! Cash hates reverting to the behaviors of his adolescence, but he decides in that instant that he will tell his mother about the stores going under and he will let Irene tell Russ. He can even tell Irene *not* to tell Russ—he can pretend he wants to break the news to Russ himself, but Irene won't be able to help herself. Those two are typical parents; they tell each other everything.

"What's good, Mama?" Cash says. "Happy New Year."

"Cash," Irene says, "where are you?"

Something is wrong with her voice. It sounds like she's being strangled.

"I'm pulling into my driveway," he says. "Just me and Winnie." Now is not the time to explain that he's going to pack up all of his worldly belongings and head for the mountains; somehow, he senses this.

"Cash," Irene says.

"Yes, Mom."

"Your father is dead."

Cash's first thought is: *I don't have to tell him about the stores.* Then, the cold, sick meaning of the words hit him. His father is dead.

Dead.

But...what?

"What are you talking about?" Cash says. "What do you mean?"

"There was an accident," Irene says. "A helicopter crash, in the Virgin Islands..."

"The Virgin *Islands*?" Cash says. He's confused. Are the Virgin Islands even a real place? He thinks they *are* real, but they sound fake and he would have a hard time finding them on a map. Are they in the Caribbean, or farther south, like the Falklands? And what do the Virgin Islands, wherever they are, have to do with his father?

A *helicopter* crash? No, there's been a mistake.

"St. John, in the Virgin Islands," Irene says, and her voice is full-on quavering now. Cash shuts the engine of his truck off and releases a long, slow stream of air. Winnie lays her head in Cash's lap. It's amazing how much dogs understand. Cash has seen and heard his mother cry on plenty of occasions—all of them happy, every tear a tear of joy and wonder. She cried when Baker and Cash graduated from high school, when Baker and Anna had Floyd, she cried every Christmas Eve when the church choir launched into "O Come, All Ye Faithful." But Irene Hagen Steele didn't cry over disappointment, or even death. When her parents died, Irene handled it with a solid midwestern pragmatism. Circle of life and all that. She arranged for proper Lutheran funerals and covered dish receptions afterward. She didn't cry.

This, of course, is something else entirely.

"St. John," Cash repeats. "In the Virgin Islands."

"Your father was in a helicopter crash," Irene says. "It crashed into the sea. Three people were on board: your father, the pilot, and a local woman."

"Who *told* you this?" Cash asks.

"Todd Croft's secretary, Marilyn," Irene says. "Todd Croft, your father's boss."

"Was Dad in the Virgin Islands *working*?" Cash asks. The exact details of his father's career have been hazy ever since he switched jobs. When Cash was young, Russ worked as a salesman for the Corn Refiners Association. Then, when Cash entered high school, Russ got a different job, a much better-paying job working for Todd Croft, who owned a boutique investment firm, Ascension, that catered to high-end clients—international soccer stars and the like, though when Cash asked *which* soccer stars, Russ claimed he wasn't at liberty to say. Russ's job was to keep the clients happy, do interface, provide a personal touch, whatever that meant. All Cash knows for sure is that they went from being the middlest of middle class to people who had money. "Having money" meant Irene could buy and renovate her dream house; it meant no college loans; it meant Russ had seed money for Cash's doomed business venture.

"I'm not sure," Irene says. "Todd's secretary, Marilyn, told me your father has a 'concern' there. She told me your father owns *property* there."

"Property?" Cash says. "Does Baker know about this?"

"I haven't talked to Baker yet," Irene says. "I called you first."

Right, Cash thinks. Their family, like every family, has its allegiances. It's Irene and Cash on one side and Russ and Baker on the other. Irene called Cash first because they're closer—and also because she fears Anna, Baker's wife.

"Maybe Baker knows what Dad was doing in the Virgin Islands?" Cash says. His father is dead. Could this possibly be *true*? His father was in a *helicopter crash*?

"I have to fly down there," Irene says. "I can't get there tomorrow. I'm leaving Thursday morning out of Chicago. I'm not sure what to do about your grandmother. This will kill her."

Cash does some quick mental calculating. It's an eleven-hour drive from Denver to Iowa City. If Cash grabs his things from the apartment and the money from both stores, he'll be on 76 by ten o'clock. Even with stops, he should be pulling into his parents' driveway before noon.

"I'm going with you," Cash says. "I'll be at your house tomorrow and I'm going down there with you."

"But how can you get away?" Irene asks. "The stores..."

"Mom," Cash says. "Mom?"

"Yes," she says.

"Call Baker," Cash says. "But don't tell anyone else about this yet. Don't call Grammie. I'll be there tomorrow. I'll help you. I'm on my way."

HUCK: ST. JOHN

Any day on St. John is better than a holiday, if you ask Captain Sam Powers, known to one and all as "Huck." Huck's first mate, Adam, is twenty-seven years old, and all he can talk about on their December 31st afternoon fishing charter (a couple from Albany, New York, and their college-aged daughter, who hasn't been off her phone since getting on the boat) is how he can't wait to go to Drink for the big party that night.

They have a ball drop and snow, and everyone is served drinks in real glasses instead of plastic cups.

"You should come with me," Adam says to the college-aged daughter. (Maybe she's older, Huck can't tell, but he thought he was clear with Adam: pursue girls who show an interest in fishing! This girl, who is scrolling through her Instaface account, is attractive, sure, but she doesn't even seem to realize she's out on the water, for Pete's sake. If it were up to Huck, he'd turn around and take her back to the dock.)

The girl raises her eyes to look at Adam, who is elbow-deep in a bucket of squid, baiting the trolling lines. "Ah-ight," she says.

Is that even a word? Huck wonders.

"Yeah?" Adam says. "You'll go? It won't get good until about ten, but we should plan to arrive around eight, eight thirty."

"We have a dinner reservation at eight in Coral Bay," the girl's mother says. The mother is attractive as well, but she isn't interested in fishing either. She brought a book—something called *Lilac Girls.* Huck isn't against books on his boat; in fact, there was a period of time when he believed that a person reading brought the fish. Huck likes to read himself, though never on the boat, but at home in his hammock, yes. When LeeAnn was alive, she got him hooked on Carl Hiaasen, and from there it was an easy jump to Elmore Leonard and Michael Connelly. Rosie is always telling him he should try some *female* writers, and he promised her he would read anything she put into his hands, as long as it didn't have the word *girl* in the title. *Gone Girl, Girl on the Train*—and now look, *Lilac Girls.* The mother—Huck has forgotten her name; he only retains the names of people interested in fishing—seems pretty engrossed, however.

"Dinner reservation?" Dan, the father, says. Dan is a name Huck remembers because Dan wants to catch fish and Dan is paying for the trip. Dan works for the state government of New York—Huck shudders just thinking about it—but he is now on his Caribbean vacation and he wants to catch a fish, preferably a wahoo or a mahi. Huck assured Dan that would happen even though he's been experiencing something of a dry spell. He hasn't had a decent haul since the high season started.

Huck has decided to stay inshore—one look at the mother and daughter told him they would *not* be up for the forty-minute ride south to blue water—so wahoo and mahi are out of the question.

"Yes," the mother says. "We have an eight o'clock reservation at Shipwreck Landing."

"Good place," Huck says.

"But I want to catch a fish and grill it up," Dan says. "That's what we agreed on."

The wife shrugs. "If you catch a fish big enough to feed the three of us, I'll cancel."

"Count me out," the daughter says. "I want to go to the party."

Huck will have to reprimand Adam for starting this mess. He doesn't get involved in other people's family drama. He focuses all of his emotional energy on his own girls—LeeAnn's daughter, Rosie, and Rosie's daughter, Maia. Maia, at age twelve, probably qualifies as Huck's favorite person in the world.

Now there's a girl who loves to fish.

Huck's mind wanders as it tends to when he's captaining his boat, *The Mississippi.* People always ask if he's from Hannibal or Natchez, St. Louis or New Orleans, but the answer is no. Huck's nickname was given to him his first week in St. John, twenty years earlier at the bar at Skinny Legs, by a West Indian fella named Rupert, who is now Huck's best friend. Rupert saw Huck's strawberry-blond hair and the nickname fit somehow. Rupert hooked him up with a boat for sale—a twenty-six-foot Regulator—that had been bought by a kid on the island who lost his shirt gambling in Puerto Rico and needed to sell it quick for cheap. The boat had been named *Lady Luck,* but Huck changed it immediately to *The Mississippi* to match his new identity.

Who wants to drink from real glasses? Huck wonders. He can do that at home. His favorite thing about this island is that it's a barefoot, casual place; there isn't a pretentious thing about it. After a full-day charter, Huck likes to hit Joe's Rum Hut for happy hour—he gets a planters punch or the local beer—and he wanders to the waterline of Frank Bay for a cigarette, then he heads down to Beach Bar with his drink and he's allowed to finish it there before he buys his next drink. He knows everyone and everyone knows him: Huck, captain of *The Mississippi.* It doesn't matter that he hasn't had a decent catch since Halloween. He always has clients because he's connected. And he also happens to know what he's doing.

Huck will spend tonight with Maia because the Invisible Man is on-island. Sometimes, when the Invisible Man is here, Maia will go along with her mother, but tonight is New Year's Eve. The Invisible Man hasn't been here for New Year's Eve in four years, and so Rosie planned a special night of champagne and romance.

Fine. Huck can think of no better person to ring the new year in with than Maia. Huck will stop by Candi's on the way home and pick up some barbecue.

He anchors the boat at the edge of Mandal Bay, off the north coast of St. Thomas, and helps Adam bait the hooks. The air has been crystalline since Christmas, and today there isn't a cloud to be seen. The sky is a deep, painterly blue. There are supposed to be thunderstorms tomorrow morning but there's no sign of them now.

"Who's casting?" Huck asks. Dan already has his rod at the ready. Mrs. Dan is reading, and the daughter is on her phone. Huck looks between the two of them. Nothing.

Hey, Huck wants to say. *You're in the Caribbean! Look at the string of palm trees backing that platinum beach over there. Look how clear the water is. Days don't get any more picturesque than this. Now, let's catch some fish.*

Adam taps the girl's shoulder. "You want to try? I can cast it for you."

"No, thanks," she says. She does manage to tear her eyes off her screen long enough to offer him a smile. "This is my dad's thing."

How can Adam possibly want to take this girl on a date? Huck wonders. He doesn't bother asking the wife if she wants to fish. He just casts the line himself.

New Year's Eve doesn't change his luck. Dan catches two blue runners and a hardnose. He's getting visibly discouraged; he's a hunter with a family to feed. Then, blessedly, he reels in a small blackfin tuna, which will be at least enough for him and

Mrs. Dan. This does double duty of making Dan feel like a success and getting the daughter off the hook for dinner.

"Everyone happy?" Huck asks. He doesn't wait for an answer. "Okay, let's head back in."

The town of Cruz Bay is more frenetic than usual. People are flooding the streets, plastic cups in hand, wearing shiny hats and feather boas; women are in black velvet dresses even though it's eighty-one degrees. Huck couldn't be happier to get in his truck, stop by Candi's for one order of ribs and one of chicken, extra comeback sauce, one side of pasta salad, one of slaw and one of plantains, then coax his aging truck up the series of switchbacks that comprise Jacob's Ladder.

"Come on, chipmunks," he says, as his engine growls in its lowest gear. He started saying this to amuse Maia when she was little—she loved thinking about a pair of little furry animals eagerly powering the engine of Huck's truck—and now when he says it out of habit, Maia rolls her eyes.

Maia is standing in the driveway wearing denim shorts that she made herself the old-fashioned way—by taking scissors to a perfectly good pair of jeans—and a gray t-shirt on which she painted what Huck refers to as an iguana on acid: the bugger is a swirl of seventeen different colors. Maia's hair is out of its cornrows in a bushy ponytail, which is how Huck likes it best. She must be 99 percent her father, whom Huck has never had the pleasure of meeting, but she was gifted with the milk-chocolate eyes of Huck's late wife, LeeAnn, which is another reason why Maia is Huck's favorite and basically can do no wrong.

"Hey, Nut," he says. "Nut" is short for "Peanut," which refers to a birthmark Maia has on her shoulder. She still tolerates the name, though maybe not for much longer. "Joanie went home?"

"Yes, but I was invited there overnight," Maia says. "I texted but you didn't answer. Drive me?" He can see the uncertainty on her face. She knows that they had plans and that she's now breaking them to go to Joanie's. What she doesn't know is whether he's going to be relieved about this change of plans—because he wants to drink some beers and fall asleep in his hammock long before midnight—or upset, maybe even angry.

She's getting older, Huck thinks. Her legs are long but still as straight as sticks; she remains a little girl for the time being. Anyone with one good eye can see what's coming down the road: bras, boyfriends, broken hearts, bad decisions, maybe not quite as bad as the ones her mother has made, he hopes.

Joanie is a good kid with nice parents. Both the mother and father are marine biologists who work for the National Park Service. They are avid hikers, naturalists, vegans. Huck can't imagine what they're having for dinner, but whatever it is, Maia will be wishing she stayed home for ribs and chicken.

He nods at his passenger seat. "Let's go," he says.

LeeAnn believed that everything happens for a reason, a theory that Huck only half agrees with, because some moments in this life seem random and senseless.

But he is very, very happy that Maia is at Joanie's house the next morning.

* * *

Huck spends his New Year's Eve eating both the ribs and the chicken and drinking a cold six-pack of Island Hoppin' IPA, then wandering down the street to have one drink with the neighbors, a local family made up of Benjamins and Singers—they're having a full-on shindig with a roast pig and homemade moonshine. Huck gets a good tip from Cleve Benjamin: there has been a school of mahi hanging six miles offshore, in the same place for the past three days. Cleve has the coordinates written in his phone; he shares them with Huck.

"There's enough fish in that spot to fill your freezer chest until *next* Christmas," Cleve says.

Huck is grateful for the information and feels lucky to be trusted and liked by his West Indian neighbors. He's accepted because he was married to LeeAnn—some of these folks grew up with LeeAnn out in Coral Bay, others knew her from church or worked with her at the Myrah Keating Smith Community Health Center, still others are distantly related to her first husband (Rosie's father), Levi Small, who left the island long ago and has never come back.

Huck wanders home and takes his last long look of the year over Great Cruz Bay; he can hear music wafting up from the Westin below. Then he goes inside and falls asleep.

He intends to sleep in but is awakened at seven by the forecasted thunderstorm, and then he can't go back to sleep, so he gets out of bed and fixes himself a New Year's breakfast of hash—made from potatoes, onions, peppers, and some of the leftover barbecued chicken—and throws two fried eggs on top. He reads his book, *The Late Show,* by Connelly. He stops every few pages to wonder about the wife from yesterday—if she enjoyed the fish or if Dan cooked it for too long and ruined it. Huck then wonders about Adam and the daughter. Did they have fun at Drink? Did Adam get lucky? Or did the girl have too much champagne, as most amateurs do on the final night of the year, and spend her night crying or puking? Huck bets on the latter.

He is having a cigarette on the front porch when the police pull up. He thinks for a second it's about Adam. But they ask him to go inside and then they tell him: there was a helicopter crash early that morning in the waters north of Virgin Gorda.

Rosie is dead.

BAKER: HOUSTON, TEXAS

Anna makes two New Year's resolutions: She's going to spend more time at home with Baker and Floyd, and she's going to become friends with at least one of the other mothers at Floyd's Montessori school, the Children's Cottage. She hands Baker a page from her prescription pad (Dr. Anna Schaffer, MD) with the two goals written down.

1. More time at home
2. Friends

Baker finds he has follow-up questions. Does "more time at home" mean she'll have sex with him on days other than his birthday and their anniversary? Does "making friends" mean that some of the "at home" time will be spent on "girls' night out," or in long phone conversations listening to Delia, mother of Sophie, air her grievances against Mandy, mother of Aidan?

Baker folds the paper in half, kisses it, and puts it in his jeans pocket. It's appropriate that Anna wrote her resolutions on the prescription pad, because their relationship is sick. These two actions will heal it, he hopes. "Good for you," he says. "What should we do today?"

A look of panic crosses Anna's face. She's a beautiful woman, with flawless olive skin; she has impenetrable brown eyes and long dark hair. She exudes serenity and, beyond that, competence. She's a natural-born perfectionist, at least when it comes to cardiothoracic surgery. It's only her personal life that she has trouble navigating.

"Today?" she says. She checks her phone. "I have to go to the hospital."

"It's New Year's Day," Baker says.

"It's *Tuesday,*" she says. "I have rounds."

"But...," Baker says, waving the page from her prescription pad in the air.

"Am I supposed to tell Mr. Kavetsky, who just had a triple bypass, that I can't check on him because I have to...what? Do a gouache project with my husband and four-year-old? Watch *Despicable Me 3* yet *again*?"

"You haven't even seen it *once*!" Baker says. His voice is defiant, verging on bratty. *He* sounds like a four-year-old. But come *on*! For Anna to represent herself as someone who is routinely subjected to children's movies is downright unfair. She *never* watches movies with Floyd; she hasn't seen *Despicable Me 3*—or numbers one and two, for that matter. On the rare occasion she does sit down with Baker and Floyd to watch a movie, she falls asleep in the comfy womb of the leather gel recliner, leaving Baker to answer Floyd's rapid-fire questions about the intricacies of character and plot. Floyd, like his mother, has a finely tuned intellect, but it's as if after physically giving birth to Floyd, after donating the genius half of his DNA, Anna decided her job was done. First, she turned the care and feeding of Floyd over to a baby nurse for the staggering fee of three hundred fifty dollars a day, and then, when Anna was done "breastfeeding"—she nearly always pumped milk, was a fiend about it, in fact, insisting that it was much more "efficient" than latching Floyd onto her actual body when he was going to switch to the bottle eventually anyway—they hired Maria José, a nanny from El Salvador. Maria José and Anna didn't see eye to eye (Maria José held Floyd all day long, and in the evenings, when Anna came home from the hospital, Floyd was set down, and he would cry)—and so Maria José was dismissed.

Then Anna hired Svana, from Iceland, who drew Floyd a bath that was too hot and scalded him the color of a lobster, necessitating a trip to urgent care. Good-bye, Svana. At that point, Baker was looking for a job in private equity, but he kept getting to final interviews and not getting hired—he suspected that Houston firms tended to hire Texas boys, especially those who had played high school football—and since Anna's career provided plenty of money, Baker thought, why didn't *he* stay home and care for Floyd? He could day-trade while Floyd napped. Day-trading encapsulated everything he loved about his field—it was a game, a gamble, a risk, a thrill—and he was good at it. He was also good at parenting. The love and joy and wonder he felt when he looked at tiny baby Floyd—a person, another *person,* he had helped create—was nearly overwhelming. Why would he pay someone else to care for their child when he could do it himself?

Anna had put up the predictable arguments: Staying home with Floyd wouldn't provide Baker with any intellectual stimulation. *You'll be bored stiff,* she said. He would be like the unfulfilled housewives of the 1950s. He would choose something inappropriate to fill his time—internet porn or marijuana, or an affair with one of the mothers he met at the playground. He would get so far behind in his career that he would never catch up. What would Baker do when Floyd was eighteen and headed to college? Even three years hence, when Floyd went to preschool, too much time would have passed for Baker to seamlessly reenter the world of high finance. He would become depressed, smoke more weed than he already did, get addicted to pills.

Baker had assured Anna at the time that she was being melodramatic. But now Floyd is four years old, and while he is a very bright, curious, and well-adjusted kid, it's true that Baker's decision to stay home has created issues. First of all, Anna has grown so comfortable with their new roles that she has nearly checked out of family life altogether. Secondly, whereas Baker has *not* become addicted to internet porn or had an affair, he does smoke a fair amount of dope, and he has developed very close friendships with a group of mothers, all of whom have sons and daughters at the Children's Cottage. His clique includes Wendy, Becky, Debbie, and Ellen. They are all single mothers—three divorced and one single by choice—which is how they became friends in the first place. They have more or less adopted Baker as their "school husband." He covers their kids when they have work emergencies, he fixes things around their houses, and he gives them free investment advice. He suspects that the other mothers—the married mothers—are critical of the relationship between Baker and his school wives, but it wasn't until the Holiday Sing that he realized just how jealous and vile women could be. One of them cornered Anna in the bathroom and told her she was very "evolved" for letting Baker have a "harem."

Anna had not been amused. Baker assured her the friendships were just that and not one thing more. He informed Anna that if she wanted to put an end to the vicious gossip, she should show her face around school more often. She should make some friends of her own, which was how she arrived at Resolution Number Two.

"Why can't someone else cover your rounds?" Baker asks now. "Why can't Louisa do it?" Louisa is another surgeon in the practice, Anna's closest friend. It feels like Anna is forever going in to cover *Louisa's* patients; surely Anna is due a return favor?

"Louisa is busy," Anna snaps. "We're all busy."

"I won't make you do gouache," Baker says. It's a very cool painting technique that Wendy taught him; she makes her own greeting cards and wrapping paper. "Or watch *Despicable Me 3.* I thought we could go to the park. It's beautiful out..."

"I'm sure Floyd will love it," Anna says. She grabs her bag and smiles. Smiles are what pass for kisses these days. "I'll be home by six. We can get pizza!" She says this, apparently not recalling that Baker has bought a roast he'd planned to serve with Boursin potatoes and sautéed asparagus. Anna isn't impressed by Baker's efforts in the kitchen. In her world, each dawning day is merely another chance to eat pizza.

"Okay," Baker says. He watches Anna's back disappear through the door—and at that moment, he knows he has no choice. He has to ask for a divorce.

Divorce, he thinks as he waits at the bottom of the big slide for Floyd. It's such a dark, ugly, complicated word.

Floyd comes whooshing down, his bangs flying. He's such a *good* kid, so cute and perfect in his boyness. "That was my tenth time down," Floyd says. "Let's go to the swings."

Always ten times down the slide, no more, no less, and slide always precedes swings, where Baker is allowed to push Floyd seven times—then Floyd takes over under the power of his own pumping legs. Baker senses some OCD tendencies in the rules Floyd sticks to at the park, although the jungle gym is a free-for-all and Floyd is very sociable and can make friends with other children in an instant, as he does today. When he's finished on the swings, he joins a game of tag, leaving Baker to lie back in the grass and let the mellow January sunshine warm his face.

Divorce.

Divorce Anna.

Will she even *notice*? She'll move out and rent one of the condos across the street from the hospital. She'll have no problem paying for the house and for Baker and for Floyd. Baker has a tidy sum in the bank as well; his luck this past year playing the market has been tremendous. All will be well. Baker's only concern is that Anna will *never* see Floyd if they don't live in the same house. And yet isn't that exactly why Baker should get out? What kind of mother doesn't love her own child? That may be too harsh. Certainly Anna *loves* Floyd. But does she *like* him? Does she enjoy one single thing about being a parent?

Baker sits up on his elbows and watches Floyd, running and laughing, right in the thick of it with a bunch of kids he just met. He's so happy and carefree. Can Baker really be considering putting the kid through the emotional trauma of a divorce? Anna's parents are divorced. Her father has been divorced *twice.* And so that is her idea of normal. But Baker's parents have been happily married for thirty-five years. Baker knows that Irene and Russ will see his divorce as a failure. *He* will see it as a failure.

It's a new year, Baker thinks. And Anna *did* make the resolutions, which is a promising start.

He'll give it more time, he decides. Maybe she'll surprise him.

Anna doesn't make it home by six, although she does call. "I'm going to be another hour," she says. "Just order the pizza without me."

Does she ever get tired of disappointing people? Baker wonders.

"Will do," he says. He won't order pizza, but neither will he go to the trouble of making the roast. Floyd has asked for pancakes for dinner, and pancakes he will get. Baker makes bacon and squeezes some fresh juice. Why not?

"Would you mind staying awake until I get home?" Anna asks. She sounds almost nervous, and Baker gets a flutter of excitement in his stomach.

"Absolutely," he says.

That simple question changes the whole tenor of the evening. Anna wants him to stay awake. She wants to spend time with him. She wants to...connect, maybe. He'll give her a massage, he'll draw her a bath, he'll wash her hair, he'll do anything she wants. He loves her so much. At times, it's like loving a shadow or a hologram. But not tonight.

Baker makes big, fluffy buttermilk pancakes and crispy bacon, and he gives Floyd two cups of juice, even though that's a lot of sugar before bed. He cleans the kitchen, does the dishes, sends Floyd down the hall to brush his teeth. He helps Floyd get into his pajamas and starts reading him *The Dirty Cowboy.* It's a long book, and Floyd falls asleep on page six, as he always does. Baker eases himself off the bed, turns on the night-light, and slips out of the room.

This is the time of night when he usually takes a few hits off his bong, but he won't tonight. He needs to stay awake!

He cracks open a beer, gets himself a bowl of Ben & Jerry's Red Velvet Cake ice cream—which his single-by-choice mom-friend Ellen turned him on to (she eats "like a long-haul trucker," in her own words)—and switches on the TV to get a recap of the bowl games. He's...just drifting off when he hears Anna coming through the door. He sits bolt upright. He's awake!

"Hey, babe," he says. "I'm in here."

He hears Anna in the kitchen, rummaging through the fridge, opening the cabinets. He hears a cork being pulled from wine. A few seconds later, Anna comes into the den. She lets her hair free of her elastic, takes a sip of wine, and regards him with an expression he can't read. Interest? Curiosity? *What does she see when she looks at him?* he wonders. Well, he's slouched on the sofa with an open beer and half a bowl of melted ice cream on the table next to him, so she can hardly view him as a sexy world conqueror.

He sits up straight, moves over, pats the sofa next to him. He is soft with forgiveness. It's as easy for him to fall into his chubby-hubby stoner-dad role as it is for Anna to default to her super-busy achieving spouse. He's guilty of smoking a joint and falling asleep on the sofa most nights. He's as much to blame for their disconnect as she is.

She reaches for the remote and shuts off the TV. In the six years of their marriage, eight years together, Baker has never known Anna to watch a single minute of television.

"How was work?" Baker asks.

"I'm leaving you," Anna says.

"What?"

"I'm in love with someone else," Anna says. "And it's beyond my control so I'm not going to bother apologizing for it."

"Oh," Baker says. "Okay." He looks at his wife. With her hair down and loose, she is at her most beautiful, which he feels is unfair, given the circumstances. But then, too, Baker experiences a strange sense of inevitability. He knew this was coming, didn't he? Earlier today, when he had thought about divorce, when he had all but decided on it, in fact, it was because he *knew* this was coming. Anna doesn't love him. She loves someone else. But who? Who is it?

"Who?" Baker says. "Who is it?"

"Louisa," Anna says. "I'm in love with Louisa."

She's in love with Louisa.

Anna doesn't bother giving him time to process, to react, to emote. No. She takes her wine and leaves the room.

Baker sinks back into the Baker-shaped and -sized divot on the couch. His phone rings. It's his mother.

His mother? No. He can't possibly speak to his mother right now. Briefly, he wonders if Anna called his parents to inform them she was leaving him, then decides the answer is no. Anna and his mother don't have a relationship. And Russ once naively referred to Anna as a "smart cookie," and Anna hasn't spoken to him since.

The house phone rings and Baker wonders who on earth would be calling the house phone at ten o'clock on New Year's night. The ringing stops. Anna calls down the hall. "Bake? It's your mom."

This is not happening, Baker thinks. Now he has to get on the phone and make at least sixty seconds of pleasant conversation without letting his mother know that his life is dissolving like an aspirin in acid. His wife is in love with her esteemed colleague, Louisa!

"Hey, Mom," Baker says, picking up the phone in the kitchen. He hears Anna hang up. "Happy New Year."

"Baker," Irene says. She's crying. So obviously Anna *did* tell her.

"Mom, listen..." Baker scrambles for a way to talk Irene off the ledge. She was born and raised in Iowa. She's the editor of *Heartland Home & Style.* Do they even *have* lesbians in the heartland? Baker doesn't mean to be a wise guy—he obviously knows the answer is yes, and Irene and Russ live in Iowa

City, which is pretty much the People's Republic of Iowa, but even so, he worries this is really going to upset her. Confuse her. She's going to ask *why* Anna turned into a lesbian. She's going to ask if it's Baker's fault.

"Baker," Irene says. "There was an accident. Your father is dead."

PART TWO

Little Cinnamon

IRENE

She wrote down everything Marilyn Monroe told her. There was a helicopter crash. Russ and a local woman and the pilot left from a private helipad at seven o'clock in the morning on Tuesday, January first. There had been a thunderstorm; the helicopter was struck and it went down somewhere between Virgin Gorda and Anegada. Anegada had been the apparent destination, Marilyn said. The helicopter wreckage had been recovered, as well as the three bodies.

"Mr. Steele's property manager traveled to the British Virgin Islands to identify the body," Marilyn said. "And Mr. Croft has arranged for cremation."

"Wait," Irene said. "What?" She knew that Russ wanted to be cremated, it's what they both wanted, but did this mean…? "Am I not going to *see* him again, then, before…?"

"I'm sorry, Mrs. Steele," Marilyn said. "You're going to have to trust Mr. Croft's judgment on this. The body needed to be identified as soon as possible, so Mr. Croft requested that Mr. Steele's property manager do it. Time was of the essence, and a decision had to be made."

"I don't understand!" Irene said. "Shouldn't *I* have been

the one to make the decision? I'm his wife. Who is this so-called property manager? What does that even mean? I don't understand!"

"I know this is coming as a shock," Marilyn said. "Beyond a shock. Again, you'll just have to trust that Mr. Croft took the appropriate measures."

Trust Todd Croft? He was a man Irene had met briefly only once, a man who had controlled their lives for thirteen years. And it wasn't even Todd himself telling Irene that Russ had died in a helicopter crash between Virgin Gorda and someplace else, a place Irene had never heard of, but, rather, his secretary, Marilyn Monroe. It was like a joke, a prank, a bad dream. Irene had gone so far as to pinch the soft skin on the underside of her wrist, hard, to make sure she was awake and cogent; that Ryan, their handsome server, hadn't slipped something into the Cakebread chardonnay earlier.

Marilyn was telling Irene that some "property manager" had ID'd the body and that Todd Croft had given the okay to cremate it. Time was of the essence and Irene would never see her husband again. "Why was Russ in the Virgin Islands?" Irene asked. "He never once mentioned the Virgin Islands. Was he there for work?"

"He had concerns there," Marilyn said. "He owned a home there."

"A home?" Irene said. "My husband did *not* own a home in the Virgin Islands. I would obviously know if he owned a home. I'm his *wife*."

"I'm very sorry," Marilyn said. She paused. "Mr. Steele owns a villa on St. John."

"A villa?"

"Yes," Marilyn said. "If you have a pen and paper, I can give you the specifics..."

"Pen and *paper*?" Irene said. "I'm flying down there."

"That's not advisable...," Marilyn said.

"You can't stop me," Irene said. "Russ was my *husband*. I've lost my *husband*." Does this secretary, Marilyn Monroe, *understand*? Irene briefly, fancifully, thinks about the husbands of the real Marilyn Monroe. Arthur Miller. Joe DiMaggio. Someone else. "I'm going down there to see about this so-called home. Because, frankly, this all sounds suspicious. Are you sure we're talking about Russell Steele, of Iowa City, Iowa? Originally from..." Where was Russ born? She can't remember. "Are you *sure*?"

"Mrs. Steele," Marilyn said. Her tone of voice made it sound like Irene was being unreasonable. "There's a woman who will meet you at the ferry if you insist on making the trip. Her name is Paulette Vickers. Her number is 340-555-6121. She'll take you to Mr. Steele's villa."

Irene's head was spinning. She had drunk too much of the Cakebread chardonnay. Dinner at the Pullman with Lydia, Brandon the barista at Prairie Lights—all of that now seemed to belong to a different life.

"I'm very sorry, Irene," Marilyn Monroe said, more gently now, and then she hung up.

Cash arrives at noon the next day. Irene wakes up sprawled across the purple velvet fainting couch in her clothes, Winnie licking her face. She languishes in the warm, wet love of her son's dog before she comes to full consciousness. Slowly she opens her eyes and sees Cash's expression, and she remembers.

Russ is dead. Helicopter crash. West Indian woman, a local, dead, and the pilot also dead. Villa. On a scrap of paper on the coffee table is the phone number of someone named Paulette. Also on the paper is Irene's flight information.

Cash has always been a free spirit, but he does a remarkably good job of taking charge. First, he sits next to Irene on the fainting couch and holds both her hands in his. He's expecting her to cry. She keeps expecting herself to cry, to gush like a dam breaking—her husband of thirty-five years is dead!—but nothing comes. She doesn't believe it. It makes no sense. There's been a mistake. Russ is in the Virgin Islands and went on a helicopter ride to an island no one has ever heard of with a local woman? And what did Marilyn Monroe say about a villa? What *is* a villa, exactly? Irene pictures a vacation home, a tropical vacation home. Marilyn had called it *Mr. Steele's home.* Which makes no sense. Russ's home is here, on Church Street. He and Irene talked about buying someplace up in Door County once Milly passed so that they could have the boys and their families come visit. Irene had pictured waterskiing, trout fishing, big family dinners around a harvest table, lighting sparklers out on the porch while they listened to the loons. She envisioned a silvered, aging version of her and Russ, side by side in rocking chairs. But that image implodes like a star.

"Milly," Irene says. They need to tell Milly.

"Not yet," Cash says. "First we're going to worry about

you." He looks at the paper on the coffee table. "These are your flights? You booked these?"

Irene nods. She booked the flights last night, although it now seems like a dream. Making plane reservations to St. Thomas has no basis in Irene's reality. (She had discovered that she couldn't fly to St. John, because St. John has no airport. Private helipads, yes, but no commercial airport. She had to take a ferry from St. Thomas.) And yet she had done it. She flew Chicago to Atlanta, and then Atlanta to St. Thomas, on Delta. She has booked herself coming back a week later, and that seems surreal. Who would Irene *be* after a week in St. John, collecting her husband's remains? Because she certainly can't do it and stay the same person she is now.

"I booked them," she says. "I have to be in Chicago tomorrow by nine."

"I'll drive," Cash says. "I'm going to book myself on the flight as well. Myself and Winnie. And I'll tell Baker to meet us in Atlanta."

"With Floyd?" Irene asks.

"No, Floyd has school. He's staying home with Anna. It'll be just you, me, and Baker. And Winnie."

Irene nods. There are so many things to think about, but none come to mind. "This woman, Paulette, is supposed to pick us up. Would you call her and let her know we're coming?"

"I will," Cash says. "I'm going to bring you ice water and aspirin. I'm going to make coffee. Can you handle toast?"

"I cannot handle toast," Irene says. She takes a deep breath and looks around the impeccably furnished amethyst parlor. How many hours did she slave over this room, this house? For the past six years, she has been married to this house. Russ came second; he used to joke about it. When she was in a good mood, she told him she was feathering their love nest. When she was in a bad mood, she told him he was never home anyway, so what did it matter if she was preoccupied?

Only now does she realize how little attention she actually paid him—the particulars of his work, where he was and what he did. When she talked to him on Monday afternoon, what had he said? He had a dinner meeting with clients. He wasn't sure if he would be able to stay up until midnight. He loved her.

Had he been *lying*?

Russ's villa. The Virgin Islands. A local woman.

Yes, he'd been lying.

When Cash comes back in with Irene's coffee, she says, "I haven't told anyone except you and Baker."

"Good," Cash says.

"I haven't told my friends. I haven't told work. I haven't told Milly. What am I going to tell Milly?"

"Let's do this," Cash says. "I'll call the magazine and tell them there's been a family emergency and that you'll be out the next week or so."

Irene nods. Work is the least of her worries, because, of course, she has just been demoted. The magazine will be fine without her. She doesn't care about the magazine. She doesn't care about anything except...this. This. Russ, he's gone.

"We can't tell Milly," Cash says.

"We can't *not* tell Milly," Irene says.

"Let's tell her together when we get back," Cash says. "We can't tell her and then leave."

"That's right," Irene says. "We can't tell her and then leave."

"Call her tonight, as usual," Cash says. "Tell her we're taking a surprise vacation."

A surprise vacation, Irene thinks.

* * *

It's a blur, all a blur, until the plane lands in St. Thomas and the other passengers erupt in applause.

Irene peers out the window. St. Thomas has verdant hills—green and lush, dotted with brightly colored buildings, yellow and pink, the color of sand, the color of shells. The water is... well, it's the brilliant turquoise you see in advertisements. Yes, St. Thomas is supposed to be a place that makes you clap and cheer.

"It's so...pretty," Irene says.

"Anna and I honeymooned on Anguilla," Baker says. "It looked like this, only flatter."

"That's right, you did," Irene says. She remembers being nonplussed when Baker and Anna chose Anguilla. Irene and Russ had offered the honeymoon as a wedding present—anywhere they wanted to go, anywhere in the *world*—and they had chosen Anguilla. It had seemed so...*unimaginative* to Irene. But Baker had said that Anna wanted to stay close to home. She had wanted sunshine, massages, a constant flow of alcohol. She didn't want to *tour* anything.

Irene, if she had her druthers, would vacation in Europe—France, Switzerland, England, places with history, places with culture. And so that was what she and Russ had done: a week in London, a week in the Cotswolds, a week in Provence, in Paris, in St. Moritz. Or they went to Colorado and skied. Irene harbors a natural prejudice against the Caribbean. Why is that? She thinks back on a trip to Jamaica when the boys were young, eight and ten, maybe nine and seven. This was before they had money, so they had booked a mediocre hotel near the airport. It had rained all week and they had barely left their rooms. Russ had finally given the boys money to go to the arcade in the hotel lobby. Baker and Cash were down there for a couple of hours—Irene had napped—and then she had woken up, alarmed to discover they still weren't back. Russ had gone down to check on them and had come rushing up, frantic. The kids were *gone.*

Irene can still recall the sheer panic she felt then. It had been like falling into a hole with no bottom. They had alerted hotel security, who had directed them to a shantytown right across the street from the hotel; sometimes women infiltrated the lobby and convinced hotel guests to shop for souvenirs. They found a mishmash of shacks with corrugated tin roofs; it was noisy in the rain. There were women cooking and men playing cards and children and chickens running around, plenty of children, so it wasn't sinister, by any means, but it had seemed so to Irene—a rabbit warren of foreignness that had swallowed her sons. She lashed out at the men, screaming, *Where are my children? My sons?* Her voice was accusatory, when really the only person Irene could blame was herself. She had been *napping*—and now her boys were gone.

They had turned up, of course, almost immediately. They were listening to a gentleman with long, graying dreadlocks play the guitar in one of the shacks. Irene had grabbed Baker so fiercely she'd nearly wrenched his arm out of its socket.

That had been it for Irene and the Caribbean. She had smiled politely whenever anyone said they were headed to Barbados or Aruba or the Dominican Republic, and she had probably said, "I'm sure it will be wonderful!" But in her head, she had been thinking, *Better you than me.*

And now here she is. They have to descend a set of stairs onto the tarmac and then walk into the terminal. The air is warm, humid, sweet-smelling. Irene is wearing a white short-sleeved blouse and a pair of khaki capri pants, sandals, sunglasses. She knows what she looks like to everyone else.

She looks like a woman taking a vacation.

AYERS

Helicopter crash off Virgin Gorda, three dead: Rosie, the Invisible Man, the pilot, whose name was Stephen Thompson. Ayers doesn't know if he was white or West Indian.

"They think the helicopter got hit by lightning," Mick says. "Did you hear the storm this morning?"

Ayers had been woken up by the thunder, but then she'd fallen right back to sleep.

"What do I do?" she asks Mick. "Where do I go?"

He holds his arms out to offer her a hug and she accepts. Out the front door she sees Gordon sitting patiently in the passenger seat of Mick's blue Jeep. No Brigid, thank God. Although what does Brigid matter anymore? Ayers thought Mick dumping her for Brigid equaled heartbreak, but now Ayers understands a new definition of heartbreak.

Rosie is dead.

"I have to go to Huck's," Ayers says.

"I'll drive you," Mick says. "Let's go."

Huck lives up Jacob's Ladder, a series of switchbacks so steep that Ayers's head lolls back and she feels like she might swallow her tongue. At the last turn before Huck's duplex, the cars are lined up: two local police cars, pickup trucks, a Jeep that belongs to Huck's first mate, Adam, a car from U.S. Customs and Border Control.

Walking down the street are the West Indian women—many of them friends of LeeAnn's, Ayers knows—some of them carrying covered dishes, some carrying flowers, one holding a Bible aloft. It's as busy as downtown during Carnival. One thing about a close-knit community like St. John: no one endures a tragedy alone. Ayers had experienced the celebration of LeeAnn Powers's life five years earlier; she hadn't realized until then that dying could be beautiful and filled with love.

LeeAnn had been sixty years old when she died, a newly retired nurse practitioner and a grandmother. She'd had congestive heart failure, so her death hadn't been a great surprise. Rosie, Maia, and Huck all had time to say good-bye.

Rosie's death is something else entirely, but the support and prayers will be great, maybe greater. Many, if not all, of these women watched Rosie grow up; a handful probably cared for her while LeeAnn worked nights and weekends up at Myrah Keating and over at Schneider Regional Medical Center on St. Thomas—until Captain Huck swept LeeAnn off her feet and married her.

Mick hits the brakes before ascending the final hill, and Ayers sees the uncertainty on his face. Do they belong here? They're locals, but they aren't native islanders; neither of them has family here, or roots. They merely have jobs. Mick has managed the Beach Bar for eleven years; Ayers has waited tables at La Tapa for nine years and been a crew member on *Treasure Island* for seven. She has never had anyone close to her die. What's the protocol?

If Ayers were to list anyone as a family member on this island, it would be Rosie. Would have been Rosie. And Maia and Huck. So, yes, Ayers is going up to the house. If she *doesn't* go, what would Huck think?

"Park up there," Ayers says, indicating a spot mid-hill. "We can walk the rest of the way."

"You go," Mick says. "I'll wait here until you want to leave. Or, if you decide to stay for a while, text me and I'll come back for you later."

Ayers nods and rubs Gordon's bucket head. She has missed him, and when human words and emotions fail, animals still provide comfort.

She climbs out of the Jeep. It's broiling in the sun, and Ayers's stomach roils with last night's tequila and that stupid cigarette. Her best friend is dead. Ayers stops. She's going to vomit or faint. Her vision splotches. One of the West Indian women—Dearie, she has a beauty shop up behind the Lumberyard building—takes Ayers's hand and all but pulls her up the hill.

"Ayers!"

She sees Huck hurrying off his porch, where a group of men—some white, some West Indian, some in uniform, some not—are gathered. A West Indian woman named Helen—she was LeeAnn's best friend—emerges from the house with a pot of coffee and starts filling cups.

"Oh, Huck," Ayers whispers. She stands with her arms hanging uselessly at her sides, tears streaming down her face as he gathers her up in a hug. He's a big bear of a man with a bushy reddish-gray beard and the ropy, muscled forearms of a fisherman. He's missing half his left pinky thanks to a feisty barracuda. He's an island character, nearly an icon. *Everyone* knows Huck, but few love him like Ayers does, and like Rosie did. He was more a father to Rosie than Rosie's own father, and the same can probably be said for Ayers.

"Is it true?" she asks.

He lets her go. "It's true," he says. His eyes shine. "Helicopter went down. They were headed over to Anegada for the day, I guess."

Ayers has questions. "They" means Rosie and the Invisible Man, but why did they take a helicopter and not a boat, like normal people? Too slow, she figures. Helicopter is faster and makes more of a statement. What happened? Who was this pilot, Stephen Thompson, and did he not check the weather report? Aren't there *rules,* the FAA and whatever?

But those questions don't matter.

"Maia?" Ayers asks.

"She's at Joanie's," Huck says. "I talked to Joanie's parents. They had planned to take the girls to Salt Pond and then to hike Ram's Head in the late afternoon once it cooled down, then have dinner at Café Concordia. I told them to go ahead with their plans. Maia may end up hating me for it, but I want her to have today. I'll tell her when she gets home. I was hoping you would be here when I tell her. She likes you. What does she always say? You're like her mom, but..."

"But better," Ayers says. "Because I'm not her mom."

"She's going to need you now," Huck says. "She's going to need you a whole lot."

"Okay," Ayers says, but she can barely get the word out because she's crying too hard. *It's fine,* she thinks. She'll cry now, she can fall to absolute pieces now, but there's a twelve-year-old girl depending on her to be strong, and, dammit, Ayers isn't going to let her down.

CASH

Cash treats his mother like she's made of bone china. She's not, he knows—she has kept a stiff upper lip thus far, and she looks pulled together. Her chestnut hair is in its usual fat braid with a swoop of bangs that dips toward her right eye. For Cash's entire life, his mother's hair has looked exactly the same. They used to tease her about it, but now Cash finds it soothing. If Irene braided her hair, some essential part of her is intact. He can't imagine what must be going through her mind. It's bad enough that Russ is dead, but to die in such a dramatic, suspicious way, in a place none of them even knew he was, and then to find out that he has "concerns" and owns property here? It's also an unusual burden to be on such a somber mission in such an achingly beautiful place. It's bright, sunny, and hot. The air is crystalline, and the water is turquoise, more beautiful than any water Cash has ever seen. The islands are green and mountainous—volcanic, he learned, when he did a little research. There are enormous yachts anchored in the harbor with people out drinking, barbecuing, playing reggae music. The ferry is abuzz with excited tourists talking about fish tacos at Longboard and snorkeling at Maho Bay. Cash picks three seats on the far right side of the boat. He and Baker have barely spoken a word to each other since meeting up in Atlanta; Russ's death hasn't changed the fact that Baker is one of Cash's least favorite people on planet Earth.

They take the seats on either side of their mother, buffering her. Winnie hangs her head over the lower railing, panting at the ocean. She's a mountain dog; this is all brand-new to her.

It takes only twenty minutes to reach St. John. Cash has

read that it's a smaller, more rustic cousin of St. Thomas. There are no traffic lights, no chain stores, and only one small casino, The Parrot Club. Seventy percent or more of the land on St. John is owned by the National Park Service. It's for hikers and snorkelers, birders and fishermen, people who love the outdoors. Cash likes the sound of it.

Or he would, under other circumstances.

Cash had spoken with Paulette Vickers on the phone. She told him she was the property manager of Mr. Steele's villa. The phrase "property manager" triggered a memory of something Irene had told him.

"Are you the one who identified my father's body?" Cash asked.

"That was my husband, Douglas," Paulette said.

"And your husband knew my father? Knew what he looked like? And my father was dead? And the man who was dead was actually my father, Russell Steele?" Cash had paused. "I know these questions sound strange. It's just that I'm in a state of suspended disbelief."

Yes, yes, she understood, she said. Though how could she, possibly? Paulette said that she took care of maintaining the villa in the summer months, when Mr. Steele was away, and that Douglas did all the handyman work. When Cash had asked how long his father had owned the villa, Paulette had been slow to answer. She said that she had "inherited" the villa from another property manager three years earlier. She wasn't certain when Mr. Steele had bought the villa; she would have to check the files.

"All right, I'll wait," Cash had said, and Paulette had laughed.

"How are you related to Mr. Steele?" Paulette had asked. "Marilyn, from Mr. Croft's office, said only that a family member would be calling."

"I'm his son," Cash had said. "His younger son. My brother will be coming as well, and my mother, Irene. Mr. Steele's widow."

This had elicited a long pause from Paulette. "I see," she said.

"Is there a problem?" Cash asked. He meant aside from the obvious problem that his father was dead under mysterious circumstances.

"Not at all," Paulette said. "I didn't realize Mr. Steele had sons, but then again, he was a very private person. He liked to keep a low profile, to be 'invisible,' he used to say. The villa, as you'll see, has everything: a pool and a hot tub, a shuffleboard court and a billiards table, multiple decks and outdoor living spaces, nine bedrooms, seven of them en suite, and, of course, a private beach. There was no reason for him to leave the property, and he rarely did."

Cash's head was spinning. Nine bedrooms? A shuffleboard court? A private beach? It just wasn't *possible.* Cash thanked Paulette, gave her the details of their travel, and hung up.

Cash and Baker help their mother off the ferry while Winnie goes nuts, pulling on the leash, intrigued by so many new smells. Cash sees a West Indian woman in a purple dress waving at him. Is that Paulette Vickers? How would she have recognized him? He wonders if Paulette had been *friends* with Russ, if maybe Russ had shown Paulette pictures of his family at home. But then Cash remembers that he told Paulette he was bringing his golden retriever.

He strides up to her and offers his hand. "Paulette, I'm Cash Steele. Can we get into your car and away from here with minimum fanfare?" It has only just occurred to Cash that there might be some attendant celebrity to being the family of the man who died in the helicopter crash on New Year's Day.

"Yes, of course," Paulette says. She waits, smile plastered to her face, while Irene and Baker approach, and then she offers Irene her hand. Irene stares.

"You knew my husband?" Irene asks. "You knew Russ?"

"Mom, let's get to the car," Cash says.

Baker smooths things over by taking Paulette's outstretched hand and saying, "Very nice to meet you. Thank you for coming to get us. What a beautiful island."

Cash gives Baker a hard stare. It *is* a beautiful island, but it hardly seems appropriate to say so.

Paulette, although she must realize that the three of them are numb with shock and grief, prattles on about the sights as though they are run-of-the-mill tourists. The town is called Cruz Bay, it's where the "action" is, the shopping, the restaurants, the infamous Woody's, with its infamous happy hour.

Happy hour? Cash almost interrupts Paulette to remind her who she has in her car, but his mother puts a hand on his arm to silence him.

Winnie's head is out the window, and Cash decides to follow suit and turn his gaze outward, tuning out Paulette. Baker can handle her.

The "town" is maybe four blocks long. It's understated and laid-back. There are restaurants with outdoor seating under awnings, bakeries, barbecue joints, shops selling silver jewelry, renting snorkel equipment—nothing gaudy or overbearing.

They pass public tennis courts and a school with children in yellow-and-navy uniforms out on the playground.

"The children are just back to school after the holiday break," Paulette says. "I have a son at that school. He's six."

"I have a son who's four," Baker says. "He's back in Houston with his mother."

Cash supposes he should be grateful that Baker's an extrovert; he will be the goodwill ambassador and Cash will tend to Irene. The family joke has always been that Cash is the daughter Irene never had; it doesn't bother Cash because he's secure in his masculinity. He knows his strengths: he's sensitive, thoughtful, introspective, a nurturer. And Baker is alpha, or he was until he married Anna. She definitely wears the pants in that family—hell, the whole tuxedo—but Cash is relieved to see that Baker has retained his charm.

Out of town, the road grows steep and curvy. Paulette is pointing out trailheads, talking about hiking, about the three-thousand-year-old petroglyphs of the Reef Bay Trail.

"Very famous," she says. "They're what St. John is known for."

On either side of the road is dense vegetation. Everything here is so green and alive, Cash can practically hear it growing. At the crest of a hill, Paulette pulls over to the shoulder. Below them is a crescent of white beach backed by palm trees. It's the most picture-perfect beach Cash has ever seen. It's so beautiful it hurts.

"That's Trunk Bay," Paulette says. "Perennially voted one of the best beaches in the world."

"Great," Baker says, nodding. He pulls out his phone, and Cash wonders if he's going to take a *picture,* but no, he's just checking the time. "Paulette, you are so kind to serve as our tour guide, and I hope you don't think I'm being rude when I suggest you take us right to my father's property. We've been traveling since early this morning."

"Of course," Paulette says. "I just thought since you were unfamiliar with the island, you might want to see what all the fuss is about."

They couldn't have sent anyone less sensitive, Cash thinks. And yet he doesn't want to alienate Paulette because she is, right now, their only link to Russ's life here.

Paulette pulls back onto the road. She's at ease on the windy, twisty, steep terrain, where there's zero room for error. One side of the road is unforgiving mountain face, and the other side is a dramatic drop to the sea. Paulette waves to the drivers of the big open-air taxis that pass them—too close for Cash's comfort—in the oncoming lane. She stops to talk to one of the taxi drivers. They speak some kind of island patois; the only words Cash recognizes are "invisible man." *Is that what they call Russ?* he wonders. He peers discreetly at his mother. Her eyes are closed.

Finally, Paulette slows down, puts on her blinker, and turns. They drive up a series of hairpin turns. The road is deserted and it's shady; there are driveways, but no houses are visible. At the end of the road is a high gate with a sign that reads: PRIVATE.

Baker laughs. "Is this where Kenny Chesney lives?"

Paulette punches a code into the keypad and the gate swings open. Cash nudges his mother awake. He knows she's tired, but she has to see this. It's like something from a movie. This is his father's *villa,* his *father's* villa, on an island in the Caribbean. Cash can't help thinking that there has been a mistake, a very large, serious, and yet simple mistake. A man named Russell Steele did die in a helicopter crash north of Virgin Gorda, but it was a different Russell Steele. Their Russell Steele—husband, father, connoisseur of arcane trivia and corny puns, fan of the Beatles and *The Blues Brothers,* is still alive somewhere, schmoozing with clients in Sarasota or Pensacola.

The driveway is long, surrounded on both sides by evenly spaced palm trees, each of which has a spotlight at the bottom. When they reach the house, Cash takes his mother's hand.

"We're here," Paulette says.

They all climb out of the car. Baker lets out a long, low whistle. He has absolutely no impulse control.

The property is...stunning. They're way, way up high, with hundred-eighty-degree views of the water and the islands beyond. Paulette leads them up a curved stone staircase to a mahogany deck, where she turns with her arms open like a woman on a game show, as if to present the view.

"That's Jost Van Dyke and, next to it, Tortola."

"What?" Irene says.

"The British Virgin Islands, Mom," Baker says.

Paulette guides them around the outside of the house. The grounds are impeccably landscaped with bougainvillea, frangipani, banana trees, and tall hibiscus bushes. There's a round aqua pool with a slide down to a second, free-form, dark-blue pool. A few yards away is a separate hot tub, water bubbling, surface steaming. There's a covered outdoor kitchen with a granite bar, a grill, an ice machine, and a glass-fronted refrigerator displaying a variety of Italian sparkling waters. Cash shakes his head. This isn't his father's house. Russ drinks tap water.

Paulette opens a sliding glass door and they all step into the house; after the heat outside, the air-conditioning is delicious. The ceiling of the living room is peaked, with thick beams jutting from the center like the spokes of a wheel. They wander into the enormous eat-in kitchen and Paulette says, "I'll let you explore in peace. I'll be on the deck if you have any questions."

"Which way to the master bedroom?" Irene asks. "And is there a study?"

"The master is at the end of that hall," Paulette says. "Mr. Steele's study is attached. All of the other bedrooms are upstairs, and there's a lower level with a billiards table and a wine cellar. That level opens up onto the shuffleboard court below. And the steps to the beach. There are eighty steps, just so you're aware."

"I'm going down to check that out," Baker says. He looks at Cash. "Do you want to come?"

"I'll go with Mom," Cash says. He can't let his mother walk into the "master bedroom"—presumably where his father slept—by herself.

Baker cocks an eyebrow, a signature expression of his, and Cash remembers just how much his brother irks him. Cash resents Baker's confidence, his smug self-assuredness, his aura of superiority. Baker is the worst kind of older brother—all alpha dominance, no support or advice. But the most frustrating thing is that despite this, Cash yearns to be just like him. "This place is unbelievable," Baker says. "And I do mean *unbelievable.*" He lowers his voice. "It can't be Dad's. They have the wrong guy."

Cash doesn't comment, though he happens to agree. He trails his mother down the long hall to the master suite. In the bedroom is a king bed positioned to face the water through an enormous sliding glass door. There are two walk-in closets—empty, both of them: Cash checks immediately—and there's a huge marble bathroom with dual sinks, a sunken soaking tub for two, and a glassed-in shower. There's a paneled study, which is where Irene has chosen to start poking around. The top of the desk is clear, so she's rifling through drawers. Cash, meanwhile, pokes through the bathroom. There are a couple of toothbrushes and a can of shaving cream, but nothing else in the way of personal items.

The place feels *staged.* It feels *cleaned out.* If Russ had been living here or even just staying here—Irene said he'd left Iowa on December 26—then wouldn't he have left behind clothes, a razor, aftershave, reading glasses?

Cash opens the dresser drawers. Empty. That's weird, right? He goes over to the bed and opens the nightstand drawer. He startles as if he's found a disembodied head.

There's a photograph staring up at him. It's a framed photograph of Russ with a West Indian woman. They're lying in a hammock. Cash turns around. It's the hammock that's hanging out on the deck right off the master bedroom. Russ is wearing sunglasses and grinning at the camera and the woman is snuggled up against him.

Cash casts about the room for a place to hide the photograph. He can't have his mother see it.

He stuffs it between the mattress and box spring, then sits on the bed and drops his head in his hands. His unspoken suspicions have been confirmed: Russ had a mistress, most likely the woman who was with him on the helicopter. The bigger shock, perhaps, is seeing a picture of his father in this house. This is real. This is his father's house. His father is dead.

Cash wants to laugh. It's absurd! He wants to scream. After all of Russ's gentle prodding for Cash to finish his education and establish an "infrastructure," it turns out his father's own infrastructure was built of lies! He had a *secret life!* A fifteen-million-dollar villa in the Caribbean and a West Indian mistress!

What else? Cash wonders. What else was Russell Steele—a

three-term member of the Iowa City School Board while Cash was growing up—hiding?

He pokes his head into the study, where his mother is sitting at the desk, staring out the window.

"I'm going out to get some air, Mom," he says. "I'll be right back."

"Was there anything in the bedroom?" she asks.

"Not really," Cash says. "This is like the house of a stranger."

"Well," she says.

He finds Paulette out on the front deck, reciting a shopping list to someone over the phone. When she sees him, she hangs up and lights a cigarette. He's encouraged by this gesture. He needs to talk to the real Paulette Vickers.

"So, what do you think of the house?" she asks.

"I have some questions." His voice is low. He leans his forearms on the railing and she follows suit. Together, they gaze out at the vista—the glittering aquamarine water, the lush green islands, the sleek boats that must belong to the luckiest people in the world. Maybe Paulette takes this landscape for granted, but for Cash it's like discovering another planet. "I'd like to talk frankly, without my mother present."

"I'll answer what questions I can," Paulette says.

"This is my father's house?"

"Yes."

"Where are all of his things? His clothes, for example? His shoes, his bathing suits, his deodorant? It's as anonymous as a Holiday Inn."

"Nicer than a Holiday Inn," Paulette says.

"Please don't dodge the question," Cash says. "If he was staying here before he left on that helicopter, where are his things? Did someone go through the house?"

"I did," Paulette says. "I had strict orders from Mr. Croft's secretary to rid the house of all personal effects." She pauses. "So as not to upset you. Or your mother."

"So where are they?" Cash asks.

"Packed up," Paulette says. "Mr. Croft sent someone to collect them this morning."

"Did he," Cash says. "Does Mr. Croft have a house on St. John as well?"

"Not to my knowledge," Paulette says.

"What does that mean, not to your *knowledge*?" Cash says. "You're a local with a child in the schools. You work for a real estate agency. It seems like you would know whether or not Mr. Croft has a house here."

"Down here...," Paulette says, "a lot of the high-end properties are owned by trusts. People come to the islands to *escape,* Mr. Steele."

To *hide,* Cash thinks.

"Can you tell me where Mr. Croft does live?" Cash says. "Where is his business located?"

"Again, I'm not certain..."

"Paulette," Cash says. He feels himself about to lash out at her. She seems nice—lovely, even—and he can't understand why she's giving him the runaround. "I'm sure you can see that we're grieving. My brother and I lost our father, my mother her husband. If he'd died of a heart attack at home, this would have been tragic enough. But he died *here,* in a place we didn't know he'd even visited, much less owned property in. The details we've received are sparse. Part of the way the three of us are going to process our loss is to find out exactly what happened. We need to talk to Todd Croft."

"That would be a start, I suppose," Paulette says.

"Do you have a phone number for him?"

Paulette laughs drily. "For Mr. Croft? No, I'm afraid not. I've never met the man. I've never even spoken to him on the phone."

"You're kidding," Cash says.

"I deal with his secretary," Paulette says. "Marilyn. She called your mother, so your mother has her number."

"But it's Mr. Croft who pays you," Cash says. "Right?" He nearly says, *It's Mr. Croft who pulls the puppet strings.* He pulled Russ's, or at least that was how it had seemed.

"I was paid by Mr. Steele directly," Paulette says. "In cash. And occasionally by Mr. Thompson."

"Mr. Thompson?" Cash says. "Who is Mr. Thompson?"

"Stephen Thompson," Paulette says. "He was their associate."

"Their associate," Cash says. He feels like he's on a detective show, only he's the new guy, first day on the job, trying to figure things out. "Do you have a number for Mr. Thompson, then?"

"I do," Paulette says. She stares at the glowing tip of her cigarette.

"Paulette, again..."

"Mr. Thompson is dead," Paulette says. "He was the pilot."

"He was the pilot," Cash says. "And the third person who died, the local woman, she and my father...were involved?"

"I'm not comfortable discussing that," Paulette says.

"I have a photograph of them together," Cash says. "It was in the drawer of the nightstand."

Paulette exhales a stream of smoke and casts her eyes down.

"What's her name?"

"Again, Mr. Steele, I'm not..."

"Paulette," Cash says. "Please. *Please.*" His voice breaks, and he fears he's going to cry. He wants to go back to New Year's Eve, or even to New Year's Day, to the mortifying and yet inevitable conversation with Glenn the accountant. He wants his father to be alive. Cash will confess his failure with the stores and he *won't* go to Breckenridge to waste away the rest of his young adulthood. He'll enroll at the University of Colorado, Denver. He'll get a degree. He'll make something of himself. But he wants his father back. His desperation creates a sour taste in his mouth and he inhales a breath—the honey scent of frangipani combined with Paulette's secondhand smoke.

Paulette looks at Cash. She must sense his pain, because her brown eyes well with tears. "Rosie," she says. "Rosie Small. She was the daughter of LeeAnn Powers, who was married to Captain Huck. LeeAnn died five years ago." Paulette taps her ashes into the bougainvillea below. "There's going to be a memorial service tomorrow at the Episcopalian church, with a reception following at Chester's Getaway. If you go to either the service or the reception, you'll find people who can tell you more. But I'd advise you to be discreet. And to go with an open mind and an open heart. Lots and lots of people on this island loved Rosie Small. And almost no one on this island knew your father. Like I said, he preferred to remain invisible."

Cash turns around to face the house. "And we can stay here a few days?"

"As long as you want," Paulette says. "It's yours now."

"Okay, thank you, Paulette," Cash says. "Really, thank you."

"God bless you boys," Paulette says. "And God bless your mother."

HUCK

Joanie's parents, Jeff and Julie—they are a self-proclaimed "J" family—pull into the driveway at six o'clock on the dot. Huck somehow managed to get everyone out of the house except for Ayers. She is sitting at the counter, wringing her hands and staring at a bottle of eighteen-year-old Flor de Caña rum like she's drowning and it's a life raft. Huck nearly suggests they both do a shot to fortify their nerves, but then he thinks better of it.

As his grandfather used to say: hard things are hard. Huck has done plenty of hard things in his life. He was drafted into the Vietnam War right out of high school. He had been born and raised on Islamorada in the Florida Keys, so he thought the U.S. Navy would be a natural fit, and he was happy because in the navy, you didn't get shot at. But choice was for those who enlisted, not for those who got drafted, and the powers that be placed Huck in the Marine Corps. His first year in Vietnam was spent facedown in the mud, in the jungle, in the rice paddies, fearing for his life every second of every day, developing an addiction to nicotine that he still can't shake.

Later, years after he got home, he had to put his then-wife, Kimberly, into rehab for drinking and serve her with divorce papers.

He buried his sister, Caroline, who died of brain cancer at forty-one, and his mother, who died of heartbreak over Caroline, and eventually his beloved father, the original captain, Captain Paul Powers, who had run a fishing charter out of Islamorada for fifty years and whose passengers had included Jack Nicklaus and Frank Sinatra. He had taught Huck everything he knew about fishing and about being a man.

It was after his father died that Huck moved to the Virgin Islands, where life was easy for a long time. He bought his boat, started his business, and met and married LeeAnn Small, an island treasure. Huck would name burying LeeAnn as the hardest thing he'd ever had to do, but only because he had loved the woman so damn much.

This would be harder.

Maia comes bounding into the house, her skin burnished from a full day outside, even though Jeff and Julie are fastidious about sunscreen and bug spray. The smile on her face is proof that he was right: she had a happy day. Maybe the last happy day for the rest of her childhood.

He doesn't want to tell her.

Maia sees Ayers and goes right to her for a hug. Huck catches Ayers's expression over Maia's shoulder; her eyes are shining. He doesn't have but a few seconds left before Ayers breaks down.

They should have done the rum shot. He's shaking.

"Maia," he says. "Please sit."

She pulls away from Ayers and looks at him wide-eyed. "Are you *mad*?" she asks. "You *said* I could go."

"I'm not mad," Huck says. "But would you please sit down? Ayers and I have to tell you something."

"What?" Maia says. She is standing, defiant now in her posture.

Ayers reaches out to take Maia's hand.

"There was a helicopter crash north of Virgin Gorda," Huck says. "Maia, your mother is dead."

There is a blankness on Maia's face and this, Huck thinks, is the soul-destroying moment: Maia taking in the words and making sense of them.

Then, Maia starts to scream. The sound is raw, primitive; it's the sound of an animal. Ayers pulls Maia close and tears stream down Huck's face and he thinks, *Hard things are hard,* and *Please, God, do not give her anything harder than this.*

The screaming morphs into crying, great ragged sobs, seemingly bigger than the girl herself. Huck goes for tissues, a glass of ice water, a pillow in case she wants to punch something. He and Ayers had made a pact that they would not shush Maia or tell her everything was going to be okay. They were not going to *lie* to the girl. They were going to let her take in what she could, and then they were going to answer her questions as honestly as possible.

The crying ends eventually. Ayers leads Maia to the sofa, and Huck plants himself in the chair, within arm's reach. He had been over at Schneider hospital with LeeAnn when Rosie gave birth to Maia. He had been the third person to hold her, red and wriggling and utterly captivating. If Huck were very honest, he would admit to feeling a quick stab of disappointment that the baby hadn't been a boy. Huck had imagined a grandson to take fishing. But Maia stole Huck's heart that first moment in his arms, and he decided that she would make a better mate anyway. The men in LeeAnn's family were either weak or absent. It was the women who were strong.

Maia blows her nose, gets a clear breath. Her face, which had been so radiant when she walked in, is now mottled, and, if Huck isn't imagining it, her dainty features have instantly aged. She suddenly looks seventeen, or twenty-five.

"Helicopter," Maia says. "So she was with my father. Is he dead, too?"

"*Father*?" Ayers says.

"Honey," Huck says. "She was with her...her friend. The one who comes to visit." The man's name is Russell Steele. Rosie told Huck the guy's name when he first came on the scene, a few months after LeeAnn died, but Rosie kept the relationship private. The fellow showed up one or two weeks a month, November through May; he had some big villa on the north shore. Huck had a pretty good idea which road it was, though he'd never been invited to the house and he'd never met the guy. Maia, he knew, went to the house sometimes when the man was on-island, though there were plenty of occasions when Rosie had asked Huck to cover so that she and her mystery lover could have some privacy.

Huck won't lie: the arrangement had troubled him. He had expected at least an *introduction.* He had expected, if not a weekly barbecue, then an invitation for a beer. But Rosie had been both stubborn and contrite when it came to the Invisible Man. She was very sorry—and Huck could see on her face that the emotion was genuine—but she wanted to keep her relationship private. The island was small, she had been born and raised there, everyone had always been right up in her business, and she just wanted one thing that would not be discussed and dissected by the community at large.

Huck had suspected this was not how Rosie truly felt. He had suspected that her plea was on behalf of the Invisible Man.

Which meant, of course, only one thing: he was married. Or he was one of those bastards who had a girl like Rosie in every port. International finance was his business, Rosie said, which meant, of course, only one thing: he was also a criminal. You want an honest business? Go out on a boat, catch a fish, and eat it for dinner.

But the Invisible Man should not be confused with the Pirate, which is what Maia is now doing. The Pirate was some other white fella who came in on his buddy's yacht, hot on Rosie—this was back when Rosie was cocktail waitressing at Caneel Bay—knocked her up and left without a trace. Rosie called him "the Pirate" because he'd stolen her heart.

And her dignity, LeeAnn had said privately to Huck.

Rosie had fallen hard for the Pirate in the four days they'd spent together. It had been over a long weekend—Presidents' Day in February. And then Maia had been born on November 15.

"If by 'friend' you mean Russ, then, yes, he's my father. Was my father. Russell Steele. So they're both dead?" Maia holds Huck's gaze. "They're *both* dead?"

"Yes," Huck says. He wonders if there's something he doesn't know. He wonders if Rosie let the Invisible Man *adopt* Maia at some point over the years without telling anyone. Without telling him. He knows the Invisible Man pays for Maia's expenses, including her tuition at Gifft Hill, but Huck had thought that was a gesture, possibly even a payment in exchange for Rosie's discretion. Rosie still had a job, paid her own bills, lived under Huck's roof whenever the Invisible Man was away, which was a lot. Had Rosie been hiding something *that* big? How had she pulled it off, legally, without someone in the courthouse in Charlotte Amalie blabbing? It eventually would have gotten back to Huck.

Impossible, Huck thinks. They must have just started calling this Steele fellow Maia's "father."

"So I'm an orphan," Maia says. "I have no one."

"You have me," Ayers says. "You're always going to have me."

"And you have me," Huck says. He gets down on his knees before Maia, which seems fitting because he has done nothing for the past twelve years so much as worship this child. He knows she's too young to understand the quality of his devotion—and this is probably for the best. She doesn't need someone to worship her. She needs someone to love her, clothe her, feed her, teach her right from wrong, someone to set limits and provide opportunities, someone to believe in her and be her champion.

And that person will be Huck. He will be her Unconditional. He will be her No Matter What.

BAKER

Anna did Baker a favor before he left. She filled a prescription of Ativan for his mother.

"I bet you she won't take them," Anna said. "But it'll be good to have them just in case."

It turned out Anna knew Irene better than Baker imagined. She did refuse the pills at first.

But Thursday night, when the sun is dropping like a hot coal into the Caribbean and Irene has refused Baker's offer of dinner three times, she says, "I think I'd like to try sleeping. Can I see those pills?"

"Do you want the master bedroom, Mom?" Cash asked.

"Heavens, no," Irene said. "I'll take one of the guest rooms upstairs." She offered them both a weak smile. "That's what I am, a guest. A guest in your father's house."

Cash helped Irene get situated upstairs while Baker checked the contents of the kitchen. Paulette had said it was "well-stocked," and she also said that she could arrange for a private chef if they so desired.

"No private chef," Baker said. "I don't think my mother wants any strangers in the house."

"The landscapers are scheduled every Friday...," Paulette said.

"Please," Baker said. "If you would just tell everyone to give us our privacy for a week..."

"Of course," Paulette said. "Call if you need anything."

Now, Baker inspects the fridge and cabinets. "Well-stocked" is an understatement. The fridge is filled with steaks, hamburgers, pasta salad, deli meats, fresh vegetables, milk, eggs, and a giant bowl of tropical fruit salad. The bottom shelf holds four flavors of local beer. The cabinets contain enough pasta, cereal, and canned goods—including, curiously, six cans of SpaghettiOs—for a small family to survive a nuclear fallout. The SpaghettiOs remind Baker of Floyd, and he thinks to go out on the deck and call home, but honestly, the only positive thing about this whole surreal trip is that he's able to leave his own problems behind. Or, rather, his "own problems" become what is happening here. His father is *dead.* Right? Baker hasn't been able to feel the reality of Russ's death, however, because nothing about this *makes any sense.*

Take, for example, the wine cellar. Russell Steele was a man who liked his Leinenkugel's, his Bud Light, and his scotch. Baker has no memory of Russ *ever* drinking wine. Champagne, maybe, at Baker and Anna's wedding. One sip. The person who liked wine in their family was Irene. She drank chardonnay from California. Her everyday wine was Kendall-Jackson, her favorite splurges Simi and Cakebread. Curiously—or not?—Baker had found one case of both Simi and Cakebread in his father's wine cellar, almost as if he were expecting Irene to visit.

Cash comes down the stairs just as Baker is cracking open what he believes to be a well-deserved beer, and he reaches into the fridge to grab one for Cash. Cash takes it from him and nods toward the pool.

"She's asleep," Cash says. "The pill knocked her right out. Which is a good thing, because I need to talk to you."

They go out to the swimming pool and sit with their feet in the shallow end. The gurgle of the fountain will drown out their voices in case Irene should appear.

"What is it?" Baker says.

"He had a mistress," Cash says. "A West Indian woman. I found a picture of the two of them in the master bedroom."

Baker takes a sip of his beer. It's good, but not quite good enough to distract him from this crushing news about his father. Is *nobody* as they seem? Does *everyone* have nefarious secrets? Okay, obviously something was going on with his father, and it occurred to Baker that the "local woman" in the helicopter was, perhaps, a damning detail. But that was only a maybe. She could have been the *pilot's* girlfriend, or a tour guide, or one of Russ's clients.

"Let me see this picture," Baker says.

Cash disappears into the house, returning with a framed photograph of Russ and a truly stunning West Indian woman, lying together in a hammock.

There is no misreading the photo.

What strikes Baker is how Russ looks. He's wearing sunglasses so it's a bit hard to tell, but the father Baker knows—the goofy midwestern salesman always ready with a quip or pun—has been replaced by a man who looks sophisticated, worldly, and most of all, confident. When Baker and Cash were growing up, Russ had been like nothing so much as a big, eager Saint Bernard who faced each day with the same quest for attention, love, reassurance. He had a list of DIY projects that he liked to tackle on the weekends. He would go in to wake the boys up on a Saturday morning, calling Baker "buddy," and Cash "pal," as he did their entire lives, but they wouldn't stir. Russ would then take a seat at Baker's desk and wait. When the boys finally woke up, he would jump up with a childlike enthusiasm. Baker understood his father's eager-to-please, don't-rock-the-boat attitude to be the result of his childhood. He had moved every eighteen months, and the quest to be found likable and to be included was constant. But Baker won't lie. Both he and Cash found their father's obsequiousness off-putting, nearly cringeworthy. There were a lot of shared eye rolls.

Once Russ got his new job, he had a new luster, certainly; there was suddenly a *ton* of money. But Russ's attention was still so intense—possibly even more intense because he was around less frequently—that sometimes Baker and Cash wanted to deflect it. They thought their father was a nice enough guy, but ultimately they preferred the cooler, more reserved presence of their mother.

This man in the photograph with the open-collared tomato-red shirt and the "I've-got-the-world-by-the-balls" smile is a stranger.

"Has Mom seen this?" Baker asks.

"No."

"Good."

Cash stands up. "I'm returning it to its hiding place."

"Get two more beers," Baker says. "Please."

Baker grills up six cheeseburgers, and he and Cash fall on the food as they used to when they were teenagers—without thinking, without conversation. Then they sit, with their empty plates before them, staring at the twinkling lights of Tortola in the distance. Baker wonders if he should tell Cash about Anna. Cash is, after all, his brother, though they aren't close; they don't confide in each other. Baker has long viewed Cash as a little punk—that was definitely true all through growing up—because Russ and Irene coddled him. And he had spent his adult years freewheeling, which always seemed more like freeloading: sleeping on his buddies' couches out in Breckenridge, teaching skiing for a pittance because the job came with a free season pass, living off the food that his roommates who worked at restaurants brought home.

Baker and his parents had been unimpressed. But then what did Russ go and do? He bought Cash a business! Handed him the keys to two outdoor supply stores! Baker had really kept his distance then, because the demonstration of blatant favoritism was so egregious. Baker had always been able to speak frankly with his father, and he nearly told Russ that sinking two hundred grand into any business Cash was going to run was as good as sending it to a Nigerian prince.

The only time in recent history that Baker had seen Cash in a more favorable light was when he had taken Anna to Breckenridge to ski, back when they were dating. Anna had been uncharacteristically effusive in her praise of Cash. She loved that he got them access to the back-of-the-mountain trails. She loved that he was dating the hostess at the hottest sushi restaurant in town and then scored them a table in the window at eight o'clock on a Saturday night.

Your brother knows everyone, Anna had said. *He's like the mayor.*

Six months later, Baker had grudgingly asked Cash to serve as best man in his wedding.

"I really wish we had some weed," Baker says now. "I need to relax. My heart has been racing since Mom called with the news. Maybe I should take one of Mom's Ativans."

Cash takes an audible breath, as though Baker has startled him out of a waking sleep-state. "Wait," Cash says. "There's more to the story about the woman Dad was seeing."

"Right," Baker says. He'd dropped the thread of their earlier conversation. The woman in the photograph.

"I asked Paulette about her," Cash says. "The woman's name was Rosie Small. There's a memorial service being held tomorrow at the Episcopal church, followed by a reception at a place called Chester's Getaway."

Baker nods. Todd Croft arranged for Russ's body to be cremated.

As for a funeral service...Irene wants to wait until they figure out what's going on before they even tell anyone that Russ is dead. They can't very well tell everyone they know that Russ was killed in a helicopter crash in the Virgin Islands when they have no answers to the inevitable follow-up questions. Baker has scoured the internet—there has been no mention anywhere of a helicopter crash in the Virgin Islands.

Baker notices Cash looking at him expectantly. "What?"

"We have to go tomorrow," Cash says. "To either the service or the reception."

"Why?" Baker says.

"To find out who this woman was," Cash says.

"I'm not sure that's a good idea," Baker says. "What would that accomplish?"

"There are so many questions," Cash says. "How did Dad meet her, how long have they been together..."

"Who cares?" Baker says. "Think about it: What is it going to benefit you or me to know the answers? She was a woman Dad was screwing down here. How will it help to know any more?" Baker leans in and lowers his voice. "How will it help Mom? The answer is, it won't. We need to get Dad's ashes and leave. Put this house on the market, if it's even ours to sell."

"Paulette said it was ours," Cash says. "I'll ask her to produce the deed. Mom will have to call her attorney and have him check Dad's will. If Dad owns this house outright and the will leaves everything to Mom and the two of us, then it would be ours to sell."

"You sound like Jackass P. Esquire," Baker says.

"We need to find Todd Croft. See what he can tell us about Dad's business. It wasn't just a 'boutique investment firm,' Baker."

No, Baker thinks. This became evident the second they pulled into the driveway of this house. This is a twelve- or fifteen-million-dollar property. If Russ did own it outright, then he was into something far bigger than he claimed to be. Shell companies, offshore accounts, hiding money, cleaning it, the things you see in movies. He had access to a helicopter.

"I really think we should leave things be," Baker says.

"I don't," Cash says. "I'm going to either the service or the reception tomorrow and you're coming with me. I'll let you pick which one."

"Reception," Baker says. "Obviously. Because there will be alcohol."

"People will be more likely to tell us things," Cash says.

Things we don't want to know, Baker thinks.

At one o'clock the next afternoon, they find themselves in one of the two gunmetal-gray Jeep Saharas that belong to their father, driving to a place called Chester's Getaway off the Centerline Road.

They told their mother they were going on a top secret investigative mission.

"We can't tell you anything else," Baker said.

"I don't want to know anything else," Irene said. "Do what you have to do. I have my own list."

Baker thought his mother looked marginally better. She had finally slept, for a full twelve hours, and then she'd eaten a few chunks of fresh pineapple and a bite of toast.

"What's on your list?" Baker asked.

Irene blinked. "I'm going to call Ed Sorley, our attorney, and ask him to fax me a copy of your father's will. I'm going to call Todd Croft and I'm going to call Paulette. I was in no shape yesterday to ask her any questions, but today I want to appeal to her, woman to woman."

Baker kissed his mother on the forehead. She was a strong woman. She should be falling apart, but instead she had made a list.

"Call if you need us," Baker said.

There are cars lined up for hundreds of yards before they reach the entrance to Chester's and so they have to turn around, double back, and park at the end of the line. They arrive at Chester's at the same time that a bus lets off a load of people—a mix of young and old, white and West Indian, most of them somberly dressed.

Chester's is a two-story clapboard building set off the road and painted ivory and dusty pink. The parking lot has been taken over by a tent. Billowing out behind the tent are clouds of barbecue-scented smoke. Somewhere, a steel band is playing.

"It's good that it's crowded," Cash says. "We won't stick out."

"Let's get a drink," Baker says. It feels wrong to be here. They didn't know Rosie Small. They are the sons of her lover, the man who was taking her to Anegada, and who was indirectly responsible for her death. Surely there are people in attendance—possibly a lot of people—who believe Rosie's death is Russ's fault.

The place is too packed for there to be any kind of receiving line, thank God, which was another reason for avoiding the service. Cash seems to think everyone here is just going to offer up all kinds of information, but Baker isn't so sure.

Baker asks a gentleman in a fedora where the bar can be found and the gentleman says, "Drinks inside but you got to pay. Food outside is free. Pig roast and all the sides, including Chester's johnnycakes. You ever had Chester's johnnycakes?"

Baker sidles away without answering. "The bar is inside," he says to Cash.

"It's hot," Cash says. He's pink in the face and sweating. He chose to wear a long-sleeved plaid shirt and a pair of jeans. Baker is in khaki shorts and a navy polo. They both look... well, the word Baker wants to use is *white*...he doesn't mean Caucasian, exactly, but rather pale and out of place, like they've just parachuted in from the North Pole. Only half the people here are West Indian, but the other white people here look tan, weathered, well-seasoned.

The inside of Chester's is mercifully cooler, and Baker immediately feels better because the bar is the kind Baker would seek out if he had time to seek out bars. There's a long counter, a few tables, a sticky concrete floor, and a room through the back that has a pool table and a dartboard. Chester's Getaway has clearly seen dramas more interesting than the one he and Cash are presently living, or at least Baker would like to believe this. Two TVs hang over the bar, but they're both shut off. The line for a drink is three deep, and Baker decides to exercise his privilege as older brother.

"You wait," he tells Cash. "I'm going to wander."

"Wander *where*?" Cash says. "There isn't room to think in here, much less *wander*."

"Over there," Baker says. He nods vaguely in the direction of an easel displaying photos. *Celebrating Rosie,* it says in bubble letters across the top. Baker hands Cash a twenty, since his brother is perpetually low on money. "And get me two beers, please, when it's your turn."

Cash shrugs and tries to shoulder his way closer to the bar. Meanwhile Baker shuffles over to the sign and the photos, wondering if there are any photos of Rosie Small with their father. There's a woman standing next to the easel behind a small table where she's encouraging people to sign the guest book.

"Hello," she says to Baker. "Would you like to sign the guest book?"

Baker's mouth falls open. It's not just that he's unsure of what to say—*No,* the answer to her question is definitely *no,* he does not want to sign the guest book—it's that she is the prettiest woman he has ever seen. Ever. She has blond ringlet curls and a smile like the sun. She's a natural beauty, and above and beyond that, she looks *nice.*

Anna is striking, certainly. There have been times in the past eight years when Baker hasn't been able to stop staring at her. But this woman affects Baker differently. She's lightly tanned, with freckles across her nose. She wears no makeup. She has blue eyes and straight white teeth. She wears five or six silver bracelets and a simple black jersey dress that clings to her slender frame. Looking at her fills Baker with wordless joy. She looks like hope.

I'm in love with you, he thinks. *Whoever you are.*

"Sure," he says. "I'd love to sign the guest book."

He accepts the pen from her, wondering what name he can possibly sign. He stalls by locking eyes with her and saying, "Can I get you a drink or anything? You seem to have pulled the short straw, being stuck back here in the corner."

"Oh," she says. "It's fine. Chester is keeping me in rum punches." She holds up a plastic cup containing an inch of watery pink liquid, a maraschino cherry, and an orange slice. "He'll be back soon, I'm sure." She sets down the cup and offers a hand. "I'm Ayers Wilson, by the way. I was Rosie's best friend." She tilts her head. "I don't think I recognize you. How did you know Rosie?"

"I...uh...I didn't, really," Baker says. "I came with someone who knew her. My brother. He's at the bar, getting me a beer, I hope."

Ayers laughs. "Nice brother," she says. "How did he know Rosie?"

"Um...," Baker says. "He worked with her."

Ayers's eyes widen. "Really?" she says. "Who's your brother? Is it Skip? Oh my God, that's right, Skip's *brother* from LA, right? But, wait...he's...she's transitioning to a woman. That's not you, I take it."

"No," Baker says. Just like that, he's been caught. "Actually, my brother *is* at the bar, but he didn't work with Rosie."

Ayers shakes her head. "Don't tell me," she says. "You guys are crashing, right?"

Baker sighs. "Kind of."

"Here on vacation, saw the crowd, smelled the pig roast,

and figured why not?" Ayers gives him a pointed look and he feels like an idiot. Before he can decide if he should tell her who he really is, she shrugs. "I honestly don't blame you."

"You don't?" Baker says. "I didn't want to come. My brother insisted."

"I'm actually happy to meet a complete stranger who has nothing to do with any of this," Ayers says. "Half the women here are pissed that I'm doing the guest book instead of Rosie's third cousin or Maia's preschool teacher, and as if that's not bad enough, over there in the doorway are my ex-boyfriend and the tramp he left me for."

Baker looks toward the doorway and sees a chunky guy with a buzz cut and a woman in her twenties who has seen fit to come to a memorial reception without either washing her hair or wearing a bra.

He turns back to Ayers. He's still holding the pen.

"Just write your name," Ayers says. "I'll remember you as the crasher and that'll cheer me up."

"Okay." Baker says. He writes: *Baker.* Then he hands the pen back to Ayers.

"Baker," she reads. "Well, Mr. Baker, it was nice meeting you."

"Baker is my first name," he says.

"Gotcha," Ayers says. "You're afraid to write your last name in case I call the police? Or do you go solely by your first name, like Madonna and Cher?"

"The latter," he says. She's flirting with him, he thinks. He stands up to his full height and squares his shoulders.

"Do you want to come outside with me and have a cigarette?" she asks. "Or are you horrified by a woman who smokes?"

He would follow her to East Japip to drink snake venom,

he thinks. He answers by scooting the table aside so she can step out. "Lead the way," he says.

She navigates around the crowd to the back of the tent, where a West Indian man with an orange bandana wrapped around his head is tending to the pig. There's a rubber trash can filled with beer and ice. Ayers grabs two, then says to the man, "You forgot about me, Chester. I'm taking these."

Chester waves his basting brush in the air. "Okay, doll."

Ayers leads Baker to the edge of the parking lot, where there is a tree with a low branch big and sturdy enough to sit on. Ayers pulls a pack of cigarettes out of a little crocheted purse that hangs across her body and lights up. "I'm horrified by people who smoke," Ayers says. "But my best friend just died and so I'm going to give myself a pass for a while to indulge in some self-destructive behavior." She hands the cigarette to Baker. "Want to join me?"

"Sure," he says. He inhales and promptly coughs. "Sorry, I'm out of practice. I haven't had a cigarette since I was fourteen years old standing out in back of the ice rink. It's been only weed for me since then."

This makes Ayers laugh. "So where are you visiting from, Baker?"

"Me?" he says. "Houston."

"Houston," Ayers says. "Never been. Are you a doctor? You look like a doctor."

No, he nearly says. *But my wife's a doctor.*

"I'm not a doctor," he says. "I used to trade in commodities but now I'm kind of between jobs. I do some day-trading and I'm a stay-at-home dad. My son, Floyd, is four."

"Floyd," Ayers says. "Cool name."

"It's making a comeback," Baker says. "Your name is pretty cool."

"My parents are wanderers," Ayers says. "They travel all over the world. I was named after Ayers Rock in Australia, which is, apparently, where I was conceived. But since then the rock has been reclaimed by the Aboriginals and now it's called Uluru. And so I am now politically incorrect Ayers."

"It's pretty," Baker says. *You're pretty,* he thinks.

"So what brings you down here?" Ayers asks. "Vacation?"

How should he answer this? "Not a vacation, exactly," he says. "I'm here with my mom and my brother."

"Family reunion?" Ayers asks.

"I guess you could say that."

"Are you married?" Ayers asks. She blows out a stream of smoke and looks at him frankly. Something inside of him stirs. Someday, he thinks, he will be married to this girl right here, Ayers Wilson. And they will remember this, their very first conversation, sitting on a low tree branch outside Chester's Getaway during the funeral reception for her best friend, who also happened to be Baker's father's mistress.

"I was," he says. "I mean, technically I still am. But my wife found a girlfriend. She announced two days ago that she was leaving me for her colleague, Louisa."

"Ouch," Ayers says.

"Don't feel sorry for me," Baker says. "It's nothing compared to what you're going through."

"That's right," Ayers says. "Thanks for reminding me."

"I heard your friend was in an accident," Baker says. He wants to tell her who he is, but he's afraid she'll run off and he'll never see her again. "What was she like?"

"Rosie? She was...she was...she just *was*," Ayers says. "You know how sometimes people just click? And there's no reason for it? Rosie and I were like that. I met her working at La Tapa."

"La Tapa," Baker says.

"It's the best restaurant on the island. When I first got to St. John, it was the only place I wanted to work, but places like that can be hard to break into. I was very lucky to get hired and even luckier that Rosie took me under her wing. Rosie was a local, she's born and raised here, her parents were born and raised here, and her grandparents. There was no reason for her to befriend me, some white chick who shows up for the season to get in on the good tips, then leaves. But Rosie was nice to me from the very beginning. She was protective. She showed me where the quiet beaches were, she introduced me to a guy who sold me a pickup truck for cheap, she took me to Pine Peace market and introduced me to her mother and her stepfather and just generally treated me like a long-lost sister."

"Wow," Baker says. He's moved by this and he wants to ask some strategic follow-up questions. Was she seeing anyone? Had Ayers known Russ? But at that moment, Baker looks up and sees Cash headed toward them, holding two beers in each hand.

Baker shakes his head at Cash in an attempt to convey the very important message: *She doesn't know who we are!* But Cash looks too hot and pissed-off to care about secret codes.

"Why the hell did you *vanish* like that?" Cash asks. "You expected me to find you all the way over here?"

"That's my fault," Ayers says, dropping the butt of her cigarette into her now empty beer. "I led your brother astray. Sorry about that."

Cash hands Baker two of the four beers and takes a long swallow of one of the beers he's holding. He seems like he's making an effort to regroup. "It's fine," he says.

"Cash, this is Ayers Wilson," Baker says. "Ayers is a friend of the deceased..."

"Best friend," Ayers interrupts. "Your brother admitted that you two are crashing."

"Um...yeah," Cash says.

"It seems like there would be better ways to spend your precious vacation days than attending a local funeral lunch," Ayers says. "Though Chester's barbecue is pretty good."

"Vacation days?" Cash says, and he gives Baker a quizzical look.

Ayers takes the awkward moment of silence that follows—during which Baker is silently imploring Cash to just *go with it*—as an opportunity to stand up. "I should get back to my post," she says. "And back to my grief, although God knows that's not going anywhere." She offers Baker her hand. "Thank you for allowing me to escape for a few minutes. Maybe I'll see you again before you leave."

"I hope so," Baker says. "What's the name of the restaurant where you work?"

"La Tapa," she says. "Right downtown, near Woody's."

"Woody's of the infamous happy hour," Baker says.

Ayers touches a finger to her nose. "You got it. And hey, go get yourself some barbecue. Anyone gives you trouble, tell them you're with me." She vanishes back into the crowd.

"What was that?" Cash asks, once she's gone. "You told her we were on *vacation*?"

But Baker is too lovestruck to answer.

IRENE

She's relieved when the boys leave the villa because she needs time and space to think, really think, and she needs room to process. There are two weighty issues Irene has to deal with. One is Russ's death, and the other is his deception.

Because this house, this island, is a very large, very real deception. Russell Steele, Irene's husband of thirty-five years, was a liar, a schemer, and most likely a cheat. Irene doesn't know what to say—words fail her, thoughts fail her, and the boys seem to expect both thoughts and words, some expression of pain, some expression of anger. But Irene is so befuddled she can't yet identify pain or anger. Her interior life is a barren wasteland.

She thinks back to the woman she was before, even hours before that blood-chilling call from Marilyn Monroe. She had been consumed with her problems at work, the demotion, the magazine moving off in a flashy new direction without her. She had gone to dinner with Lydia. Lydia had said, *You wouldn't understand because you have Russ, who dotes on you night and day.* Irene had deflected the statement, saying, *When he's around.* But she had thought, then, that Lydia was right: Irene did have a doting husband and she didn't properly understand what it was like to be alone.

Irene Hagen first met Russell Steele at a bar called the Field House during Irene's senior year in college when the University of Iowa played Northwestern in a snowstorm and that snowstorm turned into a blizzard and I-80, which led back to

Chicago, was shut down, effectively stranding all of the Northwestern fans in Iowa City. There had been a rumor circulating among Irene's sorority sisters at Alpha Chi Omega that the Northwestern boys were looking to hook up simply so they would have a place to sleep that night.

Only a few minutes after Irene heard this rumor, she felt a tap on her shoulder. "My name is Russell Steele," Russ said. "Would you allow me the honor of buying you a drink?"

Irene had scoffed. The guy was cute—brown hair, brown eyes, hooded Northwestern sweatshirt, *clean-cut*, her father would have said—and he had a beseeching look on his face, but Irene suffered no fools.

"No, thanks," she said, and she turned back to her friends.

Russell Steele had walked away. The jukebox, Irene remembered, was playing "Little Red Corvette," and Irene and her friends had stormed the dance floor. When they returned to their spot at the bar, there was a drink waiting for Irene. At that time in college, she drank something called a Lemon Drop, because she had an idea that vodka was less fattening than beer. Vanity came at a price: Lemon Drops at the Field House cost five dollars, a relative fortune.

"From that guy, over there," the bartender said. "The enemy."

When Irene looked, Russ waved.

He had stayed on the other side of the bar the rest of the night, and when it was time to go home, she had gone over to thank him for the drink.

"You didn't have to do that," she said.

"I know," he said. "But you're pretty and a way better dancer than all your friends."

"You're only saying that because you want a place to sleep tonight."

"I'm saying it because it's true," Russ said. "I'll be fine on a park bench tonight."

Irene had sighed. "You can sleep on the floor of my room," she said. "But I want you out by nine and if you touch me, I'll call security."

"Deal," Russell Steele said.

Russ had spent the night on Irene's dorm room floor—she had grudgingly given him one of the blankets and pillows from her own bed—with his arms crossed over his chest, like he was sleeping in a coffin. It was weird, Irene had thought, but also sort of endearing. At nine the next morning, when he was on his way out to catch his ride back to Evanston, she gave him her phone number. She figured she would never hear from him again, but he had called that very night, and the next day, he sent a bouquet of white calla lilies. He had noticed a poster of white callas on Irene's dorm room wall.

Because you love callas and I love you. That was what the card on the flowers said that had arrived on New Year's Day. Russ had been dead by the time those flowers arrived.

Irene thinks back on her marriage. Had she ever had reason to doubt Russ's honesty, or his fidelity? No. Russ's dominant trait had been one of utter devotion; he had never been one to flirt with other women. If Irene complimented a certain woman's figure or sense of style, Russ would say, "I didn't notice." And Irene believed him.

There was a way in which their marriage had been divided in half. The first half of their marriage, they had been normal, hardworking midwesterners, trying to raise two boys. Russ had his job selling corn syrup, and Irene was a full-time mother who picked up freelance editing work once the boys were in school. They lived in a nondescript ranch on Clover Street, a cul-de-sac east of the university, close to the high school. Irene won't lie: those had been lean years. She might even characterize them as tough. If Irene and Russ wanted to do anything fun or special—even a night out to dinner at the steakhouse in the Amanas—they had to budget. When Irene's minivan died, they had to ask Russ's mother, Milly, for a loan.

When Russ got the job offer from Todd Croft, it had seemed nothing short of a miracle, or like God's benevolent intervention finally lifting them up. Suddenly there was money—so much money! They were able to send Baker to Northwestern without taking out any loans. Then they were able to buy the fixer-upper of Irene's dreams on Church Street. A scant year after Russ got this new job, Irene was offered a full-time editorial position at *Heartland Home & Style.* Between the renovation and the new job, she had been so consumed, so *busy,* that she had barely taken notice of the dark side of their good fortune: Russ became less like a man she was married to and more like a man she dated whenever he was in town. But she had liked that, hadn't she? It had been nice to have Russ out from underfoot, to have freedom and autonomy when it came to making decisions about the new house, which was especially sweet since she no longer worried about their finances. Irene had been complicit in the change in their relationship; she had preferred their new situation to the slog of everyday married life. Irene's friends and coworkers asked why Irene never joined Russ on his business trips. He was in Florida, right? Didn't Irene want to enjoy the sun?

Irene used to answer, "I'll join him one of these days! I just need to find the time."

Deep down, she knew she should have been asking Russ questions: How did he like the new job? What were its downsides, its challenges? She should have kept track of where he was on certain days, who his clients were. She should have made plans to travel with him. But she didn't. And that's really all she can say: she didn't.

And so, as much as Irene wants to believe that Russ was an evil, deceptive charlatan with unfathomable secrets, she understands that she was partly to blame.

She is disturbed that Todd Croft made the unilateral decision to cremate Russ's body. He should have asked her permission. He should have given Irene control.

Baker spoke to someone at border control and discovered that because the crash happened in British waters, the British authorities—Virgin Islands Search and Rescue (VISAR), in conjunction with Her Majesty's coast guard—needed to give the FAA the authority to investigate the cause of the crash. But there were loopholes and regulations, as with any bureaucracy.

"I can't tell if they're giving me the runaround or if it's just a lot of red tape," Baker told Irene. "I haven't talked to the same person twice, so I don't have an ally. I did find out that the pilot's name is Stephen Thompson and he was a British citizen. The helicopter apparently belonged to him. So it's a British helicopter with a British pilot that crashed into British waters."

They are essentially being held hostage here as they wait for the ashes and the findings from the crash-site investigation. The only upside is this gives Irene time to do some detective work. She sits down at the desk in Russ's study. There is nothing in any of the drawers but pens and some paper clips, nothing on the shelves but one lonely legal pad. Someone came in and removed everything else.

The phone on Russ's desk works, and once the boys have left, Irene dials the 305 number that Marilyn Monroe called from on Tuesday night. Area code 305, she now knows, is Miami. This, at least, makes a certain kind of sense.

The phone rings three times and Irene's stomach clenches. She will demand to talk to Todd Croft. She deserves answers. She deserves *answers*! What kind of business was Russ involved in? What was going *on* down here? She fears Todd won't tell her.

The phone clicks over to a recording, telling her that the number she has dialed is no longer in service.

No longer in service.

Somehow, Irene isn't surprised.

She tries Paulette's cell phone next but is shuttled right to voicemail. There's a magnet on the refrigerator from the real estate company that provides a phone number.

A woman answers on the first ring. "Afternoon, this is Welcome to Paradise Real Estate, Octavia speaking. How can I help you?"

"Yes, hello," Irene says. "May I please speak to Paulette Vickers?"

"Paulette is out of the office today, I'm afraid," Octavia says. "Would you like her voicemail?"

"It's urgent," Irene says. "Is there any way I might speak to her in person?"

"I'm afraid not," Octavia says. "She's at a funeral. I don't expect her back in the office until tomorrow morning."

Funeral, Irene thinks.

"Okay, Octavia, thank you very much," Irene says, and she hangs up.

Funeral for the local woman, Irene thinks. The local woman who was in the helicopter with Russ and the British pilot, Stephen Thompson, flying at seven o'clock in the morning from St. John to an island in the British Virgin Islands called Anegada. Who was this local woman?

Irene isn't naive. There is no possibility that Russ lived in this house by himself, without a companion, without a woman. Irene thinks back to the day before, when Cash was searching the master bedroom. He told Irene he'd found nothing, but Irene knew he was lying.

Winnie comes banging into the study, panting and wagging her tail, sniffing at Irene's knees. Irene rubs Winnie's soft butterscotch head and says, "Come with me."

She and Winnie enter the master bedroom, and Irene says, "What are we looking for, Winnie? What are we looking for?" She stands in the middle of the room and inhales, trying to divine something, anything, using her intuition. Someone came through the house and cleared it out, sweeping away all of Russ's dirt.

But something—Cash had found something. He had that expression on his face, feigned innocence, like when he used to hide his one-hitter in his varsity soccer jacket, and years before that when he finished an entire box of Girl Scout cookies—Caramel deLites—by himself and then stuffed the box deep in the trash.

Stuffed the box deep in the trash.

Irene looks around the room for hidden nooks and crannies. She checks the drawer of the nightstand: empty.

She sees Winnie nosing the bed. Is she picking up a scent?

Winnie seems pretty interested, nearly insistent, her nose working into the gap between the mattress and the box spring.

"What are you doing?" Irene asks. She lifts the white matelassé coverlet—she has to admit there is a freshness to the decor of this house that is a nice alternative to the heavy, dark furnishings of home—and slips her hand under the mattress. Bingo. She feels the edge of something.

She pulls out a frame. A photograph.

Oh.

Oh no. God, no.

Irene sits on the bed, her hands shaking.

The photograph is of Russ with a beautiful young West Indian woman. They're lying in a hammock, their limbs intertwined. The woman's skin is the color of coffee with cream, and next to her Russ is golden, glowing. He looks healthy.

He looks happy.

Irene lets out a moan. She can't believe the agony she feels. Russ had another woman, a lover. More than a lover: Irene can tell from the ease and familiarity of their pose, from Russ's smile, from the woman's eyes shining. They were together, a pair, a couple. They were in love.

Irene wants to smash the glass. She wants to go onto the balcony and throw the offending photograph as far as she can into the tropical bushes below.

But she needs it. It's evidence.

Irene is mortified to think that Cash has seen this photo, this proof of his father's secret life. It conveys failure—on Russ's part, certainly, but also on Irene's part. She wasn't sexy, desirable, or enticing enough to have kept her husband happy at home. This photograph is proof.

Irene screams until she feels her voice reach its ragged

edge. It feels so indulgent, so childish, but it's also the release she's been waiting for. Russ was *cheating* on her, living with someone young and beautiful, having sex with her, laughing with her, kissing her, eating meals with her, curling up in a hammock with her, falling asleep next to her. For how long? For years, Irene has to assume. Every single time he told her he was "working" in Florida or God knows where else, he was here, in this house, with this woman. The depth of Russ's lies takes Irene's breath away. Hundreds of lies, *thousands* of lies. He had professed his love for Irene daily, every single time she spoke to him on the phone. He had told her he loved her so often, she had stopped hearing it. She thinks of the airplane he hired to drag a banner around Iowa City on her fiftieth birthday. At the time, Irene had been embarrassed by that blatant show of devotion. What she hadn't realized, of course, was that Russ was trying to compensate. He hadn't hired the airplane because he loved Irene and wanted everyone to know it; he'd hired it because he felt guilty.

And did this woman know? Irene wonders. Did she know that Russ was married and had two sons? Did she know that he lived in a Victorian house in Iowa City, Iowa? Had Russ shown her pictures of Irene? It's too heinous to contemplate. Irene cries, she *wails,* and Winnie starts to bark, but Irene can't stop. She's grateful that the boys are gone so she can just let go. She was such a trusting fool.

She thinks back on the many hours that she spent comforting Lydia when Lydia found out that her husband, Phil, philandering Phil, was cheating on her. Phil worked as the head of security for the University of Iowa. One night, he answered a call from a freshman named Natalie Mercer, who was receiving calls on her dorm room phone. The caller kept saying he was watching her, he could see what she was wearing, he was coming to get her when she least expected it. Irene could remember Lydia relaying these terrifying details to her, back when Natalie Mercer was a faceless university student. Phil ended up catching the guy, a doctoral candidate in psychiatry, of all things. He was expelled from the school and this was, in theory, a happy ending. Peace was restored; Phil was a hero. But then, over a year later, when Lydia sensed the temperature of her marriage cooling to a suspicious low, she did some snooping—and what did she find? Phil's cell phone documenting a lurid affair with Natalie Mercer that dated all the way back to the day Phil caught the caller.

Irene remembers feeling disgusted with Phil, but also—in her most private thoughts—a bit incredulous that Phil had been conducting an affair for over a year and Lydia hadn't noticed.

Compared to what Russ has done, Phil having an affair with a student seems almost quaint.

Irene and Russ were married at the First Presbyterian Church in Iowa City in 1984, when they were fresh out of college. They had been together for a scant year and a half, since that football game in the blizzard. Russ's father, the navy pilot, was dead by then, but Milly was there to represent the family. Milly and Irene had hit it off from the moment they met. Because Russ had grown up in so many places, he didn't have any longtime childhood friends or neighbors or members of the community attending the wedding, the way Irene did. He had Milly and Milly's two sisters—Bobbie and Cissy, whom Russ called "the aunties"—and there were also a bunch of Russ's friends and fraternity brothers from Northwestern. Nothing about Russ's background had seemed unusual, and certainly not sinister.

Irene and Russ had said their vows and kissed at the altar.

There had been a reception at the Elks Lodge, where they ate filet mignon and cut the cake and danced to "Little Red Corvette," and then after the reception, Irene and Russ ran through a shower of rice to get to the getaway car. They drove to the Hancock House, a bed-and-breakfast in Dubuque, Iowa, where they were given a suite with a library, and a claw-foot tub in front of a fireplace in the bathroom, and it was in this moment that Irene fell in love with the style and decor of Queen Anne houses. She said to Russ, "I want us to live in a house just like this one."

Russ had laughed nervously. They were renting a one-bedroom apartment in University City. They were kids. They had, Irene sees now, barely known each other then, the newly minted Mr. and Mrs. Russell Steele.

Irene had grown to know Russ the only way it could be done—by putting in the time. She had learned how Russ liked his coffee, how he liked his eggs, the way he brushed his teeth, the sound of his snoring, the habits of other drivers that made him angry, the actors he admired and found funny, the way he whistled "Penny Lane," only that song, when he was doing small home improvement projects. Irene knew his shoe size, his jacket size, his waist and inseam measurements. She knew how he had voted in every election. She knew his first, second, and third favorite flavor of ice cream. She knew he would get forty pages into a book and then abandon it, no matter how good it was. She knew that he had spent his childhood as a constant outsider because he moved so often. She also knew he never felt like his father loved him. Russ's father was a military man, a fortress, with a mind and heart that were impossible to penetrate. Irene knew that, because of his father, Russ had never wanted to serve in the military. In fact, if Irene were to disclose Russ's biggest secret, it was that he had sabotaged his chances of getting into the U.S. Naval Academy by intentionally missing his interview.

That, as it turns out, was not his biggest secret.

Irene howls. There are so many thoughts that pierce her, not least of which is her own blindness, her own myopia, her own pathetic, middle-class, middle America view that marriages are meant to last forever, through the bad times, through the boring times. They were Russ and Irene Steele, parents of Baker and Cash, owner of the stunning Victorian on Church Street. They were good, God-fearing, straightforward people. Not people with scandalous secrets.

Finally, Irene stops crying. She wears herself out. She must have worn Winnie out as well, because Winnie has fallen asleep in a sunny spot on the floor.

Irene regards the photograph. Russ has a lover, an island girl. It seems less awful than it did forty minutes earlier. One thing Irene has learned in her fifty-seven years is that no matter how hideous something seems at first, with the passing of time comes habituation and then acceptance. What Irene is living through now is abhorrent. But the world is filled with deceptions and betrayals—nearly every life has one—and yet the sun still rises and sets, the world continues on.

She sits up. The water out the window seems to wink at her, and not in a wicked, I-seduced-your-husband sort of way but in a benevolent way.

What did Paulette say? Eighty steps down to a private beach. Okay.

* * *

Irene decides to go barefoot. The stone steps turn to wood, they meander down the side of the hill until the vegetation clears and Irene steps onto a tiny, perfect crescent of white sand beach. The sand is like sugar, like flour, like talcum. She stoops to pick some up and rub it between her fingers. Is it real? Yes.

There are three teak chaises on the beach with bright orange cushions. Irene tries to imagine Russ lying on one of these chaises, with his girlfriend next to him. *And who would the third chaise be for?* she wonders.

Today it's for Irene. She lies back in the sun, absorbing the heat, which feels like a miracle after the icy winds of Iowa City. She can't stay here long, just another minute; wrinkles are multiplying on her face by the second, she's certain. Her breathing is almost back to normal. Her eyes are sore but dry.

Russ had a lover.

Deep breath.

Okay.

Irene gets up and walks to the water's edge. The color is halfway between blue and green; it's not a color found elsewhere in nature, except, in rare and wonderful cases, in people's eyes. Tiny waves lap at her feet. The water is soft and just cool enough to be refreshing. When Irene had packed, back in Iowa, the idea of bringing a bathing suit had briefly crossed her mind, part of some kind of mental checklist, but she hadn't been able to imagine circumstances in which she would want or need one. She looks both ways. This beach is secluded from view. There are a few boats on the horizon, but no one can see her here.

Irene shucks off her clothes and stands naked on the beach. Is she invisible? She feels quite the opposite. She feels exposed. Let the world see her drooping breasts, the dimpling at her thighs, the cesarean scar eight inches across her lower abdomen.

She steps into the water and all she can think is how good it feels, the coolness enveloping her. She swims out a few yards.

This is the same water that claimed Russ. Russ is dead. That's the next fact Irene has to grapple with. He's gone. He's never coming back. She will never see him again. She can't ask him why he did what he did, where she went wrong, where they both went wrong. She can't scream at him and he can't apologize. There is nowhere to put her fury, no one to answer the question of *why.*

Irene lies back in the water, floating, looking at the cloudless bluebird sky, and thinks, really *thinks,* what it was like for Russ in that helicopter. Irene has never been in a helicopter, but she has a vague notion that it's loud. Russ was probably wearing a headset. Did he see the storm approaching? Did he see flashes of lightning or hear thunder? Was he scared? When the helicopter got hit, did it go into free fall? Was it terrifying? Did Russ have a second or two when he knew they were plummeting, when the earth was getting closer and closer? Did his heart stop? Did he have any thoughts? Did he think about Irene and the boys? And what about impact? Did he burst into flames? Did he lose consciousness? Did he drown?

Irene sets her feet on the firm, sandy bottom and wades toward shore, until her toe hits something solid. She bends down and picks up a smooth gray rock the size of an egg. She drops the stone from hip-height into the water and watches it sink.

Russ's body had been lying at the bottom of the sea like that rock.

Her heart shatters. The tears she cries now aren't of anger

or indignation but of pure sadness. Russ is dead and the woman, his lover, his love, is dead. Dead. Never coming back.

I will forgive them, Irene thinks. *I will make myself forgive them if it's the last thing I do.*

Irene dries off in the sun, puts her clothes back on, and faces the eighty steps she has to climb to get back to the villa.

The woman in the photograph is young, thirty or thirty-five. She must have family, parents. And Irene is going to find out who they are.

AYERS

She wakes up the morning after the funeral hungover, no surprise there. She has to go back to work at La Tapa at four o'clock and she's due to crew a BVI charter on *Treasure Island* the next day. Her best friend is dead but that doesn't change the fact that Ayers has bills to pay.

Maia, she knows, has bravely decided to go back to school on Monday. Gifft Hill is nurturing, a nest, and all of Maia's friends are there. Her teachers will care for her and keep her busy. If she needs to take a break, she'll take a break. If she needs to cry, she'll cry. There's no point staying home to wallow, Maia said, sounding a lot older than twelve.

There's no point staying home to wallow, Ayers thinks, and so she ties up her hiking boots and throws a couple bottles of water and a baggie of trail mix into her small pack and she climbs into her truck.

She drives down the Centerline Road past mile marker five and parks. She's going to hike the Reef Bay Trail today, all the way down and all the way back up. It's not her favorite hike on St. John—it's popular and sometimes overrun with tourists—but it has the payoff of the petroglyphs carved into the rocks at the bottom of the trail, and today Ayers wants to put her eyes on something that has lasted three thousand years.

The first time she hiked this trail, nearly ten years earlier, she was with Rosie. It was their first date.

As Ayers starts down the path, she remembers Rosie asking her, *So what's your story, anyway? Where are you from and how did you end up here?*

As always, Ayers had hesitated before answering. She envied people who had *grown up* someplace—Missoula, Montana; Cleveland, Ohio; Little Rock, Arkansas. Ayers had been homeschooled by her parents, both of whom suffered from an acute case of wanderlust. She had lived in eight countries growing up and had visited dozens of others. To most people, this sounded cool, and in some ways, Ayers knows, it *was* cool, or parts of it were. But since humans are inclined to want what they don't have, she longed to live in America, preferably the solid, unchanging, undramatic Midwest, and attend a real high school, the kind shown in movies, complete with a football team, cheerleaders, pep rallies, chemistry labs, summer reading lists, hall passes, proms, detentions, assemblies, fundraisers, lockers, Spanish clubs, marching bands, and the dismissal bell.

What had she told Rosie? She had told her the unvarnished truth.

My parents were hippies, vagabonds, travelers; we lived out of our backpacks. My father did maintenance at hostels in exchange for a free place to stay, and my mother waited tables for money. We lived in Kathmandu; in Hoi An, Vietnam; in Santiago, Chile. We spent one year traveling across Australia, and when we finally got to Perth, my parents liked it so much I thought we would stay, but then my grandmother got very sick so we went back to San Francisco, where she lived, and I thought we would live in San Francisco because my grandmother left my father money—a lot of money. But the only thing my parents ever wanted to do with money was travel, and so we moved to Europe—Paris first, then Italy, then Greece. We were living in Morocco when I turned eighteen and I had applied to college without their knowledge—Clemson University in South Carolina—and I got in and I went, but I had to pay for it all myself and I worked two jobs in addition to studying, which left me no time for fun. I hated it in the end and so I dropped out and started working the seasonal circuit. I spent my summers in New England—Cape Cod, Newport, the Vineyard—and winters in the Caribbean. I spent last winter in Aruba and a guy I met there told me about St. John. So here I am.

Holy shit, Rosie had said.

I know, Ayers said. *I know.*

Ayers makes it to the bottom of the hill in no time. The trail is steep and rocky but well maintained and shaded by a thick canopy of leaves all the way down, though the sun streams through here and there in a way that turns the air emerald. Ayers is so dehydrated from the night before that she sucks down her first bottle of water in one long pull. She should have brought more than two bottles. What was she thinking? She considers her trail mix. She hasn't eaten much of anything since hearing the news; not even Chester's barbecue appealed to her.

Rosie is dead. When Ayers gets to work at four, Rosie won't be there. Her name will be off the schedule. There will be a new hire by Monday. At La Tapa, Rosie is replaceable. But not with Ayers.

Ayers hikes up to a small outcropping of rocks to see the petroglyphs. They've had rain recently—the thunderstorm that killed Rosie—so the markings in the stone are easy to see. Ayers gets up close and focuses on them. So old. So permanent. Ayers could leave St. John today and come back in fifty years and they would still be here.

Rosie had a tattoo of the petroglyph above her ankle that Ayers had always admired. *Get one,* Rosie had said. *We can match.* But Ayers had felt funny about appropriating the symbol as her own. She hadn't *grown* up here; she had merely *shown* up here. She somehow didn't think she had earned it.

Maybe now, though.

One of the rogue thoughts Ayers has entertained in the past few days is that of leaving. Without Mick and without Rosie, she wondered, what's the point?

The point, she supposes, is that St. John is as much of a home as she has ever had.

Besides, there's Maia to consider now. Ayers can't leave Maia. If Ayers is going to make a change, it should be the opposite of leaving. She needs to stay here through the year—endure the hot summer, pray through hurricane season.

There's only one other person at the petroglyphs, a guy with bushy blond hair and a gorgeous golden retriever. He looks like a hard-core hiker: he's wearing cargo shorts and a pair of Salomon boots. He's studying the petroglyphs with an intensity that discourages conversation, but the dog runs right over to Ayers and buries her nose in Ayers's crotch.

"Aw, sweetheart," Ayers says. She pries the dog's snout from between her legs.

"Winnie!" the hiker calls out. Ayers looks up and he smiles. "I'm sorry. I sent her to finishing school but still she has no manners."

"Not a problem," Ayers says. "That's the most action I've gotten in weeks."

The hiker blushes and Ayers congratulates herself on being truly inappropriate. Then she takes a closer look at him. She has seen this guy before, but where?

"Do I know you?" she asks.

"No, I don't think so," the hiker says. "I just got here a couple days..." His voice trails off. "Oh, wait."

Wait, Ayers thinks. She assumed he'd come into the restaurant or maybe even been a guest on *Treasure Island*, but no, she met him *yesterday,* at the reception. "Yeah," Ayers says. "I... you... were at Chester's, right? With...?"

"My brother," the hiker says. "Baker."

"Right," Ayers says. "Baker." She had liked Baker. He was super-handsome, tall, charming. She had thought maybe she had actually *met a man* at Rosie's funeral reception. She had thought maybe he'd been a gift from Rosie.

But Baker was a tourist and Ayers tried to stay away from tourists. This was advice she had received from Rosie. Thirteen years earlier, Rosie had hooked up with a guy who sailed in on a yacht, stayed for four days, and then left. *The Pirate,* she called him. She had never seen him again. He was Maia's father.

"Anyway, I'm Cash," the hiker says, offering his hand. "As in Johnny."

"Ayers," she says. "As in Rock."

"And this is Winnie," Cash says. "As in the Pooh."

"So you found the petroglyphs," Ayers says. "What about Baker? He didn't make it?"

"He's not much of a hiker," Cash says. "He was by the pool when I left."

"Pool?" Ayers says. "Where are you guys staying? The Westin? Caneel?"

"Villa," Cash says.

"Nice," Ayers says. "North shore?"

"I'm really not sure," Cash says. He whistles to Winnie. "We should get back, though."

"Are you catching the boat?" Ayers asks. "Or hiking back up?"

"Hiking back up," Cash says. "I didn't realize there was a boat."

"You have to set it up with the park service," Ayers says. "Or maybe it picks up at certain times. I used to know, but I've forgotten." She shakes her head and, much to her chagrin, she starts to cry. "My best friend died a few days ago in a helicopter crash. That party you and Baker stumbled upon was her funeral reception..."

"I know," Cash says. He's carrying a small pack and he pulls out a navy bandana and an ice-cold bottle of water. He offers both to Ayers.

She accepts them gratefully. "I'm sorry," she says. "I heard it would be like this. You're fine one minute and not fine the next. It's just...I came down here to see the petroglyphs because Rosie loved them. She had this tattoo..." Ayers struggles for a breath. "She was just so pretty and so *cool,* such a good friend, my only friend, really, the best friend I've ever had. My parents…we never *stayed* anywhere. I would make a friend in Chiang Mai or Isla Holbox and then we'd *leave*…" She wipes her eyes with the bandana and takes a much-needed swig of water. "I'm babbling. This awful, horrible thing happened and now I'm bemoaning my entire existence." She tries to smile. "And you're a complete stranger."

"It's okay," Cash says. "Believe me, I understand being shell-shocked." He looks like he might say more but instead, he shakes his head. "It's just…I *do* understand."

That's not likely, but Ayers isn't going to argue. "Do you want to hike back up together?" she asks. "I have to get back, too. I have work at four o'clock."

"Sure," Cash says.

"Good," Ayers says. "I'm also worried about passing out on the way back up. I only brought one other bottle of water."

Cash grins. "Ah, the truth comes out. You need me to keep you alive."

He's cute, Ayers decides. Not rock star handsome like his brother, but cute. Compact, strong, sturdy.

But again, a tourist.

They start back up the trail, Cash leading, Winnie at his heels, Ayers following. Up is way harder, her hangover is gripping her head like a tight bathing cap. She has to stop and when Cash turns around to check on her—he's very sweet to do so—he stops, too.

"You seem like a pretty experienced hiker," Ayers says.

"I live in the mountains," Cash says. "Breckenridge, Colorado. Being at sea level is new for me. Honestly, I could probably go forever without getting tired. It's amazing how nice life is with an adequate supply of oxygen."

"Yeah," Ayers says. "I guess I take it for granted." That wasn't always the case, though. She and her parents had trekked to Everest Base Camp when Ayers was thirteen. The air in the Himalayas was thin; Ayers had crazy dreams that she still remembers to this day. She and her parents spent weeks hiking in Patagonia as well. She remembers sinking to her knees in scree, scrabbling over rocks, jumping down into her father's arms off a high ledge, eating ramen noodles cooked over a camp stove for days on end, waking up at three in the morning to see the sunrise set the Torres del Paine on fire. When they finally came out of the mountains, they stayed in a town called San Carlos de Bariloche, where they took hot showers and ate a breakfast of pancakes drizzled with chocolate sauce and a big bowl of fresh, ripe strawberries.

"So do you ski?" Ayers asks Cash. He's too far ahead for casual conversation, but Ayers wants him to know she's a normal person and not just some emotional basket case.

"I do," he says. "Do you?"

"I do. Haven't been in a while but my parents and I lived in Gstaad one winter so I got pretty good. I miss it." She gazes up into the trees. "You might not think it living here, but sometimes I really miss the snow."

"I've only been here three days and I miss it," Cash says.

"So you live in Colorado and your brother lives in Texas?" Ayers says. "And you're here for a family reunion?" She's proud of herself for remembering.

"Family reunion?" Cash says. "Is that what Baker told you?"

Is that what Baker told her? Yes, she's pretty sure that's what he said. "Um . . . ?"

"I guess it is a family reunion of sorts," Cash says. "He's

right." With that, Cash seems to pick up his pace and Ayers takes the hint: he doesn't want to talk. Fair enough. She should conserve her energy and use it for making it up the hill.

This had been a stupid idea.

Once they reach the road, however, Ayers drinks the last of her water and eats a handful of the trail mix and immediately feels a sense of accomplishment. She didn't stay home and wallow. She hiked the Reef Bay Trail, wildly hungover.

"Want some trail mix?" she asks Cash.

He helps himself to a handful. "Thank you." He seems to perk up a little as well. "I don't want to pry, but your friend who died...do they know what happened?"

"Helicopter crash," Ayers says.

"I heard that," Cash says. "But do they know why? Or where she was going?"

"She was going over to Anegada for the day with her... boyfriend. The helicopter got struck by lightning."

"They both died?" Cash asks.

Ayers nods. "And the pilot."

"Do they know anything about the boyfriend?" Cash asks. "Does he have a family?"

"I don't care about the boyfriend," Ayers says. "At this point, I wish Rosie had never met him." Her voice is sharper than she meant it to be. "I'm sorry, bad topic. Listen, how long are you here?"

Cash looks at the ground. "Another couple of days, I guess," he says.

"Well, if you're free tomorrow, I'm crewing on a boat called

Treasure Island, and we're going on a day trip to the British Virgin Islands—the Baths on Virgin Gorda, snorkeling, lunch on Cooper Island. It's fun and I can bring you as my guest. Do you have a passport?"

"I do," Cash says. "I'm embarrassed to admit that I thought I might need it to come here. I wasn't sure. This trip was kind of thrown together at the last minute."

"If you have a passport, then you should definitely come," Ayers says. "Have you ever snorkeled before?"

"I haven't," Cash says. "I want to. But my mother might need my help tomorrow." He bends down to pat Winnie's head.

"Well, if you decide you want to come, just bring your passport and wear a bathing suit and come to the dock right across the street from Mongoose Junction at seven thirty tomorrow morning. I'll take care of everything else."

"Okay," Cash says. "I'll think about it." He waves as he leads Winnie back to his Jeep.

He'll think about it but he won't do it, Ayers knows. He thinks she's nuts.

And he's probably right.

CASH

There's no way Cash is going on a snorkeling trip to the BVIs, and yet he keeps thinking about Ayers and about the invitation.

Ayers is pretty, there are no two ways about it, and she was out *biking by herself,* which turned Cash on in a big way. He had thought Denver and Breckenridge would be filled with women who loved the outdoors—who liked to hike and cross-country and downhill ski—and whereas that was sort of true, none of the outdoorsy women Cash had met had struck a chord with him.

None of them had been anything like Ayers.

And Winnie had been crazy about her. A good sign.

Cash doesn't tell Baker or his mother where he's been or who he's seen, and they don't ask. His mother had taken the other Jeep and gone into Cruz Bay—for what reason, Cash couldn't imagine. She sure as hell wasn't shopping for silver bracelets or bottles of rum. And Baker was being positively useless. He'd made two or three calls to the British authorities before declaring himself stonewalled, and so he'd spent the day "waiting for callbacks," which meant sitting by the pool, staring out at the spectacular view. He didn't even seem sad to Cash. Or maybe he was sad and just hiding it—which is exactly what Cash is doing. Cash wants to cry—to put his fist through a wall or break a vase, he wants to lose his shit, exorcise the bad feelings. But the problem is that his emotions are muddy. He's not purely sad about losing his father. Nor is he purely angry that his father was a wizard of deception. His feelings are a toxic combination of both, and to head off an explosion or tantrum, he is utilizing good, old-fashioned denial. Hence the hike today.

Cash takes an outdoor shower. The walls are encrusted with shells—conch, whelk, cowrie—and there's purple bougainvillea draping in overhead, and the water is hot and plentiful, and Cash has a view of the water. He decides it probably qualifies as the best shower he's ever taken. He gets dressed as the sun sets, then he offers to grill up some steaks.

Irene says she isn't hungry. "I think I'll go up to bed."

"Do you want me to call Milly, Mom?" Cash asks. "Just to, you know, check in?"

Irene turns around on the stairs and gives Cash a plaintive look. "Would you mind?" she asks. "I can't lie to Milly. I just can't do it. You know, she did a good job with your father. This isn't her fault. I don't ever want you to think that."

"I *don't* think that," Cash says. "Dad was a grown man."

"I'm beginning to wonder," Irene says.

"I'll call Milly," Cash says.

He dials the number for the Brown Deer retirement community, but the nurse who answers in the medical unit tells him that Milly is too weak to talk.

"What do you mean too *weak*?" he asks. "Is everything okay?"

"She's ninety-seven years old," the nurse says. "Her body is shutting down."

"Well, right," Cash says. "I know, but..."

"Call back tomorrow, Mr. Steele," the nurse says. "Until then, enjoy your vacation."

Cash and Baker eat steak and potato salad out on the deck. Cash knows he should tell Baker he saw Ayers, and he should tell Baker about Milly not being strong enough to come to the phone, and he should really tell Baker about losing the stores. But before he can broach any of these topics, Baker says, "So Mom told me she has a meeting tomorrow."

"A meeting?" Cash says. "With whom?"

"She wouldn't tell me," Baker says. "She came back from town and when I asked how it went she said it was productive and that she has a meeting tomorrow."

"What time?" Cash asks.

"In the morning," Baker says. "She wasn't sure how long it would take."

"Are you worried?" Cash asks.

"No," Baker says. "It's Mom."

Right, Cash thinks. They have never had to worry about Irene in the past. But now...things have changed, haven't they?

"What are you doing tomorrow?" Cash asks.

"Same thing I did today," Baker says. "Waiting for the phone to ring, but it's Sunday so I'm sure nothing will happen. I would like to get out tomorrow night, though. What do you think about that? I want to eat at La Tapa."

"La Tapa?" Cash says.

"Do you remember that girl, Ayers?" Baker asks. "From the reception?"

Cash's heart starts bobbing up and down. Yes. Ayers. Yes. He tries to keep his expression neutral. "Yeah, why?"

"She works there," Baker says. "And I want to see her again."

"See her why?" Cash asks.

"Because she was Rosie's best friend," Baker says. "She has information."

Cash clears the plates. Ayers *was* Rosie's best friend and she possibly *does* have information, but Cash gets a very strong feeling that that *isn't* why Baker wants to see Ayers again.

You're *married*! He wants to snap. To *Anna*!

But instead, Cash makes a decision. He's going to the British Virgin Islands tomorrow.

Cash avoids group tours for a reason: they turn even the most authentic experiences into a Disneyland ride. It's unavoidable, he supposes. This tour company, Treasure Island, which takes a group of twenty people on a three-stop adventure to another country, needs to make the experience safe and user-friendly. And fun!

"Most of all," Ayers says over her headset microphone to the assembled group, after explaining where the life preservers are kept, how to disembark at the Baths of Virgin Gorda (they have to jump off the boat and swim to shore), and how to defog one's mask for maximum snorkeling visibility, "we want you to have fun. In that spirit, the bar is now open. Come get your painkillers."

Painkillers, Cash thinks. *If only.* And yet he finds himself shuffling to the bar behind a big fat guy in a HARLEY-DAVIDSON OF SOUTH DAKOTA t-shirt. There's nothing wrong with this guy or any of the other couples or families aboard the boat, except that they are taking up Ayers's time and attention. It's like she's running a day care, Cash thinks. *Everyone* has questions: What if they aren't a strong enough swimmer to make it to the shore in Virgin Gorda? Will there be gluten-free options at lunch? Is it true that the Baths have been spoiled by too much tourism? Will there be sharks? What about barracudas?

Ayers answers all the questions, and Cash surreptitiously hangs on her every word while he sips his painkiller (it's rum, cream of coconut, pineapple juice, and orange juice, with nutmeg on top). He had to go online and look up what the Virgin Gorda Baths even *were*—when Ayers said it yesterday, he pictured a cavernous building populated by overweight Slavic men—so he knows it's a rock formation that has created various "rooms" that can be toured. After the Baths, they're stopping at Cooper Island for lunch, and on the way home they'll snorkel at a spot called the Indians.

"How're you doing?" Ayers has caught him back in line for a second painkiller; the first one went down way too easily on an empty stomach, and he knows that after his second, he should avail himself of the fresh sliced papaya, watermelon, and pineapple as well as a piece of the homemade banana coconut bread. Otherwise he's going to be one of the people who doesn't make it to shore.

When is the last time I did any real swimming? he wonders. Junior-year gym class at Iowa City High School?

"I'm good," he says. He knows he should engage some of his fellow adventurers in conversation—there's a gay couple about his age who look nice—so that Ayers doesn't think he's a snob or socially awkward. Cash has been too busy feeling jealous about Ayers's relationships with her two male crew members: James, the captain, and Wade, the first mate. James is a West Indian guy built like a Greek god and Wade must be a retired Hollister model. Both of them call Ayers "baby," and when Cash first arrived at the dock, he saw Ayers and James hugging, but then he realized James was offering his condolences. Still, Cash is discomfited by the physical attractiveness of the crew; it seems designed to make Cash and his fellow adventurers feel unremarkable.

"I'm sorry I don't have time to chill with you right now," Ayers says. "It'll be different on the ride home."

"No worries," Cash says. "I'm a big boy."

Ayers gives him a nice smile, one that targets his heart. Has he ever reacted this way to a woman? Geez, not since ninth grade with Claire Bellows, who ended up being his girlfriend all through high school until she went off to Northwestern, where she proceeded to hook up with Baker. His own brother. That had been devastating, Cash won't lie, and it had led to Cash hating Baker and being very mistrustful of women. Since then, Cash's romantic life has consisted of weeklong hookups and one-night stands, usually with the women he was teaching to ski.

Cash takes his second painkiller to the upper deck and chooses a seat near the gay couple. The sun feels good, and there is something about being out on the water that reminds Cash of standing at the top of a mountain. It's elemental, he supposes, communing with the earth. Ayers, over her headset microphone, gives the group some background history—the Danish settlers, the sugar plantation, the slave revolt in which African slaves from St. John swam to the British Virgin Islands to freedom. She points out Lovango Cay, where there used to be a brothel for pirates—the pirates called it "love and go," which was then shortened to Lovango; everyone laughs at that story. Ayers shifts her focus to Jost Van Dyke, home of the world-famous bar the Soggy Dollar (Cash has never heard of it), then to Tortola, on their left, and the "sister islands"—Peter, Norman, Cooper, Salt, and Ginger—on their right. Cash goes downstairs for another painkiller, and when he comes back up to the deck, he says to one of the members of the male couple (tall, balding, pale), "So is this your first time to the BVIs?"

"Affirmative," the other man (short, dark) says. "Chris's parents just bought a timeshare at the Westin so we thought we'd come down to see what the fuss is about. How about you?"

Cash needs to pick a story and stick to it. "Here for a week with my mom and my brother. Family reunion."

Chris says, "Did they come with you?"

"No," Cash says.

"My kind of family reunion!" the short, dark-haired guy says, and the three of them do a cheer.

Thanks to another painkiller or three (Could Cash really have had five drinks already? It's not even ten in the morning), the morning passes quickly, with soft, blurred edges. Once they reach Virgin Gorda, Cash's anxiety about jumping off the boat and swimming to shore melts away. He's an athletic guy, in good shape—that should count for something—and sure enough, he makes it with ease. Ayers leads the tour through the Baths. They're not like anything Cash has ever seen: huge granite boulders that form a series of rooms and formations with shallow pools of warm turquoise water in each. They start out viewing the Whale Gallery—a rock that looks like an orca shooting out of the water—then move on to the Lion's Den and Moon rock. Cash's favorite room is called the Cathedral because of the way the light reflects off the water, spangling the rocks with color and making it look like stained glass. Ayers not only offers charming commentary, she is attentive to the older and less agile members of the group who have difficulty negotiating the rough-hewn wooden steps and squeezing through narrow passageways. Cash helps out wherever he can, offering his hand and allowing a little girl, five or six years old, to jump down into his arms. He feels like a Boy Scout, but then again, he *was* a Boy Scout.

Ayers whispers in his ear. "Want a job?"

Does he want a job? Only five days ago, Cash made what he thought was a major life decision to return to the mountains. Now his father is dead and Cash's "life," or what's left of it, has been turned on its head. What remains that is solid and reliable? Winnie. His mother. In a pinch, he supposes, his brother. There's nothing to stop Cash from moving down here and working for Treasure Island. He could live in his father's villa. As outrageous as the thought is, it holds appeal. He realizes that Ayers is only kidding, but what if she's *not* kidding?

He's drunk, he needs to slow down, but when Chris and Mike ask him if he wants to join them for a beer—there's a bar at the exit of the Baths, of course—he says yes.

He has never before seen the appeal of day-drinking. Lots of people drink while skiing; many, many folks choose to do two or three runs and then hit the bar. Cash likes his daytime hours to be productive, and so he saves his drinking for the evening, which is probably a legacy of his strait-laced midwestern upbringing. Now, however, he understands how liberating it is to get intoxicated while the sun is out. It feels decadent in the best possible way. The world seems alternately kind, forgiving, absurd, and hilarious.

"You can't drink all day if you don't start in the morning," he says to Chris and Mike. "Am I right?"

* * *

They leave Virgin Gorda and motor to Cooper Island, where there is an eco-resort with a restaurant that serves large groups like theirs. Cash orders the blackened fish sandwich with fries, and Chris and Mike do likewise. They inform Cash with a certain solemn righteousness that they're pescatarians, which Cash hears as "Presbyterians," and he says, "I'm Presbyterian, too, though I hardly ever go to church anymore." This statement cracks Chris and Mike up and Cash is nonplussed until they explain that *pescatarian* means they eat only fish—no meat or chicken. Then Cash dissolves into laughter that he can't recover from. Every time he lifts his head to take a breath, he doubles over again.

"You look like you're enjoying yourself," Ayers says. She lifts Cash's rum punch and takes a discreet sip. "I'm not supposed to imbibe until after the snorkeling."

Cash tries to sober up a little. He introduces Chris and Mike to Ayers, and then their food arrives and it turns out there's a fish sandwich for Ayers as well, which she douses with hot sauce.

"God, I love"—Cash stops. He nearly says, "you," but he catches himself—"a woman who enjoys spicy food."

"Rosie loved spicy food," Ayers says. "And she could cook, too. She made the best jerk chicken. Mmmmmm."

Cash knows he should capitalize on the topic of Rosie, since Ayers brought her up, but he's too intoxicated to think it through strategically and he feels it would be awkward to include Chris and Mike in the conversation and rude to exclude them. He takes a bite of his own sandwich. It's delicious.

Food, he thinks. He needs food.

* * *

After lunch, they head to the Indians, three rock towers jutting from the sea, where they anchor to snorkel. Cash is feeling slightly more in charge of his faculties after eating, but he continues to drink because he doesn't want to risk becoming hungover.

Ayers puts her headset microphone back on and explains the rules of snorkeling—where they can go, where they can't go, what they can expect to see. "This is the best snorkeling in the Virgin Islands," she says. "You'll see it all—parrot fish, angelfish, spotted eagle rays, sea turtles, maybe even a basking shark. The sharks aren't dangerous to humans, but I'd advise you to leave them alone nonetheless. The only thing you need to worry about is the fire coral—it's easily identifiable by its bright orange branches—and if you rub up against it, you will develop a very painful burning rash. The other danger is sea urchins. The sea urchins have sharp black spines. Please do not touch or, God forbid, *stand on* any of the coral. James and Wade and I aren't just here to make a buck, people. We're here to educate you about the natural beauty of these islands and to spread awareness about just how precious and unique this eco-system is."

I love her, Cash thinks. She's everything he has ever wanted in a woman.

Once Cash is in his flippers, with his mask secured around his head and his snorkel poised a couple inches from his mouth, he feels like a world-class fool. Does everyone else feel this way? People seem excited, maybe a little anxious—there's nothing like jumping into shark-infested waters to inspire camaraderie—but generally the mood is positive, expectant.

It's all Cash can do not to just leap off the side of the boat rather than wait his turn to go down the ladder. Once he's in the water, he should be fine. He thinks back on the hundreds of people he has taught to ski. He recalls one girl in her twenties—a nanny for one of the fancy families with a house on Peak 7—who stared right into Cash's eyes and with the purest fear Cash has ever witnessed said, "I'm terrified."

And guess what? She had made it down the mountain just fine.

Cash waits his turn behind Chris and Mike, who look like frogs that mated with ducks, and then he lowers himself down the ladder into the turquoise water. He fits the snorkel into his mouth, takes a few breaths—all clear—and then lowers his head and swims behind his fellow adventurers.

How to describe what he sees?

He can't believe it's real. There's an entire universe under the surface of the water. The coral—purple, orange, greenish-yellow—are like buildings or mountains. Fish are everywhere: The parrot fish are shimmering rainbows, there are black angelfish with electric blue stripes, schools of silvery fish that are as flat as coins, all of them swimming along, pecking here and there at the coral. It's astonishing that all this exists in pristine condition and that regular people like himself, without skills or specialized knowledge, can observe it. Why isn't everyone in the world talking about how *remarkable* this is? Why isn't a snorkeling trip to the Indians number one on everyone's bucket list? He's drunk, yes he is, but he's also blessed with a brand-new clarity. He is alive, on planet Earth, experiencing a natural wonder.

He lifts his head. Above the surface, life is the same. There's the coast of St. John in the distance, there's the boat a few hundred yards away. Cash likes the way his flippers give him buoyancy. He's barely treading water but he has no problem staying afloat.

Suddenly, there's someone next to him in a black mask. It's Ayers, he realizes. She's wearing a green tank suit, very simple and, on her, incredibly sexy. She takes his hand. They're holding hands? Or no, she wants him to swim alongside her. She wants to show him something. What? They swim for what seems like a while—away from everyone, away from the boat—then she points. On the smooth, sandy bottom, Cash sees a gargantuan silver platter with wings that ripple. It's a manta ray, gliding elegantly along the ocean floor. It's huge, way bigger than Cash expected.

Ayers stops to tread water and Cash does the same. She removes her snorkel.

"That's Luther," she says. "He's the biggest ray in the VIs. Five feet, two inches in diameter. He lives out here."

"Luther is . . . wow," Cash says.

"Let's follow him," Ayers says.

They trail Luther for a while, then Ayers makes a sharp turn—she must have seen something—and Cash kicks like crazy in an attempt to keep up. She's chasing what looks like a shark—it's sleek, silver, menacing. She takes off her silver hook bracelet and waggles it at him and he comes charging for it, then Ayers yanks it away and he darts past her.

Cash lifts his head. "What are you *doing*?"

She laughs. "Barracuda," she says. "A baby. He's harmless." She swims back in the direction of the boat and Cash follows.

They're back on the boat, headed home. Cash is bone-tired but energized. What a great day. What a transformative day. He's a convert: he loves the tropics.

"You're allowed to drink now, right?" Cash asks Ayers. She

nods and he grabs two rum punches from the bar and follows her to a bench on the shady side of the wheelhouse. The shade is a relief. He might be a convert in his heart and mind, but his skin is still that of his Scottish and Norwegian ancestors. He has been reapplying sunscreen every hour, but he's still pretty sure he's going to have a wicked sunburn.

He hands Ayers a rum punch and they touch cups. Ayers is wearing silver-rimmed, blue-lens aviators and her feet are resting up on the railing. She looks exhausted.

"To a job well done," Cash says. He takes a sip of his drink, his twentieth of the day. "You know, it's not so different from my job as a ski instructor."

"Aside from being completely different, not so different at all," she says. Together they look at the tired, sun-scorched, happy people below them on the deck—some snoozing, others forging bonds that will last all the way to the bar at Woody's, or the rest of the week or a lifetime. Cash has Chris's and Mike's numbers and promised to call them if he ever finds himself in Brooklyn, which secretly he hopes he never does.

Ayers sucks down the rum punch and seems to both relax and pep up. "You liked it, right?"

"Loved it," he says. "Can't thank you enough."

"Well, you basically saved my life yesterday by sharing your water. And you gave me your bandana. And you were nice to me when I was sad."

"Like I said, I understand."

Ayers leans her head on his shoulder. At the same time that he's experiencing pure ecstasy at her touch, he realizes she's crying again.

He hands her his damp cocktail napkin; it's all he has. "I'm happy to give you my shirt," he says.

She laughs through her tears. "I'm sorry," she says. "It's all lurking there, right below the surface. But I have to sublimate it. This job requires me to be peppy. I'm not allowed to be a human being, a thirty-one-year-old woman who lost her best friend." She sniffs and wipes at her reddened nose with the napkin. "At my other job it's different, because Rosie worked there with me, so we all lost her and every single person on the staff knows how close we were, so even though I have to smile while I'm serving, when I need a break I can hide in the kitchen and cry and do a shot of tequila with the line cooks."

Cash feels a surge of jealousy about the line cooks. He wants to ask if Ayers has a boyfriend or is married. He could be getting carried away for no reason. But instead, he asks if Ayers has a picture of Rosie.

"A picture of Rosie?" Ayers says.

"Yeah," Cash says. "I'd like to see what she looks like." It has occurred to him since their conversation yesterday that Ayers's friend Rosie might not be the same woman in the photograph with Russ. It would be better, so much better, if Rosie Small weren't Russ's lover. They would both still be dead, but maybe just friends or colleagues. It would be so much easier.

Ayers pulls out her phone. "Here," she says. "She's my screen saver." She hands Cash the phone.

On the left is Ayers in a canary-yellow bikini on a beach next to a tree that supports a tire swing. On the right is Rosie, the same woman in the photograph with Cash's father. She's wearing a white bikini and beaming at the camera.

"She's really pretty," Cash says. "Though not as pretty as you, of course."

"Oh, please," Ayers says. She tucks her phone back into the pocket of her shorts. "You know, I want to apologize about being short with you yesterday...when you asked about Rosie's boyfriend."

Cash holds his breath. *We don't have to talk about it,* he wants to say. When he'd registered for the trip, he'd been glad that Wade was handling the paperwork and not Ayers, because he didn't want Ayers to see his last name and make the connection.

He needs to tell her who he is, but he doesn't want her to know who he is. And he certainly can't tell her *now,* while she's at *work.*

"You don't have to apologize..."

"He was rich," Ayers says. "Some rich asshole who showed up every couple of weeks and completely monopolized Rosie's time, but that wasn't the problem. The problem was that he had this shroud of secrecy around him. They'd been together for six years and I'd never met him. And I was her best friend. The first few years I accused her of making him up, that's how bad it was. But he was always giving her things—silver bracelets, money, a new Jeep. He almost never left his property, and they never entertained or invited anyone over."

"Maybe he was hiding something," Cash says. "Maybe he was married."

"Maybe?" Ayers says. "Of *course* he was married. But the one time I brought it up, Rosie flipped out and wouldn't speak to me for three days. So that was the last time I mentioned it. She was two people, really: a very strong and independent woman, on the one hand—feisty, fierce, even. But when it came to the Invisible Man, she was a goner. She was so... blinded by him. So...in love, I guess you'd have to say."

"Well, then," Cash says. "He couldn't have been all bad." He tries a smile. "Right?"

HUCK

On Sunday, Huck cancels both of his charters. He'll reschedule them for the following week. Today, he just wants to go out on the water by himself, maybe see if there's any truth to Cleve's school-of-mahi story. He still has the coordinates written down, saved from New Year's Eve.

Back when Rosie was alive.

It's a cruel trick of the world, a person alive and well one minute, thinking harm will never come her way, and then dead the next.

Huck doesn't get as early a start as he would have liked, because he has to drive Maia over to Joanie's house. They are planning on starting a bath bomb business. They want to make bath bombs in tropical scents and sell them to tourists.

"Are you sure you don't want to come fishing?" Huck asks. Her company is the only person's he would relish, and he worries that Maia is returning to her regular twelve-year-old routine too soon. Tomorrow, Monday, she's going back to school.

"I'm sure," she says.

Huck reminds himself that everyone processes loss in his or her own way. After LeeAnn died, Huck had gone through a rough patch—smoking and drinking, and spending one regrettable night with Teresa, the waitress from Jake's, who everyone knew had a sleeping-around problem. And Rosie had handled LeeAnn's death by meeting, and then shacking up with, the Invisible Man.

He's going to let Maia be. If she wants to start a bath bomb business with Joanie, then Huck will be their first customer.

But today he's going fishing. And he's going to *catch* something, damnit.

He loads up *The Mississippi* with light tackle and his trolling rods, a chest of clean ice, a second chest that holds water, a case of Red Stripe, and two Cuban sandwiches from Baked in the Sun, plus one of their "junk food" cookies—the thing is loaded with toffee, pretzels, and potato chips—because those were Rosie's favorite. He's about to untie his line from the dock when he hears his name being called. His proper name.

"Mr. Powers? Sam Powers?"

He looks up to see a woman marching down the dock, waving her arm like she's trying to hail a cab. She's slender, with pretty hair—one fat chestnut braid hangs over one shoulder. She's wearing round sunglasses, so he can't get a good look at her, but as she grows closer he sees she's older than he originally thought, and her expression can only be described as All Business. That, combined with the fact that she's calling him "Mr. Powers" makes him feel like he's about to be reprimanded by his high school English teacher. What was her name? Miss Lemon. Miss Lemon had once caught Huck writing dirty limericks. Instead of tearing up the page, as he expected her to, she had insisted he go in front of the class and read them aloud.

Good old Miss Lemon, responsible for the most humiliating moment of Huck's young life.

And now here comes Miss Lemon reincarnated, although a sight better-looking. The original Miss Lemon, appropriate to her name, had a pucker face.

The reincarnated Miss Lemon marches right up to the edge of the dock. Huck has the line in his hand. All he needs to do is unloop it from the post and putter away. She can't very well follow him.

"Are you Sam Powers?" she asks.

"Technically, yes," he says. "But people call me Huck."

She nods once, sharply. "So I've heard. Mr. Powers, do you have a minute to talk? It's important."

Does he have a minute to talk? No. It's nearly nine o'clock now. He's going offshore, a forty-five-minute trip. He has to be back here by four thirty at the latest to pick Maia up from Joanie's by five. He wants to fish all day. To fish all day, he has to leave now. *It's important,* the Reincarnated Miss Lemon says, and he somehow knows this isn't a matriarch disgruntled by his postponed charters. This woman's face holds a certain tension in it that Huck recognizes. He has an idea, but he hopes to God he's wrong.

He cuts the motor, then offers the woman his barracuda hand. She takes in the sight of his half-missing pinky but doesn't flinch, which he supposes is a good sign.

"You want me to get into your boat?" she asks.

"You want to talk?" he asks.

She removes her sandals without being asked—she must be a boat person, how about that—and she takes his barracuda hand and nimbly descends into the bow.

Huck flips open the cooler. "I have water and I have beer."

"Nothing," she says. "Thank you."

Huck goes to reach for a water for himself when she speaks up. "Actually, a beer. Thank you."

Huck's eyebrows shoot up, but the Reincarnated Miss Lemon doesn't notice. Her eyes are scanning the dock. Who's watching? Well, the answer to that is: no one and everyone. The taxi drivers—Pauly, Chauncey, and Bennie—are lined up across the street from the cruise ship dock. Huck flips the top off two Red Stripes; he isn't about to let a lady drink alone, and if she needs a beer, then he probably does as well.

Huck hands the Reincarnated Miss Lemon a beer. "What can I do for you, Ms. . . . ?"

"Steele," she says. "Irene Steele."

Huck closes his eyes a beat longer than a blink. Irene Steele. His bad feeling has been proved correct.

"I guess that answers my question," he says. He offers Irene Steele one of the cushioned seats in the cockpit. He's a bit concerned about who will hear what; acoustics over the water are funny. He sits down a respectful distance away but leans in. It could still be an ex-wife, he thinks. Please let it be an ex-wife.

"Russell Steele was my husband," Irene says, immediately dashing Huck's hopes. "And I understand that you're the father of Rosie Small. Who was my husband's mistress."

Huck flinches at the word "mistress," although he realizes she could have chosen worse.

"I'm her stepfather," Huck says. "*Was* her stepfather. I married her mother, LeeAnn, nearly twenty years ago. LeeAnn passed five years back."

"But you're still close with Rosie? *Were* close with her? She lived with you?"

"You did your research," Huck says. "How did you find this out?"

"It wasn't easy," Irene says. "I don't know anyone here except for Paulette, from the real estate agency..."

Paulette Vickers, Huck thinks. He saw her at the funeral and the reception yesterday, but then again, he saw everyone.

"...but Paulette was out of the office yesterday." Irene pauses. "So I had to ask around, which didn't yield me much until I found the woman who sells mangoes next to Cruz Bay Landing."

"Henrietta," Huck says.

Irene shrugs. "She gave me the basics. When I asked if the girl who died had parents, she told me your name and the name of your boat and that you tied up here most mornings."

"I'm sorry about your husband," Huck says. He's not, though—not sorry one bit that sonovabitch is dead. He only cares about Rosie. But before Huck can tack on any more insincere statements, Irene says, "No, you're not. Nor should you be. You can tell me the truth, Mr. Powers."

"The truth?" Huck says. "I don't like being called 'Mr. Powers.' Also, I'm grieving just like you are and I plan to take today out on the water by myself so I can fish and drink beer and gaze off at the horizon and wonder what happens when we die."

"So you'd like me to leave?" Irene says.

Pretty much, Huck thinks. But he's too much of a gentleman to say it. "I'm just not sure what you want from me. I probably know as much as you do about what happened. They were traveling by helicopter from here to Anegada in the BVIs."

"Why?" Irene says.

"Day trip?" Huck says. "Anegada is pretty special. It's nothing more than a spit of pure white sand, really. It has a Gilligan's Island feel to it. There's almost nothing there, a few homes, a couple of small hotels, a few bars and restaurants, a native population of flamingos..."

"Flamingos?" Irene says flatly.

"And lobsters," Huck says. "Anegada is famous for its lobsters. So my guess is they were on a day trip. Go over, see the birds, walk the beach, eat a couple lobsters, fly home. People do it. I've done it. Of course, most people take a boat." He finishes his beer and deeply craves a cigarette. He needs this woman off his boat. He stands up, takes Irene's empty bottle from her, and throws both bottles in the trash. Hint, hint. What else could she possibly want to ask?

"Did you know Russ?" Irene says.

"No," Huck says, clearly and firmly. "Never had the pleasure. Rosie was...protective, I guess you'd say. I knew the guy existed, knew he had money...and a villa somewhere..."

Irene laughs. "Villa."

"I've never seen it, was never invited, don't know the address. Rosie kept all that private. She told me his name once, long ago. But after that she referred to him only as the Man and everyone else on this island refers to him as the Invisible Man. Because no one ever saw him."

"The Invisible Man?" Irene says. "That's ironic. I could have called him that as well." She stands up and Huck fills with sweet relief—she's leaving!—but then she opens the cooler, takes out another beer, and hands it to Huck.

He can't decide whether to laugh or cry. He needs to go. He wants to fish.

"Can we finish this conversation another time?" he asks. "I want to fish."

"Take me with you," Irene says. "I can pay."

"I had two paying charters today that I canceled," Huck says.

"But those people weren't me," Irene says. "They weren't the widow of your stepdaughter's lover."

Huck's head is spinning. He needs a cigarette and it's his boat, goddamnit, so he's going to have one. He opens Irene's beer and lights up.

"Do you fish?" he asks. "Where are you from?"

"Iowa City," Irene says.

Huck chuckles. "I doubt you're built for a day offshore."

"I most certainly am," Irene says. "I used to go fly-fishing with my father on a lake in Wisconsin. He called me…" She pauses as her eyes fill. "He used to call me Angler Cupcake."

Angler Cupcake: Huck hasn't heard that one before.

"I'm sorry," Irene says. "I don't mean to horn in on your day of solitude and reflection. It's just that I could use a day like you're about to have myself. Fishing, drinking beer, gazing at the horizon, and wondering what happens when we die."

Go to the beach at Francis Bay, he wants to tell her. Drive out to the East End—no one is *ever* on the East End. Hike to Salomon Bay. Sit at the bar at the Quiet Mon. St. John has lots of places to hide.

But instead he says, "You really think you can handle this?"

"I know I can," she says.

"Okay, then." Huck starts the engine and unloops the rope and steers them out into the harbor. There's instantly a breeze, and between the wind and the noise of the motor, the need for conversation evaporates. Still, Huck looks at Irene Steele, his stowaway, the wife of Rosie's lover—what the *hell* is he doing?—and says, "Angler Cupcake, huh?"

"I guess we'll see," she says.

Huck captains *The Mississippi* offshore to the south-southeast toward the coordinates Cleve gave him. Irene "Angler Cupcake" Steele is lucky, because the water is glass and the boat might as well have a diamond-edged hull. The ride is smooth and easy—and despite having an unwanted, unexpected passenger, Huck relaxes. Is he surprised this woman found him? He is. But then again, he isn't. He had guessed that she existed, though he never spoke the words out loud. He thought maybe a few months from now, someone from the secret life of the Invisible Man might surface.

Or was *this* the Invisible Man's secret life?

Yes, Huck thinks.

He might ask Irene some questions. Maybe by learning about Russell Steele, he'll learn about Rosie. But Huck knew Rosie. He *knew* Rosie. She fell in love with a man who had a wife elsewhere and now that wife was here on Huck's boat, expecting Huck to answer questions like he owes it to her.

Does he owe it to her? That's not a question he wants to explore right now.

He's less bothered by her presence than he ought to be. Why is that? Because she's hurting, too. Because she lost someone at exactly the same time he did, and so she also must feel like the gods have her by the head and toes and are wringing her out.

But enough. It's time to fish.

As Huck nears the coordinates Cleve gave him, he slows down. A little ways off he sees something floating on the water and directs the boat over until he can see what it is. A rectangular cut of carpet. Huck bends over to grab it.

"Someone tossed that?" Irene asks.

"Someone *left* it," Huck says. "As a marker. This is where the fish are. Or were. There's no telling now. I heard this back on New Year's Eve."

"Before," Irene says.

They're in the same emotional space. There's no way to think of New Year's Eve except as *before.*

Huck nods and grabs a rod for Irene and one for himself. He checks her lure and her line and hands it over.

"You know how to cast?" he says.

"Of course," she says.

"Would you like a beer?"

"If you're having one," she says.

Well, it's his day and he *is* having one. He happens to believe that beer brings the fish. He flips the cap off two Red Stripes and places one in the cup holder next to Irene's left hip. Then he retreats to the other side of the boat and discreetly watches Irene.

She lifts the beer to her lips and takes a nice long swallow. Then she holds the line, flips the bale, and executes a more than competent sidearm cast. *Wheeeeeeeeee!* The line flies.

Beautiful, Huck has to admit. He hasn't seen a woman—hell, a *person*—cast like that since...well, since he's not sure when.

Nearly as soon as she starts to reel the line in, her rod bows.

"Fish on," she says. Her voice is calm and assured. Most women—hell, people—get a fish on and they shout like God lost a tooth. The rod is *really* bending; there's a fish on and it's big. Huck gets a rush. He has been skunked since Halloween. He's ready—more than ready.

"You want help with that?" Huck asks.

"Not yet," Irene says.

"Come sit in the fighting chair," Huck says. "I think you're going to need it." He leads Irene over to the chair and gets her situated, pole in the holder. Meanwhile, she's doing just the right thing, letting the fish take some line and then reeling when the fish rests. Huck would normally be offering verbal instructions, but Irene is making every move at just the right time. He can't be accused of "mansplaining," which has earned him the silent treatment from both Rosie and Maia in the past.

Huck moves Irene's beer to where she can reach it and she does, at one point, take a quick swig, then gets back to reeling.

She is one cool customer. Likely she has a monster on the other end of her line, and Huck has seen men twice her size give up on light tackle. It's difficult by anyone's standards.

"You're doing great," Huck says. He feels strangely useless, the way he felt at Rosie's bedside when she was giving birth to Maia. "Just let me know if you need help."

"I'm fine," Irene says.

She *is* fine, releasing, then reeling in, two steps forward, one step back, which is what a fish like this takes, and she doesn't seem to be losing patience. Fifteen minutes pass, then twenty. She's getting more aggressive with her reeling, which is what he would have advised. The fish is getting tired.

"Anyone else would have handed the reel over by now," Huck says.

"I doubt that," Irene says.

"I only meant to say you're doing well," Huck says. He can't believe it, but he thinks of the Invisible Man, Russell Steele. *You have a wife who fishes like this and you cheated on her?*

Huck should cast his own line, he knows, but he's vested in this fight and wants to see it through. Irene lets the line go and then she reels with a grunt—she's human, after all—and just like that, Huck sees the flash of gold fins beneath the surface.

"Here we go, baby," he says. "Don't give up now. Bring him in."

Irene lets out a moan that sounds like a bedroom noise, and Huck won't lie, he gets a bit of a rise. But no time to dwell on that, thank God, because here's the fish. Huck grabs the gaff and leans all the way over the side of the boat to spear the fucker and hook it up over the railing onto the deck of *The Mississippi,* where it flops around, making a tremendous ruckus. It has gorgeous green and gold scales, Huck's favorite color in the world, and the protruding forehead of a bull fish.

"Mahi mahi," he says. "I'd say twenty-five pounds, maybe forty inches long."

Irene takes a sip of her beer. "Can we eat it?"

"For days," Huck says. Without thinking, he raises his hand for a high-five and Irene slaps his palm, square and solid. He grabs her hand.

"Congratulations," he says. "That was some skillful rod work there, Angler Cupcake."

Irene looks at Huck and she breaks into a smile and then so does Huck, and for one second, they are two people standing in the tropical sunshine while one hell of a majestic fish flops at their feet. For one second, they forget their hearts are broken.

It doesn't end there—no, not even close. Huck puts the bull on ice and then casts his own rod, and Irene casts again, and they both get fish on. Two more mahi. Again, they cast. Huck gets a hit right away, Irene a few minutes later. Two more mahi. Irene asks if there's a head and Huck says, "There is down below. No paper in the bowl, please." Irene comes up a few minutes later, pops the top off a Red Stripe, and casts a line. She gets a fish on.

It's insane. Insanely wonderful. They have six mahi, eight, twelve. Huck brings in a barracuda, which he throws back, and Irene brings in a mahi that has been bitten clean in half.

"Shark," Huck says. He unhooks the half fish and throws it back.

"Oh yeah?" Irene says. He thinks maybe he scared her, but she casts another line.

Fourteen, sixteen, seventeen mahi.

Thank you, LeeAnn, he thinks. For the past five years, every time he's caught a fish, he's thanked his wife, because he believes she's helping from above. Silly, he knows.

They take a break and Huck offers Irene one of the Cuban sandwiches, which she accepts gratefully. He thinks maybe they'll talk, but Irene takes her sandwich to the bow of the boat, on the side with the shade, and Huck lets her be. He does wonder what she's thinking about. Is she contemplating the horizon, wondering what happens when we die?

He would like to explain to her how extraordinary today is. *Seventeen mahi!* Maybe she understands, or maybe she thinks fishing with Huck is always like this. At any rate, she returns to the stern, pulls a bottle out of the water, and casts a line.

At three thirty, he tells her it's time to go.

"Yes," she says. "I'm sure my sons will be wondering about me."

Sons? he thinks. She has sons. He wants to ask how many and how old they are—but there isn't time. He has to pick up Maia. Today has been magical, nearly supernatural, and restorative the way he'd hoped. But unfortunately, real life awaits.

Forty-five minutes later, he pulls up to the dock by the canary-yellow National Park Service building. He ties up and offers a hand to help Irene out of the boat.

"Oh wait," he says. "I owe you some fish."

"Don't worry about it," she says.

"No, no," he says. He doesn't have time to fillet any right now, and he can't very well hand her a whole mahi. "I could drop some off at your villa tomorrow. Or we could meet somewhere in town?"

"You don't have to give me any fish," Irene says. She takes a deep breath. "I can't believe how therapeutic today was. I managed... somehow... to step out of myself. And it's because you let me tag along. So I'm grateful. I will forever remember today and your kindness."

It sounds like she's saying good-bye, and Huck rejects this for some reason. "Are you... leaving? Soon? Leaving the island? Heading home?"

"At some point, I guess," Irene says. "I have a life at home. A job, a house, and Russ's mother, Milly, is still alive and I'm her... contact person, her point person, the one who makes decisions for her. My sons have lives as well. We can't stay forever. But we're still waiting for the ashes and for a report from the authorities about what exactly happened..."

"Bird got struck by lightning," Huck says.

"I guess they need to confirm that," Irene says. She presses her lips together, and Huck sees her fighting tears.

"Listen, what if we met in town sometime tomorrow? We could grab a drink and I'll bring you a bag of mahi fillets." Tomorrow's Monday, and it's also the night of the Gifft Hill School's annual overnight field trip to the Maho Bay campground. They'll sleep in tents and tell ghost stories. Maia had said she still wanted to go, and Huck wasn't particularly looking forward to a night alone.

"You said you've never been to the villa," Irene says. "Is that true?"

"That's true," Huck says. "I don't even know where it is."

"I don't know where it is, either," Irene says. "But why don't you bring some of that fish over tomorrow evening and we can grill it. I'll figure out the address and I'll text you. You do text, right?"

"Of course I text," Huck says. "I have a twelve-year-old granddaughter."

Irene stares at him a second and then pulls out her phone. "Give me your number," she says.

Huck watches Irene walk away. She's not a bad-looking woman, not bad-looking at all, and, boy, can she fish. If she were anyone else—*anyone* else—Huck would ask her out. As it is, they have a sort-of date tomorrow night.

If she remembers to text him.

Which she probably won't.

Why would she?

She might, though, he thinks. She just might.

BAKER

Both his mother and his brother return to the house in the late afternoon. Both are sunburned, and they won't tell him where they've been. Baker has been home, lying by the pool, waiting for his phone to ring with some news about...about anything. He's called VISAR and gotten transferred three times, so he's had to leave messages. Then he called the Peebles Hospital on Tortola, hoping they could give him some information about Russ's ashes, but the woman he spoke to, Letitia, said she didn't have any bodies by the name of Russell Steele.

"Really?" Baker asked. "It's my father...he was in that helicopter crash off Virgin Gorda on New Year's Day."

"I was off last week for the holidays," Letitia said. "All I can tell you, sir, is that name is not in the hospital database."

"The contact name might have been Todd Croft," Baker said. "Would you mind checking Croft?"

"Not a problem," Letitia said. He heard her typing. "I'm sorry, I don't have that name in the database, either. You might check with the Americans."

Baker called the Hurley-Davis Funeral Home in St. Thomas and spoke to Bianca, who was even less helpful.

"I'm looking for my father's remains. His name was Russell Steele. He was killed in the helicopter crash north of Virgin Gorda on New Year's Day."

"Virgin Gorda?" Bianca said. "You'll need to call Peebles Hospital, then. On Tortola."

Baker hung up, confused and agitated. He tried the number his mother had for Todd Croft next, but it was out of service. Next he went to his laptop to look up the Ascension website, but the site wouldn't load. Baker couldn't figure out if his service here on the island was the problem or if something was wrong with the website. He googled the names Russell Steele and Todd Croft—his Google worked, so it *wasn't* the service that was the issue—but none of the hits matched the men Baker was looking for. He tried Stephen Thompson next—there were probably only fifty or sixty thousand people in the world with that name—so he refined it by adding *pilot* and *British Virgin Islands,* but that was a bust. There was a

Stephen Thompson, Esquire, listed in the Cayman Islands—not exactly pay dirt, but Baker had nothing else to go on, so he called the number listed on the website and that number, too, was out of service.

Coincidence? Baker wondered. Or was this Stephen Thompson the same Stephen Thompson who piloted the helicopter? It was beginning to feel like someone was trying to erase the whole situation.

Before Baker could explore further, Anna texted, asking Baker when he was coming home. *Floyd misses you,* she wrote. Baker wanted to respond that Anna would be well served to put in some quality time with Floyd now that she was going to be a single parent. But instead, Baker channeled his best self—which was easier when he remembered how he felt when he'd set eyes on Ayers—and he said, *Things here are still in flux so I'm not sure. Tell Floyd I love him.*

To which Anna responded not *Ok* (her go-to) but rather, *Do you think you'll still be there on Wednesday?*

Yes, he said. *Definitely yes. If you need a sitter, call Kelsey.*

Don't need a sitter, she said.

Yeah, right, Baker thought. In his ruminations about Anna and Louisa, he has naturally wondered how long they've been together, and when it started, and what their plans for the future entail. They'll become a regular lesbian couple, he supposes, if two in-demand cardiac surgeons count as regular.

His pain and shock have been ameliorated by his own experience. When he set eyes on Ayers, he knew instantly it was love. Why shouldn't that have been true for Anna? She might have been discussing a case with Louisa when she realized: *This* is who I want.

Cash and Irene head off to opposite parts of the house to shower. Neither of them had expressed any interest in dinner, and frankly, they had both seemed kind of off, almost as if they'd been drinking.

Well, fine, Baker thinks. Clearly they aren't a bonded band of three in their grieving. If his mom and brother can go out on their own, then so can he. He grabs one of the sets of Jeep keys. He's going to dinner at La Tapa.

Baker heads to town slowly—the steering wheel is on the left, like at home, but here everyone drives on the left instead of the right—and the roads are steep, hilly, and poorly lit. Once he gets to town, he finds that the streets are alive with people out enjoying their Caribbean vacation. Baker has an urge to grab a father walking through Powell Park holding his wife's hand while he carries a little boy about Floyd's age on his shoulders. *Do you know how lucky you are?* Baker wants to ask. Baker's envy isn't limited to just that one guy. *Everyone* who isn't mired in an emotional crisis should be grateful. Baker, while he was at the playground with Floyd on Tuesday afternoon, should have been grateful, instead of bemoaning the state of his marriage. Why hadn't he been grateful?

La Tapa is easy to find. It's right next to Woody's, which has a crowd of post-happy-hour revelers still hanging out front. Baker parks the Jeep up the street and heads back to the restaurant. His emotions quickly shift from self-pity to nerves. It's been a while since he's pursued anyone romantically. But he's an okay-looking guy, maybe a little soft around the middle, thanks to life as a stay-at-home dad and all the late-night ice cream, but he can shed the weight with some exercise. He'll go for a run tomorrow, he decides.

He steps down into a tasteful, rustic dining room. The place is charming, with its candlelight and white linen tablecloths, rough-hewn wooden bar and fresh flowers. And it smells so good—rich, layered scents of butter and roasting meat and herbs.

Baker takes an empty seat at the end of the bar closest to the kitchen, next to where the waitstaff come to pick up their drink orders. Ayers, where is Ayers?

"Hey, man, welcome to La Tapa," the bartender says. "My name is Skip. Can I get you something to drink?"

Baker has become a big fan of the St. John beers but he opts for a vodka tonic. He's out of the house, this place is really nice, and he's going to act like an adult. His drink comes and he peruses the menu, using his peripheral vision to look for Ayers. There's a tall, slender girl with cropped dark hair hanging at the service station, flirting with Skip the bartender, and there are two male servers. But Baker doesn't see Ayers.

"Can I get you something to eat?" Skip asks.

Baker scans the menu. It all looks delicious, but he can't begin to think about food until he finds Ayers. He's in the right place: she said La Tapa, and she *asked* him to stop by...

"What's good?" Baker asks helplessly. If she's not here, he should leave and come back tomorrow. He'll bring Cash with him.

"The mussels are the best in the world, and the mahi was just caught today, if you like fresh fish," Skip says. "It's done with braised artichokes and a thyme beurre blanc."

Baker raises his head to look Skip in the eye. "Is Ayers working tonight, by any chance?"

Skip's eyebrows shoot up. "Ayers? She's off tonight. It's Sunday night—she works on *Treasure Island* on Sundays. She'll be on tomorrow night. Do you want me to leave her a message?"

"No, no..."

Skip leans over the bar and lowers his voice. "I hear you, man, she's really hot. A little psycho, but all chicks are psycho. She sometimes comes in here on her night off for a glass of Schramsberg, so you might want to stick around."

Baker's heart is buoyed even as his mind is racing. Stay or go? *Stay,* he thinks. She sometimes comes in here on her night off for a glass of the whatever. But what does Baker's new best friend, Skip, mean by "a little psycho"? There's a mom named Mandy at the Children's Cottage—Baker's school wives call her "psycho" because she's obsessed with the Houston Astros, especially Justin Verlander. She wears Astros merch *every single day,* and she got a vanity plate for her Volvo that says JV-35. Maybe Skip tried to put the moves on Ayers and she turned him down, so he has categorized her as "a little psycho" to soothe his bruised ego. Guys do that. For instance, Baker might be tempted to call Dr. Anna Schaffer "a little psycho" for leaving him for Louisa, even though Anna is the most mentally stable person Baker knows.

Maybe Ayers has foibles—of course she does, everyone does. Baker vows he will love her foibles.

"I'll have the mussels," Baker says. "And the mahi, at your suggestion."

"Good man," Skip says. The tall, short-haired girl comes back, and Skip says, "Hey, Tilda, this guy is here to see Ayers. Is she coming in for a nightcap, do you know?"

Tilda turns to stare down Baker. She shakes her head in disbelief. "You do *realize* that Ayers's best friend died, like, five days ago, right?"

"Uh," Baker says. "Right..."

Tilda snarls at Skip. "And no, I don't think Ayers is coming for a nightcap, since that was only something she did *when Rosie was working*!" Tilda's voice is so loud that the entire restaurant grows quiet.

Skip pours Tilda a shot of beer, and without a word she throws it back and storms off. A few seconds later the restaurant returns to its normal decibel level and Skip leans forward.

"Sorry about that, man. That's Tilda for you. She's a little..."

"Psycho," Baker says. "Got it."

The mussels arrive, they're outstanding, the best Baker has ever had, and then the mahi comes and it's even better, fresh and moist, just cooked through, perfectly seasoned, and the sauce is so sublime, he's light-headed.

But no Ayers.

"How was your food?" Skip asks as he clears the plates.

"Unbelievable," Baker says. "So good that I think I'll be back tomorrow night with my brother."

"Cool, man," Skip says. "I'll save you guys two bar seats, and, hey—I don't do that for just anyone."

"That's great, thank you," Baker says. He pays the bill and leaves Skip a very, very generous tip—nearly 40 percent—because he can't risk Skip telling Ayers that a guy came in looking for her who seemed a little...

* * *

The next morning Baker gets up early to go for a run. He was an athlete in high school, the classic three—football, basketball, and baseball—and when he got to Northwestern, he played on his fraternity's intramural teams. In Chicago, he belonged to Lakeshore Sport & Fitness, where he went mostly to meet women. He hasn't done much in the way of exercise since moving to Houston. There was one ill-advised 5K in Memorial Park; he thought he was having a heart attack—a great irony, because Anna was supposed to come cheer him on, but she'd been called in to work, so one of his thoughts as his vision went black and he stopped dead in his tracks, bent over his knees, was that at least Anna was in a position to save his life.

But today, Baker decides, will be different. Today he is motivated. He has a mission: he is going to sweep Ayers off her feet. He laces up his sneakers and heads out to the end of his father's driveway.

While he feels okay running down his father's shaded road, when he gets to the bottom and turns right, he's in the sun and it's immediately uphill. As if that isn't bad enough, a large open-air taxi comes blazing around a blind corner, nearly forcing him over the guard rail down the side of the cliff to the sea. Baker breaks stride to flip the driver off.

Ayers, he thinks. He keeps going, shoulders back, spine straight, face stoic. The sun is broiling, it's hotter than Houston in August, and suddenly he feels last night's vodka tonics and mussels and mahi churning in his stomach. The hill grows steep. Baker sets his gaze three feet ahead of his stride—otherwise he'll give up.

Ayers, he thinks. Do this for Ayers. He hears three low

resonant notes, like a foghorn. He raises his face to see an enormous water truck barreling down the hill toward him. He jumps aside.

That's it, he thinks. He's done. He turns around.

He gets lost walking back. How can he be lost when he's only been on one road? His father's driveway is hidden and unmarked, but Baker has been able to find it when he's driving because it's a few yards after the utility pole, which has two yellow stripes. Where is that pole? Baker can't tell if it's in front of him or behind him. He didn't bring his phone; he has sweat in his eyes.

A small lizard-green pickup truck pulls up next to him.

"Are you lost?" a woman asks.

"Maybe?" Baker says. He wipes the sweat off his face with the bottom of his t-shirt and starts to laugh in a way that he knows makes him sound unhinged. But really, what is he even *doing* here? And then it hits him: *his father is dead.*

He starts to cry.

"Baker?" the woman says.

Baker's head snaps up. He looks through the open passenger window to the driver's side. It's not some random woman in a funny truck. It's Ayers.

No, he thinks. Not possible. But yes, it's her, and she's even lovelier than he remembers. Her hair is in a messy bun; she's wearing a loose tank top and yoga pants and he can see she's driving in bare feet. Bare, sandy feet.

"Hey," he says, wiping at his eyes. "How are you?"

"Surviving," she says. "Listen, can I give you a ride somewhere?"

"Oh...no," Baker says. "I'm good. I was just heading back from a run and I seem to have gotten turned around, maybe. Or maybe not. I'm not sure. But I'll figure it out."

"You sure?" Ayers says. "I just took yoga on the beach at Maho and I don't work until four. I have plenty of time to take you wherever."

"I'm okay," Baker says. "Thanks, though."

"Was it you who came in to La Tapa last night?" Ayers says. "I must have just missed you. Skip said you'd been in."

"Oh...yeah," Baker says. "Yeah, that was me. Food was fantastic. Thanks for the recommendation." He realizes he sounds like he's trying to get rid of her—and he *is* trying to get rid of her. He can't *believe* she caught him here, now, in his weakest moment. On top of everything else, his bowels are starting to rumble. He needs her to move on. Why her, of all people? Did he conjure her by saying her name so many times in his mind? Or are there really only five people on this island?

"You're welcome," Ayers says. "Hey, are you sure you're okay?"

Baker straightens up against the troublesome clenching in his gut. He tries to look like the world conqueror he wants her to believe he is. "I'm great, thanks. Hey, listen, I may..." He wants to say he may come to the restaurant again that night with Cash, but at that moment a taxi pulls up behind Ayers and the driver lays on his horn.

"Okay, bye!" Ayers says, and she drives off.

It takes him a while but eventually he finds the pole with two yellow stripes and the nondescript dirt road that is his father's.

When Baker finally makes it home, he's depleted, physically and emotionally. What must Ayers think of him? He's going to have to roll into La Tapa that night and be his most impressive self.

He enters the kitchen to find his mother standing in front of the open refrigerator, sniffing the container of pasta salad, and he's transported back a decade or so.

"Mom?" he says. He's surprised to find her in this posture; his mother has expressed no interest in food the entire time they've been here.

Irene straightens up and closes the fridge. She has an inscrutable expression on her face. Baker almost feels like he caught her at something.

"I have to ask a favor," she says.

He goes to the sink for water. "Anything," he says. "What is it?"

"I need you and your brother to go out tonight," she says. "I have a dinner guest coming at seven and I'd like privacy."

Baker takes a second to process this. She has a *dinner guest* coming? It must be Todd Croft, he thinks. Who else could it possibly be? His mother doesn't know anyone around here. He realizes her request is fortuitous. Now Baker and Cash can go to La Tapa by themselves without seeming like they're ditching her.

"You got it," Baker says.

His mother appears relieved, not only at his answer but also because he hasn't asked any follow-up questions. She has a secret, he thinks. She knows something she isn't telling them. Which leads him to the nagging guilt he feels because he hasn't told his mother about what's happening with Anna. It seems inconsequential after everything that's happened.

His mother goes back to rummaging through the fridge, inspecting this and that.

"Oh, look," she says. "Camembert."

Baker handles the news of Irene's surprise dinner guest far better than Cash. Cash barely manages to conceal his indignation. Baker has to admit that it is a little disconcerting to see his mother wearing a black gauzy sundress, her hair freshly washed and combed out long and loose (honestly, he can't remember the last time he saw it out of its braid). The dress isn't anything *new,* he doesn't think, more like something she would wear when she and Russ used to entertain the Dunns and the Kinseys by the pool back in Iowa City.

Baker watches Irene bury a bottle of Cakebread chardonnay in an ice bucket. There's no mention of how twisted it is that Russ kept Irene's favorite wine—a *case of it*—in a house that she knew nothing about. She bids both boys good-bye with a kiss, seeming like a subdued version of her former self. But it's clear she wants them to leave. It's quarter to seven.

As soon as Baker and Cash get in the Jeep, Cash explodes. "What the hell is going *on*? Cheese and *crackers*? Wine? And did you see what she was *wearing*? And what's with the secrecy? She won't tell us who's coming for dinner?"

"It must be Todd Croft," Baker says. "Right? It has to be. Which is good, because he's been unreachable and the Ascension website is down. Something weird is going on."

"Then why not just *tell* us that?" Cash says. He's on his way to a five-flavor freak-out, which is how their father used to describe Cash's tantrums growing up. It makes no sense that Cash—who doesn't have an ambitious or competitive bone in his body, who *skis* for a living—is so high-strung emotionally, while Baker, who thrives on pressure and tension, tends to be pretty sanguine no matter what. And yet that's the way it is. Maybe Cash inherited more of their hotheaded Scottish ancestors' blood and Baker the sangfroid of the Norwegians. Maybe Cash was treated differently growing up because he was the "baby." Maybe it's simply one of the unsolved mysteries of human nature: how two siblings, born of the same parents and raised in the same house, can be complete opposites. Cash is clearly bent out of shape by Irene's behavior, whereas Baker doesn't care. What he *does* care about—immensely—is seeing Ayers.

Maybe Baker is just painfully self-absorbed.

"Do you trust Mom?" Baker asks.

"Yes," Cash says. "But then again, I trusted *Dad*..."

Baker cuts him off. "We're talking about Mom. You trust her. Do you think she's likely to do anything rash or self-destructive?"

"No," Cash says.

"No," Baker agrees. Irene Steele is the epitome of level-headed competence. Her behavior today harks back to her actions on Thanksgiving Day of his senior year at Northwestern, when he brought home his friend Donny Foley, from Skagway, Alaska. Baker and Donny had been in the front yard of the Steeles' Victorian playing the traditional game of tackle football with Cash and a few of the neighbors. Donny took a hard hit and started screaming that his shoulder was dislocated. Irene had come flying out of the house in her apron—she was cooking a turkey with all the trimmings for twenty people—and with one strong twist, she had popped Donny's shoulder back in place. The entire episode took all of thirty seconds, but his mother's composure and swift act would be forever emblazoned in Baker's mind.

His mother is, in today's parlance, a badass.

If she wants privacy for dinner, it's for a good reason.

"...but I trusted *Dad* not to do anything rash or self-destructive, and *look what happened*!" Cash shouts these last three words, and, as usual when confronted with Cash's episodes, Baker shuts down. He won't say a word until they get to dinner.

But Cash's words echo in Baker's mind. *I trusted Dad not to do anything rash or self-destructive, and look what happened.*

Look what happened.

At La Tapa, Baker and Cash take the seats at the corner of the bar that Skip has reserved for them. Skip lights up as though Baker is an old friend and offers a fist bump.

"Hey, man, back again, two nights in a row, now that's an endorsement, if ever there were one." He leans in. "And Ayers is here, man, you're in luck."

"Great," Baker says, and he immediately breaks into a light sweat. There's a guy with a guitar in the corner crooning Cat Stevens, and because of the live music, the restaurant is really crowded, much more crowded than the night before. Where is Ayers? Baker casts around, then sees her pulling a cork from a bottle of red wine for a middle-aged couple on the deck under the awning. Her hair is up and she's wearing the black uniform shirt with the black apron over it. She is . . . breathtaking. There's no other word for it.

"Hey, man, I'm Skip." Skip offers Cash his hand, and Baker says, "I'm sorry. This is my brother, Cash."

Skip asks Cash where he's from and Cash says Breckenridge, Colorado, and it turns out that Skip was a snowboarder in Telluride in his former life. Cash says (as Baker knows he's going to), "To hell you ride! No way, man!" And then they're off and running, talking about how Peak 7 compares to Senior's as Baker sits anxiously by, wondering when he can reasonably interrupt to ask Skip for a vodka tonic.

He feels a hand on his back.

"Hey," Ayers says. "You came!" She looks genuinely happy and surprised, and Baker experiences a surge of pure love like a sugar high or a hit of nicotine—but then Ayers turns her attention to Cash. "Hey, stranger!"

Cash stands up and gives Ayers a hug—more like an overly familiar, overly affectionate squeeze—and Baker is confused. He recalls introducing Cash to Ayers at the reception briefly, but had they said anything more than hello?

Ayers looks at Skip. "Buy these two a round on the house." She points to Cash. "Painkiller, extra strong, for this guy."

Cash laughs. "No, thank you."

"Aw, come on," Ayers says. "How about a rum punch, Myers's floater?"

"Stop!" Cash says.

Baker is lost. What is going *on* here? He's about to ask when Ayers rests a hand on his bicep. Involuntarily, he flexes.

"Are you feeling better?" she asks.

"I . . . uh, yeah, yes," Baker says.

"If you want to run, you should drive to Maho. There's a

four-mile loop to Leinster Bay. Skip can draw you a map, can't you, Skip?"

"On it," Skip says.

"Gotta get back to work," Ayers says. "Say good-bye before you leave."

"Thanks for the drink," Cash says. Then to Skip he says, "Don't listen to her. I'll have a beer. Island Hoppin' IPA is fine."

"Did you go out on *Treasure Island*?" Skip asks.

Cash nods. "Yesterday. Poisoned myself."

"That happens," Skip says. "Did you go to Jost?"

"Baths, Cooper Island, the Indians."

"Next time, you've got to go to Jost," Skip says. "You haven't lived until you've had a painkiller at the Soggy Dollar."

Baker says, "I'll have a vodka tonic, please." He pauses. Then, at the risk of sounding like a douche bag, he says, "Pronto." He's failed: He sounds like a douche bag. But he's learning that Skip is a talker and easily distracted. And Baker desperately needs a drink if he's to process what he thinks is going on.

Skip slaps the bar. "Pronto."

The drink does arrive pretty much pronto. Baker takes a long, deep sip before he turns to his brother, who is doing his best to look nonchalant—twirling his beer bottle, humming along to the guitar player, who is doing a fair rendition of "Promises," by Eric Clapton.

"Do you mean to tell me *that's* where you were yesterday?" Baker says. "You went out on *Treasure Island*? You went on a trip to the BVIs?" Baker lowers his voice and moves in on Cash. "Our father is *dead.* I sat home waiting to hear from Her Royal Highness's blasted coast guard or what have you. I called the crematorium trying to track down the *ashes,* and you're out getting *drunk* on a *pleasure cruise*?"

"Yep," Cash says. A smile is playing around his lips and Baker wants to punch him. He was out all day on a boat with Ayers, getting drunk, getting cozy. Baker's question is: How did Cash even know Ayers worked on *Treasure Island*? He hadn't been around for that part of the conversation. Was it just dumb luck—Cash needed something to do, stumbled across *Treasure Island,* and recognized Ayers? Or is something more going on? Baker knows that Cash has long wanted to get back at him for hooking up with Claire Bellows at Northwestern. Baker had bumped into her at a Sig Ep party when he was a junior and she was just a freshman. Quite frankly, Claire had thrown herself at Baker. She had drunkenly confided that the entire time she'd been with Cash she had harbored a painful crush on Baker. Baker had pretended to be surprised by this admission, although he had certainly noticed all of the moony looks and the way, whenever Irene had invited Claire to stay for dinner, she had always chosen the seat next to Baker and "accidentally" bumped knees with him under the table. When Baker saw her at Sig Ep, he had spent a few minutes deliberating with his conscience. Could he screw Claire Bellows? He wasn't a complete asshole, and he did love his brother, deep down. But Claire's fawning attention and the number of beers Baker had drunk that night won out. He had taken her back to his room. In the morning, consumed with guilt, she had called Cash.

Cash had been pissed enough to threaten getting on a bus from Boulder to Chicago and showing up to kick Baker's ass.

Baker had laughed and said, "I can't help it if chicks like me better, dude." He had meant this as a kind of apology, but Cash had taken it as exactly the opposite. Things between them had never been the same. Baker thought, *Fine, whatever.*

He wished they were closer or at least on less prickly terms, but they were adults—or at least Baker was, with a house and a wife and a child. Cash was still a punk, mooching off their father's magnanimity, and apparently still a sore loser. It could be that Cash has been waiting all these many years to get back at Baker.

"Really," Baker says now. "How did all that come about?"

"Ayers invited me," Cash says.

Baker finishes the rest of his vodka tonic in one swallow, then holds his empty glass up to Skip, and Skip says, "Pronto, man, as soon as I finish with the sixteen orders from the service bar," a response Baker knows he deserves.

"Invited you *when*?" Baker says.

"When I bumped into her hiking," Cash says.

"Hiking."

"Winnie and I hiked the Reef Bay Trail on Saturday," Cash says. "And we came across Ayers by the petroglyphs, crying and nearly out of drinking water."

"Stop," Baker says. He can all too easily picture the scene. Winnie probably approached Ayers; Cash was fond of letting his dog introduce him to women. And then Cash wooed her by being his well-prepared Boy Scout self. "Just so we're clear on this, I'm going to ask her out."

"What?" Cash says. "You can't ask her out. You're married."

"I..." Baker realizes he hasn't told Cash about Anna, so he most definitely sounds like a world-class jerk. "Anna and I have separated."

"What?" Cash says.

Baker can't explain right now. And he can't wait another twenty minutes for a drink. And he can't sit and eat a meal with his brother, who has seen Ayers two of the past three days and now has his own private jokes with her.

Baker stands up. He sets the Jeep keys next to Cash's beer. "I'm out," he says.

He expects Cash to protest, but all Cash says is, "Good."

Baker weaves between tables as the guitar player croaks out "Thunder Road." Baker scans the restaurant and sees Ayers taking an order out on the deck. He stands a few feet behind her until she finishes and then he whispers her name.

She spins around. "Oh, hi," she says. "Are you leaving?"

"I only came for a drink," he says. He squares his shoulders. "Listen, turns out I'm here for a couple more days. I'd love to take you out."

"That's sweet," Ayers says. "But I'm pretty busy. I work two jobs and I have..."

"When are you free?" Baker asks. "I can do lunch, I can do dinner..."

Ayers chews her bottom lip and peers into the restaurant. *Is she looking at Cash?* he wonders. That's just impossible.

"Seriously," Baker says. "I can do breakfast or late drinks. Or late dinner. How about tonight, after you get off?"

Ayers looks hesitant. She's wavering. There's no way she's into Cash; Baker rejects the very idea.

"Please," he says. "Just tell me what time."

"Ten o'clock," she says. "I'll be done by ten and we can go to De' Coal Pot. They serve Caribbean food."

"Perfect," Baker says. "I'll be back at ten."

Ayers nods and hurries inside, and Baker watches her go.

Just please don't invite my brother, he thinks.

IRENE

What is she doing?

What is she doing?

What is she doing?

She is throwing away the rule book, she thinks. And it feels okay.

For the first fifty-seven years of her life, Irene stayed on script. She was a dutiful daughter, a good student in both high school and college. She got married, had children, took a job that was suited to her.

She had been a good mother, or good enough. The boys were fine.

She had been a good wife.

Hadn't she?

It's only at night, after Irene has taken one of the pills that Anna prescribed, that she allows herself to indulge in self-doubt. Where did she go wrong? She feels like she must have done Russ a huge, terrible injustice somewhere along the way for him to engage in a deception so wide and deep.

But she comes up with nothing.

She wasn't sure what to expect when she arrived here; the villa and the island are as foreign as Neptune. What she finds surprising are the small flashes of her own influence that she stumbles across. All of the beds, she's noticed, have six pillows, along with one oversized decorative pillow against the headboard, one small square decorative pillow in front, and a cylindrical bolster. This is exactly how Irene dresses the beds at home; she had no idea Russ had ever noticed. Also, the wine Russ keeps on hand—cases of it, on the ground floor—are her two favorites: Cakebread and Simi. It's almost as if Russ expected her to show up for a drink one day.

She wouldn't say these details made her feel at home, although they do provide a connection. This was her husband's house. *Her husband's house.* And now her husband is dead. These pieces of news that were, initially, so difficult to conceive, she's now finally processing.

This is Russ's house.

Russ is dead.

She's also becoming acclimatized to life here—the temperature, the surroundings, the particulars of the villa—kind of the way one gets used to the thin air at altitude after a few days. Irene remembers when she and Russ used to visit Cash in Breckenridge; she would suffer from shortness of breath, headaches, strange dreams—and then these symptoms would gradually fade away.

She supposes this goes to show that one can get used to anything.

Seeking out Captain Sam Powers—Huck—had been a bold move, Irene knows. She had desperately wanted to hold *someone* accountable. She can't confront Rosie, but why not Rosie's parents? Huck had been nothing like what Irene had expected. First of all, he was not Rosie's biological father but her stepfather, married to Rosie's deceased mother. Secondly, he was kind—gruff, yes, at first, and unenthusiastic about talking to her (can she blame him?), but he seemed to understand that they were in the same boat (so to speak). Irene had stunned herself by asking to go fishing, and Huck had further stunned her (and likely himself) by agreeing. He could easily have told her to go away and leave him alone. He owed her nothing. He had lost a daughter, and Irene could see that his pain equaled her own; he deserved a day out on his boat by himself. That they had enjoyed such a cathartic and successful outing and that this dinner had evolved from that says...what? That misery loves company, she supposes. That they are not enemies but rather casualties of the same sordid circumstances.

Huck likely has as many questions for her as she does for him, but of course, she has no answers.

She'd had such an easy time finding Huck first thing Monday morning that she tries to track down Todd Croft. Cash had checked with Paulette, who had no contact information for Croft. Paulette dealt only with Marilyn Monroe and with pilot Stephen Thompson—an associate, she said, from the British Virgin Islands.

Irene tries Marilyn Monroe's number again, but it's still disconnected.

She tries the Ascension webpage, but—just as Baker had claimed—it won't load. Someone took it down.

Russ's cell phone isn't in the house, though Irene has called it several times each day. Every time the phone starts ringing, her heart tenses in anticipation. Will today be the day that Russ answers? Is he alive somewhere? No: after two rings, it clicks over to generic voicemail. Irene doesn't even have the luxury of hearing Russ's recorded voice; if she did, she would likely scream at him each time.

She tries to access Russ's cell phone records. She knows his phone number, of course, but the phone bill was paid by Ascension, and she has no idea which carrier he used—she tries contacting AT&T, Verizon, and T-Mobile but gets nowhere.

She wonders if he used a carrier out of the British Virgin Islands, but here she grows frustrated. Even if she figures out the carrier, she doubts they'll give her access to his call log without a court order.

Russ said that he'd been acquainted with Todd Croft at Northwestern, so Irene calls the Northwestern alumni office to see if they have contact information. They don't. Irene could potentially ask one of Russ's other friends from Northwestern—Leo Pelusi or Niles Adrian—but she hasn't seen either of them since their wedding thirty-five years earlier. She has their mailing addresses—they exchange Christmas cards every year—but not phone numbers or email addresses. Russ doesn't go to reunions. The last time he went to Northwestern was eight years ago, for Baker's graduation.

A garden-variety Google of the name Todd Croft, paired with the name Ascension and then separately with Miami, yields nothing fruitful.

Irene grows frustrated. In this day and age, everyone has a digital profile. Someone just told her that, but who? Mavis Key! Mavis Key had explained to Irene and Irene's boss, Joseph Feeney, that with some new software they could learn a lot more about their subscribers' purchasing habits.

Irene is just desperate enough to do the unthinkable. She calls Mavis Key.

"Hey, Irene," Mavis says. She sounds both surprised and concerned. "I heard you had a family emergency. Is everything okay?"

Everything is the opposite of okay, Irene wants to say. *My husband is dead and he had a secret life.* She should have thought this conversation through before she dialed. She needs to convey that the family emergency is real without disclosing even a hint about what has happened.

"Things are difficult right now," Irene says. "Very difficult. But I can't get into it. I called you because I need help finding someone."

"Finding someone," Mavis says. "I'm at the Java House getting a chai." Before Irene can think that of course Mavis Key is downtown on the pedestrian mall, where all the hip university students hang out, ordering a "chai," whatever that is, Mavis adds, "Let me sit down with my laptop. I love detective work."

Irene feels herself relax. Mavis sounds self-assured. She's thirty-one years old, roughly the age of Irene's children, and she exudes both confidence and competence. Irene cherishes competence in everyone, even Mavis Key.

"The man's name is Todd Croft," Irene says. "He's in his mid- to late fifties. He's a banker—a businessman—in Florida, I think. Miami. His business is called Ascension. He went to Northwestern."

Mavis double-checks the spelling of Croft and of Ascension, then Irene can hear her fingertips flying across a keyboard. *LinkedIn*, Mavis murmurs. *Tumblr, Instagram, Snapchat, Twitter, Facebook.* This is a world Irene has actively resisted. People encouraged her to start a Facebook page about her home renovation, but she had been so immersed in the work itself that there had been no time left over to document it.

"I'm not finding him," Mavis says. "Do you know where he worked before Ascension? Do you know if he has kids, or where they went to school? Do you know where in Miami he lives? Do you know if he owns property?"

"I don't," Irene admits. She chastises herself for being so

impetuous; it isn't like her. Now Mavis will go back to the office and tell everyone that Irene is looking for a fifty-something banker from Miami—and what will people *think*?

Well, whatever they think, it won't be as awful as the truth.

"Never mind," Irene says. "I just called on a whim. I need to get a hold of this gentleman because he has some information that will assist with my family issues. But thanks anyway, Mavis."

"Oh," Mavis says. "No problem. When do you think you'll be back? The office isn't the same without you. We're kind of like a bunch of crazed teenagers when Mom is away."

Irene imagines Beyoncé and Drake playing at full blast over the office sound system, microwave popcorn ground into the rug of the common room, long, expensed lunch breaks at Formosa, and the entire staff cutting out early for craft cocktails in the name of "team building." Everyone at the magazine probably views Irene as a schoolmarm, smacking her yardstick into her palm. Irene offers a paltry laugh. "I'll be back next week to restore order," she says. "Thanks, Mavis." She can't hang up fast enough.

The boys leave for dinner. Irene asks them to stay out until eleven, a request that is met with blank stares. Neither of them has asked what she's planning. They're afraid of her, she realizes. They're afraid that at any minute she's going to crack and all of her ugly emotions are going to come flying out. That's fine—they can think what they want, as long as they give her privacy tonight.

She pulls things out of the fridge that she can serve with grilled mahi. Camembert with crackers to start, pasta salad and the makings of a green salad as sides. There's a fruit salad she can serve for dessert with packaged cookies. Food is the least of her worries.

She pours herself a glass of wine, the first since she left the Pullman Bar & Diner six days ago. Thinking about the Pullman and Prairie Lights leads Irene to thoughts of Milly. Cash called Milly on Saturday evening and Milly had been unable to come to the phone. What must Milly think? That they've abandoned her?

Irene grabs her cell phone and calls Milly while she sets the table for two. She debates setting out candles. They're more flattering than the outdoor lighting, but will Irene be sending the wrong message? The boys were kind enough not to ask why she was wearing a sundress and earrings (possibly they hadn't noticed). Irene wants to look nice and normal, though not like she's trying too hard. She has left her hair hanging down her back, still damp from the shower. No makeup; it's best if Huck sees her how she really is.

As she decides no to candles and then yes to candles—why deny herself the pleasure of candlelight?—Dot, the head nurse on the medical floor, answers.

"Dot, this is Irene Steele. I know I've been lax about calling this week..."

"Oh, Irene," Dot says. "Cash called and let us know that you all were taking a vacation. Are you back?"

"No," Irene says. "Not yet." She stands at the deck railing and looks out at the sky, striped pink as the sun sets out of sight to the left. The water has taken on a purplish hue, and pinpricks of light start to appear on the neighboring islands. This view is probably what someone like Dot thinks of when she thinks *vacation.* And yet.

"I haven't called you because I don't want to rain on your

parade," Dot says. "But Milly is failing, Irene. It's nothing dramatic, just a steady decline I've noticed since the first of the year. She's not going to die tomorrow—I don't want you running home—but I figured you ought to know."

Irene is silent. Milly has been failing since the first of the year. The day that Russ died. Her only child. It's almost as if she sensed it.

"Is she awake now?" Irene asks. "Can I speak with her?"

"She's been asleep for hours," Dot says. "But I'll tell her you called. Around lunchtime is best, if you want to try again tomorrow."

Try again tomorrow, Irene thinks. So she can lie to Milly and tell her everything is fine, Cash surprised her with a vacation, the Caribbean is beautiful.

"Okay," Irene says. "I'll do that."

Huck arrives a few minutes after seven. From her second-floor guest-room window, Irene watches his truck snake up the driveway. She checks her hair and hurries down the stairs to meet him at the door.

This is not a date, she tells herself, though her nerves are bright and jangly with anticipation. She will attempt to make Huck her ally. She needs one here on this island.

Irene opens the door. Huck has cleaned up a bit himself—his red-gray hair is combed, his yellow shirt pressed. He's holding a bag of fish fillets—more than they could possibly eat—in one hand and a bottle of…he immediately hands the bottle over to Irene…Flor de Caña rum, eighteen years old.

"Thought we might need that," he says.

Irene accepts the bottle gratefully. It solves the problem of how to greet him—air-kiss or handshake. Now neither is necessary.

"Come on in," she says. "Did you have any problem finding it?"

"You know I've lived here twenty years," Huck says. "And I never knew this road existed. Does it have a name?"

"Lovers Lane," Irene says.

"Seriously?"

"That's what the deed says." This is a development, new as of this afternoon. Paulette Vickers managed to produce the deed. The house, known as Number One Lovers Lane, is owned solely by Russell Steele. This news had come as a solid punch to the gut. Irene had secretly believed that they would discover the property was owned by Todd Croft or Ascension. If that had been the case, Irene could have believed Russ was a pawn, manipulated by his powerful boss. More than once after Russ had accepted the job from Todd, Irene had realized that he'd made a deal with the devil. But had she ever encouraged him to quit? Never. The money had been too seductive.

According to Irene's lawyer in Iowa City, Ed Sorley, Russ's will leaves everything to her should she survive him. *When had he signed the will?* Irene had asked Ed. She worried that another will would materialize, leaving everything to Rosie Small. But Ed said that Russ had come in to sign a new will in September, one that included a new life insurance policy he'd taken out, to the tune of three million dollars.

"September?" Irene said. This was news to her. She remembered them both signing new wills back when they bought the Church Street property.

"Yes," Ed says. "Why do you ask? Is everything all right?"

"Never better," Irene said, and hung up.

"Well," Huck says now, stepping into the foyer. "This is quite a place."

Quite a place. Huck follows Irene through the entry hall into the kitchen. She doesn't feel like giving him a tour—although there is something she wants to show him upstairs, after dinner.

"Let me get you something to drink," Irene says. "I have wine chilled or..." She looks at the rum; she's not sure what to do with it. No one has ever brought her a bottle of rum before. "Can I make you a cocktail? We have Coke, I think."

Huck opens a cabinet and pulls out two highball glasses; he pours some rum in each. "Let's do a shot," Huck says. "Then we can be civilized folks and switch to wine."

Throwing away the rule book. "Deal," Irene says. She lifts her glass, raises it to Huck, and throws the rum back. It burns, but not as much as she'd expected; it has a certain smoothness, like fiery caramel.

"Well," she says.

"Good stuff," Huck pronounces. "Now, if you can find me olive oil, salt, pepper, and a lemon, I'll marinate our catch."

Thirty minutes later, Irene is slightly more relaxed, thanks to the rum, a glass of the Cakebread, and a man who is as confident a cook as he is a fisherman. Irene sits at the outdoor table as

Huck grills, and when he brings the platter of fish to the table, she finds herself hungry for the first time since the call came.

Huck takes the seat next to Irene and then pauses a minute, looking at the food. It seems like he's about to speak—make a toast maybe, or say grace. Do they have anything to be grateful for?

Well, they're still here.

"To us," she says. "The survivors."

Huck nods. "Let's eat."

AYERS

The restaurant clears out by quarter of ten, as usual, though there are still a couple of people at the bar, including Baker's brother, Cash. Or maybe Ayers should be thinking of Baker as Cash's brother. She likes them both. Baker is hotter, but Ayers feels more comfortable around Cash.

She wipes down the tables, clears all the dishes, unties her apron, and throws it in the hamper. The chef hired someone to replace Rosie, an older gentleman named Dominic, which Ayers supposes is for the best. Skip pours Ayers a glass of the Schramsberg to drink as he counts out her tips.

"Ayers!" Cash calls across the bar. "Come sit!" He raises his beer aloft and Ayers drifts over but does not commit to sitting down. Baker had said he'd be back at ten, and Ayers plans on taking him to De' Coal Pot. She has been dreaming about the oxtail stew all night.

Rosie had loved the oxtail stew at De' Coal Pot. And the curried goat.

"So how was your dinner?" Ayers asks Cash.

"Wuss good," Cash says. He's slurring his words. From the looks of things, he's even drunker than he was on *Treasure Island.* Ayers notices the Jeep keys next to his place mat.

"Water here, please," Ayers says to Skip with a look. She wonders if her date to De' Coal Pot is in jeopardy. Baker will have to drive Cash home; he can't drive himself.

Ayers feels a hand on her back and turns, expecting to see Baker but—whoa! surprise!—it's Mick. He's wearing a sky-blue Beach Bar t-shirt and his hair is damp behind the ears. He's working, obviously, but what Ayers doesn't understand is why, if he's going to sneak off for a drink, doesn't he go somewhere *else*? Why not Joe's Rum Hut or the Banana Deck? Why does he have to come *here*?

"Hey," he says. He waves to Skip, and a cold Island Summer Ale lands in front of him.

"What?" she says.

"I came to see how you're holding up," Mick says. "Want to get a drink? I just got off. And actually I'm starving. Want to grab Chinese at 420?"

Chinese at 420: Their old ritual. 420 to Center is a dive bar next to Slim's parking lot where everyone in the service industry goes after his or her shift. It's owned by two guys from Boston; "420 to Center" is some reference to Fenway Park. They do whip up remarkably good Chinese food late-night. Time was, not so long ago, that Mick and Ayers were the king and queen of 420 to Center. But that time has passed. Ayers hasn't been to 420 once this season. She avoided it because she assumed Mick went there with her successor.

Speaking of which.

"Where's Brigid?" Ayers asks.

Mick shrugs.

"Trouble in paradise?" she says.

"It was never paradise."

Ayers thinks about this for a moment. Ayers would have called what she and Mick had paradise. Yes, she would have. They were in love in St. John, they had good jobs and the same days off, and they knew everyone; when they went out, it was hard to pay for a drink. They both loved the beach, the sun, sex, hiking, drinking tequila, and Mick's dog, Gordon. What could Ayers assume when Mick left but that Brigid—young, alluring Brigid—offered something *even more sublime.* To discover that this maybe wasn't true, that life with Brigid had somehow not lived up to expectations, is, of course, enormously satisfying. But only for a fleeting moment. Mick is here, she realizes, *not* to see how Ayers is "holding up." No, it's not about Ayers's emotional state, but rather, about *Mick's.* He wants her company or he wants sex—probably the latter—but Ayers doesn't have time for it.

"Oh, well," she says, and she turns back to Cash, who has consumed his water and seems reinvigorated, like the herbs in Ayers's garden after a rain. "You feeling better?"

"Yes," Cash says. "Do you know what time it is?"

"Nearly ten," she says. She can feel Mick at her back, watching her, and probably sizing up Cash. When they were a couple, Mick had been fiendishly jealous of every single one of Ayers's male customers—single or married, in the restaurant or on the boat—and yet, in the end, it was he who had put his head up someone else's skirt. "Are you calling it a night?"

"I wish," Cash says. "I can't go home for another hour. My mother has a guest for dinner and she wants privacy."

"Your mother," Ayers says. "Did she meet someone here? Or...do you know people?"

"Met someone," Cash says. "Apparently."

"So your parents are divorced?" Ayers asks.

"Divorced?" Cash says. He takes what seems like a long time to consider the question. "No. No." Another pause, during which Ayers hears Mick and Skip talking about a supposed surfable swell in Reef Bay. It was Ayers's least favorite thing about Mick: he professed to be a "surfer," and he used all the lingo, but the one time Ayers had watched him "surf," he'd fallen off the board and broken his collarbone. He'd blamed his accident on the waves. "My father is dead."

Because she's distracted thinking about the five hours she and Mick had spent in the waiting room at Myrah Keating, with Mick moaning and groaning while she smoothed his hair and brought water to his lips like a dutiful girlfriend, it takes her a moment to process this statement.

"Dead?" she says. "I'm sorry. Recently?"

Cash nods. "Really recently. That's kind of why we're down here."

Down here. Family reunion, maybe the first vacation since the father died, which is why the mother came along.

"You're still here?" a voice says.

Ayers turns around to see Baker standing behind her and also, of course, behind Mick. Baker is as big, tall, and broad as a tree. He's staring down his brother.

"Mom said stay out until eleven," Cash says. "Where else was I supposed to go?"

"Yeah, I don't know," Baker says. "But Ayers and I are going out and you're not invited." His tone is strong, nearly bullying, and Ayers feels bad for Cash. She understands now that both

Cash and Baker are interested in her, and she wished they'd sorted this out at home to save her from being stuck in the middle, although a small part of her is gloating, because what better situation for Mick to witness than two men fighting over her?

"Where are you guys going?" Cash asks.

"None of your business," Baker says, so harshly that Ayers winces, but then he softens and says, "Listen, just give us an hour, okay, man? I'll be back to pick you up at eleven. I promise."

"But where are you going?" Cash asks.

"De' Coal Pot," Ayers says. "It's Caribbean food. You're welcome to..."

Cash holds up a hand. "You guys go. I ate."

"De' Coal Pot?" Mick says. "I could go for some oxtail stew myself."

Not happening, Ayers thinks. *This is not happening.* She is smacked by a wave of devastating sorrow. The person she needs by her side right now isn't Mick or Baker or Cash. It's Rosie.

Can you see this? Ayers asks Rosie in her mind. *Please tell me you are somewhere you can see this.*

Baker swings around. "Who are *you*?" he asks Mick.

Mick, wisely, holds up his hands. "No one," he says. "I'm no one."

Baker and Ayers walk down the street toward De' Coal Pot, although Ayers finds she no longer has any appetite. She needs air, she needs space.

"I'm not hungry anymore," she says. "Let's go down to the beach."

"You lead," Baker says. "I'll follow."

Ayers takes him down past the Beach Bar to the far edge of Frank Bay, where it's dark and quiet. Out on the water, she sees the ferry making its way toward St. Thomas. On the far horizon, she spies a cruise ship, all lit up like a floating city. Ayers sits in the cool sand and Baker eases down next to her.

"Your brother is pretty drunk," Ayers says.

"I didn't realize you knew him so well," Baker says. "That came as a surprise."

"He didn't tell you we bumped into each other on the Reef Bay Trail?" Ayers says. "He saved my life, or at least it felt like it at the time. So, as a thank-you, I invited him to come on *Treasure Island* yesterday. I didn't think he'd show up, but he did."

"Of course he did," Baker says. "When a gorgeous woman invites you somewhere, you go."

Ayers smiles. She's flattered by the compliment—but then she chastises herself. She can't let herself be won over so easily.

"Your brother is nice," Ayers says.

"Very nice," Baker says. "I'm extremely jealous that he got to spend so much time with you. When I met you at the reception...I can't explain any way to say it except that I was bowled over. Blown away. I looked at you and...well, I'd better not say anything else."

"You don't even know me," Ayers says. "And I hate to tell you this, but I have a rule about dating tourists. I don't do it."

"That's good to know," Baker says.

"I'm serious," Ayers says. "Guys like you and your brother come here, you're on vacation, on the beach all day, hiking, snorkeling, happy hour, out to dinner, and that's all great. That's what you're supposed to do. But then you get back on the ferry to St. Thomas, where you board the plane home to your real life. And I stay here." She opens her arms wide, aware that the back of her right arm is now touching Baker's chest. He gently reaches around her and pulls her close. She lets him. She wants physical contact, meaningless though it may be. It's really not fair that Mick showed up and then admitted that life with Brigid was never paradise. It's not fair that Rosie is dead because *she* fell in love with a tourist—or if not a tourist exactly, then a visitor, and if not a visitor, then... Ayers doesn't quite know *how* to categorize the Invisible Man, but she does blame him for stealing her friend. And, just say it, for *killing* her friend. Her best friend.

Baker senses something in her breathing, maybe, or he reads minds, because he touches her chin and says, "Hey, are you okay?" And the next thing Ayers knows, she's kissing him. She tells herself to stop, this is irrational, self-destructive behavior; she knows exactly nothing about this guy. But the kissing is electric, just like it was the very first time she kissed Mick, maybe better. Chemistry, she has learned, is either there or it isn't and wow, yes, it's there, this guy knows what he's doing, his tongue, she can't get enough of it, his arms are so strong, his hands, every cell of her body is suddenly yearning for more. She's going to sleep with him, maybe right here on the beach—no, that would be bad, what if someone sees, it'll be all over town by tomorrow, but she doesn't want to break the spell to go to her truck and drive to her house, it's too far, she wants this now. Does he want it now? He's being shy with his hands, one is on the back of her head, one on the side of her neck, she wants him to put his hand up her shirt. She guides his hand, he just barely fingers her nipple, she groans, she reaches over into his lap, he's hard as a rock, practically busting through his shorts. Oh yes, she thinks, this is happening *right now.*

He pulls away, out of breath. "We have to stop."

"We can't stop," she says. She strokes his erection through his shorts and he makes a choking sound, then says, "You're killing me. But I like you, I like you so much, Ayers, and I don't want it to be like this, here on the beach, over quickly and then I go home and you go home and I'm just the tourist you let through the net because you're sad about your friend and because I told your ex-boyfriend off."

She draws back. She only had one sip of Schramsberg after service but she feels light-headed, not drunk exactly but addled, mixed-up, off-kilter, and yet she knows he's right. She's startled, in fact, at just how right he is.

"You knew that was my ex-boyfriend?"

"You pointed him out at the reception," Baker says. "He was with that unwashed trollop."

"Yes," Ayers whispers. "Brigid."

"Let's spend the day together tomorrow," he says. "Can we?"

"We can," Ayers says. "I have the whole day off tomorrow. Day and night—"

He squeezes her. "Beach during the day...

"Wait," she says. She's supposed to take Maia tomorrow after school and overnight. It's the first time since Rosie died. Ayers can't cancel. She *won't* cancel. "Actually, I'm only free tomorrow until three."

He stiffens. "Hot date?"

"Something like that," Ayers says. She doesn't elaborate; she wants him to be jealous. "But we can still do beach. I'll meet you around ten, we'll get sandwiches. I know a place out in Coral Bay that's always deserted. I swim naked."

"Yes!" Baker says. "I'm in!" He stands up, offers her a hand, pulls her in close, and kisses the tip of her nose. "I don't want you to think I meant anything by stopping. I just want this to be memorable. I want it to be perfect. You deserve that."

He's saying all the right things. But he's a tourist. A tourist! He lives in...she tries to remember. He has a child somewhere and a wife who left him.

"How much longer do you have here?" Ayers asks. "When are you leaving?"

Baker pauses. "I'm not sure."

"You're not sure?" Ayers says. She suddenly gets the feeling he's hiding something, and she realizes that she felt that way while talking to Cash as well. As if not everything added up. They're here for a family reunion, the father is dead, but the mother has a date tonight. They don't know the address of where they're staying and Baker seemed pretty dead set against Ayers driving him home that morning. He was lost, he said. "Well, you rented a villa, right? How long is the rental?"

"It's not a rental," Baker says. "The villa belongs to my father."

He and Ayers have made their way back up to the road. At the Beach Bar, a band is playing a Sublime cover. "But isn't your father dead?" Ayers asks.

Baker stops in the street. "Did Cash tell you that?"

"Yes?" Ayers says. "He said your mother has a date tonight and I asked if your parents were divorced and he said no, your father was dead."

"Did he say anything else?"

"Anything else like *what*?" Ayers says. It's now more than a feeling; it's a certainty. Something is going on with these two guys that they're not telling her.

"Well, first of all, my mother does *not* have a date," Baker says. He takes Ayers's hand and they head back in the direction of La Tapa. "But we do, tomorrow at ten. Right?"

Ayers takes a deep breath of the sweet evening air. The problem, she realizes, is Mick. Mick has made her mistrustful. He cheated on her with Brigid and now Ayers is destined to think *everyone* is hiding something.

"Right," she says.

CASH

At five minutes to eleven, Cash finishes his beer, leaves a tip for Skip, and stumbles out to the front of the restaurant. He has called Baker three times but gotten no answer, which is really making Cash's blood boil, because while Baker is out putting the moves on Ayers—on *Ayers,* the first woman Cash has been attracted to in *years*—Cash has no way to get home.

What is he supposed to do? He has twenty-six dollars left to his name; all the rest of the cash from his now-defunct stores is gone. To live another day, he's going to have to ask his mother or brother for money. He can maybe pass off his flat-broke state as a logistical situation, claiming his bank card doesn't work down here, but there are enough cover-ups and lies in this family as it is. He needs to come clean: the stores are gone.

It seems like a minor problem. He tried to be someone he wasn't, he failed, and now he will go back to being the person he is. A ski instructor. For some reason, the idea doesn't hold as much appeal as it did before all this happened.

He tries Baker again: voicemail. He feels himself about to

snap. But then he hears his brother's voice and sees Baker waving an arm.

"Back in five!" Baker says. He's with Ayers; they're holding hands. They walk down the street to a green pickup and then Cash is treated to the sight of them kissing, really kissing. Cash feels sick.

"He's married!" Cash calls out. But they don't hear him.

On the way home, Baker is giddy. He sounds like a teenage girl. He kissed Ayers on the beach, he could have done more, way more, but he stopped her. *He* stopped *her.* She was totally into it, eager, ready, but with a woman like Ayers, a quick hookup on the beach isn't good enough. She deserves a bed. A suite at Caneel Bay. He's going to look into it.

"Look into a *suite* at *Caneel*?" Cash says. The words leave his mouth just as they happen to drive past the grand landscaped entrance of the Caneel Bay Resort. None of the resort is visible beyond the gatehouse, but Cash imagines it's pretty opulent. Like his father's house, only sexier. "You're married."

"I told you, Anna and I separated," Baker says. "She came home on New Year's Day, I kid you not, like five minutes before Mom called with the news, and she said she was leaving me. She said she was in love with someone else."

"Really?" Cash says. He has never thought of Dr. Anna Schaffer as someone who would be "in love" with anyone, Baker included. She had appeared decidedly unenthusiastic at the wedding, but Cash understood that Anna was in thrall to her work. People took a distant second. Irene had long intoned her concern that Anna didn't even have warm feelings for Floyd. Her own child. "Who is she in love with?"

"Dr. Louisa Rodriguez," Baker says. "Another cardiothoracic surgeon. Friend and colleague."

"Luis?" Cash says. He's confused. "Or Louisa?"

"Louisa," Baker says. "Woman."

"Really?" Cash says. "Anna's a lesbian? I guess I can see that."

"I'm not sure we need to label her," Baker says. "It might just be that she has feelings for Louisa in particular."

"Fair enough," Cash says. At that moment, his phone starts ringing and he thinks it must be his mother, calling to say the coast is clear and they are free to come home—because who else could it be? When he checks the display, he shakes his head. *Anna*, it says. Wait. He looks at Baker, then back down at his phone. It's almost as if she heard them talking about her.

"Hello?" Cash says.

"Cash," she says. "Hey, it's Anna. Anna Schaffer. Baker's wife."

"Hi," Cash says. It speaks volumes that she has to explain who she is. Still, he tries to keep his voice neutral. "How are you?"

"Do you know where Baker is?" she asks. "I've been calling him all night but he won't answer."

Cash nearly says, *Yeah, Baker is right here*—but something stops him. "Is everything okay?" he asks.

"Everything's fine," Anna says. "Would you please let Baker know that Floyd and I are flying down there tomorrow? We land at one fifteen and should be on the two o'clock ferry out of Red Hook that will get us to St. John by three."

To St. John tomorrow by three.

"Okay," Cash says. He can't believe this. Didn't Baker say he had a date with Ayers tomorrow?

"You really need to remember to tell him," Anna says. "Baker has no idea we're coming. It was basically impossible for me to clear it with work until the very last minute."

"Will do," Cash says.

"I can count on you?" Anna says.

"Absolutely," Cash says.

"Okay," Anna says, and she sounds happier, maybe even a little excited. "See you tomorrow!"

Cash hangs up the phone. He can't believe this is happening. He can't believe it.

"Who was that?" Baker asks.

"That?" Cash says. "No one."

HUCK

This is right up there with the craziest things Huck has ever done. A dozen times on the way over, he thought, *For the love of Bob, turn around, go home to your book and your beer. Getting mixed up with this woman, the wife, is going to be nothing but trouble. Rosie is dead and nothing will bring her back.* The voice in Huck's head was one of reason, loud and clear, and yet still he drove to the north shore and found the utility pole with the two yellow stripes. Still he ascended the steep, winding road—there were no other homes, only dummy driveways that led to nowhere, until you reached the gate at the top, which had been left open. Huck wondered if this bastard had enough money to buy up the entire hill, just to make certain he had no neighbors.

Still he knocked on the door.

Irene looks pretty. It's not a thought he should be having about Russell Steele's widow, but there it is, plain and simple. Huck is a man, built like other men, and so he appreciates Irene's chestnut hair hanging loose and damp down her back, and the black sundress that shows off her arms, her neck, and her pretty feet.

She's nervous, he can tell—her hands are shaking as she accepts the rum. Huck thinks, *Better do a shot right away.* Why did God provide humans with alcohol if not for situations like this?

They make casual chitchat while Huck prepares the mahi. Irene pours white wine, it's her favorite, from Napa, she says, and Huck makes a sound of general appreciation, as if he cares where the wine is from. Irene has set out cheese and crackers but she doesn't touch them, and Huck holds back to be polite. Or maybe it's rude not to eat? He can't tell; he should have reviewed his Emily Post before coming up here. Huck asks Irene if she has a job. She says yes, she's the editor of something called *Heartland Home & Style*. It's a glossy magazine, she says, with a hundred seventy-five thousand subscribers and a quarter-million in advertising each month.

"So it's like *Penthouse,* then?" Huck says.

This gets a laugh out of her, which must come as a surprise, because she claps a hand over her mouth.

"It's okay," Huck says. "You're allowed."

This is the exact wrong response, because Irene's eyes fill with tears, but she takes a breath, recovers, and says, "I'm sorry. It's kindness that undoes me."

"Understood," Huck says. "From here on out, I'll try to be more of a bastard."

Irene smiles. "Thank you. Anyway, a day or two before all this... I had something happen at work. They named me 'executive editor,' which is technically a rung up the masthead, but for all intents and purposes I was fired. They relieved me of all my important duties, my decision making..."

"Turned you into an editor *emeritus,*" Huck says.

Irene's eyes grow wide. "Exactly."

"They're giving you an honorary title, hoping you'll retire," Huck says.

"They couldn't fire me because then advertisers would have made noise, so they got sneaky instead."

"You should quit," Huck says. "Move down here. I'll hire you as my first mate. You're one hell of a good fisherperson."

Irene laughs again, not happily. "Not a chance," she says.

He gets back in her good graces once he sets down the grilled mahi. He waits until Irene takes a bite.

"Wow," she says.

"Really?" he says. "Good?"

She takes another bite and he takes the hint: she's not there to plump his ego. He tastes the fish: yes, perfect. Huck is something of a fanatic about grilling fish. In his opinion, you have a sixty-second window with fish. You take it off a minute too early, it's translucent and not quite *there.* But this is preferable, in his mind, to a minute too late. A minute too late and the fish is dry, overcooked, ruined. Three generations of Small women—LeeAnn, Rosie, and Maia—have been schooled in Huck's feelings about grilled fish, and they all reached a point where they were as discriminating as he was. Huck's fish is always on point, because he stands at the grill like the Swiss Guard and doesn't let anything distract him. He'd worried that tonight would be an exception, because there are a host of distractions here, but, praise be, the fish is correct.

Irene eats only the fish—the pasta salad and greens remain on her plate—then she helps herself to seconds. "I have no appetite," she says. "Except for this fish."

"Because you caught it yourself," Huck says. "Because you pulled it out of blue water." He catches her eye. "Angler Cupcake."

She pours more wine. They're at the end of the first bottle and without hesitating, Irene opens a second. Okay, then, it's going to be that kind of night. Huck has questions, but he won't ask them yet.

"Powder room?" he asks, standing up.

Irene says, "Through the living room to the back corner down a short hall."

Huck takes his time wandering. The house is grand but the furnishings are impersonal. He had hoped to see something of Rosie, some indication that she spent time here. There are no photographs; there's no art at all, really. It looks like any one of a thousand rentals. On the other hand, Huck is glad about this for Irene's sake. How unpleasant it would be for her to have to live, even briefly, in the love nest Russell Steele once feathered with his mistress.

Huck isn't sure when he started taking Irene's feelings into account. Probably when she took the second helping of fish.

As Huck washes his hands, he stares at himself in the mirror and asks himself the hardest question.

Did Rosie know the Invisible Man was married? Huck desperately wants to believe the answer is no, but...come on! Russell Steele shows up here a week or two per month; the rest of the time he's ostensibly "working," but he's never here at Thanksgiving or Christmas. Is he "working" on Thanksgiving or Christmas? No! He's with his family, his other family, his real family.

Rosie was sweet, but she wasn't naive.

When Huck gets back to the deck, Irene is standing at the railing with her wine, staring at the water.

It's time now, he supposes. He joins her.

"Tell me about your children," he says.

She shakes her head. No, she doesn't want to tell him, or she doesn't believe he deserves to hear. But then she says, "Baker is thirty. He lives in Houston. He's married to a heart surgeon and has a four-year-old son named Floyd. He's a stay-at-home dad, runs the household, does all the things I used to do when the boys were small. He day-trades in tech stocks, too, on the side, but Anna makes most of the money."

"Do we like Anna?" Huck asks. Something about the way she said the woman's name makes him curious.

"Oh," Irene says. "She's fine."

"That bad?" he says.

"She's an excellent surgeon. She makes all the Houston Best-of lists, and her patients love her. But you don't have that kind of demanding career without some personal sacrifice."

"The sacrifice in her case...?"

"She's never home. She isn't much of a mother to Floyd. She's a bit dispassionate. It's hard to pierce her armor, to get any kind of human response out of her at all. Now, in her defense, she deals with life and death all day, every day, so telling her about finger-painting projects or playground squabbles falls on deaf ears."

"That's too bad," Huck says. "I love hearing the day-to-day details about my granddaughter Maia's life. She and her friend Joanie are starting a bath bomb business. They're making them in tropical scents to sell to tourists. I had to order citric acid crystals from Amazon—the package will probably take several months to get here. But I treasure all the little stuff. Because then they get older and they stop telling you things."

"Amen," Irene says.

"I didn't mean to hijack the conversation," Huck says. "Tell me about your other son."

"Cash," she says. "Short for Cashman. The boys were given the maiden names of my two grandmothers. Cash owns and operates a couple of outdoor supply stores in Denver. Savage Season Outdoor Supply, they're called. Russ gave him the seed money. Russ wanted to see Cash do something with his life other than be a ski instructor."

"Nothing wrong with teaching people to ski," Huck says. "Honest living."

If Irene notices the archness in his voice, she doesn't let on. "So those are the boys. They're good kids. They don't know what to make of all this. They know about Rosie, although we haven't discussed it. I should tell them I know—it would probably be a weight off their minds. They want to protect me from it, I'm sure. I suppose I'll tell them in the morning."

"Always best to be open," Huck says.

"Is it?" Irene asks. "I made them leave the house tonight because you were coming. They don't know I've made contact with you. They don't know about the fishing." Irene throws back what's left of her wine. "It's like Russ had this giant secret, which, in turn, is causing the three of us to keep our own smaller secrets." She looks Huck in the eye for the first time, or the first time without her guard way up. Her eyes are steel-blue, the color of a stormy sea. "I can't believe this happened to me. And I can't believe I tracked you down, forced you to take me fishing, and then invited you to dinner."

"If it makes any difference," Huck says, "I'm glad you did."

"Are you?" she says.

He wants to kiss her. But he is too old and out of practice to know if she would welcome this or slap him.

Slap him, he thinks. She's been a widow for less than a week.

"Yes," he says. "I am." He rips his eyes away from her and focuses on Jost Van Dyke, twinkling in the distance. The view is quite something from up here.

"Tell me what you know," Irene says. "Tell me about Rosie."

"All right," Huck says.

Should he go all the way back to the beginning?

Huck is new to the island, but not brand-new. He has his boat and he has his best friend, Rupert, out in Coral Bay. Coral

Bay is different from town: folks out there keep to themselves, West Indians and whites alike. Honestly, as soon as you came down the other side of Bordeaux Mountain, it was as though you were on a different island. When Huck wanted to see Rupert, he had to drive to Coral Bay; Rupert simply refused to come west. They would drink at Skinny Legs or Shipwreck Landing and then, half in the bag, Huck would drive home.

Stay left, Rupert used to say. *And look out for the donkeys.*

It was at a full-moon BBQ at a place called Miss Lucy's that Rupert introduced Huck to LeeAnn. There was a three-piece steel band and she was right in front, dancing in the grass. Love at first sight? Sure, why not.

LeeAnn had a daughter, fifteen years old and beautiful, which meant trouble. Rosie's father was long gone, but his people were still around, and while LeeAnn was working her long hours as a nurse practitioner, Rosie sometimes visited her Small aunties and cousins out in Coral Bay—or at least that's what she said she was doing. Part or most of that time, she was, instead, falling in love with a fella named Oscar from St. Thomas who was twenty-four years old and bad news. Oscar worked "security" for Princess cruises—Huck suspected he also supplied the staff and passengers with drugs—and as such, he was flush with cash that he liked to show off. He drove a Ducati motorcycle and came over to St. John every chance he got to take Rosie for a ride.

Rosie sneaked over to St. Thomas to attend the Rolex Regatta. She had begged LeeAnn to be allowed to go and LeeAnn had said no, she was too young, period. But Rosie had gone anyway. When LeeAnn found out, she dispatched Huck to find her and bring her home. Huck and LeeAnn had been together only a few months at that point, and Huck was still completely infatuated. He would do whatever LeeAnn asked without question, even though he knew he held no sway over Rosie.

He had loaded his truck on the car barge and driven to the St. Thomas Yacht Club, where he paid twenty-five dollars to park and another five for a couple of beers to walk around with while he hunted for LeeAnn's child. Because Huck had been born and raised in the Florida Keys, he was no stranger to regattas. They were only nominally about sailing; really, they were about drinking. Huck took in the well-heeled crowd holding their cocktails aloft as they danced to the band playing vintage Rolling Stones, and the pervasive sense of joy and revelry—because what better way to spend an afternoon than drinking rum and dancing under the Caribbean sun while a bunch of white guys in five-million-dollar boats negotiated wind and water in the name of an overpriced watch?

He was cynical because he was jealous. It looked fun, and he had come to be a buzzkill.

Huck found Rosie sitting on Oscar's lap at a picnic table crowded with other West Indians, all of them nattily dressed, all of them wearing Rolexes themselves. They were eating chicken roti and conch stew, drinking Caribes. Huck was bigger than Oscar, just barely, but there were some other gentlemen at the table who were bigger than Huck and Oscar combined, with Rosie thrown in.

Huck saw no way to tackle his assignment other than head-on. He approached the table—the men and Rosie were all speaking patois, Huck could barely decipher a word—and said, "Rosie, I've come to bring you home."

Rosie, he remembered, had blinked lazily, unfazed, and had burrowed like a sand crab into Oscar's arms. "I'm not going anywhere. I'm staying here."

"No," Huck said. "You're not."

"Hey, man," Oscar said. "You heard the lady."

"She's not a lady," Huck said. "She's fifteen years old."

This caught the attention of the other gentlemen at the table. They started lowing and whoa-ing. Oscar knew how old Rosie was—maybe he thought she was sixteen or seventeen. However, the others likely thought Rosie was nineteen or twenty, maybe even older. She was wearing iridescent-blue eyeshadow and a halter top the size of a handkerchief.

Huck squared his shoulders. "I'm not leaving without her." He hadn't been sure how intimidating he seemed, but he had been to Vietnam before any of these guys were born and he would remind them of that if he needed to. "I'm going to have a cigarette while you say your good-byes."

Oscar had eased Rosie off his lap and then held her face and talked to her gently while she cried. But it was clear Oscar wasn't going to put up a fight, and Huck felt proud of himself, thinking how relieved LeeAnn would be when both Huck and Rosie pulled in the driveway. As long as he found the girl some other clothes.

Huck was ready for Rosie's anger. She climbed into Huck's pickup and slammed the door so hard it nearly fell off. That hadn't surprised him. When they pulled up to Route 322, the sounds of the reggae band still wafting in through Huck's open window, Rosie said, "I hate you." That hadn't surprised him, either.

"I don't know who you think you are. Maybe you think you're some kind of god because you're white. But no white man tells me what to do."

Huck said, "There's a popular phrase that goes, 'Don't shoot the messenger.' I came at the request of your mother. She had to work, and so she sent me. Frankly, I think you got off easy."

"I still hate you," Rosie said.

Huck doesn't think Irene needs or wants to hear all this, so he just says, "I married LeeAnn when Rosie was a teenager. She was a rebellious child. She dated a West Indian fella, older, from St. Thomas named Oscar. That went on for too long, but it ended when Oscar went to jail."

"Lovely," Irene says.

"Tell me about it," Huck says. "He got drunk and stabbed one of his friends. Though not fatally."

"Did Rosie go to college?" Irene asks.

"She did, at UVI in St. Thomas. It's funny, some kids who grow up here can't wait to get away, and some can't bear to leave. Rosie was the latter. She loved it here. She and her momma used to fight like half-starved hens over a handful of feed, but there was a deep emotional attachment. So she stayed. For a long time, she waited tables at Caneel Bay. That's where she met the Pirate."

"The pirate?" Irene says.

"It was...let's see...thirteen years ago, Valentine's weekend. Some guy, rich, white, showed up on a yacht for the weekend and swept Rosie off her feet."

"What was his name?" Irene asks.

"Never learned it. He came and went. It was just a weekend fling. Rosie called him the Pirate, though, because he stole her heart."

"So she had a history of this?" Irene says.

"If by 'this' you mean poor choices in men, then yes," Huck says. "I actually suspected the Pirate was a made-up story. I thought Rosie was back with Oscar—this would have been after he was released from jail. But when the baby was born, she was very light-skinned. No doubt the father was white."

Irene backs away a fraction of an inch. "Baby?"

"Maia," Huck says. "Rosie's daughter. My granddaughter. She's twelve."

"Oh," Irene says. "I didn't put...I didn't realize..." She tears up, then starts to soundlessly cry. Huck pulls a handkerchief out of his pocket, which is actually just one of the bandanas he likes to tie around his neck when he's fishing, and hands it to Irene. She shakes it out over the railing like a woman bidding her loved ones good-bye on an ocean liner, then dabs at her eyes. "I'm sorry. I didn't realize Rosie left behind a child."

"That's the real tragedy here," Huck says. "Me, I'm old. I've known loss. But Maia..."

"She's twelve, you say? And never knew her father? So Rosie was all she had?"

"Rosie and me," Huck says. "Now there's just me. But people will step up. Maia won't get lost. I won't let her get lost. I don't care if I have to keep myself alive until I'm a hundred years old."

"When did Russ come into the picture?" Irene asks.

"I couldn't be sure..."

"But if you had to guess," Irene says. "The deed says he bought this house three years ago. Had their relationship... been going on for *three years*?"

Here is where things get thorny, Huck thinks. Here is where he profoundly regrets his decision to let this woman ever set foot on his boat. They have been acting like they're on the same side. In some sense, they are. They're the bereaved. The survivors.

But Huck is Rosie's family and Irene is Russ's family. Irene wants this whole mess to be Rosie's fault and Huck wants it to be Russ's fault. Irene is making it sound like *three years* would be nearly inconceivable—but Huck knows that their relationship went on longer than three years. Rosie met the Invisible Man right after LeAnn died—five years ago.

"I'm really not sure, Irene," Huck says. "What I know about their relationship I could write on my thumbnail and still have room for the U.S. Constitution. Rosie told me next to nothing. And like I said, I never had the pleasure of meeting..."

"My husband."

"Mr. Steele." Huck clears his throat. "Your husband."

Irene steps back to the table, fills her glass with more wine, and regards Huck over the rim, as if trying to gauge whether or not he's telling the truth.

He is. He knows it sounds unusual. It *was* unusual. And part of what's at work in Huck is guilt. He should have nipped the relationship—or at least the secrecy about it—in the bud. But like he said, Rosie met the guy right after LeeAnn died, when Huck was in bad shape. LeeAnn had been sick, sure—her death hadn't come as a total shock. And yet Huck had been left feeling like his entire right side had been amputated.

He'd been glad that Rosie had found someone to distract

her from her grief. By the time he realized how pathological the relationship was, it was too late. Rosie was in love. All the way.

"I should have done more," he says. "I should have tried to stop it. I should have hired a private investigator."

Irene sets her wineglass gently down and lets her hands drop to her sides. "You showed up here," she says. "That's more than a lot of men would do."

True, he thinks. But he says nothing.

Irene reaches out…and takes his hand. "Will you come upstairs with me?"

He's speechless.

"There's something I need your help with," she says.

Huck follows Irene up the stairs, his mind racing. Is she making advances? Is the "something" that she wants help with getting out of that black dress? This is all moving a little fast for Huck. But he won't say no. She's a grieving widow and he has lost his daughter. Now that he has allowed himself to travel back in time, he realizes that Rosie became his daughter the second he yanked her out of the regatta. Or maybe it was when he paid twenty bucks for a regatta t-shirt to put on over the hankie she was wearing. Or maybe it was when she told him she hated him.

Irene needs physical contact and Huck needs it too, doesn't he? And she's a good-looking woman.

They walk down a long white hallway with a vaulted ceiling ribbed with exposed beams. There are rooms off to both sides, bedrooms. Huck peers into each one. They're similar; it feels like a fancy hotel. At the very end of the hall is a closed door. Irene turns the knob. Locked.

"When we got here on Thursday, the house had been cleaned out," Irene says. "Every personal item removed. Russ's clothes, gone. All the papers from his office, gone. Someone came and took it all away, probably his business partner, Todd Croft. Ever heard that name?"

Huck shakes his head. "No."

"This door is locked. And I was hoping you could force it open for me."

"Okay." Huck says. The door is solid wood, the handle is heavy. Nothing about this house is cheap. "Have you asked your sons?"

"I didn't ask them," Irene says. "And they obviously haven't been blessed with any natural curiosity, because neither of them has noticed. I'm afraid of what we're going to find inside."

Huck presses against the door. He's a big guy, but breaking down this door is beyond him; he'll have to pick the lock. The nice thing about owning a boat for forty years is that he can tinker with the best of 'em. He is a world champion tinkerer.

"Do you have a hairpin?" he asks. "Or bobby pin?"

"I do," Irene says. "Hold on."

She's back in a few seconds with an ancient, sturdy steel bobby pin that looks like it came straight from the head of Eleanor Roosevelt. It takes Huck a few moments of poking and twisting—he doesn't have his reading glasses, and the wine has gone to his head somewhat—but then, *click,* he gets it. Lock popped. He hesitates before turning the knob, because he's also afraid of what they're going to find inside. More dead bodies? Assault rifles and refrigerators full of money? Who was this guy Russell Steele, and what was he *into*? Irene clearly doesn't have the first idea.

* * *

Huck opens the door and the first words that come to him are those from "Sugar Magnolia," *Sunshine, daydream.* It's a bedroom with a huge white canopy bed decorated with turquoise and purple pillows. The wallpaper is a swirl of purple, green, and turquoise tie-dye. There's a white powderpuff beanbag chair, a desk, and a dressing table. Maia would love this room, Huck thinks. Then he sees the letters painted on the length of one wall. M-A-I-A.

"Oh," he says. "This is Maia's room."

Irene slips past Huck into the room and starts poking around. Hairbrush and pick on the dressing table, a bottle of shea butter lotion. A book on the nightstand entitled *The Hate U Give.* Huck thinks to speak up on behalf of Maia's privacy; she's only twelve, but she still deserves respect. Huck understands why the door was locked—it would have been impossible to "undo" this room on short notice.

How must Irene feel, knowing her husband decorated a room like this for his lover's daughter? Is it salt on the wound? Huck supposes so, although he, for one, is happy to see that Maia had a safe space of her own in this house. He will be Maia's champion to the end.

"There can't be anything too important in here," he says. "She hasn't mentioned it."

Irene spins around. "Do you have a picture of her?"

"Of Maia? Yes, of course." Huck takes his phone out of his pocket. There she is, a close-up of her face, his screen saver.

Irene takes the phone from Huck and studies the photograph. He expects her to comment on how pretty Maia is, exquisite really, and elegant in a way that belies her years.

But when Irene looks up, her steel-blue eyes are spooked. Like she has seen a ghost.

No, Huck thinks. *Please, no.*

BAKER

He can't have Ayers pick him up at the villa—he's savvy enough to realize at least this much—and so he plans to have her pick him up at the Trunk Bay overlook.

"I don't get it," Ayers says. "Why don't I just come to the house?"

For all he knows, Ayers has been to his father's villa with Rosie. He isn't willing to risk it. "I hate to be the bearer of bad news," Baker says. "But my brother, Cash, also has a crush on you, and I think you coming to the house to pick me up for our romantic beach date would be...uncool and probably also unkind. I'll be at the Trunk Bay overlook at ten."

Baker isn't completely lying: Cash *does* have a thing for Ayers. When Baker comes down dressed in swim trunks and a polo shirt, holding a couple of towels he lifted from the pool house, Cash shakes his head.

"I can't believe you."

"It's not like we're eloping. We're going to the beach."

"If you were eloping you'd be breaking the law. You're *married,* Baker."

Baker lowers his voice. He's not sure if Irene is awake yet or not. "I told you, Anna left me. She's in love with Louisa

Rodriguez. Do you not remember having this conversation? Were you too drunk?"

"I remember," Cash says. "But still."

Still, Baker thinks. You're jealous.

"She doesn't know who you are, does she?" Cash asks. "Who *we* are?"

"No," Baker says. "I haven't told her."

"If she knew who you were, she wouldn't go out with you," Cash says. "But she's going to find out sooner or later. You should cancel now to save yourself the heartache."

Baker feels an uncomfortable pinch of conscience. "Don't tell me what to do."

"Fine," Cash says. "What time are you going to be home?"

"She has a previous commitment at three. So I'll be home around then."

"Previous commitment meaning another date?" Cash asks.

"She didn't say."

Cash takes two bananas from the fruit bowl, pulls them apart, and hands one to Baker. "I have an errand to run around then. Why don't you have Ayers drop you at the ferry dock at that outdoor bar, High Tide? We can grab a drink and you can tell me about your date."

Something about this sounds fishy. "What kind of errand?" Baker asks.

"The only kind of errand there is," Cash says. "A boring one. I have to pick up something coming from the States."

Money, Baker hopes. Cash was ironically named because he's the brokest SOB Baker has ever known. However, meeting Cash at the ferry dock saves him from having to give Ayers another excuse about why she can't come to the house.

"Okay," Baker says. "I'll meet you at High Tide at three. And I'll tell you about my date."

As Baker hikes up the unreasonably steep hill to the Trunk Bay lookout in the gathering heat of the morning—the trade winds, he's learned, don't kick in until the afternoon—he has upsetting thoughts. His father is dead and the list of questions surrounding his death is long, and nearly all of them are unanswered. On the one hand, Baker feels like he's put in a good-faith effort. He's made calls, he's left messages, and he's followed up with more messages. Short of hiring a private investigator—which isn't a step his mother is ready to take—he has done all he can do. On the other hand, his efforts feel meager. He doesn't deserve a day at the beach. He should be at home to support Irene, whether she wants it or not.

There are the additional issues of Ayers not knowing who Baker is, and—as Cash so emphatically pointed out—of the pesky fact that Baker is still married to Anna and hardly in a position to jump into a new relationship.

To all of this, Baker says: *Too damn bad, I'm going anyway.* It's half a day of pleasure. Cash went out on *Treasure Island;* he has no right to point fingers.

Baker is panting by the time he reaches the lookout. He needs to get in shape! He has time to gaze down over the white crescent of Trunk Bay, backed by an elegant stretch of palm trees. He thinks about snapping a picture and sending it to Anna so she can show Floyd—half the fun of seeing something so breathtaking is letting other people know you've seen it—but he doesn't want Anna to question his real reason for being here on St. John while she's out saving people's lives. And there's no time, anyway, because at that moment, Ayers pulls up in her little green truck.

Baker folds himself into the passenger side. It's small; he's chewing his knees, even when he puts the seat all the way back.

"Your first ride in Edie," Ayers says. "I'm so happy you fit. I was a little worried."

He *doesn't* fit—he has to hunch over and his thighs are cramping—but he's so happy to be in Ayers's presence, he doesn't care. "Edie? That's the truck's name?"

"Short for Edith," Ayers says. "Rosie named her. She had a pet gecko named Edith when she was a kid that was this color."

"Gotcha," Baker says. There was no room for his backpack up front, so he put it in the back, and he checks the side view nervously, expecting it to go flying out when Ayers takes the steep, twisting turns at breathtaking speed.

"Don't worry," she says. "Your bag is fine. I stopped at Sam & Jack's for sandwiches. I got three because I wasn't sure what you liked, and I got some of their homemade potato chips and a couple of kosher dills. And I went to Our Market for smoothies!"

Baker looks down in the console to see two frosted plastic cups, one pink, one pale yellow. He was too nervous to eat the banana Cash gave him so he threw it to the iguanas on the way down the hill. But now he's both starving and dying of thirst.

"Which one is mine?" he asks.

"Take your pick," Ayers says. "There's strawberry-papaya and pineapple-mango." She turns up the music—it's Jack Johnson singing "Upside Down," and Baker surprises himself by singing along. Until this very moment, Baker *hated* Jack Johnson, harbored an almost personal vendetta against him, in fact, because one of Baker's former girlfriends from Northwestern, Trinity, had loved Jack Johnson so ardently. She would only have sex with Baker if Jack Johnson was playing in the background. Needless to say, this had made Baker jealous, and because of this jealousy, he declared Jack Johnson overrated. Now, however, sitting next to Ayers, who is singing along with gleeful abandon, sometimes in key, sometimes not so much, Baker fully understands the appeal. The music is happy, undemanding, and full of sunshine. It's going-to-the-beach music, the same way that Billie Holiday is rainy-Sunday-morning music and George Thorogood is drinking-at-a-dive-bar music. Thanks to the many hours Baker spent with Trinity in bed, Baker knows all the words. He chooses the pineapple-mango smoothie, it's delicious, and he finds a magic arrangement for his legs so that he can relax. He was right to come, he thinks. He's happy.

They twist and turn and wind around until they're somehow back on the Centerline Road. To the right is a stunning view of the turquoise water and emerald mountains.

"Coral Bay," Ayers says. "Fondly known as the Other Side of the World."

They cruise down hairpin turns until they reach a Stop sign, an intersection, a little town on a harbor filled with boats.

"Skinny Legs is that way," Ayers says, pointing left. "Legendary. I wish I could say we'll have time to stop for a drink on the way home but we probably won't." She turns right and they meander past colorful clapboard cottages, a convenience store called Love City Mini Mart, a round open-air restaurant called the Aqua Bistro. "Best onion rings on planet Earth," Ayers says. She hits the gas and they fly up around a curve and nearly collide with three white donkeys standing on the side of the road.

"Donkey!" Ayers cries, and at first Baker thinks she's as

surprised to see them as he is. What are three donkeys doing on the side of the road? Ayers pulls to the shoulder and the donkeys leisurely clomp over to the car. Ayers reaches across Baker, grazing his leg with her arm, which sends an electric current right to his heart, and she pulls a withered apple from the glove box.

"Do as I say, not as I do. We're not supposed to feed them." Ayers sticks the apple out and the alpha donkey eats it from her outstretched palm. She looks at the other two and sighs. "I wish I had three. Sorry, guys!"

When they pull back onto the road, Baker says, "Whose donkeys are those? Do you *know* them?"

"There's a population of wild donkeys across the island," Ayers says. "I do have one favorite. I call him Van Gogh—he only has one ear, and I keep the apple for him. But I wanted you to see them up close. You haven't been to St. John until you've seen the donkeys!" She throws her hands up. She seems positively radiant, and Baker hopes it's because of him. She's wearing a crocheted white cover-up with a white bikini underneath and her blond hair has been wrangled into a messy bun. She is so pretty it hurts, and she keeps an apple in her glove box for a donkey with one ear. Baker can't imagine anyone being more infatuated than he is with Ayers Wilson right now.

He feels a buzzing against his leg and the sound of bongo drums. It's his phone. He has to re-contort himself to slide it out of his pocket. He checks the display: *Anna.* He hurries to silence it, then to turn the phone off completely. He'd like to chuck it out the window. When he got home the night before, he saw he had six missed calls from Anna, but there was not a single voicemail. Anna doesn't believe in voicemail; it can too easily be ignored.

What's up? Baker had texted first thing that morning, but he had received no response. That was Anna's way of punishing him for not answering his phone. But Baker didn't *want* to talk to Anna on the phone and now that she had confessed to falling in love with Louisa Rodriguez, Anna no longer got to say when and how they communicated.

"Who was that?" Ayers asks.

"My brother," Baker says quickly. "He probably wanted to remind me that I'm meeting him at High Tide around three, or whenever we get back. I forgot to ask you, is that okay? Can you drop me at High Tide?"

"Works for me," Ayers says.

Finally they reach the beach, and, as promised, theirs is the only vehicle around.

"Sometimes there are snorkelers," Ayers says. "But hopefully not today."

In the back of her truck, she has two beach chairs, the picnic, and two pool rafts. She and Baker carry everything out onto the "beach," which is a half-moon of smooth blue cobblestones. Baker has never seen a stone beach like this one before. It's tricky to walk, but Ayers strides ahead sure-footed and Baker attempts to follow suit. She places the chairs down, hides the picnic in the shade of the chairs, and slips off her cover-up; it's like a veil falling off a piece of art.

She picks up one of the pool rafts and heads for the water, which is a bowl of crystalline blue.

"Come join me when you're ready," she says.

"Oh, I'm ready," Baker says. He shucks off his polo shirt, takes off his watch, puts his phone and his watch in his backpack, rubs sunscreen on his face, hoping he worked it all in. There is nothing less attractive, Baker's school wives have informed him, than a lapse of personal grooming in a man—back hair, yellow teeth, unclipped toenails. It has led him to become overly sensitive about how he presents himself. Anna, of course, wouldn't notice if he had hot dogs growing out of his ears, but now there is someone new to impress.

Baker grabs a float. The water looks inviting, but there's a slight downward incline and the rocks are difficult to negotiate, and they're burning hot besides. Baker decides to run for the water, praying he doesn't break an ankle, and then throw himself and his raft facedown onto the water's surface. This works, sort of, he's in the water now, half on the raft, half off. He probably looked like a buffoon. He made a huge splash and now there's a wake undulating through the water that reaches Ayers. She laughs.

"Come over here," she says.

He paddles over to her and flips onto his back without too much trouble. Ayers reaches for his hand. They hold hands, drifting across the surface of the bay. From here, Baker can better appreciate the beach. The stones are backed by scrub brush and the occasional palm tree, and on either side of this bay are rocky outcrops. It's silent and deserted. They might be the last two people on earth.

Baker closes his eyes, feels the sun warm his skin. This is delightful. He doesn't go to the beach enough. Why is that? Probably because the closest beach to Houston is Galveston, with its sour brown water. Floyd loves it, of course, and clamors to go whenever there's a break from school. But that's because he doesn't know any better. When Baker and Anna were in Anguilla on their honeymoon, she was stung by a jellyfish during their first dip into Meads Bay, so for the rest of the week they hung by the resort's pool.

When he and Cash were kids, Baker remembers, their family went to Jamaica. Russ had been keen to go, but this was back when he was still a corn syrup salesman, and so they had traveled on a budget; even at ten years old, Baker had realized this. They had stayed at a hotel not far from the airport, and for the first few days, it poured rain. Baker remembers watching television, exactly as he would have done at home. His father walked out onto the balcony every time the rain abated, thinking it would clear, but it never did. Finally, Russ had broken down and given the boys each three dollars for the arcade in the lobby, even though Irene believed video games corrupted children. Baker and Cash had quickly tired of the pinball and Ms. Pac-Man, and they decided to sneak out of the hotel. They darted across a busy road to a real Jamaican village, where people were selling crocheted hacky sacks and bootleg Bob Marley tapes. A goat was being grilled on a half-barrel grill, and a man was playing the guitar and singing in a language Baker and Cash didn't quite understand. Irene and Russ had shown up a little while later, Irene plainly frantic at first and then relieved and teary, then more furious than Baker could remember ever seeing her. When the sun came out the next day, it didn't matter: Irene stayed in the room. But Russ, not wanting the vacation to be a complete loss, had rented a car and driven the boys all the way to Dunn's River Falls; on the way home, they stopped at Laughing Waters beach. Baker remembers racing for the waves, screaming and splashing, with Russ right alongside him, giddy as a little kid. Later, they had dried off with the threadbare towels they'd taken from the hotel and stopped at Scotchie's for jerk chicken and rice. Baker can practically see Russ, glowing from a day in the sun, throwing back a Red Stripe to cool the spice of the chicken. His father had been happy. His father had loved the tropics.

"My father loved the tropics," Baker murmurs.

"Oh yeah?" Ayers says. "What did your father do?"

"I'm not really sure," Baker says. "He was in business."

Suddenly Baker hears a splash. He opens his eyes. Ayers has flipped off her raft into the water. Before Baker can blink, Ayers's bikini top lands on the raft and another second later, her bikini bottom.

"Whoa," Baker says. "Wait a minute."

She swims away, leaving Baker to grab hold of her raft and glimpse the curves of her naked body beneath the surface. He scans the beach—no one around.

"Come back here!" he says.

She floats on her back so that her breasts break the surface of the water. They're small and firm, her nipples hard. Baker is so aroused he aches. Her gorgeous wet breasts glisten in the sun; this is happening in real life—he can't believe it, but he isn't quite sure what to do. He decides to sacrifice the rafts; he'll swim after them later. He flips off his raft, takes off his trunks underwater and enjoys the feel of being naked in the Caribbean. It's liberating. He belongs here. He swims after Ayers. She treads water, waiting.

They kiss in the water for a while and then Ayers reaches down to stroke Baker; the sensation of her warm hand in the cool water is almost too much to bear, he's about to pop, but no, he doesn't want it to go this way.

"Let's swim back to shore," he says. He heads for the beach, hoping she's following, but once he clambers out of the water onto the hot stones, he sees this is going to be a logistical nightmare. Why couldn't she have picked a sandy beach?

Probably because sandy beaches are populated, whereas stone beaches—nearly impossible to walk on and impossible to have sex on—are unpopulated.

Baker sits in one of the beach chairs and spins Ayers around to sit on his lap. She slides right down on him and the sensation is too amazing to describe. He has never more fully inhabited his body; every cell swells with desire, every nerve ending is shimmying.

"Don't move," he whispers. He reaches forward to gently touch her breasts. He pulls her down onto him and groans. She is a goddess. He wants her to crush him, to subsume him; he wants to become her.

She lifts herself an inch then slides back down, and Baker tries to control himself, to feel the sun on his back and neck, to move his hands down to the curve of her waist.

She is divine.

And then, without warning, the earth shakes, it slams up to meet them and Baker is thrown backward. There is pain, instant and rude.

The chair has broken under their weight. Ayers scrambles away, reaches for towels, tosses one to Baker. *NO!* he thinks. They can't just stop. He feels nauseated. Ayers wraps herself up; her head is turned. Sure enough, another car has pulled into the small dirt lot.

"You stay here," Ayers says. "I'm going to make a dash for it." She walks to the water's edge, drops her towel, and executes a shallow dive into the lapping waves. She swims for the rafts, which have drifted to the right side of the beach, out near the rocks.

Meanwhile, Baker secures a towel around his waist and fixes the chair, waving to the approaching couple, who are all decked out for snorkeling. Ayers has reached the floats; Baker watches her put her suit back on.

The couple is approaching him. "Beautiful day," the man calls out. Baker has never hated anyone more in his life.

"Isn't it?" he says.

Plan B: Baker and Ayers pack up and drive the short distance to Salt Pond.

"The good news is we can snorkel with the turtles!" Ayers says.

"Great," Baker says, but he can't conceal his crushing disappointment. Sex, he wants sex. The thirty or forty seconds inside her weren't enough. But where can they go? Her truck isn't an option; it's way too small. Baker's spirit sags as Ayers pulls into a different sandy parking lot, this one packed with cars.

"Let's snorkel first," Ayers says. "Then we'll eat." She seems unfazed by their reversal of fortune, and Baker tries to discern if this is a good thing or a bad thing. Maybe she didn't like the way it felt, maybe the position was uncomfortable, with her feet resting on burning rocks. Maybe she was so mortified by the collapse of the chair that her way of dealing with it is just to pretend it never happened. Baker is with her on this final option. They should reset, start over. Third time's a charm. As soon as Baker gets to High Tide, he's going to call Caneel and book a room.

His mood improves after the short hike to Salt Pond. He has always been a reasonably good sport, able to deal with pitfalls and move on, and today will be no exception. He's carrying the chairs and his backpack; Ayers has the picnic and the snorkeling gear. She has a mask, snorkel, and fins for Baker, left behind when her ex-boyfriend moved out of her apartment. Baker is such a good sport he's going to calmly accept the fact that he's using Mick's old snorkel equipment. He's going to relish it, even. After all, it saves him from having to rent, and the fins fit.

Ayers wades into shallow water, secures her mask, and grins at Baker. Then she takes off swimming and Baker follows. He has used a mask before in swimming pools growing up but never in open water. (They were supposed to go snorkeling on a day trip in Anguilla, but Anna had nixed it.) If Cash snorkeled, then Baker can snorkel. Cash is the better skier, but Baker is a far better swimmer. He takes off after Ayers and soon is right by her side.

The water is clear; the bottom is white sand covered by a carpet of sea grass. They swim a little farther and Baker expects the scenery to change. Cash described "cities" of colorful coral and thousands of multicolored fish. Baker sees only sand and sea grass and Ayers's body, which is sweeter than anything Jacques Cousteau could dream up.

And then he hears Ayers make a sound. She's gesticulating wildly, pointing—and Baker will be damned: A few yards ahead of them, nibbling on the sea grass, is a turtle! A real turtle, one that looks exactly like Crush from *Finding Nemo.* That's backward: Crush is a cartoon and this is nature—this is real! Floyd would... well, his little mind would be blown.

Ayers swims on and Baker follows, waving to Crush, studying the pattern on the back of his shell, watching the way his neck stretches as he feasts on the grass. Ayers finds a second turtle and this one has a baby turtle with him—Crush *and* Squirt! Floyd would love this! Ayers swims alongside the father-and-son turtles and soon Baker is, too. He is so close he could reach out and touch the back of the father's shell, but he's guessing that's against the rules, like feeding the donkeys. He's content to just glide along with the turtles and Ayers until the turtles dive to eat again and Ayers takes Baker's hand. They both surface. Ayers lifts her mask and says, "Cool, huh?"

"So cool!" he says. "I can't believe they're just... hanging out."

"This is where they live," she says. She pulls Baker in to kiss him, which makes Baker very, very happy, and then she says, "I'll race you back. I'm starving."

They sit on a towel in the sun and eat their sandwiches—turkey with arugula for Ayers, rare roast beef with BBQ sauce for Baker. When she's finished, Ayers lies back on her towel and says, "I'm going to take a nap. Then we should probably head out."

Head out? Baker thinks. But she's right: It's quarter of two already. The day flew by and now their date is almost over, so he will have to ask her about Caneel on the way home. Tomorrow night, if she's free.

Ayers closes her eyes and Baker props himself on his elbow and watches her sleep.

On the way home, Baker feels a leaden sense of melancholy. Despite the mishap with the chair, it was a great date and he doesn't want it to end.

"Are you sure you can't go to dinner tonight?" he asks.

"Positive," she says.

"Because you have another date," Baker says. "Just tell me one thing, is he bigger than me?"

Ayers's laugh is musical, like a bell. He loves her laugh. He loves her smooth tan arms. He loves her jangling silver bracelets. There are five, all variations of the St. John hook, including one she had custom-made with an "8" and a hook because every February she runs a race called "8 Tuff Miles"—the length of the satanically hilly Centerline Road from Cruz Bay to Coral Bay. The race ends at Skinny Legs, hence the name of the bar. (Things here are finally starting to click for Baker.) He loves her blond curls, her sense of adventure, her taste in music, and her enthusiasm about the natural world.

"I have another commitment," she says. "And I'm not telling you what it is, but you don't have to feel threatened."

"I do feel threatened," Baker admits. "I don't want to share you."

"Hey now," she says. "Aren't things moving a little fast?"

"Sorry," Baker says. "I just had a really good time today. I enjoy being with you."

"I had a good time, too," Ayers says. "But you're a tourist, so we can't get too serious. Let's just have fun while you're here, okay? Let's not attach too many feelings to this."

Baker takes this like a poison dart to the throat. No feelings? He is nothing *but* feelings.

"Let's not *not* attach feelings," he says. "Besides, I don't know when I'm leaving. I might be here for a while yet."

"I guess I don't understand that," Ayers says. "Do you not have a return ticket?"

"It's open-ended," he says.

"Really?"

"Really."

"Why did you get an open-ended ticket? I mean, I realize you don't have a traditional job, but you do have a child, right, and a life in... Austin?"

"Houston," he says.

"We had a wonderful day," Ayers says. "And it was exactly

what I needed. But we barely know each other. And I also don't understand why you don't want me to come to your villa. It's like you're hiding something."

"*You're* hiding something," Baker says. "You won't tell me what you're doing tonight."

Ayers takes an audible breath. "My ex-boyfriend, Mick? He cheated on me. He told me he was working late 'training' Brigid, and I went down to the Beach Bar at two in the morning and found them together. *Very* together. So I'm sorry, but I can't handle a man who isn't absolutely forthcoming and transparent. If you have secrets, that's fine, that's great, good for you, but I'm not interested." She grins at him. "I'm dead serious. I will never let myself get hurt like that again."

"I would never," Baker says. "Will never." He needs to keep himself in her present, in her future, but her words make him realize that he needs to tell her about his father. It will take just one sentence: *My father was Russell Steele.* Baker worries she will freak out, maybe even leave him on the side of the road and drive off. The time to have told her was right at the beginning, at the memorial service, when they were sitting on the branch. But the situation had been so raw then; they had been at Rosie's funeral lunch. He had been right to keep quiet. He could have told her last night on the beach. That was a missed opportunity. He doesn't want to tell her now because she hasn't quite fallen for him yet. He'll take her to Caneel Bay, he decides, he'll consummate the relationship properly, he'll make her fall in love with him, and *then* he'll tell her. And she'll have no choice but to process and accept the news. It might not even matter.

All right, he's not naive, it will matter. But he still thinks it's best to wait.

"I want to take you to Caneel Bay," he says. "Take you to dinner, get a room, spend the night. Would you do that with me? When's the next night you're free?"

"Caneel?" she says. She drops the tough-girl attitude and lights up. Baker has stumbled across the magic words, apparently. "I've never stayed there, though I've always wanted to. And ZoZo's, the restaurant, the osso buco is... wow, are you sure that's what you want to do? It's not exactly cheap."

"Who cares?" Baker says. "It's a splurge. You're worth it. I would love to stay a night away from my mother and brother."

"I would love a night with reliable air-conditioning," Ayers says. "Can we turn it all the way up?"

"All the way up," Baker says. "What night are you free?"

"Tomorrow night," Ayers says. "I work on *Treasure Island* tomorrow, I'll be back around four."

"I'll make a reservation," Baker says. "And meet you there around five."

"I probably shouldn't go on such an extravagant date with a tourist," Ayers says. "But it's too tempting to resist. And I don't have to be at La Tapa on Friday until four, so maybe we can sleep in, get a late checkout?"

"Anything you want," Baker says. "Breakfast in bed, midnight swim, a marathon of Adam Sandler movies..."

Ayers grabs his hand. "I can't believe it. Thank you. I'm..."

"Say no more. It's happening. Caneel Bay, tomorrow night."

At three o'clock, the traffic in town is at a standstill. A ferry has just unloaded, and some of the all-day charters have come in, and happy hour at Woody's is beginning and...yeah. Cruz Bay is a blender.

"Is it okay if I just drop you here?" Ayers asks. They're in front of a restaurant called the Dog House Pub. "That way I can avoid going all the way around the block. I really have to be somewhere."

"No problem," Baker says. "I'll grab my backpack when I get out, so don't drive away." He leans over to kiss her goodbye and the kiss goes on and on until the taxi driver behind them honks his horn. Ayers pushes Baker away. "Go," she says. "I'll see you tomorrow at five."

"Thank you for lunch," he says. He doesn't want to get out of the truck.

"Yeah, yeah," she says. "Go!"

He hops out of the truck, grabs the backpack, blows Ayers a kiss, then blows a kiss to the disgruntled taxi driver. He is so happy that he floats around the corner and down to the ferry dock. Next to the dock is High Tide.

Caneel, he has to call Caneel. What if they're fully booked? It's high season, but at least it's after the holidays. They'll have a room. He'll pay whatever it takes.

Baker strides into High Tide, half hoping that Cash is a little late—that way he can order a drink and regroup, maybe even take care of the hotel reservation right there at the bar. But no such luck, he sees Cash right away—that bushy blond hair is impossible to miss. Baker blinks. Next to Cash is a woman who looks a little like Anna. The woman has long, dark hair like Anna, but it's loose and she's wearing a lavender tank top, drinking what looks like a margarita.

Not Anna.

But then Cash waves and the woman turns and a wave of

nausea rolls over Baker. *Run!* he thinks. *Hide!* He hears a familiar voice and feels a pair of small arms wrap around his legs.

"Daddy Daddy Daddy, we're here!" the voice says.

Instinctively, Baker bends down to pick up his son.

IRENE

After Huck leaves—the door to Maia's room closed and locked again for the time being—Irene does the dishes, takes an Ativan, takes a second Ativan, then goes to bed.

She wakes up early, very early; the sky is just beginning to turn pink. She slips from bed and heads down the eighty steps to the beach. She sits on one of the orange-cushioned chaises. Now at least, she understands why there are three chaises—one for Russ, one for Rosie, one for Maia.

Russ's daughter.

Irene takes off her tank top and sleep shorts. She steps into the water. And then she starts to swim.

She learned to swim in Clark Lake, in Door County, Wisconsin, which is also where she learned to fish. The water of Clark Lake has little in common with the Caribbean, and yet the swimming clears Irene's mind, just as it used to the summer she was sixteen. That was the summer she witnessed her family falling apart. Her grandmother, Olga, was dying of lung cancer in the gracious old lakefront cottage where Irene had spent every summer of her life. Irene had wanted to go to bonfires with her best summer friend, Caris, and listen to Lynyrd Skynyrd and talk to Davey Longeran, who had just bought his first car, a Pontiac Firebird. She had wanted to ride through the back roads of Door County in Davey's Firebird more than she wanted the sun to rise in the mornings. But she was stuck in the house with her mother, Mary, and her mother's sister, Aunt Ruth. Mary and Aunt Ruth fought nonstop about who was doing more for Olga, and who Olga loved better. Irene was assigned the bottom-rung jobs: emptying the bedpans and the bucket Olga coughed into, washing the soiled sheets and hanging them on the line and riding her bike—two point nine miles each way in the hot sun—to the pharmacy, where Mr. Abernathy would occasionally ask Irene to "spin around" so he could see how big she'd gotten.

When Irene's father showed up on the weekends, they went out on the boat to fish for smallmouth bass and walleye, and he took over Irene's unpleasant tasks so that she could swim in the lake. She swam the crawl, arms pulling, legs like a propeller, breathing every third stroke, alternating sides.

The movement comes right back to Irene, even though it has been a while since she really swam. She spent nearly a hundred thousand dollars on the pool in her Iowa City backyard, forty feet long, but she only did what Russ called the "French dip"—into the water to her neck and then back out in a matter of seconds. She would hold her braid up so that it didn't get wet; the chlorine gave her hair a greenish tint. There had been a time—in the mid-nineties, maybe—when she had gone to the community pool on Mondays, Wednesdays, and Fridays to do laps—thirty-six laps, half a mile, in the name of physical fitness. But that lasted only a couple of months, the way those things do.

Irene swims out at first, toward Jost Van Dyke. Then she finds a calm swath of water and starts to the east. When she catches sight of the neighboring bay, she turns around and heads back.

There isn't time to think while she's swimming except about her heart, her lungs, her eyes, which are stinging, and her arms and legs.

She misses her father. He was a man of few words but he loved her; she is named after his favorite song, "Goodnight, Irene." Irene even misses her mother, though her mother had turned bitter and hard after Olga left the house on Clark Lake to Aunt Ruth. Irene's mother had never forgiven Olga or Ruth; her last words to her sister were at Olga's funeral. Irene has often wondered why Olga made the decision to leave the house to one daughter instead of the other. Did she, in fact, love Ruth more? Or were they simply closer, the way Irene is closer to Cash and Russ was closer to Baker? Or did Olga feel sorry for Ruth because she was single and childless, while Mary had a husband and a daughter? Maybe the house was meant to be an attempt to make up for the bad luck life had dealt Ruth. Irene, of course, will never know, just as she will never know why Russ engaged in such a tremendous deception. It's newly astonishing to Irene that as much as we know about the world, we still can't see into another person's mind or heart.

Irene remembers when she introduced Russ to her parents. His ardor for Irene had been on grand display, and Irene wondered how her emotionally reserved parents would view a man who was so outspoken about his feelings. Mary, Irene recalls, had said, "That young man certainly wears his heart on his sleeve."

Before the cataclysmic revelations of this past week, Irene had agreed with that statement: Russell Steele was a man who wore his heart on his sleeve. But, as it turned out, it wasn't his real heart.

Russ loved Rosie. To deny this in the name of self-preservation is folly. Fine, then, Irene thinks. She can accept it but she is allowed to be hurt and angry.

And now, for the next revelation.

Maia is Russ's daughter.

Irene had looked at the picture on Huck's phone and she had very nearly fainted. The girl, although only twelve years old and half West Indian, *was* Russ. She looked *exactly* like him. She looked more like him than either of the boys did.

That's Russ's daughter.

It can't be, Huck said. *It was years before…*

Huck had calculated back. Maia was seven when his wife, LeeAnn, died, and the one thing he knew for sure was that Rosie started seeing "the Invisible Man," Russ, *after* LeeAnn died. The other fella, Maia's father, was years before.

That's Russ's daughter, Irene insisted. She showed Huck the photograph she'd found wedged under the mattress in the master bedroom, but in that photo, Russ was wearing sunglasses, and so Irene had pulled up a picture from off her phone. She had to scroll all the way back to the summer before, a picture of Russ and Irene at the magazine's annual cookout. Before handing the phone over, Irene marveled at how normal they looked—Russ with his silvering hair and his dad shorts, Irene with her braid, wearing the very same dress she had on right then. Did she remember anything peculiar about that cookout? Not one thing. The cookout was always potluck. Irene brought her corn salad with dill, toasted pine nuts, and Parmesan, and people raved over it; she told them the secret was just-picked corn. *Go to the stand just off I-80*, she said. *It's so much better than the Hy-Vee*! She drank the fruity sangria that Mavis Key brought in an elaborate glass thermos with a nickel-plated spout and a cast-iron stand. Irene had gotten a little tipsy. She and Russ had danced to the bluegrass band; Irene fell asleep on the way home. It was one night of a thousand nights where she was just a regular married woman, maybe one with a grudge against the shiny, newfangled ways of Mavis Key.

When Huck looked at that picture, he pressed his lips into a straight line.

Irene swims until it feels like her arms might break and then she heads for shore. She staggers out of the water, wraps herself in a towel, and bends over, staring at her feet.

Maia is twelve, born in November. The story that Rosie told Huck is that the Pirate came in on a "big yacht" over Valentine's weekend and stayed for four nights. Rosie was working as a cocktail waitress at Caneel Bay. She served the Pirate and his "friends," the Pirate took a liking to her, things went from there. The Pirate left on Tuesday morning, never to be heard from again, according to Rosie. A month or two later, when Rosie discovered she was pregnant, this was the story she told. She had never given the man's name. Huck said that, on the birth certificate, the father's name was left blank. *I was at the hospital when Maia was born,* he said. *I was there.*

Thirteen years ago next month. February. Irene squeezes her eyes shut and tries to concentrate.

When had Russ taken the job with Todd Croft? Thirteen years ago? Irene and Russ had bumped into Todd in the lobby of the Drake Hotel in Chicago. They had been in the city for the Christmas party given by Russ's biggest corn syrup client. So that would have been December...and Todd had called Russ up a few weeks later.

Yes. Irene raises her head. Russ flew down for an interview in February. The meeting was at Todd's office, which Irene understood to be in southeastern Florida somewhere—Miami, Boca, Palm Beach. It *had* been over Valentine's Day, which also fell during Presidents' weekend; they had planned to drive up to St. Joseph, Michigan, to ski. Irene had ended up taking the boys alone. Baker met a girl and vanished, Cash took half a dozen runs with Irene the first morning, and then he went off to snowboard. Irene had headed back to the hotel, wishing she were in Vail or Aspen and that she were returning to a lodge with a roaring fireplace instead of the Hampton Inn. She had wished she could get a hot stone massage instead of taking a lukewarm bath in a cramped fiberglass insert tub. She had indulged these longings because Russ was away, interviewing for a new job, a whole new career. Irene had prayed he would get an offer. She had prayed so hard.

The following Tuesday or Wednesday, Russ had come home, with the first of many suntans, triumphant.

They're going to give me a bonus just for signing the contract, he said. *Fifty thousand dollars.*

Irene had let out an uncharacteristic whoop. Her entire view of Russ had changed in that moment, *because of the money.* Their struggle was over. Irene could throw away the envelope stuffed with grocery store coupons in the junk drawer; she didn't have to steel herself for Russ's reaction when the Visa bill came and he saw that Irene had bought Cash a new pair of ski goggles for fifty-five dollars.

That was what she had been thinking of thirteen years earlier—her liberation from coupon clipping, the dread she felt every time she handed her credit card to a merchant. She hadn't asked Russ how his weekend was, where he went, what he did. She didn't ask if he'd sailed to the Virgin Islands on a yacht, met a cocktail waitress, and impregnated her.

But that, apparently, is what happened.

What Irene does *not* want is to become a slave to her rage and her jealousy. She does not want to become her mother.

I will forgive them, Irene thinks once again. *If it's the last thing I do.* And it might be the last thing. Because the burden keeps getting heavier.

A daughter. A twelve-year-old daughter, Maia Rose Small. In sixth grade here on St. John at the Gifft Hill School. A good student, Huck said, and an entrepreneur. She's starting a bath bomb business. She's making them in tropical scents to sell to tourists.

Russ had never wanted a daughter. He had been hoping for

a boy both times Irene was pregnant, and both times he got his wish. The person who had wanted a daughter was . . . Irene. Irene had wanted a daughter.

She climbs back up the eighty steps, wrapped in just a towel; her legs are so fatigued they're shaking. Both the boys are in the kitchen, but Irene walks right past them, up to her room.

She had told Huck she wanted to meet the girl, Maia. *Please,* she'd said.

He told Irene he would think about it. *Give me a couple days,* he said. Which Irene knows was the right answer.

AYERS

She pulls up in front of the Gifft Hill School just as Maia is emerging. Maia sees her and breaks into a shy smile. Ayers lets go of the breath she has been holding since she pulled out of town onto the Centerline Road. She thought she was going to be late, late for her first sleepover with Maia, late because of some incredibly handsome, charming, and sexy *tourist.*

But no. She is here as she said she would be. She is a reliable, steady force during this tumultuous time for Maia.

Another mother—Swan Seeley is her name; Ayers has served her at the restaurant—comes over to Ayers's open window and squeezes her forearm. "You're here to pick up Maia? You are. Such. A. Good. Person." Swan's eyes shine. "I asked Beau just last night: *Who* is going to be the female influence in Maia's life? She needs one, you know—every girl needs a positive role model. Especially. These. Days. I'm so glad it's you, Ayers. Rosie was lucky to have a friend like you. This community is lucky to have you."

Ayers blinks back her emotion. Secretly, Rosie found the other mothers at Gifft Hill a little too touchy-feely for her taste, although it was unfair to criticize them because they were all. Just. So. Nice. They wore no makeup, bought organic produce, dressed in natural fabrics in neutral colors, volunteered at the animal shelter, lobbied for more efficient recycling, and were generally tolerant and thoughtful. Every so often, one of these mothers would show up at La Tapa and have a couple of glasses of wine and loosen up, and that was when Rosie liked them best. Swan Seeley, Ayers happens to know, even enjoys the occasional Marlboro.

"Thank you. There was no question. Maia is"—Ayers grabs Maia's ponytail because now she has climbed into Edith beside her—"my best girl."

"Well," Swan says. She's clearly overcome, and her son, Colton, is tugging on her arm. But Swan seems hesitant to end the conversation, and Ayers fears the question that might be coming. *Have they figured out what happened?* Ayers refuses to address that topic in front of Maia, or at all, and so she just gives Swan a wave and backs Edie out into the street.

"Thank you for saving me," Maia says. She pulls out her phone. "I'm tired of people asking me how I'm doing."

Ayers is astonished by, and maybe even a bit uneasy about, how well-adjusted Maia seems. Ayers was expecting a sadder girl, possibly even a broken girl. She hopes Maia isn't burying her feelings, which will then fester and come spewing forth later in some toxic way, like lava out of a volcano. Ayers wants to ask Maia how she's doing, but then it will seem like Ayers isn't listening. Maia is sick of that question. She probably doesn't want to be seen as a twelve-year-old girl whose mother just tragically died; she wants to be seen as a twelve-year-old girl.

"Mrs. Seeley was lending her support," Ayers says. "She thinks I'm a positive role model in your life. Ha! That shows how little *she* knows!" There's no response. Maia is down the rabbit hole. Ayers grabs Maia's phone away without taking her eyes off the road and says, "Hey, where to? Happy hour at Woody's?"

"Pizzabar in Paradise," Maia says. "Then Scoops."

"Pizza and ice cream on opposite sides of the island," Ayers says. "I feel like you're taking advantage of me because you know I would do absolutely anything in the world for you. What did Huck pack you for lunch?"

"What do you think?" Maia says.

"A leftover fish sandwich on buttered Wonder bread?" Ayers says.

Maia pulls a greasy paper bag from her backpack and Ayers can smell the fish. "First order of business, throwing that away."

"Facts," Maia says. She reclaims her phone, and Ayers understands what it's like to be the parent of a teenager.

They pull into Pizzabar in Paradise at three thirty, which is a time that nobody other than a sixth grader with a stinky lunch wants to eat, and so they have the place to themselves. Maia orders the margherita pizza. "Why mess with perfection," she says.

Ayers nearly orders the bianco, which was Rosie's favorite. She thinks it might be a tribute of sorts, but she doesn't want to seem like she's trying to *be* Rosie, and besides, she isn't hungry at all. She had a turkey sandwich on the beach with the tourist.

She says, "Will you think I'm a bad influence if I order a glass of wine?"

"You're my surrogate mom now, right?" Maia says. "Moms have wine."

"Perk of the job, I guess," Ayers says, trying to keep things light. She waves to the owner, Colleen, and orders a glass of the house white with a side of ice to water it down. She's keyed up and she needs to relax. She should ask Maia about school, about things at home, about her *feelings,* but Maia is into her phone, which gives Ayers a few minutes of freedom to think about the tourist.

Baker.

She rummages through the factoids: Houston, son Floyd, wife left him, brother Cash, mother here at the mysterious villa, father dead, father loved the tropics. Ayers realizes she doesn't know Baker's last name. She remembers that at the reception, he signed only "Baker" in the guest book. Ayers had made a joke about it. Madonna. Cher.

Had *Cash* mentioned their last name? Ayers doesn't think so. But they'll have it in the files at the Treasure Island office. Ayers will have to remember to check tomorrow.

She sips her wine, watches Maia scroll through other adolescent girls performing lip-sync on musical.ly, and tries to talk herself out of her feelings for the tourist. Yes, he's tall and super-hot; yes, he's charming and a really, really good sport.

The circus act of trying to have sex on Grootpan Beach, the slapstick of the chair collapsing—that might have sapped anyone's confidence. But Baker had rebounded like a champ.

And now they have a date at Caneel Bay. Ayers is embarrassed about how excited she is, and she issues herself a stern warning: she is *not* to fall in love with the tourist! And yet, an overnight date at a five-star resort like Caneel, with a candlelit dinner at ZoZo's first and a midnight swim and uninhibited, unimpeded hotel sex and a breakfast in bed of percolated coffee and banana French toast might tempt her down that forbidden path. Ayers's life is so devoid of luxury and, even some days, comfort, that the allure of a splurge is strong. Baker wants to treat her like a queen, and that is a powerful aphrodisiac.

That, Ayers thinks, is how the Pirate stole Rosie's heart. And later, the Invisible Man. It's not necessarily the creature comforts themselves, it's that someone thinks you deserve them.

Maia's pizza arrives, fresh and hot.

"Want a slice?" Maia asks.

"Duh," Ayers says, because who can resist a piping hot pizza?

Ayers lifts a slice, and strings of cheese stretch all the way to her paper plate. Then she feels something warm and hairy crawling around her ankles and she shrieks and looks down. It's Gordon, Mick's dog. Ayers watches Maia's eyes widen. She fully expects to find Mick and Brigid behind her. A split second later, the stool next to Ayers's is yanked out and Mick sits down. He helps himself to a slice of pizza.

"Hey!" Quick surveillance tells Ayers there's no Brigid. "That's Maia's."

"It's okay," Maia says to Mick. "You can have some."

"It's okay," Mick says to Ayers. "I can have some." He chucks Maia on the arm. "How you holding up, bae?"

Maia turns pink and Ayers remembers that Maia has always been smitten with Mick. He's nowhere near as good-looking as Baker, but Mick has that something, a magnetism, a masculinity, a sly sense of humor that makes him appealing to women of all ages.

"I'm okay," Maia says.

"Oh yeah? Really? I'd say you're better than okay. I'd say you're the coolest young lady on the whole island." He winks at her. "And of course, the prettiest."

Maia fist bumps him. "Facts."

This makes Mick laugh. He turns to Ayers. "Yeah, I'd say she's okay. Self-esteem fully intact."

"What are you doing here?" Ayers asks. Without thinking about it, she finds herself rubbing Gordon's sweet bucket head, and he closes his eyes in ecstasy. Gordon feels about Ayers the way Maia feels about Mick: pure devotion.

"Hangry," Mick says. He devours his slice in three bites and reaches over to take what's left of Ayers's slice, and she lets him. "I have to be at work in an hour."

Right, Ayers thinks. The only other people who eat at three thirty in the afternoon? Everyone in the restaurant business.

"So how was your *date* last night?" Mick asks.

"What date?" Maia asks Ayers.

"Friend of mine, Baker," Ayers says. "We went to dinner."

"I call shenanigans," Mick says. "I swung by De' Coal Pot. You weren't there and you hadn't been there. I asked."

"We went somewhere else," Ayers says.

"Where?" Mick says.

"Who's Baker?" Maia asks. "Do I know him?"

"You don't," Ayers says. "He's visiting."

"He's a tourist," Mick says.

Maia tilts her head. "I thought you didn't date tourists."

"There's an exception to every rule," Ayers says.

"So you're *dating* that guy, then?" Mick asks. "Seriously? He looks like . . . a banker."

Ayers throws back what's left of her wine. Oh, how she would love to order another, but she can't. She has to drive all the way across the island to Scoops, and then drive home.

"He's taking me to Caneel Bay tomorrow. The hotel. Overnight."

Mick cocks an eyebrow. "Really? So he *is* a banker."

"None of your business," Ayers says.

"Are you jealous?" Maia asks Mick. "Do you still love Ayers?"

"Maia!" Ayers says.

"Yes," Mick says. He turns to Colleen and orders a pizza—the pepperoni and ham, which Ayers could have predicted. Mick is a devout carnivore. "Yes, I do still love Ayers."

"Mick, stop," Ayers says.

"Do you really?" Maia asks.

"Yes, I do, really."

"Oh," Maia says. "I thought you broke up with her."

"I did something wrong and Ayers broke up with me," Mick says. "I made a huge mistake and I'll regret it for the rest of my life. But just because I made that mistake doesn't mean I don't still love Ayers."

"Love is messy," Maia says. "My mom used to tell me that. She said love is messy and complicated and unfair." Maia rolls her eyes. "I'll take a no-thank-you helping."

Mick laughs again, and Ayers asks Colleen for a box to take the rest of Maia's pizza to go.

"On that note," Ayers says. "We're leaving."

"Ayers . . . ," Mick says.

Ayers bends down to kiss Gordon between the eyes. Then she turns to Maia. "Ready for ice cream?"

"Facts," Maia says.

CASH

He is so juiced about taking Baker by surprise with the arrival of Anna and Floyd that he has ignored the fact that they will have another situation on their hands.

That situation is named Irene.

But first, *first,* Cash takes a moment to savor Baker's shock and obvious discomfort at seeing his wife and son. He looks *caught.* He *is* caught. The only thing better would have been if Ayers had come with Baker to the bar. But no—that would be cruel to Floyd. Cash will avoid compromising Floyd at all costs. He's learning what it's like to be the son of a philanderer.

If it were only Floyd who had arrived unexpectedly, the scene would have been touching indeed. Floyd grabs Baker around the legs and Baker, although seeming disoriented at first, squeezes Floyd tight, kisses the boy on the cheek, then squeezes him again. Cash has to admit: Baker is a good dad, very open with his affection, just like Russ used to be.

Baker and Floyd go down to look at the water, and Cash turns to Anna. She seems different here, on the island. Her hair is down and she's into her second margarita, so she is super-relaxed. Has Cash ever seen Anna relaxed? Maybe once, when she and Baker came to Breckenridge, but that time, Cash remembers, she had turned her hyper-competitive nature toward skiing. She was faster than Baker and more technically sound than Cash, and she had taken great pride in her superior speed and prowess. Now, she is only competitive about her margarita drinking, and Cash can get behind that—especially since Irene, who is unaware of Anna and Floyd's arrival, waits at home.

"Floyd missed him," Anna says to Cash. "It wasn't until Baker left that I realized how much he does—the cooking, the cleaning, the shopping, the laundry. He coaches Floyd's basketball team, takes him to chess club on Sundays, and he's on the fund-raising committee of Floyd's school, so the phone kept ringing with people donating things for a silent auction that I knew nothing about. I haven't given him nearly enough credit."

"He told me you left him," Cash says. He eyes his own second margarita, half gone.

"Am leaving," Anna says. "I told him just seconds before your mother called with the news."

"Ah," Cash says. He finds he's disappointed that Baker was telling the truth. "It's a...colleague of yours?"

"Louisa," Anna says. She raises a palm. "Don't ask me why, because I don't know. I like men, I'm attracted to men. This came out of nowhere, but it's big and it's real."

"No judgment here," Cash says. "Any chance this might be a phase? Any chance you might salvage the marriage?"

"Nope," Anna says. "But we can salvage the family, I'm pretty sure. We can have a functional divorced relationship, with shared custody."

Baker and Floyd reappear. "I'd love to join you two for a

drink," Baker says, "but I think we should get Floyd home. He's overheated."

Anna pulls out a fifty and leaves it on the bar, much to Cash's relief. "I made a reservation at a place called St. John Guest Suites," Anna says. "I didn't want to assume there would be room for us at the villa."

"Oh, there's room," Cash says. "You can cancel your room." He then thinks of Irene. "Or keep it—you may want privacy, and you probably won't get your money back anyway."

"Nonrefundable," Anna confirms. "But I'd love to see the place. And to see your mom, obviously."

"Obviously," Cash says.

He tries to text Irene about their impending arrival, but his phone has no service on the north shore road. *Oh well,* he thinks. His mother has been through a bigger shock than this; she'll be fine. Then again, his mother has been through such a big shock that it feels unfair to pile on more. Cash is sitting in the backseat of the Jeep with Floyd as though he, too, is a child—but he is also the architect of this mess. He alone knew Floyd and Anna were coming. He could have—*should have*—given Baker and Irene fair warning.

Baker turns right and they wind up the hill and pull up to the gate, which they've left open since their arrival. The house comes into view.

"Wait," Anna says. She turns to Baker. "This is where you're staying?"

"This is the villa," Baker says flatly. "My father's villa."

"I don't believe it," Anna says.

Baker doesn't respond. He parks and gets out of the car. "Come on, buddy," he says to Floyd. "You want a tour?"

Baker and Floyd head up the stone staircase to the main deck, with Anna and Cash following a few steps behind. Anna is plainly floored. Cash tries to remember what he felt like six days ago when he saw this place for the first time. He had been gobsmacked. Now he takes it for granted.

"Outdoor kitchen," Baker says. "Pool, hot tub..."

"The pool has a slide!" Floyd shouts. "To another pool! This house has two pools, one on top and one at the bottom!"

Anna stands on the deck and takes in the view. "What was going on?"

"We're still not sure," Cash says. "The helicopter crashed in British waters. Dad's boss, Todd, signed off to have his body cremated. We're waiting for the ashes and for a report from the crash site investigators, but it's tricky because the Brits are the authority, not the FAA or the coast guard. The pilot was killed—he was British—and a local St. John woman."

"Local woman?" Anna says. "Did your father have a mistress here? Was he *that* cliché?"

"I think he might have been, yes," Cash says.

They step into the kitchen, where Irene is sitting at the table. Her head is buried in her arms. She's asleep.

"Your poor mother," Anna says. "Don't wake her."

Irene raises her head, blinking. "Oh," she says. She gets to her feet and offers a hand. "Hello, I'm Irene Steele."

"Irene," Anna says. "It's Anna. Anna Schaffer. Baker's wife."

Irene steadies herself on the back of a chair. "Anna," she says. "What are you doing here?" The question comes out as accusatory, just as Cash feared it might, but Anna wears a heavy suit of armor, so Irene's tone bounces right off of her.

"I brought Floyd down," she says, and she opens her arms. "I am so sorry about all of this. How awful it must be for you."

Irene stares at Anna for a moment and then she walks right into Anna's arms and the two women embrace, and Cash is as amazed that his mother is accepting comfort as he is that Anna is offering it—but he is also relieved.

Baker and Floyd enter the kitchen, Floyd gets a hug and a kiss from Grammie, and Baker announces that he's taking Floyd down to look at the beach.

"That's fine," Anna says. "Then someone should probably drive us to our hotel."

"Hotel?" Baker says.

"I got a suite at a boutique place in Chocolate Hole," Anna says. "I'm sorry, I wasn't sure how big this home was."

"There are nine bedrooms," Irene says. "Stay here, please."

"Floyd will stay here," Baker says. "Anna can go to the hotel." With that, he takes Floyd's hand and leaves the kitchen, shutting the side door firmly for emphasis.

Irene raises her eyebrows. "Is something going on?"

Anna says, "Baker and I are splitting. I've met someone else. Another surgeon at the hospital, actually. Her name is Louisa."

Cash wishes he'd had a third margarita, or even a fourth, although he admires Anna's ability to just come out with the plainspoken truth. Her tone is matter-of-fact and holds not even a hint of apology.

Irene opens her mouth, then closes it, then starts to laugh. Cash cringes. Why is *he* the one who has to bear witness to this confession? Why didn't he go to the beach with his brother and nephew, or run upstairs to the guest room he has claimed as his own and hide under the bed? Why does he have to be standing here, watching his mother laugh at Anna's moment of coming out? Irene laughs so hard that tears leak from her eyes. She's trying to stop herself; she struggles to catch her breath.

"I'm sorry," Irene says finally. "It's just I didn't think anyone else in the whole world could take me by surprise, but you've gone and done it. You're leaving Baker for a woman?"

"A person," Anna says, and Cash wants to applaud. "Another doctor, who also happens to be female, yes. I'll apologize for being the one to break up the family, Irene, but I won't apologize because Louisa is a woman."

Irene nods. "I didn't mean to laugh at you. I'm a bit self-absorbed these days, but I appreciate your being direct. Would you like to stay for dinner?"

"I'm tired," Anna says. "But thank you for asking."

"It's just as well," Irene says. "I have a delicate matter to discuss with the boys."

"Delicate matter?" Cash says. "Did you get news?"

"Something like that," Irene says. She smiles at Anna. "Thank you for bringing Floyd down. It's a lovely surprise. Now, if you'll excuse me." Irene leaves the kitchen.

When Anna turns to Cash, he expects her to be angry or offended—but she's beaming. "That went much better than I expected," she says.

* * *

Baker and Floyd come up from the beach and the adults agree that the best course of action is for all of them to drop off Anna at the St. John Guest Suites and then for the menfolk to pick up dinner at Uncle Joe's B.B.Q. Baker seems nervous and agitated. He drives like a bat out of hell all the way to Chocolate Hole, and when he pulls into the driveway to drop Anna off, he says, "How many nights did you book?"

"Two," Anna says. "And I thought you would come back with us."

"No!" Baker says, his voice like a hammer. "As you can see, my mother needs me."

"Cash is here to care for Irene," Anna says. "But you have a child who needs you. I need you."

"What you mean is that you need me to come home and be a parent because you're too busy to do it."

Cash glances at Floyd. He has earbuds in and is fully engrossed in his iPad, but still.

"Don't do this here," Cash says. "I don't want to hear it, and neither does you-know-who."

"Cash is right," Anna says.

"I'm not leaving in two days," Baker says.

"We'll discuss later," Anna says. She gets out of the Jeep, grabs her bag, pokes her head in the backseat window. "Thanks for coming to get us, Cash. Floyd, I'll see you at some point tomorrow." Floyd doesn't look up. Anna removes one of his earbuds. "See you tomorrow."

"Okay," Floyd says. "Bye."

Maybe she's not the most maternal presence, but Cash still finds his sister-in-law impressive. He notices her posture as she goes to greet the owners, trailing her roller bag behind her, the picture of extreme self-confidence, uncompromising in her principles.

A person, Anna said to Irene. *Another doctor, who also happens to be female.* Cash chuckles and moves to the front seat, next to Baker.

"Don't kill me," he says.

Turns out Baker isn't angry. Scratch that: he is angry, but his anger is secondary to his panic. He had told Ayers he would take her to Caneel Bay the following night—dinner, hotel, the whole enchilada.

"I had to text her and cancel," Baker says. His voice is low, even though Floyd still has his headphones in. "I told her our sister showed up unexpectedly."

"Our *sister*?" Cash says. "You *lied* to her?"

"I didn't lie," Baker says. "She's your sister."

"She's my sister-in-*law,*" Cash says. "She's your wife."

"I couldn't very well tell Ayers my wife showed up."

"Estranged wife," Cash says. "You could have said your estranged wife showed up with your child out of the blue and you need a few days to deal with it. Ayers is cool. She would understand."

"*Ayers is cool,*" Baker mimics. "You have no idea whether she's cool or not cool. Stop pretending like you know her better than I do."

"I wasn't saying that. But I have spent time with her, and I do happen to think she's cool. I hiked with her, and we went on *Treasure Island* together. I'm sure it comes as a crushing blow, but she likes me."

"She may like you just fine," Baker says. "But she likes me more. All women like me better, Cash, starting with that sweet little... what was her name?"

Claire Bellows, Cash thinks.

"Claire Bellows," Baker says. "I bet you still haven't forgiven me for Claire Bellows."

"Claire Bellows was my girlfriend," Cash says. "And you slept with her—not because you liked her, but because you wanted to prove to me that you could."

"You knew Anna and Floyd were coming," Baker says. "And you didn't tell me."

"If you'd answered your phone, you would have known."

"You're in love with Ayers yourself," Baker says. "And that's why you didn't tell me Anna was coming."

"You shouldn't have been on a date with Ayers," Cash says. "You're pretending you're a single man, but you're far from it."

Baker pulls up in front of Uncle Joe's B.B.Q. and puts the car in park. "Get chicken and ribs," Baker says. "And a bunch of sides."

"I need money," Cash says.

"You've got to be kidding me," Baker says. "I've paid for everything on this trip. You haven't paid once."

"I told you my bank card doesn't work down here."

"That's bullshit and you know it," Baker says. "What's the issue? You own a business, right? A business that Dad handed you on a silver platter. Are the stores not making money?"

Cash stares at the dashboard. He's going to punch his brother. He clenches and unclenches his fists. They are right downtown, people are everywhere, Floyd is in the backseat, he has to control himself.

"The stores failed," Cash says. "They're gone. The bank owns them now."

Baker throws his head back to laugh. Cash gets out of the Jeep, but instead of going to Uncle Joe's B.B.Q., he storms off toward the post office and the ferry dock.

Baker yells from the car. "Cash! Where are you going, man? Listen, I'm sorry."

Cash doesn't turn around. He ducks behind a tree and watches Baker drive past, looking for him.

Cash isn't flat broke. He still has twelve dollars, which, because it's now happy hour at High Tide, will buy him another margarita.

An hour later, he's buzzed and indignant. The heinous things Baker said roll through his mind, one after the other. *You're in love with Ayers yourself... a business that Dad handed you on a silver platter... she likes me more. All women like me better... Are the stores not making money?* Baker thinks he's better than Cash. He has always thought that, and maybe Cash had thought it, too. But Baker isn't going to win this time, not if Cash can help it.

He calls Ayers's cell phone. He vaguely recalls that she's busy tonight, not work, some other commitment—but she answers on the second ring.

"Cash?" she says. "Is that you? Is everything all right?"

He breathes in through his nose. He tries to sound sober, or at least coherent. "Baker canceled your date for tomorrow night?" he says. "He told you our sister arrived on the island?"

"He did," Ayers says. "I didn't realize you guys had a sister. Neither of you mentioned her before..."

"We don't," Cash says. "We don't have a sister. Baker was lying."

"Oh," Ayers says.

"The person who showed up was his wife, Anna. And she brought their son, Floyd."

"Oh," Ayers says. "He told me they'd split. That she left him."

"She's leaving him, yes," Cash says. "That part is true. For another doctor at the hospital where she's a surgeon. But she's here now, with Floyd. Baker didn't know they were coming."

"He didn't?" Ayers says.

"He didn't at all," Cash says. "He was blindsided and he didn't want you to know, so he lied and said it was our sister."

"I see," Ayers says.

"I'm pretty drunk," Cash says. He's standing in Powell Park near the gazebo. The sun is setting and the mosquitoes are after him. "Do you think you could come give me a ride home?"

"I wish I could," Ayers says. "I'm busy, I'm sorry."

Cash takes a breath. He's come this far; he might as well go the rest of the way. "Ayers, I have something to tell you. I'm in love with you."

"Oh, Cash," she says. "Please don't make this complicated. You're a great guy, you know I think that..."

"But you have the hots for Baker," Cash says. "Because that's how things always go. Women think I'm a great guy but they have the hots! For! Baker!" He's shouting now, and he has attracted the attention of a West Indian policewoman, who crosses the street toward him. "You really shouldn't be interested in either of us. Do you know why?"

"No," Ayers says. "Why?"

"Russell Steele? Rosie's boyfriend? The Invisible Man?" Cash says.

"Yes?" Ayers says. She sounds scared now. "Yes?"

"He was our father," Cash says. And he hangs up the phone.

HUCK

Hard things are hard. And there's no instruction manual when it comes to parenting—or in Huck's case, step-grandparenting—a twelve-year-old girl.

His dinner with Irene, instead of heading in an amorous direction, as he had hoped, ended with a quandary. Irene was dead certain Maia was Russ's blood daughter. Huck had been skeptical. Why wouldn't Rosie have just said so? Why make up the story about the Pirate and then pretend the Invisible Man was a different guy? Rosie *was* prone to drama; maybe she *wanted* her life peopled like a Marvel comic.

To prove her point, Irene brought Huck a framed photograph: Rosie with an older gentleman, lying in a hammock. Russell Steele. But in the photo, Russ was wearing sunglasses. There was something in his face that was replicated in Maia's face, but without seeing his eyes, Huck couldn't be 100 percent sure. Then Irene scrolled through the pictures on her phone and found a good, clear picture of her husband's face.

Yes, Huck thought. There was no denying it. Maia had the

same half-moon eyebrows, the same slight flange to the tip of her nose, the exact same smile.

"Uncanny," Huck said.

"She's his," Irene said.

"Yes."

"Yes, you see it?"

"Impossible not to see it." Huck remembered back to when he and Ayers told Maia that Rosie was dead. She had asked about her father. She knew. They'd told her, maybe. She was twelve, old enough to understand. It also explained why Russell Steele paid for Rosie's living expenses and Maia's tuition. Huck had checked Rosie's bank account balances. She had seven thousand in her checking and a whopping eighty-five thousand in savings, and it looked as though she might have some kind of account in the States. Huck would need to hire a lawyer to get access to that money on Maia's behalf, and he supposed he would need to legally take custody, although his distrust of lawyers and his distaste for paying their exorbitant fees had kept him from doing anything just yet. The custody question was a moot point—or so he had assumed. No one on this island was going to dispute his claim to the girl, not even the Smalls, Rosie's father's people. So there was no sense of urgency. Until now. Maybe.

"I'd like to meet her," Irene said.

Huck could not put the inevitable off any longer: he needed a cigarette.

"I'd like to smoke," he said.

"I'll join you," she said.

They stepped out onto the deck and Huck lit up. He took a much-needed drag, then handed the cigarette to Irene. "Or I could light you your own."

"A whole cigarette would be wasted on me," Irene said, though she inhaled off his deeply. "I know she's not related to *me*."

"Just let me think a minute," Huck said. "I need to consider Maia. Maia's emotional state, Maia's best interests."

"I don't think there are blueprints for this," Irene said. "The circumstances are unique. I, for one, can't accept the information that Russ has a child, a daughter, without wanting to meet her."

"What do you hope to get out of it?" Huck asked.

"I'm not sure," Irene said. "I loved him. She's his. I think my motives are pure."

"You *think*?"

"The boys—Baker and Cash—are her brothers."

"Half brothers."

"Fine, half brothers. But that's still blood. That's still family."

Huck didn't like where her reasoning was headed. *He* was Maia's family! He had been the third person to hold her after she was born. He had taught her how to cast a line, bait a hook, handle the gaff. He drove her to school, packed her lunches, signed her permission slips. It rankled him that "the boys, Baker and Cash," shared blood with Maia when he did not.

Irene was a perceptive woman. She put a hand on his arm. "I'm not going to take her from you, Huck. I just want to meet her. Let her know we exist. She's twelve now. Even if we don't tell her, she'll find out eventually and there will be resentment. Aimed at you."

"Let me think about it," Huck said. "I'll call you by Wednesday night."

"Thank you, Huck," Irene said. "Thank you for even considering it." She gazed up at him, her eyes shining; she looked, in that moment, as young and hopeful as a woman in her twenties. Huck flicked the butt of the cigarette over the railing. It was time for him to leave.

Irene stood on her tiptoes and kissed his cheek. It was official. Despite the bizarre, twisted chain of events that had brought them both there, he liked her.

On Wednesday, he picks Maia up from school at noon. She has a half day and he didn't schedule an afternoon charter because they have an important mission.

They stop by home to grab the things they need. Huck loads the buoy, rope, and anchor into the back of the truck. Maia emerges with a paper lunch bag.

Thirty minutes later, they are in *The Mississippi,* heading for the BVIs. It's a clear day, cloudless; the sun is so hot it paints fire across the back of Huck's neck. He pulls his bandana out and imagines it's still damp with Irene's tears. He hasn't been able to think of much besides Irene—half because he's starting to feel something for her, half because she has asked him to make an impossible decision.

"How was your night with Ayers?" Huck has been so preoccupied with Irene that he has neglected to ask until now.

Maia is facing into the wind, wearing an inexpensive pair of plastic sunglasses that she decorated with seashells she and her mother collected on Salomon Beach. "Impossible-to-reach-Salomon-Beach" had been Rosie's favorite. Maia has a faraway expression on her face, and Huck wonders what's going on in that mind of hers. He nearly repeats the question, but then Maia says, "It was fine. I think Ayers is having man problems."

"Oh really?" Huck says. "Someone new, or is she still hung up on Mick?"

"Someone new," Maia says. "A tourist, I think."

"Bad news," Huck says. He casts a sidelong glance at Maia. "You're not allowed to date until you're thirty, by the way."

"We saw Mick at Pizzabar in Paradise," Maia says. "He told me he still loves Ayers."

"Oh boy," Huck says. "Sounds like you had an educational night."

"She likes the tourist," Maia says. "But they had a date for tonight, and he canceled. She was upset. I told her she should go back out with Mick. I like Mick."

"I know you do," Huck says. Huck likes Mick, too. Mick always buys him a round at the Beach Bar, and he buys Huck's fish for the restaurant. But Mick had gotten mixed up with one of the little girlies working for him and Ayers gave him the boot.

Now she's interested in a tourist? No, Huck thinks. Not a good idea. Although Huck, of course, has no say.

Huck steers the boat past Jost and up along the coast of Tortola. He's in British waters now and he expects to be stopped by Her Majesty's coast guard; Huck isn't allowed to be over here without going through customs. But the border control and BVI police boats must all be at lunch or at the beach, because he moves toward their destination unimpeded.

North of Virgin Gorda, southeast of Anegada. It's a haul—

which, he supposes, is why Russ and Rosie decided to take a bird. It was only an irresponsible decision because of the weather; it must have seemed like a good gamble, though, and if Huck had all the tea in China and a bird at his disposal, he might have chanced it as well.

They pass *Treasure Island,* which is on the way from Norman Island to Jost Van Dyke, and Maia starts waving her arms like crazy.

"Ayers is working today," she says.

"Does she know what *we're* doing today?" Huck asks.

"I didn't tell her," Maia says. "I didn't tell anyone." *Treasure Island* is past them now, and *The Mississippi* catches some of her choppy wake. The boat bounces, but Maia enjoys it the way she might a ride at the amusement park. She's his girl.

Hard things are hard. Maia asked to see the place where the helicopter went down. At first, Huck had resisted. What good would come from seeing the place where Rosie died so violently? But then Huck reasoned that any real-life visual would likely be less horrific than the pictures Maia held in her mind.

They reach the general area of the crash, according to the coordinates Huck had gotten from Virgin Islands Search and Rescue when they had delivered Rosie's body—a huge favor pulled by Huck's best friend, Rupert, who grew up in Coral Bay with the governor; bodies are notoriously hard to recover from the Brits—and Huck cuts the engine. The water is brilliant turquoise; the green peaks of Virgin Gorda are behind them. Huck picks up the mooring—a white spherical buoy that Maia painted with a red rose and Rosie's name and dates.

Huck had told Maia that the mooring isn't legal; it will likely be pulled within twenty-four hours. Maia doesn't care. She wants to go through the ritual of marking the spot.

"We're here," Huck says.

Maia stands, holding the buoy, and kisses it. Huck picks up the rope and tosses the anchor overboard. Maia throws the buoy over. The rose is pretty; she did a good job.

"Should we say something?" Huck asks.

"I love you, Mama," Maia says. "And Huck loves you, too, even if he is too manly to say it."

"Me, too manly?" Huck says. He clears his throat. "I love you, Rosie girl. I'll love you forever. I just hope you're with your mama now. My precious LeeAnn."

"Amen," Maia says.

Huck smiles, though a couple of tears fall. LeeAnn was the only one of them who ever went to church—Our Lady of Mount Carmel: she loved the priest, Father Abraham, who has an enviable charisma—but some of the faith must have rubbed off on Maia.

She opens the paper lunch bag and produces a pink sphere. She holds it above the water with two pincer fingers and lets it go right next to the buoy. The water fizzes, just as it used to back in the day when Huck would make himself an Alka-Seltzer.

"What is that?" Huck says. He's an ecologist by nature, so he's concerned.

"Bath bomb, rose-scented," Maia says. "Don't worry, it's organic."

They both peer over the side of *The Mississippi* until the rose-scented bath bomb dissolves.

"For you, Mama," Maia says.

Huck waits a respectful moment. Just as he's about to start the engine, Maia pulls out a second bath bomb, this one pale yellow.

"What's that?" Huck asks.

Maia brings it to her nose and inhales deeply. "Pineapple mint," she says. "My favorite. It's for Russ." She drops it in the water. "For you, Russ."

He couldn't hope for a more natural segue, and yet when he starts to speak there's a catch in his throat. He's about to change this kid's entire life. But he won't live forever. He's sixty-one now, and who's to say he won't drown or get struck by lightning, or die of a heart attack, or get bitten by a poisonous spider, or have a head-on collision on the Centerline Road? If there's one thing Huck can say about Rosie, it's that she firmly believed she would live forever. And she didn't. So it's best to err on the side of caution. If Huck dies, the girl will have no one. Ayers, maybe, if Ayers doesn't move to Calabasas or Albany, New York, with some tourist—but Ayers has no legal claim of guardianship.

Maia needs family—a chance at family, anyway. And Irene is right—if Huck doesn't tell her now, she'll find out when she's older. And hate him.

"Speaking of Russ," Huck says.

"Uh-oh," Maia says. She puts her elbows on her knees, rests her chin in her hand.

"Back when I told you the news," Huck says, "you said that Russ was your father."

"He is," Maia says. "Was. They told me the truth on my birthday, back in November. Russ is the Pirate. We have the same birthmark."

Huck shakes his head. "Russ has the birthmark?"

"The peanut," Maia says. "In the exact same spot on his back."

"No kidding," Huck says. Maia's birthmark, on the back of her shoulder, is the shape and size of a ballpark peanut.

"No kidding," Maia says. "He was my birth father after all. I kind of already knew. We have the same laugh, we both love licorice, we're both left-handed."

"Do you know...anything else?" Huck asks. *Like where the guy was the first seven years of your life?*

"No," Maia says. "Mom said she would tell me the whole story when I was older. Fifteen or sixteen. When I could handle it better, she said."

"Okay," Huck says. His job has been made both easier and more difficult. On the one hand, there's no need to pursue a DNA test if the birthmark story is true—Irene should be able to confirm—but on the other hand, Maia may not want to know the truth about her father. "Well, I've made a new friend recently."

"Seriously?" Maia says. "I thought you hated people."

Huck gives a dry laugh. "My friend, Irene, Irene Steele, actually, used to be married to Russ."

Maia's face changes to an expression that is beyond her years. It's wariness, he thinks, the expression one gets when one senses a hostile presence. "Used to be?" she says.

"Honey," he says. "Russ was married. While he was with your mom, the whole time, he was married to someone else. A woman named Irene. She flew down here when she learned he was dead, and she found me. She has two sons, one thirty years old, one twenty-eight. They are your brothers."

"My brothers?" Maia says. "I have brothers?"

"Half brothers," Huck says. "Russell Steele is their father and he's your father. Their mother is Irene. Yours is... was... Rosie."

"Okay," Maia says. She bows her head. "Wait."

Wait: Huck has done irreparable damage. Something inside of her is broken... or altered. Innocence stolen, spoiled. She now knows she's the daughter of a cheat and a liar.

"He loved Mama," Maia says.

"I know," Huck says.

"But love is messy, complicated, and unfair," Maia says, like she's reciting something out of a book.

"That's a dim view," Huck says. "I loved your grandmother very much. We were happy."

"Mama used to say that."

Rosie might have known about Irene—must have known, Huck thinks. It was one thing for Russell Steele to keep Rosie a secret from Irene. Could he really have kept both sides in the dark? "Did they ever explain where Russ went when he wasn't around?"

Maia shrugs. "Work."

"Did they ever say what kind of work?"

"Business," Maia says. "Finance, money. Boring stuff."

"Boring stuff indeed," Huck says. He takes a sustaining breath. He has not ruined her. She had a clue, an inkling, that Russ was keeping secrets. Huck is grateful that Rosie and Russ didn't see fit to burden Maia with any information about Russ's business, even though Huck is dying to know what the guy was into. "Okay, now for the tricky part."

"Tricky?" Maia says.

"My new friend Irene, Russ's wife, wants to meet you. And

she'd like you to meet her sons. They aren't taking you from me, they're not taking you anywhere, they just want to meet you."

"But why?" Maia says. "Wouldn't they hate me? I'm the daughter of Russ's girlfriend. Even though Mama is dead, wouldn't they want...I don't know...to pretend like I don't exist? Wouldn't that be easier?"

Easier, for sure, Huck thinks.

"Part of it is that they're curious. Part of it is that...well, your mother was right about love being complicated. Irene loved her husband and you're his child, so"—Huck can't quite make the transitive property work here, much as he wants to—"she's interested in you."

Maia blinks. If she were any older, she might take offense at how objectifying that sounds: "interested," the way one becomes interested in astronomy or penguins.

"Okay, let me ask you this. Let's say we found out that your mom had another child, a son, say, that you never knew about until now. You love your mother and maybe you feel betrayed that your mother kept this big, important secret. You would still want to meet your brother, right?"

"I guess," Maia says. "Do I have a secret brother?"

"Not on your mother's side," Huck says. "I can vouch for the fact that your mother was pregnant only once, and that was with you. But what I'm telling you is that you have two brothers. They want to meet you and their mother, Irene, wants to meet you. But you're in control. If you say no, I'll politely decline."

"Will they be upset if we decline?" Maia asks.

"Maybe," Huck says. "But that shouldn't affect your answer. You wouldn't be meeting them so they feel better. You'd be meeting them because you want to." Huck pauses. The sun is bearing down on him. "I know that may sound selfish, but you have to trust me here. If you want to meet them, we'll meet them. If you'd rather not, that's fine. More than fine."

Maia leans over the side of *The Mississippi* and peers into the water. Both the bombs have dissolved; all that remains, on the surface, are soap bubbles, like one would find in dish-water. Huck doesn't want Maia to contemplate this particular spot for too long—the depths of this sea; the darker water below, where Rosie's body landed.

"I'll meet them," Maia says. "But if I don't like them, I don't ever have to see them again, right?"

"Right," Huck says.

"You promise?"

"I promise." Huck is proud of her. She is brave and fierce and incorruptible. Huck can't believe he thought that either he or Irene Steele or her sons could ruin Maia Small.

No matter what happens with all of this, Huck thinks, Maia is going to be fine.

BAKER

At eight thirty at night, after Floyd and Baker have eaten the barbecue—chicken, ribs, pasta salad, coleslaw with raisins, rice and beans, and fried plantains—there's a knock at the door. Somewhere in the house, Winnie barks.

Who could it be? Baker wonders, and he wishes they'd left the gate down. He feels ill. He just indulged in some world-class stress eating, shoveling food in without even tasting it, and he can't imagine who could be at the door this late. It's not Cash; he would have sauntered right in. Maybe the police have shown up with Cash in custody? Maybe something happened to Cash: he hitchhiked home with the wrong person, or he was trying to hitch a ride and a driver didn't see him and mowed him down. Maybe he did something desperate. Baker shouldn't have teased him about Ayers, or about Claire Bellows, and he should *never* have forced a confession about the business. *The stores failed. They're gone.* Even though Baker had predicted that would happen, he feels no joy in the reality. Poor Cash. He just wasn't meant to run a business.

It could be Anna at the door, Baker supposes, although she would have to be a homing pigeon to find this place in the dark. There are no neighbors on this road.

He asks Floyd to run upstairs, brush his teeth, and put on his pajamas.

"No," Floyd says.

Normally, Baker has a deep well of paternal patience, but he senses that this knock means bad news of some kind. "Please, buddy," Baker says.

"I'm scared," Floyd says, and Baker realizes that Floyd has every reason to be scared. This is a huge, unfamiliar house. Even Baker can't recall which room he put Floyd's suitcase in. Baker wants to tell Floyd that he, too, is scared—of things far more terrifying than shadows and strange noises.

It's probably a taxi driver who picked up Cash and now is demanding to be paid.

Baker opens the door to find a tall, hulking West Indian man, and initially he thinks his guess is correct.

"Hello?" Baker says. He searches the darkness beyond the man for signs of his brother.

The man thrusts forward a square cardboard box. "For you," he says. "Mr. Steele's remains."

Mr. Steele's remains? Baker reaches out to accept the box and the man turns to go.

"Wait," Baker says. "Who are you? Where did you come from?"

"I'm Douglas Vickers, Paulette's husband," the man says. "Those came to her office today and she asked me to deliver them here."

"Oh," Baker says. In the moment, this makes sense. "Thank you." Douglas gives Baker and Floyd half a wave and disappears down the stone staircase, leaving Baker to hold what remains of his father. The ashes have been delivered to the door like a pizza.

"Daddy?" Floyd says. There is likely a barrage of questions coming as soon as Floyd can figure out what to ask, but for now, he just seems to need reassurance.

"Everything is okay, bud," Baker says. "I'll be back in one second. You stay right here." Baker turns to check that Floyd is standing in the doorway, then he goes flying down the curved stone staircase after Douglas. He catches the man just as he's climbing into a white panel van. "Excuse me? Mr. Vickers, sir?"

Douglas Vickers stops, one leg up in the van, one on the ground, his face framed by the open driver's-side window. "Yes?"

"You were the one who identified my father's body, is that right?" Baker asks.

Douglas Vickers nods once. "I did."

"You...*saw* him?" Baker asks. "And he was dead?"

Douglas Vickers gives Baker a blank stare, then he hops into the truck and backs out through the gate.

* * *

Once Baker gets Floyd to sleep—thankfully, Anna remembered to pack a few picture books, including *The Dirty Cowboy,* which reliably knocks Floyd out by the end of page six—he heads down the hallway to the room Irene has been using and knocks on the door.

"Come in," Irene says.

His mother is sitting on the side of the bed, fully dressed, as if she has been waiting for Baker to knock.

"Is Floyd asleep?" she asks.

Baker nods.

"Good," Irene says. "Because I have to talk to you and your brother."

"Um, okay?" Baker says. "Cash isn't home. I left him off in town when I got the barbecue."

"Whatever for?" Irene asks.

"He jumped out of the car, actually," Baker says. "We had an argument. I wasn't very nice. I was upset...he knew Anna and Floyd were coming and he didn't tell me."

"He didn't tell me, either," Irene says. "I had no idea who Anna was when I saw her. I *introduced* myself to her. She was so out of context and I haven't laid eyes on her for so long..."

"Three years," Baker says. Anna hasn't been back to Iowa City since just after Floyd's first birthday. "Listen, Mom, Anna and I are getting a divorce."

"She told me," Irene says. "She's fallen in love with a person named Louisa."

Baker's eyebrows shoot up. "She told you that?"

"She did."

Well, yes, Baker thinks, she should have. It was Anna's

news. The dismantling of their family was Anna's doing. "I'm sorry. I'm sure you're disappointed."

"Hard to register any kind of feeling about Anna, I'm afraid," Irene says. "She's always been a mystery."

"You should probably also know...if he hasn't told you already...that Cash lost the stores. They went belly-up."

Irene gives Baker a sharp glance. "He hasn't told me, no. I figured as much, but it's Cash's responsibility to tell me, not yours."

"Right," Baker says. He knows his mother favors Cash, or feels more protective of him than she does of Baker. "None of my business, sorry. So listen, Mom, a gentleman just stopped by..."

"Gentleman?" Irene says. "Was he older, with a reddish beard?"

"Huh?" Baker says. His mother is on her feet now, at the front window, searching. "No, it was a West Indian gentleman. Paulette's husband, Douglas. He brought Dad's ashes."

"Dad's ashes?" Irene says. "Where are they?"

"Downstairs," Baker says.

They get to the kitchen just as Cash stumbles through the door. Baker can smell him from across the room—tequila.

He opens the refrigerator door. "Any barbecue left?"

"Plenty," Baker says. He's relieved that Cash seems to be either numbed or neutralized by alcohol and that there will be no rehashing of their earlier argument.

As Cash pulls the various to-go containers out of the fridge, Irene cuts open the cardboard box.

"Actually, Cash, you may want to wait on eating," Baker says.

"Fuck you," Cash says. "I'm starving."

"How'd you get home?" Baker asks.

"That tall chick that works at La Tapa picked me up outside Mongoose Junction," Cash says. "Tilda, her name is."

"Yeah, I know who you mean," Baker says.

"I guess she has the hots for Skip, the bartender," Cash says. "Funny, we've been here less than a week and we know everyone else's personal drama..."

There's a sound.

It's Irene, wailing in hoarse, ragged sobs. She's holding a heavy-duty Ziploc bag that contains white and pale-gray chunks. Without warning, she collapses on the kitchen floor.

For an instant, both Baker and Cash stare. They are grown men and they have never seen their mother act like this. Baker, although not surprised—he's been wondering if his mother would break, if she would finally act like a woman who has tragically lost her husband instead of a woman moving around in an extended state of shock—doesn't know what to do. Cash is holding the take-out containers of food and a bottle of water, seemingly paralyzed.

Cash is better at dealing with their mother. *Do something!* Baker thinks.

Cash sets the food down and approaches Irene cautiously, as if she's a ticking bomb or a rabid dog.

"Mom, hey, let's get you up. Can you sit at the table?"

Irene cries more loudly, then she starts to scream—words, phrases, Baker can't make sense of much. He keeps checking the stairs; the last thing he wants is for Floyd to wake up and see his grandmother like this.

"…I trusted him! Bad back…clients in Pensa*cola*! I never checked! Never questioned! Never suspected a thing…greed…the money…the house! I was married to the house! Secrets are lies! They're lies! I never suspected…why would I suspect? Your father was so…effusive…so loving…it was too much, sometimes, I used to *tell* him it was too much…I told him to *tone it down,* it was *embarrassing…*" She stops. "Can you imagine? I was embarrassed because your father loved me too much. Because I wasn't raised like that. My parents told me they loved me…once a year, maybe, and I never heard them say it to each other. Never once! But they did love each other…they just showed the love in their actions, the way they treated each other…honor, respect. They didn't keep secrets like this one!"

"Mom," Baker says, but he doesn't know what to add. She's right. Their father was demonstrative, verging on sappy. He exuded so much *I love you, please love me back* that Baker at least, and probably Irene and Cash as well, saw it as a weakness.

Had it all been an act, then? Baker wonders. Or had the three of them done such a pitiful job of returning Russ's love that he'd sought affection elsewhere?

Irene holds up the plastic bag. "This is all that's left. All! That's! Left!" She flings the ashes across the kitchen. The bag hits the cabinets and slaps the floor. Thank goodness the seal held, Baker thinks. Otherwise they would be sweeping Russ up with a broom and dustpan.

Cash gets Irene to a chair at the kitchen table while Baker picks up the ashes. Across the label of the bag it says: STEELE, RUSSELL DOD: 1/1/19.

Baker sits down beside his mother. Cash has brought a pile

of paper napkins to the table. He's trying to put his arm around Irene, but she's resisting—possibly because he smells like a Mexican whorehouse.

"Just let me...just let me...," Irene says.

Baker studies the contents of the plastic bag. The pieces are chalky and porous; the "remains" look like a few handfuls of coral on the beach in Salt Pond. It's a sobering, nearly ghastly, thought: You live a whole life, filled with routines, traditions, and brand-new experiences, and then you end up like this. Baker can't let his mind wander to the mechanics of cremation—your body, which you have fed and exercised and washed and dressed with such care, is pushed into a fiery inferno. Baker shudders. And yet there is no escaping death. No escaping it! Every single one of us will die, as surely as every single one of us has been born. Baker is here today, but one day he will be like Russ. Gone.

He, for one, is glad the ashes have finally arrived. They all needed closure.

Baker checks the cardboard box for the name or address of the funeral home but finds neither. It's just a plain box, sealed with clear packing tape. The bag is just a bag, labeled with Russ's name and date of death.

How do we know this is even Russ? he wonders. It could be John Q. Public. It could be coral from Salt Pond. Baker had asked Douglas point-blank, Did you see my father, was he dead? And Douglas had stared. Now, maybe he'd stared at Baker like that because he thought the question was rhetorical. Maybe he thought the question was coming from a man half-crazed with grief, ready to grasp at any straw. But maybe, *maybe,* the stare meant something else.

Irene blots her nose and under her eyes with a paper napkin. "I need you boys to promise me something," she says.

"Anything," Cash says. But Baker refrains. Cash can be his mother's acolyte, but Baker is going to hear what Irene is asking before he commits.

"What is it, Mom?" Baker says.

"Don't be like him," Irene says. "Don't lead secret lives."

Cash laughs, which Baker thinks is in poor taste.

"No one *intends* to lie," Irene says. "But it happens. Sometimes the truth is difficult and it's easier to create an alternate reality or not to say anything at all. I can't imagine how soul-shredding it must have been for Russ to…to go back and forth. Rosie here, me in Iowa City."

Baker looks at his brother. Irene knows about Rosie. Did Cash tell her?

"Mom…," Baker says.

Irene barks out a laugh. "I found the photograph. Winnie helped me. And then I did some sleuthing. It must have destroyed your father deep inside to know he was betraying me and betraying both of you…" She stops. "Just promise me."

"Promise," Cash says.

"Promise," Baker says.

"And yet, you've both spent the better part of a week with me. Baker, you didn't tell me that you and Anna had split. Cash, you didn't tell me you'd lost the stores."

The kitchen is very, very quiet for a moment.

Baker says, "I didn't want to make you even more upset…"

"I thought it was irrelevant," Cash says. "Petty, even, to bring it up when you had so much else going on…"

"So you said nothing, time passed, and I had no idea about

either thing. Which is why I'm asking you now to please not keep any secrets. Secrets become lies, and lies end up destroying you and everyone you care about."

"Okay," Baker says.

"Okay," Cash says. He rises to fetch Irene some ice water. He is such a kiss-ass, Baker thinks, but really Baker is just jealous because he's better at anticipating Irene's needs.

"Thank you," Irene says. "I haven't exactly been forthcoming, either, as I'm sure you both realize..."

Cash says, "Mom, you don't have to..."

"Let her finish," Baker says.

"I tracked down Rosie Small's stepfather," Irene says. "He's a fishing captain by the name of Huck Powers. He was the one who came for dinner last night. He helped me jimmy the door to the bedroom at the end of the hall."

"What bedroom at the end of the hall?" Baker says.

Cash shrugs.

Irene says, "The door at the end of the hall was locked, and I wanted to see what was in it. I thought maybe I would find something that would explain all...this." She holds up her arms.

"What was in it?" Cash asks.

"A bed," Irene says. "Furniture."

"Oh," Baker says. "With that kind of buildup, I thought maybe you'd discovered something."

"I did," Irene says. "Because painted on the wall, in decorative letters, was a name: Maia."

"Who's Maia?" Baker asks.

Irene takes another sip of her water. "Maia is Russ's daughter," she says. "Your sister."

* * *

Funny, we've been here less than a week and we know everyone else's personal drama...

Those words, spoken by Cash, contain some truth, but who are they kidding? Nobody can hold a candle to the Steele family when it comes to personal drama.

Russ has a daughter, twelve years old, named Maia.

He was not only hiding this home, a mistress, and whatever it was he did for a living—he was hiding a child.

Okay, fine, it happens. Baker knows it happens. There was a guy in Iowa City—Brent Lamplighter, his name was, he used to belong to the Elks Lodge—who had gotten a waitress in Cedar Rapids pregnant. That child was in kindergarten before anyone realized that he was Lamplighter's son.

But Russ with a daughter? It's a punch to the gut. Another punch to the gut.

Russ's deception knew no bounds.

The only thing more shocking than the news of Russ's daughter, Maia, is the revelation that Irene wants to *meet* Maia. She wants them *all* to meet Maia. Irene has asked Huck, Rosie's stepfather, if that would be possible. He's going to let her know by tomorrow.

Before Baker goes up to bed, there is something he has to do.

He steps out to the deck beyond the pool to call Ayers. The call goes straight to voicemail, which isn't surprising, given the hour. It's nearly eleven. It also isn't surprising because when

Baker texted Ayers—*My sister showed up out of the blue and I can't do Caneel tomorrow night. What's the next night you're free?*—there was no response. Maybe Ayers was busy with her other "commitment," or maybe she was angry. Maybe she thought Baker was just another tourist who made pretty promises he had no intention of keeping.

Baker can't let himself care why Ayers hasn't responded. He has feelings for her, but those feelings are cheapened because he hasn't been honest.

"Ayers, it's Baker. I'd like you to listen carefully to this message. I lied today when I said my sister showed up out of the blue. It wasn't my sister. It was my wife, Anna, and my son, Floyd. Anna and I are estranged. She's staying at the St. John Guest Suites, so there was no reason I couldn't be honest about that other than I thought you'd be angry or think some kind of reconciliation was going on—which, I can assure you, is *not* the case."

Baker takes a breath. He hates when people leave him lengthy voicemails. He should hang up now and explain the rest when she calls him back.

But what if she doesn't call him back?

"The bigger issue is more than a lie. It's a deception. I never told you the real reason I'm on St. John. The real reason I'm here is because I'm Russell Steele's son. Russell Steele, your friend Rosie's lover, was my father. Cash and I had no idea he owned a villa here, no idea about Rosie...it's been a confusing time for us, and for my mother. Despite the lie and the deception, I want you to know that my feelings for you are genuine. It was love at first sight."

Baker wonders how to sign off. *Call me if you want to? Talk to you later? Good luck and Godspeed?* In the end, he just hangs up.

When he steps back inside the house, he's surprised to find his mother is still awake. She's at the kitchen table in her pajamas, with the bag of ashes and her phone in front of her. When she hears the slider, she raises her head.

"I just got a text from Huck," she says. "He's going to bring Maia by tomorrow after school."

"Great," Baker says. He has no idea if this is great or not, but his mother seems buoyed by the news. "I'm happy to meet Maia tomorrow. But I'm flying back to Houston with Anna and Floyd on Friday."

Irene nods. "That's the right thing to do."

It *is* the right thing to do, Baker tells himself. No matter how much it feels like just the opposite.

Part Three

Love City

MAIA

What's a love child?" Maia asks.

Ayers hits the brakes and they both jolt forward in the seats. She reaches an arm across Maia.

"Sorry, Nut," Ayers says. "That just surprised me. Why are you asking?" She seems halfway between horrified and amused. This is one thing Maia has noticed about adults: they never feel just *one* way. Kids, on the other hand, are simpler: they're angry, they're sad, they're bored. When they're angry, they yell; when they're sad, they cry; when they're bored, they act out or play on their phones.

"I overheard someone say it, and I think they were talking about me."

"Who?" Ayers says. "Who said that?"

Maia doesn't want to get anyone in trouble. It was Colton Seeley's dad. He was talking to Bright Whittaker's father in the parking lot of Gifft Hill and he said something about the "love child of Love City," and Maia had felt that the words were aimed at her. "Just tell me what it means, please."

"It means what you'd think it means," Ayers says. "A child conceived in love."

"But does it have a negative connotation?" Maia asks.

Ayers laughs. "You know what's scary? How precocious you are."

"Tell me."

"Well," Ayers says. "I think it's often used to describe a child whose parents aren't married. So, way back in the olden days, having children was seen as a biological function to propagate the species. People got married and had children so that mankind survived. Whereas a love child is special. Its only reason for being is love."

"And so that's what I am?" Maia asks. "A love child? Because my parents weren't married?"

"I've got news for you, chica. My parents aren't married, either."

"They're *not*?" Maia says.

"Nope. They've been together a long, long time, thirty-five years, but they never got officially married. And guess what? I never think about it. Nobody cares."

Maia loves that she is still learning new things about Ayers. Ayers is *interesting*—and Maia's greatest desire when she grows up is to be interesting as well. She knows that to become interesting, she must read, travel, and learn new things. Maia is pretty much stuck on St. John for the time being, but she does love to read and she watches a fair amount of YouTube, which is how she and Joanie learned to make bath bombs.

"So if you and Mick had a baby, it would be a love child?" Maia asks.

"If Mick and I had a baby, it would be a grave error in judgment," Ayers says, and she turns in to Scoops. "I'm getting the salted peanut butter. What are you getting?"

"Guava," Maia says. Before she gets out of the truck, she notes that she must be growing up, because she feels two distinct emotions at this moment: She is happy to be getting her favorite ice cream with Ayers. She loves Ayers. And she feels empty—like if someone did surgery and cut her open, they would find nothing inside her but sad, stale air. Her mother is dead.

Maia's mother, Rosie, is dead. Some days, Maia can't accept this truth, and so she pretends her mother is on a trip, maybe the trip to the States that Russ was always promising but which never came to fruition. Or, she pretends that Rosie and Russ made it to Anegada, have gotten a beachfront tent at the Anegada Beach Club, and are so taken with the flat white sands, the pink flamingos, and the endless supply of fresh lobster that they have simply decided to stay another week.

Other times, reality is dark and terrifying, like the worst bad dream you can imagine, only you can't wake yourself up. Rosie is gone forever. Never coming back.

Lots of people offered their support—Huck, obviously, and Ayers. Also Joanie's parents, especially her mom, Julie. Julie pulled Maia aside to talk to her alone.

"I lost my mother when I was twelve," she said. "She died of a brain hemorrhage while she was asleep. So as with Rosie, there was no warning."

Not knowing what to say, Maia just nodded. The no-warning part was important. No-warning was the worst. LeeAnn had died, but she had been very sick, and they'd all had time to prepare. They said good-bye. LeeAnn knew they all loved her.

Maia worries: Did Rosie know how much Maia loved her? Did she know she was the start and end of everything for Maia? Did she know she was Maia's role model?

Julie continued. "It's going to be hard for the rest of your life, but it'll also define who you are. You're a survivor, Maia."

There have been plenty of moments when Maia hasn't felt like a survivor. There have been moments when she wished she'd gone down in the bird with her mother, because how is Maia supposed to go through *the rest of her entire life* without Rosie? It feels impossible.

"But it'll get easier, right?" Maia said. Other people had reassured her that the nearly unbearable pain Maia was feeling now—worse than a side stitch, more torturous than a loose molar—would mellow with time. Maia repeated that word, *mellow*.

"Yes, it'll get easier," Julie said. "But certain days will be more difficult than others. Mother's Day is always tough for me. And when Joanie was born"—here Julie welled up with tears, and Maia wanted to reach out and hug her—"...when I had Joanie, I wanted my mom. I wanted her to see her granddaughter. I wanted her to tell me what to do." Julie had then taken a deep breath and recovered. "What helped me was looking outward, and thinking about the other people who missed my mom. You're mature enough for me to suggest that you keep an eye on Huck and Ayers, because they're hurting, too, and they're trying to stay strong for you. But you have something they don't. You have your mother inside of you, half her genes, and as you get older, you'll likely become more and more like your mother, and that will bring people comfort. It'll be like getting Rosie back, in a way."

Maia liked that idea enormously. Her mother was alive inside of her. Maia was her own person, but she was also a continuation of Rosie.

"But don't put pressure on yourself to be perfect in order

to make your mother proud," Julie said. She lifted Maia's chin and gave her a very nice smile. "I assure you, Maia Small, your mother was proud of you every single second of every single day, just for being you."

Maia has never been religious, but now it's helpful to imagine her mother and her grandmother in the sky, in a place Maia thinks of as heaven, where they lie back on chaise longues, like the ones they used to relax in on Gibney Beach. Maia's grandmother, LeeAnn, was friends with Mrs. Gibney, and she was allowed to sit in the shade in front of the Gibney cottages whenever she wanted.

"I hope heaven looks like this," LeeAnn used to say. White sand, flat, clear turquoise water, the hill of Hawksnest and Carval Rock in the distance.

When Maia can keep her mother and grandmother in those chaises in the sky, watching over her, cheering her on, keeping her safe, then she can move—nearly seamlessly—through her days.

She tries to remember her mother in full, fleshy detail, because one of the things she has heard is that once people die, they fade from memory and become more of an idea than a person. Maia and her mother were so connected, so attached, that Maia can't imagine forgetting her, but she replays certain moments and images again and again, just in case.

Her mother was beautiful—short, trim, perfectly proportioned. She had cocoa skin, darker than Maia's, and a flash of orange in her brown eyes, which caused people to stare. Her eyes were *arresting,* Russ said once, meaning they made you stop. Maia didn't inherit the orange; her eyes are regular dark brown like her grandmother's. LeeAnn claimed the orange was a Small trait—it meant fire, and the fire meant trouble.

Rosie worked four evenings a week at La Tapa. She was a great server, the kind returning guests requested when they called to make their reservations. Having dinner at La Tapa wasn't enough of a tradition; they had to have dinner at La Tapa with Rosie as their server—otherwise their trip wasn't complete. Rosie knew a lot about wine and even more about food, and she liked to hang out with the kitchen crew to see how they prepared things. Rosie was a really, really good cook, and at home she made mostly Caribbean food, recipes she had learned from LeeAnn and that LeeAnn had learned from *her* mother—conch stew, jerk chicken, Creole shrimp over rice. She put peas in her pasta salad and raisins in her coleslaw just like everyone else in St. John, but Rosie's versions of these dishes were better because she added a teaspoon of sugar.

Maia is old enough to wonder if her mother had aspirations. She sometimes talked about opening a food truck, but she thought it would be too much work. More than anything in the world, Maia knows, her mother had been passionate about the Virgin Islands—the USVI and the BVI—and when she was working at La Tapa, she was always giving people at her tables excellent tips, such as go to the floating bar, Angel's Rest, in the East End; don't miss the lobster at the Lime Inn; there's yoga on the beach at Cinnamon and a really cool church service on the beach at Hawksnest. She could have been a tour guide, Maia thinks, or a yoga instructor, or owned a food truck, but Rosie had lacked ambition, whereas Maia has ambition to spare. She will need two or three lifetimes to reach all of her goals. Maia doesn't like to think badly about her mother, though, so instead of believing her mother *lacked* something, she has decided to categorize her mother as content. She was so happy with her life—in love with Russ, absorbed with Maia, good at her job, and living in a place she adored, with friends everywhere she turned—that she had no reason to make any changes.

Maia tells Huck about her plan for a memorial ceremony out on the water, in the place the bird went down, and he agrees, as she knew he would. Huck has always been Maia's favorite. Her mother and grandmother loved her because they had to. Huck loves her because he wants to.

Originally, she was only going to honor Rosie, but at the last minute, she chose a bath bomb for Russ as well.

Maia's feelings about Russ are mixed. She first remembers him as the man with the lollipops—flat, oval Charms pops, strawberry, Maia's favorite. Then Maia remembers him teaching her to swim at their private beach. Then, when she was nine, he let her decorate her room in his house however she wanted. But there was a part of Russ that made Maia uneasy. He didn't stay on St. John; he came and went. When he came, Maia's mother was happy—ecstatic, even. Impossible to bring down! And when Russ left, Rosie was devastated. It broke her every time, she said, and the leaving, the worrying that he would never be back, never got any easier.

Normally when he came, Rosie and Maia went to his villa. They swam in the pool or at the beach, they ate at the house—food Mama fixed or that Miss Paulette dropped off from different restaurants. Russ liked the lobster tempura from Rhumb

Lines and the key lime chiffon pie from Morgan's Mango. They read books and watched movies and played shuffleboard. But they didn't go anywhere, and once they returned to their own lives, to the house where they lived with Huck, Maia wasn't allowed to talk about Russ or the villa at all. She had heard Huck and other people refer to Russ as the Invisible Man, and it did sometimes seem to Maia that Russ only existed for Rosie and Maia. It was as if they and Miss Paulette and her husband, Douglas, and the man who came to do the landscaping and service the pool, were the only people who could see him. Maia wondered how Russ got on and off the island. Did he take the ferry, like everyone else? It seemed inconceivable. Maia had asked her mother, and Rosie had said, "Sometimes he takes the ferry, yes. Sometimes he flies in a helicopter. Sometimes his business associates pick him up by boat down on the beach." The helicopter and the private boat sounded reasonable; Maia could not imagine Russ waiting in line at the ferry dock, or sitting on the top deck, the way Maia liked to, or disembarking in Red Hook. She thought Rosie was trying to make Russ seem like a normal person, when it was quite obvious to Maia that he was not.

When Maia got older and had friends and activities and plans of her own, she started opting to stay at Huck's when Russ came. But she still wasn't allowed to talk about him or the villa, or the location of the villa.

I deserve privacy in one area of my life, Rosie would say. *I don't need every damn person all up in my business. And you know that is what would happen.*

Maia *did* know. If the citizens of St. John found out about the huge villa overlooking Little Cinnamon, they would treat

Rosie differently; they would ask for favors and loans—especially Rosie's Small relatives.

Love is messy and complicated and unfair, Rosie would say—but only on the days that Russ left.

The last time Maia saw her mother was midday, New Year's Eve. Rosie had come home from Russ's villa, where she had been staying for the past few days, solely to give Maia "the last kiss of the year." Rosie looked supremely gorgeous, like a goddess, in a new cream-colored sundress (Christmas present from Russ) and a new leather and black pearl choker (ditto). Seeing these gifts made Maia check out her mother's left hand, but it was still unadorned, which Maia knew meant that, deep down inside, her mother was disappointed. What Rosie wanted from Russ, more than anything, was an engagement ring.

Maia and Joanie hunkered down in Maia's room, making a list of tropical scents for their nascent bath bomb business. They were also talking about a boy in their class, Colton Seeley, because Joanie was obsessed with him. Joanie had been snapchatting with Colton, using Maia's phone. Joanie's parents were strict and protective; they treated Joanie like she was six years old instead of twelve. Joanie had a *flip phone,* for phone calls only. It didn't even text.

When Rosie knocked and then entered Maia's room without waiting for a response, Maia made a noise of protest.

"What?" Rosie said. "You hiding something?"

"No," Maia said defensively. She had never hidden anything from her mother. There was no reason to: her mother was a very lenient and permissive parent. But Maia didn't want to give away Joanie's secret. Joanie only pursued her crush on Colton while she was in the free world that was Maia's house.

But Joanie seemed eager to tell the truth. "I'm snapchatting with Colton Seeley," she said. "He's so hot."

"Colton *Seeley*?" Rosie said. "I've known that child since he was in his mama's belly. Let me see what's so hot."

Rosie sat on the bed between them and inspected picture after picture of Colton while both Maia and Joanie snuggled up against her. Maia was happy that Joanie felt comfortable admitting her crush to Rosie and proud of Rosie for being the kind of cool mom that her friends could confide in. For those few moments on the bed, Maia's world was golden.

Then Rosie stood up. She told the girls she was going to "the villa," shorthand for Russ's house, and that she was headed to Anegada the next day. So she was there to give Maia the last kiss of the year.

"What if *we* want to come to Anegada?" Maia asked. She knew she was pressing at a boundary by asking, because Russ didn't socialize with anyone, not even Joanie. But Maia thought maybe this year would be different.

"Sorry, Nut," Rosie said. "We're taking a helicopter." Rosie had caressed Maia's cheeks and kissed her flush on the lips. "I love you and I'll be back late tomorrow night. Happy New Year." Then she turned to Joanie. "You're right, Joan, Colton Seeley is a hottie in the making. Bye, girls. Be good."

Joanie had fallen back on the bed, returning to her rapture over Colton. She didn't see Rosie peek her head back in the room to mouth to Maia, *I love you, Nut.*

Love you, mama, Maia mouthed back.

Rosie blew a kiss and was gone.

* * *

When Huck tells Maia, as they're bobbing out on the water that claimed Rosie, that Russ had a wife and other children, sons, Maia is stunned breathless, but on the other hand it feels like Huck is telling Maia something she had already guessed. All Rosie had wanted was an engagement ring. But Russ was already married.

"They want to meet you," Huck says.

Maia has an adult moment: she wants to meet them because she's curious. At the same time, she doesn't want to meet them because she's scared.

In the end, she decides to meet them. Otherwise, she'll always wonder. But she has a couple of conditions. She wants Huck there, obviously, but she also wants Ayers there.

"This may be putting Ayers out of her depths," Huck says.

"I need her," Maia says. "The two of you are my squad."

"Joanie is your squad," Huck says. "But you would never invite Joanie, because she's not family."

Maia considers this for a moment. When she tells Joanie that this is happening—she's meeting her father's wife and his sons, who are, in fact, Maia's half brothers—Joanie will be fiendishly jealous. A secret in Joanie's family is that her father, Jeff, occasionally goes to Greengo's in Mongoose Junction for carnitas tacos. Joanie has to whisper *carnitas tacos* so Julie doesn't overhear.

My father is only pretending to be vegan, Joanie said.

"Ayers is family," Maia declares. "I need her there."

"I'll ask her," Huck says, but he still seems uneasy.

"*I'll* ask her," Maia says with a martyr's air. She sends Ayers a long text, the gist of which is that it has been revealed that Russ (the Invisible Man) has a wife and two sons and they just found out about Maia and want to meet her, and Maia would like Huck and Ayers to go with her tomorrow after school.

Kind of like a king needs tasters, Maia says. She's proud of herself because she just learned about this courtly detail that very morning—the tasters sampled the king's food to make sure it wasn't poisoned—and now she is applying it to her own life. *Only you won't die.*

I have work at four, Ayers texts back initially. But then, a few seconds later, she says: *I switched nights with Tilda. Ask Huck to pick me up at home.*

Yay! Maia responds. *TYVM!* She's relieved Ayers is going, but she also feels guilty that she has to miss work. Having adult feelings is exhausting, she realizes.

Driving to the villa the next day, Maia is petrified. She's shaking, a phenomenon she has never experienced before but that is beyond her control. She holds her hand out, palm facing down, and tries to steady it—but to no avail.

"Do you want me to turn around?" Huck asks.

"No," Maia says with more certainty than she feels. She won't back away from something because she's afraid of it.

"If it makes you feel any better, I'm nervous, too," Ayers says.

"And me," Huck says.

What is Maia afraid of, exactly? Last night, on the phone,

Joanie helped Maia break it down. They were taught in school that fear often derives from ignorance. Once you understand a situation, it becomes far less intimidating.

"What's the worst that could happen?" Joanie asks. "They aren't going to *hurt* you."

Maia had written a list:

1. They're mean.
2. Awkward silence.
3. They don't like me.
4. They will say unkind things about Rosie. They will call Rosie names. They will say the crash was Rosie's fault.

Bingo: It's the last one. Maia can't bear to hear her mother maligned by people who didn't even know her. And yet that's also why Maia has to go. Someone has to defend Rosie's honor.

Huck makes the turn—he knows where it is without Maia even telling him—and they crawl up the hill.

"Come on, chipmunks," Huck says, but his heart isn't in it, Maia can tell. He would probably be okay with the chipmunks quitting altogether.

Finally, they pull into the driveway. The gate has been propped open; that never happened when Russ was here. Of course, the people Russ was hiding from are now inside the house.

Maia takes a deep breath. Ayers is squeezing her hand. "You're okay," Ayers says. "You've got this."

When Maia climbs out of the truck, the enormity of what

is about to happen strikes her. She runs over to the bougainvillea bordering the driveway and throws up her lunch—fish sandwich. Huck hands her a bottle of water from the fishing trip supply he keeps in the back of the truck.

Tomorrow, she'll tell Huck she's becoming a vegan. She'll accept only peanut butter and jelly for the rest of the year.

That decision made, they ascend the stone staircase.

Before they enter the house, Ayers takes in the view. "It's so weird," she says. "This is Little Cinnamon, or close. The house has this view and yet you can't see it from the road."

"Only from the water," Huck says. "I'm sure that was by design." He strides right up to the slider, knocks on the glass, and opens the door. "Hello!" he says. "We're here."

There are three people sitting at Russ's kitchen table—a woman and two men. When Maia, Huck, and Ayers walk in, they all stand.

One of the men, the really tall, good-looking one, says, "Ayers?"

"Here we are," Huck says. He strides over to the men and offers a hand. "Captain Huck Powers."

"Baker Steele," the tall one says.

Baker: Maia has heard this name before. Then it clicks. Baker is the tourist, Ayers's tourist.

"Cash Steele," the other man says. He's shorter, with a head of bushy blond hair like a California surfer. His face is sunburned, which makes his eyes look fiercely blue.

"This is our friend Ayers Wilson," Huck says. "And this is Maia."

The woman steps forward and offers Maia her hand. "I'm Irene," she says. "It's nice to meet you, Maia. You're even prettier than the pictures your grandfather showed me."

"Oh," Maia says. "Thanks." She gives Irene her firmest grip and manages to look her in the eye. She's old, Maia thinks, way older than Rosie. She's pretty, though in a mom/grandma kind of way. Her hair is reddish-brown and styled in a braid. She's wearing a green linen sundress, no shoes.

Baker looks at Ayers. "I didn't realize you'd be coming."

"Last-minute decision," Ayers says.

Irene says, "Do you two know each other?"

The other brother speaks up. Cash. Cool name, Maia thinks. She loves last-names-as-first-names and has long wished her name, instead of Maia, was Rainseford. Or Gage. Maia is boring and soft.

"Baker and I met Ayers when we went to dinner in town," Cash says. "She works at La Tapa."

"Guilty as charged," Ayers says, but her tone sounds forced.

Did Ayers know the tourist was Russ's son? Maia wonders. Her mind goes one crazy step further: If Ayers and the tourist get married, Ayers will be Maia's half sister-in-law!

This thought serves as a distraction from Maia's prevailing emotion, which is one of bewilderment. This is the kitchen of the villa, in some sense Maia's kitchen, or at least a kitchen where she has spent a lot of time—and maybe as much or more time pretending it didn't exist. If she opens the cabinet on the far left, she knows that she will find half a dozen cans of SpaghettiOs, which Maia loves but which Huck doesn't allow at home because he had to eat them cold out of the can in Vietnam. Now, Maia is here with Huck. And Ayers. If Rosie is watching from her beach chaise in heaven, she is very, very upset. Maia is suffused with a sense of disloyalty. She's betraying her mother—and her father—by being here.

But maybe not. Maybe Russ, anyway, is happy his two families are finally meeting each other. Maybe this was supposed to happen.

Maia studies the three strangers, and she can tell they are studying her.

What do they think? she wonders.

IRENE

The girl is beautiful and she has a grace you can't discern from a picture. She is light-skinned, her hair gathered in a frizzy ponytail. She has brown eyes, but her nose and smile are all Russ, and more than Russ, they're Milly. Looking at Maia is like looking at Milly at age twelve, if Milly were half West Indian.

Irene needs to get a grip, offer everyone a drink and put out some snacks, but she is hobbled by thoughts of Milly. When she goes home—which will be very soon, maybe as soon as the weekend—she will go to see Milly. That morning, she decided that she needs to tell Milly the truth: Russ is dead, Russ had a home and a second family down in the Caribbean. Irene lectured the boys about not keeping secrets, and she can't be hypocritical. Milly needs to know. Milly needs to know, too, that she has a granddaughter who so strongly resembles her.

"What would you like to drink?" Irene asks Maia.

"Ginger ale, please, if you have one," Maia says, and she places a hand on her stomach. "I'm feeling a little green."

Poor thing, Irene thinks as she pulls a ginger ale out of the fridge. This defines what it feels like to be thrown for a loop.

Winnie saunters into the kitchen, wagging her tail. She heads straight for Ayers, who bends down to rub Winnie under the chin. Irene isn't quite sure who Ayers is or why she's here. She's a friend of Rosie's, maybe? If so, she may have some of the answers Irene is looking for.

Cash says to Ayers, "You've never been to this house before?"

"Never," Ayers says. "I didn't even know where it was."

"I'd never been here before, either," Huck says. "Until the other night, when Irene invited me for dinner."

"Really?" Baker says. "Didn't either of you wonder...?"

"You've been here before, right, Maia?" Irene asks. She catches a warning look from Huck. He told her that under no circumstances was she to grill the child.

"Yep," Maia says. "I have my own bedroom here, upstairs at the end of the hall."

Irene knows she's pushing her luck but she has to ask. "Do you have any idea what Russ did for a living? Who he worked for or what kind of business he was in?"

"Not really," Maia says. "Money or something. All I know is he was away a lot."

This last statement makes Irene laugh, but not in a funny ha-ha way. "You mean he was home a lot."

Maia blinks, uncomprehending.

"At home in Iowa City," Irene says. "With me. His wife. Us, his family..." She nearly says *his real family*, but she stops herself. She will not vent her anger at the girl. The girl is innocent.

She wants to ask, *Did your mother know about me?* Did she know about the woman she was betraying? Did she know about Baker and Cash, Anna and Floyd? Did. She. Know. Irene realizes she can't ask; Huck will whisk Maia out of here faster than you can say Jiminy Cricket.

However, Maia is intuitive.

"My mother used to tell me that love was messy, complicated, and unfair."

"Well," Irene says. "She was right about that."

"Amen," Baker says.

"Amen," Ayers says.

"Amen," Cash says.

Winnie stands at the sliding door and barks.

AYERS

Thank God for dogs, she thinks. No matter how tense a situation humans find themselves in—and the situation in the kitchen of the Invisible Man's villa, with his decidedly visible wife and his *sons,* Baker and Cash, is an eleven out of ten on the stress scale—a dog lightens the mood.

When Winnie enters the kitchen, she comes right over and buries her nose in Ayers's crotch, her tail going haywire.

Everyone is trying to act normal, to pretend this visit isn't completely messed up. Irene says she'd like to talk to Huck and Maia alone, and Baker takes the opportunity to invite Ayers outside. Cash follows with Winnie.

"Go away," Baker says to him. "Please."

"Cash can stay," Ayers says. "I'd actually like to talk to you both."

They wander over to the pool. There's a shallow entry where they can all sit with their feet in the water. Winnie lies down between Ayers and Cash, and Ayers strokes her head.

"Let me start," Baker says. "I owe you an apology."

"Stop," Ayers says. She marvels that her parents took her to the rice paddies of Vietnam, the red desert of the Australian outback, and the snow-capped peaks of the Swiss Alps, all with the aim of making her "worldly," and still she has no idea how to negotiate this emotional landscape.

"Ayers is talking now, Baker," Cash says. "Respect."

"Thank you," Ayers says. She bows her head and smells Mick's scent on her clothes. When she'd gotten off the phone with Cash the afternoon before—*You really shouldn't be interested in either of us*—she had flipped out. She had been blindsided. But once that piece clicked, everything else made sense.

Baker and Cash came to Rosie's memorial lunch on purpose—because they wanted to gather intel on the woman their father was keeping on the side.

Even saying that phrase in her head fills Ayers with fury. Rosie was nothing more to Russell Steele than a side piece, a baby mama, an island wife. What can she think but that Russell Steele was a despicable human being? And yet she has to be careful, because he was Maia's biological father. The Invisible Man was also the Pirate, which is sort of like finding out that Santa Claus is the Tooth Fairy.

"You're both liars," Ayers says. "Like your father."

Cash holds up his palms as if to protest his guilt, and Ayers pounces. "Neither of you told me who you were at the memorial reception. You let me believe you were crashing."

"We *were* crashing," Baker says.

"And then I bumped into *you* on the Reef Bay Trail," Ayers says to Cash. "Did you *follow* me there?"

"*Follow* you?" Cash says. "No, that was a coincidence."

Ayers narrows her eyes.

"I swear," Cash says. "I've never been here before, I'm an outdoors person, I wanted to get out of the house, *see* something, take Winnie for a walk. Bumping into you was totally random. How could I possibly have followed you?"

Fair enough, Ayers thinks. Maybe it was just really terrible luck. "But you came on *Treasure Island* because you wanted to ask me questions about Rosie. Admit it."

"I came on *Treasure Island* because I wanted to see *you,*" Cash says. "Because I thought you were pretty—scratch that, I thought you were *beautiful,* and I thought you were cool. And you invited me."

"Sheesh," Baker says.

"And you!" Ayers says. "You were so much worse."

"I admit, we went to the reception to do some detective work," Baker says. "But when I saw you, Ayers...I could barely remember my own name. It was love at first sight."

"You *used* me," Ayers says. The sun is directly in her eyes so she squints, which suits her mood. "You say you like me, you say you love me, but both of you lied to me about who you were or weren't. And the thing is...I *knew* something wasn't right. I *knew* it." She drops her voice. "I never met your father, but he spent years lying to my best friend. All I can think is not only did he have no scruples, he had no soul."

"Whoa," Baker says.

"She's right," Cash says. "I offer no excuses for my father. None."

Ayers wants to land one more punch. "The two of you are just like him. You're sneaky."

"I called you and told you the truth," Cash says.

"You did not," Baker says. "I did."

"You did?" Cash says. "I did, too."

"Too little, way too late," Ayers says. She never wants to see either of them again, and this really hurts because she liked them both. She's also worried that she'll never be rid of them now because *they're Maia's brothers.* "It doesn't matter, anyway. I'm back together with Mick."

"No," Baker says.

"Yes," Ayers says. "I was with him last night."

She relishes saying this, even though a part of her is ashamed about taking Mick back so readily. She called him, and he was at her house half an hour later with an order of oxtail stew from De' Coal Pot, plus a side of pineapple rice, plus one perfect red hibiscus blossom, which he stuck in a juice glass. He'd begged her for another chance. He'd made a mistake and it would never happen again.

Ayers had succumbed, even though she knew it *would* happen again—just as soon as he hired the next girl who looked like Brigid. But unlike these two, Mick was a known quantity. And he lived here.

Tourists, she thinks, are nothing but heartbreak.

CASH

The bad news is, he can't have Ayers.

The good news is, Baker can't have her, either.

She hates them both.

It's a knockout punch, but Cash admires Ayers's principles. He would hate them, too, if he were her.

They leave the pool and head back to the kitchen, where Irene, Huck, and Maia are sitting at the table in silence. It feels like they've interrupted something, or maybe they came in on the tail end of a conversation.

Huck stands. "We should probably go."

"But wait," Irene says. "The ashes."

"I'm leaving," Ayers says. "I'll walk to the bottom of the hill and call my boyfriend to come pick me up."

"I'll drive you home," Huck says. He looks at Irene. "I'll run Ayers home and then I'll come back to pick up Maia. Forty minutes. Will that be enough time to do what you have to do?"

"Plenty," Irene says.

Cash, Baker, and Maia follow Irene down the eighty steps to the private beach. A few minutes later finds the children of Russell Steele, along with the wife he betrayed for thirteen years, tossing chunks and silt into the Caribbean. No one says anything. No one cries.

Irene saves a handful of ashes in the bag. "I'm taking these home for Russ's mother." She smiles at Maia. "Your grandmother. She's ninety-seven."

"Really?" Maia says.

"And you look just like her," Irene says.

Cash has tried not to study Maia's face too carefully—he doesn't want to make her uncomfortable or self-conscious—but he agrees with Irene: there is something about Maia that strongly resembles Milly.

He replays Ayers's words in his head. *I never met your father, but he spent years lying to my best friend. All I can think is not only did he have no scruples, he had no soul.*

Cash feels that's too harsh. He wants to think that Russ was more than just what happened down here. Russ had spent years and years providing for their family in a job he disliked, and he had always been an involved, enthusiastic father. When Cash was little, Russ would hold on to his hands, let Cash walk up his legs, and then flip him over in a skin-the-cat. Two years ago, Russ had handed Cash the keys to two prime pieces of Denver real estate. He hadn't objected to the name Savage Season Outdoor Supply; he had even come to Denver for the ribbon cuttings. He had believed in Cash more than Cash had believed in himself.

And yet there's no denying that Russ made a terrific mess of things. The money for those stores had come from... where?

Cash is the first one back up the stairs.

He may feel differently at some point, but for now, he's glad to be rid of the man.

HUCK

When Huck and Maia are alone with Irene, she says, "I want to talk about money."

"Maybe you and I should have that talk privately," Huck says.

Irene ignores this suggestion. "I'm guessing Russ probably gave Rosie support," she says. "And I just want you to know that I want to continue. Do you go to private school?"

Maia nods. "Gifft Hill."

"And do you want to go to college?" Irene asks.

"Of course!" Maia says. "My first choice is NYU and my second choice is Stanford. I'm interested in microlending. That's where you lend a small amount of money to help people get local businesses started. I want to help Caribbean women."

"Well," Irene says.

"I'm an entrepreneur," Maia says. "My friend Joanie and I started a bath bomb business. They're six dollars apiece, if you'd like to buy one."

"I'd like to buy several," Irene says.

"Let's keep the transactions simple, like that," Huck says. "I'm perfectly capable of supporting Maia and sending her to college."

"Of course," Irene says. "I didn't mean to offend you."

"Not offended," Huck says, though he is, a little. The emotional terrain here is difficult enough without bringing up money, although he understands that Irene is trying to provide reassurance: She isn't a witch, she isn't vindictive. Maia will continue to have what she needs.

"I don't want to impose myself on your life," Irene says.

"But I wanted to meet you, as strange or unconventional as that choice might have been. I want to stay in your life, as little or as much as you want me. Maybe I leave here on Friday and I don't see you again until you're on your way to NYU or Stanford. But I want you to know I'm here, and if you ever need anything, I want you to be comfortable asking me. I would be *honored* if you asked."

"Thank you," Maia says.

"You're leaving Friday?" Huck says.

"I am," Irene says. "The boys and I will spread most of the ashes today and Maia, I hope you'll join us, but then I need to get back."

"What are you going to do about the house?" Huck asks.

"Nothing, for the time being," Irene says. "I have a lot of decisions in front of me, but, thankfully, they don't have to be made today." She reaches over to squeeze Maia's hand. "I am so glad you came today, Maia. You are a very special person."

"Thank you," Maia says. "I try."

Irene laughs then, for real, and she says to Huck, "You have your hands full with this one."

"Wouldn't have it any other way," Huck says.

Their conversation must have been far more pleasant than the one going on outside, because Ayers, Baker, and Cash walk into the kitchen looking like three kids whose sandcastle just washed away.

Huck offers to give Ayers a ride home so that Maia can scatter the Invisible Man's ashes with Irene and her brothers.

Irene and her brothers. Huck wonders how long it will be until he gets used to the way things are now.

When they reach the north shore road, Huck turns to Ayers. "You okay?"

"I guess," Ayers says.

"I'm sorry if that was awkward for you," Huck says. "Maia really wanted you there."

"I met both the boys this past week," Ayers says. "I went on a date or two with Baker."

"Is he the tourist Maia was telling me about?" Huck says.

"He's the tourist," Ayers confirms. "I knew better, but I fell for him anyway. And he's leaving tomorrow."

"Irene is leaving Friday," Huck says, and he realizes he sounds wistful.

"I guess it would be easier if we didn't like them so much," Ayers says.

Huck nearly clarifies that he doesn't "like" Irene, at least not in the way Ayers is describing, but then he thinks, *Why lie?*

"I've decided to get a tattoo of the petroglyphs," Ayers announces.

"One like Rosie had?" Huck asks. Rosie's tattoo, which she got without permission when she was fifteen—before Huck came on the scene, he would like to point out—was just above her left ankle.

"Yes," Ayers says. "I used to think I didn't deserve one because I didn't grow up here, I don't have family here..."

"You loved someone deeply here," Huck says. "And you lost her. I think that makes this home for you."

"Thank you for saying that." Ayers is openly weeping. "Would you come with me when I get it?"

"I would be honored," Huck says.

IRENE

She sits in the same spot on the plane home, next to Cash, with a scant cup of Russ's ashes in her purse. She has been in the Virgin Islands for seven days and eight nights. She knows more now than she did when she arrived, although far from everything she needs to know. When she gets home, she has to call Ed Sorley, her attorney. She has to let everyone know that Russ is dead. She has to hire a forensic accountant and, most likely, a private investigator.

The Virgin Islands used to be rife with pirates, or at least the lore of those charming swashbucklers, with their skulls and crossbones and their hidden treasure. An aura of lawlessness still pervades the islands: that much Irene has learned. It's as if the sun has melted away the rules, and the stunning beauty of the water and the islands has dazzled everyone into bliss. The soundtrack says it all: "The Weather Is Here," "You and Tequila," "One Love."

Before she left, Huck had insisted on taking Irene out on *The Mississippi* again. She knew he had most likely canceled a charter in order to do so. He said he wanted to give her a proper island good-bye.

If I do a good job, you might even find you like it here, he said.

There wasn't enough time to fish, because Huck had to pick Maia up from school at three, so instead, Huck gave Irene a round-the-island tour. They puttered out of Cruz Bay harbor and headed northeast. Huck pointed out each beach and provided a running commentary.

"First on your right are Salomon and Honeymoon. You'd think Honeymoon would be the nude beach, but you'd be wrong. Salomon is nude, and Honeymoon has water sports."

Irene couldn't help herself: She squinted in the direction of Salomon, but it was deserted.

"There's Caneel Bay, the resort. If we had more time, we could dock and go in for a bottle of champagne."

"You don't seem like much of a champagne drinker," Irene said.

"True," Huck said. They rounded the point. "On the right is Hawksnest, popular with the locals, although I wouldn't be caught dead there, and on the left is Oppenheimer, named after Robert Oppenheimer, father of the atomic bomb. He used to own the land. Coming up is Denis Bay, below Peace Hill. My first mate, Adam, calls it 'Piece of Ass' beach."

Irene shook her head and smiled.

"There's Trunk Bay, our pageant winner, followed by Peter Bay, where all those fancy homes are...and now we are approaching...Little Cinnamon."

"Little Cinnamon?" Irene said. "Where's the house?"

Huck had to cut the engine and pull out his binoculars. He studied the hillside for a moment. "There. The outside of the house is meant to blend in with the surrounding bush, but if you look closely and hold the glasses exactly where I have them, you'll see it."

Irene accepted the binoculars. She had a hard time finding anything resembling a house, but then she picked out the curve of the upper stone deck. A man and a dog were outside: Cash and Winnie.

They proceeded past Cinnamon to Maho and went around Mary's Point to Waterlemon Cay ("great snorkeling—we'll have to do that the next time you come") and Francis Bay ("buggy"), and all the way around the East End ("nothing out there but a great floating bar") to Coral Bay. They headed back along the south-facing beaches: Salt Pond ("guaranteed turtles"), Lameshur Bay, Reef Bay, Fish Bay. Irene followed their progress on the map. She was awed by the size of the island and by the homes she saw tucked into crevices and hanging from cliffs.

There were a lot of places to hide in St. John.

Huck guided the boat toward an island called Little St. James. "What do you like on your pizza?" he asked.

"My pizza?" Irene said.

He pointed a few hundred yards away to a sailboat flying a pizza flag. PIZZA PI, the sign said. As they got closer, Irene could see a menu hanging on the mast. It was a pizza boat in the middle of the Caribbean.

"Let's have a lobster pizza," she said. "Just because we can."

"Woman after my own heart," Huck said. "All the pizzas are made to order, but the lobster is my favorite." He dropped the anchor, shucked off his shirt, and swam over to place their order.

Irene vowed that if she ever came back, she would bring a bathing suit.

She and Huck devoured the entire pizza, then she lay back in the sun. She was about to doze off when she heard Huck start the engine.

"Are we leaving?" she asked. Her heart felt heavy at the thought.

"We have one more stop," Huck said.

He drove them due west, pointing out Water Island, "the

little-known fourth Virgin," and then he cut the engine, threw the anchor again, and fitted on a mask and snorkel.

"Back in a sec," he said.

Irene leaned over the side of the boat to watch his watery form shimmering beneath the surface. At one point he swam under the boat, and just as Irene started to wonder if she should be worried, though she couldn't picture Huck as the kind of man who would ever need to be rescued, he popped up.

"Got a beauty!" he said.

What kind of beauty? Irene wondered.

He climbed up the ladder on the back of the boat with a brilliant peach conch shell in his hand.

"Oh!" Irene said. The shell was perfect; it looked like something she would buy in a gift shop.

Huck brought out the cutting board that he used to fillet fish and pulled the live conch from the shell and sealed it in a clean plastic bag.

"Maia loves my conch fritters," he said. He then dropped the shell in a bucket of water and added bleach. "That'll be clean by the time we dock."

"You're giving the shell to Maia?" Irene asked. She thought how wonderful it must be to have a grandfather who produced surprise gifts from the sea.

"No," Huck said. "It's for you."

It turned out Huck was giving Irene more than just a conch shell. With a few flicks of his fillet knife, he transformed the shell into a horn. He held his lips up to the hole he'd just cut, wrapped his fingers into the glossy pink interior, and blew. The sound was far from lovely. It was low, sonorous, mournful. It was the sound of Irene's heart.

Huck handed Irene the shell. "Take this home," he said. "And when you need a friend, blow through it."

"You won't hear it, though," Irene said.

"No, but you'll hear it, and you'll remember that there's a tiny island in the Caribbean, and on that island you have a friend for life. Do you understand me, Angler Cupcake?"

Irene nodded. She forced herself to look into Huck's eyes and she thought back to her last innocent hour, ten days and another lifetime ago, when she was at the Prairie Lights bookstore and noticed Brandon the barista gazing at her dear friend Lydia. Huck was gazing at Irene now in much the same way. She wasn't an idea or an outline or a mere distraction from a younger, prettier woman.

Huck saw her.

He saw her.

When Irene and Cash land in Chicago, Irene sees she has three missed calls from the Brown Deer retirement community and one voicemail.

"Milly," Irene says to Cash.

She listens to the voicemail. It's from today. "Hi Irene, Dot from Brown Deer here. I'm not sure if you're still on vacation? But I needed to let you know that Milly has lost consciousness and Dr. Adler thinks it's likely she'll let go tonight." There's a pause; Irene can practically hear poor Dot trying to choose the right words. "I didn't want to have to deliver this news while you were away, but I also can't have you not knowing. Thanks, Irene, and I'm sorry. Call anytime."

* * *

It turns out that Milly Steele does not let go that night. She holds on until Monday morning. By Monday morning, Irene and Cash have unpacked, thrown their clothes in the laundry, and made it over to Brown Deer to take turns sitting with Milly in case there's a miracle and she wakes up.

Irene and Cash have also had time to talk. Cash confided that Baker had feelings for the woman, Ayers, who was such good friends with Rosie, but that Cash liked her, too.

"Women always pick Baker over me," Cash says.

Irene shakes her head. "Baker isn't a free man yet, and you are. You are every bit as handsome and charming as your brother." Irene brightens. "If I remember correctly, Ayers seemed quite fond of Winnie. I think you should pursue her." Irene doesn't offer any thoughts about how Cash might go about this when Ayers is on St. John and Cash is in the American Midwest.

It just so happens that both Cash and Irene are sitting at Milly's bedside on Monday morning. It has been an arduous overnight vigil and now the eerie breathing known as the death rattle has set in. It won't be long now.

Irene is relieved that she has been spared telling Milly the truth about her son.

Because there are no cell phones allowed in the medical unit and certainly none allowed in a room where a ninety-seven-year-old woman is trying to seamlessly transition to the next life, neither Irene nor Cash sees the calls come in from an unknown number with a 787 area code: San Juan, Puerto

Rico. The call to Irene's phone comes in at 8:24 a.m. The call to Cash's phone comes at 8:26 a.m.

Missed.

Milly passes away at two minutes past ten in the morning. Dot comes in to record the time of death.

"Life well-lived," she says.

Irene and Cash make the necessary arrangements. Milly's body will be cremated. Her ashes, along with what remains of Russ's ashes, will be buried together in the cemetery at the First Presbyterian church once the ground thaws in the spring.

"What do you want to do now?" Irene asks Cash.

"Honestly?" Cash says. "I want to go back."

Irene nods. She doesn't have to ask what he means by "back." She knows.

"Me too," she says.

At 8:27 on Monday morning, Baker is having breakfast at Snooze in Houston with his school wives: Wendy, Becky, Debbie, and Ellen. They had been very worried about him. Baker had been gone for over a week without warning and they had seen Dr. Anna Schaffer herself delivering Floyd to school *and picking him up.*

"I knew something was wrong," Debbie says. "I didn't want to pry, and Anna isn't approachable even if I *had* wanted to pry."

Baker told his friends that his father died and he'd taken a week with his mother and brother. That's why they're all at breakfast. They want to comfort him.

"Your mother lives in Iowa, doesn't she?" Becky asks. Becky is in HR and remembers every personal detail Baker has ever told her. "How'd you come back with a suntan?" She is also, like any good HR executive, naturally suspicious.

Baker can't begin to explain that his father was killed in a helicopter crash in the Caribbean, where he happened to own a fifteen-million-dollar villa, keep a mistress, and have a love child. Baker also can't say a word about the beautiful woman—body and soul—that he fell in love with during his week away.

He can, however, tell them the truth about Anna. They're going to find out sooner or later.

"I have more bad news," Baker says. "Anna announced that she's leaving me."

"Whaaaa?" Debbie says. "Just as you found out your father was dead?"

"She found someone else," Baker says. "Another doctor at the hospital." He waits a beat. "Louisa Rodriguez."

There is a collective gasp, then some shrieking, then a declaration from Ellen that this is, hands down, the best gossip of the entire school year. Baker gets so caught up talking with his friends that he misses the call that comes in to his phone from an unknown number, area code 787, San Juan, Puerto Rico, at 8:32 a.m.

At 8:34 a.m. on Monday, Huck is dropping Maia off at school. They're four minutes late, but better late than not at all, which was what Maia was lobbying for. She was tired, they both were, because they'd accompanied Ayers over to Red Hook in St. Thomas the evening before so that she could get her petroglyph tattoo.

The tattoo had taken longer than they'd anticipated, but it was a beauty—an exact replica of the petroglyphs of Reef Bay, left there by the Taino three thousand years ago.

"It's so *cool,*" Maia said.

"Don't even think about it," Huck said. After the tattoo adventure, he'd treated both of them to dinner at Fish Tails, next to the ferry dock. Ayers had been a little subdued at dinner, as had Huck. He couldn't pinpoint the exact cause of his malaise. If it wasn't such a cockamamie notion, he would say he missed Irene. But how could he miss someone he'd only known a week? He wondered if Ayers was suffering from a similar affliction, if she missed either or both of Irene's sons. She *said* she was getting back together with Mick. However, she didn't sound too excited about it.

Noting their glum faces, Maia had reached out for each of them and said, "I want you guys to know I'm here for you if you ever need to talk."

She had sounded so earnest that both Huck and Ayers had been helpless to do anything but smile.

"What?" Maia said. "What?"

Maia is gathering her things—backpack, lunch, water bottle—when Huck's phone rings. It's an unknown number, 787, San Juan, Puerto Rico. It's probably Angela, the travel agent who sends Huck group charters, which is all well and good. He needs to get his head back into his business.

"Hello?" he says. He shoos Maia out of the truck; she's dawdling.

"Mr. Powers?" a woman's voice says. The voice is too young to be Angela's; she's a grandmother of fifteen and her voice is raspy from cigarettes and yelling. "Mr. Sam Powers?"

"Yes?"

"My name is Agent Colette Vasco, with the FBI, sir. I've just had a call from VISAR in the British Virgin Islands. They were investigating a helicopter crash on January first, a crash in which your daughter was one of the deceased?"

"Yes," Huck says. Reluctantly, Maia climbs out of the truck. She eyes him through the windshield as she walks to the front gate of the school.

"That investigation has been passed on to us," Agent Vasco says. "What was initially thought to be a weather-related incident now looks like it involved foul play."

"Foul play?" Huck asks.

"Yes, sir," Agent Vasco says. "Any chance you're available to answer a few questions about your daughter and her friend Russell Steele?"

Huck puts the window down. He needs air. He notices Maia standing at the entrance of the school, staring back at him. She senses something.

Huck sets the phone down on the passenger seat. Agent Colette Vasco can wait. Right now, Huck has to tend to his girl. He is her Unconditional. He is her No Matter What.

"See you at three!" he calls out. "I'll be right here, waiting."

ABOUT THE AUTHOR

Elin Hilderbrand is the mother of three 3-sport athletes, an aspiring fashionista, a dedicated jogger, a world explorer, an enthusiastic foodie, and a grateful seven-year breast cancer survivor. She spends part of every winter writing on St. John. *Winter in Paradise* is her twenty-second novel.

What Happens in Paradise

ALSO BY ELIN HILDERBRAND

The Beach Club

Nantucket Nights

Summer People

The Blue Bistro

The Love Season

Barefoot

A Summer Affair

The Castaways

The Island

Silver Girl

Summerland

Beautiful Day

The Matchmaker

Winter Street

The Rumor

Winter Stroll

Here's to Us

Winter Storms

The Identicals

Winter Solstice

The Perfect Couple

Winter in Paradise

Summer of '69

28 Summers

Troubles in Paradise

Golden Girl

What Happens in Paradise

A Novel

Elin Hilderbrand

BACK BAY BOOKS
Little, Brown and Company
New York Boston London

Back Bay Books / Little, Brown and Company
Hachette Book Group
1290 Avenue of the Americas, New York, NY 10104
littlebrown.com

Originally published in hardcover by Little, Brown and Company, October 2019
First Back Bay trade paperback edition, September 2020
Boxed-set edition, October 2021

ISBN 978-0-316-43557-4 (hardcover) / 978-0-316-42607-7 (large print) / 978-0-316-53651-6 (Canadian) / 978-0-316-42807-1 (signed) / 978-0-316-42808-8 (Barnes & Noble signed) / 978-0-316-42809-5 (Barnes & Noble signed Black Friday) / 978-0-316-43554-3 (paperback) / 978-0-316-37146-9 (boxed-set edition)

LCCN 2019943388

Printing 2, 2023

LSC-C

Printed in the United States of America

This novel is for St. John, U.S. Virgin Islands—the island itself and everyone who lives there.

Thank you for the revelry, and thank you for the refuge.

AUTHOR'S NOTE

What Happens in Paradise is the second book in a planned trilogy. While this book can, most certainly, be read as a standalone, a richer and more textured reading experience will be had by starting with book one, *Winter in Paradise.*

In the author's note in *Winter in Paradise,* I explained that the St. John portrayed in the novel is the one that existed before September of 2017, when Hurricanes Irma and Maria created such widespread devastation. There are businesses and restaurants mentioned in both books that now exist only on my fictional St. John. Thank you.

Part One

A Rooster and Two Hens

IRENE

She wakes up facedown on a beach. Someone is calling her name.

"Irene!"

She lifts her head and feels her cheek and lips dusted with sand so white and fine, it might be powdered sugar. Irene can sense impending clouds. As the sun disappears, it gains a white-hot intensity; it's like a laser cutting through her. The next instant she feels the lightest sprinkling of rain.

"Irene!"

She sits up. The beach is unfamiliar, but it's tropical—there's turquoise water before her, lush vegetation behind, a rooster and two hens strutting around. She must be back on St. John.

How did she get here?

"Irene!"

A man is calling her name. She can see a figure moving toward her. The rain starts to fall harder now, with intention; the tops of the palm trees sway. Irene dashes for the cover of the tree canopy and wishes for a towel to wrap around her naked body.

Naked?

That's right; she forgot to pack a swimsuit.

The man is getting closer, still calling her name. *"Irene! Irene!"* She doesn't want him to see her. She tries to cover up her nakedness by hunching over and crossing her arms strategically; it feels like an impossible yoga pose. She's shivering now. Her hair is wet; her braid hangs like a soggy rope down her back.

The man is waving his arms as if he's drowning. Irene scans the beach; someone else will have to help him because she certainly can't. But there's no one around, no boats on the horizon, and even the chickens are gone. There will be a confrontation, she supposes, so she needs to prepare. She studies the approaching figure.

Irene opens her mouth and tries to scream. Does she scream? If so, she can't hear herself.

It's Russ.

She wipes the rain out of her eyes. Russell Steele, her husband of thirty-five years, is slogging toward her through the wet sand, looking as though he has something urgent to tell her.

"Irene!"

He's close enough now for her to see him clearly—the silvering hair, the brown eyes. He has a suntan. He's had a constant tan since he started working for Todd Croft at Ascension, thirteen years ago. Their friends used to tease Russ about it, but Irene barely noticed, much less questioned it. He was on business in Florida and Texas; the tan seemed logical. She had chalked it up to lunch meetings at outdoor restaurants, endless rounds of golf. How many times had Russ told her he would be unreachable because he'd be playing golf with clients?

Now, of course, Irene knows better.

"Irene," he says. His voice frightens her; she digs her heels into the sand. Russ's white tuxedo shirt is so soaked that she can see the flesh tone of his skin beneath. His khaki pants are split up one leg. He looks like he's survived a shipwreck.

No, Irene thinks. *Not a shipwreck. A plane crash. A* helicopter crash, *that's it.*

"Russ?" she says. He's getting pummeled by rain, and Irene flashes back twenty years to a Little League game of Baker's that was suspended due to a violent midwestern thunderstorm. All the parents huddled in the dugout with the kids, but Russ, in a show of gallantry, ran out onto the field to collect the equipment. Another father, Steve Sonnet (Irene had always rather disliked Steve Sonnet), said, *Reckless of him, picking up those metal bats. He's going to get himself killed.*

There was another time she remembers Russ soaking wet, a wedding in Atlanta. The Dunns' daughter Maisy was marrying an executive at Delta Airlines. This was five or six years ago, back when Irene and Russ found themselves attending more weddings than they had even when they were young. The reception was held at Rhodes Hall, and when she and Russ emerged from the strobe-lit dance floor and martini bar, it was to a downpour. Again, Russ insisted on playing the hero by tenting his tuxedo jacket over his head and dashing across the parking lot to their rental car. When he'd pulled up to the entrance a few moments later, his shirt had been soaked through, just like this one is now.

"The storm," Russ says, "is coming."

Well, yes, Irene thinks. *That much is obvious.* It's a proper deluge now, and the darkest clouds are still moving toward them. "I thought you were dead," she says. "They told me…" She stops. She's speaking, but she can't hear herself. It's frustrating. "They told me you were dead."

"It will be a bad storm," Russ says. "Destructive."

"Where should we go?" Irene asks. She turns to face the trees. *Where do the chickens hide from the rain?* she wonders. Because she would like to hide there too.

At eight o'clock on the dot, Irene wakes Cash. He has started calling her Mother Alarm Clock.

"I had another dream," she says.

Cash props himself up on his elbows in bed. His blond hair is messy and he's growing a beard; he hasn't shaved since they left the island. Irene has put him in the grandest of her five guest rooms, the Excelsior suite, she calls it. It has dark, raised-panel walls with a decorative beveled edge at the chair rail and an enormous Eastlake bed with a fringed canopy. There's also a stained-glass transom window that Irene got for a steal at a tiny antiques shop in Solon, Iowa, and a silk Persian rug in burgundy and cream that she purchased from a licensed dealer in Chicago. (She'd thought Russ might veto a five-figure rug, but he told her to go ahead, get it, whatever made her happy.) Irene's favorite piece in the room is a wrought-iron washstand that holds a ceramic bowl edged in gold leaf; above it hangs a photograph of Russ's mother, Milly, as a young girl in Erie, Pennsylvania, in 1928. Irene remembers the joy and pride she'd felt in refurbishing this room—every room in the house, really—but at this instant, she can't understand why. The Victorian style seems so heavy, so overdone, so tragic.

Irene has abandoned the master bedroom; she will never be able to sleep there again. Since she returned from St. John, she's been using the smallest guest room, originally meant to be quarters for a governess. It's up on the third floor, across from the attic. The attic is crammed with the bargains Irene scored at flea markets but couldn't find a place for in the house along with all the furniture from their former home, since Russ refused to let her take it to Goodwill. Russ had remarked many times that he would have been just as happy staying in their modest ranch on Clover Street, and Irene had thought him crazy. Of course, that was before she realized that Russ had a second life elsewhere.

The governess's room had been all but neglected in the renovation. Irene had simply painted the walls sky blue and furnished it with a white daybed and a small Shaker dresser. Now she appreciates the room's simplicity and its isolation. She feels safe there—although she can't seem to hide from these dreams.

"Dad was alive?" Cash asks.

"Alive," Irene says. This is the third such dream she's had since returning from St. John. Irene and Cash and Irene's older son, Baker, all traveled down to the Virgin Islands upon receiving the news that Russ had been killed in a helicopter crash off the coast of Virgin Gorda. He had been flying from a private helipad on St. John to the remote British island Anegada with a West Indian woman named Rosie Small. Irene then discovered that Rosie was Russ's lover and that Russ had left behind a fifteen-million-dollar villa and a twelve-year-old daughter named Maia. It was a surreal and traumatizing trip for Irene and her sons, and yet now, a week later, all of these shocking facts have been woven into the tapestry of Irene's reality. It was incredible, really, what the brain could assimilate. "He was talking about a storm. A bad storm, he said. Destructive."

"Maybe he meant the lightning storm," Cash says.

"Maybe," Irene says. The helicopter had been struck by lightning. "Or maybe it's what lies ahead."

"The investigation," Cash says.

"Yes." The week before, only a couple days after they'd arrived home from St. John, an FBI agent named Colette Vasco called Irene, Cash, and Baker to let them know that the Virgin Islands Search and Rescue team had contacted the Bureau with suspicions that there might be more to the helicopter crash than met the eye.

What does that mean, *exactly?* Irene had asked.

The damage to the helicopter doesn't match up with a typical lightning strike, Agent Vasco said. *There was lightning in the area, but the damage to the helicopter seems to have been caused by an explosive device.*

An explosive device, Irene said.

We're investigating further, Agent Vasco said. *What can you tell me about a man named Todd Croft?*

Next to nothing, Irene had said. She went on to explain that she had tried any number of ways to reach Todd Croft, to no avail. *I probably want to find him more than you do,* Irene said. She gave Agent Vasco the number that Todd Croft's secretary, Marilyn Monroe, had called Irene from. Agent Vasco had thanked her and said she'd be back in touch.

More to the helicopter crash than met the eye. An explosive device. This was turning into something from a movie, Irene thought. Yet she suspected that it was only a matter of time before the next dark door into her husband's secret life opened.

"Also, there were chickens in the dream," Irene says to Cash. "A rooster and two hens."

Cash clears his throat. "Well, yeah."

Well, yeah? Then Irene gets it: Russ is the rooster, Irene and Rosie the two hens.

* * *

Other than Cash and Baker, no one here in Iowa City knows that Russ is dead; Irene hasn't told anyone, which feels like a huge deception, as though she stuffed Russ's corpse into one of the house's nineteen closets and now it's starting to stink. Irene quiets her conscience by telling herself it's her own private business. Besides, no one has asked! This isn't strictly true—Dot, the nurse at the Brown Deer Retirement Community, asked where Russ was, and, in a moment of sheer panic, Irene lied and told Dot he was on a business trip in the Caribbean.

And he couldn't get away? Dot asked. *Even for this?* Dot was fond of Russ; she cooed over him at his every visit as though he had forded rivers and climbed mountains to get there, although she took Irene's daily presence at Brown Deer for granted. Irene perversely enjoyed watching the shadow of disillusionment cross Dot's face when she learned that Russ had put work before his own dying mother.

Russ's footprint in Iowa City all but disappeared after he took the job with Ascension thirteen years ago. Russ used to know everybody in town. He worked for the Corn Refiners Association and was a social creature by nature. He would drop off Baker and Cash at school and then go to Pearson's drugstore on Linn Street for a cup of coffee with "the boys"—the four or five retired gentlemen known as the Midwestern Mafia, who ran Iowa City. Russ's coffee break with the boys was sacred. They were the ones who had encouraged him to run for the Iowa City school board, and they'd suggested he join the Rotary Club, where he eventually became vice president.

All of the boys were now dead, and Russ hadn't been involved with local politics or the Rotary Club in over a decade. Irene occasionally bumped into someone from that previous life—Cherie Werner, for example, wife of the former superintendent of schools. Cherie (or whoever) would ask after Russ and then add, "We always knew he would make it big someday," as though Russ were a movie star or the starting quarterback for the Chicago Bears.

But who from Iowa City remained in Russ's everyday life? No one, really.

Now that the business of Milly's death has been handled—her body delivered to the funeral home, her personal effects collected, the probate attorney from Brown Deer enlisted to settle her estate—Irene has no choice but to face the daunting task of contacting the family attorney, Ed Sorley, to tell him about Russ.

"Irene!" Ed says. His voice contains cheerful curiosity. "I didn't expect to hear from you again so soon. Everything okay?"

Irene is in the amethyst-hued parlor, pacing a Persian rug that the same Chicago carpet dealer who'd sold her the Excelsior-suite rug had described as "Queen Victoria's jewel box, overturned." (Irene had bought it immediately despite the fact that it cost even more than the other rug.)

"No, Ed," Irene says. "It's not." She pauses. Russ has been dead for ten days and this is the first time she's going to say the words out loud to someone other than her sons. "Russ is dead."

There is a beat of silence. Two beats.

"What?" Ed says. "Irene, what?"

"He was killed in a helicopter crash on New Year's Day," Irene says. "Down in the Virgin Islands." She doesn't wait for Ed to ask the obvious follow-up question: What was Russ doing on a helicopter in the Virgin Islands? Or maybe: Where *are* the Virgin Islands? "When I called you last week to ask about Russ's will, he was already dead. I should have told you then. I'm sorry. It's just...I was still processing the news myself."

"Oh, jeez, Irene," Ed says. "I'm so, so sorry. Russ..." There's a lengthy pause. "Man...Anita is going to be *devastated.* You know how she adored Russ. You might not have realized how all the wives in our little group way back when thought Russ was an all-star husband. Anita used to ask me why I couldn't be more like him." Ed stops abruptly and Irene can tell he's fighting back emotion.

Anita should be glad you weren't more like him, Irene wants to say. Anita and Ed Sorley were part of a group of friends Irene and Russ had made when the kids were small—and yes, Anita had been transparently smitten with Russ. She had always laughed at his jokes and was the most envious on Irene's fiftieth birthday when Russ hired an airplane to pull a banner declaring his love.

"I need help, Ed," Irene says. "You're the first person I've told other than my kids. The boys and I flew down to the Caribbean last week. Russ's body had been cremated and we scattered the ashes."

"You *did?*" Ed says. "So are you planning a memorial, then, instead of a funeral?"

"No memorial," Irene says. "At least not yet." She knows this will sound strange. "I can't face everyone with so many unanswered questions. And I need to ask you, Ed, as my attorney, to please keep this news quiet. I don't even want you to tell Anita."

There was another significant pause. "I'll honor your wishes, Irene," Ed says. "But you can't keep it a secret forever. Are you going to submit an obituary to the *Press-Citizen*? Or, I don't know, post something on Facebook, maybe?"

"Facebook?" Irene says. The mere notion is appalling. "Do I have a legal obligation to tell people?"

"Legal?" Ed says. "No, but I mean...wow. You must still be in shock. I'm in shock myself, I get it. What was...why..."

"Ed," Irene says. "I called you to find out what legal steps I need to take."

There's an audible breath from Ed. He's flustered. Irene imagines going through this ninety or a hundred more times with every single one of their friends and neighbors. Maybe she *should* publish an obituary. But what would she say? Two hours after the papers landed on people's doorsteps, she would have well-intentioned hordes arriving with casseroles and questions. She can't bear the thought.

"When I called you before, Ed, you said Russ signed a new will in September." Irene had shoved this piece of information to a remote corner of her mind, but now it's front and center. Why the hell did Russ *sign a new will* without Irene and, more saliently, without *telling* Irene? There could be only one reason. "You said he included a new life insurance policy? For three million dollars?" She swallows. "The life insurance policy...who's the beneficiary?" *Here is the moment when the god-awful truth is revealed,* she thinks. Russ must have made Rosie the beneficiary. Or maybe, if he was too skittish to do that, he made a trust the beneficiary, a trust that would lead back to Rosie and Maia.

"You, of course," Ed says. "The beneficiary is you."

"Me?" Irene says. She feels...she feels...

Ed says, "Who else would it be? The boys? I think Russ was concerned about Cash's ability to manage money." Ed coughs. "Russ did make one other change. After you called me last week, I checked my notes."

"What was the other change?"

"Well, you'll remember that back when you and Russ signed your wills in 2012, you made Russ the executor of your will and Russ made his boss, Todd Croft, the executor of his. In my notes, I wrote that Russ said his finances were becoming too complex for, as he put it, a 'mere mortal' to deal with and he didn't want to burden you with that responsibility. He said Todd would be better able to deal with the fine print. Do you remember that?"

Does Irene remember that? She closes her eyes and tries to put herself in Ed Sorley's office with Russ. She definitely remembers the meeting about the real estate closing—she had been so excited—but the day that they signed their wills is lost. It had probably seemed like an onerous chore, akin to getting the oil changed in her Lexus. She knew it had to be done but she paid little attention to it because she and Russ were in perfect health. They were finally hitting their stride—a new job for Russ, a new house, money.

No, she does not remember. She doubts she would have objected to Russ making Todd Croft the executor of his will. Back then, Todd had seemed like a savior. *Todd the God.*

"So Todd was the executor," Irene says.

"And when Russ came in to sign the new will this past September, he changed it," Ed says. "He made you the executor."

"He did?" Irene says.

"Didn't he tell you?" Ed says.

"No," Irene says. Then she wonders if that's right. "You know what, Ed, he might have told me and I just forgot." *Or I wasn't listening,* she thinks. It's entirely possible that back in September, Russ said one night at dinner, *I saw Ed Sorley today, signed a new will with extra life insurance protection, and I made you executor.* And it's entirely possible that Irene said, *Okay, great.* Back in September, this information would have seemed unremarkable, even dull. Life insurance; executor. Who cared! It was all preparation for an event, Russ's death, that was, if not exactly inconceivable, then very, very far in the future.

Now, of course, the will has red-hot urgency. Irene is the beneficiary of the life insurance policy and she's the executor of the will. This is good news, right?

"I have something else in my notes," Ed says, and he sounds on the verge of getting choked up again. "When I asked Russ if he was concerned that being executor might be a burden for you, considering the complicated nature of his finances, he said, 'Irene is the only person I trust to do the right thing.'" Ed pauses. "Those were his exact words. I wrote them down."

Irene is the only person I trust to do the right thing. That seemingly simple sentence has a lot to unpack. Russ didn't trust Todd Croft to do the right thing—no surprise there. Had Russ assumed that Irene would find out about Rosie, Maia, the villa in St. John? And if the answer was yes, did he expect that Irene would have enough forgiveness in her heart to make sure that Rosie and Maia were taken care of financially? If again the answer was yes, he had given her a lot of credit.

Irene sighed. Russ was right. Rosie is no longer an issue, but Irene most certainly plans on providing for Maia.

"What do I do from here, Ed?" Irene asks.

"I'll need at least ten copies of the death certificate," Ed says. "I'd like one as soon as possible so I can start the probate process."

"Where do I get a death certificate?" Irene asks.

"Um... no one provided one for you? You should have been issued one from the state where Russ died."

"He died in the British Virgin Islands," Irene reminds him. "Between Virgin Gorda and Anegada."

There's silence from Ed. She might as well have named two moons of Jupiter.

"Baker was in charge of figuring out exactly who claimed the body," she tells Ed. "And who performed the cremation. He had some trouble. It's apparently very hard to get a body back from another country, and it was over the holidays. The regular people were on vacation."

"I'm not going to lie to you, Irene," Ed says. "My experience with this is limited. But you're saying you didn't get a death certificate while you were down there?"

"We didn't," Irene says. "Baker called the Brits, who directed him to the Americans, who sent him back to the Brits. Todd Croft had someone go down and identify the body—that was before we arrived—and he ordered the cremation without even asking me."

"What?" Ed says.

Irene has opened the proverbial can of worms now; she may as well keep going. "Todd Croft has, essentially, vanished. I can't reach him or his secretary, and the Ascension web page is down."

"Jeez, Irene," Ed says. "This is like something out of a movie."

"Ed," Irene says. "You didn't know anything about Russ's owning property in the Caribbean, did you?"

"In the Caribbean?" Ed says. "Heck no!"

"How much did you understand about his job?" Irene asks. "Did the two of you ever discuss it?"

"He worked for Croft's hedge fund, right?" Ed says. "He was the front man?"

"Right," Irene says. She relaxes a little. The way Russ had described it to her, the Ascension clients were investing such large amounts of money in such a high-risk environment, they needed a dedicated person just to put them at ease, and that person was Russ. Up until this very second, Irene wondered if maybe Ed Sorley was in on the whole mess, but now it's clear from his earnest tone that he's just as bewildered as she is. Ed wears sweater-vests. He handles wills, trusts, real estate closings, and the occasional dispute over property lines for the farmers of Johnson County. Russ and Irene hired him for their legal matters because he's their longtime friend. Irene realizes Russ must have had a second lawyer, one provided for him by Ascension.

Real estate, though.

"I'll call our bank, obviously," Irene says. They used to keep a checking and savings account at First Iowa Savings and Loan, where their friend Jerry Kinsey was the president. But shortly after Russ started working at Ascension, they switched to the behemoth Federal Republic Bank because Russ insisted that that bank was better equipped to handle Russ and Irene's "change of circumstance." Irene recalls pushing back on this. Just because Russ had a shiny new job didn't mean they had to change their small-town ways, did it?

Russ had looked at her like she was naive and Irene had capitulated. They opened a joint brokerage account at Federal Republic, although Irene defiantly kept a smaller account at First Iowa in her own name; that was where her paychecks from the magazine were deposited.

Now that Irene thinks about it, she realizes she never saw a balance of more than fifty thousand dollars in the Federal Republic account. They have several million invested, or so Irene has been led to believe, and the amount in the Federal Republic account was obviously replenished by Russ's paychecks and bonuses. So there should be a money trail that leads to Todd Croft and Ascension. Irene never delved into the particulars of their new financial situation because, quite frankly, she had done her share of worrying—creating budgets, stretching their meager resources—for a long time, and it was a relief just to know that there was money now, so much money that Irene could take a bath in French champagne every night if she wanted.

Back when Irene was renovating the house, Russ had transferred money into an account dedicated solely to paying the contractors and estate-sale managers and rug dealers. But that account had been closed for a while now. "We bought the house and the lot here on Church Street outright," Irene says. "That money was wired to our Federal Republic account from somewhere else. Would you look into it?"

"I can certainly do that," Ed says. "It was seven years ago? We've gotten a whole new computer system since then, but we must still have the paperwork in a box in the attic. I'll go upstairs and check."

"Thank you, Ed," Irene says.

"Aw, Irene," Ed says. "It's the least I can do."

"Please don't say anything to Anita," Irene says again. "I'll tell people when I'm ready."

"You have my word," Ed says. "Your job is to get a certified copy of the death certificate. Without that, Russ is technically still alive."

Still alive, Irene thinks. Just like in her dreams.

Irene's next move is a trip to Federal Republic. There's a branch in Coralville, although she has never set foot in it. She manages to find the most recent statement, which shows a balance of $46,270.32. There was a deposit of $7,500 on Monday, December 10, and another deposit of $7,500 on Monday, December 24, at eleven o'clock in the morning. The withdrawals are automatic payments for the household bills—electricity, cable, heating oil. There's a $3,200 payment to Citibank—that's Irene's credit card—an amount that was a little higher than normal due to Christmas.

Irene approaches the teller with trepidation, even though she has never seen the young woman before. She's Asian and far younger than either Cash or Baker, which is good. Irene craves anonymity. The last thing she wants is to deal with someone who knows her family, even slightly. Irene checks the woman's name plate: JOSEPHINE.

"Good afternoon, Josephine," Irene says. She stretches her face into a smile, but she suspects it looks like a grimace. "I have some questions about my account."

"Certainly," Josephine says. She accepts the statement from Irene, then starts tapping at her computer keyboard. "Let me just bring this up on my screen." She pauses. Her eyes grow wide.

What? Irene thinks. She's worried she's going to be exposed on the spot. She'd have to say, *I'm here because my husband died under mysterious circumstances. I've just discovered he had a second life but I was never suspicious because, honestly, Josephine, I paid very little attention to him. And I know next to nothing about our current financial situation.*

"You're a valued and trusted account holder here at Federal Republic," Josephine says. "With us since 2006?"

"Yes," Irene says. She points to the amounts she underlined on the statement. "I was wondering if you could tell me where these two amounts were wired from? I don't see any other account number or the name of the bank."

Josephine checks the amounts on the statement, then blinks at her screen. "You're referring to the seventy-five-hundred-dollar deposit on Monday, December tenth, and the seventy-five-hundred-dollar deposit on Monday, December twenty-fourth?" Josephine's voice is very loud, Irene thinks. She seems to be intentionally drawing attention to her teller window. Irene quickly casts a glance around the bank. She lives in mortal fear of seeing someone she knows.

"Yes," Irene whispers, trying to telegraph the delicate nature of the situation.

"Those deposits were made in cash," Josephine announces brightly.

"Cash?" Irene says. She nearly adds: *You mean to tell me Russ walked in here with seventy-five hundred dollars on his person and then did it again two weeks later?*

"Yes, cash!" Josephine says with such gusto that Irene thinks, *Why not just broadcast over the bank's PA system that Russell Steele was a drug dealer?*

"Okay," Irene says. "Thank you. One more quick question." She leans in, locking eyes with Josephine, hoping that Josephine will finally understand the need for discretion. "Are there any other accounts at this bank under my name or my husband's name?"

Josephine pulls back a couple of inches. "Do you have the account numbers?"

"I don't," Irene says. She's trying to choose her words carefully here, though really what she's tempted to do is tell young Josephine a cautionary tale: *I let my husband take over our finances and now I don't know what I do or don't have!* "I think I may have a second account here, one I haven't been keeping close tabs on. Would you be able to check using my name or my husband's name, our address, or our Social Security numbers?" Here, Irene slides Josephine a piece of paper with both Socials clearly labeled. "I can't find any paperwork on our other accounts but it's a new year, so one resolution I made was to figure this out."

Josephine presses her lips together in a way that lets Irene know she's growing suspicious. Still, her fingers fly across the keyboard. She slows to punch the Social Security numbers in carefully, then waits for the results. Blood pulses in Irene's ears, and her shearling coat feels like it's made of lead.

"I don't see another account under either name or Social," Josephine says. "Nothing's coming up. Would you like me to call over my branch manager?"

"No, thank you, that's okay," Irene says. "For all I know, the account I'm thinking of could be at a different bank altogether."

Josephine tilts her head. "A different *bank?*"

Irene backs toward the door. She can't get out of there fast enough. "Well, like I said, it's my New Year's resolution to get organized."

"All righty!" Josephine says. "Good luck with that."

AYERS

Huck has asked Ayers to help him go through the things in Rosie's bedroom during the week, while Maia is at school. Ayers doesn't make it up to the house on Jacob's Ladder until the Thursday before the Martin Luther King Day weekend.

"I'm sorry I didn't come sooner," Ayers says. "My life just got really busy all of a sudden."

"Don't apologize," Huck says. "You have two jobs, and now that you're back with Mick, I'm sure he wants your attention as well."

Ayers sighs. She *is* back with Mick and he *does* want her attention. He admitted that seeing her with Baker (Mick calls him "Banker") drove him crazy with jealousy, and he vowed not to let anything—or anyone—get between them again. Since they've been back together, Mick has stopped by La Tapa at the end of Ayers's shift each night and walked her to her truck before heading back to Beach Bar until closing. He's abandoned his usual ritual of late-night drinks at the Quiet Mon and instead drives straight to Ayers's apartment in Fish Bay, where he spends the night. When Ayers works on *Treasure Island,* he meets her at the customs dock at four o'clock with a pineapple-banana smoothie from Our Market. On the one day off they've had together so far, Mick borrowed his boss's boat and they cruised all the way up the north shore to snorkel at Waterlemon Cay. They spotted three basking sharks and two spotted eagle rays. Mick is as much of a snorkel-nerd as Ayers. When they saw the second spotted eagle ray rippling along the sandy bottom, Mick dived down and undulated right along top of it. When he and Ayers surfaced a few moments later, he pulled off his mask and grinned like a kid with a shiny new bike, and Ayers felt a wave of the familiar adoration. This was her guy.

They'd left Waterlemon and headed to Gibney for an hour on the beach. When Ayers's stomach started to rumble, they climbed back into the boat and tied up to the dock at Caneel Bay. They strolled hand in hand, salty and sandy, to the Beach

Bar, where Mick ordered a bottle of Moët, the conch fritters, and four sushi rolls.

Ayers had craned her neck to ogle the hotel rooms that lined the beach, each of them as luxurious and appealing as pearls on a string.

"I'm dying to stay here," she said, then instantly regretted it. The champagne had gone right to her head.

"Guess you'll have to wait for your banker to come back," Mick said.

"Guess so," she said lightly. Mick dipped a fritter in aioli and let the topic go. Maybe he was consciously avoiding a fight or maybe he wasn't as jealous as he'd claimed to be. Maybe he was content to let the past be the past. Maybe he thought Baker Steele would never return to St. John. Maybe he thought he and Ayers could just continue their relationship where they'd left off, as though neither Baker nor Brigid had ever existed.

Ayers wasn't so sure.

Huck leads Ayers to Rosie's room and opens the door. Ayers has been in Rosie's room only twice before, both times years ago. The first time was when they swung by after work so Rosie could change before they went dancing at Castaways. The other time, Rosie was at work and Ayers was off and Rosie had texted Ayers and begged her to grab her bottle of Percocet—she had just had all four wisdom teeth removed and was crying in pain. But that was it. They were grown women; they hung out in bars, not in each other's bedrooms.

Ayers remembers, however, that while the rest of the house looked like it was shared by the protagonist of *The Old Man and the Sea* and the Little Mermaid (Huck and Maia), Rosie's room was a sanctuary, cool and elegant, and it still is. The wallpaper is printed with pink hibiscus blossoms, and the hibiscus theme is echoed by a bush outside the open window. The queen-size bed has at least a dozen pillows artfully arranged against the rattan headboard. Rosie was a fastidious bed-maker, whereas Ayers sleeps in a tangle of sheets every night and sees absolutely no point in making a bed that she's only going to climb right back into the next night. (Ayers gets a sudden vision of Rosie folding napkins at La Tapa. She was careful and precise in the task, like she was doing origami.)

Against the wall is a large teak bureau; over it hangs a giant, round silver-framed mirror. The door to the closet is closed tight. The only personal touches that Ayers can see are a trio of framed photographs in one corner and a copy of *Jane Eyre* on the nightstand. Rosie was a sucker for the classics, especially the novels of Edith Wharton, George Eliot, and the Brontë sisters, and it was nearly impossible to get her to read anything contemporary, though she and Ayers had made a deal: Ayers would read *Middlemarch* if Rosie would read *Eat, Pray, Love*. (Ayers hadn't kept her end of the bargain, which she feels awful about now.)

Huck asked Ayers to "help" him go through Rosie's things, but it's clear he hasn't been in here even once, and Ayers suspects Maia hasn't either. The room is undisturbed, as if Rosie might walk back in at any moment, straw market bag over her shoulder, singing Aretha Franklin.

That, probably, is the point. If they go through everything and sort out what to keep and what to throw away, they're admitting Rosie is gone.

"I'll get started, I guess," Ayers says to Huck. "I'll make four piles—to keep, to give away, to throw away, and undecided."

"Ayers," Huck says.

She turns to him. She's afraid he's going to break down, and if *he* breaks down, she will too. They both vowed to be strong for Maia, and they have been, but this hasn't left a lot of time for them to tend to their own grief. Ayers can practically hear the texture and timbre of Rosie's voice: *You make me feel like a nat-u-ral wo-man!*

"Last Friday," Huck says, "the FBI called."

Ayers snaps back to reality.

"Virgin Islands Search and Rescue contacted them about the wreckage. The agent I spoke to said it looks like there might have been foul play."

Ayers nods but says nothing. After she and Mick had left Caneel Bay and returned the inflatable dinghy, they'd continued on to Joe's Rum Hut for happy hour, then they stopped at Woody's for a drink, then they strolled down to Morgan's Mango to have dinner. By that time, Mick was drunk enough to engage in some pretty wild theorizing. *The bird Rosie was on did not go down by accident,* Mick had said. *I guarantee you that.*

"Turns out the damage to the helicopter wasn't consistent with a lightning strike," Huck says. "They think there might have been a bomb aboard or that maybe someone tampered with the wiring to cause an explosion."

Ayers blinks.

"I just thought you should know," Huck says. "They're still investigating."

"Maia?"

"I didn't tell her," Huck says. "The less she thinks about the actual crash, the better."

"Agreed," Ayers says. "What about…I mean, do we know if…" She swallows. "Have you heard from Irene?"

"I made her promise she would text me once she made it

home," Huck says. "And she did. Then a day or two later, she texted to let me know that her mother-in-law, Russ's mother, had passed away. Which I guess was something of a blessing. Though I don't know...that's a lot of loss for one week. I sent my condolences, then decided I'd leave her be for a while. So I'm not sure if she knows about this. Though I assume so. Have you heard from the boys?"

Ayers has not, which bothers her more than it probably should. Especially since she told both Baker and Cash to leave her alone. She was disappointed that they had lied to her about who they were, and besides that, she was back together with Mick. There was no reason for either of them to reach out to her, but their silence chafes nonetheless. They had both claimed to have feelings for her. Baker used the phrase "love at first sight," and Cash said he thought he was in love with her. But now that they're back in America, living their lives, Ayers has been forgotten.

Which is why she never dates tourists.

She is especially peeved at Cash because she had texted him the day before with a link to a job opening on *Treasure Island*. Wade, the first mate, was moving back to the States to manage a marijuana dispensary outside of Boston, and they needed to hire a replacement before he left in two weeks. Skip, the bartender at La Tapa, had expressed interest, but Ayers didn't think she could handle dealing with Skip at both of her places of employment, and she suspects that James, the captain, would throw Skip overboard before they made it into British waters. The problem is that everyone on St. John already has a job, and anyone who's not on St. John doesn't have housing. Then Ayers thought of Cash. He had been a big help on that trip to Virgin Gorda. And he'd had years of experience as a ski instructor, which, as he pointed out, was exactly the same thing, only completely different. He's probably certified in CPR. He would have to get his lifesaving certificate, take a marine-safety class, and, literally, learn the ropes. But all of that stuff is easy. The most attractive thing about Cash, other than his charm and love of the outdoors, is that he has a place to live.

Maybe it was a bit of a stretch to imagine that Cash would drop everything and move to the Virgin Islands in order to crew on *Treasure Island.* Maybe he thought Ayers was teasing him or taunting him, but if so, wouldn't he have shot back a snappy response?

"Not a word," Ayers tells Huck. She tries to make this sound like a good thing, but he must know better, because he pats her shoulder.

"Holler when you get hungry," Huck says. "I'll bring you some lunch."

"Great," Ayers says weakly. She thinks of the awful fish sandwiches on buttered Wonder Bread that Huck packs for Maia.

"I'm picking up barbecue from Candi's," he says, and Ayers perks up. "Thank you for doing this." He casts his eyes upward. "I'm sure Rosie would prefer to have you discovering her secrets rather than me."

Discovering her secrets makes the work sound intriguing when in fact it's merely heartbreaking.

Ayers starts with the closet. Rosie loved to wear white; it made her skin look luminous. The clothes in the right half of the closet are all white. Shades of eggshell, ivory, ecru, and pearl mix with the most blinding of whites. Everything is crisp and ironed, even her jeans. The clothes in the left half of the closet are full of color—Rosie's bright printed handkerchief halters, her bohemian blouses, her simple cotton tank dresses. Nobody rocked a jersey patio dress like Rosie Small. Ayers's favorite is a ribbed cotton racerback in brilliant marigold. She fingers it, remembering some special occasion at Chateau Bordeaux. The two of them had gone for cocktails to enjoy the spectacular view over Coral Bay, and Rosie had been wearing that dress.

Beneath the clothes are shoes—sandals, wedges, and the pair of black Dansko clogs marked with green tape that Rosie wore when she waited tables at La Tapa.

Ayers inhales through her nose, trying to stave off the tears. Everyone at La Tapa wore black clogs, and on Ayers's very first day of work, Rosie had advised making hers distinguishable in some way. She showed Ayers the green tape. *Looks like we wear about the same size,* Rosie said. *But if I ever see these on your feet, I'll cut you. Hear?*

Ayers could take the clogs now, of course, and wear them as a tribute—but is she worthy? Rosie was hands down the best server at La Tapa, the best server on the island, period. The guests clamored for her; her name was mentioned something like a hundred and seventeen times on TripAdvisor. Ayers would also like the marigold dress and all of the pristine white jeans. The handkerchief halters are so quintessentially *Rosie* that Ayers can only imagine giving them to Maia to wear when she's older. Much older.

Ayers throws herself down on the bed. She'd look awful in the yellow dress. But maybe she'll take it anyway and hang it in her closet, a reminder of her beautiful friend.

Foul play. The FBI. Russell Steele was into something illegal. He had enemies. Someone wanted him dead, and Rosie was collateral damage.

Ayers pushes herself up and goes to the corner to study the photographs. The top is a photo of Rosie with LeeAnn and Huck. Rosie is wearing a white cap and gown; it's her graduation from the University of the Virgin Islands on St. Thomas. Huck looks pretty much the same as he does now, maybe a few pounds lighter then with a bit more red in his beard. Ayers studies LeeAnn, Rosie's mother. She was tall and statuesque and wore her reddish-brown hair in a braided topknot. Ayers had heard all about the glamorous LeeAnn—that she had modeled as a teenager and gotten as far away as the fashion shows in Milan but had come home to marry her childhood sweetheart, Levi Small, who'd ended up leaving the island for good shortly after Rosie was born. LeeAnn had then gone to school to become a nurse practitioner. To hear some people tell it, LeeAnn was the most qualified caregiver at the Myrah Keating Smith Community Health Center, even better than the doctors. Ayers had found LeeAnn intimidating—initially, anyway. She exuded competence as well as something Ayers could only describe as a regal bearing. When LeeAnn first met Ayers, she'd seemed disapproving that Ayers had no college degree and no way to support herself other than the hand-to-mouth existence that waiting tables afforded. *Don't your parents want more for you?* LeeAnn had asked. Ayers had tried to explain that her parents were wanderers without a home, without possessions, really, and that they counted wealth by life experiences. LeeAnn had met this news with a skeptical arched eyebrow. *Don't you want more for yourself?* LeeAnn asked. Ayers had shrugged; she was twenty-two years old at the time. But it was LeeAnn Powers's questions that led Ayers to get her second, slightly more professional job on *Treasure Island.* After that, LeeAnn's opinion of her had seemed to improve. *Learn every-*

thing you can about the business, LeeAnn said. *Then save your money and buy it.*

LeeAnn had been even tougher when dealing with Rosie. The worst insult LeeAnn could dish out was to say that Rosie took after her Small relatives. That look in Rosie's eyes, for example, that fire, that defiance, was pure Small, LeeAnn said, and it had to be contained or the girl would ruin herself.

What would LeeAnn have made of the Invisible Man? Nothing good, Ayers guesses.

Ayers hasn't said this out loud to anyone but she doesn't think it's a coincidence that Russell Steele, the "Invisible Man," reappeared in Rosie's life just after LeeAnn died. A few weeks ago, Ayers had learned that Russ was Maia's father, meaning he had been in Rosie's life a lot longer than anyone knew.

Oh, how Ayers longs to ask Rosie herself. *You could have told me everything,* Ayers thinks. *I was a safe place for you.*

The center photo is of Maia, taken outside the Gifft Hill School. She's very small, wearing a backpack that is nearly as big as she is, and in the photo she's on her tiptoes, reaching for the latched gate of the fence to let herself in. The picture is precious and Ayers can imagine Rosie in the parking lot, possibly crouched down between two cars so Maia wouldn't see her, capturing this early expression of independence.

Maia's relationship with Rosie had been less contentious than Rosie's with LeeAnn, but that's not to say it was all milk and cookies after school and snuggles and stories at bedtime. There was a ferocity that ran through the female line of that family—maybe LeeAnn, Rosie, and Maia were all too similar—and Ayers had seen Rosie and Maia butt heads again and again. When Ayers was called on to referee, she usually sided with Maia, causing Maia to utter the famous line that Ayers was like a mother to her but better, because she wasn't her mother.

The third photograph is of Rosie and Ayers on Oppenheimer Beach, back when the tire swing still hung from the crooked palm that stretched out over the water. The tire swing was more fun to look at than actually ride on, as Ayers had learned the hard way, but this picture of the two of them in bikinis is the best picture of them ever taken. Ayers keeps the same photo on her phone as her screen saver, and she will never replace it.

She feels honored that she has earned a spot on Rosie's bedroom wall. It seems to mean that Rosie considered her family.

Ayers can't help but notice that there is no picture of Russell Steele on the wall.

If there are secrets to discover, Ayers predicts she'll find them in the top drawer of the dresser. That's where people put intimate things, right? Women their lingerie and men their condoms. Rosie's top drawer holds the expected collection of bras and panties, some functional, some recreational, as well as teddies and slips, cotton socks, a box of tampons, two full carousels of birth control pills, and a plastic bag containing six tightly rolled joints, which Ayers slips right into her purse. Rosie would definitely want Ayers to take those so Maia doesn't find them and get thoughts about experimenting.

The middle drawer is a jumble of bikinis, nearly all of which Ayers recognizes; at least half a dozen are white. The rest are black, red, blue gingham, kelly green with hot-pink piping. There's a pink smocked top that Ayers loves, and then she remembers a supercool turquoise crocheted bikini that Rosie got from Letarte. Ayers digs for it, but it's not there—maybe Rosie wore it to Anegada? A sobering thought. Then

Ayers finds something intriguing. Beneath the bikinis is a layer of clothbound books. But they're not books, Ayers realizes when she opens one and sees Rosie's handwriting. They're journals.

Ayers extracts the journals like she's unearthing the bones of ancient peoples on an archaeological dig. She reads from the one on top.

January 1, 2000

It's not only a new century but a new millennium. I, Rosalie Veronica Small, am seventeen years old, a senior at Charlotte Amalie High School. I'm in love with Oscar Cobb and nothing my mother or Huck can say will keep us from getting married on my eighteenth birthday.

Ayers shuts that journal and scrambles for one closer to the bottom of the pile, from 2015. Her breathing is shallow.

January 1, 2015

R. has stayed in Iowa through the holidays because his older son is visiting from Houston with his new baby. I wanted to text him a picture of me and Ayers doing tequila slammers up at the Banana Deck but of course the rule is "no texting."

Ayers closes the journal, then her eyes. Tequila slammers at the Banana Deck, New Year's Eve four years earlier. Yes; they had stopped there after the end of service at La Tapa but before they went to the Beach Bar to dance to Miss Fairchild. It had been a fun night, recklessly wild. They had closed the Beach Bar, gotten high, skinny-dipped in Frank Bay, then crashed a party all the way out on Ironwood Road in Coral Bay and stayed up to watch the sun rise. Ayers knew then about the Invisible Man, but he was just some guy who showed up every now and then to wine and dine Rosie and give her lavish presents. If Ayers is remembering correctly, it was right after that New Year's that Rosie got a new Jeep, a four-door Wrangler in stingray gray with all the bells and whistles.

Whose is that? Ayers had asked when Rosie pulled up in it.

Mine, Rosie said without another word of explanation. Ayers had known then that it was from the lover, the Invisible Man, and that was when Ayers started to wonder just how serious that relationship was.

Ayers turns around to make sure the bedroom door is closed. How is she going to smuggle the journals out of there? If there's any question as to whether she's the right person to read them first, she pushes it aside. God only knows what kind of details they contain; Ayers can't risk letting Maia read them before she does. And Huck made his feelings clear.

Despite this, Ayers doesn't want to tell Huck she's found them.

Why?

Well, she's not sure why. It's just a gut instinct. What if curiosity or ego gets the best of Huck and he decides to read them himself?

Ayers can practically hear Rosie saying, *Nooooooooo!*

Ayers looks under the bed and on the floor of the closet for a duffel or a suitcase but finds nothing. Then she hears a car and peeks out the window to see Huck pulling out of the driveway. He must be on his way to get lunch from Candi's—perfect. Ayers heads out to the kitchen and pulls a reusable shopping bag off the hook next to the sink. She loads the journals up and hurries them out to Edith, her truck. She throws a beach towel over them for good measure.

She goes back to Rosie's room, replaces all the bikinis, and shuts the drawer. She sits on the floor. She's short of breath. She has discovered all of Rosie's secrets. They're waiting like a time bomb in Ayers's truck.

A few minutes later, Ayers hears the front door open and then Huck calling out, "Grub! Come and get it!"

Ayers is too keyed up to eat. She wants to get home and read the journals! She's going to have to hide them somewhere Mick won't find them or see her reading them.

Huck knocks on the bedroom door and swings it open just as Ayers pulls out the third dresser drawer, so they both see what's inside at exactly the same time.

Ayers shrieks.

Huck says, "What the hell is that?"

It's money. The bottom drawer is filled with money.

CASH

He's having dinner with his mother at the Pullman Bar and Diner when she asks the question he's been dreading.

"So what's next for you? Back to the mountains?"

"Trying to get rid of me already?" he says.

"Not at all," Irene says. "It's just that I thought this"—she indicates the restaurant and their server, Ryan, whom she seems to be on pretty familiar terms with—"was the stuff of your nightmares. Stuck in Iowa City, eating the early-bird special with your mother."

"It's been only five days," Cash says. "And Milly—"

"Milly is handled," Irene says. "I don't mean to make your grandmother sound like a loathsome errand. But I also want you to know that you don't need to stay here on my account. Surely you have better things to do than listen to me describe my crazy dreams."

His mother is right. Cash should load Winnie into his truck and return to Denver to clean up what's left of his life there before he heads to Breckenridge for the remainder of the winter. But what had seemed so appealing before he got Irene's phone call informing him his father was dead has lost its luster. He received no fewer than ten panicked voicemails from Dylan, the manager of Cash's Belmar store, asking why there are chains on the door and why no one is answering the phone at the Cherry Creek store. (Cash finally responded: *Business went under. I would offer you a reference but I know you've been skimming from the register. Sorry, bro, good luck out there.*) Cash is two payments behind on his truck so he needs a job right away. But because it's already January, all of the positions at the ski school have been filled. Cash called his buddy Jay, and he said Cash could sleep on his sofa for a week but that would be all his new girlfriend would tolerate and finding other housing at this point would be tricky, especially with a dog.

"You might want to cool your heels there," Jay said. "And try coming out in March when everyone else gets cabin fever and leaves."

Cool his heels in Iowa for *two months?* In winter? There's no way he can do it, can he? And yet, what choice does he have? Living with his mother is free, the house is comfortable and plenty big enough, and she gives him twenties and fifties every time he goes out. She would probably make his car payment in exchange for him doing some simple handyman work.

But would his morale survive? He fears not. Earlier that day, his mother pressed two hundred dollars into his hand and sent him to the Hy-Vee for groceries, which he didn't object to as he needed dog food for Winnie and some shaving cream for himself. And who should he run into at the deli counter but his high-school girlfriend Claire Bellows, the one who went to Northwestern and promptly slept with Baker?

"Cash?" Claire said, blinking like he was an apparition. "Cash *Steele,* is that you?"

Cash forced a smile while he cursed his truly terrible luck. And yet, this was what happened when you returned to your hometown: you bumped into the people you used to know. Claire Bellows looked basically the same, maybe a little older, maybe a little washed out; her face was wan, her hair colorless and pulled back into a sad little bun. She was pushing a cart that held two children, a toddler who was standing up among the groceries—his left foot perilously close to a carton of eggs—and a baby in a bucket seat that snapped onto the front of the cart. The toddler was a boy; the baby was swaddled in a pink fleece sack, her face obscured.

"Hey, Claire." Cash said it casually, as though he'd just seen her the week before. He *felt* like he'd just seen her the week before because he and Baker had spent so much time talking about her. The good news was that the bad mojo of Claire Bellows had been exorcised. Cash felt nothing when he looked at her. He leaned in to kiss her cheek. "How are you?"

"This is like that song!" Claire exclaimed. *"Met my old lover in the grocery store, the snow was falling Christmas Eve!"*

Cash nodded along, trying to be a good sport. The lyrics rang a distant bell—Gordon Lightfoot, maybe? Simon and Garfunkel? Cash was reminded that Claire used to be a lyrics wizard, especially when it came to the music of their parents' era, because Claire's mother, Adrienne Bellows, was a disc jockey on the local easy-listening station. When Cash and Claire were in high school, Adrienne worked the evening six-to-ten shift; she was eastern Iowa's answer to Delilah. While Adrienne Bellows was comforting the heartbroken and lovelorn who called in with their requests and sappy dedications, Cash and Claire were making out and, eventually, having sex in Claire's bedroom.

"And who do we have here?" Cash asked in an attempt to be gallant. He was trying, he really was.

Claire looked confused until she realized he meant the children. "Oh!" she said. "This is Eugene and the baby is Mabel."

Cash tried not to grimace. Claire had followed the trend of naming her children as though they'd been born a hundred and twenty years ago. "Nice," he said. "Hi, guys." The toddler turned to look at Cash, missing the eggs by a fraction of an inch, and Cash couldn't help himself—he moved the carton to safety. "So you're back in Iowa City?"

"Temporarily," Claire said. "For the next five or six years. My husband is doing a fellowship in endocrinology at the university."

Cash nearly said, *And you?* But he was afraid Claire would tell him that she'd given up her job as a marketing executive with Colgate-Palmolive in Chicago in order to follow her husband back to Iowa and then add that she was "okay" with it or else openly express bitterness. To extract himself from that awkward topic, Cash would then ask about her mother, and

Claire, realizing that she was doing all the talking, would take the reins and say, *What about you? Why are you in town?* Cash could then say he was visiting his parents, which would be half a lie, although lying would be preferable to telling Claire that Russ was dead. Claire had loved Russ. She and Russ had had a thing where they told each other knock-knock jokes, which Cash had found annoying even at the height of his passion for Claire.

Knock-knock.
Who's there?
A broken pencil.
A broken pencil who?
Never mind, it's pointless.

He might be able to successfully evade the topic of his parents but there would undoubtedly be follow-up questions about where he was living and what he was doing—and then finally, as if it had just occurred to her for no particular reason, Claire would ask about Baker.

To avoid that inevitable moment, Cash smiled at Claire and said, "Well, at least Iowa City is a good place to raise kids. We learned that firsthand. See you later, Claire."

"But—wait," Claire said.

Cash did not wait. He sacrificed the half a pound of sliced turkey on Irene's list and sauntered off in the direction of the bakery. Claire had always been socially awkward in a sweet way. When Baker hit on her at that frat party at Northwestern, it must have been like taking candy from a baby.

But, really, what did Cash care? He was over it.

Thinking about it now in the Pullman Diner, he can't imagine spending two to three months here in Iowa City dodging land mines like his ex-girlfriend Claire.

To Irene he says, "I'm going to stay a few days longer. At least."

She gives him a tight smile and Cash wonders if maybe she *wants* him gone.

"Let's order," she says.

He's nearly asleep, sprawled across the massive acreage of the guest-room bed, when he gets a text on his phone.

Who would be texting him so late? Cash figures it must be Dylan again, telling Cash that he left his one-hitter behind the counter or complaining because he's still owed for a day and a half of work. The first thing Cash notices when he picks up his phone is the time. It's not late at all; it's only ten o'clock. It just feels late because it gets dark at four thirty in the afternoon and there's nothing to do in this town after the dinner hour. The second thing Cash notices is that the text is from Ayers.

Ayers.

Cash stares at the phone, wondering if it's a trick. Did Baker somehow figure out a way to send Cash a text that looks like it's from Ayers? Cash hesitates a moment, then swipes to open. The text isn't a text but rather a link, and when Cash clicks on the link, it opens to the website for Treasure Island Cruises—*Day Trips to the BVIs, St. Thomas, Water Island, and Beyond!*

Beyond? Cash thinks. *Beyond* must be that place you visit in your mind after nine or ten painkillers.

This section of the website starts with *Join the* Treasure Island *crew!* In smaller print beneath that is *We are currently seeking a first mate for our BVI routes. Must possess strong administrative skills and CPR and lifesaving certification; must enjoy working with people. Valid passport required, boating experience preferred. To apply, contact Ayers Wilson, ayers@treasureislandcruisesvi.com.*

Did Ayers send this to him for a reason? Cash wonders. Does she think he should... apply? He has been boating exactly once in the past ten years—when he went on *Treasure Island* as Ayers's guest. Yes, he'd enjoyed it, and yes, Ayers had asked him if he wanted a job. But that had been a joke. Right? And yet now, apparently, they were looking for someone.

CPR certification he has; lifesaving, not a chance—unless you considered avalanche-rescue certification "lifesaving." Well, it was, but it wouldn't help him save someone who was drowning. Cash is an okay swimmer and he does have years of experience working with people, but in his heart, he's a mountain boy.

His thumbs hover over the keypad. It doesn't matter why Ayers sent this; it only matters that she's reaching out. She's thinking of him.

He lies back in bed and tries to lasso his bucking bronco of a heart. Ayers had been so angry the last time he saw her, so indignant that two people she'd befriended had deceived her about who they were and what they were doing on St. John. In retrospect, Cash doesn't blame her. They—meaning Baker—should have told Ayers who they were at Rosie's funeral lunch. But okay, let's say that would have been in poor taste. Fine. Cash should have told her who he was when he bumped into her on the Reef Bay Trail. No excuses; he should have and he hadn't, and then once he'd spent the day with her aboard *Treasure Island,* he'd become infatuated with her and didn't want to ruin his chances. The same had been true for Baker. And guess what—they both lost out. Ayers told them she had gotten back together with her old boyfriend, Mick.

Cash reads the link she'd texted him again. She must have sent it to him because she thought it would be a good fit. Right? *Right?* Or maybe it was a joke. For all Ayers knows, Cash is back in Colorado, skiing the bowl on Peak 8.

But he's not. He's in Iowa City without a job, without prospects. He closes his eyes and tries to imagine a life on the water.

With Ayers. He would agree to live in the space station if it was with Ayers.

He decides not to respond to the text right away. He wants to sleep on it.

In the morning, the text is still there and Cash is proud of himself for exercising restraint and not sending a knee-jerk response.

Winnie is asleep at the foot of the bed. When she feels Cash stir, she lifts her head.

"You liked St. John, right?" Cash asks. "Wanna go back?"

Of course, it's not Winnie's permission that he needs. Cash pads down to the kitchen in his pajama bottoms and a decade-old Social Distortion T-shirt he found in the bureau in his room. Irene is juicing oranges the old-fashioned way—by crushing the hell out of the buggers with a galvanized-steel juicer that had belonged to her own mother. Cash watches her as she presses and twists the orange under her palms. All of that energy for a dribble of juice. Though it's probably not the worst way to release pent-up frustration.

"Mom," he says. "I'm not going back to Colorado."

"You're not?" she says, relaxing her death grip on the orange in her hand and then tossing the rind in the sink.

"With your permission..." he says. His voice sticks. Asking her this is harder than he thought it would be. "I'd like to go back down."

"Down?" she says, though he can tell she understands.

"To St. John," Cash says. He clears his throat. "I have a lead on a job there. And I was hoping I could just stay in the villa."

Irene abandons the juice project altogether in order to stare at him. He can't tell what she's thinking, but then, his mother's expressions have always been inscrutable. Against all odds, they had both sort of fallen in love with St. John—at least, Cash did. He knows Irene had warmed to it as well; she went out fishing with Huck once in an attempt to get information, but she also took a second boat trip with him before she and Cash left. He supposes it's possible that her feelings have changed since they've been back home and now the whole Caribbean represents an enormous, ugly deception that she doesn't want to revisit. And maybe she'd prefer that Cash not revisit it either.

It's the idea that Irene might say no, might ask him nicely not to go or forbid him to stay in the villa, that makes Cash realize how badly he wants to return and give life down there a shot. He won't stay forever. Maybe just until summer.

"Is this about the girl?" Irene asks.

"What?" Cash says. He can feel his face turning red. "No, of course not."

"Oh," Irene says. "That's too bad. I like her for you, you know."

"So...is it okay?" Cash asks.

"Yes, honey," Irene says. "It's fine. The villa is just sitting there empty. Someone should use it. Let me buy your plane ticket and give you some money to get started."

Cash wants to tell her she doesn't have to—he's too old to be taking handouts from his mother—but the fact is, he's flat broke. Broker than broke.

"Thank you, Mom," he says. "Thank you so much."

Irene gives him a sad smile. "I'm jealous," she says.

HUCK

One hundred and twenty-five thousand dollars; this is how much cash Huck and Ayers discover in the bottom drawer of Rosie's dresser. It's all banded up in neat bricks, just like in the movies. After they count the bricks, they count them again, announcing the amounts out loud as they go so they don't lose track. Then Huck says, "Come into the kitchen."

"I don't think I can eat," Ayers says.

"I'm not talking about barbecue," Huck says. "I'm talking about rum."

Ayers shuts the drawer, and the blue Benjamins disappear; Huck ushers her down the hall. In the kitchen, he takes two shot glasses out of the cabinet and brings his trusty bottle of eighteen-year-old Flor de Caña—useful in most emergencies—down from the shelf.

He pours two shots and gives one to Ayers. "I don't know what to say," he admits, raising his own glass.

"Me either."

They clink glasses and drink. He notices Ayers eyeing the

barbecue spread out across the counter. She grabs a drumstick dripping with comeback sauce. Huck follows suit. No matter what the circumstances, Candi's is too tempting to resist.

After Ayers leaves, taking one yellow dress and three pairs of white jeans with her—the rest of the clothes they should let Maia go through, Ayers said, as soon as she's old enough—Huck picks up the money, armful by armful, and stashes it under his bed. He's aware that it has remained undetected in Rosie's room, but he figures it's only a matter of time before Maia goes snooping. Maia will never voluntarily enter Huck's room. He's messy, and Maia has declared on numerous occasions that, despite Huck's valiant effort with the laundry, his room smells like fish guts, *rotten* fish guts.

After the money is beneath the bed, he stacks all the issues of *Field and Stream* and *National Geographic* that he's collected over the past twenty years around the bed so that if Maia does come poking around, she will see only that Huck is a packrat.

Money hidden, he feels a little better. He drives to Gifft Hill to pick up Maia from school.

A hundred and twenty-five grand. In cash. In a dresser drawer.

It's a lot of money, but it's not enough to kill two people over; that's Huck's thought as he pulls into the school parking lot.

Maia is lingering by the gate with her friend Joanie and two boys Huck recognizes but can't put names to. All four kids have their phones out and they're laughing at something on the screen. Huck knows Maia sees him and he also knows enough to be patient and not tap the horn or, God forbid, call out to her. That would be *so embarrassing*.

Maia runs over to his window and he cranks it down.

"Hello there," he says. His voice sounds normal to his own ears, gruff, grandfatherly. All of his internal panic about having so much cash hidden under his bed is, he thinks, undetectable. "Are you not getting in?"

Maia bites her lip. "Would you take me and my friends into town so we can walk around?"

"Walk around and do what?" Huck asks. Cruz Bay is a small town consisting mostly of bars. Three o'clock is when happy hour at Woody's starts, luring people off the beaches in the name of good, cheap rum punch, and at four o'clock, all of the excursion boats pull in and disgorge people who have been drinking all day, most of whom are interested in continuing their drinking on land. This is all well and good for the island economy—Cruz Bay in the late afternoons is one of the most festive places on earth—but it's not exactly a wholesome environment for a bunch of twelve-year-olds.

Maia shrugs. "Get ice cream at Scoops, walk around Mongoose, maybe listen to the guitar player at the Sun Dog. He knows some Drake songs."

Huck is pretty cool for a grandpa; he, too, knows some Drake songs. "All right. Pile in, I guess. What time should I plan to pick you up?"

"Joanie's mom will bring us home," Maia says.

"Fine," Huck says. If Julie is on board with the kids going into town, then Huck figures it must be all right. Joanie climbs into the truck, giving Huck a fist bump, but the boys offer him scared sideways looks, like he's Lurch from *The Addams Family*. This actually cheers Huck up a bit.

"Hey, fellas," he says. "I'm Captain Huck. Remind me of your names."

"Colton," says one.

"Bright," says the other.

Colton and Bright—Huck has definitely heard both names before, so that's good. The four kids wedge themselves into the back seat of the truck's cab, leaving Huck to feel like very much the chauffeur. He nearly asks Maia to move up front, but he doesn't want to embarrass her and he supposes that part of the fun is being smushed up against a boy. This is how it all starts, Huck thinks. One minute you're leg to leg with a boy in your grandpa's truck during a ride into town, and the next minute you're hiding a hundred and twenty-five thousand of that boy's illegally gotten dollars in your dresser drawer.

Huck heads up the hill to Myrah Keating, then takes a left on the Centerline Road. At every curve and dip, the kids hoot as though the thrill of the ride is brand-new, even though they've all grown up driving on this crazy road. When they descend to the roundabout and Huck signals to go right toward Mongoose Junction, Maia says, "Actually, Gramps, can you drop us off at Powell Park? We're waiting for some Antilles kids to get off the ferry."

"*Antilles* kids?" Huck says. Antilles is the private school over on St. Thomas. "Not *those* rascals."

One of the boys guffaws and Huck can practically hear Maia rolling her eyes. Waiting for the Antilles kids is fine, Huck supposes. Powell Park attracts a colorful cast of characters but it's perfectly safe to hang out there in the midafternoon. So why does Huck feel uneasy? He knew these days were coming; Maia wasn't going to stay a child forever. But he's not ready. He should probably acknowledge that he'll never be ready. He needs Rosie back from the dead; he needs LeeAnn. Ayers has offered to serve as a surrogate mother but she has her own life, two jobs and a boyfriend, so how much can he really ask of her?

Huck has gotten used to the solo life, but right now he could really use a partner.

Irene? He immediately chastises himself for the thought. He must be out of his mind.

That night, after Maia shows Huck her completed homework and then goes into her room to FaceTime Joanie and giggle about God knows what—probably Colton and Bright or possibly a boy who goes to Antilles—Huck climbs into bed with his Michael Connelly novel. He's been reading this book since before Rosie died, which is an addling thought. When he first cracked open *The Late Show* a couple weeks ago, his life was one way, and now that he's on page 223, it's completely another. Now Rosie is dead—*dead!*—and he's hiding a hundred and twenty-five grand under his bed. The book does the trick, though—keeps him engrossed for a few chapters until his eyelids start to feel heavy. He closes the book and turns off the light.

Sleep, he thinks.

But he can't sleep. He might as well have a pile of uranium under the bed; the money feels radioactive.

A hundred and twenty-five thousand dollars. In cash.

Why?

Eventually, he drifts off; when he's awakened by his alarm, his head aches and he's in a foul mood. In his day, this was known as getting up on the wrong side of the bed.

"Let's go!" he calls out to Maia. "I have a charter at nine. A bachelor party."

Maia emerges from her room wearing a pink jean skirt, a black tank top, and black Chuck Taylors. She looks older, as though she aged three years overnight.

"I thought you hated bachelor parties," she says.

"Put on something else," Huck says. "That top is too revealing and that skirt is too short."

"What are you talking about?" Maia says. "I wear this outfit all the time."

"You do?" Huck says. He has to admit, he doesn't usually notice what Maia is wearing and he has never commented on it before. "I guess maybe you're growing, because it looks too small."

"Maybe you need new glasses," Maia says with a grin. She peers into the frying pan, where he's scrambling eggs. "Cut the heat. They're perfect now."

Huck snaps the burner off. It's an ongoing joke that Huck tends to overcook the eggs, and Maia feels about dry eggs the way that Huck feels about dry fish. No *bueno*.

"Serve them up yourself," Huck says. "And make your own toast. I have to get ready."

Maia stares at him. "Is this about yesterday?"

Huck stops in his tracks. He's facing the refrigerator, where he's about to grab Maia's lunch box—packed with a peanut butter and jelly as per her request because all of a sudden sandwiches made from freshly caught fish aren't good enough. "Yesterday?"

"Taking my friends to town," Maia says. "You've been in a weird mood since then."

She's intuitive, he'll give her that. He can't very well tell her the truth—that what has put him in a "weird mood" is the hundred and twenty-five grand he found in her mother's room—but neither does he want her to think that he minds driving her and her friends around. If she believes that, she'll start asking someone else for rides, and he'll lose his window into her world.

"That's not it," Huck says. "I enjoyed taking you to town."

"Oh," Maia says. "What is it, then? Is it Irene?"

At this, Huck does turn around. "Irene?"

"You miss her, right? That's why you're grumpy?"

Huck opens his mouth but for the life of him, he can't think of how to respond. The night following Irene's departure, he made the mistake of drinking a couple of shots of Flor de Caña and saying some things to Maia that he should have kept private. What exactly did he say? Maybe something as innocuous as *I've never seen a woman fish like that before*. Maybe something more revealing. But did he say he had *feelings* for Irene? No. Did he ever say he'd *miss* her? No.

Huck nearly snaps, *I'm not grumpy!* But he is, and it's not Maia's fault.

"Sorry, Nut," he says. "I'm just tired, I'm missing your mom—and your grandma too, for good measure—and I'm dreading this bachelor party."

Maia opens her arms to give Huck a hug, which he gratefully accepts. He loves this child to distraction, she's all he has left, and he'll be damned if he's going to let whatever mess Rosie was involved in affect her.

"Eat your breakfast," he says.

Adam is late getting to the boat, which normally ticks Huck off, but today, he's grateful. He has to think. What does he do about the money? He's a human being, so part of him fantasizes about keeping it and slipping five hundred here and three hundred there into Maia's college fund. He's not rich, he might not even qualify as "comfortable," but his house is paid off and so is the boat. He has money saved for a new truck once his old one finally dies and he has a fund for boat repairs. The money, if he kept it, would be a cushion. A really soft cushion.

He can't keep it. He has to report it. But to whom? He'll call Agent Vasco, he decides. He'll call her today, after the charter.

But maybe he'll call Irene first.

A dinghy putters up to the *Mississippi*. It's Keegan, the first mate from *What a Catch!*, a friendly-rival fishing boat, dropping off Adam.

"Sorry, Cap," Adam says, climbing aboard.

"He was up late talking to Marissa," Keegan says.

Huck pretends not to hear this last comment, as though ignoring it might make the situation go away. Marissa is the daughter of Dan and Mrs. Dan, the Albany couple from Huck's charter on New Year's Eve. Marissa is the girl who did not cast a line, the one who barely took her eyes off her phone's screen the entire time they were out on the water. Adam asked the girl out for New Year's Eve, an act of desperation if Huck had ever seen one. But the date must have been a humdinger because after that, they'd been inseparable until Marissa left a few days ago.

The day before yesterday, Huck said to Adam, "Why pick a girl who doesn't like to fish?"

Adam scoffed. "You know how hard it is to meet a chick who actually *enjoys* fishing?"

Huck nearly spoke up about Irene—the woman seemed to have taken up permanent residence in the front of his mind and on the tip of his tongue—but instead he said, "Maia likes to fish."

Adam said, "Maia is twelve. She'll grow out of it."

Keegan putters away in the dinghy. Adam removes his visor, runs a hand through his hair, and gazes in the direction of St. Thomas, where they both see an airplane taking off, probably going back to the States.

"Head in the game," Huck says. "Check the lines."

"I have to talk to you, Cap," Adam says.

Huck shakes his head. "Afterward, please. We have a bachelor party today, and you know how I feel about bachelor parties."

Huck hates bachelor parties. Nine times out of ten, if someone calls looking to book the *Mississippi* for one, Huck will tell the person his boat is unavailable for the foreseeable future. With bachelor parties, something bad always happens. Huck keeps one case of Red Stripe on ice at all times—and one case only. Bachelor parties often bring an additional thirty-pack of Bud Light (undrinkable, in Huck's opinion) as well as rum or tequila or sometimes punch in a plastic gallon jug. Huck gives extra alcohol the side-eye, but he has never flat-out forbidden it—that would be a fatal move for his TripAdvisor ratings—although he thinks to himself that what these kids really want is a booze cruise, not a fishing trip. He nearly always ends up with one participant completely jack-wagon drunk, puking off the back. He's had guys fall off the boat, and he's had fistfights. Huck never gets involved in the fistfights; he just turns the boat around and drops the group at the National Park Service dock without a word, regardless of whether they've caught any fish.

Huck agreed to book this bachelor party because he has been all but ignoring his business since Rosie died and he needs to get back into some kind of groove.

He pulls up to the National Park Service dock at ten minutes to nine but the only people waiting are four gentlemen, Huck's age or maybe older. They're in proper fishing shirts and visors and they have bags from the North Shore Deli, home of a roasted pork and broccoli rabe sandwich that Huck dreams about. He wonders if these guys are waiting for *What a Catch!* and feels a stab of envy.

Huck gives them a wave as he ties up and considers just poaching this foursome and letting Keegan and Captain Chris from *What a Catch!* handle the bachelor-party guys—who, Huck guesses, will show up late and hung over after a raucous night at the Dog House Pub.

One of the gentlemen, full head of snowy white hair, steps forward. "Captain Huck?" he says. "I'm Kyle Maguire."

Kyle Maguire? That's the name of Huck's guy. These four geezers *are* the bachelor party! Huck laughs with relief. He'd been expecting Millennials with their hashtags and their GoPros and their swim trunks printed with watermelon margaritas.

"Welcome aboard!" Huck says.

It's the charter of Huck's dreams. The four geezers—Kyle Maguire, his brother Harry, and Grover and Ahmed, childhood friends from Worcester, Massachusetts—are in their sixties, like Huck, and Huck can tell right away that they are *good* guys. They grin with just the right amount of eager enthusiasm as they kick off their shoes without being asked, shake Huck's hand, and climb aboard the boat.

Kyle, the groom-to-be, tells Huck he's a hospital administrator at Mass General and that he has a home on Nantucket, where he goes fishing two or three times a summer. "Up there, it's striped bass, bluefish, maybe bonito and false albacore if you're lucky."

Harry is a lawyer, Ahmed a retired ophthalmologist, and Grover a professor of business at the Kellogg School at Northwestern. Grover asks Huck about his USMC hat and Huck talks about his tour in Vietnam. Turns out, Grover was over there around the same time.

"Are you gentlemen okay with going offshore?" Huck asks.

"Let's do it!" Kyle says.

Huck decides to take the boat out to the spot that he and Irene fished, what the hell, why not give it a try. The day is sunny and the water is flat; the men relax with beers, Ahmed chats with Adam, and Huck plays music—the Doors, Led Zeppelin, the Rolling Stones. They reach the coordinates where they found the school of mahi before and start trolling.

C'mon, fish! Huck thinks. Maybe the luck he had with Irene will repeat itself.

Kyle gets a bite first. He reels it in as Huck stands alongside in case he needs any help. It's a barracuda; they all gather around to admire it, then Huck throws it back. After that, it's quiet for a while, which is when some people on these trips grow antsy. Often, that's when Huck has to tell them, "That's why it's called *fishing*, not *catching*." Huck nearly describes to these four men the day that he and Irene had out here—seventeen mahi!—but he holds his tongue because it doesn't seem like history will repeat itself.

"So you're getting married," Huck says. "Is this your first time?"

"No," Kyle says. "Been married twice before. First time to my college sweetheart. I have two boys from that marriage, but we split after five years. Then I met Jennifer and we were married for twenty-two years. She died in 2014."

This story eerily parallels Huck's own. He'd married his first wife, Kimberly, when he got home from Vietnam, and they divorced six years later, after her second unsuccessful stint in rehab. Then he met LeeAnn and they'd spent twenty blissful years together before she died in 2014.

"So who's the new gal?" Huck asks. He knows that Maia would likely object to his use of the word *gal,* finding it old-fashioned or, possibly, offensive.

"Her name is Sheila," Kyle says. He gives Huck a sheepish grin. "We met on the internet. Match dot com."

"Really?" Huck says. Rosie used to encourage Huck to try one of those dating services, but to him it was utterly pointless. Who was going to want to move to St. John? A week's visit, sure, two weeks maybe, but that didn't make a life together. And no way was Huck moving back to the States. He didn't care if Christie Brinkley came calling.

"Yep," Kyle says. "She's a civil engineer. She builds bridges in the Bay Area, the kind of bridges that can withstand earthquakes. Her husband died of Lou Gehrig's disease two years ago. She has one son, grown up, who lives near me outside of Boston, so Sheila is moving east from Oakland and we're tying the knot."

"If you don't mind my asking, how long have you been dating?"

"Nine months," Kyle says. He waves his beer can in the direction of his friends. "They all thought I was rushing into things when I bought the ring after only six months. I can't describe it. We just clicked. I flew out there one weekend, she came to see me on Nantucket a couple weeks later, then we went to Chicago, where she met Grover and he approved, then we did a week in Napa. At Thanksgiving she came to Boston and I introduced her to my kids. They loved her right away. I proposed when I dropped her off at the airport."

"Are you worried about her moving in with you?" Huck asks. A week in Napa is one thing, he thinks; sharing closet space is another.

"I know it's a gamble," Kyle says. "But I'm sixty-four years old and life gave me another chance to be happy. Only an idiot would say no to that out of fear."

Huck stares over the turquoise sheet of the water toward the verdant hills of St. John. Kyle must sense that his words have stirred something up in Huck because he claps Huck on the shoulder and says, "You hungry? We got enough sandwiches for everyone."

They catch another barracuda, then Adam suggests heading over toward Little St. James and Huck agrees; the spot he picked has lost its magic, apparently. In the next place they troll, Ahmed catches a decent-size tuna, then Harry brings in a wahoo big enough to serve as dinner and Huck relaxes. He cracks open a Coke and turns up the Who's "Baba O'Riley" and casts a line himself. He gets a fish on almost instantly and hands the line over to Grover, who reels in a second wahoo, bigger than the first. Then Kyle catches a tuna. Ahmed takes a nap in the shade. Huck overhears Adam talking to Grover about business school, and suddenly Huck knows what Adam wants to tell him—but he won't let it ruin the afternoon.

At quarter past two, it's time to turn the boat back. Kyle passes out Romeo y Julietas and Huck gratefully accepts one. He loves Cuban cigars. LeeAnn absolutely forbade them, so Huck can't light up without feeling like he's indulging in a guilty pleasure.

How does Irene feel about them? he wonders.

Life gave me another chance to be happy. Only an idiot would say no to that out of fear.

Huck thinks of the first time he saw Irene, her chestnut braid draped over one shoulder as she marched down the dock calling him "Mr. Powers." Now that he knows her a little better, he realizes she doesn't mess around nor suffer fools—but still, it was impressive, the way she talked herself onto his boat.

We just clicked.

Had Huck and Irene *clicked?* He would have a hard time saying they hadn't.

Angler Cupcake.

There's nothing like the wisdom of a twelve-year-old, Huck thinks. Maia was right. Huck misses Irene and that's why he's grumpy.

When they tie up back at the dock, Adam fillets the fish for the gentlemen and Kyle pours a shot of tequila for everyone. They clink glasses and throw back the shots. Kyle thanks Huck profusely and slips him a generous tip, which Huck nearly refuses because the guy has given Huck so much already. If nothing else, he has changed Huck's mind about bachelor parties.

Temporarily, anyway.

They shake hands and say their goodbyes and Huck says maybe he'll see them in town over the next few days, it's not impossible, although Huck hasn't been out since Rosie died.

"They were terrific!" Huck says to Adam once they're gone. He slips Adam one of the hundreds that Kyle gave him. Those are the kind of men Huck would have as friends, if he had time for friends.

Adam stuffs the hundred in his pocket. "Cap," he says. The boy looks green around the gills, downright seasick, as though *he* will be the one to upchuck off the back of the boat. And just like that, Huck is snapped out of the golden reverie that a good day out on the water provides. He's back to real life: the money under his bed, the FBI, and whatever Adam has to tell him.

Huck decides to cut the kid a break and do the hard part for him. "You're leaving me?" he says.

Adam nods morosely. "I'm moving to upstate New York to be with Marissa."

Upstate New York? Huck thinks. What did this girl Marissa *do* to him?

"It's cold in upstate New York," Huck says. "It snows. A lot. And there's no ocean."

"I love her," Adam says, and he swallows. "I'm in love with her."

Huck nods. He yearns to tell Adam that, more than half the time, love dies, and it probably dies quicker in places like Oneida and Oneonta. But Huck won't be that curmudgeonly skeptic today.

"They have lakes," Huck says. "*Great* lakes. You can fly-fish."

Adam looks so relieved that Huck's afraid the boy might try to kiss him. "Yeah, that's what I thought I'd do," he says. "In the summer."

Huck lights a cigarette and inhales deeply. "So you'll leave in May, then? Or June?"

"A week from Tuesday," Adam says.

A week from Tuesday, Huck thinks.

"Oneonta in January," Huck says. "Must be love."

That night after dinner—fresh, perfectly grilled wahoo that even Maia agrees is sublime—Huck heads out to the deck with his pack of Camel Lights and his cell phone.

Agent Vasco or Irene? He decides on one, then changes his mind and decides on the other. Then back, then back again.

Irene.

He's almost more nervous about calling her than about calling the FBI. He *is* more nervous about calling her because he has no idea how the conversation will go.

She answers on the first ring. "Oh, Huck, is that you?"

Her voice stirs something in him. He exhales smoke. "It's me." He pauses. He had planned to say, *I'm calling to check on you.* Or *I'm calling to see how you're doing.* But instead the words that fly out of his mouth are "I have a business proposition. My first mate, Adam, quit on me today and I can't properly run my charter without a mate. So I'm calling to offer you a job."

There's a pause long enough for Huck to take a drag off his cigarette, consider the lights of the Westin below and the cruise ship headed to St. Croix in the distance, and castigate himself for acting like a fool. He should have gone with *How've you been?*

"What does it pay?" Irene asks.

He grins and tells her the truth. "Hundred bucks for a half day, two hundred for a full day," he says. "Plus tips." He clears his throat. "Plus fish."

"That sounds fair," she says. "When do I start?"

He has to rein in the joy in his voice before he makes the second call. He clears his throat, takes a cleansing breath, lights another cigarette, and dials.

"Colette Vasco."

"Agent Vasco, this is Sam Powers calling from St. John. I'm Rosie's—"

"Yes, hello, Captain Powers," Agent Vasco says. "I'm sorry, I don't have any further news—"

"*I* have news," Huck says. He lowers his voice in case Maia happens to pop out of her room in search of some Ben and Jerry's Brownie Batter Core. "I found a hundred and twenty-five thousand dollars hidden in a dresser drawer in Rosie's room. I thought you would want to know."

"Yes," Agent Vasco says. "Yes, you're certainly right about that. What would be a good time tomorrow for me to stop by?"

BAKER

When he tells his "school wives"—Wendy, Becky, Debbie, and Ellen—that Anna has asked him to get a sitter for Floyd so that she and Louisa can take Baker to dinner at Indigo and "civilly discuss arrangements," they all start talking at once.

"Don't let them railroad you," Wendy says. "Ask for full custody if that's what you want."

Debbie slides a business card across the table: Perla Piuggi, Esq. "My divorce attorney," she says. "Pitbull."

"We've agreed to do mediation," Baker says.

"Using words like *civilly* and *mediation* nearly always means an ambush is coming," Becky says.

Baker slips the card into his pocket.

"I'm dying to eat at Indigo," Ellen says. "Their tasting menus are the talk of the city. It's neo–soul food."

"I'm in," Wendy says. "Let's book a table the same night."

She cackles. "That way if things go south, you can come sit with us."

"I thought Anna ate only pizza," Debbie says. "Didn't you tell me Anna hated going out to fancy places?"

"She was always too tired," Baker says.

"But not anymore," Ellen says with an eye roll.

"Call the lawyer," Debbie says.

"And report back," Wendy says.

"Also, take a picture if you can," Becky says.

Debbie swats her hand. "We sound like a pack of catty teenagers."

"I want to see if Anna looks happy," Becky says. "I want to see if she has that glow."

"Imagine," Wendy says. "Anna, happy."

Ellen wasn't wrong; Indigo is a unique experience with its own set of rules and a robust social conscience—which must be why Louisa picked it (Baker assumes that Louisa picked it, since what Debbie said is true—Anna eats only pizza). There are only thirteen seats at a horseshoe-shaped bar, making for a communal experience, which Baker figures is both good and bad. On the one hand, things can't possibly get too ugly in such a controlled environment, but on the other, their civil discussion of arrangements might become a group-therapy session. They are, blessedly, placed at the far side of the horseshoe with Baker agreeing to take the seat on the end, in a relatively dim corner. Louisa is next to him, Anna on the other side of Louisa. This feels weird and wrong—shouldn't he be sitting next to Anna so they can talk about Floyd? And yet, it's also symbolic; Louisa is, in fact, the person who came between Baker and Anna, as the seating now illustrates.

They're asked to select their tasting menu; they can choose carnivore, omnivore, or pescatarian-chordate.

Pescatarian means fish, Baker knows. He hasn't a clue about *chordate,* but listed underneath is the word *amphibian,* which probably means frogs' legs, but it's too risky to chance it. Baker chooses carnivore with a first course called Turtlenecks and Do-Rags, and the ladies—women!—choose omnivore and will enjoy a first course called Descendants of Igbo, which is apparently yams with marshmallows.

This place is truly an alternate universe, but at least it serves as a distraction.

Anna, not one for small talk, leans forward and says, "Louisa was offered a position in the neonatal cardiothoracic surgery department at the Cleveland Clinic and she's going to take it, and she persuaded them that two heart surgeons are better than one, so they've offered me a job as well."

"Turns out, they're even more excited to get the great Anna Schaffer than they are to get me," Louisa says, and she covers Anna's hand with her own.

Baker gazes at the two of them. They seem like strangers to him, like people he's met at jury duty. Anna is wearing her hair down and it looks lovely, like a dark velvet curtain. Louisa's hair used to be dark and long like Anna's—Baker has known her long enough to remember this—but now she has cut it very short and dyed it platinum blond. They're both glowing; they're both happy. It's obvious that they're in love, that they're a couple. None of the other ten diners tonight would ever guess that Baker and Anna are the people who are married.

Immediately after making this observation, he processes the

words *Cleveland Clinic.* They're both taking positions at the Cleveland Clinic, which, if Baker isn't mistaken, is in Cleveland.

He feels like he has to double-check. Hospitals all have satellite campuses these days.

"Are you talking about the Cleveland Clinic in... Cleveland?" he asks.

Louisa's head bobs and he notices her grip on Anna's hand tighten. "Yes, Baker," she says. It's probably not her intent to speak to him like he's a moron but that's pretty much what she's doing. "We're relocating to Cleveland."

"Not with Floyd," Baker says. "You aren't taking my son to Cleveland."

"That's what we wanted to talk to you about," Anna says. "There's more than one way to look at this."

"Oh, really," Baker says. He runs his eyes along the horseshoe to the opposite side, hoping that he will see his four friends eating amphibians. He needs them now because it's becoming clear that this *is* an ambush. Anna and Louisa have accepted positions at the Cleveland Clinic. They're moving to Cleveland, Ohio!

"Yes, really," Anna says. The server arrives with Anna's and Louisa's Descendants (yams) and Baker's Turtlenecks and Do-Rags, which appears to be a crab dish (not actual turtles' necks). Louisa and Anna dig in, but Baker can't even remember how to use his cutlery. "Our first choice would be for you and Floyd to come to Cleveland."

"What?" Baker says.

"You can do your job from anywhere," Anna says. "You don't have to be in Houston."

"But... we have a house, Floyd has school, we have friends in Houston. A community. A life."

Anna scrapes yams out of the bowl. "The deepest roots we have in Houston are mine, at the hospital. And I'm willing to pull those up for this opportunity."

Baker stares at his crab, fervently wishing that Wendy, Becky, Debbie, and Ellen were here so he could inform them that his friendship with them is, according to Anna, shallow—or at least, not as deep as Anna's career. The woman is so *cold,* so dispassionate, Baker can't believe he ever decided to marry her. Good luck to Louisa!

"You and Louisa go to Cleveland," Baker says. "Floyd and I will stay here. I'll send him up to you on his vacations."

"That's our third choice," Louisa says. "A distant third, because we'd obviously like to remain a cohesive family unit." Baker very much resents her chiming in at all. She stole Baker's wife and now she's dragging her to Ohio. It's clear that Louisa is maintaining some kind of utopian vision of the three of them as the parents in this "cohesive family unit," with Anna and Louisa as the breadwinners and Baker as Floyd's primary caregiver. "But we want to keep the transition as harmonious as possible, for Floyd's sake. So we can try that option for the first year if you insist upon it. You and Floyd stay here and we'll set up a realistic visitation schedule—holidays and summers."

"Great," Baker says. "You can be the Disneyland parents." This is Debbie's term. Her ex-husband, Jaybee, takes her kids only three weeks per year—to Martha's Vineyard over the summer, to Aspen at Christmas, and to a different European city each spring. Baker considers the two very serious, accomplished women—people!—on his left. Sorry to say, they are no one's idea of Disneyland parents.

And yet, this plan works for Baker. Because he is *not* moving to Cleveland.

"You should also know..." Anna says, and for the first time during this unpleasant and confusing dinner, she seems ill at ease.

"That I'm planning on getting pregnant," Louisa finishes. She considers the yams and marshmallows on the end of her fork. "Using a sperm donor."

The words *sperm donor* should never be uttered during dinner, Baker thinks. He has just lost his appetite.

Their server takes advantage of the pause in their conversation to whisk away their first-course dishes—Baker's untouched—and set down the Homogenization of Mandingos (venison sausage with beets) for Baker and the Belly of the Beast (boar ribs) for the ladies. Women. People. Baker has some other words to describe them at this point, words that don't fall in the category of "civilly discussing arrangements."

"So Floyd will have a half brother or half sister, in a sense, and we obviously want them to have a relationship," Anna says.

"Cohesive family unit," Louisa says again. Those are her buzzwords, and it takes all of Baker's willpower to keep from shouting at her that Anna, Baker, and Floyd are—were—the family unit. Louisa is the interloper. The homewrecker!

Baker reaches for his beer, which he's been too distracted to drink. He takes a long sip, buying himself time. Anna has left herself wide open here.

"I thought you said you didn't want any more children," Baker says. "You were adamant about it, in fact. And now you're talking about a baby."

"Louisa will have the baby," Anna says.

"And yet you want a cohesive family unit," Baker says. "So you'll be co-parents."

"Of course," Anna says, shrugging. She doesn't meet Baker's

eyes because, very likely, she doesn't want to provoke him into describing what having Dr. Anna Schaffer as a co-parent was like. It was like…having no co-parent at all! But Baker decides he *won't* tell Louisa this; he'll let her find out on her own. Two busy surgeons at the Cleveland Clinic, one baby—what could go wrong?

"Well," Baker says. "Congratulations." He picks up his fork. Suddenly, the whole situation seems amusing—and maybe even fortunate? Anna and Louisa are leaving town. Floyd will see them for vacations and holidays, which on the surface appears sad and pathetic. He's a four-year-old boy; he needs his mother. But Baker is in a position to know that Floyd *doesn't* need Anna. He's been fine this long without her. Maybe Anna will be more engaged as a parent when the job is taken in small bites.

Anna smiles at him; her glow returns. "Thank you for being so understanding," she says. "And please know that whatever financial resources you want, we'll provide. You can keep the house; there will be support for Floyd and support for you as well."

He's being paid off, but he doesn't care. He cuts into his venison sausage. He can't wait to get home and call his friends.

He starts with Ellen because, really, theirs is the closest relationship, and Ellen is a single mother by choice, so she is savvy and resourceful by nature.

He tells her *everything*—including the esoteric menu items at dinner—and with each new revelation, she gasps.

Louisa offered job at Cleveland Clinic.

Anna offered job at Cleveland Clinic.

Louisa and Anna moving to Cleveland.

Louisa and Anna offering to move Baker and Floyd to Cleveland.

Louisa and Anna offering to take on the role of Disneyland parents while Baker keeps Floyd in Houston.

Louisa having a baby with sperm donor, Anna agreeing to co-parent. Anna and Louisa promising to support Baker and Floyd financially.

At the end, Ellen says, "On the surface, this sounds...great for you. Really *great*. Anna and Louisa are out of your hair, you get to keep Floyd and the house, *and* they're going to pay you..."

"But?" Baker says.

"Doesn't it seem too good to be true?" Ellen says. "Like something doesn't add up? I know Anna isn't the most hands-on mother, but is she really going to move twelve hundred miles away from her son and see him only at Christmas?"

"And summers," Baker says weakly. He, too, feels uneasy now, but he can't tell if it's because he thinks Anna is going to renege and possibly sue him for custody—which is what it would take for her to get Floyd—or if he's just embarrassed about marrying a woman who really just *isn't* maternal. At all. "Listen, I know it sounds unconventional, but think about Anna. This scenario is perfect for her. She doesn't have *time* to parent. I'm concerned about Floyd spending the entire summer with her because you and I both know that means he'll have a full-time nanny. He's better off with me."

"Agreed," Ellen says. She takes a sip of what he can only assume is 8th Wonder IPA (she's a craft-beer *fanatic*) and says, "So my brilliant-best-friend mind now wonders why you would even stay in Houston. With Anna leaving, you're free to go wherever you want."

Ellen's tone is heavy with innuendo. She's the only one in the group that he's told about his father dying *in the Caribbean,* the fifteen-million-dollar villa, and...Ayers. She's the only one he's told about Ayers.

That night, the carnivore tasting menu churns in Baker's stomach as he scrolls through every reason why he *shouldn't* leave Houston for good and move down to St. John. He starts with the reasons he gave Anna.

They have a house here.

Well, the house is a house. He can sell it or rent it or leave it be until he sees how things work out down in the islands. He and Anna bought it outright when they moved from Chicago, so there's no mortgage, only taxes, insurance, and maintenance.

Floyd has school. They have friends, a community, a life.

Floyd is four. He goes to Montessori. He's not a sophomore in high school; he's not even in middle school. If they leave Houston now, it's possible Floyd won't have any memories of the place, much less feel resentful about moving. Floyd can already read and count to a hundred. Baker should investigate the schools in St. John, make sure there's somewhere suitable.

Friends. Community. Baker is chairperson of the Children's Cottage annual benefit auction, which is in two weeks. Baker's work on the auction is basically done; all of the items have been solicited. He bought a table for three thousand dollars and invited all his school wives. He should really attend.

But it's not necessarily a reason to *stay*. The auction will happen, the school will make money, the auction will be over.

Would Anna object to Floyd living in the Virgin Islands? She's seen the villa; she knows it's comfortable. She'd be concerned about the schools. Baker will look into it first thing in the morning. Maia goes to school. Maia is…Floyd's *aunt*. Okay, that's a little weird. But maybe not. It's late, Baker is tired, everything seems weird.

Louisa wants to have a baby, essentially a half brother or half sister for Floyd.

Baker would love to have more kids.

Ayers. Baker knew the instant he saw her that he wanted to marry her. They'd ended on bad terms—really bad—and she said she was back with Mick. *That means she's having sex with Mick,* Baker thinks, *maybe even this very second,* which is enough to make him sick. But he needs to think realistically about sex. Sex is ephemeral. Once it's over, it's over. Sex is not a lasting connection; it's only real while it's happening. It's not love.

Besides, Mick cheated on Ayers, and once a cheater, always a cheater. If Baker is confident of anything, it's that Mick will blow it and Baker will be there to show Ayers how she deserves to be treated.

Ayers hadn't wanted to get serious about Baker because he was a tourist.

If Baker moves into his father's villa, he will be a tourist no longer.

Bright and early the next morning, Baker books two tickets to St. Thomas with a return flight in two weeks so that he and Floyd will arrive back the day before the auction. Then, assuming all goes well on St. John, after the auction they will move back permanently. This trip will be an exploratory mission, a toe dipped in to test the waters.

He calls Paulette Vickers to let her know that he and Floyd will be down on Saturday to stay at the villa for a couple of weeks, and might she be able to meet him at the dock with the keys?

"Certainly, Mr. Steele," she says. "I'm happy to know you're using it. A beautiful villa like that shouldn't sit empty. I asked your mother if she wanted me to rent it and she said to hold off for the time being."

"My mother is overwhelmed," Baker says. "She doesn't need more to worry about. I'll handle all things relating to the villa from now on." He wonders if he's overstepping, but all of the goodwill he's put in with Paulette is paying off because she doesn't question it.

"Very good," she says. "I'll meet you at the ferry dock on Saturday with the keys."

Baker hangs up and feels an elation so strong he could levitate. The only string tying him to earth is...Irene. Baker should call her and tell her his plans.

But...what he just told Paulette is true—Irene *is* overwhelmed. She doesn't need one more thing to worry about. She doesn't need to fret about Baker and Floyd on St. John or about Anna relocating.

Then again, Irene had been perfectly clear that she would not tolerate any more secrets. Secrets are lies, Irene said.

Baker's trip to St. John isn't a *secret*. Of course it's not a secret. Paulette knows he's coming, and before he and Floyd leave, Baker will have to tell Anna.

Once Baker is down there and settled in, he'll call Irene. This will give her a few more days of relative peace. That's the kind thing to do.

ROSIE

February 21, 2006

My life is a house that has been ransacked. My heart, which I had so recently reclaimed as my own, has been stolen again. Some might say I'm being careless with it.

Friday afternoon was the start of Presidents' Day weekend, which brings nearly as many tourists as Christmas and Easter now because schools in the Northeast—Massachusetts, New York, and a few of those other densely packed states—give their students a winter break. The problem with the visitors who can afford to come when the weather is the most inhospitable at home is that they tend to be demanding. They want their Caribbean experience to be just so—the sky must be clear, the mangos ripe, the cocktails strong and delivered right away.

Caneel Bay was at maximum capacity. Every room was booked at high-season rates, and along the front row on Honeymoon Bay, it was all return guests, the ones Estella calls "the patronage": Mr. and Mrs. Very Important of Park Avenue, the Big Deal Family from Lake Forest, Illinois, the New Moneys from La Jolla. I recognized them (and yes, I called them by their real names: Mr. and Mrs. Vikram, the Caruso family, the Burlingames). Their eyes lit up when they saw me but I always reintroduce myself, just in case.

"Oh, yes, Rosie, how are you! Wonderful to see you again! How has your year been?"

I said my year had been good, though nothing was further from the truth. But there was no way I could tell the New Moneys about my excruciating breakup with Oscar and how disappointing that had been because he'd promised me that once he got out of jail he would work in a legitimate business, maybe even get a job alongside me at Caneel, but instead he was back to selling drugs to people on the cruise ships. I didn't complain that I was still living at home with my mother and Huck. The returning guests, the patronage, loved coming back and seeing a familiar face because it made Caneel feel like home; it made it feel like a private club where they were members. For me, it was primarily a business relationship. The tips were double what they would have been with complete strangers.

In most cases, anyway.

The guests at Caneel are 95 percent white. There are a few Japanese here and there, a couple of rich South American businessmen (rum, casinos), and the occasional black American couple or Indian family, so when Oscar came in for drinks with Borneo and Little Jay, they stuck out. They wore baseball hats on backward, heavy gold chains, those ridiculous jeans that drooped in the ass.

Estella saw Oscar first. She came over while I was at the bar getting cocktails for a trio of pasty-white gentlemen who had just anchored their enormous yacht out in front of the resort, and she said, "Oscar here, Rosie-girl, with his clownish friends."

"Send him away," I said.

"I wish I could, Rosie-girl, but they're paying customers just like the rest."

"Keep them out of my section."

"Oscar asked for you."

"All the more reason."

"Okay, I'll give them to Tessie."

I loathed Tessie, so this was killing two birds.

I dropped the drinks off with the yacht gentlemen. Yacht Gentleman One was tall and bald with a posh English accent and what I knew to be a forty-thousand-dollar Patek Philippe (I'd picked up some useless knowledge on this job). Yacht Gentleman Two had dark, slicked-back hair and such distracting good looks that I nicknamed him "James Bond" in my mind. Yacht Gentleman Three was a doughy midwesterner with silvering hair. I knew he was midwestern because he stood up and introduced himself.

"Russell Steele," he said. "Iowa City."

His manners caught me off guard. Normally, men like the ones he was with either ignored me, made a pass at me, or snapped their fingers so I would move faster. They did not stand up and offer their names like they were crashing a party and I was the hostess. And thank goodness they didn't—on an average holiday-weekend night, I had over a hundred customers. How could I possibly remember them all?

"Rosie Small," I said. "Pleasure." I had already forgotten his last name, but I did retain his first name, Russell, and Iowa City, because the place sounded so…American, or what I always thought of as American. Iowa City *evoked cows in pastures, silos, corner drugstores where kids bought malted milkshakes, church socials, marching bands, and grown men wearing overalls. "Enjoy your drinks. Let me know if you're interested in ordering food. The conch fritters are very good."*

"Conch fritters, then," Russell from Iowa City said. "I'm not sure what they are but if you say they're good, I'm up for trying them. In fact, bring two orders. That okay with you guys?"

The other two gentlemen were poring over a sheaf of papers printed with columns of figures. James Bond looked up. "Yeah, yeah, Russ, get whatever you want. Bring some sushi too, you pick. Enough for three, please." James Bond handed me his AmEx Centurion Card and said, "Start us a tab, doll."

I wanted to tell James Bond that I was not a doll, I was a person, but I figured I'd get back at him by ordering the most expensive sushi on the menu—sashimi, tuna tataki, hamachi, unagi. I could see poor Russell looking very uncomfortable, like he wanted to stick up for me but didn't know how. He was, quite clearly, low man on the totem pole of this particular triumvirate as he had neither the flashy watch nor the movie-star good looks (nor the Centurion Card). He might have been the brother-in-law of one or the other, a sister's husband whom they had brought along to the Caribbean as a favor or because they lost a bet.

He didn't know what conch fritters *were!*

I went to the register to put in an order for the fritters and two hundred dollars' worth of sushi—I could have doubled that; James Bond wasn't the kind of man to complain about his bill or even check it—and studied the name on the Centurion Card.

Todd Croft. *It was a solid, whitewashed name, symmetrical and masculine, like the real name of a secret superhero—Clark Kent, Peter Parker. I wondered if it was made up. I didn't care as long as the card worked, which it did.*

I kept tabs on Oscar out of my peripheral vision. He ordered a bottle of Dom Pérignon, which Tessie made a big production of carrying out in front of her, label displayed, like she was one of those chicks on a game show giving away the grand prize. The pop of the cork cut through all the chatter and the restaurant quieted so that I could clearly hear Harry Belafonte singing, "Yes, we have no bananas." People whispered and sneaked glances at Oscar and I yearned to tell them to stop. Couldn't they see that was what he was after?

I then watched the Big Deal Family's daughter, Lucinda

Caruso, who has made sure to tell me every year for the past three years that she "recently graduated from Harvard" (which I take to mean that she has yet to find a job, a theory reinforced by the fact that she signed every charge to her father's room), approach Oscar's table and proceed to take the fourth seat. Lucinda was wearing a very short, sequined cocktail dress that would have been better at an event where she remained standing. I overheard her say, "Are you guys rap *stars?" I rolled my eyes, not only because Lucinda was feeding the beast but also because she probably couldn't imagine a black man having the money to order Dom unless he was a rap star or a professional athlete. I could have shut her up by telling her the truth.* He sells drugs, Lucinda! *But it was none of my business.*

The yacht gentlemen's food was up. I set one order of conch fritters—piping hot, golden brown, and fragrant, served with a papaya-cayenne aioli—in front of Russell from Iowa City. This is my favorite part of the job, other than the money, introducing the Caribbean to people who have never experienced it. I plunked the tower of sushi—the way Chef had arranged it was quite impressive, and the fish was so plump and fresh, it looked like art—in front of Todd Croft.

"There you go, doll," I said. "Enjoy."

Russell from Iowa City barked out a laugh so surprised and genuine that I gave him a wink.

The night progressed. It was busy. I kept one eye on the yacht men—after all that, they barely touched the sushi—and one eye on Oscar and his friends. Lucinda stayed at the table; they ordered another bottle of Dom. Mr. and Mrs. Big Deal stopped by the table and tried to entice Lucinda to go with them to the Chateau Bor-

deaux, but she refused to leave, and the second her parents were out the door, she rose from her chair and sat on Oscar's lap.

At that point, I turned away. I knew Oscar was showboating just to goad me into reconsidering my decision, but I hadn't done all my soul-searching only to cave because I couldn't stand to see him with a silly rich girl on his lap.

I tended to my other tables. I was even nice to Tessie. When I saw her heading out with a third bottle of Dom, I said, "Tonight is your lucky night. Oscar is an excellent tipper."

Around ten, things started to quiet down. Two of the yacht men—Todd Croft and the tall, bald Brit—left, and Russell from Iowa City moved to the bar and planted himself in front of the television to watch a basketball game. When I checked the screen, I saw Iowa was playing Northwestern. I went up to him because I had a minute and also because Todd Croft had left an even five hundred dollars for a three-hundred-and-twenty-dollar check.

"You're rooting for Iowa?" I asked.

"Northwestern, actually," he said. "My alma mater."

"Ah." I knew more about football than basketball, and nearly all my basketball knowledge was limited to the San Antonio Spurs in general and Tim Duncan in particular because he hailed from St. Croix and some of my Small cousins had actually played a pickup game with him once on the courts in Contant. But it was best I change the subject. "So, your friends left you behind?"

"They went into Cruz Bay," Russell said. "Looking for women." He held up his left hand. "I'm married, with two boys."

"Well, your wife is a very lucky woman," I said, and I patted his shoulder. "Your next drink is on me. How did you like the conch fritters?"

"I loved them!" he said. "I was meaning to ask if you knew a

place I could get some real Caribbean food. I have the day to myself tomorrow and I want to explore."

"Well," I said, "if you want local flavor, go to the East End. There's a place called Vie's on Hansen Bay."

He took a pen out of his shirt pocket and pulled a cocktail napkin off the stack. "Vie's?"

"She makes some mean garlic chicken and the best johnnycakes," I said. "For a few dollars, you can rent a chaise on her beach."

"Is there shade?" Russell from Iowa City asked. He held out a pale, freckled arm and I thought, This poor guy. God bless him.

"There's shade," I said. "Here, I'll draw you a map."

I clocked out at eleven, sorted my tips, marveling at my windfall from Todd Croft, and decided that I would stop by the Ocean Grill at Mongoose for a drink on my way home. I headed past the Sugar Mill on my way to the parking lot and stopped to say hello to my wild donkeys, Stop, Drop, and Roll. They always looked a little eerie at night, more like ghost horses than white donkeys, and the backdrop of the stone ruins of the sugar mill only heightened the otherworldly effect. But I thought of these three like pets—they rarely wandered off the grounds of Caneel—and I couldn't ignore them.

In retrospect, I should have realized that Oscar knew this. He jumped out of the shadows and grabbed my arm.

"Baby."

I gasped, though I wasn't exactly surprised. A part of me knew there was no way he'd left. I had already planned to turn on the flashlight of my phone and sweep the back of my car before I climbed in. "Let me go, Oscar."

He held tight. I checked behind him for Borneo or Little Jay or even Lucinda Caruso, but there was no one on the path in either direction. If I screamed, Woodrow or one of the other security guards would hear me and escort Oscar off the property but the last thing I wanted was everyone all up in my business. As soon as it got out that Oscar had shown up at the restaurant and made trouble, my mother would hear about it and somehow twist it into being my fault. She would say that I had led Oscar on or had acted recklessly by walking to my car by myself.

Oscar didn't let go. He pulled me to him so close that I could smell the champagne on his breath. "I need you to come back, baby."

I said, "We've been over this, Oscar. I'm not changing my mind."

"You got another man, then? That brother from Christiansted?"

He was talking about Bryson, a guy I'd gone out with a few times in college. Bryson lived on St. Croix.

"It's none of your business, Oscar." I succeeded in reclaiming my arm. "I'm tired, I'm going home, good night." I turned around. "And you know that if you come anywhere near the house, LeeAnn will call the police and you'll go right back to jail."

Oscar said, "I'm going to Christiansted tomorrow to kill that brother."

I stopped in my tracks. Had anyone else said something like that, I would have scoffed, but what had landed Oscar in jail was stabbing his friend Leon for borrowing his Ducati without permission.

"You'll do no such thing," I said.

"Try me," Oscar said. Then he suddenly dropped the tough-guy act and sounded like himself. "Rosie. Try me."

"Why can't you just leave me alone?" I said. "Why do you come here when you know I'm working? There are ten other places you and your friends can hang out. Why come to Caneel? Because you want me to know you have the money to order Dom Pérignon? I don't care! You want me to see that girls throw themselves at you? I care even less! I loved you when I was a girl—fifteen, sixteen, seventeen. But I'm a woman now, Oscar, and I'm moving on."

"Baby," Oscar said, and he grabbed the strap of my purse.

"Get off *me!" I said. I put a hand against the unyielding muscles of his chest.*

"Stop bothering the lady!"

Both Oscar and I turned to see who *jogging toward us? Russell from Iowa City, that's who.*

Oscar laughed and I thought, Oh, dear Lord, no. *It was probably a midwestern thing to defend a woman's honor but it would end in disaster for Russell from Iowa City. I would have to call out for Woodrow after all.*

"What you gonna do about it?" Oscar said. He kissed his teeth. "You gonna stop me?"

To his credit, Russell from Iowa City did not appear even a little afraid. He looked serious and disappointed, as though he were an assistant principal who had found his favorite student misbehaving and a suspension was coming.

"Yes," Russell said coolly. "I'm going to stop you. Rosie, are you heading home? Can I escort you to your car?"

I tried to give him a look that said he didn't have to defend me and he shouldn't *defend me because the consequences would be dire. Oscar would beat him to a pulp, or maybe just hit him once, or maybe just humiliate him, but whatever course of action Oscar took, it wouldn't be worth it. I could handle Oscar; Russell from Iowa City most certainly could not.*

Russell held out his arm like an old-fashioned gentleman caller. I sighed and hoped that maybe, just maybe, Oscar would be more afraid of violating his parole than of being shown up. I linked my arm through Russell's.

From there, things happened fast. Oscar pushed Russell from behind and Russell let go of my arm and grabbed the front of Oscar's shirt and they tussled while I searched the shadows for Woodrow on his golf cart—where was he?—and then, the next thing I knew, Russell from Iowa City had Oscar in a death grip and Oscar was gasping for air. It looked like Russell was about to snap his neck and I found myself fearing that Russell was going to kill Oscar instead of vice versa.

"Now," Russell said in a calm-but-disappointed-assistant-principal voice, "I'm going to let you go. But you are to leave Rosie alone. Do you understand me?"

Oscar choked out an affirmative and Russell tightened his grip so that Oscar squeaked like a chew toy.

"It's okay," I said. "Thank you."

Russell let Oscar go. Oscar buckled at the knees, stumbled a few yards away, and bent over in the grass, turning his neck to be sure it still worked.

Russell offered me his arm again.

"Where did you learn to do that?" I asked him once we were safely at my car.

"My father was a navy man," Russell said.

I stood on my tiptoes and kissed his cheek. "My hero," I said.

The next day, almost without thinking, I drove to the East End to Miss Vie's at Hansen Bay. I was like a woman possessed because there was no good reason to go all the way out to that side of the island; normally, if I wanted to go to the beach, I parked at the National Park Service sign and hiked down to Salomon Bay. But I somehow convinced myself that, on the Saturday of the holiday weekend, even Salomon would be overrun and that the only way to escape the crowds would be to go to Hansen Bay. Besides which, now that it was in my head, I couldn't shake my craving for Miss Vie's garlic chicken and johnnycakes.

I told myself it had nothing to do with Russell from Iowa City. I wasn't attracted to him, or I hadn't been until the incident with Oscar—but having one's honor defended is a mighty aphrodisiac. Still, Russell was old enough to be my father (I now know he's forty-five, double my age), but that, in a way, was also attractive because what I was looking for was someone older, someone responsible and stable, someone adult. *Oscar was older than me by seven years but emotionally he was a little boy who had a bone to pick with everyone.*

I wore my white bikini and a white T-shirt knotted at the midriff and a pair of white denim shorts. White is my color.

There was a line of cars, all rentals, parked along the road near Vie's. There was no telling if one of them was Russell's or if he'd taken a taxi or if he was even there at all. The East End was a hike from everywhere and he might have decided to go fishing with his buddies or cruise over to the BVIs for lunch at Foxy's. The second I stepped onto the beach and scanned the chaises in the shade, I saw him, settled back with a rum punch in hand.

When he spotted me, he smiled, and by smiled, *I mean he* beamed *like I was the only person in the world he wanted to see.*

"Rosie!" he said.

We hugged and he kissed my cheek and it was like seeing a friend, even though I barely knew him. He called over Flora, whom he already knew by name, and said he would pay for a sec-

ond chaise and Flora waved a hand and said, "Rosie don't need to pay, she's family." Which was actually true; Flora and Vie were second cousins of my father, Levi Small, and for that reason, they didn't speak to my mother, so I didn't need to worry about news of me visiting a white gentleman out at Hansen Bay getting back to her.

I ordered a Coke because I had to work at five and Russ ordered another rum punch and then together we ordered garlic chicken with rice and beans and johnnycakes. We stuffed our faces and we talked. I told Russ the long story of my relationship with Oscar and then he told me that he was down in the Virgin Islands because he had been offered a job with a hedge fund that was owned and operated by Todd Croft, whom he had known during his college years.

"At Northwestern?" I said, proud of myself for remembering.

"Todd flunked out freshman year but he hung around Winnetka and we had some business dealings."

*I laughed. "*Business *dealings? At eighteen?"*

Russ sighed. "I haven't even told my wife this story…"

"What?"

"Todd had a contact who wanted to sell alcohol to underclassmen in the dorm. My sophomore year, I was an RA—resident adviser—and in exchange for me looking the other way, Todd gave me a cut of his profits."

"Russ!" I said. "I wouldn't have pegged you as a criminal."

"We never got caught," Russ said. "I have a trustworthy face, I guess."

"So I take it Todd has moved on from the smuggling business?" I said.

"High finance," Russ said. "And I mean high. *Todd is an impressive guy, though. He got a job working in one of those*

boiler rooms, calling people cold and encouraging them to invest money…and now his hedge fund is worth nearly three billion dollars."

"No wonder you're going to work for him," I said. "What an opportunity."

"For the past seventeen years, I've worked for the Corn Refiners Association," Russ said. "But the pay is peanuts and my wife, Irene, is unhappy. She keeps a stiff upper lip. She's from some pretty hardy Scandinavian stock, but I can tell she thinks I'm a failure. And most days I'm pretty sure she thinks about leaving me."

"Oh my God," I said. "She would have to be crazy to think about leaving you."

He stared at me a second with a look of utter amazement and something changed between us then. I felt equal parts terrible and triumphant about it, but terrible won out and I didn't even stay for a swim. I plunked down ten bucks for the food, offered Russ my hand, and said, "I wish all visitors to our fair island were like you, Russ. Thank you for your help with Oscar. I will forever be grateful."

Russ held my hand and said, "Stay a little longer, can you?"

"Sorry," I said. "I have some things to take care of before work." My words were rushed and I tripped over a tree root as I hurried off the beach but I had to get out of there before I crossed a line. Though I knew a line had already been crossed. I had sought him out, worn my sexiest outfit, and said the words that I knew he needed to hear. I would like to say this was unwitting, but working in the service industry has given me keen people skills. I could tell that Russell from Iowa City was a people-pleaser and that his wife, Irene, made him feel like a disappointment and that hearing me say he was the opposite would all but make him fall in love.

He was married. Irene was waiting for him back home in Iowa. There were women on St. John—Tessie among them—who thought nothing of sleeping with men who were here on vacation. Tessie routinely had one-night stands with gentlemen who were staying at Caneel by themselves; that was one of the reasons I disliked her.

I was not going to sleep with Russell from Iowa City.

And yet, when I got to work at five o'clock and noticed the yacht was gone, I felt something like sorrow. My hero had left, and I couldn't remember his last name. I would never see him again.

So imagine my surprise when, at seven o'clock, as the hibiscus-pink ball of the sun was sinking into the water and Lucinda Caruso was shooting me a smug glance from the table where her Harvard-educated ass was sitting with her Big Deal parents—a look that I could only assume meant that she had slept with Oscar after all, poor girl—Russ walked across the beach and into the restaurant. I blinked, wondering if it was a trick of the blinding light of the sun just before it set, but then he waved at me and I hurried over. "I thought you left," I said. "The yacht—"

"Todd and Stephen headed over to Virgin Gorda," Russ said. "They have business. I told them I wanted to stay here and mull over their offer. They're coming back Monday to pick me up."

"Stay here on St. John?" I said. I was so happy that he wasn't gone forever that I wasn't quite following.

"At Caneel," Russ said. He pulled a key out of his pocket. "Honeymoon 718."

"How did you manage that?" I asked. "I thought we were full."

"I put the general manager in a headlock," he said.

We laughed. I said, "I'd put you in my section but you'll probably be more comfortable at the bar."

He said, "Bar is fine but I'll miss you bringing me my conch fritters."

I said, "If you think I'm going to let someone else bring you your conch fritters, you're crazy."

He gave me a look then that was so long and deep, my legs grew weak and my face grew hot and never in my life had I been more aware that I was a human being—powerful and fallible.

Part Two

Lawyers, Guns, and Money

IRENE

She drives Cash and Winnie to the airport in Cedar Rapids. From Cedar Rapids, they will fly to Chicago, and from Chicago to St. Thomas. Irene is tempted to tell Cash that she received her own job offer on St. John but he's so excited about getting back down there that Irene decides not to steal his thunder or distract from his anticipation.

Besides, she isn't at all sure Huck was serious.

Still, it was nice to hear his voice.

Cash's departure turns out to be the impetus Irene needs to get things done. On the way home from Cedar Rapids, she calls Ed Sorley.

"Oh, Irene," he says. "You must have read my mind. I just dug up a photocopy of the check that Russ gave me when we closed on the Church Street house. Turns out, it was a cashier's check drawn on a bank called SGMT in the Cayman Islands."

"The *Cayman* Islands?" Irene says. "Not the Virgin Islands?"

"The Cayman Islands," Ed says. "I double-checked that myself."

"But it cleared, right?" Irene says. "We did actually pay for the house?"

"Yes, yes," Ed says. "I'll try to see if maybe this SGMT has a phone number or a website, but even if it does, it might be difficult to track down. It's a cashier's check, which is almost like Russ showed up at the bank with six hundred grand in cash...but that's obviously impossible."

Is it, though? Irene wonders.

"He might have an account at this bank," Ed says. "I'll try to figure it out."

"Thank you, Ed," Irene says.

She hangs up and calls Paulette Vickers. Paulette is out of the office—is Paulette ever *in* the office? Irene wonders—and so Irene leaves a voicemail.

"Paulette, it's Irene Steele," she says. "I need a copy of Russ's death certificate. I can't do anything without it. My attorney said that until it's issued, Russ is technically still alive." Irene gives a weak laugh and flashes back to her dream about the chickens. "So if you would please send me a certified copy, I would greatly appreciate it. That's apparently what I need. You have my address and if there's a fee, I'm happy to send a check, or maybe you can take it out of your operating account for the villa." Irene pauses. "Thank you, Paulette. If this is an issue, please call me back."

Irene hangs up and thinks, *Please don't call me back. Just send the death certificate.* Paulette's husband, Douglas Vickers, was the one who identified Russ's body and delivered his ashes to Irene. He's her only hope of getting this documentation.

She feels a small sense of accomplishment—*really* small, because she has learned nothing except that Russ apparently had a relationship with a bank in the Cayman Islands. Irene doesn't have the foggiest idea where the Cayman Islands are. If she were to visit, would she find that Russ also has a mistress and child there? She laughs at the absurdity of the thought—and yet, it's not out of the question!

The road home from the airport brings Irene perilously close to the offices of the magazine *Heartland Home and Style,* her place of employment. Irene hasn't been to work in three weeks. She has two voicemails from Mavis Key on her cell phone; in the second of these, Mavis announced that she "did a little detective work" and learned that Milly had passed away—which, Mavis assumed, was the reason for Irene's "extended absence." Mavis offered her condolences, then asked if Irene would prefer the magazine to send flowers or donate to a particular cause.

Irene had ignored the message. She didn't want to think about work.

But she can't ignore it forever. Impulsively, Irene turns into the parking lot of the magazine and pulls into her spot. Already the signage has been changed to read EXECUTIVE EDITOR. She cuts the engine and checks her appearance in the rearview. Her hair is braided, her bangs long but not ratty. She's not wearing any makeup but she still has a little bit of color on her nose and across her cheeks from the sun in St. John.

In she goes.

The first person she sees is the magazine's receptionist, Jayne. Jayne decorates the reception desk herself using the magazine's small slush fund; she follows the lead of all the major retailers and really gets a jump on things. Now that Christmas and New Year's are behind them, Jayne has her area decked out for Valentine's Day. There's an arrangement of red and white carnations on the desk and, next to that, an enormous bowl of candy hearts.

"Irene!" Jayne shrieks. She leaps out of her chair and comes running to give Irene a maternal embrace; Jayne has five children, seventeen grandchildren, a pillowy bosom, and soft downy cheeks.

Irene allows herself to be swallowed up in Jayne's arms and soon the rest of the staff—bored or easily distracted, even though they should be hard at work on the April issue—come trooping out, all filled with joy (or maybe just relief) at Irene's unexpected return.

Happy New Year, we've missed you, is everything okay, we've been so worried, it's not like you to take unscheduled time off, we knew something must be wrong, we heard about your promotion, and then Mavis gave us the news about Milly. God bless you, Irene, she was so lucky to have a daughter-in-law like you.

Bets, from advertising, says, "How's Russ handling it?"

At this, Irene separates herself by an arm's length. She can't lie, but neither can she tell them the truth.

She says, "Is Mavis in her office? I really need to talk with her."

Yes, yes, Mavis is in her office. Jayne takes it upon herself to personally escort Irene up the half-flight of stairs to Mavis's office, which happens to be right next door to Irene's own office, the door of which is shut tight.

Jayne raps on Mavis's door, then swings it open and announces, "Irene is here!" As though Irene is the First Lady of Iowa.

Irene steps in. Mavis is on the phone. Jayne whispers, "Mavis is always on the phone." As if this is Irene's first time in the office, her first time meeting Mavis. "She shouldn't be long. I'll give you two your privacy." And she closes the door.

Mavis is wearing a silk pantsuit in what must be considered winter white. She's not wearing a blouse under the blazer, though Irene spies a peek of lacy camisole. In an office where most of the employees are women and most of those women wear embroidered sweaters or Eileen Fisher *schmattas*, Mavis is a curiosity indeed.

Mavis raises a finger (*One minute!*), then lowers a palm (*Please sit!*). She has decorated her office in eggshell suede and black leather, an aesthetic previously frowned upon as "modern" and "urban" by the executives at *Heartland Home and Style*. Irene helps herself to one of the Italian sparkling waters in Mavis's glass-fronted minifridge. Why not enjoy the pretensions that are on offer?

She decides to remain standing.

Mavis says, "Thanks for your help with this, Bernie. I'll circle back next week." She hangs up. "Irene?"

"Mavis," Irene says. She turns back to make sure that the office door is closed and that Jayne isn't stationed outside with her ear to the glass. "I need to talk to you. Can I trust you to keep what we say confidential?"

The question is rhetorical. Mavis doesn't trade on gossip like the other people in the office because Mavis has invested only her head here, not her heart. She was hired to be a problem-solver and a moneymaker. She's an ice queen, which, under the present circumstances, is a tremendous asset.

Irene lets it all out as concisely as possible: Russ has been killed in a helicopter crash in the Virgin Islands; Irene's trip down to St. John with the boys revealed evidence of a second life—an expensive villa, a mistress (also dead), a twelve-year-old daughter. Russ's body was identified and cremated before Irene arrived. Russ's boss, Todd Croft, the apparent puppet master of this whole grotesque theater, can't be reached, and the business's website is down.

"I'm...I'm speechless," Mavis says. "Your *husband* is dead? He had a secret *life?*"

Irene blinks.

"I'm sure you don't want to go into the gritty details. Who can blame you. But...wow. I thought maybe you were angry about your new role here."

"Oh, I was," Irene says. "But then all this happened and..." She studies the bottle of fancy water in her hands because it gives her something to do other than cry.

"Irene," Mavis says. "What can I do to help?"

"I'm giving you my notice," Irene says. "I can't come back to work. I thought maybe, with time...but no." Irene sighs. "I'm not even sure I'll stay in Iowa City."

"What?" Mavis says. "What about your house?"

Irene shrugs. Three weeks ago, leaving behind the house would have been *unthinkable*. That house took six years of her life to complete; it's a work of art. Now, of course, Irene sees how blindly devoted she was to the project, how she sweated over the details and completely ignored her marriage. It's entirely possible that Irene had been standing at her workspace in the kitchen poring over four choices of wallpaper for the third upstairs bath and Russ had come to her and said, *Honey, I have a lover in the Virgin Islands and I've fathered a daughter,* and Irene had said, *That's great, honey.*

What Russ did was wrong. But Irene is not blameless.

"You know, I've been to St. John," Mavis says. "I stayed at the Westin with my parents. It's beautiful."

"I'd like you to pass my resignation on to Joseph," Irene says. "I'll call him myself eventually, but right now..."

Mavis waves a hand. "I got it. Consider it handled."

"And would you smooth things over with the rest of the staff?"

"I certainly will," Mavis says. "They'll all miss you, of course. And they'll assume it's my fault you're leaving. The good news is I don't think they can hate me any more than they already do."

"They're midwesterners," Irene says. "A bit resistant to change."

"You think?" Mavis says. "I tried to win them over with team building—lunches at Formosa, happy hour at the Clinton Street Social Club—but I'm pretty sure they talk about me behind my back the second I pick up the check."

"At least they see you," Irene says.

Mavis cocks her head. She's not pretty, exactly, but she's young, strong, and vibrant. She has presence. But someday, Mavis Key, too, will find herself leaving less of an impression. She'll be overlooked, shuffled aside, forgotten.

Or maybe Irene is just bitter. She tries to regain the feeling she had as she stood on the bow of Huck's boat, but it's gone. She wants to go back down to the islands, she realizes then, if only so she can feel *seen* again.

"I'll come back for my things another time," Irene says. "On a Saturday. Or after hours."

Mavis says, "Whatever you need, Irene. Please ask me." She opens her arms and Irene allows herself to be hugged. "I hope you figure this out."

"Me too," Irene says.

Back at home, Irene sits at the kitchen table with her list in front of her. *Death certificates*—being pursued. *Resignation*—tendered.

Obituary. Irene flips to the next page of her notebook and writes, *Russell Steele died Tuesday, January 1. He is survived by his wife of thirty-five years, Irene Hagen Steele, and his sons, Baker and Cashman Steele.*

Is that all? Irene can't mention his job at Ascension. She could maybe say that he worked for the Corn Refiners Association for two decades. She could mention Rotary Club and his years of service to the Iowa City school board.

She drops her pen, picks up her phone. She sends a text to her best friend, Dr. Lydia Christensen.

Lydia, the first text says.

Irene feels like she's falling backward in one of those Outward Bound games where you're supposed to trust your comrades to catch you.

Russ is dead. He died on New Year's Day but I didn't find out until I got home from our dinner. The circumstances were so extraordinary and, honestly, so baffling that I didn't know how to tell you or anyone else. I'll call you later, I promise.

Irene presses Send.

Okay, she thinks. It's officially out in the world. Unlike Mavis, Lydia is not a vault.

A little while later, the doorbell rings. The doorbell is an antique, salvaged from a convent in Vicenza, Italy, and it makes quite a formal sound, somewhere between a gong and cathedral bells. Irene hurries down the hallway, hoping and praying it's FedEx with the death certificates but knowing that, unless Paulette read Irene's mind before she left the voicemail, that's logistically impossible. It might be Lydia, though Lydia normally flings open the door and walks right in. Maybe Lydia called the Dunns and the Kinseys and this is the start of the onslaught. Bobbi Kinsey will have pulled a casserole from her freezer or stopped by the Hy-Vee for a deli tray.

Irene pauses before opening the door and takes a sustaining breath. She'll tell people the truth—helicopter crash, Virgin Islands, work, but leave out the villa, the mistress, and Maia.

Strong, beautiful Maia.

Irene opens the door. It's not Lydia, and it's not Bobbi. It's four men in dark suits, trench coats, and impractical shoes for the weather. The man in front—African-American, tall and broad, with a grim facial expression—flashes a badge.

"Irene Steele?" he says.

Irene is so stunned, she can't speak. Is she being arrested?

"Are you Irene Steele?" the man says. "Is this the Steele residence?" He glances above the door frame, then down toward the corner of Linn. "Thirty Church Street?"

Irene nods. "Yes, it is. I am."

"Agent Kenneth Beckett, FBI, white-collar crime division. We have a search warrant for this address. If you'll kindly step aside."

White-collar crime. Irene steps aside.

Three of the agents start searching the house. Irene's instinct is to follow them—not to hide anything but to make sure they're careful with her things. However, Agent Beckett wants to talk to Irene in private. She leads him to the amethyst parlor. It's chilly and she offers to lay a fire.

"Just please sit down, Mrs. Steele," Agent Beckett says. He's stern and serious, like an FBI agent on television. Irene notices a black and gold knit cap sticking out of his briefcase.

"Iowa grad?" she asks. "I'm the class of '84."

"Class of '91," Beckett says. For a second, his eyes smile. "Go Hawks."

"They aren't going to break anything, are they?" Irene asks. "This house... well, it took me six years to renovate and the antiques are real. There's a mural in the dining room; the moldings and trim have all been restored to period. The carpets..." She stares down at Beckett's wet and icy wingtips on the Queen Victoria jewel-box carpet. "They'll be careful, right? Respectful?"

Quick nod. "We're professionals."

"Of course."

"Your husband was Russell Steele?" Beckett says. "Died January first in a helicopter crash off the coast of Virgin Gorda?"

"Yes."

"And what did your husband do for a living, Mrs. Steele?"

Irene briefly wonders if she needs a lawyer present. She tries to imagine Ed Sorley in his sweater-vest dealing with these gentlemen. The idea is nearly laughable.

The fact is, *Irene* has done nothing wrong. *Irene* has nothing to hide.

"He worked for a hedge fund called Ascension," Irene says.

"What was his position there?"

"My understanding was that he was in customer relations."

Beckett looks up. "Customer relations."

"Not like he answered the phone and took complaints," Irene says. "He wined and dined the clients, played golf, a lot of golf, made them comfortable. Russ was a very... *nice* guy. Nonthreatening, friendly, engaging. He told a lot of corny jokes, asked to see pictures of your kids, remembered their names." Irene had been jealous, at times, of how good with people Russ was, how generous with his attention. All of their friends and acquaintances liked Russ better than her. And that was fine, Irene understood; they had their roles. Irene let Russ do the talking because he liked it and she didn't. She enjoyed quieter things—reading novels, cooking, nurturing one-on-one friendships, achieving goals in a timely and organized fashion, whether it was renovating a room in this house or putting an issue of the magazine to bed. She enjoyed fishing, the peace of being out on the water with a single simple mission.

Why is she thinking about fishing?

Well, she knows why.

"And where is this company, Ascension, based?" Beckett asks.

"Miami?" Irene says. "I'm not sure, though. Russ did a lot of traveling for work. He told me he was in Florida, Texas..."

"*Told* you?" Beckett says.

"Yes," Irene says. "But I now have reason to believe he spent most of his time in the Virgin Islands. In St. John."

Beckett scratches down a note.

"You know my husband owns property in St. John."

"Yes," Beckett says. "Federal agents are searching that house now."

"Oh, dear," Irene says.

Beckett looks up. "What?"

"I put my son Cash on a plane to St. Thomas this morning," Irene says. "He'll arrive at the house in St. John sometime tonight."

Beckett nods. "They should be finished with the search by then."

"But if they're not?"

"They'll let him know and he can make other arrangements."

Huck, Irene thinks. *Maybe he can stay with Huck for a night or two.* Which is a crazy thought. Huck isn't *family;* he's merely a sort of friend.

"I guess I'm confused about what you're after. Is this part of the investigation about the helicopter?"

"Possibly related," Beckett says. "Do you know a man named Todd Croft?"

"Russ's boss," Irene says. "I met him once, December 2005, in the lobby of the Drake Hotel in Chicago. That was right before he offered Russ the job at Ascension. They knew each other at Northwestern. Or at least, that's what Russ said."

"Do you have contact information for Mr. Croft?" Beckett asks.

"I don't. Mr. Croft's secretary, Marilyn Monroe, called here on the night of January first to tell me Russ had died. I've tried calling her back since then but that number has been disconnected and the Ascension website is down."

Beckett says, "Your husband made quite a good living, isn't that right?"

"Yes," Irene says. "After he took the job with Ascension."

"This house must have been expensive to renovate."

"It was."

"And how did you think your husband was earning so much money?"

"He worked at a hedge fund," Irene says. "And I thought that provided a good salary. I didn't know about St. John. I didn't know about the other house..."

"You went down there recently, though? After he died?"

"Yes. That was my first time. We went for a week and returned home last Friday. My mother-in-law, Russ's mother, was failing. Now she's passed away so I have that to deal with."

"I'm sorry," Beckett says. He looks at her again, this time more sympathetically.

"Would you like some tea, Agent Beckett?"

"No, but thank you."

"*I'd* like some tea," Irene says. "Is it all right if we go into the kitchen so I can make some? I mean, I'm free to move around the house, right?"

"Just stay where we can see you," Agent Beckett says. He rests his hands on his thighs and pushes himself to a stand. "Actually, some tea might warm me up."

Irene makes a pot of Lady Grey, and while she's at it, she prepares a tray of sandwiches and rinses two bunches of grapes. Agent Beckett accepts a ham and cheese and a cup of tea. An agent who looks like Tom Selleck pops into the kitchen to report that they have found nothing.

"Did you remove or destroy any of your husband's papers or personal belongings after he died?" Beckett asks.

"I did not," Irene says. "I searched through both this house and the house on St. John, looking for clues."

"Clues?"

"What he was into," Irene says. "Certainly, Agent Beckett, you realize that I think all this is suspicious as well. My husband was killed in a place I didn't know he was visiting, then I found out he *lived* there. He owned *property* there. I was looking for answers."

"What did you find?"

A mistress, Irene thinks. *A love child.* "Nothing," she says.

The youngest agent—a baby-faced ginger—pokes his head into the kitchen. "Nothing in the master bed or bath," he says. He eyes the tray of sandwiches. "Are those for everyone?"

"Help yourself," Irene says. Then she thinks of something! A hiding place! She looks at Beckett, who is reviewing his notes as he eats his ham and cheese.

No, she won't tell them. Maybe they'll find it. Maybe they won't.

Irene wonders if this investigation can work both ways. "I called my real estate contact in St. John to request a death certificate." She blows across the surface of her tea. "My family attorney here says that until I produce it, Russ is technically still alive." She pauses, waiting for a reaction, but none comes. "Which would be quite something, because we've already scattered the ashes. Or what we thought were Russ's ashes. I never saw the body and I wasn't consulted about the cremation until after it was a done deal. Is there any chance... I mean, do you think my husband might still be alive?"

Beckett stands up to secure the door to the hallway and then the door to the dining room. "You've been very accommodating," he says. "And we appreciate it. I'm sure you realize that we're here because we have reason to believe your husband had illegal business dealings. The one thing I *can* assure you"—Agent Beckett holds Irene's gaze—"is that your husband is dead."

"He is," Irene says. Yes, he is, she knows this. She has been processing this news for over two weeks. And yet hearing Beckett say the words comes as a fresh shock. Irene's eyes sting with tears. The dreams were just that—dreams—but Irene must have been hanging on to a thread of hope. None of this added up. From the beginning, it felt like a hoax. The person who told Irene that Russ was dead—Marilyn Monroe—wasn't someone Irene had ever met face to face. Paulette had been professional to the point of seeming insensitive, nearly as if she was just going through the motions because she knew Russ would turn up eventually. "You're sure?"

"Yes," Beckett says. He must have definitive proof, Irene

thinks, but he isn't sharing it. "We're going to need your cell phone and your computer. They'll both be returned to you."

"Yes, of course," Irene says. She pulls her cell phone out of her purse just as it lights up and starts chiming with a call from Lydia. Of course it's Lydia. Irene hits Decline and hands it over. She nods at her laptop on the desk in the corner. "When you say my husband had illegal business dealings, you mean *Ascension* had illegal business dealings, right? *Todd Croft* had illegal business dealings. I can tell you right now that Russ just wasn't the kind of person who would—" She notices the expression on Agent Beckett's face and stops talking. Russ wasn't the kind of person who would...what? Have a mistress, a secret daughter, and a nine-bedroom villa down in the Caribbean? It's pretty clear that Irene doesn't know what kind of person Russ was. She is as clueless as Ruth Madoff was. Irene remembers back when that news story broke. She had thought, *Of course the wife knew her husband was running a bazillion-dollar Ponzi scheme. How could she* not *know?* But now that Irene is in a similar situation, she's certain Mrs. Madoff had no idea what was going on. She probably spent all her time at the club lunching with her friends and meeting with her personal shopper. And if Ruth Madoff—or Irene—had asked her husband questions about his business, who's to say either woman would have been told the truth?

Irene, for one, hadn't asked any questions. She had happily accepted the money Russ deposited into her renovation account and turned her attention to wallpaper and crown molding. "Are you looking for Todd Croft?"

Barely a nod from Beckett. "Not at liberty to say."

Yes; the answer was yes. "He's drinking a daiquiri on some remote island without a name," Irene says.

"That actually happens less than one would imagine," Beckett says. "Men like Todd Croft can't just drop out of society. They're too power hungry." Beckett pops the last bite of sandwich into his mouth and polishes off his tea. "Don't worry. He'll turn up."

"I did learn two things on my own," Irene says, "that you might find helpful." She's hesitant to hand over what she knows, but Russ's words have taken root inside of her. *Irene is the only person I trust to do the right thing.* He probably meant the right thing for Rosie and Maia but he most certainly also meant the right thing morally, which was to cooperate with the FBI, tell the truth, preserve her own integrity, protect the boys. "We have a bank account at Federal Republic. I have a statement I can give you. And the teller informed me that Russ made the last two deposits of seventy-five hundred dollars apiece...in cash." Irene searches Agent Beckett's face to see if this news startles him as much as it startled her, but he doesn't even blink. Of course, he's in the FBI. He has seen...Irene can't even imagine what. "And I asked my attorney, Ed, Edward Sorley, to find the account that Russ used to pay for this house when we bought it. He has a copy of a cashier's check drawn on a bank—MGST or something like that—in the Cayman Islands."

Agent Beckett's left eyebrow lifts a fraction of an inch. "Sounds about right," he says. "Would you give me Mr. Sorley's contact information, please?"

The FBI agents leave at eight thirty that night. As they're finally heading out the door—with far less evidence than they anticipated, Irene can tell by their dejected demeanors—she suggests that they go to the Wig and Pen for dinner.

"Great wings," she says. "My mother-in-law..." But she can't finish the sentence.

Agent Beckett shakes her hand. "Thank you for your help today."

Irene finds herself uncharacteristically craving validation. She *was* helpful, right? They're aware from how cooperative and accommodating she's been, from the details she's shared, and from her general demeanor that she had no idea what Russ was involved with. *She* is innocent. She should not be held accountable—and yet she fears that she'll see these men again storming her house in the predawn hours with a warrant for her arrest.

Their visit today has taken its toll; she's scared.

"Will you be back tomorrow?" she asks.

"Someone will be by to drop off your phone and your computer," he says. "Here's my card. Don't hesitate to call if you think of anything else you want to tell us."

Irene waits ten minutes, then fifteen. When she's positive the agents are not coming back, she snaps off the porch light and heads for the library.

The house phone rings, startling her.

Should she answer?

It's probably Cash, wondering why she isn't answering her cell phone. *Well, honey, the FBI has it...*

"Irene?"

"Lydia," Irene says. She carries the phone into the library, where she snaps on the Tiffany lamp and collapses in her favorite reading chair. "Hi."

"I got your texts," Lydia says. "But then you didn't answer

when I called. You can't...be serious? Russ is not dead! You would have told me right away if you'd found out he was dead. It was just hyperbole, right? You wish he were dead. What did he do wrong? He was away somewhere, right?"

"The Virgin Islands," Irene says. The conversation feels like a hill she doesn't want to climb.

"The...where? Did you *tell* me Russ was in the Virgin Islands? You *didn't* tell me that. I would have remembered."

Irene closes her eyes. This is just as excruciating as she feared it would be. She has made things far worse by waiting for so long. Lydia doesn't believe her; Irene should have called her right away. Irene should have brought her—or someone—in at the beginning. But she hadn't. It had been so sudden and so bizarre, so inexplicable. It was *still inexplicable*—and yet, here they are.

"Lydia," Irene says. "Russ is dead. He was killed in a helicopter crash in the Virgin Islands on January first. He was there on business. The rest of the details are too painful to share right now. His body was cremated and the boys and I flew down to scatter his ashes."

"What?" Lydia shouts. There's a muffled voice in the background. "Brandon and I are on our way over right now."

"No," Irene says. "Please, I was just heading up to bed. We'll talk tomorrow, I promise." She thinks for a second. "Brandon who?"

"Brandon the barista," Lydia says. "We're dating. We've been dating since...that night."

Irene supposes it's too late to ask Lydia to keep the news of Russ's death to herself. "I'll call you tomorrow, really. I...I have to go."

"Okay," Lydia says. She sounds put out, and then she starts

to cry. "I'm so sorry, Irene. I'm sure you're destroyed. Russ was...well, you know he was the most devoted husband."

Wasn't he just, Irene thinks. "Good night, Lydia." She punches off the phone, sighs deeply, then turns her attention to the library shelves. Three shelves in from the right, three shelves down from the ceiling, Irene finds the *Oxford English Dictionary* that she lugged to college, *Roget's Thesaurus,* and *Bartlett's Familiar Quotations* in a solid, scholarly stack. She moves the three massive tomes onto the brocade sofa and slides the panel out of the back of the shelf to reveal a secret compartment. And voilà! There's a manila envelope, stuffed full.

Irene had forgotten all about the secret compartment until she started thinking about hiding places. The secret compartment had been original to this room, and even though the library had undergone a complete overhaul, Russ had insisted the compartment stay. It added character and history—they agreed it had probably been used to hide alcohol during Prohibition. It was one of the only aspects of the house Russ had taken a personal interest in.

What will we hide in there? Irene had asked.

Love notes, he'd said.

She remembers that, clear as day. *Love notes.*

She pulls out the manila envelope and empties the contents onto the coffee table. It's a stack of postcards secured with a rubber band. For one second, Irene holds out hope that the postcards are family heirlooms, maybe the correspondence that Milly conducted with Russ's father while he was away in the navy. But once she wrangles the rubber band off, she sees the pictures on the postcards are all of St. John—Cinnamon Bay, Maho Bay, Francis Bay, Hansen Bay.

None of the cards is addressed. On the back of each is a

short, simple message. *I love you. I'll miss you. You are my heart. I'll be here waiting. I love you. I love you. I love you.* All of them are signed with the initials *M.L.*

M.L.? Not Rosie? She thinks of Maia, but these notes feel, almost certainly, like declarations of romantic love. So they have to be from Rosie. M.L. must be a nickname.

These are the love notes Russ was talking about then, years earlier, when he insisted they keep this compartment.

Irene feels a wave of anger and disgust—he kept these *in the house!*—but she also feels implicated. If she had to guess, she would say Rosie tucked these cards into Russ's luggage for him to find once he'd arrived home. Or maybe she slipped them into his jacket pocket as he was leaving. Instead of throwing them away, as Russ certainly knew he should, he'd kept them. He'd wanted—or needed—to save this proof that someone loved him because so little love was shown to him at home.

Irene has heard that love is a garden that needs to be tended. And what had Irene thought about that? She had thought it was sentimental nonsense, the stuff of sappy Hallmark cards. Love, for Irene, was a daily act—steadfastness, loyalty, devotion. It was raising the boys, creating a beautiful, comfortable home, stopping by to see Milly three times a week because Russ was too busy to do it himself. It was ironing Russ's shirts, making his oatmeal with raisins the way he liked it, taking his Audi to the car wash so it was gleaming when he returned from his trips.

She tosses the postcards in the air and they scatter. She would like to burn them in one of her six fireplaces; nothing would give her greater satisfaction than watching Rosie's declarations of love for Russ curl, blacken, and go up in smoke.

Forgiveness, she thinks. She will save the postcards and give them to Maia someday.

She picks up the landline and dials, and Huck answers on the first ring. "Hello," he says. "Who's calling me from Iowa City?"

"It's me," Irene says, which she knows is presumptive. They haven't been friends long enough for her to be "me."

"Hello, you," he says, and she feels better. "What's up?"

What should Irene tell him first? That she spent all day with the FBI? Or that she found an illicit cache of postcards from his stepdaughter to her husband?

"Adam leaves a week from Tuesday?" she says.

"Yep," Huck says.

"All right," Irene says. "I guess that means I'll be down a week from Monday."

"You serious?" Huck says. She hears him exhale, presumably smoke. "Angler Cupcake, you serious?"

She squeezes her eyes shut. "Yes," she says.

AYERS

You're hiding something," Mick says. It's one of their rare nights off together and they're having dinner at the bar at Ocean 362, where they can watch the sun set. Ayers spent the afternoon on Salomon Bay by herself; Mick asked to come along but Ayers said she wanted to be alone. It was important, this time around, to preserve her me-time.

I want to lie in the sun and think about Rosie, she said.

You can think about Rosie with me right next to you, Mick said. *You can even talk about Rosie. I'll listen.*

It's not the same, Ayers said. *You'll distract me.* What she didn't tell Mick, couldn't tell him, was that she needed time to read Rosie's journals. She had made it from the year 2000—Rosie at age seventeen—all the way through her tumultuous relationship with Oscar to the weekend in 2006 when she met Russ. Ayers was just getting to the good stuff, the important stuff—but it was tricky, finding blocks of time to read.

"If you're suspicious," Ayers says now, "it's probably because of your own guilty conscience." She digs into the walnut-crusted Roquefort cheesecake.

"What?" he says.

"Don't act offended," Ayers says. She lowers her voice because the bartender, Alex, is a friend of theirs and she doesn't want him to hear them squabbling. "We agreed we wouldn't dance around the topic of your infidelity. We agreed you would own it and that I was free to bring it up at any time."

"Within reason. We said 'within reason.' "

"You're accusing me of hiding something," Ayers says. "Meanwhile, you haven't even fired Brigid."

"I can't fire her just because we broke up," Mick says. "That's against the law." He pulls his phone out because the sun is going down and one of Mick's passions is photographing the sunset every night, then posting it on Instagram as #sunset, #sunsetpics, #sunsetlover. Ayers has forgotten how this annoys her. She enjoys a good sunset as much as the next person, but she finds pictures of the sunset #overdone.

"You can fire her because she's a terrible server," Ayers says. "She's the worst server I've ever seen."

"You're biased."

Ayers carefully constructs a bite: a slice of toasted baguette smeared with the Roquefort topped with the accompanying shallot and garlic confit. "How do you think I feel knowing that she's right there under your nose every single night? The answer is: not great. But do I complain? Do I sniff your clothes or show up at the restaurant unannounced? No. Do I *accuse* you of hiding something? I do not."

"You're right," Mick says. He's distracted by his sunset posting. "I'm sorry."

Ayers lets the topic drop because guess what—she *is* hiding something! She's obsessed with Rosie's journals, and she isn't using that word cavalierly like the rest of the world now does ("I'm obsessed with AOC's lipstick" or "mango with chili salt" or " 'Seven Rings' by Ariana Grande"). If Ayers didn't have two jobs and a boyfriend, she would lock herself in a room and binge on the journals until she had the whole story—but there is pleasure to be had in pacing herself. Read, then process.

Of course, it's more difficult to hold back now that Russ has entered the picture.

Ayers and Mick finish dinner and decide to end the evening by going to La Tapa for a nightcap. To an outsider, it might seem pathetic that Ayers can't stay away from her place of employment on her night off, but the fact is, La Tapa is her home and her coworkers are her family. Skip and Tilda finally hooked up—they've been circling each other since October—and Tilda told Ayers that for three days straight, they did nothing but drink Schramsberg, eat mango with chili salt, and have wild sex. But on the fourth day, Tilda woke up at Skip's place and wondered what the hell she was doing there.

It was like the fever broke, Tilda whispered to Ayers as they polished glasses before service. *I'm over him. In fact, looking at him makes me feel kind of sick.*

Human nature being what it is, when Tilda's enthusiasm

cooled, Skip's grew more intense, and Tilda confided to Ayers—yes, somehow Ayers and Tilda were becoming confidantes—that Skip followed her home to her parents' villa one night after work. (Tilda's parents are quite wealthy and have a home in Peter Bay. Tilda doesn't *have* to work at La Tapa but she's determined not to "play the role of entitled rich kid," so she hammers out four shifts a week and also volunteers at the Animal Care Center, walking rescue dogs. The more Ayers learns about Tilda's life outside of work, the harder it is not to admire and even like her.) When Tilda explained to Skip in her parents' driveway—she was *not* about to invite Skip in—that she thought maybe they had gotten too close too quickly, Skip had started to *cry*.

Now, apparently, he's venting his anger at the restaurant during service; he's been acting erratically with the customers.

And sure enough, after Ayers and Mick claim two seats at the bar and order Ayers's favorite sipping tequila, Ayers overhears Skip describing a bottle of Malbec for the couple sitting a few stools away like this: "This wine is a personal favorite of mine," Skip says. "It has hints of hashish, old piñata candy, and the tears of cloistered nuns."

"What?" the woman says. "No, thank you!"

Ayers waves Skip over. "You okay?"

"Great, Ayers, yeah," Skip says, scowling. "Seriously, never better." He looks over Ayers's shoulder and his expression changes. "Hey, man, how're you doing? Good to see you! It's...it's...I'm sorry, bud, I've forgotten your name."

"Cash," a voice says.

Ayers whips around. "Cash!" she says. She hops off her stool. It's Cash Steele, here at La Tapa! Ayers remembers too late that she's angry with him. She finds that she's happy, really happy, to see him. She inadvertently checks behind him to see if maybe Baker followed him in.

No. But Ayers finds her heart bouncing around at the prospect of his being here.

"Hey, Ayers," Cash says. He offers Skip a hand across the bar. "Good to see you, man. Just got in on the ferry. I'm starving. Can I get an order of mussels and the bread with three sauces?"

"You got it, Cash," Skip says.

Cash eyes the stool next to Ayers. "This taken?"

Mick clears his throat. Ayers says, "No, no, sit, please. Cash, this is…Mick. And Mick, this is Cash Steele."

Mick raises his tequila and slams back the whole thing. Cash nods in response.

"So what are you doing here?" Ayers asks. "I thought you guys went back to your lives in America." Which is how it always happens, she thinks. Which is why she doesn't date tourists.

"My life in America kind of fell apart," Cash says. "So that text you sent me was pure serendipity."

On the other side of Ayers, Mick sounds like he's choking. Ayers watches Skip set a glass of water in front of him.

"Text?" Ayers says, though she knows exactly what Cash is talking about.

"About the job on *Treasure Island,*" Cash says. "Have you filled it?"

"Uh…no," Ayers says. "We haven't. We're pretty desperate, actually. Wade leaves in another week."

Cash slaps some paperwork down on the bar. "I can fast-track my lifesaving certification," he says. "I should be good to go in another week."

"Seriously?" Ayers says. "You want the job on *Treasure Island*?"

"I'd love it," Cash says.

Ayers hears Mick muttering on the other side of her. She would be lying if she said she wasn't taking some satisfaction in his discomfort. She must be angrier at him than she realized.

"Cash!"

Tilda swoops in and throws her arms around Cash's neck, then gives him a juicy kiss on the cheek.

"Hey, Tilda," Cash says.

Across the bar, Skip holds Cash's order of bread with three sauces. He glares at Tilda and Cash, then comes just short of slamming the plate down.

"I thought you were in Colorado!" Tilda says. "I've been trying to figure out how to tell my parents that I'm taking a trip to Breckenridge to ski with you."

"No Breck for the foreseeable future," Cash says. "I'm moving down here. And hopefully working on *Treasure Island* with Ayers."

" 'Working on *Treasure Island* with Ayers,' " Mick mimics under his breath.

"Moving down here?" Tilda says. "That's hot."

Skip huffs. "Hot?" he says. "Get back to work, Tilda."

Tilda appears unfazed. "Call me later," she says to Cash. She sashays off to give table eight dessert menus.

Ayers says, "I didn't realize you knew Tilda."

"You sound jealous," Mick murmurs. "How about you let lover boy eat his bread and we get out of here?"

"She gave me a ride home when I was here the last time," Cash says. "She's cool."

"She's *taken,*" Skip says. He's holding Cash's mussels and looks like he might dump them over Cash's head.

"She's *not* taken," Ayers says. She waves Skip away. "Get back to work yourself."

"You're not my boss," Skip says.

Mick stands up. "I'm going home. Are you coming?"

Ayers looks from Cash to Mick. It's a standoff, she realizes. To Cash she says, "Hey, I'm picking up Maia tomorrow morning and we're hiking from Leicester Bay to Brown Bay, then swimming after. Do you want to join us?"

"Do you think Maia would mind?" Cash asks.

"Are you kidding me? She'd love it."

"I'm in," Cash says. "I have Winnie with me. She's tied up outside."

"Winnie!" Ayers says. "This is so great! I'll text you in the morning. How are you getting to the villa? I mean, we can wait until you're finished and give you a ride."

"No, we can't," Mick says. "We have to get home. I have work tomorrow."

"At four o'clock," Ayers says. "Chill."

"Don't tell me to chill," Mick says. "Please."

"No problem," Cash says. "I'll see if Tilda can give me a ride home. If not, I'll take a taxi."

Skip leans across the bar. "How are those mussels?" he asks aggressively.

"I'll see you tomorrow," Ayers says. "Welcome back."

Ayers weaves her way out of the restaurant. Mick is already on the sidewalk, lighting a cigarette. Ayers stops to rub Winnie's head. She seems to recognize Ayers; her tail is wagging like crazy.

Mick takes a deep drag of his cigarette, then exhales. "I guess I'm confused. That's Banker's brother, right?"

"Cash. Right."

"And you guys are buddy-buddy as well?"

"Mick, stop."

"You texted him," Mick says. "You told him about the opening on *Treasure Island*."

"That was a Hail Mary," Ayers says. "He came out on *Treasure Island* a few weeks ago, he was good with the guests."

"The plot thickens," Mick says. "Why am I just hearing about this?"

Ayers shrugs. "Why would I have told you? We were broken up."

Angry exhale of smoke.

"You know we need to hire someone who already has a place to live," Ayers says. "Like Cash. And I think he'd be excellent on the boat. Not okay, not good, *excellent*. He likes people. He's a ski instructor—"

"Did you not hear him say his life fell apart?" Mick says. "Doesn't that send up a red flag?"

"His father died, Mick. He found out his father had this whole other life. That's enough to throw anyone into a tailspin."

"Yeah, but wouldn't you think he'd want to stay as far away from here as possible?"

Ayers inhales the night air. There's guitar music floating down from the Quiet Mon. Across the street, the lights twinkle at Extra Virgin Bistro. "I think he came down here and fell in love with the place," she says. "Just like I did. Just like you did."

"As long as he didn't fall in love with you," Mick says. "But who are we kidding? Of course he did. There isn't a woman in Colorado or anywhere else that's as beautiful and sexy and cool as you."

Ayers climbs into Mick's blue Jeep. She's still bothered by

the memory of Brigid sitting in this seat. "Honestly, I barely know him."

"And yet you invited him hiking with you and Maia tomorrow. You didn't invite me; you invited Money."

"Cash," Ayers says, trying not to smile. Mick is good with nicknames and it'll be hard for her now not to think of Baker and Cash as *Banker* and *Money*. "You don't like hiking. And I'll point out that Cash is Maia's brother."

"Half brother."

"Whatever. He and Baker are Maia's only blood relatives, aside from whoever is left on Rosie's father's side."

"I don't want you hiking with him."

"You don't have any say."

"But we're in a relationship," Mick says.

"We're dating. You don't own me. I'm sorry that you don't like it. I don't like it that Brigid still works for you. I didn't like driving down to the Beach Bar at three o'clock in the morning and seeing you—"

"Stop," Mick says.

"I'm going hiking with Cash and Maia," Ayers says. "And Winnie!"

"Great," Mick says. "You're cheating on Gordon as well."

"Just drive," Ayers says. She leans back in the seat, marveling at the unexpected turn the night has taken and how buoyant she now feels. Mick is jealous, but Ayers doesn't care. Cash is here—and tomorrow, Ayers will ask him about Baker.

CASH

His mother called to tell him about her visit from the FBI, so Cash isn't surprised when the taxi turns onto his father's road and he sees a dark SUV parked in one of the dummy driveways.

They're watching the house. Well, he can't blame them.

It's been nearly three weeks since he left. The villa seems basically the same, although Cash can tell things have been gone through. The bed in the guest room he used last time has been hastily made and all of the drawers in the adjacent bath are ajar. Cash does a quick check of the house and this seems to be the case throughout. Irene said they found nothing at the house in Iowa City and Cash imagines the same is true here. There was very little of a personal nature in this house to begin with. When they arrived the first time, reeling from the news of Russ's death, it seemed more like a hotel than someone's house.

It feels good, though, to have the place to himself. It feels better than good; it feels luxurious. Cash stands out on the deck bare-chested while Winnie goes nuts sniffing everything and chasing after geckos. Cash gazes down the lush, leafy hill over the moon-spangled water. He's king of the castle! He wants to howl, he wants to sing. The villa is his!

His exultation is tied to seeing Ayers. He wondered if he'd built her up in his mind—but when he saw her from behind, her curly blond hair hanging loose and crazy down her back and the silhouette of her body in that halter top and white jeans, he felt like he was being swallowed up. She had been so happy to see him, happier than he would have predicted, and she had seemed nearly jealous when Tilda came over to give Cash a hug. The interaction had been great, great, great, everything Cash could have dreamed of.

Today was the first day of the rest of his life, Cash thinks. It's a tired phrase—and yet so true, so true! He has never been more certain of anything: his life began today. He swung down here on a slender filament of hope that a potential job on *Treasure Island* offered and now it looks like it will all work out.

He wants to beat his chest! He has escaped the doom of a lonely winter in Iowa City, shoveling snow and bumping into ex-girlfriends at the grocery store. Tomorrow he has plans with Ayers and Maia, and Monday he starts his lifesaving course, which Irene has given him more than enough money to pay for.

"I'm so happy!" Cash cries out. He wonders if the FBI has bugged the house. Well, if they have, they are going to hear the twenty-nine-year-old son of Russell Steele talking to himself. And maybe it will seem strange or even cruel that Cash is so jubilant only a few short weeks after his father died. Cash misses his father; he's mourning his father, and he's angry and resentful and disappointed in his father. But all of that feels like a pot Cash can pull off the stove for now. His excitement about this island and this girl and this sense of freedom and opportunity win out.

"It's going to be epic!" Cash says. Winnie barks and comes trotting over; she noses around Cash's legs and he bends to rub her soft butterscotch head. "Right, Winnie? Right?"

* * *

The next morning Cash winds his way down the hill in one of his father's gray Jeeps, stops at the black SUV, and rolls down his window. "I'm Cash Steele," he says. "Russell Steele's son."

The man sitting in the front seat—shaved head, blond Hulk Hogan mustache—flexes one of his enormous biceps as he brings a cup of coffee to his lips. "I know," he says.

Cash waits a second, thinking maybe there will be more, but the guy looks down into his lap; he's reading the paper. Cash is the one with questions—who is this guy? Why is he watching the house?—but Cash is certain he'll be stonewalled and he doesn't want to be late, so he carries on.

He meets Ayers and Maia in the parking area on Leicester Bay Road. In Cash's backpack are three towels, nine bottles of water, and three sandwiches from the North Shore Deli. He's wearing trunks under his cargo shorts, his Social Distortion T-shirt, and his lightweight hiking boots. Both girls are standing next to Ayers's green truck, tying bandannas around their foreheads.

"Hey," Cash says as he climbs out of the Jeep. Winnie heads straight for Maia, who crouches down to pet her. Winnie is an excellent ambassador; as always, she smooths over a potentially awkward situation. Cash follows, tentatively offering Maia a fist bump. Ayers said that Maia would be cool with Cash joining them, but will she? Cash knows nothing about the psyches of twelve-year-old girls.

"Hey, bro," Maia says. She bumps knuckles with him, then grins. "You came back! And Ayers tells me you're going to work on *Treasure Island*."

"That's the plan," he says. He glances quickly at Ayers in her white tank and light blue Lululemon running shorts; he can see the outline of a bikini underneath.

"Ayers's boyfriend, Mick, is really jealous," Maia says.

"Maia!" Ayers says. "Hush!"

"What?" Maia says. "He is. He's even jealous we're taking this hike."

"Well, he doesn't need to be jealous," Cash says. "Ayers and I are just friends."

"That's what I told him," Ayers says. She drops her blue aviators down over her eyes. "Are you sure you don't mind carrying the pack? It's got to be heavy."

"Please," Cash says. "I hike at eight, nine thousand feet with a pack that's three times this weight."

"Ayers doesn't like hiking," Maia says. "But she's my parent now, so she has to do enriching things with me."

"Mangrove snorkeling is enriching," Ayers says. She looks up at the brilliant blue sky. "And a far more appropriate activity than hiking on an eighty-degree day."

"Next week," Maia says. She strides toward the trailhead. "Come on, Winnie, let's go."

The Johnny Horn Trail has five spurs, Maia explains. The first spur, a flat, sandy walking path, leads to a narrow beach hugging a bay that has a rugged island a hundred yards offshore.

"Waterlemon Cay," Ayers says. "Best snorkeling on St. John. How about I stay here and you guys keep going?"

"We've only been hiking thirty seconds," Maia says. She turns to Cash. "See what I have to deal with?"

The second spur takes them up a steep, rocky incline that requires a fair amount of scrambling and careful foot placement before it levels out, when they reach stone ruins. This is the guardhouse, Maia tells them, built in the 1840s, back when slavery had been abolished in the British Virgin Islands across the Sir Francis Drake Channel but was still legal on St. John.

"There were sixteen soldiers stationed here," Maia says. "And their job was to keep watch for runaway slaves."

Cash is impressed. "You have quite the body of knowledge," he says. "How did you learn all this?"

"My mom," Maia says. "She knew everything about the Virgin Islands."

Cash nods as the peculiarity of what he's doing hits him. He's hiking with a half sister he never knew he had. Maia bows her head and is quiet and Ayers places a hand on the back of her neck and draws her in. They're thinking about Rosie; Cash can feel how much they miss her. A twelve-year-old girl lost her mother, lost both of her parents, and yet here she is, bravely soldiering on with her mother's best friend and a strange man she has gamely decided to accept as "bro."

"Did your mom like to hike?" Cash asks.

"No," Maia says, and she and Ayers laugh. "She was more like Ayers; she preferred the beach. But, I mean, she brought me up here a few times because she wanted me to experience the place we lived."

"I wish I'd been able to meet your mom," Cash says honestly. More than once over the past couple of weeks, Cash has imagined this whole thing unfolding differently. What if, at some point, Russ had just come clean about his life, said that business had taken him to the Caribbean and he'd met a woman and fallen in love. Cash and Baker would have been furious at first, incredulous, resentful on Irene's behalf. They probably would have refused to speak to Russ for a while. But eventually, Cash suspects, they would have come to terms with the situation and flown down to visit Russ here. They could have met Rosie. It might have taken time, but they could have accepted her as part of the family.

Cash shakes his head. *That* is a trail spur that never was; there's no use dwelling on it.

"Shall we go?" Ayers asks. "Get this over with?"

After the guardhouse, they begin to hit their stride. There's not much canopy cover but even so, Cash finds himself slowing down so he can enjoy just being. His breathing steadies. He reminds himself he doesn't need to be anywhere; he has nothing else to do today. Ayers is here, Maia is here. Ayers is right, it's hot, but just then, the sun disappears behind a cloud, so there's a brief respite.

Maia not only knows history, she is also quite the naturalist. She points out a genip tree—in the summer it produces a fruit similar to a lime. Cash has never heard of it.

"In the summer, I eat elk jerky," Cash says.

Maia shoots him a look. "I'm a vegetarian," she says.

"You are?" Cash says. "Ayers told me to get you a pastrami melt."

"I make an exception for pastrami," Maia says. "And Candi's barbecue."

Maia points out wild tamarind, cassia trees, and something called catch-and-keep, which is a cute name for a nefarious pricker bush. They eventually reach a scenic overlook where each of them—Winnie included—sucks down a bottle of water. Maia points across the way to Jost Van Dyke and Tortola.

After the lookout, the trail heads downhill and it's fully shaded. Everyone seems a little happier.

"So I guess I'll address the elephant in the room," Maia says. "How's your brother?"

Cash isn't sure he's heard right. "Is Baker an elephant?"

"I don't know, Ayers, *is* Baker an elephant?" Maia says.

"Stop being precocious for one minute, please," Ayers says. She turns to Cash and he can see the hopeful expectation in her face, even with her sunglasses on. "How is Baker? He...went back to Houston, I take it? I haven't heard from him."

Cash can't look at her. He concentrates on walking, left foot, then right, steady in his boots, moving down the dirt trail over rocks and around the tentacles of catch-and-keep. Ayers likes Baker. She's hung up on him; Cash can hear it in her voice. He can't *believe* it. He'd met Mick the night before, and Mick is who she's with now, but Cash isn't intimidated by Mick. Mick is ridiculous, a clown, a clown who cheated on Ayers once and who would most certainly do it again.

"I haven't heard from him since our grandmother died a few days after we all got home," Cash says.

"Milly?" Maia says. "The one I look like?"

"Yes," Cash says. He chastises himself for being insensitive. Milly was Maia's grandmother too—how weird is that? "I'm sorry. I should have broken the news in a different way. She was really old. Ninety-nine."

They are all silent for a moment, then Ayers says, "So you don't know if Baker is pursuing a divorce or—"

"No idea," Cash says, cutting her off. "If you're curious about Baker, just call him. You have his number, right?"

"Right," Ayers says.

"Uh-oh," Maia says. "Sounds like somebody needs lunch."

When they reach Brown Bay, Maia shows them a little cemetery. "These are the graves of islanders from long ago," Maia says, which is obvious, as the modest headstones are so old and weathered they're barely legible. "But I kind of wish my mom had been buried here. Look at this view, and it's so peaceful and shady under these trees."

"She would have liked it here," Ayers says.

"Where..." Cash starts. He has no idea where Rosie is buried.

"She's with my grandma in the cemetery in Cruz Bay," Maia says. "Or that's where her body is. Her spirit is wherever spirits go when people die."

They march single file onto a ribbon of white-sand beach. It's completely deserted and the water is a clear, placid turquoise. Cash can't recall ever seeing such inviting water. He shucks off the backpack and strips out of his shirt and shorts. Winnie is already splashing in, barking with joy and, probably, relief. Cash follows and soon he's floating on his back, staring up into the cloudless sky. He hears Maia and Ayers get into the water as well. Cash tries to readjust his frame of mind. He's not going to let his brother ruin a perfectly good day when he's a thousand miles away in Houston.

Cash likes Ayers. Ayers likes Baker. It's a classic like triangle. But Cash has the advantage because Cash is here and Baker isn't. Cash has a further advantage because he will soon be working with Ayers. After spending some time with him, Ayers will realize that he's the superior Steele brother. She'll fall in love. He will, somehow, make her fall in love.

After swimming, he joins Ayers and Maia, who are drying off on a flat rock—Picnic Rock, Maia calls it. Cash passes out the sandwiches and gives Winnie the biscuits he brought. Maia slips Winnie some of her pastrami, which makes her Winnie's new best friend. The silence is companionable, Cash thinks, or maybe it's awkward; he can't tell. It's true that, among the three of them, there are a number of taboo subjects.

"How's Huck?" Cash asks.

"Grouchy," Maia says.

"Yeah?"

"Part of it is that I've started going to town with my friends and he doesn't like it."

"I don't like it either," Ayers says.

"We're just hanging out," Maia says.

"Who's 'we'?" Ayers and Cash say at the same time. They exchange a look and for a second, Cash feels like he and Ayers are Maia's parents instead of her half brother and sort of aunt.

"Me and Joan," Maia says.

"And?" Ayers says.

"And Colton Seeley and Bright Whittaker," Maia says. She licks some mustard off her thumb. "Joan has a crush on Colton."

"And you have a crush on Bright?" Ayers asks.

"No," Maia says. "Bright isn't my type. Plus, he has a crush on Posie Alvarez."

"Do I know Posie?"

"She goes to Antilles," Maia says. "She's friends with a kid named Shane who's a year ahead of us."

"I'm going to take a wild stab in the dark here," Ayers says. "You have a crush on Shane."

Maia shrugs. "I might."

"I can't believe it," Ayers says. "Your first crush! I have to meet this kid. I'm going to come find you guys in town one day before work. And Cash, you have to come with me. This is your little sister. You need to protect her. You need to be a lieutenant in the cause."

Cash opens his mouth but he's unsure of what to say. *Your little sister. You need to protect her.*

The FBI are staking out the house. Russ was conducting illegal business. He likely got Rosie killed. Do Ayers and Maia know this? If they don't know and they find out, will they hate Cash? Isn't it better to prepare for this eventuality and remain aloof?

Cash focuses on Ayers for a second. She's sitting on Picnic Rock, wearing a white bikini and a towel around her waist. Her blond hair is drying in the sun. She takes a bite of her Cuban sandwich, waiting for him to answer.

They won't hate him, he realizes. They know his heart is pure, that he's as bewildered as they are, maybe more so. He's a good guy. He doesn't know a thing about having a "little sister"—both the phrase and the notion are completely foreign to him—but he wants to learn. He wants some good to come out of the choices Russ made. Their relationship—his and Maia's—can be part of that good.

"I would certainly like to meet Shane before this goes any further," he says.

Maia rolls her eyes theatrically, and although Cash knows exactly nothing about twelve-year-old girls, he can tell that beneath the surface of her exasperation, she's grateful. Her mother is gone, but she's not alone. She has Ayers and now she has Cash, and they're here to pay attention. They're here to care about her.

"Just please, *please,* don't tell Huck," Maia says.

"You have my word," Ayers says.

"And mine," Cash says.

"So I told my secret," Maia says. "Now it's your turn. Cash, who do you have a crush on?"

"Okay," Cash says, standing up. "Time to head back." He

whistles for Winnie, who is down on the beach, chasing stray chickens.

He has a crush on Ayers; more than a crush. When they get back to the parking lot, it's difficult to say goodbye. Ayers has to work at La Tapa that night and on *Treasure Island* the next day, and Maia is going fishing with Huck. Then, next week, Maia has school and Cash starts his lifesaving classes. He can begin crewing on *Treasure Island* a week from Sunday; Wade will still be around to train him.

A week from Sunday feels awfully far away.

"Maybe you and I can hike again sometime," Maia says. "I'll take you to the Esperance Trail. There's a baobab tree."

"It's a date," he says. He peers over Maia's head at Ayers. "Thanks for inviting me along today."

"Of course," Ayers says. She and Maia hop in the little green truck and wave. "See ya later."

Cash and Winnie watch them drive away.

There's no reason to feel down, and yet he does. He drives back to the villa, knowing he can crack a beer and spend what remains of the afternoon by the pool, and then he should take a trip to the grocery store because he can't eat at La Tapa every night or he'll quickly burn through the money Irene gave him.

He passes the black SUV in the dummy driveway—different guy, dark-complected. Cash waves.

When he gets up to the house, he hears voices, splashing. Someone is in the pool.

Whoa! Cash's crazy first thought is that it's FBI agent number one. His second thought is that the house has been rented and Paulette forgot to tell Irene, or maybe she thought it wouldn't matter since they'd gone back to the States. That must be it. What is Cash going to do? He doesn't have money for a hotel and his lifesaving class starts Monday. He sends Winnie up the stairs ahead of him. Paulette will have to come up with a solution. Find these people another house.

Cash is nearly at the top step, prepping himself for an uncomfortable confrontation, when he hears a young voice say, "Winnie! Uncle Cash!"

It's Floyd, bobbing in the pool. And Baker, sitting on the edge in just his bathing trunks.

"Hey," Baker says.

"What—" Cash shakes his head. Winnie's tail is going nuts; she barks. "What are you doing here?"

"We're moving here!" Floyd announces. "To live!"

HUCK

Agent Colette Vasco is a serious woman, though not unkind. She has a niece Maia's age, her sister's daughter, and they're very close. Agent Vasco knows that being twelve isn't easy, and she understands how difficult things must be for Maia right now with the sudden loss of her mother. She agrees to come get the money while Maia is at school.

"I'm sorry to say, I have to bring a search team, including a drug dog, but if all goes according to plan, Maia will never know we've been there."

Huck is grateful. A team of four show up, along with a German shepherd named Comanche. Comanche does a quick, frenetic tour of the house, although he's in and out of Huck's room in a matter of seconds, which makes Huck wonder if maybe it *does* smell like rotting fish.

Comanche is tied up in the shade outside while the team comes in to retrieve the money from under Huck's bed. Then they systematically search the rest of Huck's house. Huck would be worried about them invading Maia's room but it looks like it's already been ransacked. There are clothes *everywhere;* supplies for Maia's bath-bomb business are spread across her desk, and hair products and makeup cover the surface of the dresser. There's also a fair amount of trash—wrappers from Clif Bars, half-full cans of LaCroix coconut seltzer.

"Maybe you could clean up while you're in there," Huck jokes. The FBI agents don't so much as crack a smile. They aren't humans, they're robots, Huck thinks. Robots on a mission. Fine; Huck will leave them to it. He peers into Rosie's room—Vasco herself is on her knees, pawing through the dresser drawers—then he goes into the kitchen, does a shot of Flor de Caña, and heads out to the deck, where he smokes three cigarettes in quick succession and keeps an eye on the southern waters for the *Mississippi.* Adam is taking the charter by himself today; Huck called and told him that something came up and he couldn't get away.

Agent Vasco lets Huck know that they haven't found anything else of interest. They are taking the cash, and Vasco asks for the numbers of Rosie's savings and checking accounts.

"I realize how difficult it must have been to call us about that money," Agent Vasco says. She lays a hand on Huck's arm. Her nails are polished shell pink and she wears no wedding ring; Huck checks out of habit. Agent Vasco is an attractive woman, a redhead like Huck, and she has a salty-sweet aspect that reminds Huck of his ex-wife, Kimberly. And, for that matter, LeeAnn.

Huck puts Agent Vasco at about thirty-five, still young enough to want children, which is too young for Huck. He's encouraged that he's even thinking this way; it's taking his mind off Irene.

When he next talks to Irene, he'll tell her how attractive Agent Vasco is. Maybe she'll get jealous.

"That wasn't money I earned and I doubt it was money Rosie earned," Huck says. He hands over the statements from Rosie's bank accounts. "If Rosie is guilty by association of something...well, it's my job to make sure it doesn't affect Maia in any way."

"I understand," Agent Vasco says. "I was really hoping I might find something of a more personal nature in Rosie's room. Letters, or a diary."

Diary, Huck thinks. Rosie kept a diary when she was younger. She used to threaten LeeAnn with it, saying that future generations would someday learn what a mean witch LeeAnn was, how harsh and unfair she was to her only child. Huck has no idea if Rosie kept up her diary-writing into her adult years. Because she worked nights at La Tapa, most of her downtime was during the day, when Huck was at work and Maia at school.

Letters? Well, there might be letters from Russell Steele if this were 1819 or even 1989, but nowadays people didn't write letters; they wrote to each other on their phones.

"I'm sure Rosie had her phone *with* her."

"Yes," Agent Vasco says. "We've subpoenaed the records."

Subpoenaed sounds serious, but of course, Rosie had a huge amount of cash stuffed into a drawer.

"If you don't mind my asking, what kind of crimes are you investigating?" Huck is thinking drugs, obviously. It's the Caribbean.

"I'm not at liberty to say. Also, we aren't really sure what we're dealing with here." Agent Vasco offers Huck a tight smile. "If we have any further questions, I'll be in touch."

"That's it?" Huck says. "You're leaving me?"

"Yes," Agent Vasco says. "You should be happy." She gathers the goons and they follow her out to the car with two black duffel bags filled with the money.

Easy come, easy go, Huck thinks.

Agent Vasco and company drive down Jacob's Ladder's series of switchbacks; Huck spies the car once, twice, three times—then they disappear. At nearly the same moment, Huck sees the *Mississippi* gliding across Rendezvous Bay. Today's charter was a couple of state troopers from Alaska. Apparently, these two are famous; they're featured on some reality-TV show, which Huck has a difficult time fathoming. Huck has less than no interest in celebrities; what makes him regret missing today is that these gentlemen really wanted to fish. Huck nearly calls Adam to tell him to turn around and pick him up at the Westin dock, but that's impractical, a waste of time and gas.

It's only ten o'clock and Huck doesn't have to get Maia until three. He could read his book—he still hasn't finished the Connelly—and, he supposes, he could go to the beach. He hasn't been in a long time; whenever Maia wanted to go, Rosie would take her. LeeAnn used to love sitting on Gibney, and Huck loved LeeAnn so he would join her there, though left to his own devices, he would go to Little Lameshur, far, far away from the crowded north shore. Should Huck pack up a fish sandwich and drive out to Little Lameshur? Maybe live really large and stop at the Tourist Trap for a lobster roll on the way? The idea is novel enough to be intriguing, but then Huck thinks about one of Agent Vasco's comments: *We aren't really sure what we're dealing with here.*

Huck isn't sure what they're dealing with either, but he does know one thing: he was relieved when the dog didn't go pawing at the floorboards and they didn't discover blocks of cocaine or heroin to go along with all that money.

Someone on this island must know more than Huck does. The coconut telegraph is real. Huck picks up his phone and calls Rupert.

Because Rupert doesn't like to leave Coral Bay, he and Huck meet at Skinny Legs. It turns out, it's as good a place as any to have a quiet conversation in the middle of a gorgeous sunny day. Skinny Legs is the quintessential Caribbean bar. It's tucked into a grove of shade trees a few hundred feet from the lip of Coral Bay. The bar itself looks like a lean-to built by Robinson Crusoe after a few rum punches. It's open to the air on one side and features picnic tables thick with paint and a little stage for live music from happy hour until last call. There's an adjacent gift shop that sells souvenirs celebrating all things Skinny Legs; Huck has never set foot in it. In Huck's opinion, Skinny Legs' only fault is that it's gotten so famous. The best way to ruin a place is to make it popular.

One of the things that keeps Skinny Legs authentic is that characters like Rupert still hang out here. Rupert is the prince of the establishment, if you can call a sixty-something-year-old man a prince. He's in his usual spot, corner stool on the right-hand side; he has a Bud Light in front of him. Huck checks the time: eleven fifteen. He still has more than three hours before he has to pick up Maia from school, and for this conversation, he probably needs something stronger than an iced tea. He flags down Heidi, the bartender.

"Painkiller, please," Huck says.

Rupert chuckles. "That's a woman's drink."

"I'm not allowed to say things like that in my house," Huck says. "Don't you know any better?" He takes a stool and rubs the top of Rupert's bald brown head.

They fall into their usual pattern of conversation, which is distinguished by long pauses and subsequent non sequiturs. Rupert doesn't like to be rushed; he's retired now and has earned the right to mull things over, and if his mind wanders in the process, oh, well. Rupert has lived on St. John his entire life; his family goes back generations, and Huck teases him by saying that Rupert's ancestors invented the concept of island time, but Rupert is the one who perfected it.

Huck drinks one painkiller and waves to Heidi for another before Rupert finishes summarizing his list of physical ailments: his back has been giving him trouble, his right toe throbs in the rain, he can't sleep more than three hours without having to get up to take a piss. Then it's Huck's turn to talk about how the fish are running. Better since the new year, he says—meaning since Rosie died, meaning since Irene set foot on his boat and into his life.

"Good to hear it," Rupert says. "And how's Maia?"

Huck tells Rupert about taking Maia to town with her friends and how that bothers him.

Rupert laughs. "It's a goddamned island, Huck. How much trouble can she get in? All the West Indian ladies who grew up with your wife have eyes in the backs of their heads. If Maia takes so much as a puff of a cigarette, you'll hear the crowing all the way up on Jacob's Ladder."

Huck shakes his head. "They don't smoke anymore, Rupert. They vape. It's electronic, thing looks like a pen. They put a pod in it—"

"Don't tell me," Rupert says. "I don't want to know."

"It's all happening so fast. And I don't like the timing, her getting so independent right after her mother dies." This is when Maia would be most vulnerable to vaping and drinking and—Huck can barely let himself think it—*sex.* He has to find a way to make sure she grows up responsibly. Honestly, he could use some help.

They're quiet a few minutes. The song in the background is Warren Zevon's "Lawyers, Guns, and Money." Huck isn't sure Rupert is listening to the music, but it feels like a natural segue. "So I had a visit this morning," Huck says. "From the FBI."

Huck can sense his friend's invisible antennae rising.

"That's why I called you, actually," Huck says. "To see if you know something I don't."

"Funny you should ask," Rupert says. "Because I heard federal officers paid a visit to the Welcome to Paradise Real Estate office."

"Really?" Huck says. "Paulette Vickers—"

"Paulette and Doug Vickers and the little boy are gone," Rupert says. "Rumor has it they left last night on the car barge."

"*Left* as in …"

"*Left* as in *left,*" Rupert says.

Left *as in* left. Paulette and Douglas Vickers, who owned Welcome to Paradise Real Estate, pulled their young son, Windsor, out of school and packed what they needed into Doug's pickup and left twelve hours before the FBI showed up. That was the story Rupert heard from Sadie, one of his many girlfriends, and Sadie's gossip was generally known to be reliable.

On his way home, Huck drives past the office, and sure

enough, there's the black SUV parked out front, its presence as ominous as a hearse.

The question that bothers Huck is this: How did Paulette and Douglas Vickers know that the FBI were coming? Did they find out Huck had contacted Agent Vasco? Was Huck's phone compromised? Was there a bug somewhere *in his house?* If so, would the FBI have found it this morning in their search? Huck lights a cigarette. He needs to get a grip. This is the stuff of movies and Connelly novels. This is not daily life in the Virgin Islands.

At three o'clock, he's waiting out in front of the Gifft Hill School when Maia emerges with her cronies Joanie, Colton, and Bright.

Here we go again, Huck thinks.

Maia studies his expression. "You okay, Gramps? You in a bad mood again?"

He meant what he told Agent Vasco. He is determined to keep whatever Rosie was involved with away from Maia. She's a twelve-year-old girl who wants to hang out with her friends. It's a goddamned island. She's safe here.

But really, he could use some help.

"I'm fine," he says. He won't smile because then Maia will *know* there's something wrong, so he adopts the air of a weary chauffeur. "You guys can all hop in."

BAKER

He knows he shouldn't be surprised that his brother came back down to St. John and, apparently, plans to make it his permanent home, sponging off Irene, but he is. He tells Cash as much, though instead of using the word *sponging,* he calls it "taking full advantage of Mom's generosity." It's marginally kinder; after all, Floyd is listening.

"I'm not taking advantage any more than you are," Cash says with what Baker can only assume is a phony smile. "And I found a job."

"So soon?" Baker says. "Where?"

"First mate on *Treasure Island,*" Cash says.

First mate on *Treasure Island*? It takes Baker a second, but he puts it together. *Treasure Island* is the boat that Ayers works on.

"You have got to be"—he swallows the swearword because of Floyd—"kidding me."

"Not kidding," Cash says.

Not kidding; of course not kidding. Somehow Cash weaseled his way onto that boat and into near-daily interaction with Ayers.

"I didn't realize you liked the water," Baker says. "I thought you were more of a mountain guy." He says this with relative equanimity. What he's thinking is this: *You hate water unless it's frozen! You're ten thousand feet out of your comfort zone! The only reason you're here is to try and steal my girl!* "How did you find out about the job, anyway?"

"Ayers texted me," Cash says. He rubs Winnie under the chin. "Winnie and I just went for a hike and a swim with Ayers and Maia on the Johnny Horn Trail. It was beautiful, but man, was it hot. I was dreaming about this pool the whole way back." Cash pries off his hiking boots and strips down to his swim trunks. Baker tries to look at his brother objectively. Cash is in good shape; he has six-pack abs and really strong legs from all the skiing, but he's not quite six feet tall, so Baker has always discounted him as a possible rival. But now, Baker has all kinds of troubling thoughts. Maybe Ayers is into the short, stocky, and (admittedly) super-cut look as opposed to the tall, broad-shouldered, and (admittedly) dad-bod look. (Baker flexes his arm behind him to see if he still has triceps. Maybe; it's hard to tell.) Cash went hiking and swimming with Ayers and Maia—he's been the recipient of Ayers's smile. It's Baker's fantasy.

He's jealous.

His first instinct is to be a jerk about it. But honestly, he doesn't want to do battle with Cash over Ayers. He doesn't want to do battle with Cash over anything. He finds he's actually psyched—and relieved—that Cash is here. Baker talked a big game about moving down here but he doesn't know a soul except for Ayers and, sort of, Huck, and he has nothing in the way of a support system. He can continue to day-trade and he can accept Anna's offer of financial help, but he needs to see if life here is sustainable—school for Floyd, some kind of job for himself that's part-time with flexible hours that will get him out of the house and into the community. He could even volunteer.

"How's Maia doing?" Baker asks. "Was she…okay seeing you?"

"Surprisingly, yes," Cash says. "She seems great. I mean,

don't get me wrong, she had a moment or two where she almost broke down—"

"I'm going down the slide," Floyd announces. "Uncle Cash, are you getting in?"

Cash jumps into the pool and swims over to a spot where he can watch Floyd go down the slide to the lower pool.

"But, I mean, generally, she was okay. She's a smart kid. She was teaching me about the island's history and the plants and trees—"

"Maybe I'll apply for a job with the National Park Service," Baker says.

Cash gives him an incredulous look and Baker thinks it's probably justified. Being a park ranger must require years in forestry school or some such.

"And before you ask, Ayers is still with Mick. I saw them together at La Tapa last night."

"He'll cheat on her again," Baker says.

"Agreed," Cash says. He holds Baker's gaze for a second and Baker can tell they're thinking the same thing: Once Mick cheats on her again, it'll be brother against brother.

Or maybe not, Baker thinks. Maybe Cash will realize that he and Ayers should just remain friends. Maybe Cash will fall for one of the young, single women who climb aboard *Treasure Island*.

"What's up with Anna?" Cash asks.

"She and Louisa have accepted positions at the Cleveland Clinic," Baker says. "They're moving to Shaker Heights. Floyd will go there holidays and summers. That's why we decided to move down here. There's nothing tethering us to Houston anymore."

"Great minds think alike," Cash says. "I was going to head to Breck to ski but it's too late in the season for me to get a decent job. Then Ayers told me about *Treasure Island*. I start my lifesaving classes on Monday."

Baker is surprised that Cash is so organized; it sounds like he's thought something through for once. Objectively, Baker has to admit that Cash would be great as a first mate on a tour boat. When Baker and Anna visited Cash in Breckenridge, they had a chance to see him in action as a group ski instructor and they had both been impressed. Cash was friendly, engaging, funny, kind, and paticnt—his patience had been astonishing, in fact.

"What would Dad think," Baker asks, "if he could see us together right now?"

Cash raises his eyebrows. "The more relevant question is, what would *Mom* think? I talked to her yesterday and she didn't tell me you were coming down. Does she even know?"

Baker eases himself into the pool and swims over to Cash. He peers down at Floyd, splashing in the lower pool. "She doesn't."

"Why didn't you *tell* her?"

"I'm not sure," Baker says. "Probably because I didn't want her to stop me."

"Legally, it's *her* house," Cash says. "I'm not trying to be a jerk but my advice is to call her and tell her you're here."

Baker knows Cash is right. "I will," he says. "I'll call her tonight after Floyd is asleep."

Before Cash can respond, Baker hears the strains of "Blitzkrieg Bop," by the Ramones—and Cash pushes himself up out of the pool. He pulls his cell phone out of his hiking shorts, looks at the screen, and says, "Well, guess what, it's Mom."

"Good," Baker says. "Tell her I'm here. She'll like it better coming from you anyway."

Cash says, "Hello, Mother Alarm Clock, what's up? Good,

yeah…I saw Maia today. Ayers and I took her on a hike, or she took *us* on a hike, actually…yeah, I start Monday, they said I'll be good to go in a week. Hey, listen, I have some news…oh, all right. No, you go first."

There's a pause during which Baker can hear the tinny sound of Irene's voice over the phone and Baker grows hot and uncomfortable. He just wants Cash to spit it out already! Baker checks on Floyd, who is splashing around, happy as can be, like a model only child. Baker will check out preschools for Floyd.

When Baker phoned Anna and told her that he and Floyd were considering moving down to St. John on a somewhat permanent basis, Anna had accepted the news the way she accepted everything he said: with indifference.

"It's nice there," Anna said. "I'll have to see what Louisa thinks—"

"It doesn't matter what Louisa thinks," Baker said. "She doesn't get to weigh in on my decisions."

"But Floyd…" Anna says. He recognized her distracted tone of voice; she was probably writing in someone's chart while she was talking to him.

"Louisa isn't Floyd's mother," Baker said. "You are. Now, assuming I find a suitable school for our child, do you have any objections to Floyd and me spending some time in St. John? The vacation schedule will be the same. Nothing changes except he won't be in Houston. Do you object?"

"No," Anna said. "I guess not…"

"Wonderful, thank you," Baker said, and he hung up before she could change her mind.

Baker is yanked back into the present moment when he hears Cash say, "A week from *Monday?*"

A week from Monday what? Baker wonders.

"Well, you're in for a nice surprise," Cash says. "Because guess who else is here—Baker and Floyd!"

Pause. Baker hears his mother's voice, maybe a little more high-pitched than before.

"Yep, I guess Anna took a job in Cleveland and so Baker and Floyd are...yep, they're here now. Yes, Mom, I think that's the plan." Cash locks eyes with Baker and starts nodding. "Yes, it *will* be so nice, all of us together."

All of us together? Does this mean what Baker thinks it means?

"Just text to let us know what ferry you'll be on," Cash says. "And one of us will be there to pick you up. A week from Monday."

That night, they grill steaks and asparagus and Baker makes his potato packets in foil and he and Cash and Floyd devour everything and Baker remembers that it's nice cooking for people who actually appreciate it. Floyd goes inside to watch *Despicable Me 3* for the ten thousandth time and Baker and Cash stare out at the scattering of lights across the water.

"So Mom is coming a week from Monday," Baker says. He's not sure how he feels about this. "There are obviously pluses and minuses to this situation."

"Agreed," Cash says. "On the plus side, we have been through a family crisis. If Mom stayed in Iowa, I would worry about her."

"I can't believe she quit her job," Baker says.

"She wants a change, she says."

"But working on Huck's fishing boat? Mom? She's a fifty-seven-year-old woman. She must have been kidding about that."

"Don't you remember the way she used to wake us up at dawn on Clark Lake to go out on Pop's flat-bottom boat to fish for bass? Mom took us, not Dad. Mom baited our hooks. Mom taught us how to cast."

"Yeah, I do," Baker says. He hasn't thought of it in eons but suddenly he has a vivid picture of being out on Clark Lake before the sun was even fully up, Irene yanking on the starter of the outboard motor, then Irene driving the boat to the spot where the smallmouth bass were biting. Irene had indeed taught both Baker and Cash to cast. She had shown them how to reel in a fish after they felt a tug on the line. She had deftly worked the hook from the fish's mouth, using one gloved hand to hold the fish and one hand to maneuver her Gerber tool. Irene could snap fishing line with her teeth. She could fillet a bass or a perch so expertly that there were no bones to worry about when it came off the charcoal grill that evening at dinner. Baker had forgotten that his mother liked to fish, but even now that he remembers, he wonders if this is really what she wants to do for a living. Maybe she needs a break, a respite, a time to recharge and reset.

Maybe that's what they all need.

"On the minus side," Cash says, "we'll be grown men living with our mother."

"Sexy," Baker says.

"But the house is big," Cash says.

"The house *is* big," Baker says. And it'll be nice to have an extra person to watch Floyd. He won't mention that, however, lest Cash call him a self-involved bastard.

Later that night, Baker wants to go out. The dishes are done and Baker has read to Floyd and tucked him in. Baker also showed him how their bedrooms connect; the house feels more familiar this time around.

Baker finds Cash collapsed in a heap in front of a basketball game. He considers slipping out the door—he needs to go to town; he needs to see Ayers—but he can't just leave with Floyd asleep upstairs. "Hey, Cash?"

"Yeah." Cash doesn't move his eyes from the TV.

"I'm going out for a little while, man," Baker says. "Or I'd like to. If you could just…keep one ear open in case Floyd wakes up?"

"Yeah, of course," Cash says.

Baker lets his breath go.

"Are you going into town to see Ayers?" Cash asks.

Baker considers lying, but what can he say? That he's going to the grocery store? Out for a nightcap? Cash will know better.

"Yeah," Baker admits.

"She asked about you today on the hike," Cash says.

Baker's heart feels like a speeding car without brakes. "She did?"

"She said you didn't call her after you left." Cash pauses. "Were you really that stupid?"

Yes, Baker thinks, he was. There had been dozens of times when Baker thought to reach out, but, honestly, he hadn't seen the point. He had been stuck in Houston…until Anna announced she was leaving. "I was that stupid," Baker says.

"My guess is she has a thing for you," Cash says. "Don't mess it up."

Cash's tone indicates that he fully believes Baker *will* mess it up. It's true that Baker's track record with women hasn't been great. He chose to marry a woman who didn't love him, who may or may not have liked men at all. But Ayers is different. It's as though Baker had been on a quest without even realizing it—until he found exactly what he was looking for.

He's not going to mess it up.

Baker wonders why Cash is being so cool about Ayers. He seems relaxed and at ease in a way that is very un-Cash-like. Maybe it's some kind of trap. Or maybe the island is working its magic.

"Thanks, man," Baker says. "I mean it, Cash. Thank you."

"Good luck," Cash says.

Good luck. Baker turns up the radio in the Jeep; the excellent station out of San Juan—104.3 the Buzz—is playing the Red Hot Chili Peppers. Baker sings along, woefully off-key, but who cares; he's got the windows open and the sweet night air is rushing in. Baker hasn't felt this sense of freedom, this sense of *possibility,* since he was in high school. He's nervous. He has *butterflies.*

He drives into town at ten thirty and things are still lively; it's Saturday night. He worries that to see Ayers, he'll have to go to La Tapa for a drink—he really wanted to be sober and clear-headed tonight—but then he spots her leaving the restaurant, wearing cutoff jean shorts and a T-shirt and a pair of Chucks, a suede bag hitched over her shoulder.

She reaches up and releases her hair from its bun. She is so strong and composed and self-possessed. Baker is dazzled. He has been dazzled by women before, of course—when he watched Anna pull a splinter out of Floyd's foot with one quick, precise movement; when his old girlfriend Trinity knotted a cherry stem with her tongue (Baker still doesn't understand how people *do* that)—but Ayers is different. She's flawless.

Baker drives up alongside her and rolls the window down.

He thinks about trying to be funny—*Hey, little girl, want some candy?*—but there's no way he'll be able to pull it off.

"Ayers," he says. "Hi."

She stops, ducks her head to peer into the car. They lock eyes.

"Baker," she says. She holds his gaze and the two of them knit together somehow. He can't speak so he nods his head toward the passenger seat. She runs around the front of the car, opens the door, climbs in, and fastens her seat belt.

"Wow," she says. "I can't believe I'm doing this."

"Where to?" he asks.

"Hawksnest Beach," she says. "I'll show you the way."

ROSIE

February 22, 2006

I'm afraid to write down exactly what happened with Russ but I'm afraid not to write it down because what if I forget and my weekend with him is washed away like a heart drawn in the sand?

There was sex, a lot of sex, and it was the best sex of my life, but I have only Oscar to compare it to and if there's one thing I can say about Oscar, it's that he's selfish and greedy and arrogant and any time I opened my mouth to ask him to change his style, he took offense and kept on doing things the same way because in his mind, he knew the path to my pleasure better than I did.

I faked a lot with Oscar. I faked so much that I got quite skilled at it and I assumed I would have to fake it with Russell from Iowa City because, well, let's just say he was older and grayer and not at all in shape. But, man, was I surprised at how…good he was to me. He was gentle and firm and confident when he touched my body and he was also appreciative, maybe even reverent. The sex was so sublime that I started to feel both jealous of and guilty about his wife, Irene.

At one point I said to Russ, "I hope your wife knows how lucky she is to have you."

Russ laughed. "I doubt she would describe herself that way. And not that you asked, but my wife and I don't have sex like this. We don't have sex much at all. Like I said, in Irene's eyes, I'm a day late and a dollar short in nearly everything I do. Her main attitude toward me is weary disappointment. Which kind of kills the magic."

On Saturday night I sneaked out of his room at three o'clock in the morning and got back to Jacob's Ladder at three thirty. I somehow managed to get in the house without waking Mama, who is a very light sleeper.

Russ and I had planned to spend the day together on Sunday but I had to be careful, so careful, because the island has eyes and very loose lips. Turns out, Russ's friend and potential new boss, Todd Croft, had left behind the skiff from the yacht for Russ to use, although Russ admitted he didn't feel comfortable navigating in unfamiliar waters. "Leave the driving to me," I said. I was off all day Sunday and Sunday night, so I went to church with Mama, which normally I hated, but I needed to ask forgiveness for the sins I had already committed as well as the ones I was about to commit. I told Mama I was going to Salomon Bay for the day, then straight to a barbecue, and I'd be home late.

Mama said, "You got home late last night, mon chou.*" (She uses the French phrases that she picked up in Paris when she's displeased; it's a signal I alone understand.) "I want you to tell me right now that you are not back involved with Oscar. I've heard he's been sniffing around."*

Estella must have been talking to Dearie, who did my mother's hair. I faced her on the stone walk outside the Catholic church and said, "Mama, I am not involved with Oscar."

Her expression was dubious but my words contained conviction. "Better not be," she said.

Even though we were traveling over water, which was a lot safer than land, I had to be sneaky. I left my car at the National Park Service sign as though I had indeed headed to Salomon Bay, but instead I hiked down to the public part of Honeymoon Beach and cut through the back way so that I popped out of the trees in a place where I could wade to the skiff, which I did, holding my bag above my head. Russ was waiting for me with a cooler and a picnic basket he'd asked the hotel to pack. I started the motor on the first try, and we were off.

It was an idyllic day. The water sparkled in the sun; the air had a rare scrubbed-clean feel, as though it had just received a benediction. It was as fine a performance by planet Earth as I had ever seen. Russ had on bathing trunks, a long-sleeved T-shirt, and a baseball cap that said IOWA CITY ROTARY CLUB, *which made me chuckle because, really, what was I doing with this guy? And yet I liked him. Just as I thought I had him pegged as one kind of person—he had just ended his second term on the Iowa City school board; he was encouraging his mother, Milly, to move into a retirement community but she was having none of it—he would pull out a surprise. Like the way he stroked be-*

hind my knee in a spot so sweet and sensitive, I had a hard time concentrating.

We anchored off of Little Cinnamon because the cliff above was undeveloped so no one would be spying on us with binoculars for voyeuristic purposes. Russ unpacked the cooler—there was a nice bottle of Sancerre for me, the Chavignol, which I loved, and a couple of cold beers for Russ. There were slender baguette sandwiches with duck, arugula, and fig jam, and as I ate one, all I could think of was Remy the chef preparing them, having no idea that one was for me. There was also a container of truffled potato salad and a couple of lemon tarts, and I thought of how nice it was to be on the receiving end of Caneel's hospitality for once.

We puttered along the north shore as far as Waterlemon Cay, where we stopped again because, although we hadn't brought snorkeling gear, you could watch turtles pop their heads above the surface for air and Russ loved that. It was hot enough that we both decided to jump in for a swim and Russ held me in the water, his arms incredibly strong for a corn-syrup salesman or whatever he was. We kissed, and I thought, What are we doing here at Waterlemon Cay when we have a perfectly good hotel room?

I said, "Do you think you'll take the job?"

"It's hard to say no. The signing bonus is nearly as much as I make in a year right now."

"If you take the job, will you spend more time down here?" Unfortunately, my voice betrayed what I was really asking: Would I ever see him again? I was afraid the answer would be no; I was afraid the answer would be yes. What we were doing was wrong. He was married with two sons in high school and he must have been trying not to imagine what they would think if they could see him at that moment. But…it was as if we were living in a sealed bubble. One weekend in February in the sixth year of the

new millennium, this happened. I had a vague idea that affairs like this could actually improve a marriage. Russ would return to Iowa City with not only a big job offer but also a sense of power and virility, and Irene would see him in a new light. They would renew their vows, go on a second honeymoon.

And for me—well, things wouldn't be awful for me either. I had faith in men again. The ghost of Oscar was permanently banished; every time I thought of him helpless and whimpering in Russ's grip, I thought, How pathetic. *I would venture forth with my self-esteem and self-worth restored. I would meet someone like Russ—kind, thoughtful, secure, adult—and that would blossom into the relationship that this could never be.*

Our affair would be almost excusable if this all turned out to be the case. But even as I had these pretty and nice thoughts about us both going our own ways after this without any looking back, I felt my heart stirring up trouble. Maybe Russ was experiencing the same thing, because he looked genuinely crestfallen as he said, "You know, I'm really not sure. I know there will be travel with this job but I think it'll be in dull places like Palm Beach and Midland, Texas. I think Todd just brought me down here to woo me."

"Okay," I said, trying to keep my tone light and unconcerned. "Let's go back to the hotel, then, and properly enjoy the time we have left."

We did just that, and it was wonderful—not only the sex, but also falling asleep in that luscious bed with our limbs intertwined.

When I woke up, he was staring at me just like the leading man in the movies looks at his leading lady—right before he betrays her or kills her or carries her off into the sunset.

"You're exquisite," he said. "And just now, watching you sleep, I felt so... privileged. *Like I've been granted a private viewing of the* Mona Lisa.*"*

"Everyone says the Mona Lisa *is so beautiful," I said. "But frankly, I don't get it."*

This made Russ laugh and he reached over to the nightstand and plucked a pale pink hibiscus blossom out of a water glass. He tucked it behind my ear.

"You're right," he said. "You're far prettier than the Mona Lisa.*"*

I swatted him to downplay how happy that made me—show me a woman who doesn't like being compared to a masterpiece—then said, "I'm starving."

It was dark outside. The bedside clock said twenty past nine. It was too late to get dinner anywhere on this sleepy island, besides which I was basically in hiding. So we ordered room service, lavishly, recklessly, like we were rock stars on the last leg of a world tour—one bacon cheeseburger, one lobster pizza, French fries, a Caesar salad, the key lime pie, a hot fudge sundae, and, of course, conch fritters, because now that was our "thing." I would never see Russell Steele again but every time I put in an order of conch fritters, I would think of him. I told him this and he threw me down on the bed and said, "God, Rosie, how can I ever leave you? I'm... different now, in such a short time. I'm changed." He was putting words to what I felt as well. I had tears in my eyes as I tried to control my crazy, runaway heart.

Don't leave me, *I nearly said—which would have been pathetic after a relationship of only twenty-four or forty-eight hours (depending on how you looked at it)—but I was saved from myself by a knock at the door.*

It was room service with our food, which I knew would be delivered by Woodrow, so I had to go hide in the bathroom while Russ answered the door.

* * *

I stayed overnight Sunday; Todd Croft and the other guy, the company lawyer, Stephen, were due to pick Russ up at noon. I had been up since dawn worrying about how the goodbye would go and I even brazenly wandered out to the beach where I saw my donkeys, Stop, Drop, and Roll, eating grass at the edge of the beach. I decided to take their presence as a positive omen. This is my home, this is where I belong, and I need to find someone who calls St. John home as well. The reason that getting involved with a married man is wrong is that it hurts. I knew that if it continued one minute past noon today, it would be destructive. What did I want Russ to do? Go home and tell his wife that he was leaving her for some woman half his age with whom he'd had a fling in the Caribbean?

Hell no!

We lay in bed together until the last possible minute. Then Russ showered and dressed and I thought, What can I give him to remember me by? *I wished I'd dived down at Waterlemon and picked up a shell or a piece of coral—some island token—but I hadn't. And so I rummaged through the desk in the room and found a postcard with a picture of the Sugar Mill on the front, and I wrote,* I'm going to miss you. *I signed it with the initials* M.L., *for* Mona Lisa. *I wasn't sure he would figure that out, but I enjoyed imagining him puzzling over it. I stuck the postcard in the side zip pocket of his bag and right as he was gathering up his things to go, I told him I'd left him a surprise in that pocket that he should look at before returning home. The last thing I wanted was for Irene to find it.*

He held my face in his hands. Out the window I could see the yacht anchored and a crew member pulling the skiff around (it fit, somehow, underneath the boat or inside of it). Russ kissed me hard and deep. It was the kiss you give someone when you're absolutely, positively never going to see her again.

"I don't have anything to leave you with except for that," he said. Then he turned and left the room and I was so addled, so undone, *that I hung in the doorway and watched him trudge through the sand. He raised an arm to Todd Croft, who was standing on the deck of the boat.*

Bluebeard *was the yacht's name. I hadn't noticed that before.*

I saw Todd Croft see me; his head tilted and his smile grew wider, and I disappeared into the shadows of the room, cursing myself. I was wearing my swim cover-up. If Todd asked, Russ could say we'd struck up a friendship and I'd come to say goodbye. It didn't matter, I would likely never see Todd Croft again, but I regretted not leaving first. I should have headed for home an hour or two earlier, but that would have meant losing time with Russ, and I hadn't wanted to do that. For my greed, then, I was punished. I became the one who was left behind.

As I drove home, I thought of how the weekend had been a Cinderella story, minus the part with the glass slipper. I was returned to my ordinary self, in my proverbial rags, facing my scullery work. The only part of that magical story I could claim was that I had enjoyed a night (in my case, two nights) of bliss. I had successfully charmed a prince, only the prince was a midwestern corn-syrup salesman. A married corn-syrup salesman.

Mama was at work when I got home, despite the holiday, and I was momentarily relieved. Now I'm locked in my room, writing this down, because supposedly "getting it out" is a kind of catharsis. I have an hour left to get ready before I have to go back to Caneel, where I will work and pretend that everything is just fine.

February 23, 2006

I've decided that Bluebeard *is an appropriate name for the yacht that delivered Russ to me and then took him away.*

He was a pirate.

He stole my heart.

March 30, 2006

Mama was the one who noticed that I looked peaked and that I wasn't eating much. When had I ever said no to her blackened mahi tacos with pineapple-mango salsa? Never *was the answer. But they just didn't seem appealing. Nothing seemed appealing.*

She said, "Do you want to come to the clinic at lunchtime tomorrow and I'll slide you in?"

I couldn't tell her that I was suffering from a broken heart, and there's no cure for that except time, and for all the technological advances going on in the world, no one has figured out how to speed time up or slow it down—or stop it. Whoever figures out that trick is going to be rich. "Nah," I said.

"No, but thanks for offering," Mama prompted.

I retreated to my room. I needed to put less energy into pining for the pirate and more into saving money so I could get a place of my own.

Then, a couple of days ago, I woke up feeling dizzy and nauseated and I thought, Damn it, I really am sick. *I had planned to go to Salomon Bay—the best thing for me to do was get back into a routine—but it looked like it would be the clinic instead.*

I raced to the bathroom and puked into the toilet. I heard Mama knocking on my bedroom door, asking if I was all right, and then I heard Huck say, "LeeAnn, leave the poor girl alone, no one likes to be bothered when they're praying to the porcelain god."

And Mama said, "You're right, handsome. I'll leave her be. She'll be okay as long as it's not morning sickness."

Morning sickness, *I thought.*

It was off to the Chelsea drugstore for a test, but I had to wait until my mother's friend Fatima left for lunch because Rosie Small buying a pregnancy test would win Fatima a gold medal in the Gossip Olympics.

I hurried home, praying, praying, *and then I peed on the stick.*

I'm pregnant.

April 30, 2006

Today a package addressed to me was hand-delivered to the house. The package contained ten thousand dollars in cash.

I'm being bought off.

There wasn't a note but I don't have to be a wizard to know the money is from Todd Croft. But has Todd Croft told Russ that I'm pregnant?

Let me go back.

When I found out I was pregnant four weeks ago, all I could think was that I needed to tell Russ. I was pretty sure he would offer to help. And by help, *a part of me was thinking he would leave his wife, move to St. John, and raise this baby with me. It was a long shot, I knew, but not impossible. Maybe instead of making Russ's marriage stronger, the weekend affair (I'm shying away from the word* fling*) had been a breaking point. Maybe Russ would say yes to the job and goodbye to Irene and start a whole* *new life. The boys were teenagers; the older boy was headed to college in the fall and the younger one was only a year or two behind, so they were nearly out of the house. If anyone was poised for a second act, it was Russ.*

Or so I let myself momentarily believe.

I called Iowa City information and asked for the phone number for Russell or Irene Steele.

"Irene Steele," the operator said. "Hold for the number."

I hung up the phone. The listing was under Irene's name. She paid the bills. She was in charge of the household. She intimidated me—indeed, scared me—even from afar. I would never call the house, I decided. I wasn't that desperate.

I had to somehow circumvent Irene. I needed an e-mail. I knew there was probably an e-mail attached to the room reservation at Caneel. I had worked at Caneel long enough to know that all reservations were kept in a database, but that database couldn't be accessed on any of the restaurant computers.

So I would have to ask the restaurant manager, Estella, to get it for me.

I said to her, "Please don't tell my mother"—Estella rolled her eyes as if to say, Rosie-child, no matter how you implore me, you know I could never keep a secret from LeeAnn—*"but a gentleman who stayed here over Presidents' Day weekend begged me for the conch-fritter recipe. He wants to give it to the chef at his country club so they can serve them at his wife's surprise birthday party and I promised him I'd send him the recipes for the fritters and the aioli. He gave me his e-mail, but I lost it, Estella. And I feel terrible. I remember he said his wife's birthday is May twenty-third because that's a day after mine and so time is of the essence. Can you help me find the man's e-mail, please, Estella? I want to provide the kind of service Caneel is famous for."*

Estella huffed for a minute. Didn't I know that accessing the guests' personal information was forbidden?

I said, "But he already gave *it to me and I lost it! It's his wife's fortieth birthday!"*

Estella hesitated, then she ushered me into the back office, and together, we looked. The name Russell Steele didn't turn up in the system, which was perplexing. Had he used a fake name? Was he not only a pirate but an impostor?

Then I said, "Let's check the name Todd Croft." And it popped right up—room 718 for two nights, total bill $1,652. There was an e-mail, but it was Todd's, and my heart sank, though I did think it was encouraging that it was a BVI e-mail address.

I copied it down and thanked Estella, who closed the file and hurried us out of the office, saying, "That was the easy part. Good luck convincing Chef to hand over his recipes."

I wrote to Todd Croft, explained who I was, and said merely that I would like an e-mail address for Russ so that I could send him the conch-fritter and aioli recipes that he'd requested.

But I guess Mr. Croft saw right through my ploy because here I am, holding ten large.

I know I should feel insulted but all I feel is relieved. Because if Mama kicks me out, and she very well might, I'll have money to get a place for me and the baby.

I'm telling her tomorrow.

May 1, 2006

I was so nervous that I got out of bed early after barely sleeping all night. I couldn't wait another hour, another minute. Once I heard both Mama and Huck in the kitchen, I walked down the hall, comforted by the idea that in thirty seconds, the secret would be out. They could holler; they could scream, call me names, and cast me out, but all of that would pale against the relief of speaking the truth.

When Mama saw me, she was shocked. "Rosie? What are you doing awake? Is everything all right?"

In that second, everything was *still all right. Mama was dressed for work in her raspberry scrubs and her white lab coat, her towering bun wrapped in a brightly patterned scarf. She'd had her nails done—she was vain about her nails, and they were the same shade of raspberry—and I noticed her fingers against the white porcelain of her coffee cup. Every morning, Huck makes her coffee, one poached egg, and a piece of lightly buttered wheat toast. Huck was standing at the stove tending to the egg. He was wearing cargo shorts with a lure hanging from the belt loop and a long-sleeved T-shirt advertising the* Mississippi. *He had a bandanna wrapped around his neck and was ready for a day of fishing. I didn't dread Huck's anger; what I dreaded was his disappointment in me. We'd had a rocky start to our relationship. When he started courting Mama seven years ago, I resented him. I thought,* He sees a single woman and her wayward daughter and thinks they need to be saved—but we *don't* need to be saved. *But I quickly grew to love Huck and, yes, to count on him. I remember one time when he'd told me to help myself to twenty bucks from his wallet so I could go into town to meet my friends, I found a folded-up, faded picture of Huck with another woman. The picture was obviously old, from the seventies or eighties. In it, Huck was a young man. He had a full head of strawberry-blond hair and a mustache but no beard; he wore jeans with what looked like a white patent-leather belt and a Led Zeppelin T-shirt. The woman was in a crocheted chevron-print dress and had on white patent-leather boots. Her blond hair was feathered and she wore too much black eyeliner.*

I took the picture to Huck and said, "Who's this?" Huck had had a sister who had died of cancer and I thought maybe this was her; he rarely talked about her but I knew her name was Caroline.

"Her?" Huck said. I thought he might be angry that I'd snooped in his wallet for more than just the twenty, but he didn't seem angry. "That's my first wife, Kimberly."

I was shocked *by this. I didn't know Huck had been married before. I felt affronted, maybe even betrayed—for Mama's sake, but also my own. He and Mama had been married a year or two when I found this picture and the three of us had become a happy family. I didn't like the idea of sharing Huck with anyone. "I didn't realize you'd been married before." I swallowed. "Does my mother know?"*

"Yes, of course," he said. He smiled sadly. "Sorry, Rosie, I should have told you. There just never seemed to be an appropriate time and it doesn't matter anyway."

"If it doesn't matter, why do you keep the picture?" I asked. I handed it back to him, though really I wanted to tear it to shreds.

"Well," Huck said. He thought about it for a minute. One thing I love most about Huck is that he's a straight shooter. He doesn't candy-coat the truth or brush it away because he doesn't want me to see it. "Kimberly ended up being a disappointment to me. She was an alcoholic, a really, really mean drunk, and that destroyed our marriage. It destroyed just about all of her relationships, actually. But in this picture, we were happy, so I keep it as a reminder that my time with her wasn't all bad." He slipped the picture back into the wallet. "In even the bleakest situations, there's usually some good to be salvaged."

Facing Mama and Huck to tell them I was pregnant was a bleak situation. Would any good be salvaged from it?

"I'm pregnant," I said.

Huck turned from the stove.

"What?" Mama said.

"I'm pregnant."

She set down her coffee cup and stood up. Her face was unreadable. Shock, I suppose. Huck was watching her.

"Oscar?" she said.

"Not Oscar," I said. "It was a man at the hotel, someone you don't know. I was stupid. He's gone now and I don't know how to reach him."

There was a moment of such profound silence that I felt like the world had stopped. She was probably deciding whether or not to believe me.

Then, finally, she opened her arms, and I entered them.

Part Three

The Soggy Dollar

IRENE

Before she leaves for St. John, Irene has some loose ends to take care of.

A death certificate issued by the Department of Vital Statistics of the British Virgin Islands arrives in the mail in an unmarked envelope. Is it authentic? It seems so, though Irene has no way of knowing for sure.

So, obviously, Paulette received her message. There's no note, no invoice, no mention of a fee. Irene has assumed that Paulette is the one who pays to maintain the villa—taxes (do they *have* taxes in the Virgin Islands?), insurance, landscapers, repairs, et cetera—probably out of a fund that Russ or Todd Croft set up . . . with cash.

She takes the death certificate to Ed Sorley's office and drops it off with the receptionist, then leaves before Ed appears with questions.

She withdraws eight thousand dollars from the account at Federal Republic, using the drive-through window. The cash and the postcards from M.L. go right into Irene's suitcase.

* * *

At Lydia's insistence, Irene puts an obituary in the *Press-Citizen,* and she phones her close friends and neighbors to invite them to the house for a memorial reception. She tells them that Russ was killed in a helicopter crash; lightning was the cause. He was down in the Virgin Islands for work. He's been cremated and the ashes scattered. This is a small gathering so his friends can pay their respects.

"No food and no flowers," Irene told them. "I'm taking some time away, leaving Monday. If you feel you must do something to honor his passing, you can donate to the Rotary Club scholarship fund. It always goes to some terrific kid who really needs it."

Lydia arranges for the Linn Street Café to cater the reception and Irene is grateful. Under normal circumstances, she would insist on doing everything herself—but these aren't normal circumstances. The people from the café will drop off sandwiches, quiche, salads, and urns of coffee. Irene chills wine and rolls her drinks trolley into the parlor. With so many people in the room, it will be too warm to light a fire and Irene will be so busy visiting that she won't have time to tend it.

Irene is anxious about facing everyone. She doesn't want to be the recipient of sympathy or to be asked any probing questions. She nearly succumbs to the temptation of taking an Ativan right before the reception begins. She has the prescription bottle in her hand, but the doorbell rings and Irene hurries downstairs.

It's Lydia, attended by Brandon the barista, who looks far more distinguished out of his leather apron. He's holding Lydia's hand, and with his other hand he offers Irene a platter of cookies.

"Homemade," he says. "Lemongrass sugar."

Irene tries out a smile. Lydia looks radiant. She and Brandon are delirious with infatuation, and Irene is, of course, happy for her friend. Brandon and Lydia take charge of setting out the food and cups for coffee and filling buckets with ice, leaving Irene idle to steep in her dread and count the minutes until she boards the plane.

The doorbell rings again. Irene mentally pulls herself up by her bootstraps. Compared to what she's been through already, this is nothing. This is easy.

And for a while, it's not so bad. The Kinseys arrive, followed by the Dunns; Ed Sorley and his wife, Anita; Dot, the nurse from Brown Deer; and some of the neighbors. Nearly everyone from the magazine attends, including Irene's boss, Joseph Feeney, Mavis Key, and the receptionist, Jayne, who brings her newly retired husband, Rooney. Rooney is something of a blunderbuss. He's always the first to get drunk and obnoxious at the holiday party. He speaks without thinking, he's a know-it-all; honestly, Irene can't stand him. Thankfully, he leaves Jayne to gush out the condolences.

"I'm so sorry, Irene, none of us had any idea! But it was unusual for you to be out for an entire week without any notice. Of course, once we learned that Milly had passed, it all made sense...none of us knew that Russ...I mean, you've had *such* a double whammy!"

A little while later, Irene notices Rooney pouring himself a scotch at the drinks trolley. She needs to find Lydia and tell her to keep an eye on him. But she's too busy. She has to spend time with everyone, nodding her head and lying by omission.

Why is it the people you'd like to leave the party first are always the last to go? The party has thinned out to just Irene, Lydia and Brandon, Dot, Ed and Anita Sorley, and Jayne and Rooney. Irene finally allows herself to eat something—a lemongrass sugar cookie—and Brandon, ever the barista, steeps her a tea that he thinks will complement the cookie. Irene nearly laughs at the absurdity of the notion. *It's a cookie, Brandon,* she wants to say. Irene hasn't tasted anything since Russ died—except the fish that Huck grilled. That had been delicious.

Her thoughts are interrupted by Rooney, who raises his voice above the others and says, "Russ worked for a hedge fund, right? You're aware, I assume, that the Virgin Islands were recently added to a blacklist of tax havens by the EU? What kind of business was Russ involved in? Are you sure it was aboveboard?"

Brandon, possibly attempting to head Rooney away from the topic, makes things worse. "What does that mean, a blacklist of tax havens?" He looks around the room and shrugs. "I can explain the difference between a latte and an Americano, but tax havens confound me."

"What does it *mean?*" Rooney asks in a way that makes it clear he isn't sure what it means. He's sitting in the velvet-upholstered bergère chair, holding court now. "It means they conduct business without obeying the tax code. We're talking money-laundering, numbered accounts at banks in Switzerland and the Cayman Islands, shell companies, dark money, terrorists, drug dealers, human traffickers..."

Irene shoots a look at Ed Sorley. *The Cayman Islands?*

Jayne emits a nervous laugh. "Rooney, *stop,*" she says. "You knew Russ. He was...well, he was the nicest man in the world is what he was."

"I second that," Dot says.

"Sometimes it's the nice guys who are the worst criminals,"

Rooney says. "Because they're the ones you'd least suspect of anything."

Irene stands up. "I'm feeling a little worn out," she says, and everyone takes the hint.

Monday afternoon, Irene's ferry pulls in among the powerboats and catamarans moored in Cruz Bay, and Irene scans the crescent of white sand that's home to a string of open-air restaurants backed by palm trees. She feels like she can breathe again. It's bizarre that the place her husband conducted his wild and massive deception has become her refuge. Irene doesn't want to overthink this and she doesn't want to fight it. She's now experiencing the emotions one *should* feel upon arriving on St. John: anticipation and joy.

Both of her boys are here, and her grandson. It feels like an embarrassment of riches, all of them choosing to be together this time, choosing to be in the paradise Russ unwittingly brought them to.

Cash had texted Irene the night before to let her know that today was his first day as a crew member aboard *Treasure Island*. He thought he'd be back in time to pick Irene up, but if not, he'd send Baker. However, when Irene steps off the ferry and grabs her luggage—two rolling suitcases that contain sundresses, sandals, plenty of bathing suits, and some old fishing shirts that she used to wear out on Clark Lake—she doesn't see either Cash or Baker, and she's annoyed. Have they forgotten her?

"Irene!"

Irene looks around. Huck is in the parking lot, standing in front of his truck. Irene can't believe the feeling that overcomes her. She ducks her head so he can't see her smiling.

Get a grip! she thinks. *It's just Huck.* "Oh, hi," she says. She grabs her luggage and starts rolling it over to his truck. "Are you here for me?"

"Baker took Floyd to the Gifft Hill School and Maia wanted to show them around," Huck says. "So that left me free to pick you up."

Things are really happening, then—Cash started a job, Floyd will go to school. Irene opens the passenger door to Huck's truck.

"Wait a minute," Huck says. He strides over and puts his hands on her shoulders and looks her in the eye. "It's good to see you, Angler Cupcake. I'm glad you're back."

Irene feels herself reddening. "Stop it," she says. "You're embarrassing me."

On the way to Russ's villa, Irene thinks it best to fill Huck in on what's been happening.

She says, "I've had a visit from the FBI."

Huck says, "I'm afraid that might have been my fault. I had a call from an agent down here right after you left to let me know that they'd opened an investigation into the crash—"

"Yes," Irene says. "The boys and I received calls as well—"

"And then I contacted Agent Vasco myself last week to let her know that... well, we found money in Rosie's room."

Irene gazes out the window, trying to focus on the views. The vista of the neighboring islands across the turquoise water is nothing short of spectacular. Less than a month ago, Irene made the same drive but she saw nothing, noticed nothing.

Money. "How much?"

"A lot."

"How much, Huck?"

"A hundred and twenty-five grand."

A hundred and twenty-five grand. A hot, nauseating panic rises in Irene's chest. "In cash, you mean?"

"Yes, in cash. Bricks of it."

"And they took it?"

"They took it," Huck says. He lights a cigarette and blows the smoke out his window. "And I heard they paid a visit to Welcome to Paradise Real Estate."

"Dear God," Irene says. "Paulette?"

"She left the island. Her husband and her son too."

"She left the island?" Irene says. "I called and left a message asking for a certified copy of the death certificate and she never returned my call, but then, voilà, a copy came in the mail."

"Well, that's good," Huck says. "Right?"

"I thought Russ was still alive somewhere," Irene says. "I had these dreams where he was so...*vivid,* so present, so whole. He was there, three-dimensionally, in my mind. And when I'd wake up, I'd think, *He made it out of that helicopter and Croft plucked him out of the sea and whisked him away.*" Irene is mortified when her voice breaks. "I thought he was just hiding somewhere. I thought I'd see him again."

Huck takes Irene's hand. Irene looks down to see their fingers intertwined, her hand slender and wrinkled and white, his large and wrinkled and brown.

"The FBI didn't find anything in Iowa," Irene says. "Did they find anything in your house, other than the money? Did they find anything in Rosie's room?"

"Not that I know of," Huck says. "I had Ayers go through Rosie's things while Maia was at school. Ayers was the one who discovered the money."

"But not anything else?" Irene says. "No clues? No...explanations?"

"No," Huck says.

"And we can trust Ayers?" Irene asks. "We don't think she knows more than she's saying, do we?"

"I trust her," Huck says. "She's just as in the dark as you and me."

"But she was Rosie's best friend," Irene says. "Her confidante. Surely..."

"Where the Invisible Man was concerned, Rosie was a brick wall," Huck says. He signals to turn up Lovers Lane. "Sorry—I mean Russ."

"It's okay," Irene says. "The nickname fits."

When they get to the house, they see both Jeeps are gone; the boys must still be out. Huck brings Irene's luggage up the stone steps to the deck.

"Will you stay for a beer?" Irene asks.

"I should go collect Maia," he says.

"No, of course," Irene says. She needs to shower and unpack. The news of the FBI, the cash, and Paulette *leaving the island* has Irene rattled. "Are you *worried,* Huck? Does it feel like the fire is getting a little close?"

"I'm concerned," Huck says. "I want to remain informed and aware, but I'm not going to let this whole mess control me. This has nothing to do with us, AC. I have a clean conscience and I know you do as well."

"I do," Irene says.

"I'll tell you if we ever have reason to worry," he says. "Will you trust me on that?"

Irene nods. It's remarkable how much better she feels knowing Huck's on her side. If he's not going to worry, she isn't either.

"I'll take a rain check on the beer," Huck says. "I promise.

And hey, we have an afternoon charter on Wednesday. Two couples from Wichita."

"So you haven't had second thoughts?" Irene says. "You still want me to be your first mate?"

"I *need* you to be my first mate," Huck says.

"I'll come on Wednesday and we'll see how I do, okay? But I promise I won't be offended if you want to hire some young guy." She winks at him. "Or young woman."

"Agent Vasco was quite attractive," Huck says. "I nearly offered *her* the job."

"Oh, *was* she," Irene says. She sounds jealous to her own ears.

"Are you jealous?" Huck asks.

"Are you trying to make me jealous?" Irene says.

"I dunno. Maybe."

"Well, maybe it worked," Irene says. She's afraid to look Huck in the eye so she busies herself by rolling her suitcases over to the slider. "Thank you for coming to get me. I'll see you Wednesday."

Huck smiles at her, shaking his head, and she thinks, *What? What?*

She shoos him away and he heads down the stairs. Only once he's gone can Irene get a clear breath. She is so keyed up when he's around, both agitated and happy.

Agent Vasco was attractive. Bah!

Before she goes into the house, Irene stands at the stone wall and inhales the sight of the sea and the verdant island mountains and the lush hillside below. It's the prettiest place she's ever seen, but what is she doing here? It's truly insane, this decision to move down to work on a fishing boat. Has she lost her mind?

Well, yes, Irene thinks. She probably has. And good for her.

AYERS

On Tuesday night, Mick announces that he's going over to St. Thomas the next morning and he won't be back until late, so he can't meet Ayers after her charter with a smoothie.

"I guess the honeymoon is over," Ayers says. "I knew it wouldn't last. What's happening in St. Thomas?"

"Picking up some stuff for the bar," Mick says.

"Really?" Ayers says. "Like what, from where?"

"Stuff, from places," Mick says. "Paper straws, for one thing. I have to take all the plastic straws to recycling and replace them with paper straws. Which, although environmentally friendly, disintegrate once they come in contact with liquid, thereby providing a poor straw experience."

"And what else?"

"What's with the third degree?" Mick asks.

She didn't sleep with Baker. When he pulled up alongside of her out of the blue, she thought, *Is this really happening?* And then, without thinking twice, she'd climbed into the car with him and directed him to Hawksnest. She thought they would just sit in the parking lot and talk but that wasn't very romantic, so she led him down the path toward the beach, which was deserted, and she thought, *Is that what I want? Romantic?*

The truth is, she hasn't stopped thinking of him since he left. She doesn't want to like him, but she does. And reading Rosie's journals is screwing with her head. *Rosie willingly had an affair with a man she knew was married.* Ayers's own dear, sweet friend, a person Ayers admired and respected, did that. The story in the diary is, at least, providing some context. Russ was unhappy, at a crossroads career-wise, and he'd been dropped into paradise for the weekend, where he'd met Rosie, who even on her worst day was achingly beautiful. Something had sparked between them—then ignited. It's the spark and the flame that intrigue Ayers. Did two good people do something they knew was wrong because there was some kind of magical chemistry involved? Or was it plain old human fallibility, weakness in the face of temptation?

Ayers isn't sure. What she is drawn to in Rosie's journal is the rawness of Rosie's desire for Russ and her pain when he leaves.

Has Ayers ever felt that way about *anyone?* Does she feel that way about Mick? She was hurt and angry—really angry—when she found Mick with Brigid, but that pain might simply have been the blow to her self-esteem and the sting of being rejected. The truth is, the way she feels about Mick now has changed. She still loves him but she doesn't trust him and she doesn't trust herself, and sometimes she thinks she went back to him only because it was comfortable and familiar, whereas the idea of embarking on a whole new relationship with Baker Steele is terrifying. And unrealistic. He's still married. He lives in Houston.

Once they were on the beach, Baker reached for Ayers's hand, but she batted him away, then turned to confront him. There wasn't a moon; it was really dark. Ayers could barely see Baker, but despite this, there was an instant pull of attraction. He was so tall and broad; she loved having to crane her neck to look up at him. He had a fresh haircut, she'd noticed; it looked good with his chiseled features and his dimple. He'd gone soft around the middle and there was something dad-like and a little nerdy in his demeanor. But these things set her at ease.

"I didn't bring you here for that," Ayers said. "I want to talk."

Baker nodded. "Yeah, me too. Sorry, it's a beach, we were walking, I've been thinking of you every second of every day since I left, so believe me when I say that reaching for your hand was something I did instinctively."

"I need to know a couple things," she said. "One, are you still married?"

"Legally, yes," Baker said. "It's only been a few weeks. But Anna, my wife, accepted a surgical post at the Cleveland Clinic with her girlfriend, Louisa, so they're moving and giving me physical custody of Floyd."

"Have you started divorce proceedings?" Ayers asked. "Have you spoken to a lawyer?"

"We're using a mediator," Baker said. "And yes, I've spoken to her. This is happening. There's no going back. I actually had dinner with Anna and Louisa a few days ago, and, wow, they're *together*. Two peas in a pod. An intimidating pair."

Intimidating, Ayers thought, because they weren't sexually attracted to men. Ayers let Baker's typical attitude slide because she had a more pressing question. "How long are you staying down here?"

"We're moving here," Baker said. "I have Floyd with me. I want to put him in school."

This wasn't the answer Ayers was expecting. "So you packed up all your stuff and shipped it down here?"

"Well..." Baker said.

No, she didn't think so. It would have been too good to be true.

"We're here for two weeks. Then I have to go back to Houston for this event at Floyd's school."

Which he was supposedly pulling Floyd out of.

"And then I'll take care of packing up the rest of what we need."

"So it's your *intention* to move down here," Ayers said. "But if after two weeks you aren't feeling it, you'll go back to Houston."

"It's my intention to stay," Baker said. "Cash is staying. And tonight I found out my mother is coming down. So I'll have a built-in support system."

Irene, Ayers thought. She had a whole new set of feelings about Irene now that she'd read Rosie's journals—mostly fear that she, Ayers, could someday be duped and blindsided as badly as Irene had been. It was so important to stay vigilant where your heart was concerned. Why didn't they teach you that in school?

"What about a job?" Ayers said. "Cash has a job, with me." Even in the darkness, she could see Baker wince. "I won't believe you're staying until you have something tethering you to this island."

"I'm going to look for a job," Baker said. "I day-trade for money, I can do that anywhere, which is how I'm able to pick up and leave Houston. But I want something part-time here, something flexible so I can still be around for Floyd. I admit I don't have any leads yet. I just got here today. The first thing I wanted to do was find you."

"I'm still with Mick," Ayers said.

"I know," Baker said. "Cash told me." He reached out and touched a strand of her hair. "I'm not going to put any pressure on you. I just want you to know that I'm here because of you."

Against her wishes, this affected her. "I'm with Mick," she said again, weakly.

"Well, if things don't work out with Mick, I'll be here waiting." He grinned. "Like a complete idiot. An utter fool."

She laughed, then they stood smiling at each other and she thought, *He's going to try and kiss me.*

He bent down toward her—but stopped. "Come on," he said. "I'll take you back to town."

Wednesday morning, Ayers drives down to *Treasure Island* and Mick follows behind her in his blue Jeep with Gordon hanging his head over the side. They're on their way to the ferry; Mick honks as he peels off.

They have a full boat today, twenty people, six of them kids, and handling that is a tall order, especially because it's only Cash's third day of work, his first without Wade there to train him. But Cash seems to be a natural when it comes to managing groups of strangers all keyed up for an adventure. He's courteous and convivial, he has the gift of gab, and it's clear that he takes his procedural responsibilities—the passport paperwork, tying up at the docks, cleaning and prepping all the snorkel equipment, and assisting with any young, old, or infirm guests—very seriously. Of course, this job offers a different roll of the dice each and every day; that's one of the things Ayers likes about it. Occasionally there are mechanical issues with the boat or the weather isn't great, but that's for Captain James to deal with. Ayers and Cash handle the humans.

Ayers goes to the top deck to put out the seat cushions. Six kids is a lot, she thinks, especially if the parents start drinking.

She decides to tell Cash that she'll manage the kids and he'll be in charge of the adults.

Adults are easier. Most of the time.

From her perch, Ayers spies Mick on the top deck of the ferry, Gordon with him on a leash, garnering attention from every dog lover on the boat. Mick took Gordon with him because, with both Ayers and Mick gone all day, there'd be no one to let him out. Still, Ayers suspects Mick also brought Gordon because Gordon is a chick magnet. And sure enough, a girl with long brown hair in a cute white sundress takes the seat next to Mick. The girl puts her arm around Mick and lays her head on his shoulder, so it must be someone they know. Ayers squints; the girl lifts her head and turns.

It's Brigid.

To get some stuff for the bar, Ayers thinks. *Paper straws.* This is such bullshit, Ayers can't believe she bought it! Well, she didn't quite buy it, did she? She'd had a funny feeling because Mick *hated* going to St. Thomas. If there was a reason to go, he'd send one of his employees. But when Ayers asked follow-up questions, he'd accused her of giving him the third degree, and she hadn't argued the point because she was feeling guilty about the journals and about seeing Baker.

Brigid! Where is he going with Brigid? To the recycling center and the restaurant-supply store? Or to the Tap and Still for a long boozy lunch followed by... what? Not back until late, he said. What a jerk!

Gordon puts his paws up on Brigid's knees and starts licking her face, and Ayers turns away; if she watches any longer, she's going to be sick. She pulls her phone out of her shorts pocket and as she's wondering what to text to Mick—what can she say that will make him feel as nauseated as she feels right now?—Cash calls up the stairs.

"Paperwork is ready," he says. "Permission to board?"

"Permission granted," James says from the wheelhouse.

Ayers's phone says it's ten past eight. Time to get everyone on so they can leave. She shoves her phone back into her shorts pocket, then whips it back out and shoots a quick text to Mick: I saw you with Brigid. Please don't ever call me again. It's over.

She feels triumphant, but it lasts only an instant.

Brigid!

The six children are all in the same family, the Dresslers, and they're all boys, towheaded and tan, ranging in age from fourteen to six. They all have D-names: DJ, Danny, Damian, Duncan, Donner ("Like the reindeer," the mother says), and Dougie.

Who names a child after a *reindeer?* Ayers wonders. She's in a foul mood.

The kids seem relatively well behaved, and the parents—Dave and Donna—are a striking couple, tall and superior-looking. Donna carries a bag (as big as Santa's!) that holds the entire family's snorkeling equipment.

You just never know what you're going to get, Ayers thinks. Today it's a cross between the von Trapp children and Russian matryoshka dolls.

She finds Cash in the cabin; he's setting out the platter of fruit and the sliced coconut-banana bread. The greatest thing about Cash is he doesn't mind the menial jobs. He thinks it's a privilege! And Cash is clearly skilled with a knife. The fruit is uniformly sliced and spread out in an appetizing pinwheel.

Ayers pulls Cash aside. "I'll keep a close eye on the boys. You take the so-called grown-ups."

"Got it, boss," he says. He turns from Ayers and smiles at a young woman who is hanging by the counter. "What can I get for you?"

"When does the bar open?" the young woman asks.

Ayers has to wait a beat before she answers. This happens every day, but Ayers is in no mood right now for someone whose sole reason for coming aboard *Treasure Island* is to get shitfaced.

"No alcohol until we're under way," Ayers says. "And even then, I'd urge you to be prudent until the snorkeling portion is over."

"Prudent is my middle name," she says. "But snorkeling is quite a while from now, isn't it?"

"Yes," Ayers says. "Baths first—including travel, that takes two hours—then the captain will pick a snorkeling spot. We should be finished snorkeling by eleven or eleven thirty."

"That's a long time to be prudent," the woman says.

Ayers feels herself about to snap. "Once we are on our way to Jost, you can drink as much as you want."

Cash says, "If Prudent is your middle name, what's your first name?" He sticks out a hand. "I'm Cash."

"I'm Maxwell," she says.

"That's your *first* name?" Cash asks.

"'Fraid so," she says. "It's kind of confusing, but don't worry, I'm *very* female." She sticks her chest out at Cash, and Ayers notices a tattoo of a keyhole between her breasts. Ayers gets it—she's waiting for the person who holds the key to her heart.

Cash must notice the tattoo at the same time—how could he not; it's nestled right there between her boobs, which are straining against the green cups of her bikini—because he says, "Cool tattoo."

Maxwell glances down at her chest as if she has no idea what he's talking about. "Oh, thanks," she says. Over the bikini, she's wearing a sheer green paisley peasant blouse. She gives a tiny shrug, and the blouse slips down off her shoulder. This girl has all the moves and she has her bright gaze trained on Cash. "I hope you don't mind my hanging around. It's just that I came on this trip by myself. I'm visiting a friend of mine from high school who lives here but she said she has a lot of errands today because she works at night—"

Ayers can't stop herself from jumping in. "Is your friend named Brigid, by any chance?"

"No," Maxwell says.

"Long shot, I know," Ayers says. "You just remind me of someone."

"Anyway," Maxwell says, now showing Cash one creamy shoulder, "she encouraged me to come out on this tour. She said it's the *best*." She beams at Cash, as though *Treasure Island*'s sterling reputation is all Cash's doing. "I think she was trying to get rid of me. I can be a lot."

"You?" Ayers says.

The boat engine starts. Cash says, "I have to go tend to the ropes. Excuse me, Maxwell."

"Just call me Max," she says. "When you're finished, will you come back and make me a painkiller, extra strong?"

"You got it," Cash says. He gives her a wink and shoots out a finger like Isaac, the bartender from *The Love Boat,* a cultural reference Ayers suspects is lost on Max.

Ayers wrestles with her wandering mind. She told Cash she would keep an eye on the kids and let him handle the adults, but by now, all six of the boys might have drowned.

Ayers puts on her headset. "I'm about to give the safety talk," she says to Max. "You should listen."

* * *

The ride to Virgin Gorda is smooth. Ayers makes herself notice how glorious the water, the sky, and the emerald-green islands are. She is so lucky to live here, to have this job and her job at La Tapa, her friends, her community, Maia and Huck. Rosie is gone, but at least while Ayers is reading the journals, it feels like she has Rosie back. It feels like Rosie is, finally, telling her everything.

But then she succumbs to the red, hot, itchy temptation of thinking about Mick and Brigid. *Brigid!* If Ayers had seen Mick with anyone else—Emily Ratajkowski, Scarlett Johansson with her tongue in Mick's ear—it wouldn't have sickened Ayers the way seeing him with Brigid has. Why did he even bother getting back together with her? Because she was hurting? Because he felt *sorry* for her? Because her apartment was far more homey and comfortable than the rat hole where he and Gordon lived? Is he using her? Preying on her pain and her wobbly judgment? She's actively mourning the loss of her best friend and she has been trying to hold it together so she can be whole and strong for Maia. How *dare* Mick go behind her back *again* after all Ayers has just been through. That is what makes this unforgivable.

She scans the boat, looking for anyone who seems to be suffering from seasickness, but the passengers look calm and happy, their faces turned toward the sun, hair blowing back in the breeze. The six boys are sitting on a bench between the statuesque bookends of their parents, and there isn't a single electronic device among them, which Ayers finds impressive.

She leans toward the mother, Donna, and says, "Your boys are so well behaved."

Donna wraps her arm around the youngest, Dougie, who is

sitting next to her, and kisses the top of his head. "Believe me, this is a rare moment of peace. We told them if they behaved today, we'd rent a dinghy tomorrow and go to the pizza boat in Christmas Cove."

"Good bribe!" Ayers says. "I love Pizza Pi." Mick had said something the night before about borrowing his boss's boat so they could raft up in Christmas Cove on Monday—eat pizza, listen to live music.

Maybe now he'll take Brigid.

"How do you manage six boys?" Ayers asks. Because she's an only child, she has always been fascinated by big families and she still harbors a fantasy of having a bunch of kids herself someday. Which will probably never happen, seeing as how she can't even sustain a relationship. (She has to lasso her psyche! Stay in the moment!) "Isn't it a lot, to keep track of their sports and activities and their dental appointments and haircuts and stuff?" Just looking at the Dressler family brings up visions of reminders written on a chalkboard in the mudroom, a color-coded calendar, baskets labeled with each boy's name to hold hats and gloves and rainboots.

"They're all swimmers," Donna says. "I just drop them off at the Y on Saturday morning and collect them at the end of the day. I go to some of the meets, though I've learned to pick and choose. I used to go to every single one and my hair turned green just from sitting in the pool balcony for so long." She laughs. "They aren't interested in impressing me, anyway. They want to impress their coach, their teammates, and each other. They all swim freestyle and do the IM, so it's pretty intense competition." She looks down to the end of the bench and whispers, "DJ has just committed to swim at Stanford."

"That's so cool," Ayers says. "Where are you guys from?"

"Philadelphia," Donna says. "The Main Line."

Sure, of course, Ayers might have predicted that. The Dresslers probably live in an old stone house that has a creek running behind it. The husband, Dave, probably takes the train downtown to work, and Donna probably makes enormous dinners—Taco Tuesdays!—that the boys devour, exhausted from a day of school and swimming the fifty-free in under a minute. Ayers feels herself falling in love with the Dressler family. *Adopt me, please,* she thinks.

But maybe there are secrets, like soft spots on a seemingly perfect apple. Maybe Donna is having an affair with the kids' swim coach; maybe Dave is a degenerate gambler who has lost the college savings; maybe the oldest boy got his girlfriend pregnant, which he'll reveal the day they get home from this vacation, and suddenly, Stanford will be called into question.

Ayers shakes her head. What is *wrong* with her today? She suspects it's a combination of the diaries and seeing Mick and Brigid together. It feels like the whole world is hiding something.

Ayers lifts her gaze from Donna to the cabin of the boat. The past two days, Cash has circulated around the boat and introduced himself to the guests, but there he is, behind the bar, making that chick Max another drink.

In the seven years that Ayers has been working on *Treasure Island,* she has seen a spectrum of eye-popping outfits, which she and Wade have put into three categories. Category one, the most popular, was the Siren. This included teensy bikinis and wet T-shirts. Category two was the Riviera Gigolo, a gentle way of describing men who wore, instead of trunks, European-cut briefs—nut-huggers, grape-smugglers, banana hammocks. Category three was the Vampire. These folks showed up in head-to-toe Lycra—usually black, for some reason—because they couldn't risk exposure to the sun. (The Lycra suits were always accompanied by wide-brimmed floppy hats.) Ayers was all about SPF but in her opinion, if exposure to sunlight was *that* verboten, then a day trip on *Treasure Island*—hell, a vacation on a Caribbean island in general—probably wasn't for you.

Once Max takes the paisley peasant blouse off and slides out of her jean shorts, Ayers sees that the green bikini consists of only three tiny triangles of iridescent material (possibly meant to reference fish scales) and some string. It's a dental-floss thong, leaving the pale orbs of Max's buttocks exposed. Ayers notices a tattoo on the right cheek—a pair of lips.

Kiss my ass, Ayers thinks. *Got it.* Max's body is a living rebus.

Ayers is dismayed that Max chose to wear such a revealing suit on a family-oriented boat trip. What must the six boys think? At least half of them will be ogling her all day; it's impossible *not* to ogle her.

Donna gives Ayers a sympathetic smile. "If you've got it, flaunt it."

That's a generous perspective, Ayers thinks. She will bet anyone the keys to her truck that Max is going to lose her bikini when she jumps off the boat to swim into the Baths.

Ayers puts on her headset and runs through the drill: Jump in, swim to shore, here are the life vests, and does anyone need a noodle?

Everyone does just fine—including six-year-old Dougie—and then Max climbs up to the edge of the bow and turns around in a panic. "Where's Cash?" she says. "I want Cash to go with me."

"He's onshore already, Max," Ayers says. "See him there?" Cash is standing on the small golden beach herding everyone toward the entrance of the Baths. He's going to lead the tour today and Ayers is bringing up the rear. "Just jump in and swim right for him, okay?"

"Oh, okay," Max says. She waves both arms overhead. "Cash! Cash!" She loses her footing and falls in. Ayers peers over the edge, checking to see whether Max can swim or if Ayers will have to save her.

To be safe, Ayers jumps in a few feet away. "You okay?"

Max is busy doing the doggie paddle, eyes squeezed shut, and because she is, actually, making forward progress, Ayers lets her be, swimming behind her just in case.

She can't believe this chick isn't a friend of Brigid.

"Looks like you have a barnacle on your boat," Ayers says to Cash once they're all back aboard *Treasure Island*. Max had trailed Cash through the Baths so closely that whenever he stopped, she bumped into him. At Cathedral, she jumped off the ledge into his arms and clung to him far longer than was necessary.

"Huh?" Cash says. "Oh, yeah. She's harmless." They both turn to see Max standing at the bar, waiting for Cash so he can make her another drink and she can show him her chest.

James anchors off the coast of Norman Island for snorkeling because there are already three boats parked over at the Indians. Cash helps everyone with equipment, and Ayers goes to see how the Dressler boys are faring.

"They're all set," Donna says. "But thank you."

Ayers finds herself with a free minute and she's in a spot that has reliable cell service. Should she check her phone? See if Mick responded?

No, she decides. If he knows what's good for him, he'll ditch Brigid and be waiting at the dock for Ayers, smoothie in hand.

Is that what she wants?

She checks her phone despite herself. There are two texts from Mick, but Cash has started sending people into the water. She has to go.

Ayers snorkels with the Dressler boys and encourages two of the middle ones to follow her over to a rocky outcrop of Norman where the spotted eagle rays like to hang out. She can hear the boys oohing and aahing through their snorkels, and as always, this makes her happy. Some things are more important than her romantic trials and tribulations. Things like wonder.

Ayers raises her head and sees everyone heading back to the boat. She lets the boys swim ahead and she brings up the rear, scanning the water for the fluorescent orange tape on the tips of their snorkels.

When she climbs up to the deck, she says, "Everyone accounted for?"

"Yes," Cash says.

Ayers signals James, who starts the engine, and Cash goes to pull the anchor, which makes his muscles pop in a way that is undeniably attractive. Ayers can't believe Max isn't right beside him, taking pictures for her Instagram account: #coldhardcash.

When the anchor is up and they're moving, Ayers says, "Where's the barnacle?"

"Wait," Cash says. "What?"

Panic in the form of absolute stillness seizes Ayers. "Stop the boat!" she yells.

* * *

Max is not dead and Max is not lost. Ayers repeats this like a mantra, though for the first thirty seconds after Ayers realizes Max isn't on the boat (how can she not be on the boat? And why did Cash say everyone was present? Did he not do a head count?), these are Ayers's prevailing thoughts, that Max is dead or Max is missing and will turn up dead.

James cuts the engines and Ayers races up to the top deck with the binoculars, trying not to exude any sign of the sheer terror she is feeling. But the rest of the guests realize something is wrong. Ayers overhears Cash say, "We're missing someone, the woman in the green bikini." Then everyone starts looking. They spread out around the port side and starboard side and the bow. Ayers's main concern is that Max is *under* the boat, that they unwittingly ran over her when they lifted anchor and started toward Jost Van Dyke.

Max is not dead and Max is not lost, Ayers tells herself.

Cash appears next to her. "I'm so sorry, I thought—"

"There's no *time* for sorry!" Ayers says. She mentally breaks the water into a grid and starts scanning it square foot by square foot. In seven years, she has never lost a swimmer. She has had to do only five rescues—five, in seven years. Today will be her sixth rescue, she tells herself. Today, she will rescue Max.

Someone calls out, "Over there!"

Ayers follows the pointing arm of Mr. Dressler. Yes, she sees a piece of fluorescent tape about two hundred yards away. Before Ayers knows what's happening, someone dives off the lower deck of the boat and starts swimming toward the snorkeler. It's the oldest Dressler kid, DJ, Ayers realizes. She strips off her shorts, and, although it's forbidden, she dives off the top deck, hits the water with so much force that her nose and ears flood with water, and swims after him. A second later, she feels the concussion of someone else plunging in nearby and she envisions everyone on the boat trying to be a hero.

She raises her head in order to get her bearings. Cash goes thrashing past her. He's moving so fast he nearly catches DJ. Ayers sees DJ and then Cash reach the snorkeler and Ayers hears shouts. She swims closer, and only then does she realize that the snorkeler isn't a she. The snorkeler isn't Max. It's some guy from another boat who has also gone rogue.

"Go back to your boat!" Ayers yells to the other snorkeler. She casts about helplessly. Where is Max?

She hears the air horn and swivels her head to see Captain James on the top deck windmilling his arm to beckon her back.

What? Ayers thinks. *We can't just leave her here.* Or...has Max turned up? DJ and Cash are already swimming back to the boat and Ayers puts her head down and powers forward with everything she's got left, thinking, *Please let her be okay, please let her be alive.* If she's injured, they can get her to Schneider Hospital on St. Thomas in half an hour.

When Ayers is only a few yards from the boat, James calls out, "She's aboard."

"She is?"

"She was in the head," James says. "Why didn't you guys check?"

In the head. Max was using the bathroom. Why didn't Ayers check?

Sure enough, Max is sitting on the stairs to the upper deck (which isn't allowed) drinking what's left of a painkiller when Ayers hauls herself up the ladder.

Ayers can't bring herself to say anything to the girl. What would she say? *We thought we'd lost you. We thought you drowned.* At which point, Max would say, *I went to the bath-*

room. Sorry, I didn't know I needed to report in. I wanted to change my swimsuit. Because, yup, Max is wearing a new bikini, white, which Ayers will (again) bet the key to her truck becomes completely see-through when wet.

Ayers climbs past Max without a word and goes into the wheelhouse to apologize to James.

"I'm sorry," she says. "I should have checked the head. I..." Ayers tries to explain what made her jump to the conclusion that Max was still in the water. All Cash had said was *Wait. What?* Ayers was the one who had panicked. "She'd been drinking. More than everyone else combined. I guess my mind supplied the worst-case scenario, that she went out snorkeling while drunk and she drowned."

James gives her the eyebrows. He's a man of few words, though he's been blessed with wisdom beyond his years—he's thirty-five; he went to high school with Rosie—and a dry sense of humor. "If I didn't know you better, I'd say you were jealous."

"Jealous of Max?" Ayers says. "Please give me some credit."

"She's been hanging on your boy," James says. "And we both know it's not like you to fly off like that."

"First of all, he's not my boy," Ayers says. "Is that what you think?"

James starts the engine.

"I'd like permission to cut her off," Ayers says. "She's had enough to drink."

"She didn't do anything wrong," James says. He leaves it unspoken that this whole event was Ayers's fault. Ayers can only imagine what kind of dramatic retelling the fourteen adults will provide on TripAdvisor.

"I'm sorry," Ayers says again. "I'm having a bad day."

James nods. "You're allowed," he says. He laughs. "Tell you what, though—your boy sure can swim."

Ayers puts on the headset. "Sorry about that, folks," she says. She notices that the Dressler kids are all lined up at the railing seeing who can spit the farthest and there's now a queue at the bar three-deep.

Right, she thinks. Crisis averted, people are getting bored, time to drink. "We're on our way over to Jost Van Dyke, named for the man who discovered it in the early seventeenth century. It became a center of custom shipbuilding, but now, however, Jost is most famous for its world-class beach bars, including Foxy's, One Love, and...the Soggy Dollar!"

Everyone claps. She's forgiven.

There's no happier place on earth than White Bay on a sunny day. The stunning crescent of powder-fine sand is lined with palm trees and funky, bare-bones beach bars. *Treasure Island* slips in among a flotilla of boats. There are people splashing in the shallows, tossing a football; there's reggae music and the smell of jerk chicken and the low buzz of blenders making Bushwackers and piña coladas.

"Please get yourself some lunch," Ayers says. "And try not to wander off. We'd like you back on the boat at two thirty sharp."

Ayers counts the Dressler kids as they jump off the boat in succession. There's a bit of a wade required, which the boys don't seem to mind. To DJ, Ayers says, "Thank you for your help. You're a fast swimmer."

DJ shrugs and Donna Dressler puts a hand on Ayers's shoulder and says, "That was some unexpected drama, huh?"

Ayers spies Max walking down the beach—with Cash, of

course—toward the Soggy Dollar. "I don't know if I should feel angry or relieved."

"Sounds like being a parent," Donna says. "You're not sure whether to ground them or hug them."

Grounding sounds good, Ayers thinks.

Lunch isn't a bad idea, and Ayers is a big fan of the Soggy Dollar lobster roll, so she walks down the beach and into the bar. Her favorite bartender, Leon, is pouring something pink and fruity out of the blender and into two cups, which he delivers to Max and Cash, who are sitting together at the end of the bar.

Cash says, "I'm on the clock," and passes his drink to Max.

"Awwww," she says. "Thanks." She leans her head on Cash's shoulder and closes her eyes.

Did Ayers give Cash "the talk" about not fraternizing with the guests? She knows she didn't. It never occurred to her that it would be a problem. Cash had been so earnest, so eager to please—please her, Ayers—that she hadn't realized that many if not all of the available women (and maybe even those who weren't necessarily available) would find Cash sexy and attractive and throw themselves at him as inelegantly as moths beating themselves against a screen.

Cash nudges Max's head off his shoulder and orders a Coke and a blackened mahi sandwich with coleslaw. He says, "So what do you do for work?"

"I sell drugs," Max says. She waits a beat, then honks out a laugh. "Not what you're thinking! I'm a pharmaceutical rep."

"Did you grow up in the Midwest?" Cash asks.

"Peoria," she says, diving nose-first into her pink drink.

"I'm from Iowa City!" Cash says.

Ayers isn't eavesdropping; she's just waiting to get Leon's attention. It's like she's invisible today. She debates interrupting the happy couple to remind Max to eat something, but she's not the girl's mother and she's afraid of sounding like a schoolmarm or a scold.

Max says something under her breath and Cash laughs. *Is* Ayers jealous? Maybe she is. She had thought Cash was in love with *her*. She thought Cash had taken the job on *Treasure Island* because he wanted to work with her. And yet he hasn't looked over at her even once. He's completely entranced with Max!

Ayers can't believe she's having these thoughts. She doesn't like Cash in that way—does she? She didn't think so, but right now, there's no denying she's jealous.

No, Ayers thinks. She enjoys being the object of Cash's affection. It's flattering, a boost to her ego. What's really going on is that she's upset about Mick and Brigid and confused about her feelings for Baker. Baker, who is maybe staying on St. John but also maybe not staying. Ayers would bet the keys to her truck *and* her apartment that Baker will go back to Houston for the school fund-raiser and never return. He'll find relocating too complicated. He'll spend two weeks on St. John and become bored; without a job to do, it's just sun, sand, and water. There are no museums or movie theaters, there are no professional sports teams or shopping malls. There isn't even any golf.

He won't stay. The schools won't be good enough for Floyd. Baker won't be able to find a fulfilling job; St. John isn't Wall Street. There will be some solid reason why he has to go back to the States. St. John is paradise when you visit, but when you live here, it becomes very real very quickly.

Ayers can't risk getting involved with Baker.

"Ayers," Cash says suddenly, yanking her out of her mental quicksand. "Would you like to join us?"

Ayers assesses her options. Cash's sandwich has now arrived and he offers some to Max, who slowly, *slowly,* shakes her head. She's slipping down her stool, melting like a candle.

Leon finally gives Ayers a wave. "I see you, darling. Just gonna be a minute."

"That's okay, Leon," Ayers says. "I'm not staying." She steps back out onto the sand. She'll head down to One Love, she decides, and get some jerk pork.

At a quarter after two, Ayers is feeling a little better. She has eaten and taken a ten-minute chair nap, and now she combs the beach for her guests, urging everyone to head back to the boat. If they get out of here at two thirty, there will be less of a line at customs.

Ayers has never so badly wanted a charter to end.

Coming toward her down the beach are Cash and Max. Max is stumbling and bent over; she's so drunk she can barely walk. Cash has to take her by the hand once they're wading back to the boat. If she fell over, she would drown in only two feet of water. Ayers wants to say something to Cash, something like *Why did you let her get so drunk?* She wants to point to Max and say to James, *We should have cut her off after snorkeling!* But instead, Ayers helps Cash get Max up the three-step ladder and onto the boat. Max heads toward starboard and Ayers thinks maybe she's going to the bar for another drink, but she bypasses the cabin, pushes little Dougie Dressler out of the way, and starts puking over the side of the boat.

Ayers bows her head. It would be very unprofessional to let the others see her smirking.

CASH

He's not sure how he got saddled with the drunk, and now crying, young woman named Maxwell—well, yes, he does know, he enabled her drinking and indulged her little crush on him because she's attractive and flirtatious, and both of these things seemed to bother Ayers, which was, he thought, a very good sign—but now he's responsible for making sure she gets home safely.

"Find her friend, her people, whoever," Ayers says. "I'll clean the boat by myself."

"But—"

"And, please, Cash, don't let this happen again. These are our guests, not our friends."

"You're right," he says. "It won't happen again."

He half leads, half carries Max off the dock and into the streets of St. John. As they pulled into port, he'd asked Max the name of her friend from high school, but all she'd said was *I dunno,* and then she groaned and started vomiting again.

It hadn't been a good look for her, for him, or for *Treasure Island,* though everyone else on the boat seemed to take it in stride. The parents of the six boys used it as a cautionary tale. "That," Cash overheard the father whisper to the Stanford-bound DJ, "is what happens when you decide three shots of tequila sound good after midnight."

There was a couple on the boat, keen snorkelers who'd brought a checklist of fish they were hoping to see, and the man said, "I could have told you how this was going to end up, but she was having so much fun, I hated to put a damper on it."

"We've all been there," his wife said. "For me, it was the Sig Ep house at West Virginia University in 1996."

Cash tended to agree; many people at some point in their lives had overdone it like Max. Cash had sampled his father's scotch and smoked one of his cigars when he was a week away from graduating high school, and that had ended badly. And he had taken care of Claire Bellows after she drank Jägermeister from a flask in the bathroom during their junior prom.

The town is teeming with people. All of the tour boats have just disgorged their passengers and it's happy hour at nearly every bar in Cruz Bay. Cash has no leads on who he should hand this chick off to. No one seems to be waiting for her. Cash then tries to imagine bringing Max home to the villa, where Baker, Floyd, and his mother will all be waiting.

Nope. No chance.

"Cash!"

Cash cranes his neck, trying to figure out who's calling his name. Then someone appears under his nose.

It's Maia. With a boy in tow—a handsome young man with dark hair that has been highlighted in the front. He's a couple inches taller than Maia.

"Hey," Cash says. He's more than a little uncomfortable bumping into…well, his little sister…with Max draped over him like a fur coat. "What are you doing?"

Maia shrugs. "Hanging out." She nods at the boy next to her. "This is my friend Shane. He goes to Antilles."

"Hey, Shane," Cash says. Shane is the kid that Maia has a crush on; Cash remembers this much. It's nice that they're hanging out together—alone, from the looks of it; is that okay?—

and Cash feels honored to be introduced, but he really wishes it wasn't under these circumstances. Any minute, Max might projectile-vomit onto Shane's shoes.

"What are *you* doing?" Maia asks, taking an appraising look at Max.

"I'm...well, this woman was a guest on the boat and I'm trying to find her friend. She has a friend who lives here, she said, but I have no idea who it is or what to do."

"Is it Tilda?" Maia asks. "She was just here, looking for her friend who was visiting...from Chicago." Maia turns to Shane. "Did she say Chicago?"

Shane nods. "Definitely Chicago," he says. "But I thought her friend was a boy."

"Was she looking for a Max?" Cash asks. "Maxwell?"

"Yes!" Maia says.

"*Tilda* is her friend?" Cash says. "Really? The Tilda that I know? Tilda from La Tapa?"

"Yeah," Maia says. "She worked with my mom."

"Right, yes, yes," Cash says. He's forgotten that everyone on this island is connected. "I'm going to sit with Max on this bench. Can you guys go find Tilda and tell her where we are?"

"Come on," Shane says, clearly energized by this mission. He takes Maia's hand and leads her across the street toward the docks. Is it okay that they're holding hands? Cash wonders. They look pretty darn cute.

"This way, Max, easy does it, here we go," Cash says. He sighs. He would give anything to be twelve again.

"I am *so* sorry about this," Tilda says. "I'm mortified. I told her to behave herself. I told her I worked with Ayers. And I'd forgotten that you were working on the boat now too. That makes it so much worse!"

"You don't have to apologize," Cash says. "It's not your fault." Cash offered to help Tilda get Max settled at home, and now he leans back into the soft leather seat of Tilda's Range Rover and enjoys the air-conditioning blowing full blast. Max is lying across the back seat, moaning. Tilda laid a beach towel across the floor of the car in case Max throws up again, although she's been at it for so long that Cash doesn't see how there could be anything left in her stomach. "I think maybe she was just nervous about going on the trip by herself."

"She should have made some friends," Tilda says.

"She sort of... attached herself to me," Cash says.

"Of course she did," Tilda says. "You're superhot and you're her type. You look *exactly* like her boyfriend in high school. Freddy Jarvis."

Cash isn't sure how he feels about being the reincarnation of high-school boyfriend Freddy Jarvis. If he'd seen a woman who looked like Claire Bellows, he would have steered clear. "I don't think Ayers was too happy about it."

"Oh, please," Tilda says. "As if Ayers isn't hit on herself every single charter."

"Is she?" Cash says. "She wasn't today."

"That's rare," Tilda says. "But Ayers is used to it. She never succumbs to temptation because she loves Mick." Tilda pauses. "Did you hear me, Cash? She loves Mick."

"I heard you," Cash says.

Tilda pulls up a steep incline called Upper Peter Bay and they go up, up, up until they can't go any farther. There's a gate; Tilda punches in the code and then they shoot down a driveway that's so steep Cash feels like he's on a luge or a log flume in the amusement park. They arrive, finally, at the villa, which is absolutely stunning. It's three separate buildings in the Spanish-mission style attached by arched, columned walkways.

"Um... okay?" Cash says.

"It's my parents'," Tilda says. "As is this Rover. They only come three times a year, and I have the west wing to myself." She parks the car. "Max is staying in the guest wing."

Cash follows Tilda through the main entrance into a foyer that's two stories high. Everything is white, with accents of palm green and the palest blue. To the right is a sweeping curved staircase; above it hangs a long, dripping chandelier that looks like crystal rain. In front of them is a white and pale blue living room and a white kitchen with a very cool curved bar around which are pale blue suede stools. Beyond the kitchen are floor-to-ceiling sliding doors that open out onto a patio and a T-shaped pool.

"That pool," Cash whispers. He's carrying Max like a bride over the threshold. She's snoring.

"The pool is for Granger, my dad," Tilda says. "He's very intense about his swimming. About everything, actually." Tilda sighs. "The only person who makes him seem relaxed is my mom. Now, *she's* a maniac."

Cash wants to hear more but Max is getting heavy. "Which way?"

They head out a side door and down one of the covered walkways into the guest wing. It's two stories, complete with its own garden and plunge pool. They are so high up that Cash can see all of Jost Van Dyke and Tortola.

The bedroom is on the first floor. Tilda throws Max's bag down and hurries to sweep back the white sheers from the side of the mahogany four-poster bed so Cash can set Max on it. It's like they're in some kind of weird fairy tale.

Max rolls onto her side and continues to snore.

"She needs to sleep it off," Tilda says. "Wanna go get a drink?"

"Yes," Cash says. "As a matter of fact, I do."

They go back to town and Tilda picks a place called the Lime Inn, where they sit at the open-air horseshoe-shaped bar. Tilda orders them each a cocktail called the Danger, which is probably the exact opposite of what Cash needs right now, but he rolls with it.

"So your parents..."

"Run an international headhunting firm," Tilda says. "Specializing in IT. My mother is the owner and CEO and my father is the CFO. I'm proud of them. When I was young, my mother worked in HR at a software company in Peoria and my father was a financial adviser for a lot of the top execs at Caterpillar. Then, when I was eight, my mother had an idea for this business. We moved to Chicago right before I started high school and by the time I was a freshman at Lake Forest, their company was everywhere—India, Australia, Eastern Europe, South Africa."

It's not so different from Cash's own story. Russ took the job with Ascension when Cash was sixteen and life changed—for the better, he'd thought at the time.

"My parents want to invest in a business for me," Tilda says. "But I'm not sure what I want to do yet. So I'm living down here, waiting tables at La Tapa, and I volunteer at the animal shelter."

"You do?" Cash says.

"I love dogs," Tilda says. "But I can't have one because... a white house."

"I have a golden retriever named Winnie," Cash says. "She's my world."

"I'd love to meet your world sometime," Tilda says. "Should we have one more Danger or do you have to go?"

Cash thinks about it for a second. "Let's have one more," he says.

Tilda is cool. And she's really smart. She has a degree in economics from Lake Forest. She gave business school some thought, but she's grown attached to St. John.

"I'm thinking about starting an eco-tour company here," she says. "Hiking, kayaking, snorkeling. But I'd want to provide lodging too, I think, so I've been checking out real estate. I'm not going to jump into anything."

"I wish I'd been as savvy as you," Cash says. He taps his fingers alongside his glass, wondering how in depth he wants to get with Tilda. "You know that my father was killed in the helicopter crash with Rosie?"

"You told me," Tilda says. "A few weeks ago, when you were hitchhiking and I picked you up. You remember that night, right?"

"Kind of," he says. He remembers Tilda picking him up; he hadn't recognized her as working at La Tapa until she reminded him. That was the night he'd gotten drunk at High Tide after his fight with Baker. He can't recall a thing that he and Tilda talked about. At that point, Tilda had been a minor character, someone in the background. But now that Cash is getting to know her, he's intrigued. It's enough of a plot twist that she's a child of enormous wealth, but it's an even greater twist that, despite this, she works her ass off and volunteers and is researching business ventures. "So what did I tell you about my dad?"

"That he had been killed in the copter crash, that he was Rosie's lover, and that he'd bought you two outdoor-supply stores in Denver that went under."

"I told you that? Ouch. I can't believe you're still sitting here with me."

"You invited me to Breckenridge to ski!" Tilda says. "You made me promise I would come."

Cash laughs. "Did I?"

"And..." Tilda fiddles with the straw in her drink. "You told me that both you and your brother were in love with Ayers."

Cash drops his head into his hands. "Idiot," he says. "I'm an idiot."

They decide to stay at the Lime Inn for dinner. Tilda gets the grilled lobster, which she says is the best on the island, and Cash gets the guava pork ribs, and when their food comes, they push their plates together and share.

"Eco-tourism, huh?" Cash says. "Do you like to hike?"

"Obsessed," Tilda says. "I'm trying to do every hike on the island this year."

"I told Maia I'd do the Esperance Trail with her," Cash says.

"To see the baobab tree?" Tilda says. "I haven't done that one yet!"

"Well, let's plan a time and you can come with us," Cash says.

"Are you asking me on a *date?*" Tilda says. She leans into him, much like Max did at lunch, but instead of being irritating, it feels nice. Tilda smells good. She's tomboyish, which he finds sexy. Her short hair draws attention to her light brown eyes.

"A date?" Cash says. "Aren't we on a date now?"

"Are we?" Tilda says.

"I don't know, aren't we?"

"Maybe we shouldn't examine it too closely," Tilda says.

"Maybe you're right," Cash says. "The hike would be with Maia. So I don't know how romantic it would be."

"No kissing under the baobab tree?" Tilda says.

Cash puts his hand over Tilda's. "I wouldn't rule it out."

Tilda turns her hand so that it's clasping his. Cash feels a rush. Does he *like* Tilda?

"Just do me one favor," Tilda says.

"Okay?" Cash says.

"Don't use me as a substitute for Ayers."

"What?" Cash says. "I know what I supposedly told you in the car, but I was very drunk. Ayers and I are just friends."

"I'm not stupid, Cash," Tilda says. "And I don't blame you. I get it. Ayers is a queen. She's the complete package. I know you and your brother both have a thing for her—"

"Baker might," Cash says. "But I—"

"You do too," Tilda says. "Trust me, I get it. If I were still in my lesbian phase, I'd go after Ayers."

Cash takes a deep breath. This has been a very long, very strange day. "Lesbian phase?"

"High school," Tilda says.

"Max?" Cash asks.

Tilda swats him. "Come on, let's get a nightcap."

They walk hand in hand over to La Tapa.

"It's kind of a thing we do," Tilda says. "Whenever we're out on our nights off, we stop in for a drink."

"I would think it'd be the last place you'd want to go," Cash says.

"Except we all love it," Tilda says. "It's so gratifying to watch everyone else work."

"Ohhhhkay," Cash says. He wonders if Ayers will be there and, if she is, what she'll think when she sees him with Tilda. Will she be jealous? She had been jealous of Cash's attention to Max, that's for damn sure.

Cash worries that he *is* using Tilda. But he likes Tilda and he doesn't want to stop holding her hand.

Maybe he shouldn't examine it too closely.

By the time they reach La Tapa, service has ended. Ayers is nowhere to be seen, though there are still a few people sitting at the bar. Cash and Tilda take seats on the corner and Skip, the bartender, looks between the two of them and glowers.

"Hey, Skip," Cash says.

"So, what, are you two *together* now?" he asks. He glares at Tilda.

"I'll have a glass of the Schramsberg, please," Tilda says.

"Beer for me," Cash says. "Island Hoppin'. Please."

"I'm helping these people right now," Skip says. He holds up a bottle of wine for the couple sitting next to Cash to inspect. "This is the Penfolds Bin Eight Cab. It has notes of imitation crabmeat, hot asphalt, and a one-night stand."

Nervously, the couple laughs.

Tilda says, "Don't do this, Skip."

Skip opens the bottle with a flourish and pours some in the woman's glass. She brings it to her lips. "I can definitely taste the one-night stand," she says. "The asphalt is harder to detect."

"He's a maniac," Tilda whispers.

"What's going on with you two?" Cash asks.

"Nothing," Tilda says. "And I do mean *nothing.*"

"But something did happen, right?" Cash says. "Let me guess. You had a thing, then you broke it off and he's pissed. That's the vibe I'm getting."

"A very *short* thing," Tilda says. "A very *insignificant* thing."

Cash puts his hand on the slender stalk of Tilda's neck and pulls her in close. "Tell you what," he says. "I promise not to use you as a substitute for Ayers if you promise not to use me as revenge for old Skippy here. Deal?"

Tilda pantomimes picking up a glass—her champagne has not yet, and may never, arrive—and raises it to Cash. "Deal," she says.

HUCK

At the end of his first week of fishing with Irene, he writes down the following in his ledger:

> Monday: 3 adults, 1 child; last name Ford; Calabasas, CA. 2 hardnose, 1 blue runner, 2 blackfin (1 keeper)
>
> Tuesday: 2 adults; last name Poleman; Winchester, MA; 2 mahi (2 keepers)
>
> Wednesday: 2 adults, 3 children; last name Toney; Excelsior, MN; 2 barracuda, 3 wahoo (3 keepers)
>
> Thursday: 2 adults, 4 children; last name Petrushki; Chapel Hill, NC; 4 wahoo (4 keepers), 2 barracuda; 1 mahi (keeper)
>
> Friday: 4 adults; last name Chang; Whitefish Bay, WI; 3 barracuda, 3 mahi (3 keepers), 1 wahoo (keeper)

These are the usual details that Huck records, along with the credit card numbers or a notation that the client paid with cash. He used to include where the clients were staying on the island

and how they'd heard about his charter, but then he decided it didn't make any difference. Nearly everyone finds him one of two ways: word of mouth or the GD internet. Huck pays a computer whiz named Destiny over in St. Thomas to make sure that when someone types in *deep-sea fishing* and *St. John USVI,* the *Mississippi* is the first link to pop up. Destiny also runs the cards and sends Huck a brief text the night before a charter so he knows what he'll be dealing with the following day.

What Huck doesn't write down is the way that having Irene on the boat has changed the experience of going to work. Adam was good. Adam was great. He was technically sound with the rods and the gaff, he was excellent when driving the boat, and he was usually pretty friendly with the clients—some more than others, of course, but that's true of Huck as well. Huck doesn't need to be friendly; he's the captain. His only responsibilities are keeping everyone safe and putting people on fish.

If Huck had any reservations about hiring Irene—and yeah, there had been a couple moments when he'd wondered if he was making a giant mistake—they were erased on the very first day. Irene showed up at the boat even before he did, bringing two cups of good, strong, black coffee and two sausage biscuits from Provisions. She was wearing shorts with pockets and a long-sleeved fishing shirt and a visor and sunglasses; her hair was in that fat braid of hers and she looked every inch like the fisherwoman of Huck's dreams. He had forwarded Destiny's text to Irene so she knew they were expecting three adults and one child from Calabasas, wherever that was, someplace in California.

"Los Angeles suburb," Irene said. "The Kardashians live there."

"I don't know who that is," Huck said gruffly, though he did, sort of, because he lived with a twelve-year-old girl.

The three adults turned out to be a gay couple, Brian and Rafael, and a drop-dead gorgeous Swedish au pair who wore only a bikini and a sarong. They wandered down the dock with an eight-year-old boy who was crying.

Irene looked at Huck and said, "We'll stay inshore?"

I love you, Huck thought. "You bet," he said.

The charter—one Huck and Adam might have written off as a bad blind date due to the crying child and uninterested nanny—had been a big success. Brian was an interior designer to the stars who had zero interest in fishing. Rafael was Brazilian and had grown up fishing in Recife, so he was enthusiastic. The au pair lay across the bench seating in the sun and Irene—somehow—worked magic with the kid, whose name was Bennie. She not only got him casting but helped him when he got a bite. Together, Irene and Bennie reeled in a blue runner; it wasn't a keeper but it was a good-looking fish in pictures. Rafael caught two hardnoses and a blackfin that was too small to keep, but all that action made him happy. While checking everyone's lines, Irene chatted with Brian about restoration glass (whatever that was) and epoxy floors (whatever those were). The coup de grâce, however, came near the end of the trip when Irene encouraged the au pair, Mathilde, to cast a line and she caught a nice-size blackfin that they could take home. It was big enough for a sushi appetizer.

"That's the first useful thing she's done all week," Brian whispered. Huck watched him slip Irene a hundred-dollar bill.

Huck figured that was beginner's luck. However, the entire week had gone smoothly. No matter who walked down the dock, Irene was ready, friendly but not too familiar (Adam would have fallen all over himself with the Swedish au pair). After the first day with Bennie, Irene made a habit of bringing snacks—boxes of cheese crackers, bags of hard pretzels. On Friday, Irene showed up with two dozen lemongrass sugar cookies and after Huck tasted one, he took the whole bag from her and said, "These are too good to share."

Irene laughed and tried to take the bag back and soon they were in a tug-of-war and Irene shrieked, "Huck, you're going to turn them to crumbs!" Her tone was playful and the delight on her face made her look even younger and more beautiful than the Swedish au pair and Huck had relented because at that moment, all he wanted to do was kiss her.

He didn't, of course. He couldn't—not on the boat, not while she was working for him.

That wasn't the first time he realized he might be falling in love with Irene. The first time it hit him was Thursday, when they had the family from Chapel Hill on board. The Petrushkis were a mixed-race couple—husband a big white dude, wife a dark-skinned lady—and they had four children: twin fourteen-year-old girls, Emma and Jane, a ten-year-old son, Woody, and a four-year-old son named Elton. Huck had no opinion, really, when it came to children; all he wanted to know was whether they were interested in fishing and, if not, whether they were able to sit on a boat for six or eight hours without causing trouble. If a child was "cute" or not didn't enter his brain. All children were cute, except for Maia, who was exquisite. But even Huck would have had a hard time saying that Elton Petrushki wasn't the cutest child he'd ever seen. He had café-au-lait skin, like Maia, big brown eyes, and chubby cheeks, and as soon as he climbed aboard the boat, he attached himself to Irene and started asking, "We gon' fish? We gon' fish?"

Irene said, "Yes, yes, Elton, we gon' fish."

"We gon' fish!" Elton announced to Huck.

Elton sat with his mother for the trip offshore. Huck was always worried about taking children offshore but Mr. Petrushki assured him that the kids had grown up on the water. The Petrushkis owned a vacation home on Wrightsville Beach on the North Carolina coast and they boated around Cape Fear.

When they slowed down to troll out at Tambo, the fertile spot where Huck and Irene had had such phenomenal luck just after the new year, Huck ran through the drill with Mr. Petrushki and the older kids. He was extra-kind and solicitous—maybe he was trying to show off for Irene—while she dealt with little Elton, who was dead set on catching a fish of his own.

"He gets a fish on, you hold his rod," Huck said. "Wahoo gets a hold of that line, kid's going in. Shark bait."

"Understood, Captain," Irene said. "Nothing is going to happen to this child in my care."

The Petrushki family had, in fact, enjoyed a banner day. Mr. Petrushki got a fish on first—Huck was secretly relieved because plenty of time, he had seen grown men bitter about being shown up by their own children—then Huck tossed chum into the water and they got more hits. Mister brought in a wahoo, then one of the twins brought in a smaller wahoo, then a few minutes later, the other twin brought in a wahoo exactly the same size. It was almost eerie. With the appearance of each fish, Elton Petrushki would jump up and down and yell, "Got fish! Got fish!" He stood over the hold staring down with wide eyes as Huck tossed the fish in.

There was a little bit of a lull at one point but Huck saw birds diving and directed the boat over. Sure enough, the ten-year-old Woody caught a barracuda, and then Mr. Petrushki caught a barracuda.

Mrs. Petrushki was reading a book bigger than the Bible, the *Collected Works of Jane Austen*.

"I love Jane Austen," Irene said.

"So do I!" Mrs. Petrushki said. "I'm a professor at UNC. I teach the Austen survey course."

"Oh, I get it now," Irene said. "The children's names! Emma, Jane, Wood for Woodhouse, and Elton."

"Yes, I did my thesis on *Emma,*" Mrs. Petrushki said. "I'm a bit obsessed, as my girls like to say."

Huck was in awe at the same time that he felt like an illiterate dummy.

Mrs. Petrushki closed her book and beamed. "Looks like wahoo for dinner."

Elton gazed up at Irene. "We gon' fish?"

"We gon' fish," Irene said. She got a determined set to her mouth. "Elton is taking the next fish."

A few minutes later, they had a bite. Irene steered Elton to the port rod. "We have a bite, Elton," she said. "We are going to reel in your fish. But you have to do exactly what I say."

"Listen to Miss Irene," Mrs. Petrushki said.

Irene showed Elton how to spin the reel; meanwhile, she had her hand firmly on the rod. Huck could see the tight clench of her fingers and he was glad. The rod bowed dramatically; this was a big fish.

"Irene," Huck said.

"We've got it, Captain," she said. "This is Elton's fish."

The fish put up a terrific fight, Huck thought, and by *terrific,* he meant terrible. Irene could maybe have brought the fish up alone but she had Elton squeezed between her legs and her hand over his hand on the reel. Huck was about ready to suggest she pass the kid off to his mother when he saw the flash of green-gold under the surface. He grabbed the gaff and brought up a gorgeous bull mahi that was nearly as big as the one Irene had brought up their first time out.

The other kids were impressed and Elton was beside himself. "My fish! My fish!" As soon as Huck yanked the gaff out and extracted the hook, they all watched the fish flop on the deck while Elton danced alongside it, yelling his head off with joy.

Elton decided he wanted to sit next to Irene going home and it was then, as Huck caught a glimpse of the two of them—Irene with her face raised to the mellow late-afternoon sun, Elton Petrushki tucked under one arm—that he realized he was in serious danger of falling in love with the woman. When Huck looked at Irene, he could see the future. That could be her, fifteen years from now, with Maia's child.

After their charter on Friday with the Changs (who had wanted to stay inshore and fly-fish), Huck and Irene clean the boat (the boat was never this spick-and-span when Adam did the cleaning), and then Huck hands Irene her first paycheck, which he wrote out that morning at home, and says, "Good job this week, Angler Cupcake."

She looks at the check, raises one eyebrow, and says, "I had so much fun, I feel bad taking your money."

"You earned it," Huck says. He wants to tell her how different work was this week compared to every other week of the past six years since LeeAnn died, but he finds a lump in his throat. "I couldn't ask for a better mate."

"Really?" she says.

Huck fears if he gives her any specific compliments, all of his feelings will come tumbling out and he'll embarrass them both. "Next week, we have driving lessons."

"I signed up for the online marine-safety class," she says.

"Good girl," Huck says. He unties his neckerchief and wipes off his forehead. The sun is starting its descent and Huck can already hear the hooting, hollering, and steel-drum music that characterize Cruz Bay on a Friday night. "So, do you have big plans for the weekend?"

"I'm going to sleep in," she says. "Go for a swim or two. Read. Spend time with the boys. And check in with my attorney at home."

"You... haven't heard any news, have you?" Huck asks.

"No." She pauses. "Huck, I have to say it. I'm haunted by all that money in Rosie's dresser."

"That makes two of us." Huck is uncomfortable talking about the Russ-and-Rosie mess at all, and he's glad they've avoided it all week.

"Cash said there were FBI agents watching the house when he got here, but I guess they've decided we're harmless because they haven't been back."

"I told you, AC, nothing to worry about," Huck says. "Hey, listen, Maia is with Ayers tonight. Do you want to go to dinner? Say, Morgan's Mango?"

Irene sighs. "I'm just not ready to go out," she says. "It's too soon."

"I get it," Huck says. "I have some of that wahoo from yesterday and I hid those cookies. Why don't you come to my place and I'll cook for you?"

"I should probably go on home," Irene says. "But thank you."

He nearly offers to grab some barbecue from Candi's—

enough for everyone—but then he thinks, *She's telling you no, Sam Powers.* And can he blame her? She's just spent five days straight trapped with him out at sea on a twenty-six-foot boat. Is it any wonder she wants to get away and have some time to herself?

This is what Huck should want as well. After all, the last person he'd wanted to spend his free time with during the past three years was Adam. When he bumped into Adam at Joe's Rum Hut or the Beach Bar—which happened plenty of times—they would wave and not say a word to each other.

But what Huck wants now…is to see more of Irene. In fact, he feels bereft at the idea of an entire weekend without her. Maia is with Ayers tonight, which means Huck will be home alone. He can, in theory, crack open a cold beer and try to finish his damn book. Or he could wander over to the Rum Hut, then to the Beach Bar, then go up to the Banana Deck—he hasn't been up to the Banana Deck since the new year. *Well, yeah,* he thinks. Because Rosie died. Maybe Irene is right; maybe it *is* too soon to go out to dinner and have a nice time. Maybe they should just stay home and reflect, confer with their attorneys, and wonder what the hell happened.

Then Huck remembers that Maia and her little friend who goes to Antilles, Shane, are planning to see the baobab tree with Cash.

"I heard Maia is planning a hike with Cash," Huck says.

"That's nice," Irene says. "They're forging a relationship."

It *is* nice, Huck agrees. He notices that Irene doesn't suggest *they* forge a relationship outside of work, off this boat, and what can Huck conclude but that Irene isn't interested in him? Somehow, he never considered this. Somehow, he'd let himself believe that her interest in him matched his interest in her.

Was it strange as all get-out that Irene's husband and Huck's stepdaughter had been in a secret relationship and had a love child? Hell yes.

Too strange, maybe. Huck should just forget about it. He should be grateful that he and Irene are friends and now coworkers and that they don't hate each other and aren't in litigation over God knows what—money or the villa or Maia.

Huck watches Irene as she strolls off the dock carrying her reusable shopping bag filled with snacks.

He scratches his face. Maybe he should shave his beard. Or read some Jane Austen.

The next morning the phone rings, and Huck assumes it'll be Maia asking to stay with Ayers a little longer. If that's the case he might see if Irene wants to take a drive out to the East End. He'll offer to bring Floyd and Baker along if they're looking for something to do.

He's making a nuisance of himself; he's aware of this, but he can't help it.

It's not Maia calling, or Ayers. It's Rupert.

"Huck."

"Rupert."

"You been drinking yet today?" Rupert asks.

"No," Huck says. "Not yet." His eyes graze his trusty bottle of Flor de Caña up on the shelf. Is he going to need it? Or is Rupert about to invite him to meet for lunch at Miss Lucy's—an invitation Huck just might take him up on?

"You remember talking the other day about Paulette Vickers?"

"Yes," Huck says warily. The Flor de Caña, then. He brings the bottle down to the counter.

"She and her husband were arrested over on St. Croix. You know how Doug Vickers has a sister there? FBI, two, three cars, pull into Wilma Vickers's driveway in Frederiksted and Paulette and Doug get led away in handcuffs."

"This reliable?" Huck asks.

"Sadie went to school with Wilma," Rupert says. "Wilma called Sadie herself. She has the little boy. Parents went to jail."

"Did they say why?" Huck asks. "What were they charged with?"

"Conspiracy to commit fraud, Wilma said. Real estate fraud. Financial fraud." Rupert pauses. "The guy they were in business with, and the Invisible Man, too, were doing laundry."

"Laundry?" Huck says.

"They were cleaning money," Rupert says. "Head honcho had a yacht, *Bluebeard,* and Wilma told Sadie that she knows for certain that boat used to pull into Cruz Bay with a hold full of cash. From guerrilla groups in Nicaragua, Wilma said. And the Marxists in Cuba and Argentinean soccer stars trying to avoid taxes and God knows who else. And Paulette and Douglas Vickers were helping them."

When Huck hangs up with Rupert, he calls Agent Vasco but is shuttled immediately to her voicemail. It's Saturday, so maybe she's off duty—but who is he kidding; she's probably waist-deep in the Vickers morass.

Huck has known the Vickerses for twenty years—not well, he's never been invited to their home, never done any direct business with them, but he knows them. Croft must have made them an offer they couldn't refuse; they must have thought they would never get caught. Huck understands what it's like to live here as a local person and see the big boats roll in and watch the enormous villas go up and wonder, *Why them and not me?* Maybe Paulette let herself get into a compromising spot with her family's business; God knows, real estate is risky everywhere. Huck could call some of LeeAnn's friends—Dearie and Helen come to mind—and ask what they've heard. But it's possible that what they heard came from Sadie via Wilma as well, and it's possible that Dearie and Helen haven't heard a thing but will start jabbering as soon as they realize it's a topic of interest. The Vickerses got mixed up with Russell Steele and his boss, Todd Croft, and they were helping to launder the money.

Huck's next instinct is to call Irene. He's been looking for a reason and now he has one. Paulette and Doug Vickers arrested on St. Croix. That much he could share. The rest of it—the laundering and *Bluebeard*—that all sounds suspiciously like gossip. Still, Huck feels the seed of fear that has been in his gut since Rosie died start to grow. Russ was involved in illegal and dangerous business dealings. Guerrillas in Nicaragua?

What Huck wants to know is if he or Maia—or Irene—will somehow be implicated in a crime.

We didn't know anything, Huck thinks. Surely the FBI realizes this. Huck has done nothing wrong, Maia has done nothing wrong, and Irene has done nothing wrong. They're innocent—but does that mean they're safe?

Getting Paulette and Doug Vickers can't possibly be the FBI's endgame, Huck thinks. They want to find Todd Croft. And Paulette will sing—of this, Huck is certain. She has her child to think about.

From this perspective, maybe Irene would be intrigued by the news, possibly even happy to hear it. They're tracking down answers. What were Croft and Russell Steele doing? Where was all that money coming from?

No, it will *not* make Irene happy, Huck decides. It will make her agitated, especially since all they can do until they get official word from Agent Vasco is speculate. And so Huck decides *not* to tell Irene until he's had a conversation with Agent Vasco.

Huck sets the Flor de Caña back up on the shelf. He heads out onto the deck to have a cigarette. He imagines Irene lying on the beach in Little Cinnamon, thinking about little Elton Petrushki or about how cold it is back in Iowa City or about what she's going to make for dinner. But she will *not* be thinking about Paulette Vickers sitting in an interrogation room and giving the FBI who knows what kind of information about her husband. Huck's silence is a gift. Irene is sure to find out at some point; hell, maybe she'll find out tomorrow. But at least she has today in peace. At least she has right now.

BAKER

Baker is so excited after their meeting and tour at the Gifft Hill School that he texts Anna from the parking lot.

Found a school for F. They ran assessments, he can start kindergarten now. V. advanced, they said. Happy to have him and he loved it.

"Bye!" Maia calls out. She's staying at the school to hang out with friends and then someone's mother is taking them to town.

"Thank you, Maia!" Baker says.

"Thank you, Maia!" Floyd says, waving like a maniac. Then he turns to Baker. "Daddy, how do we know Maia?"

"Oh," Baker says. Floyd is probably confused because Maia introduced Floyd to the head teacher, Miss Phaedra, as her "sort of nephew," a phrase that elicited an expression of surprise and suspicion from Miss Phaedra. Apparently, the phrase didn't get past Floyd either. Baker was glad Maia threw the *sort of* in there because it could be explained any number of ways; they wouldn't have to tell Miss Phaedra that Floyd is, in fact, Maia's actual nephew, the son of Maia's brother Baker.

Sometimes Baker wishes Floyd weren't so "advanced."

"She's our friend," Baker says. Not a lie.

"I like her," Floyd says. "I like the Gifft Hill School. Why are there two Fs?"

"No idea, buddy," Baker says. He checks that Floyd's seat belt is fastened, then heads for home.

He doesn't hear back from Anna until two days later, Wednesday.

K, the text says.

K? Baker thinks. He hadn't expected a fight, necessarily, or even a debate, but he *had* anticipated something more than just *K.* They're talking about Floyd's education! Baker was armed with the school brochure and the notes he'd taken in the margins, and he has the website for backup as well as his own impressions, which he'd spent the past two days organizing into a sales pitch. The school is nurturing (but not indulgent), inclusive, tolerant, and forward-thinking. (Anna will love all of this.) The sky is the limit for Floyd! The classes are small and they have an island-as-classroom initiative that gets the kids outside studying nature and history and Caribbean culture.

But…Anna doesn't care. Anna is relocating to Cleveland, learning the ropes at a new hospital, meeting her colleagues, reviewing protocols, buying furniture, and maybe even getting excited for Louisa to become pregnant.

Baker tries not to feel like he and Floyd have been brushed off, forgotten.

He doesn't bother telling Anna that he also got good news during the visit to the Gifft Hill School—he'd received a job offer. The upper school, Miss Phaedra said, desperately needed someone to coach basketball and baseball as well as do some administrative work for the athletic department. She mentioned this because Baker was so tall and "fit-seeming" (the "seeming" being key) and she wondered if maybe he had any background in either sport and might want a chance to get involved in the community, seeing as how he was new to the island. It was like she'd read his mind. Baker said that he did indeed have some background in both sports; he'd played basketball and baseball in high school and in college at Northwestern on the intramural level.

"Which means, essentially, that I haven't used my skills in almost ten years. I've been waiting for Floyd to be old enough so I could coach his teams."

"The job does come with a stipend, and the hours would be after school during the respective seasons," Miss Phaedra says. "I'd love to be able to pass your name on to the head of school, and she can talk with you more about it."

It's exactly what Baker is looking for, and yet he doesn't commit right away because he still has to go back to Houston for the auction this coming weekend. There's a quiet but persistent voice in Baker's head telling him that it's crazy—and, worse, irresponsible—to move to the Caribbean with Floyd.

He came down here for one reason only and that's Ayers. But Ayers is with Mick. And Ayers was clear that she wouldn't even entertain the possibility of a relationship with Baker until he had a job or an opportunity here on St. John.

The whole thing is risky. Baker can leave Houston, take the job at Gifft Hill, and move here, but Ayers might still stay with Mick.

The evening that Anna responds with *K,* Irene comes home from work with some fresh wahoo steaks from her charter. She grills them for Baker and Floyd, and because Cash is out somewhere, it's just the three of them eating dinner on the deck. It's nice. Irene is in a good mood; her frame of mind seems better now that she's working on Huck's fishing boat, though she's not her old self by any means. Baker tells her that Floyd liked the school but he doesn't say anything about the job offer yet. He reminds his mother that he and Floyd are headed back to Houston on Friday for the auction.

"Right," Irene says, though it's clear she's forgotten about it. "But you're coming back, yes?"

"Yes?" Baker says. "I think so. I mean, yes." He wants to sound definitive but the truth is, he's not sure. He's packing everything they brought down, just in case.

"When?" Irene says. "When will you be back?"

"I don't have return tickets yet," Baker says. "Though I can get them, of course, at a moment's notice. I have to figure some stuff out when I get to Houston. What to do about the house, my car, that kind of thing."

"Of course," Irene says. "No one expects you to drop everything and move down here. Though that's what I did." She laughs—at her own crazy spontaneity, maybe. "And that's what your brother did."

"Where *is* Cash tonight?" Baker asks. He suddenly gets a bad feeling. Cash didn't come back after *Treasure Island.* Did he go somewhere with *Ayers?* Out to dinner? This is what Baker has privately feared about Cash and Ayers working together, that they would become chummy, that Cash would, somehow, manage to charm her.

"He had an incident on the boat today, I guess," Irene says. "Passenger got drunk and Cash was called on to help get the girl home. Turned out the girl had a friend that Cash knew. From that restaurant you both like so much?"

"La Tapa?" Baker says.

"That must be it," Irene says. "And I think he went out with the friend. Something like that."

Baker pushes his chair away from the table. "Was it Ayers, Mom? Is he out with Ayers?"

"It wasn't Ayers," Irene says. She throws Baker an exasperated look. "You boys, honestly. No, it was some other name. British, unusual..."

"Tilda?" Baker says.

"Yes!" Irene says. "He went out with Tilda."

"Who's Tilda?" Floyd asks.

"A friend of your uncle's," Irene says.

Baker can't describe his relief. He tousles Floyd's hair. "You want some ice cream, buddy? They had red velvet cake at the Starfish Market."

Baker puts Floyd to bed, then decides to turn in himself, mostly because there's nothing else to do. Cash is still out and Baker has no other friends. If he were at home in Houston right now, he would smoke some weed and crash out in front of the TV—he needs to catch up on *Game of Thrones*—but he can't watch *that* with Irene around.

His phone rings. This, he thinks, will be Anna, just getting home from work at nine o'clock at night. He steels himself. It would be just like Anna to have glanced at his text distractedly and responded with *K,* but then, after running the whole thing past Louisa, suddenly have a list of objections.

Baker should have texted Louisa.

But his display says Ayers.

"Ayers?" he says.

"Hey." Her voice sounds funny—sad, trembling, like she's been crying. "Are you busy?"

"Not at all," he says. "I just put Floyd to bed so I can talk. What's up?"

There's a pause. "Can you get out? Is Cash there? Or your mom? To watch Floyd?"

"Uh…yeah. Cash is out but my mom is here." Baker stands up and checks himself in the mirror. He hasn't shaved—or showered, for that matter, unless swimming in the pool counts as a shower—since the day he went to Gifft Hill, Monday. He does have a nice tan now, but he looks like a Caribbean hobo. "Do you want to meet somewhere?"

"Can you just come here, to my place?" Ayers asks. "There's something I want to talk to you about."

"Your place?"

"Fish Bay," Ayers says. "It'll take you fifteen minutes if you leave right now."

"Right now?" Baker says. And before he can explain that he needs to shower and change, she's giving him directions.

* * *

Unlike the rest of the island, Fish Bay is flat. And really dark. Ayers said she lived past the second little bridge on the left, but Baker would have missed her house if he hadn't caught a flash of green, her truck, out of the corner of his eye.

She's standing in the doorway, backlit, hugging herself. He doesn't need to feel bad about not showering, he sees. She's still wearing her *Treasure Island* uniform and her hair is wild and curly.

"Hey," he says. "You okay?"

She moves so that he can step past her, inside.

Her place is small, cute, bohemian. There's a tiny kitchen with thick ceramic dishes on open shelves. There's a papasan chair, a bunch of houseplants, a glass bowl filled with sand dollars, and a gallery wall of photographs from places all over the world—the Taj Mahal, the Great Pyramids, the Matterhorn. Ayers is in every picture; in many, she's a kid.

"Have you *been* to all these places?" Baker asks.

"Story for another day," she says. "Come sit."

Baker picks a spot next to Ayers on a worn leather sofa draped with a tapestry. There's a coffee table with three pillar candles sitting in a dish of pebbles, and lying across the pebbles is a joint.

Are they going to smoke?

"Would you like a glass of water?" Ayers asks.

"Maybe in a minute," Baker says. "Why don't you tell me what's going on."

Ayers folds her legs underneath her. How is it possible that even when she looks awful, she's beautiful?

"This morning—" She laughs. "Which now feels like three

days ago." She picks up the joint and lifts a barbecue lighter off the side table, then seems to think better of it and sets both down. "It's been a very long day."

"Some days are like that," Baker says. "Start at the beginning."

"Last night Mick told me he had to go to St. Thomas to get restaurant supplies today," Ayers says. "Whatever, I found it a little strange, but I didn't question it. Too much." She throws her hands up. "Anyway, then this morning, I saw him on the ferry with Brigid."

Baker makes a face like he's surprised. But he's not surprised. He knew Mick would screw it up. He actually wishes Cash were here to listen to this. Baker leans in. "You're kidding."

"Not kidding. I saw them sitting together and I was . . . pissed. Livid. Suspicious."

"I bet."

"So I sent him a text telling him never to call me again."

Baker spreads his palms against the cool, cracked leather of the sofa. This is real? He didn't fall asleep in bed next to Floyd? Ayers is telling him exactly what he's been waiting to hear, only much sooner than he had hoped. Her timing couldn't be better.

"Then Cash and I had this weird, awful thing happen at work."

"Yeah, I heard, sort of."

"This girl got really drunk, and I thought she'd tanked while snorkeling. We stopped the boat, I dove off, your brother dove off, this other kid who's probably going to be in the Olympics dove off, it was a total circus, and in the end the chick was in the head changing out of one inappropriate suit into a second, even more inappropriate suit, and this was all before we even got to

Jost. The girl continued to drink and then puked off the side the whole way home." Ayers sighs. "And I left your brother to handle it because guess who was waiting for me at the dock."

"Mick," Baker says, and he suspects that maybe this story isn't going to have the ending he wants it to.

"Mick," Ayers says. "He just left here a little while ago. Right before I called you. We broke up."

"You broke up?" Baker says. He's afraid to go back to feeling optimistic. "What did he say? Why was he with Brigid?"

"He *said* they bumped into each other. Unplanned. A coincidence. She was headed over to St. Thomas to get a tattoo of the petroglyphs."

"Okay?" Baker says.

"I just got a tattoo of the petroglyphs a few weeks ago," Ayers says. She holds out her ankle so Baker can see the tattoo; it's a curlicue symbol in dark green. "We're hardly the only two people in the universe with a petroglyph tattoo. Rosie had one. But still, I was chafed."

"Understandably," Baker says.

"Mick says they only talked for a couple of minutes, then Mick took Gordon, that's our dog, *his* dog, up to stand at the bow and he didn't see Brigid again."

"Do you believe him?"

"I don't want to believe him," Ayers says. "But I do."

"You do?"

"I do."

"So...why did you break up?"

"Two reasons," Ayers says. "Both are secrets that I'm keeping from him. One is this...project that I'm working on. I can't tell him about it, and I can't tell you about it yet either. Maybe in the future, once I'm finished, but not right now."

"Secret project," Baker says. "I won't ask."

"Please don't," Ayers says. She seems to shrink under her *Treasure Island* T-shirt and when she gazes at him, her eyes appear robbed of their pigment. They are very, very pale blue. "The second reason is...that I have feelings for you."

"For me?"

"For you," Ayers says. "I haven't been able to stop thinking about you."

"You haven't?" Baker says.

She shakes her head and presses her lips together like she's embarrassed.

"So, wait," Baker says. Is this really happening? Him and Ayers? Does she want him to kiss her? Does she want him to—finally—make proper love to her? Baker can't find the words to ask, he's too overwhelmed, but it turns out it doesn't matter.

Ayers stands up, takes his hand, and leads him to her bed.

He wakes up in the middle of the night; 4:20 a.m., his phone says. Ayers is naked in bed next to him. He's in love. He's beyond in love.

But he has to get out of there. He can't have Floyd waking up and finding his dad gone.

Baker eases out of bed and uses the bathroom. He sees a clothbound book balanced on the edge of the sink. Ayers's journal? Baker is, of course, tempted to open it and read Ayers's innermost thoughts, presumably about how she's stuck with crappy cheater Mick but can't get Baker Steele out of her mind. However, back when Baker was in college, he read his girlfriend Trinity's diary and all hell broke loose. That was why they'd split. Trinity had called it a "devastating breach of personal trust."

If you learn one thing from me, Baker Steele, she'd said, *I hope it's never to read a woman's private thoughts without her express permission.*

No matter how tempting, she'd added. *And, oh yes, it* will *be tempting.*

It *is* tempting—the journal with the red floral cover, demure and innocent with the look of a colonial-era recipe book.

But Baker leaves it be.

In the end, Trinity taught him a lot. He must remember to hit her up on Facebook and thank her.

Back in the bedroom, he runs a finger down the length of Ayers's spine and she shivers awake and opens one eye. "You leaving?"

"I have to," he whispers. "Floyd."

"Okay," she says.

Baker clears his throat. "And, uh, you remember that I'm leaving tomorrow for Houston? I have that thing on Saturday? But I'm coming right back. So you don't have to worry."

"What day?" Ayers asks. "What day are you coming back?"

Baker does a quick calculation. The benefit auction is Saturday night. Sunday he's on cleanup duty. He needs at least two additional days to get the move organized, maybe three; honestly, he could use a week, but now that this has happened, all he can think about is how to get back here as quickly as possible. But then again, he has a life to dismantle—Floyd's medical records need to be transferred (to where?); Baker needs to forward his mail (to where?) and figure out what to do about his income taxes. There's stuff. "Wednesday," he says. "Thursday."

"Wednesday or Thursday?" she asks.

"Thursday," he says. "Week from today."

"I'm working at La Tapa Thursday night," she says. "Come by after work. We can celebrate your move."

He kisses her temple. "You got it," he says. He puts his clothes on and runs both hands through his hair. "Oh, by the way, the chick who got drunk on your boat was a friend of Tilda's."

Ayers rolls over and squints at him. "Really?"

"Yeah, that's what my mother told me Cash said. I guess Cash and Tilda went out last night."

"They *did?*" Ayers says, sitting up.

"Yeah," Baker says. "I think so." He wonders if hearing this bothers Ayers for some reason.

She smiles. "They're perfect for each other." She falls back into her pillows. "When you get back, we can double-date."

"Great," Baker says sardonically—although, actually, it sounds like fun.

The theme for the Children's Cottage benefit auction is Monopoly. This was Debbie's idea. She was in charge of dreaming up something to top Oh, the Places You'll Go!, which was last year's theme. Although Baker was skeptical about the appeal of Monopoly—it evoked nothing so much as the rainy afternoons of childhood, trapped in a never-ending game of being sent to jail, paying other people rent, and eventually going bankrupt due to real estate failures—the execution is brilliantly done. Baker has dressed up as Rich Uncle Pennybags, in a vest with a pocket watch, and people are chattering with anticipation as they leave the school parking lot. (FREE PARKING signs abound, which is cute, even though parking is always free at the Children's Cottage.)

The event is being held in the school gymnasium (built back in 2000 by one of the owners of the Houston Rockets), but the board of directors, naturally, have created a path that takes attendees through the school so that they can see where their donations will be going. Baker, with Ellen at his side, walks through the reading nook filled with picture books, the numbers room with boxes of manipulatives, the science room where kids study birds' nests and leaves and different kinds of rocks, the social studies room, festooned with flags of the world, and last, and most popular, the water-table room. They then pass through the courtyard with the outdoor playground into the gym, which has been transformed into a Monopoly board for the evening.

At the front table, everyone picks up a plastic top hat and mustache on a stick (each stick has a number printed on the back; it doubles as an auction paddle) and proceeds to one of the tables, all of which are named for Monopoly properties and sheathed in tablecloths of the corresponding colors. Baker and his school wives are, naturally, at Boardwalk, with a tablecloth of Columbia blue. The centerpiece is a flour-sack money bag filled with pebbles and holding a bouquet of gold dahlias. The photo booth is decorated to look like the Jail square, so once Baker's friends choose seats, he suggests they get their pictures taken, then go find glasses of the event's signature cocktail, the Chance Card, which is a lurid orange. They're being served by Vicki Styles, who likes to expose her cleavage whenever she can.

"That was a good choice," Becky says. "The Chance Cards are being served by the Community Chest."

Baker loves his school wives. How will he ever leave them?

The event swims along. People drink, eat hors d'oeuvres, bid on silent-auction items. Baker really wants to get Floyd tickets to the first Texans game, but then he remembers that he's not going to be around for it. Wendy wants them all to chip in on a house in Galveston in May—but Baker won't be here for that either. He needs to tell his friends about his plans, and soon; the only person who knows is Ellen.

Standing in the strobe-lit school gym surrounded by people he has known for years—and even psycho Mandy in her little black dress with her satin Justin Verlander team jacket on top seems endearing tonight—Baker has a hard time believing that he was in Ayers's apartment only two days earlier. He has switched worlds. Which one of them is real?

He could easily make the argument that this world is real. This is Houston, a real place; the Children's Cottage is a real school. Baker is a part of this community. He is known. He's Floyd's dad. No one misses Anna, though they all know that she's a big deal, if not a particularly hands-on mother. Baker's friends are real friends, there when he needs them. He's giving up a lot by leaving—his house, his autonomy. There's a way in which moving to St. John feels like regressing. He'll be back living with his mom and brother.

All of this is on one side of the scale—and Ayers is on the other.

Dinner is served. It's boardwalk food, which sounds iffy but ends up being delicious: jumbo hot dogs with a variety of toppings, skinny truffle fries, and Mexican street corn. Then the live auction starts and Baker zones out, thinking he'll tell Debbie, Becky, and Wendy his plans after the auction but before the dancing. They'll be upset initially but then one of them will request "We Are Family" from the DJ and they'll all cluster together to dance and all the married parents will be jealous. Nothing new there.

Baker perks up only when the auctioneer announces a superspecial item, added at the last minute by an anonymous donor. It's one week in a villa on St. John with 180-degree views over the Caribbean Sea. Nine bedrooms, dual-level pool, private beach and shuffleboard court, outdoor kitchen, and the use of two 2018 Jeeps. July or August dates only.

Ellen nudges Baker's leg under the table. "This is you?"

He gives the slightest of nods.

The bidding is robust. It starts at five thousand and skyrockets from there—ten, fifteen, twenty thousand dollars. July or August is the perfect time of year to escape the beastly heat of Houston, and when Baker ran the idea past Irene and Cash, they'd agreed that July or August would be an ideal time to take a break from St. John and fly to Door County (Irene) and Breckenridge (Cash).

Twenty-five thousand dollars. Thirty thousand.

"Jeez, Baker," Ellen murmurs.

"It's Nanette's husband bidding," Wendy says. "Oil."

"Against Beanie O'Connor's grandmother," Becky says. "Oil."

Thirty-five thousand. Forty thousand.

"That's going to buy a lot of manipulatives," Debbie whispers.

Forty-five thousand.

Fifty thousand. Going once, going twice…sold, for fifty thousand dollars.

"Are you going back?" Ellen asks. "For good?"

Baker sighs. He hasn't even told Ellen about his night with Ayers. He hasn't told anyone. "I am," he says.

"Good for you," Ellen says.

The auction is over, the DJ gets warmed up with "Celebrate," and all of Baker's friends go to the ladies' room, leaving him sitting at the table alone.

First order of business on getting back to St. John: Find some *male* friends. Other than Cash.

When the ladies reappear, they envelop Baker in a group hug. Wendy is crying. Baker gives Ellen a quizzical look and she shrugs as if to say, *Sorry, not sorry*. The thing that Baker has long suspected happens in ladies' rooms has happened. The truth has come out.

"I'm going to miss you guys," Baker says.

Turns out that when Nanette's husband, Tony, lost out to Beanie O'Connor's grandmother in the auction, it lit a fuse. Nanette and Tony have a raging, alcohol-fueled fight in Free Parking (though, thankfully, no one ends up dead like in that book all Baker's friends read three or four years ago), and Nanette announces that she wants a divorce.

"The auction was just an excuse," Debbie says when she comes over the next day to help Baker get organized. "She's been sleeping with Ian for years." Ian is Wendy's ex-husband.

Yes, true, everyone knows this.

Nanette sends Baker a text less than an hour later: I hear you have a place for rent?

He texts back, Just so happens, I do.

On Sunday, Debbie helps Baker clean out his fridge and cabinets. Becky helps him figure out his tax returns. Wendy comes over with her daughters, Evelyn and Ondine, and they play with Floyd while Baker packs Floyd's suitcase.

Ellen stops by with a goodbye present, a Rawlings alloy baseball bat for his new coaching duties.

"You won't hit the ball if you don't swing," she says.

Baker books tickets for Wednesday. Debbie drives a minivan; she's going to take Baker and Floyd to the airport after she drops Eleanor and Gale at school.

Monday after school, Baker and Floyd sit in the kitchen eating pizza because Baker doesn't want to dirty any dishes. It's ironic that they're eating pizza, Anna's favorite meal, when Anna is so far away.

Baker decides to reach out to Anna. He snaps a selfie of himself and Floyd and the sausage and pepperoni pie from Brother's and texts it to her with the words Miss you, Mom!

She'll probably respond to the text sometime next week, Baker thinks.

A few minutes later, Baker's phone beeps and he checks it, expecting Anna's response to be *Okay* or *Sounds good* or maybe even *Miss you 2*.

The text isn't from Anna, however. It's from Cash. Baker reads it, then drops his phone.

ROSIE

July 31, 2006

I should have known that telling Mama and Huck had gone too easily.

Mama read my diary and found out about Russell and found out about Irene—and one night after work, I walked in the door expecting to find her asleep or, possibly, waiting up with a plate of chicken, beans, and rice—she was concerned that I wasn't eating enough for two—but instead she was in the doorway, my diary in her hand, her eyes popping.

"A married man?" she said. "Have you no shame, *Rosie?"*

I grabbed the diary from her. "Have you *no shame?" I asked. I went into my room and slammed the door behind me, my heart cowering in my chest because I had left it exposed and my mother had found it.*

I'm going to set the diary on fire, *I thought.* And if the whole house goes up in smoke, so be it.

There was a light knock on the door and I figured it was Huck, there to try and fix what my mother had broken. But when I opened the door, it was Mama herself. I tried to slam the door in her face but she pushed back—for a second, our eyes locked, and it was a test of strength. I was younger but pregnant; Mama was Mama. Then she put a finger to her lips and I relented.

She entered, closed the door quietly behind her, sat on my bed, and patted the spot next to her.

I shook my head, lips closed in anger.

"I'm sorry," she said. "I had to be sure."

What she meant was that she had to be sure the baby wasn't Oscar's.

I wasn't naive. I knew there was talk across the island. Who is the father of Rosie Small's baby? *The odds were on Oscar. It was possible that Oscar had even claimed it was his, though we hadn't been together since he'd been out of jail.*

"My word isn't good enough?" I said.

"It's not," Mama said. I gave her a look, which she brushed

off. "You're young, you're afraid, you might have said anything to keep a roof over your head."

"I don't need this roof," I said. "I have money saved."

"Oh, that's right," she said. "The ten thousand dollars. Where is it?"

*She knew about the ten thousand dollars, of course. She knew everything now: Vie's Beach, the sex, the room service, the wife and sons in Iowa, the name of the boat—*Bluebeard.

"I kept a thousand in cash," I said. "The other nine I deposited a little at a time along with my paychecks."

She nodded like she approved. "Good."

"I haven't contacted him," I said. "I have no intention of ever seeing him again, Mama. Like I said, it was a mistake."

"Your voice is saying it was a mistake but your face is telling a different story."

I almost broke then. I almost said that it wasn't a mistake, that I didn't regret being with Russ, that there had been something between us and that something was real. But my mother was Catholic; she believed in the sanctity of marriage. A married white man having a baby with an island girl was no good. I could tell, however, by her mere presence in my bedroom that it was far, far better than me being pregnant by Oscar.

"What does Huck think?" I asked. I wondered if he might be more sympathetic to my situation. He had been married, then divorced. He, maybe, understood that relationships didn't always fit into neat boxes—though it would be very unusual for him to battle Mama.

"Huck doesn't know."

"You didn't tell him?" I said. It was even more unusual for my mother to keep a secret from Huck.

"I told him the man was white. A pirate."

Pirate *had been the word I used in my diary.*

"That's the story from here on out," Mama said. "Pirate came in on his yacht, you had relations, then he left, never to be seen again." *She clasped my hand. "Do you understand me, Rosie? Never to be seen again. You see this man again, I phone the wife. Irene Steele from Iowa City. I called Information. I have the number."*

Hearing Irene's name come out of my mother's mouth gave me chills. I knew she was serious. I could never see Russ again, even if he did someday return.

August 22, 2006

It was as though we'd conjured him. Three weeks after my mother confronted me, I was at work—still cocktail waitressing, even though my belly was enormous and my ankles swollen—when Estella tapped me on the shoulder and said, "There's a man at the bar who wants an order of the conch fritters."

"Isn't Purcell on the bar?" I asked.

"He is, child, but this gentleman asked for you."

I was punching in an order and I had a table with food up and a table still waiting to order drinks and Tessie was taking a leisurely cigarette break as always and I was about to snap. The restaurant was closing September first for two and a half months—hurricane season—so I only had to make it through another week. I gathered my wits, delivered one table their meals, took the drink order, ran quickly to the ladies' room, and then, feeling relieved and refreshed, I lumbered over to the bar to see which gentleman at the bar wanted the conch fritters.

Honestly, I didn't even think.

Russ was sitting at the corner seat.

I was torn between running straight into his arms and running for the parking lot.

His eyes became round as plates when he saw my belly. He knew, Todd Croft must *have told him, but maybe he didn't believe it or maybe he was overwhelmed to see evidence of his child with his own eyes.*

"Mona Lisa," *he said.*

"Stop," I said.

"Mine?" he said.

"Don't insult me," I said. I turned and gazed out at the water in front of Caneel, but I didn't see the yacht.

"Bluebeard *is on Necker Island today," he said. "I came over in a helicopter. We have...a client...with a helicopter." He seemed proud to be telling me this, like I would care about a helicopter, of all things.*

"Must be nice," I said. My voice was stony, nearly icy, but my insides were molten. He came back. He was here. As discreetly as I could, I checked his left hand—ring still in place. At least today he was dressed appropriately. He wore stone-white shorts and a navy gingham shirt, crisp and expensive-looking, turned back at the cuffs. A new watch, a Breitling. He had a tan, a fresh haircut; he had lost twenty pounds. He looked great; there was very little trace of the sweet, bumbling man I had known. I was even more drawn to this sleeker, more confident version.

"What time are you off?" he asked. He nodded down the beach. "I got our room."

Our room, 718. I had avoided going anywhere near the hotel rooms since he left.

"I can't," I said.

"Why not?"

Why not. I thought about telling him that my mother had

read my diary and was threatening to call Irene, but I didn't want him to know how much control my mother had over me. I thought he'd be angry that I'd written about our relationship and been stupid enough to leave the diary in a place where Mama could find it. I thought he'd think poorly of my mother for blackmailing me—and I couldn't bear that. Mama was looking out for me.

"You're married," I said. "To Irene. You have children already. I'm not going to disrespect that. You can't ask me to. It's not fair."

"Rosie..." he said.

"It happened," I said. "But it can't continue."

He nodded at my midsection. "Except it is continuing. You're having my baby."

I nearly surrendered to him right then and there. My baby. *Here he was, willing to claim the child so that I wasn't alone in all of this. And in the months since he'd left I had felt very, very alone. Mama and Huck would help me. I would live with them and bank the money that Todd Croft had given me to get me through the first year.*

"I have to get back to work," I said. I left Russ and put in an order for conch fritters.

He stayed until service ended. His mere presence at the bar—he was watching the Braves-Phillies game—made my pulse quicken and my breathing get shallow and I feared this reaction would affect the baby so I tried to stop and rest, drink plenty of ice water, and get to the ladies' room often to splash my face.

Finally, I was finished. It was time for me to leave. I walked over to him.

"I'm going home," I said. "It was nice to see you again."

"Please, Rosie," he said. "Just come to the room."

I wanted to, if only for the air-conditioning and because I knew he would order me whatever I wanted from room service. But then it occurred to me that Russ might have been after sex and sex alone; maybe he saw me as a girl in a port, an island wife. I was nobody's island wife.

"No," I said. "I'm sorry. You're married."

He nodded. "That I am."

It pained me to hear him say it, but it also gave me resolve.

"Please don't come back here," I said. "Unless you get divorced and you have bona fide legal documents to prove it. It's difficult for me to see you." I spread my hands across my stomach. "I had feelings for you."

"Had?"

"Had, have, it doesn't matter because you don't live here and you aren't mine."

"I'd like to support the baby," he said.

"I received money already," I said. I wasn't sure if this would come as news to him or not.

He said, "Todd showed me your e-mail last week. He told me he sent you money back in May. He told me he came down to Carnival in July and that he checked in on you and that his hunch was correct: you were pregnant. The instant he told me, I made plans to come down here. I'm here only to see you, Rosie."

Todd Croft had come during St. John's Carnival and had spied *on me? I didn't like that one bit.*

Russ had found out only last week?

"I have everything I need," I said. "But thank you."

"You don't have to forgive me but you do have to let me support that child," Russ said.

"I don't, though," I said, and I walked out of the restaurant,

past the Sugar Mill, and into the parking lot, where I climbed in my car and cried.

The following week, a package arrived containing five thousand dollars in cash. An identical package came the week after that. And the week after that.

October 29, 2006

Today at 5:09 a.m., Maia Rosalie Small entered the world weighing six pounds and fourteen ounces and measuring twenty inches long. She is the most beautiful creature I have ever laid eyes on.

The nurse brought me a form to fill out so she could make the birth certificate. On the line where it asked for the father's name, I wrote Unknown.

November 1, 2006

Maia is three days old. Today, I sent an e-mail to Todd Croft at Ascension letting him know that I'd had a baby girl and that her name was Maia Small.

September 4, 2012

Today is Maia's first day at the Gifft Hill School. She marched into the classroom, head held high, shoulders back, with barely a wave to me and Mama and Huck, all of us standing in the doorway, watching her go.

Huck had a charter and Mama was due at the health center and I thought, What am I going to do now? *Then I realized this was the perfect time to start journaling again. Because if you don't write down what happens in a day, you forget—and that day becomes a blur and that blur becomes your life.*

If I had to describe what has happened in the past six years, what would I say?

I quit my job cocktail waitressing at Caneel and got a job waiting tables at La Tapa, but only four nights a week because of Maia.

I have a best friend named Ayers Wilson, who's another waitress at La Tapa. She's like a sister to me and an auntie to Maia. She dates Mick, the manager at the Beach Bar, so we stop by there after our shift and sometimes there are cute guys and a live band and sometimes I dance and a date comes out of it—but there has been no one special because the first thing I say is that I have a daughter but the father isn't in the picture and the second thing I say is that I was born and raised on the island and will never leave.

This scares everyone away. Everyone.

On the first day of each month, cash arrives in a package and I put it in the bank for Maia. It's how I can pay for Gifft Hill. I won't say I'm not grateful, but receiving the packages also fills me with anger, shame...and longing.

Unbelievably, after all this time, I still think about Russ. I wonder how he's doing. I can only assume he's still married to Irene, trying in earnest to make the marriage work.

I hope he's happy—because if he's not happy, then what's the point of staying with her?

February 9, 2013

Journaling is like exercise; it's hard to keep it up. You have to make yourself do it, and ultimately, I don't see the point of Went to work, played Tooth Fairy, went to bed.

Tooth Fairy because Maia lost her first tooth, bottom front left.

It popped out when she bit down on a piece of breakfast toast, then it skittered across the floor and Huck found it.

I sometimes wish I had an e-mail or a cell phone number for Russ. I would tell him: Your daughter lost her first tooth. *What would he do with that news? I wonder. He has no one to share it with.*

February 13, 2014

Two things happened today, almost at the same time. One, I was on Salomon Beach, finally reading Eat, Pray, Love, *the book that Ayers holds above all others. (She has been to Italy, India, and Bali, so it resonates with her.) Anyway, I was in the midst of the India section when I looked up and saw that yacht,* Bluebeard, *sailing past Salomon toward Caneel.*

No, *I thought. But then I remembered that it was this time eight years ago that I met Russ.*

I stood up. I was wearing a white bikini, just like I had been when I met Russ at Hansen Bay. I wondered if Russ was on the boat and, if so, whether he could see me. I was tempted to drive to Caneel to check if Bluebeard *had anchored out front, but while I was in my car, debating, my phone rang and it was Huck.*

It was midafternoon. This was very unusual.

"It's your mother," he said. "She's sick and I'm taking her over to Schneider."

"What do you mean?" I said. My mother didn't get sick. My mother was a nurse practitioner who, after years of treating everything from head colds to herpes, had developed a force field around her. Nothing got through.

"She's being admitted," he said. "It's her heart. It's failing. You and Maia should plan to come over and see her after school lets

out. I'll handle today, get her settled, talk to the doctors, see if it's better for us to go to Puerto Rico or the States."

I could have told Huck then and there that Mama would never agree to be treated in the States, but I didn't want to start a health-care debate.

Her heart failing? It seemed impossible. My mother had the strongest constitution of anyone I knew, and that didn't even take into account her iron will.

For years I would have said it was impossible for my mother's heart to fail—because she didn't have a heart.

March 3, 2014

My mother, LeeAnn Small Powers, died at home with Huck and me by her side. We'd let Maia have her first sleepover, an overnight with her little friend Joanie. We explained the situation to Joanie's parents and they were very kind.

We'll tell Maia in the morning.

March 10, 2014

My mother is dead and, now, buried in the Catholic cemetery. We had a service, led by Father Abrams, my mother's favorite, followed by an enormous reception on Oppenheimer Beach. The community center was open, everyone brought a dish to share, the men got the grill going, my mother's friends sang some gospel hymns followed by some Bob Marley. There were children running in and out of the water and down the beach. It was as much a celebration of life as it was a memorial.

When the sun set, the rum came out and a steel band set up, and once I made sure Maia was safe, under the watchful eyes of her aunties, I found Huck and he poured some Flor de Caña and we did a shot together.

"We're going to make it," he said.

"Are we?" I said. I knew it was the right time for me to find a home of my own. I had plenty of money in the bank to rent a nice place, maybe even buy, but I knew that if I moved out, my heart would break and so would Huck's. My mother was gone. We needed to stick together.

I found Ayers and Mick sitting on the beach together and I joined them and Mick's dog, Gordon. We were such good friends that we didn't have to speak; we could just be.

Mick whistled, snapping me out of my daydream. "Would you look at that," he said. "Bluebeard."

I made a sound, words trying to escape that I caught at the last second. Bluebeard? *I stood up and, sure enough, there was the yacht, cruising across the horizon in front of us. Headed away from Tortola, it looked like, and toward... well, toward Caneel. Where else?*

I stayed on Oppenheimer until the very end, helping to clean up until every trace of the celebration was swept away. Ayers and Mick offered to take Huck and Maia home. I wanted to stay there and hang out by myself for a while. They hugged me. They said they understood.

They did not understand. Ayers was my confidante but I hadn't even told her *the truth. I feared she would tell Mick, and Mick would tell someone who worked at the Beach Bar, and the next day, the whole island would know. Ayers thought Maia's father, someone I called the Pirate, had come in on a yacht one weekend and then left, never to return.*

Ayers hadn't given a second thought to a yacht called Bluebeard.

By the time I got to Caneel, it was very late. I still knew people who worked there—Estella, Woodrow, and Chauncey, the night desk manager. I knew that Chauncey had grown complacent at his job. Absolutely nothing happened at Caneel between the hours of midnight and five a.m. Chauncey slept in the back on a cot.

I parked in the lot and sneaked across the property in the shadows, going past the Sugar Mill, the swimming pool, and tennis courts, across the expanse of manicured grass, to a string of palm trees that lined the beach.

Bluebeard *was anchored offshore.*

Honeymoon 718. I stood in front of the room trying to summon my courage. If I knocked and it wasn't Russ's room, whoever was in there might call security—and what would they think, seeing me there? They'd escort me off the property or they'd call the police or... Huck. Maybe someone would know me and realize I'd just lost my mother. They would chalk it up to grief.

The worst outcome would be if Russ did answer the door and he had a woman in there.

Irene.

Someone other than Irene.

I knew it was naive, but for some reason, I didn't think Russ would take Irene or another woman to our room.

I stepped up and knocked.

Nothing. No rustle, no voices, no footsteps.

I knocked again, louder—and then I turned to look at the boat. Bluebeard. *I could swim out to the boat, climb up the ladder at the back, ask for Todd Croft. I laughed. I was losing my mind.*

The door to 718 opened.

It was Russ standing before me, blinking, befuddled.

"Rosie?" he said.

"Hi."

"You're real? I'm not dreaming?"

"My mother died," I said. "Today was her service."

"Oh, Rosie," he said. "I'm so, so sorry." His voice was thick with sleep.

I peeked behind him. The room was dark, the bed empty. "Can I come in?"

"Yes," Russ said. His eyes filled and I could see my own emotions reflected back at me. For eight years I'd told myself that staying away was for the best, that denying what we'd shared was for the best, that sacrificing this man was for the best.

I had lived with agony, with sadness, with longing.

I had been such a fool.

I stepped inside.

Part Four

Christmas Cove

IRENE

Lydia sends Irene a text asking how things are going.

Irene replies: As well as can be expected.

This is a flat-out lie.

Things are going *far better* than could have been expected. It's unsettling, almost, how well Irene is adjusting to life in the islands.

To start with, she loves her job on the *Mississippi.* She loves being out on the water; she loves the clients; she gets a rush every single time someone gets a bite. She has mastered stringing the outrigger and using the gaff. Huck has promised to teach her how to read the GPS and drive the boat. Irene bragged about her ability to fillet a fish, though Huck isn't ready to relinquish that duty yet. Still, Irene tried to buy a proper fillet knife on Amazon but her credit card was declined and a call to Ed Sorley confirmed that now that Russ was "officially dead," her account at Federal Republic would be frozen until they sorted out his estate. Her account at First Iowa S & L in her own name is still active, but it has less than three thousand dollars in it. Just as Irene was about to fret, she received an e-mail from Mavis Key asking where Irene would like her final check and year-end bonus sent.

Year-end bonus? Irene thought. They never received bonuses at the magazine.

"It's a gift from Joseph Feeney," Mavis said. "As a thank-you for all your years of hard work. You built *Heartland Home and Style* from the ground up."

Irene asked Mavis to send the check to St. John. It was twelve thousand dollars! Irene still had seventy-two hundred of the eight thousand in cash she'd brought from Iowa City, plus a check from Huck on her dresser. She decided to open an account at FirstBank next to Starfish Market—with the Lovers Lane address printed on her checks.

"I'm becoming a local," she told Huck.

"Can't be a local if you don't show your face around town," Huck said. "Come to dinner with me tonight at Extra Virgin."

Irene declined. She wasn't ready.

Against all odds, Irene loves the villa. She has locked the door to the master suite where Russ slept with Rosie, even though it's the best-appointed room with the most dramatic views. Frankly, Irene would like to lop it right off the house, though this isn't an opinion she shares with the boys.

The boys—Cash, Baker, and Floyd—have all chosen bedrooms and Irene is comfortable at the opposite end of the hall, next to Maia's room.

She thinks about redecorating the entire house. The décor now is functional but uninspired. It needs brighter colors, some original and surprising elements; it needs personality. Once Russ's estate is settled and she has access to some funds, she plans on turning the house into a tasteful, tropical dream home.

Maybe when it's done she'll pitch it to Mavis Key for the magazine's Escapes feature. *Irene Steele, editor emeritus of* Heartland Home and Style, *opens up about redecorating the St. John villa that her late husband, Russell, shared with his mistress and love child.*

Irene also toys with the idea of turning the house into an inn, just as she'd considered with the Iowa City house in the minutes before she found out Russ was dead. What if she "rented" rooms free of charge to women who, like herself, had discovered a husband's infidelity or who, like her cousin Mitzi Quinn, had lost a husband and were having a challenging time bouncing back. Irene and these women could bond over iced coffee, papaya smoothies, and wine. They could gain strength from one another here in paradise, make it a sort of emotional convalescent home.

Irene loves the idea, though she knows it will never come to pass. She enjoys having the boys here. They have developed an easy routine and the house is big enough that they can all do their own thing without stepping on one another's toes. Irene is still Mother Alarm Clock; she rises before the sun and makes sure Cash is up in time for his charters. When Baker and Floyd went back to Houston, Irene was sad to see them go, but Baker assured her they'd be back the following week.

Overall, Irene is far happier than she should be. It's not lost on her that, ultimately, this is because of Huck. He's a wonderful, kind, supportive boss and he's becoming a better friend each day. Irene assumes that they share the same emotional space; they're still in mourning, still dealing daily with the shock of their situation. But because they are also mature adults, they soldier on.

And then on Monday, the beginning of Irene's second week of work, things fall apart.

It starts with the text that Irene receives Sunday evening about the next day's charter. It says: 1 adult, 2 children, last name Goshen, New York, NY—D!

Irene texts Huck. What does "D" mean? She wonders if it was just a typo or maybe Destiny's new sign-off.

Huck texts back: "D" for difficult. She must have been a real humdinger on the phone because Destiny is tough.

Great, Irene thinks. *D* for *difficult.*

She starts the day with a positive attitude. The Goshens are from New York City. Possibly, they're caught up in the rat race that is Manhattan. The father works in finance or advertising, maybe the mother is a fashion editor. Do people in New York have other kinds of jobs? Irene tries to think of characters in movies she's seen—architect, elite private-school headmaster, museum curator, bohemian artist, editor in chief, publicist, restaurateur, Broadway actress.

Irene gets two coffees and two sausage biscuits from Provisions. Meredith, the owner, has seen her enough times that she now waves. Irene stops there as a show of kindness toward Huck—he makes breakfast for Maia every day but many times forgets to eat himself—and besides, the sausage biscuit is delicious. Irene is starting to gain back some of the weight she lost.

The boat is tied up at the dock before Irene arrives, which has never happened before. Huck is watching her as she approaches. She figures he's here early because of the difficult clients. He takes the coffee and biscuits from her, then helps her down into the boat.

"There's something I need to tell you," he says.

Something about the clients? She raises her eyebrows.

"My friend Rupert called over the weekend to tell me that Paulette and Douglas Vickers have been taken into custody by the FBI."

"What?"

"They were on St. Croix with Doug's sister," Huck says. "The FBI tracked them down and arrested them."

"On what charges?"

"Real estate fraud," Huck says. "Financial fraud."

Well, yes, Irene thinks, *of course.* She wonders if the Vickerses were somehow responsible for the helicopter crash. Was Paulette Vickers the kind of person who could kill three people, then pick up one of the men's widows at the ferry and describe the delights of the island?

"They'll find out what she knows," Huck says. "She'll likely lead them to Todd Croft."

"Real estate fraud," Irene says. She thinks about the dummy driveways on the way up to Russ's villa. "Financial fraud."

"I didn't want to tell you anything until I heard back from Agent Vasco," Huck says. "She left me a message late last night, after I was asleep. I thought it might be time to start worrying..."

"Is it?" Irene says. Her wheels are spinning. Of course it is! Real estate fraud, Todd Croft, the money in Rosie's drawer. Paulette knows far, far more than she's saying, although likely she's just a pawn manipulated by Todd Croft and maybe Russ as well.

"No, AC," Huck says. "No. Agent Vasco told me it's an ongoing investigation and if she has any other questions, she'll be in touch."

"So there's nothing we should do?" Irene says. She wonders if the FBI knows she's working with Huck. And if so, what do they think about *that?* Does it seem suspicious? Does it seem like Huck and Irene are part of the conspiracy with Russ and Paulette Vickers? Should Irene quit? She doesn't want to quit. She takes a breath of the morning air and tries to calm down. She has done nothing wrong; Huck has done nothing wrong. The FBI agents know this.

"Nothing we should do, nothing we can do," Huck says. "We just have to wait until they find Croft. But I wanted you to be aware."

"Yes, thank you," Irene says. She takes Huck's left hand, the one with the missing pinkie, and squeezes it. "Please tell me everything you know. Don't spare me because you think I can't handle it. I'm tough."

"That you are, Angler Cupcake," Huck says. "But I'm happy to give you today off if you want to go home and mull this over."

"Don't be ridiculous," Irene says. "If I do go home, I *will* mull this over, and what good will that do? I'd much rather be on the boat."

"I feel exactly the same way," Huck says. "Even if these people *are* difficult."

Irene holds the ropes, smiling, as the Goshens approach. What she told Huck is true: She is tough. This family can't throw anything at her that she can't handle. But when she sees them, her heart sinks. There's the mother, a pretty but sour-looking woman—blond, thin, midforties. She's followed by a teenage daughter, a younger, prettier, angrier version of the mother. Trailing behind them with a bounce in his step is the son. He's maybe thirteen or fourteen years old and he's completely bald.

The mother's name is Galen Goshen, the daughter is Altar, and the son is Niles; Niles, Galen announces, has just finished eighteen rounds of chemo. He has leukemia, Galen informs Irene, and this last round of chemo is either going to put him in remission or it isn't. She says this right in front of Niles, who shrugs.

"I want to catch a fish," he says. "A big one. Something I can hang on the wall."

"He's frail," Galen says.

Yes, Irene can see that. He's white as chalk and his arms and legs are like sticks. His blue eyes are sunken on his face but they're bright and lively and he hasn't stopped smiling.

Huck says, "Four to six feet today."

Four to six feet isn't terrible, but going into the wind, it will be a jarring ride. Even Irene hasn't gotten used to the teeth-rattling that occurs when the boat smacks the trough of a wave. More than once she has gone home sore from tensing her muscles for so long. She can't imagine this kid surviving the ride to the drop-off six miles south. He'll be broken into pieces by the time they're ready to cast a line.

But if they stay inshore, they won't catch a big fish. Nothing big enough to mount, anyway.

"Four to six feet is too big for an offshore trip," Irene says. "We'll stay inshore today and catch plenty of fish."

Niles seems happy with this and Galen and Altar look like they couldn't care less.

Galen says, "Certainly you have a life preserver for Niles?"

"Life preservers are under the seat behind me," Huck says. "We have one to fit the boy, though for an inshore trip, we won't go faster than ten knots, so he probably won't need it."

"I was clear with the woman on the phone—" Galen says

and before she can finish her sentence, Irene is pulling out a life preserver for Niles. *D* is for *difficult*.

Niles sits next to Huck at the wheel as Huck explains the dash, shows Niles the fish finder, and points off the port and starboard sides, identifying the other islands. Irene checks the light tackle rods, then sits on the stern bench next to Galen and Altar, who are whispering angrily back and forth. Irene doesn't want to eavesdrop—as Huck told her early on, family drama rarely stops because people are out on a fishing charter, and it's absolutely none of their concern. However, it's impossible not to overhear. The daughter, Altar, is turning eighteen sometime after the family returns to New York, and Altar wants her mother to allow her to throw a party in the—house? Apartment?—for a hundred people with a DJ and a keg.

"No, no, and no," Galen says. "It's me saying no but it's also building security saying no. A DJ won't work, a hundred kids dancing to a DJ won't work. We'll get evicted."

"What about Pineland?" Altar says. "She had that exact party on the fourth floor two years ago."

"Pineland's father bribed Mr. Soo," Galen says.

"So there's the answer," Altar says. "*You* bribe Mr. Soo."

"I have neither the desire nor the spare cash," Galen says. "Your brother's treatment."

"I knew that was the real reason," Altar says. "It's Niles's fault I can't have a party."

"Well, what exactly are Niles and I supposed to do while you throw this party in our home?"

"I don't know," Altar says. "Check into a hotel?" She laughs. "Niles will probably be in the hospital anyway, and you'll be at his bedside, so what does it even matter?"

Irene can't stand to hear another word. She moves to the

captain's seat. Niles is now on his knees on the bow banquette, earbuds in. He's as still and majestic as a figurehead.

The earbuds, she supposes, are useful for blocking out his mother and sister.

Irene leans in to Huck. "They're fighting back there."

Huck nods to let Irene know he's heard her, but he doesn't seem to care. Maybe he's thinking about Agent Vasco. Or, more likely, he's trying to pick a good spot to anchor and cast. The engine noise makes most conversations impossible and yet the mother and daughter's discussion has escalated to a screaming match. It's impossible to ignore them.

"I'll just ask Dad to pay for it, then!"

"Be my guest! See how far that gets you!"

"...bitter because Misty is way cooler than you..."

"Misty is twenty-six years old. She *should* be cooler than me..."

"I'm calling him now and telling him to book me a plane ticket home. I don't want to be here! The only reason we're here is because of Niles!"

"...selfish little..."

"...I have children, I'm going to love them all equally..."

"...*sick,* Altar..."

"I don't care!" Altar screams. "I hate you and I hate Niles!"

Finally, Huck leans over to Irene. "I know it's difficult, but you have to let them go. They obviously have things to work through."

Irene wipes away the tears that are rolling down her cheeks. She's crying for them but also for herself and for all families that have been broken.

Turns out, she's not as tough as she thought.

When it sounds like Galen and Altar might actually come to

blows—Galen grabs Altar's phone and holds it over her head, threatening to throw it overboard—Irene moves up to the bow with two light tackle rods. She touches Niles on the back.

When he turns to see Irene holding both rods, his face lights up. Irene feels more tears building behind her eyes but she'll be damned if she's going to cry in front of Niles.

This last round of chemo is either going to put him in remission or it isn't.

It's going to put him in remission, Irene thinks. And right now, she's going to put this kid on a fish.

A higher power must be with them because on his third cast, Niles gets a bite, and Irene can tell just by the bow of the rod that it's something big—but what? There aren't too many big fish to be found inshore, at least not that Irene has experienced firsthand.

Niles has a natural instinct for what to do. He reels with surprising tenacity and lets the spool go when the fish runs. He keeps the rod tip up and the handle pressed into his jutting hipbone. "What's it gonna be?" Niles asks.

"I'm not sure," Irene says.

Huck comes to check on them. "Tarpon, from the looks of it," he says. "Big one."

Sure enough, a little while later, Niles Goshen reels in a tarpon that is a big fish by anyone's standards.

"I didn't think it was the season for tarpon," Irene says.

"It's not, really," Huck says. "But once in a while, the universe throws you a favor."

They're going to take the tarpon home. Huck gives Galen the card of a taxidermist who can stuff and mount it. Galen looks relieved and defeated. Altar is either asleep or pretending to be asleep behind her sunglasses.

Galen pulls Irene aside. "You have a good man there," she says, nodding at Huck. "It's clear how much he cares about you. I hope you don't take that for granted."

Irene can't think of how to respond. *He's not my man? We're not together? I'm just the mate on his boat?* What if Irene were to tell Galen that, back on the first of the year, she had been a married magazine editor living in Iowa City, but then her husband was killed in a helicopter crash, and his secret life was revealed. Galen wouldn't believe it. But if she did believe it, she might understand that everyone has her baggage and her sad stories. What differentiates people is how they choose to deal with them. Irene has done pretty well, she thinks, assuming the FBI aren't waiting on the dock when they get back.

"I take nothing for granted," Irene says.

On the way back to Cruz Bay, the sky darkens and there's one loud thunderclap, followed by a torrential downpour. Irene hands the Goshens a couple of waterproof ponchos to hold over their heads; they are squeaking and squealing like they're going to melt. As Irene stands under the canvas Bimini with Huck, she catches sight of Niles kneeling on the bow. His arms are open, his head back. He's embracing the earth and all of her aspects.

It's just rain, he seems to be saying. *I will survive it.*

The Goshens disembark early—they've barely been on the water for two hours—and Irene feels a strange melancholy, watching them go. She realizes she'll never know what happens to the Goshen family. Will Altar have her birthday party? Will Niles live to be an adult? Will he hang the tarpon he caught off the coast of St. John in his home and gaze on it with pride in his fifties, in his sixties? Irene will be forgotten, lost, as soon as tomorrow or the next day. He will never know how hard Irene was rooting for him.

"Wow," she says to Huck. She's wet—and cold for the first time since she's been here.

"D," he says. "For *difficult*."

"There's no charter tomorrow, correct?"

"Correct," Huck says. "You get a day off, unless something comes up at the last minute, which has been known to happen."

Irene nods and wraps her arms around herself. She's shivering.

Huck notices and holds his arms open.

She stares at him.

"I'm just offering you a hug," Huck says. "That was tough on you and the news I greeted you with was no picnic either."

Irene takes a tentative step toward him. He wraps his arms around her. It has been . . . well, a *long* time since a man held her like this. Russ, before he left for his "business trip" after Christmas? Had he hugged Irene or kissed her goodbye?

No, she remembers. She had been in Coralville returning some Christmas presents for Milly. She had been angry at Russ for leaving over the new year, and as punishment, she had denied him a proper goodbye.

She tries to remember what Christmas had been like. It was just the two of them in the morning in front of the tree, opening gifts. They had talked to each of the boys on the phone and they had joined Milly for the Christmas lunch served at Brown Deer.

Had they been intimate? Had they hugged and kissed? They'd held hands, she remembers, during the Christmas Eve service at First Presbyterian.

That had been nice, Irene supposes, but it hadn't offered the comfort or the rush of this hug. Irene fits into Huck's arms perfectly. His body is solid and warm. Can she trust him? She feels like the answer is yes—but she would have said exactly the same thing about Russell Steele. She would have said Russ was beyond reproach.

"Let me take you to dinner tonight," Huck says in her ear. "Maia is with Ayers and I have an idea. We'll go over to St. Thomas."

St. Thomas is bigger, and they can be anonymous. For some reason, this suits Irene better than being seen out in Cruz Bay, where everyone knows Huck and might guess who Irene is.

"Okay," she says.

Irene meets Huck back at the dock at six thirty. He told her to dress up and so she's wearing a spring-green linen sheath with a belted middle, a dress she bought for Baker's high-school graduation thirteen years earlier—right around the time that Russ met Rosie, although she tries to put this thought out of her mind.

Huck is wearing a blue button-down shirt, ironed khakis, and if Irene isn't mistaken, there's a navy blazer folded across the back of the captain's seat.

This is a real date.

Huck has wine on the boat. He pours her a glass of Cakebread chardonnay—she can't believe he remembered what kind of wine she likes—and he opens a beer for himself.

"We aren't going far," he says. "Just over to the yacht club in Red Hook. Fifteen minutes."

They cruise out, nice and easy, across Sir Francis Drake Channel as the sun sets. Irene considers sitting in the bow and letting the wind catch her hair—it's out of its braid tonight—but instead, she sits next to Huck where she can listen to the music, Jackson Browne singing "Running on Empty." The sky glows pink and blue and gold; Huck is humming; Irene's wine is crisp and cold. There is nothing wrong with this moment.

The world is a strange and mysterious place, Irene thinks. How is it possible that Russ's web of deceit and his secret second life led Irene here? She laughs at the absurdity of it. Huck never met Russ but Russ certainly knew that Huck existed. What would Russ think if he could see Huck and Irene now? It turns Irene's mind into a pretzel just considering it.

They pull into a slip at the St. Thomas Yacht Club and a cute young man in white shorts and a green polo hurries over to help with the ropes. He offers Irene a hand up to the dock.

"Captain Huck," he says. "Good to see you again, sir. It's been a while."

"Good to see you, Seth," Huck says. "Are we all set inside?"

"Yes, sir," Seth says. "They're ready for you. Enjoy your dinner."

Huck offers Irene his arm and walks her down the dock. He's wearing his blazer now and Irene is soothed by how at ease he seems and how gentlemanly he is as he opens the door to the club and ushers Irene inside.

The hostess, a stunning young West Indian woman, greets Huck with a kiss and introduces herself as Jacinda to Irene, then leads Huck and Irene to a table by the front window that overlooks the docks and the water. Irene can see the twinkling lights of St. John in the distance.

Theirs is the only table set. They are the only people in the dining room.

"Is it...always this empty?"

"The kitchen normally isn't open tonight," Huck says. "But they owe me a favor."

So they are having a private dinner. The whole club, all to themselves.

"The prime rib is very good here," Huck says. "I don't know about you, but I'm sick of fish."

They eat like royalty: Warm rolls with sweet butter, organic greens with homemade papaya vinaigrette, prime rib, baked potato with lots of butter and sour cream, and, for dessert, sabayon and berries. Huck and Irene drink wine with dinner, then end with a sipping rum, a twenty-five-year-old El Dorado that is even better than the Flor de Caña, Huck says.

They do not talk about the Vickerses' arrest or what it might mean. They don't talk about Russ or Rosie or real estate fraud or Todd Croft or frozen accounts. Irene pushes all that away, though during the natural lulls in the conversation, it feels like she's holding an unruly mob behind a door. It feels, as they finish up dinner, like Agent Vasco has just taken a seat at the table; that's how badly Irene wants to talk about it.

Instead, she says, "The mother on the boat today thought we were married. She said, 'You have a good man there.' She said she could tell how much you cared for me." The instant these words are out, Irene feels her cheeks burn.

"I hate to break it to you, AC," Huck says. "Everyone who gets on that boat thinks we're married." He reaches for Irene's hand. "And everyone can see how much I care for you."

They head back to the boat, hand in hand. There are stars overhead and it feels like there's a bright, burning star in Irene's chest. What is happening?

Huck helps Irene down into the boat. Before he turns on the running lights, he takes Irene's face in his hands and he kisses her. The kiss is sweet but intense—and there is no room for thoughts of anything or anyone else, not even Agent Vasco.

AYERS

There's no such thing as a clean breakup, Ayers thinks.

When she and Mick hashed it out, Ayers told him exactly how she felt—his infidelity with Brigid was insurmountable. Mick said that he had bumped into Brigid on the ferry and Ayers believed that—but she still didn't trust him, with Brigid or with anyone else.

"I can't do this anymore," she said.

Deep down, she acknowledges that the fault is not entirely Mick's. Ayers wanted a chance to be with Baker and she refused to sleep with him while she was still with Mick. She had only gotten back together with Mick as a way to exact revenge on both Baker and Cash for withholding the truth about who they were, and then once she and Mick—and Gordon—were back in their routine, Ayers was comfortable, if not particularly happy.

Now that she has slept with Baker—and without protection, like an irresponsible idiot—and now that Baker has left to go back to Houston, Ayers is neither comfortable nor happy.

She had meant to take it slow and steady with Baker. She had vowed to wait until he came *back* from Houston to consummate their relationship. But passion and high emotion had ruled and although their night together had been unforgettable—at least for her—now the anticipation is gone. Baker might decide Ayers isn't worth returning for.

Monday morning, there's a knock on her door. Ayers is in bed. Mondays she's off from both jobs, though she has Maia tonight. Ayers is picking Maia up in town at six and they have plans to get takeout from De Coal Pot.

Ayers doesn't like unexpected knocks at the door. Who could it be at nine thirty in the morning? Her landlady? Jehovah's Witnesses?

She pulls a pillow over her head. The door is locked. *Whoever you are,* she thinks, *please go away.* Monday is her day of rest.

"Hello?" a voice says, loud and clear. "Ayers?"

It's Mick. He still has a key. Why didn't she ask for her key back?

A second later there's a flutter of footsteps as Gordon comes running into the bedroom and jumps up on Ayers's bed. Mick is no dummy, she thinks. He sent his goodwill ambassador in first.

But Mick soon follows. "Get up," he says.

Ayers flips over and partially opens one eye. "What are you doing here?" Does she need to remind him that they've broken up? What if she had company?

"It's Monday," Mick says. "We're going to Christmas Cove. The boat is anchored in Frank Bay. I have rum punch, I have water, I have snacks, I have your snorkel and fins."

"It's over, Mick," Ayers says. "We're through."

Mick sits on the bed and brushes Ayers's hair out of her eyes. "We're not through," he says. "We'll never be through."

He looks unreasonably good, for Mick. He has a day's worth of scruff, which is how she likes him best, and he's gotten some sun on his face, making his eyes look very green. Gordon has already snuggled against the curve of Ayers's back. Ayers closes her eyes for one second and travels back in time to before the disgusting discovery of Brigid, back when Mick and Gordon were "her boys," back when life was calm and happy.

But she can travel backward only in her mind. In real time, she has no choice but to move forward. Baker. And Floyd too, she supposes. Assuming they come back.

"I slept with Baker last week," Ayers says. "The night we broke up."

Mick's eyebrows shoot up in an expression of surprise, and then a split second later, Ayers sees the hurt, which was her aim. "Banker? Wow. You wasted no time."

Ayers props herself up on her elbows. "I like him," she says. "He's a grown-up. He doesn't *lie* to me."

"Doesn't he?" Mick says. "He didn't tell you who he was. And his father"—Mick whistles—"didn't exactly serve as a role model in the honesty department."

Ayers should never have told Mick anything about Baker. "He's not his father," she says. "I'm nothing like my parents. You're nothing like yours."

"Point taken," Mick says. "I'm sure you want me to be angry or jealous about your tryst with Banker, and I am." He takes a couple of deep breaths and Ayers can see his Irish temper eddying beneath the surface. Baker is bigger than Mick, but Mick is fiercer; if they ever came to blows, Baker would lose. "But I'm glad you got it out of your system. I had my fling and now you've had yours—"

"It doesn't work like that, Mick," Ayers says. "I didn't do it for revenge. This isn't a tit for tat. And by the way, I *waited* until we were broken up—"

"You waited, what, an hour? And we aren't really broken up. We had a misunderstanding, and you overreacted. Bumping into Brigid on the ferry doesn't warrant a breakup. Check the relationship rule book. Ask your friends."

"I don't have any friends," Ayers says.

"That's what this is really about," Mick says. "Banker, Money…they're attractive to you because it's a connection to Rosie."

"Baker is in love with me," Ayers says.

"Oh, really?" Mick says. "Well, where is he now? Is he here with a pineapple-banana smoothie, waiting for you in the Jeep? Has he planned the best day off imaginable, complete with a new Jack Johnson Spotify playlist and a solemn promise that we can order the carbonara pizza *and* the bloomin' onion pizza *and* the chocolate-banana Pizza Stix? Did he arrange for Captain Stephen from the *Singing Dog* to play his guitar for three hours this afternoon? Did he make a reservation for tonight at the Longboard?"

"I have Maia tonight," Ayers says.

"I know," Mick says. "I made the reservation for three people."

Ayers has to give him credit for that. Maia will die of happiness, eating at the Longboard with Mick. She loves the lobster tacos.

"It's over, Mick," Ayers says, though even she can hear that her voice lacks conviction. "Go to Christmas Cove by yourself and when everyone asks where I am, tell them we broke up. Or better still, take Brigid with you so they figure it out on their own."

"I called Bex at Rhumb Lines," Mick says. "I begged her to take Brigid off my hands, but she says she's fully staffed. Then I heard Robert and Brittany at Island Abodes were looking for someone to help out with the villas. Brigid has an interview with them on Thursday."

"Poor Robert and Brittany," Ayers says. They're one of the nicest, coolest couples on island, and they have a cute baby. "But it'll be good for Brigid to get a different kind of job. She's a terrible server."

"Agreed," Mick says. "I wish I'd never hired her. I wish I'd never met her. But what's done is done. She'll be out of the Beach Bar by next week."

Ayers can't deny it—this news pleases her.

"Back to Banker," Mick says. "Does he know that you're ticklish right here?" Mick digs his fingers into Ayers's ribs. She shrieks and soon they're tussling in bed and Mick crawls on top of her and she lets him rest on her for a couple of seconds before pushing him off.

"I have a surprise for you," Mick says. "Two surprises. One for now and one for later. Does Banker know how much you love surprises?"

Ayers *does* love surprises. "Okay," she says. "I'll come."

It's a swan song, she tells herself, *a last hurrah.* Because she has Maia tonight, there's no danger of her *sleeping* with Mick. There's no reason they can't go out together in public as friends.

The second Ayers sits in Mick's Jeep with Gordon perched in her lap, she feels happy about her decision. The day is crystal clear, sunny, and hot—and what else would Ayers have done with her time? She would have holed up at home and read Rosie's diaries. She has been so engrossed in the story about Russ, she's on the verge of becoming addicted. She has finally gotten to the part where they're reunited. Russ knows about Maia. Rosie knows about Irene and the boys.

They're going to be together.

It's good for Ayers to leave the diaries alone for a while. She sips the smoothie Mick got her from Our Market and sings along to Chesney on the radio. This is what a day off is supposed to feel like.

Mick turns onto Great Cruz Bay Road and Ayers says, "Where are we going?"

"Surprise number one," Mick says. Great Cruz Bay Road is one of Ayers's favorite places; it has views northwest over the Westin toward St. Thomas and Water Island. Mick follows the road almost to the tip of the point, then he signals and turns into a driveway marked with a sign that says PURE JOY. This leads to an adorable white cottage with bright blue shutters. It reminds Ayers of the months that she and her parents spent living on Santorini.

They climb out of the car. "Follow me," Mick says. He steps up onto the wraparound porch that has an uninterrupted water view.

"What are we doing here?"

"This is my new place," Mick says.

"You bought it?"

"Renting," Mick says. "Long-term. But it's mine. You want to see the rest?"

He leads her inside, and everything is picture-perfect. There's a bedroom, living room, dining nook, kitchen, and a brand-new, sparkling-white-tiled bathroom; every room in the house has a view of the water. On the deck is a grill and a hot tub, and around the corner is an outdoor shower painted the same blue as the shutters.

It's a real *place*. Not a hole-in-the-wall like where Mick lives now, which meant that he was always crashing at Ayers's in a way that felt like he was infringing on her space. For years, Ayers has been begging him to find someplace better. And now he has. This cottage—Pure Joy—is a dream.

"This is amazing," Ayers says. "You'll be much happier here."

"*We* will be happier here," Mick says. "I got it for us. See those chairs?" He points to two stools, upholstered in blue, in front of a bar counter. "Those are what convinced me to take it. I pictured the two of us coming home from work late at night and having a drink there together—and can you imagine the sunset from here?"

"Hashtag sunset," Ayers says. "Your Instagram account will blow up."

"We can have our coffee out here in the mornings," Mick says.

We broke up, Ayers thinks. But Mick's expression is so earnest that she doesn't have the heart to say it.

"It's nice," she admits.

One last hurrah, she tells herself again, though Mick is slowly but surely wearing down her resistance. Her night with Baker—which had seemed so vivid and unforgettable right after it happened—is now fading from her mind.

Has she merely fallen prey to the sexual attraction she feels for Baker because it's bright, shiny, and new? Her relationship with Mick is deep and long and intense. Mick is the person Ayers tells things, even the small, inconsequential things, because he's the one who has shared her history. He has context.

If she starts something new with Baker, she would have to go back to square one. The thought is, frankly, exhausting.

Ayers wades through the crystal water of Frank Bay and climbs into the boat. Mick is borrowing *Funday,* a thirty-two-foot Grady-White, from his boss for the day, something he normally does only on special occasions. Mick loads Gordon in and turns up the music and they go zipping across the surface of the water at breathtaking speed. Ayers loves nothing in the world more than being out on a boat—*Treasure Island* included—though the experience is much better when she isn't working. She fills a Yeti cup with rum punch—Mick makes the best—and belts out, *"Save it for a rainy day!"*

It's well known that Monday is the weekend for people in the service industry. La Tapa closes on Monday nights after the holiday rush, as do a bunch of other restaurants, so when Mick and Ayers arrive in Christmas Cove, it's a Who's Who of St. John hospitality all rafted together on either side of the Pizza Pi boat. The guys from 420 to Center are there and so is Bex from Rhumb Lines and Mattie the bartender from the Dog House Pub with his girlfriend, Lindsay, who works at the Beach Bar with Mick, and Colleen from Pizzabar in Paradise and Jena from Extra Virgin Bistro. Alex the bartender from Ocean 362 is on a catamaran—with Skip. From the looks of things, Skip is pretty far along in the partying department. When he sees Mick and Ayers pull in, he raises his arms over his head and hollers at the top of his lungs, "They're here!" As though Mick and Ayers are the king and queen of this particular St. John prom.

Ayers grins at everyone and waves. This is her family.

Mick and Ayers tie up to a sleek, black Midnight Express that has a woman on board who looks familiar. She's wearing a tropical-print bikini and enormous sunglasses. She waves and says, "Hey, Ayers!" and then she helps Mick with the ropes and the bumpers while Ayers racks her brain for how she knows this woman.

She leans over to hug Ayers. "I suppose you've heard that Brent and I are getting a divorce?"

Who's Brent? Ayers thinks. The woman pulls a cigarette and a lighter out of a pair of teensy white shorts lying at her feet and Ayers realizes the woman is Swan Seeley, the mother of Colton Seeley, Maia's little friend. Swan has traded in her reusable shopping bags and sustainable vegetable gardening for day-drinking and lung cancer.

Ayers laughs. This is fabulous! She always liked Swan best when she was breaking the rules anyway. But a divorce is sad, right? "I'm sorry to hear that," Ayers says.

Swan waves the sentiment and her exhale of smoke away. "Don't be," she says. "He's got a gambling problem. I had to cut bait before he sank us."

"Good for you, then."

Swan smiles. "There are eligible men *everywhere,*" she says. "Just look at this place!" Her eyes scan the now-impressive raft of boats. "What about Skip? He's single, right?"

"He's single," Ayers says. "But I'm not sure he's your type." *Or anyone's type,* she thinks. Although who's to say that Skip, who's coming off his weird thing with Tilda, and Swan Seeley, freshly separated, wouldn't be a good match for each other?

"There's the hottest new dad at the school," Swan says. "He's brand-new to the island, relocating from Houston. I saw him last week when I was picking up Colton. Maia seemed to know him, though of course I couldn't ask who he was with Colton in the car."

Hottest new dad. That would be Baker. Ayers feels herself *bristling.* Naturally Swan Seeley and all the other Gifft Hill mothers will pant over Baker. Ayers wants to inform Swan that Baker is *taken,* by *her,* but she can't very well do this when she's here with Mick.

At that moment, who should step onto Swan's boat but Skip,

holding a chilled bottle of Dom Pérignon and a bouquet of plastic flutes.

"Champagne, ladies?" He pours some for Swan and some for Ayers. "This storied bubbly has notes of Canadian pennies, your dad's Members Only jacket, and..." He glances over Ayers's shoulder. "'We Are Never, Ever, Ever Getting Back Together.'"

Why does he keep *doing* this? Ayers wonders, but Swan laughs. "Ha! You can say *that* again!"

Ayers turns to see a cute little speedboat pull up. Tilda is at the wheel and Cash is next to her.

Ayers is seized with panic. *Cash* is here? What's *Cash* doing here? It's obvious, hello, that he came with Tilda, that's her parents' little runabout, though they also have a sixty-two-foot single-hull sailboat. Tilda and Cash? Yes, Baker told her this the other night. It's good, it's great, Tilda and Cash together isn't the problem—except, maybe, for Skip. The problem is that Cash will see Ayers here with Mick and report back to Baker.

Ugh! Arrgh! What can she do? Can she pretend she's here with Swan? Maybe Cash and Tilda won't stay; there are a lot of boats here already, maybe they want privacy, maybe they'll head over to Mermaid's Chair where they can be alone. Or to Dinghy's on Water Island.

Go to Dinghy's! Ayers thinks.

But Tilda has earned her place at this party; she works just as hard as everyone else. Ayers notices she gets a sadistic grin on her face when she sees Skip. She must want to gloat.

Cash and Tilda raft up with Mick. Ayers watches Mick and Cash shake hands. Ayers offers a lame little wave.

Captain Stephen starts playing the guitar and singing "Southern Cross."

Think about how many times I have fallen…

Mick's hand lands on the back of Ayers's neck. He knows how much she loves this song.

The pizza arrives—one carbonara with lobster, one bloomin' onion drizzled with lemon aioli, and Ayers's ultimate splurge, the chocolate-banana Pizza Stix. She drinks her champagne—Skip has, generously, left the bottle for her and Swan to split—and she eats some pizza, plays tug-of-war with the crust with Gordon, and dives off the boat for a swim.

Tilda and Cash have noodles. They're floating in the water, interested in no one but each other.

Mick is gone somewhere. Ayers cranes her neck to see if, by chance, Brigid has arrived on any of the boats. Captain Stephen stops playing and there's the spine-chilling shriek of microphone feedback, then she hears Mick's voice.

"You guys, can I have your attention please? Hey! Everyone, please quiet down."

Ayers sees Mick heading toward her with the microphone. Is he going to sing to her or ask *her* to sing, maybe something from the Jack Johnson Spotify playlist?

It all happens so fast. A hush blankets Christmas Cove, and all eyes are on Mick, now standing in the bow of *Funday* in front of Ayers, who is dripping wet in her bikini.

He drops to one knee and only then does Ayers get it: the second surprise.

"*This* is why I went to St. Thomas," he whispers. He pulls a box out of the pocket of his swim trunks and says into the microphone so that every single person they work and live with on the tiny island that is St. John USVI can hear, "Ayers Wilson, will you marry me? Will you be my wife?"

Ayers isn't sure where Cash is, but she can feel his eyes boring into her. Swan Seeley claps a hand over her mouth and then everyone starts chanting, "Say yes! Say yes! Say yes!"

Gordon, who never barks, is pressing his flank against Ayers's leg, barking.

A public proposal is never a good idea, Ayers thinks. Or is it? She can't say no. She can't dive off the boat and seek asylum on Little St. James Island. She could, she supposes, beg Cash and Tilda to take her back to Cruz Bay. Yes, that's what she should do.

But what a buzzkill. What a depressing end to such a well-executed surprise. Ayers realizes that a good number of these people must have been in on it. Nobody knows that Ayers and Mick broke up and that Ayers embarked on a new relationship. They're all caught up in the theatrics.

Rosie? Ayers thinks with a glance skyward.

But there's no answer.

Ayers presents her left hand to Mick and he slips the ring on her finger, then stands and pulls her in for a kiss.

The crowd cheers. Ayers studies the diamond. It's a beautiful ring; she has to give him that. The stone sparkles so brightly that Ayers is, temporarily, blinded.

CASH

Cash takes a picture of Mick down on one knee, holding out a ring to Ayers. He sends it to Baker with a caption that reads She said yes, dude. Sorry.

Maybe, just maybe, it was all for show. Cash always wondered about guys who thought it was a good idea to propose during the seventh-inning stretch of a Colorado Rockies game or up on the stage during a Jason Aldean concert. Was it to guarantee a yes because most women wouldn't say no in front of twenty thousand people? But then, later, was the ring pulled off the finger, put back in the box, and taken to the nearest pawnshop? Ayers looked surprised but not necessarily *happy*.

On the boat ride home, he asks Tilda for her opinion.

"She looked dazzled," Tilda says. "In the best possible way. And who can blame her? Those two have been together *forever,* they've had their issues and come out the other side. They'll get married and have kids. They'll be great parents. They dote on Mick's dog, Gordon."

"Okay," Cash says.

"Please don't tell me seeing that *upset* you," Tilda says. "If it did, I'll drop you off at the National Park Service dock right now and you can walk home. Or find another unsuspecting woman to pick you up hitchhiking."

"It didn't bother *me* in the slightest," Cash says. Which is true. His feelings for Ayers have changed dramatically in the past few days. "I'm worried for my brother. He really likes her. Maybe I shouldn't have sent him that text."

Sure enough, as soon as they get back to Cruz Bay, Cash's phone starts ringing. Baker.

Cash sends him to voicemail. He and Tilda are going to her villa to "hang out," then they're heading into town for dinner.

La Tapa is closed so they decide to go to the Longboard—Tilda is in the mood for their frozen rosé—and who should they happen across but Ayers, Mick, and Maia, who are enjoying more champagne and platters of tacos.

When Maia sees Cash, she jumps to her feet. "Bro!" she says. "Did you hear the news?"

"I did," Cash says. He smiles at Mick and Ayers. "Congratulations, you two."

Mick puts an arm around Ayers and squeezes her. "I should have done this a long time ago."

Ayers's expression can only be described as dazed. Or maybe she's just drunk. "I meant to text you," she says. "The boat has a mechanical issue and we had to cancel the charter for tomorrow."

"She wouldn't have been able to go anyway," Mick says. "I want to keep her in bed all day."

"Really?" Maia says. "We're eating!"

Yeah, Cash thinks. The idea of Mick and Ayers in bed is enough to turn his stomach as well. He can feel his phone buzzing away in his pocket. Baker. Baker. Baker.

"Well, if I don't have work," Cash says, "that means we can finally hike to the baobab tree."

"After school?" Maia says. "Can we leave at four so my friend Shane can come?"

"Works for me," Cash says.

"And me," Tilda says.

"Pick us up at the ferry dock, please," Maia says. "And bring plenty of water."

"Yes, ma'am," Cash says.

"She's a force," Ayers says. Her eyes mist over. "Just like her mother."

At four o'clock the next day, Cash and Tilda pick up Maia and Shane in Tilda's Range Rover, which both kids find impressive;

immediately, they start taking pictures of themselves in the back. Cash has probably overprepared for the hike. In his backpack, he has eight bottles of water, two of them frozen, as well as trail mix, four Kind bars, two spare clean bandannas, and a first-aid kit. He and Tilda are both dressed in hiking shorts and boots. Tilda has six bottles of water in her pack, plus sunscreen, bug spray, peanut butter–filled pretzels, a selfie stick, and a paper map from the National Park Service.

"You guys are so...gung ho," Maia says. She holds her phone over her head and snaps a photo of herself making a fish face. "We're just gonna hike in our Chucks."

"Yeah," Shane says. They all climb out of the Rover and Shane gives Cash and Tilda the once-over. "But when I climb Everest, I'm bringing you guys with me."

"Smart aleck," Tilda says.

Chucks aren't really the proper footwear for a hike but Maia and Shane have youth and exuberance on their side. They bound down the trail, and in a couple of minutes, they're so far ahead, they're out of sight.

"Hey, wait up!" Cash calls out. "It's not a race!" He would like to look around, take in the scenery, maybe stop to identify some plants—though that clearly isn't happening.

"So this company I want to start," Tilda says, "would provide guides for every hike on the island. You wouldn't need a map, and you'd have someone there to point out the pineapple cactus and the catch-and-keep, and someone to explain the historical significance of the ruins. The National Parks just aren't staffed to keep up with demand."

"I should quit *Treasure Island* and come work for you," Cash says. "I'm much more comfortable on land."

"We should be partners," Tilda says.

"I have no money," Cash says. "I might get some once my father's estate is settled." This isn't something Cash lets himself think about often, but it's always there, twinkling like a star in the distance—a possible inheritance.

"Sweat equity," Tilda says, then she nods down the trail. "Look."

Maia and Shane are up ahead, holding hands. Cash says, "I saw them holding hands last week in town. It's cute, as long as that's all they're doing."

"Don't be naive," Tilda says. "Do you *think* that's all they're doing?"

"Yes," Cash says, because he can't stand to think otherwise. "I'm new at this big-brother thing, but my natural instinct is to be overprotective. If he tries anything more, he'll have me to deal with."

"You're adorable," Tilda says. She turns, stops in the middle of the trail, and gives him a kiss.

Because they're losing daylight and the mosquitoes are coming out, once they reach the baobab tree by the Sieben plantation ruins they decide to turn around—but first they give the tree the reverence it deserves. The tree is extraordinary in breadth and height. It's the only one of its kind on the island.

"The seeds are edible," Maia says. "They were brought over from Africa by Danish slaves."

They use Tilda's selfie stick to take a picture of the four of them standing at the base of the tree. After Maia inspects the picture, she turns to Shane. "We're a cute couple," she says. She looks over at Cash and Tilda. "And so are you guys." She pauses a beat. "You two *are* a couple, right?"

"Uh..." Cash says.

"Right," Tilda says, and they all head back up the hill.

When they reach the Range Rover, both Cash's and Maia's phones start going nuts. Cash ignores his—it's Baker, of course. Maia does not ignore hers.

"Would you guys please drop us in town?" she asks after she checks her texts.

"Are you sure?" Tilda says. "I'm happy to take you all the way home."

"I live on Jacob's Ladder," Maia says. "Trust me, you do *not* want to drive the Rover up Jacob's Ladder."

"You're probably right," Tilda says. "Town it is."

"And how will you get home from town?" Cash asks.

"You're being overprotective," Tilda murmurs.

"I'm being responsible," Cash says. "She's twelve." He looks at Maia in the rearview mirror. "How are you getting home? Shane's parents?"

"Huck is coming to get me," Maia says. "His charter ran late."

"Okay," Cash says. Reluctantly, he pulls his phone out. He has two missed calls from Baker and one missed call from Ayers, which he hopes is work-related. He shoots her a text: What's up?

A second later, she responds: I need your advice.

No, Cash thinks. He's not getting in the middle of this.

As soon as the kids climb out at Powell Park, Cash reaches over and pulls Tilda in for a kiss. "So we're a couple, huh?"

"Yes," Tilda says. "We are."

Cash becomes so light-headed thinking about this that they get all the way to Jumbie Bay before he realizes that Maia was lying to him. Huck's charter didn't run late. Huck didn't *have* a charter today. Irene told Cash that this morning. She was home all day.

"Turn the car around," he says to Tilda.

They head back to Powell Park, where they dropped Maia and Shane off, but of course the kids are gone. Cash calls Maia and gets her voicemail.

"What do you want to do?" Tilda asks.

"Loop around, please," Cash says. He hangs out the window of the Rover scanning the ferry dock, which is packed with workers headed back to St. Thomas. Did Maia and Shane get on the ferry? The thought makes Cash ill. They pass the jewelry store, the timeshare office, Slim Man's parking lot. Then Tilda has to make a decision—right toward Drink and Gallows Point or left past the Lime Inn and De Coal Pot?

"Arrrgh, I don't know," Cash says. "I should never have let her get out of the car in town. It's just, I knew she and Shane had hung out in town together before, but now it's dark and she lied to me, so she must be doing something she doesn't want Huck to know about."

Tilda turns left. They pass the Dog House and the Longboard and Our Market and Cap's, then Tilda takes a right and says, "Maybe they went for pizza. Let's check Ronnie's."

Yes, Ronnie's Pizza, bingo, brilliant, Cash thinks. They're twelve.

Tilda pulls up out front and Cash runs in, looks around. No Maia, no Shane.

"She likes Candi's Barbecue," Tilda says. "I remember Rosie telling me that. Let's swing by and if she's not there, we'll call Huck."

"I don't have Huck's number," Cash says. "I'll call my mother if she's not at Candi's."

Maia is not at Candi's. Cash climbs back into the Rover and stares at his phone. He calls Maia's phone again and again, it goes directly to voicemail.

"She's ghosting me," he says.

Tilda laughs. "Maybe. Or maybe her phone died. Or maybe she turned her phone off because she wants to kiss Shane in peace."

"You're not making me feel any better," Cash says.

"Sorry, sorry," Tilda says. "Okay, let's think. Do you want me to take you home or run you up to Huck's?"

"Home," Cash says. "The last thing I want to do is face Huck."

When Cash and Tilda arrive at the villa, Irene is sitting at the kitchen table, paging through a *House Beautiful.*

"Cash," she says, standing up. "And you must be..."

"Tilda. It's nice to meet you, Mrs. Steele."

"Are you kids hungry? I haven't given a single thought to dinner, though I probably should, it's getting late—"

"Mom," Cash says. He's not sure why he feels so panicked. Maia has probably already made it home. Shane's parents probably came and picked them up. But what if they didn't? Cash should have insisted on taking Maia straight home. She acted like a full-blown teenager but she's only twelve. Twelve! "We hiked the Esperance Trail with Maia and her friend Shane."

"Oh, that's nice," Irene says.

"Then she asked us to drop her off in town," Tilda says.

"She told us Huck would pick her up," Cash says. "She told us it wouldn't be an inconvenience because his charter was running late..."

"Wait," Irene says. "What?" Cash watches Irene snap into parenting mode and it's like being transported back in time fifteen years. "Let me call Huck." Irene fishes her cell phone out of her bag and dials. Cash can hear her reach Huck's recording.

"He's not answering," she says. "And I don't want to leave a message and panic him. Maybe Maia is home and they're sitting down to dinner."

Maybe, Cash thinks. He pictures Huck and Maia at a table, Maia describing the baobab tree.

Cash needs her to be home, to be safe. He can't handle losing anyone else.

HUCK

When he gets out of the shower, he sees Irene has called.

Prayers answered, he thinks.

It was bad luck that there had been no charter today—or maybe it was good luck. Huck isn't sure.

Huck has done nothing all day but think about kissing Irene. He kissed her on the boat, then he kissed her in his truck, and finally he walked her up the steps to the villa and kissed her next to the sliding glass door. He thought that maybe, just maybe, he'd get an invitation to come inside, upstairs—but eventually, Irene had put her index finger to his lips and slipped inside alone.

He understood. It was too soon to go any further. She was newly widowed and so much still remained a mystery.

But he had hoped.

If they'd had a charter, would they have gone back to their normal, pre-kiss selves? Would it have been like the kiss never happened? What torture. Huck wouldn't have been able to focus on fishing for one second. Who cared about fishing? Love was the only thing that mattered.

He prefers to think there would have been a new energy between him and his first mate, barely sublimated. Huck would brush against Irene, their hands would touch, she would sit next to him behind the wheel of the boat. He would count the hours and then the minutes until the clients were walking away down the dock so that he could kiss Irene again.

People would assume they were newlyweds.

It's been so long since Huck has felt this way about a woman that he hardly recognizes himself. He feels twenty-five again.

But they hadn't had a charter and so Huck was left in a vacuum of solitude. He wanted to call Irene and invite her to do something. There was a new floating taco bar in the East End called Lime Out. They could drive to Hansen Bay, rent a kayak, and paddle out for tacos. Would Irene like that? Or maybe a simple lunch would be better, at Aqua Bistro in Coral Bay. Huck could introduce Irene to Rupert—but no, Rupert would be smitten immediately and Huck would have to beat him back.

In the end, Huck lay in his hammock and finally finished the Connelly book. After enjoying a brief sense of accomplishment, he'd stared at his damn phone, willing it to ring, willing it to be Irene inviting him to the villa for a swim in the pool.

Three o'clock didn't even provide its usual respite because Maia was going hiking with Cash so she didn't need a ride home from school.

Huck figured Maia would be hungry when she got home and so at five thirty, he went to Candi's for barbecue, then he got the text from Destiny about the next day's charter and he assumed Irene had received it too. They would be together tomorrow on the boat.

Huck tried Maia to get her ETA but was delivered straight to her voicemail. She always let her phone run down at the end of a day; it was frustrating. He decided to take a shower—and now that he's out, he can see he has two missed calls, both from Irene, which at this time of day is strange—and maybe troubling.

"Maia?" Huck calls out, but there's no answer. Huck pokes his head out into the hallway. The house is quiet; Maia's bedroom door is open. She's not home yet, but she should be any second, so his privacy is limited. He closes the bedroom door and prepares to call Irene back, but something stops him.

She has called twice without leaving a message, so clearly there's something she wants to tell him in person. He fears—he can barely say the words in his mind—that the kissing changed things for the worse and that Irene no longer feels she can work on the boat. He'll be crushed. He has relived the kissing so many times in the past twenty-one hours that it has taken on the quality of a dream. Irene *was* enthusiastic about kissing him back, right? In his mind, she has her hands in his hair; she's pulling him closer, wanting the kiss to be deeper. But Huck had been drinking and he has seen far too much on the news not to have doubts about even the most consensual-seeming of acts. Huck shouldn't have gotten so carried away. There was a moment at the villa where he'd wanted very badly to press his body against hers, but he hadn't done it. There had been the impulse and then maybe the start of a movement but he'd stopped himself in time. Still, he worries she read his mind, sensed the power of his urges, and now is afraid and maybe even repulsed by him and thinks that working together is no longer a good idea. In fact, it's inappropriate. In fact, the friendship has to go as well.

As Huck is spiraling down into bleaker and bleaker depths, his phone rings. It's Irene.

Hard things are hard, he thinks. He'll just have to apologize and promise to be a gentleman from here on out. But he cannot, *cannot,* let her quit.

"Hello?" he says, as jolly as Santa Claus.

"Huck," she says. "It's Irene."

"I already knew that," he says. "The marvel of cell phones."

"I'm calling to see if Maia has made it home?" Irene says.

"What?" Huck says. He's confused. "Not yet, no. Why? I thought she was with Cash."

"Oh, dear," Irene says.

Huck hangs up the phone, calls Maia, gets her voicemail, then climbs into his truck and slams the door so hard his ears ring.

Late charter? Since when has Huck ever, ever come home *late* from a charter?

Never, that's when.

He wants to wring Cash Steele's neck!

Put your son on the goddamned phone! Huck had shouted at Irene. *I need to know exactly where he dropped her off.*

Irene gave the phone to Cash. Cash sounded worried and kept apologizing; he should have brought her straight home, he said.

You're goddamned right you should have brought her home! Huck said. *You should have checked with me. I'm her family. I'm her only family!*

You're not, though, Cash had said. *I'm her brother. You can't possibly be accusing me of intentionally putting her in danger.*

I'm accusing you of being thoughtless, Huck said. *And negligent. She was a child in your care.* Huck slammed down the phone; he was livid. The Steele family, one and all, are pirates, he decides. And now they're trying to steal Maia. Well, Huck won't allow it.

He sits in his car, fuming, wondering who to call. Joanie's mother? Shane's parents?

As he's wondering about this, his phone rings. Irene, it says.

"What?" he barks.

"Huck, please, calm down," Irene says. "Whatever you said to Cash really upset him. You and I both know it was an innocent mistake. Why don't you come pick me up and we'll look for Maia together? Or I can take one of the Jeeps and meet you in town?"

"How about you and your family stay away from my granddaughter?" Huck says. "Assuming I can even find her. Your numbskull son dropped her off at Powell Park when it was nearly dark. She's twelve years old, Irene. Twelve! That is called gross negligence in my book. Now, I'm going to hang up and find my granddaughter. She's mine, Irene. Not yours, not Cash's—mine. Goodbye." Huck ends the call and feels much better for one second, then much, much worse. He dials Joanie's mom, Julie.

"I hate to bother you," Huck says.

"Oh, Huck," Julie says. "I was just about to call you. We're frantic. We can't find Joanie."

Julie is an organizer, so with a few calls, she discovers that they're all missing: Maia, Shane, Joanie, Colton, and Bright Whittaker. But Julie doesn't have eyes and ears the way Huck does. He calls Rupert, tells him Maia and her little friends are at large, probably somewhere in Cruz Bay, and asks him to alert his lady friends.

Meanwhile, Huck drives into town and checks first at the little beach in Chocolate Hole and then at the basketball courts across from the gas station.

No Maia.

As Huck is heading into the roundabout, his phone rings. It's Mick. Huck heard from Maia that Ayers and Mick got engaged—which, Huck has to admit, he found startling—and he wonders if Mick is calling to give him the news. Huck nearly sends the call to voicemail, but at the last second, he answers. "Hey, Mick, what's up?"

"Hey, Huck," Mick says. "Just thought you should know that Maia and her friends are hanging out on the edge of Frank Bay. I...was taking a little walk, and I saw them down there. It's pretty late, so I thought—"

"Yes, thank you," Huck says. "I'm on my way."

Huck drives to the Beach Bar, double-parks, and strides out onto the sand. He doesn't see Maia. He heads to the left, spies a couple of kids—it's pretty far away from the Beach Bar, Huck wonders what Mick was doing all the way down here—and whistles. Even in the dark, he can see Maia jump to her feet. She comes running through the sand toward him.

"Uh-oh," she says.

"Uh-oh is right," he says. "Follow me. We're going home." Over Maia's head, Huck calls out, "Party's over, kids. I'm calling everyone's parents."

Maia sits in the truck while Huck leans against it. He really wants a cigarette right now, but he can't set that kind of poor example until every child is claimed. This gives Huck a chance to calm down and second-guess himself. Did he overreact? No; it's nearly nine o'clock on a school night and they were having a kumbaya sit-in on a deserted section of beach. God only knows what they were doing.

"What were you doing?" Huck asks Maia once he gets behind the wheel. "Other than trying to send me to an early grave."

"Talking," Maia says. "And I know I was wrong and I know I owe you an apology. I'm sorry. I also know it's not going to make any difference and that I'm grounded. But we had a crisis."

"Crisis?"

"Colton's parents are getting a divorce," Maia says. "He needed us."

Huck sighs and lets the rest of his anger go. One of the things he likes best about St. John is exactly what Maia is describing: in times of trouble, people come together. That was true when LeeAnn died and even more true when Rosie died. Why should it be any less true for Maia and Colton just because they're kids?

"You should have called me," Huck says.

"My phone was dead."

"Not everyone's phone was dead," Huck says.

"I didn't want to call," Maia says, "because I thought you'd make me come home. We all made a vow we wouldn't tell our parents where we were until we knew Colton was going to be all right."

"Colton is going to be just fine," Huck says. He nearly points out that Maia just endured something far worse and she's okay, but Huck doesn't want to bring up Rosie right now, even though he misses her very, very much at this moment. Rosie would have been far more understanding than Huck about this little powwow. Rosie might have invited all the kids to pile into her car and then taken them all home herself, encouraging them to share their feelings as she drove. "He has two parents who love him."

"Facts," Maia says. "Unfortunately, while we were on the beach, I discovered another problem."

"Oh, really."

"I saw Mick," Maia says. "He walked all the way down from the Beach Bar."

Huck nearly says, *Yes, he was the one who called me*—but he doesn't want to reveal his sources.

"And he was with Brigid. Brigid was crying hysterically. Mick had his arms around her trying to comfort her—this was before he noticed me sitting with my friends..."

"Yeah?" Huck says.

"And then they started *kissing!*" Maia says. Her voice is shaky. "I'm so disgusted with him. He pulled away after a minute, but not soon enough. As soon as I get home and charge my phone, I'm calling Ayers."

For Pete's sake, Huck thinks. *Does the drama never end?*

"They're adults, Nut," he says. "I think maybe you should let them work it out."

"He'll never tell her," Maia says. "Ayers will never know if I don't say something."

"Maybe that's for the best," Huck says. He lights a cigarette and takes a long, much-needed drag. "Maybe he and Brigid needed closure."

"Closure?" Maia says, and she laughs like a full-grown woman. "Spare me."

When they get back to Jacob's Ladder, Huck says, "Grounded for a week. No town for two weeks."

Maia nods.

"You lied to Cash," Huck says. "You told him I had a late

charter. So then I turned around and ripped him a new one for believing you. Now your own brother can't trust you."

"I'm sorry," Maia says.

"Your mother hid a lot of things from me," Huck says. He hadn't wanted to bring up Rosie, but here she is, showing up anyway. "Probably because she didn't think I could handle the truth." Huck clears the lump in his throat. "I've learned my lesson. You promise to tell me the truth, whatever it is, and I promise to handle it. Understand?"

"Yes, sir," she says.

"Go inside, please. There's Candi's on the table with extra comeback sauce. Then straight to bed."

"Where are you going?" Maia asks.

"I have some apologizing to do myself," Huck says.

He drives to the villa even though it's late and Irene might be in bed. Both Jeeps are in the driveway, which Huck supposes is a good thing. He needs to apologize to Cash; he shudders when he thinks how hard he was on the poor guy.

But it was Maia. When Cash has a child of his own, he'll understand.

Huck trudges up the stairs and sees a light on in the kitchen. Cash is sitting at the kitchen table with his phone in front of him.

Huck knocks on the sliding door and Cash jumps, then hurries to let Huck in. "Did you find her?"

"I did," Huck says. "She's safe." He can see the relief wash over Cash's face and Huck feels ashamed. He's so afraid of losing Maia, even of sharing her, that he's ignoring the best part about her newfound family: there are more people who care about her. "Listen, I'm sorry."

"*I'm* sorry," Cash says. "I've been beating myself up since I dropped her off, wondering how I could have been so gullible—"

"You trusted her," Huck says. "That's a good thing. I had no right to speak to you the way I did, and I hope you can forgive me."

"My mom gave me your cell number," Cash says. "If you ever let me hang out with Maia again, I promise I'll follow the rules and drop her only at home."

"She's grounded for a week," Huck says. "But I'm sure she'll be bugging you as soon as she's a free woman."

"I hope so," Cash says. He offers Huck his hand. "Thanks for coming all the way up here to apologize, that was above and beyond. But I have an early morning tomorrow..."

"Right," Huck says. He turns toward the door, then stops. "Is your mom still awake, do you think?"

"Probably," Cash says. "She just headed upstairs a minute ago. Do you want me to check?"

Huck hesitates. He could just wait and talk to Irene on the boat tomorrow.

"I'll get her," Cash says. "I'm sure she wants to know about Maia."

Cash disappears up the stairs, and a moment later, Irene comes down. Her hair is out of its braid, wavy over her shoulders. She's wearing gym shorts and a gray Iowa Hawkeyes T-shirt. Huck feels himself trembling.

"I owe you an apology, AC," he says.

Irene points at the door. "Let's go outside."

This is a good sign, he thinks. He holds the door open for her and she heads out to the railing at the edge of the deck, where they can look out over the water. The pool is gurgling to their right and glowing an ethereal blue.

"Maia is okay?" she asks.

"She was at the beach with her friends," Huck says. "I'm sorry I lost my temper."

"It was understandable," Irene says. "She's your girl."

"That she is," Huck says. "I vowed she would be my first and only priority. I can't let anything happen to her."

"She's lucky to have you," Irene says.

Huck throws caution to the wind and gathers Irene up in his arms. She allows this, but he can feel tension in her body.

"What's wrong?" he says.

"The other night was magical..." Irene says.

Huck loosens his hold on her. "But?"

"Meeting you, becoming friends with you, has been nothing short of miraculous. That first day of fishing...it saved me."

And me, he thinks.

"I love working on the boat. Not just because I like the work but because I enjoy your company—"

"Did I mess things up by kissing you?" he asks. Meeting him was miraculous, he saved her, she enjoys his company...but that doesn't mean she feels romantic about him.

"Yes and no," Irene says. Without warning, tears pool in her eyes. "When we kissed...I never thought I'd feel that way again." She sniffs. "There's a way in which I've never felt that way before, ever."

"That's good, right?" Huck says.

"It's too soon, Huck," she says. "This whole situation is still so fresh. I know you don't think we need to worry about the authorities hauling us off to jail like they did the Vickerses, but I do anyway."

"I'm not going to let anything happen to you," Huck says. "I care for you."

Irene reaches up to touch his face. "And I care for you. But I need more time. I just...I need time." She rests her hand on the side of his neck. "I want you to promise you won't give up on me."

Huck isn't sure he can speak. He's disappointed. Crushed. Can she not feel the chemistry here? The love? He's not sure how he'll be able to hold himself in check. And yet he's also relieved. Irene is nothing if not a woman of her word. She does have feelings for him. She's not ready. Is Huck going to give up on her? Hell no.

"You have my word, AC," he says.

She pulls him close and rests her head on his chest for a moment. "We have an early day tomorrow," she says.

"You're right," he says. "I should go." It's difficult, but he releases her. "See you tomorrow, AC." He strides across the deck without looking back, but he hopes it's like the movies and Irene is staring after him with longing, telling herself she's made a mistake, that she is in love with Huck and should chase after him and let him know.

Huck is halfway down the stairs when he sees a pair of headlights winding up the hill toward the villa. Then he sees another pair, and another and another. Four vehicles are winding their way up Lovers Lane.

BAKER

On Tuesday, he calls an emergency breakfast meeting at Snooze. Once his friends are assembled and they all have coffee—he can't expect them to provide any kind of decent advice without coffee—Baker passes around his phone.

On the screen is a picture of Mick on one knee, proposing to Ayers, with Cash's text: She said yes, dude. Sorry.

Debbie says, "Wow, she's hot. I know you said she was hot, but...wow."

"Wow," Wendy echoes when she gets the phone. "Debbie's right."

"That's not helpful," Baker says morosely.

"Can we talk about the manipulative nature of public proposals in general?" Ellen says. "Why do people do it?"

"Insecurity?" Becky says. "Fear? Or is it the opposite—hubris."

"I think it's romantic," Wendy says. "And fearless. Don't you think it takes courage?"

"You're off topic," Baker says. "I'm now moving myself and my four-year-old son down to a remote Caribbean island for a woman who just agreed to marry someone else."

"This is Mick, right?" Ellen says. "The guy who cheated on her?"

"Yes."

"Ew," Debbie says.

"He's not bad-looking," Wendy says. "But he's not you."

"Cool dog," Becky says. "Is that Mick's dog? Or Ayers's dog?"

"Mick's," Baker says. "He has a cool dog but I have a cool kid."

"That's a pizza boat in the background?" Ellen says. She looks at the others. "A pizza boat! We need to plan a trip to St. John."

"We'll come visit you," Debbie says. "The villa has room, right?"

"Nine bedrooms," Baker says. "But again, off topic. Should I even go? Or should I stay here?"

"Wearing my human-resources hat, here's what I think,"

Becky says. "I like this move for you. It's not necessarily permanent. You go down there, you coach at the school, you get Floyd situated. He's a bright, perceptive, resilient kid and he's a sponge. I think it'll be good for both of you to live somewhere else for a while. You're renting your house, not selling it, so you can always come back. Think of it as a sabbatical of sorts. And then if Ayers sees the light and you two get together, you can make it more permanent."

The other women nod their heads.

"What did I tell you before?" Ellen says. "You won't hit the ball if you don't swing."

Baker appreciates his friends' advice, but there's no way he's making such a huge leap of faith without talking to Ayers.

But first, Baker tries Cash. He would like some intel. Has his brother talked to Ayers about the engagement? What does he know? Cash doesn't answer his phone; either he's very busy or he doesn't want to get involved. Baker assumes it's the latter, but why did he send the photo, then? To be informative or to be a jerk?

Baker tries Ayers on Tuesday evening, a full twenty-four hours after he received the photo. It doesn't seem quite as horrific now that some time has passed. Engagements get broken every day, right?

She doesn't answer either, which could be a bad sign—she's with Mick, she's finished with Baker, she wants him to go away—in which case, Baker will just stay in Houston.

He doesn't leave a voicemail—no one ever listens to them—but he does shoot her a text. Any chance I can talk to you tonight?

A little while later, there's a response. I'm at work. I'll call on my way home.

Baker stares at the words for a long time, trying to imagine what Ayers is thinking.

Well, he'll know in a few hours.

He feeds Floyd and reads him three stories, but Floyd is keyed up because they're supposed to leave in the morning. Floyd has already said goodbye to his friends and his teachers. He's excited to live on an island.

"Dad," he says. "Islands are surrounded by water."

"That's right," Baker says.

"Gramma has a job on a boat," Floyd says. "Catching fish. And Uncle Cash has a job on a boat, giving tours to people from other places." Floyd closes his eyes. "I want to work on a boat."

"Okay, buddy," Baker says, ruffling Floyd's hair. "We'll get you a job on a boat."

Floyd's eyes fly open. "Really?"

Baker laughs, and he thinks of what a unique and amazing experience it would be for Floyd to grow up on a Caribbean island. He'll learn to sail and navigate; he'll become familiar with the natural world. And maybe he will grow up to be a person who contributes so much to the island that it makes up for his grandfather's wrongs—whatever those turn out to be.

Baker indulges in some red velvet–cake ice cream but resists the temptation of marijuana.

At nine fifteen, his phone rings. It's Ayers.

"Hey," she says.

"Hey."

"You heard?"

"I did. Cash sent me a picture of Mick slipping the ring on your finger." Baker pauses. "I guess the breakup didn't last long."

"I was taken by surprise," Ayers says.

"But you said yes, right?" Baker says. "And it was still a yes once you were alone with him? I mean, I understand the manipulative nature of public proposals..." He shakes his head; he's parroting Ellen.

"Yes," Ayers says. "It was manipulative. Good choice of words."

Ellen has never steered him wrong, he thinks. "You're going to marry Mick? Even though he cheated on you? Even though you said yourself that you can't trust him?"

"Do you have time for a story?" Ayers asks. "This is something I've never told anyone—not Mick, not Rosie, not anybody."

"I have all night," Baker says.

She takes a breath. "When I was Maia's age—younger even; ten or eleven—I lived in Kathmandu with my parents."

"Kathmandu." Baker remembers all the photographs on Ayers's wall. *Story for another day*. "In Nepal?"

"Yes," Ayers says. "Kathmandu used to be this frenetic, dirty, dusty, poverty-stricken place where emaciated cows roamed the streets along with the cars and the motorbikes. My parents and I lived in a backpacker hostel. My mother, Sunny, tended bar at an expat pub, I can't remember the name, only that it had a snooker table, and while my mother worked, my father would try to teach me to play, but my arms were too short to hold the cue stick. Anyway, the manager of the pub was this guy named Simon and he was the most handsome man I have ever seen in my life—and he liked my mother. Even at my tender age, I figured out that was why my father kept me in the pub playing snooker rather than exploring the city." She sighed. "But my father couldn't keep me there too late, so eventually every night we'd go back to the hostel. One night, something must have happened with Simon because my mother didn't come home. For three days, we didn't see her."

"What did your dad do?" Baker asks.

"He moved us to this place called the Hotel Vajra, which looked like it was pulled out of a fairy tale. The beds had crimson silk spreads and the doors were made of carved teak. At night they lit pillar candles up and down the hallways, and my father and I would go to the rooftop terrace restaurant and eat lamb *momos*. It was a big change for me, having a hotel room to myself and eating out in a fancy restaurant, and I knew, somehow, that we were doing it only because my mother wasn't there. I think I even knew that we were doing it to get back at her." Ayers sighs. "Anyway, one morning as we were headed over to Mike's, this place that served a real American breakfast, we saw my mother sitting in the front garden, waiting for us. She linked her arms through ours and we all went to Mike's and ordered big stacks of pancakes."

"Did she say where she'd been?"

"No," Ayers says. "Nothing was ever mentioned about it to me. My mother quit the job at the pub and we moved to Vietnam." She pauses. "Now, as an adult, I can only assume my mother had a fling with Simon and my father waited it out."

"Are your parents still together?" Baker asks.

"Yes," Ayers says. "They're very happy. To my knowledge, nothing like that has ever happened again, on either side. It was like a hiccup."

"A hiccup," Baker says. "And that's how you see Mick's behavior with Brigid? As a hiccup?"

"Mick took a detour," Ayers says. "But he found his way back to me. And I truly believe it was a one-and-done. He knows what he lost and he won't risk it again. I've asked him for years to find a better place to live, and on our way to the boat yesterday, he drove me past this house he rented. It's gorgeous."

"Where is it?" Baker says. "I'll buy it right out from under him."

"Baker," Ayers says.

"You said you have feelings for me," Baker says. "You said you couldn't stop thinking about me."

"That's true," Ayers says. "Even on Monday before Mick proposed, one of the mothers from Gifft Hill was talking about this hot new dad, and I knew it was you and I was . . . *jealous*."

"Think about that," Baker says.

"I have been thinking about it!" Ayers says. "But Mick and I have been together a long time. He knows me. We have a life here that we built together, month by month, year by year. I can't just throw that away for something new."

"You can, though," Baker says. "Because I'm moving to St. John tomorrow and I'm going to stay. I got a coaching job at Gifft Hill. I'm going to take scuba lessons . . . " He doesn't know where this idea comes from, it just pops into his head, but it sounds good. "I'm going to work on getting my real estate license down there. I'm going to build a life, month by month, year by year, and I want you to be in that life. When I first saw you, I felt like *I* was the one who had been struck by lightning—only instead of dying, I came to life." Is this corny? He can't tell. "I made a decision then and there that I was going to marry you. So you can hang up with me now thinking you're going to marry Mick. But I promise you, I *promise you,* Ayers, that I can do better than Mick. I will be true and steadfast and devoted and crazily in love with you until the day I die. I will never have any hiccups. Ever."

Ayers is quiet.

"If a proposal is what you want, then you have one from me. I want to marry you as soon as I'm legally able."

"You barely know me," she says, but her voice is softer. He's getting to her, maybe.

"We can worry about that later."

Ayers laughs, but her laugh is cut short. "Oh, hey," she says. "Maia is calling in on my line, and I should take it. It's late and she never calls me this late. She never calls me at all, she only texts."

"By all means, take it," Baker says. "I hope everything is okay."

"Me too," Ayers says. "I'll let you know. Bye."

Baker stares at the blank screen of his phone. If Floyd weren't asleep, he would play the Clash's "Should I Stay or Should I Go?" at top volume. What the hell—he finds his AirPods and cranks the song up.

If I go, there will be trouble.

And if I stay it will be double.

Repeat song, repeat song, repeat song.

During his fourth time through—Baker is still waiting for the answer to be revealed—he sees a text from Anna. What does she want? he wonders.

Louisa and I have some concerns about you uprooting Floyd, the text says. Please hold off on your move until we talk. I should have some time for a conference call next week.

"Ha!" Baker says to the empty living room. "That's rich. That's *really* rich!" 'Louisa and I have some concerns' means that *Louisa* has concerns, because Anna said she was 'K' with it last week."

Baker knows the text should persuade him to stay put, but it does exactly the opposite. Louisa has concerns about Baker uprooting Floyd to take him to St. John, but Anna and Louisa uprooting Floyd to take him to Cleveland was fine?

Ha!

Ha!

Another text comes in, and Baker assumes it's Anna burying herself even further—she doesn't even have time to talk about it until next week!—but the text isn't from Anna.

It's from Ayers.

Maia saw Mick kissing Brigid on the beach tonight. I'm giving the ring back.

Baker shuts the music off and heads upstairs to bed. He has an early flight in the morning.

ROSIE

January 1, 2015

Love is messy and complicated and unfair.

I see Russ when he's here, which is every few weeks for a couple of days. I'm elated for forty-eight hours before he arrives and devastated for forty-eight hours after he leaves. Actually, the leaving part is getting worse.

I see him often enough that it's getting hard to keep secret. I have to lie to Huck, say I have friends from the States in town and would he mind watching Maia for a couple of days? Huck is always happy to do this. I think being with Maia helps get his mind off Mama. He's started taking Maia out on the fishing boat. Even though she's only eight, he says she's a natural, and it's important for her to get her sea legs. Huck asked the names of my "friends from the States," and I said Rachel, Monica, and Phoebe. He didn't pick up on my joke—I knew he wouldn't—but he must be getting suspicious. Since when do I have friends from the States, or friends at all except for Ayers? I'm sure he suspects it's a man.

Russ and I can't go anywhere or do anything; he doesn't even want to risk a trip back to Miss Vie's on Hansen Bay. I visit him in room 718 at Caneel, which requires me to sneak in the back way from the parking lot, or, if Russ has the yacht to himself, I visit him there.

I show him pictures of Maia. He wants to meet her but I'm not allowing that. Every time he leaves, I know I might never see him again.

Once you prove to me you're staying here, I said, you can meet her.

June 24, 2015

Russ is leaving right before Carnival and he says he won't be back again this summer, which means the earliest I'll see him is September, but September is hurricane season and Caneel is closed, so it'll most likely be October or possibly even November.

I considered traveling to the States for the summer. Lots of people here do it. But Russ says that he has some meetings with clients in Grand Cayman and Miami and then he and Irene are spending two weeks in Door County, Wisconsin.

I had never heard of Door County, Wisconsin, so I looked it up on my computer and what I found were photographs of lakes and barns and orchards and cute little towns with church steeples, ice cream parlors, and antiques stores. It looks like America in the 1950s. When I asked Russ what he and Irene did there, he said they hung out on the lake—fishing, water skiing, swimming. And then in the evenings they played cards, attended fish boils, listened to the loons.

He asked me how I would spend the summer and I tried to explain about Carnival—it's a week of music, food, and dancing when nobody sleeps—and then the entire island needs a week to recover. I explained that Huck fished for blue and white marlin in the summer, which brought in a different kind of fisherman. And then in September, Maia would go back to school and everyone would pray there were no storms.

I told him four months was a long time to be apart. He said he knew that. Then he took me in his arms and kissed me and said that he realized our "arrangement" was unfair to me and he would understand if I wanted to find someone who could give me all the things I deserved—an engagement ring, a home, a future.

I said, "Yes, I should find someone else." But I knew I wouldn't. Because I love Russ. I didn't tell him that. I want him to say it first. He didn't say it, however, and what could I think but that he only loved Irene?

I kissed him goodbye and told him to have a wonderful summer. Enjoy the fish boils in Door County, Wisconsin, and the sound of the loons. I did slip another postcard into his duffel bag saying I would miss him. I didn't warn him about it. If Irene happened to discover it, oh, well. Russ would have to explain or lie about who M.L. was.

I'm glad I didn't allow him to meet Maia. My heart is in danger, but at least hers is safe.

November 9, 2015

Russ came back and he had good news, such good news that I'm almost afraid to believe it. His company, Ascension, was looking for investment opportunities and they partnered with a "local real estate concern" (he wouldn't tell me which one) to buy a hundred and forty acres in west Cinnamon, an area known as Little Cinnamon. They plan to develop the hillside, hire someone to build luxury villas. But the even better news was that the local real estate concern had built one home on spec and lost a lot of money on it, so Russ had bought the villa himself.

I had questions. Why had Russ been the one to buy it and not Todd or Stephen?

"They don't want a house," Russ said.

"Really?" I said. Then I thought: Who doesn't want a house?

"Really," Russ said. "They have homes elsewhere. They offered it to me because they know I have interests here."

"Interests?" I said. "You mean me."

"Yes."

"They know about us."

"They do."

"How?" I said. "Did you... tell them?"

"No," he said. "But they're not naive, Rosie."

They weren't naive; I'd never thought that. In fact, I'd always worried about it. This was a holdover from years earlier, the first time I laid eyes on the three of them, when it seemed like Russ was a sheep running around with a couple of wolves.

"The bigger news is that we're doing more business down here. In both the USVIs and the BVIs. Maybe we could even go to the BVIs together."

"You mean... Jost?" Jost Van Dyke was a party island. That

was true when I was growing up but it's even more so now. Everyone loved Foxy's and the Soggy Dollar.

"I mean Anegada," he said. "Have you ever been?"

I had been to Anegada once, long ago. Before Mama met Huck, she had briefly dated a lobsterman who took us to Anegada for the day on his fishing boat. Anegada is the most remote of the British Virgin Islands and unlike any of the others in that it's just a spit of flat white sand. There are a few businesses, a few bars, a few homes, hundreds of flamingos, thousands of lobsters, and not much else. I hadn't been impressed with it at thirteen, but now, as a lovers' getaway, it held enormous appeal.

"When can we go?" I asked.

December 18, 2015

Russ and I celebrated Christmas and New Year's rolled into one during our three days on Anegada. We went over on Bluebeard *on Monday and the captain said he'd be back for us on Thursday. We stayed in a simple white clapboard cottage on the most pristine beach imaginable. I thought the sand on St. John was white but it looks positively dingy compared to Anegada's. The cottage had a big white bed and a tiny kitchen that Russ had arranged to have stocked with provisions. Our mornings consisted of sleeping in, followed by coffee, fruit, and toast on the balcony overlooking the sea. Unlike on St. John, there were no other islands on the horizon. It was a bizarre feeling, even for me, to stare out at nothing but water. At least on St. John, I felt connected to a larger whole, seeing St. Thomas, Water Island, Little St. James, and St. Croix in the distance. Here, we might have been perched on the edge of the world.*

We made love, we walked on the beach, we fell asleep in

the sun. In the late afternoons, our supper was delivered: lobster fritters; lobster bisque; baked, stuffed, or boiled lobster with butter. We drank champagne with our lobster; it seemed only fitting, and there were a dozen bottles of Krug in the refrigerator.

I used to drink champagne with Oscar and I had forgotten how tipsy it made me.

"Now that you've bought the villa in Little Cinnamon," I said, "will Irene come down?" This was my biggest fear. I could handle the idea of Irene but I could not handle the reality of Irene coming to stay on my island.

"No," he said. He went on to tell me a story about an ill-fated trip to Jamaica when the boys were young. They had wandered off, gotten lost in a shantytown near the hotel. Irene had been frantic; the trip left her scarred. She hated the Caribbean.

"Besides, she's consumed with our project at home," Russ said. He cleared his throat. He knew I disliked it when he used words like we *and* our *to describe him and Irene. The project he was referring to is a Victorian fixer-upper that Irene had begged him to buy; she was desperate to restore it "to period."*

I sipped my champagne and thought about Irene immersed in a home-renovation project in Iowa City. How vastly different that life was from my own. I suppose that's part of the appeal for Russ, part of the point. He has a wife and a mistress—I'm not sure what else to call myself—and I suppose that we nourish different parts of him. I'm sex and lobster and champagne-drinking under a blanket of stars. Irene is home and hearth, mother of the boys, keeper of the traditions that make a family.

Can I lure Russ away from her? Can I make him feel his family is here? I can try.

In the new year, I decided, I'm going to introduce him to Maia.

February 11, 2016

I told Maia she was going to meet a friend of mine but that it was a secret and she wasn't to talk about this friend to anyone, including Huck.

Then I hated myself.

But I can't have it both ways. I can let Maia meet Russ and make sure she keeps it quiet, or I can not introduce them at all.

Maia said she understood. She looked at me with her wise-child eyes and repeated what I'd told her: Russ was a friend of mine but I didn't want the whole island talking about it and I didn't want Huck to know because he wouldn't like it.

Why wouldn't he like it? Maia wanted to know. I could see her backing away from any situation that Huck might not approve of. Maia is devoted to Huck. He is God, Santa Claus, and Justin Bieber rolled into one.

"He would *like it," I said. "He wants me to be happy. But I'm not ready to tell Huck about it, only you. Russ is a person for just you and me, okay?"*

"Okay," she said.

We visited Russ at the villa in Little Cinnamon. When he shook Maia's hand, he slipped her a cherry lollipop, which she accepted only after I said it was okay. He asked her if she wanted to play Chutes and Ladders. She said yes, then added, "But just so you know, I always win."

I won't go so far as to say it was an instant success. Maia didn't care about any old white guy except for Huck. But I will say they got along fine. Russ was charmed, maybe even smitten, and as I watched them play their game—Maia won handily, landing on only ladders while Russ's rolls put him on only chutes—it struck me how much they looked alike, how their mannerisms were similar, their earnest, goofy enthusiasm matched.

She is his daughter. No doubt about it.

April 8, 2016

Maia and I went back to the villa in Little Cinnamon last week.

Russ asked Maia if there was anything he could add for her at the villa and she said a shuffleboard court.

Russ said, "I will tell the architects tomorrow to add a shuffleboard court, as long as you promise to play with me."

Maia said, "I'll play with you, but just so you know, I always win."

May 23, 2016

Love is messy and complicated and unfair.

Russ's grandson, Floyd, is getting baptized in Iowa City, which is something of an issue because Baker's wife, Anna, isn't religious and has only grudgingly agreed to the ceremony.

"Anna is a doctor," Russ said. "A real smart cookie."

"Smart cookie?" I said. "Please promise me never to use that term in front of her."

"I already did," he admitted. "It didn't go over well."

I don't know anything about the baptism except that it is happening. I imagine a church full of people with Russ and Irene sitting up front, holding hands. Everyone gazes on them with admiration, not one soul guessing that Russ has a mistress and a daughter in the Caribbean.

Does he think about us? I wonder. Or does he have a vault in his brain where he locks us, and all the feelings he has for us, away?

May 30, 2016

The villa needs some sprucing up, and Russ asked me to make the decorating decisions.

"I have no taste," he said. "At home, Irene handles these things." As soon as he said this, he knew it was a mistake.

The at home *bothered me more than* Irene. *His home is in Iowa. This is... well, I'm not even sure what to call it. His second place, I guess. I live in second place.*

I told Russ I want no part of any decorating decisions. It's his villa, not mine. In truth, I don't want to pick things and then have him compare my taste to Irene's. Russ asks Paulette Vickers to handle the decorating. It's Paulette and Douglas from Welcome to Paradise Real Estate who built the villa in the first place, and just as they were about to lose it to the bank, Todd Croft and Russ swung in on a vine; Russ bought the villa and Ascension the hillside. They asked Paulette and Douglas to stay on as property managers. I know them both but I'm not worried about Huck finding out because Paulette is a distant cousin of my father, Levi Small, and the Smalls did not speak to Mama, and they do not speak to Huck.

I was *concerned about what would happen once the other houses were built and sold and suddenly we had neighbors watching my car coming and going from the best villa.*

When I shared this concern with Russ, he said, "We won't have any neighbors."

"We won't?"

He clammed up then, which is something he's been doing more and more frequently, every time I ask him about his work. He'd told me early on that Irene didn't have the first idea what his work entailed. She couldn't care less, he said. All she cared about was the money.

"She wouldn't care if I were a paid assassin," he said.

To differentiate myself from Irene, I tried to understand what Russ does for work. He is executive vice president of customer relations for Ascension, which means, essentially, that he does exactly what he'd done in college when Todd Croft was selling beer in the dorms—he lends him his trustworthy face, his cheerful good-guy demeanor, and his sterling personal reputation. Ascension invests in "high-risk, high-yield" investment opportunities for very wealthy clients, many of them foreign.

"Why won't we have neighbors?" I asked. We were down on the private beach—I had decided to leave Maia with Huck so we could have some alone time—sitting together on one of the brand-new chaise longues that Pauline had bought. We were drinking champagne, the Krug. "Russ?"

I was leaning back against Russ, tucked between his legs, and he murmured into my hair, "We sold those lots to fictional entities. Shell companies that we set up..."

"So, wait," I said. "Is that legal?"

"People do it all the time down here," Russ said. "To clean money, to hide money."

"That wasn't my question."

Russ squeezed me tight. "This is the Caribbean, Rosie," he said, as if it weren't the only home I'd ever known.

Russ is in the business of money-laundering and tax evasion. I said I didn't believe him capable of it, and once I pried a little more, he admitted that he'd taken the position at Ascension thinking it was 100 percent aboveboard, but once he'd figured out it wasn't (in addition to everything else it did, the company invested money for some bad people—bad both morally and politically), it was too late. He was in too deep to protest.

"Then there's the fact that both Todd and Stephen know about you," he said.

Without a word, I got to my feet and bent down to kiss Russ on the cheek. "Be right back," I said. I ascended the eighty steps to the villa, got in my car, and drove home.

I hate that I now know Russ is cheating the system—and yet, what did I expect? He's cheating on his wife. I'm an integral part of the grand deception. I'm a lie. Maia is a lie. Mama was right, so *right, to tell me to stay away from him. But had I listened? No. Three days after she was gone, I was back in his bed.*

It's over, I've decided.

When I kissed Maia as she lay sleeping, I thought, I am going to find a man who deserves to be your father.

February 14, 2017

The money still arrives in packages, only instead of depositing it in a bank account for Maia's college, I've started stacking it neatly in the bottom drawer of my dresser. If the money is illegal, someone will trace it to my bank account eventually. Cash is safer.

Then, this weekend a text came to my phone from a foreign number. It said: Please come to the villa. I want to see you. Things will change, I promise.

I blinked, read the text again, read the text a third time. Russ had never texted me before. We'd both agreed cell phones weren't safe.

Things will change, I promise. *It wasn't a text saying he had left Irene, but I gave in anyway. I ached with missing him.*

March 2, 2017

Love is messy, complicated, and unfair.

Things have not changed in any way except that the villa is newly redone and Maia has been allowed to decorate one of the rooms as her own. Also, I finally came clean with Huck and Ayers and told them that, yes, there was a man—I even said his name out loud once—but my relationship was nobody's business but my own.

Huck and Ayers disagreed. Huck wants to meet the guy and so does Ayers; I've put them both off, saying that when the time is right, introductions will be made. When the time is right will be when Russ leaves Irene. He says he's getting closer to making a clean break. They live separate lives. Baker and his family are happy in Houston, and Russ has just set his son Cash up in an outdoor-supply business in Colorado. Once Irene finishes working on the house in Iowa City—it still *isn't done—he'll move down here full-time.*

He doesn't talk about work and I know enough not to ask. He spends a lot of time in the Cayman Islands as well as the BVIs—in Anegada, specifically. He asked me if I wanted to go back to Anegada; it's the one place he's not afraid to be seen with me.

"Maybe?" I said the last time he asked. I worry that he has business interests in Anegada, and I can't risk getting mixed up in them.

Huck calls Russ the Invisible Man, and I don't object. That's exactly what he is.

November 3, 2018

I haven't written in ages, and usually when I take breaks like this it's because too much is going on for me to stop and write about it.

But life has been relatively placid, if also topsy-turvy. When Russ is away, I work at La Tapa, live with Huck, hang out with Ayers, and take care of Maia, who is growing into a very cool young person. When Russ is here, I live with him. Sometimes Maia comes with me; sometimes she decides that she would rather stay home.

"It's not that much fun watching you guys kiss all day," she said. "Even if there is shuffleboard and SpaghettiOs."

We didn't tell Maia that Russ was her father; she told us. One day when it was pouring rain and there was nothing else for Maia to do, she deigned to come to the villa with me, and while she and Russ were playing Scrabble (they had graduated from Chutes and Ladders), Maia looked up and said, "You're my father, right?"

Russ had searched my face in wild panic. "Uh..."

"Right," I said. "How did you know?"

"How did I know?" Maia rounded the table and put her face cheek to cheek with Russ's. "Come on, Mom. Really?"

I'm writing now not because of any great upheaval in my life but because Ayers and Mick broke up. What happened was that Mick hired a girl named Brigid to work at Beach Bar and something about Brigid set off warning bells with Ayers. Sure enough, a couple nights ago, at three in the morning, Ayers drove into town and caught Mick and Brigid together. Mick was basically living at Ayers's place in Fish Bay, but Ayers threw him and his dog, Gordon, out. For the past two days I've had to listen to what a disgusting liar and cheat Mick is and what an unforgivable harlot Brigid is because Brigid knew Mick was in a committed relationship and still she fooled around with him. While I do agree that Mick is weak and Brigid doesn't deserve to have another female friend as long as she lives, this situation has also led me to some painful introspection.

I am Brigid. I know Russ is married and still I am involved with him. Deeply involved.

Russ showed up a few days ago—hurricane season is now officially over and the island is gearing up for the holidays—and I told him about Ayers breaking up with Mick because she had caught him cheating. Russ nodded distractedly.

I said, "These aren't fictional characters from a book I'm reading or a show I'm watching, Russ. These are my friends. You don't know them because you can't meet anyone in my life, but they're real to me, they're important to me."

"I know, Rosie," he said. "I've been hearing about them for years. They're real to me too."

"I want an engagement ring," I blurted out. "By the new year. Otherwise I'm done for good. Maia just turned twelve. She's a young woman, Russ. She's been very accepting of our arrangement, but someday soon she's going to start asking the hard questions."

"I know," he said. "And believe me, I want to give you an engagement ring. Things are tough at work right now..."

Tough at work. That old chestnut.

"I'm thinking about quitting," he said. "I love my income, but if I left, I'd have a shot at getting my integrity back. The things we're doing... they aren't right, Rosie."

"Don't tell me!" I said. I have this notion that if I don't know any particulars, I'll be safe. I have almost a hundred and twenty-five thousand dollars in my bottom drawer. It's a lot, but is it enough to live on for the rest of my life? I thought about Maia going to high school—I want to be able to send her to Antilles on St. Thomas—and then to college in the States. Russ must have

savings, right? If not, we could sell the villa and move someplace smaller. We don't need nine bedrooms; we never have guests. Seven of the bedrooms have never even been slept in.

Russ said, "If I quit, things will change. For the worse, initially, and then for the better."

"Quit," I said.

November 19, 2018

My hand is shaking as I write this. I'm thinking about calling the police, but the police here on St. John won't be able to do anything. I need to call the FBI. But if I do that, I might get Russ in trouble.

I was waiting tables at La Tapa tonight when Tilda told me there was a one-top, a man, who had asked for me specifically. This was the downside of being mentioned by name so frequently on TripAdvisor. Complete strangers pretended they knew me.

"He's ridiculously hot," Tilda said. "In a Clooney-meets-Satan kind of way."

That description should have tipped me off but it was a busy night and I didn't have time to think. I approached the table and noted only that Tilda's description was accurate; the guy was attractive but scary-looking. Sharply dressed, too sharp for the Virgin Islands.

"Hello," I said. "Welcome to La Tapa." I handed him a menu and the wine list. "Can I get you started with sparkling, still, or tap water?"

He looked up. "Hello, Rosie," he said.

"I'm sorry," I said. "Do I know you?"

In the split second before he spoke, it clicked: Todd Croft.

"Todd Croft," he said.

I wanted to scream. I did a quick survey of the restaurant. Who could help me? Skip was behind the bar. There was no way he could handle this. Ayers could, maybe. Or Tilda.

Or me. I could handle this.

"What are you doing here?" I said.

"How old is your daughter now?" he asked. "Twelve?"

The mention of Maia made me bend down and get in his face. "Get out of here," I whispered. "This is my island. Mine, not yours. If your intention was to come in here and threaten me or threaten my family, I would think again. I know people."

He seemed amused by that. "Do you?"

"Yes," I said. "I do." I was thinking of Oscar. If I took twenty or thirty thousand dollars from the drawer, could I get Oscar to board Bluebeard *in the middle of the night and shoot Todd Croft, or at least scare him to death?*

I half feared Todd would try to hire him. They were both pirates.

"Russ is finished with you," I said.

"He's not, though," Todd said. He pushed back from the table and stood. "That's what I came to tell you. Russ isn't *finished with me. He doesn't seem to see it that way, however, so I need you to talk some sense into him." He gave me a tight smile. "There's big money in it for you if you're persuasive."*

"If you want a burger," I said, in a voice loud enough to draw attention from nearby tables, "you should try the Tap and Still across the street. Thanks for stopping in."

With that, I snapped up his menu, corralled Ayers from table 11, and dragged her into the kitchen to do a shot of beer.

"Who was that?" she asked. "He was hot."

I longed to tell Ayers the truth. She's my best friend and she doesn't know the first thing about me. By choosing to be with Russ, I'm hiding from everyone else.

"Some creeper," I said. "I sent him packing."

December 31, 2018

Russ came back the day after Christmas with a leather and black pearl choker for me—not an engagement ring. I gave him a framed photograph of me and him in the hammock that I had taken with Maia's selfie stick. He was happy with his present. I was less happy with mine, which he could tell.

"I have until the new year, January first," he said. "Right? That was the ultimatum?"

I didn't like the word ultimatum *or the fact that I had issued one, but I nodded.*

I'd told him about Todd Croft coming to La Tapa, and Russ had assured me that everything was going to be all right. He'd had a confidential talk with Stephen Johnson, Todd's partner, and he'd told Russ that he would smooth things over with Todd. There was no reason Russ couldn't make a seamless exit as long as he signed a confidentiality agreement and a noncompete.

This came as a relief to me, and it made sense. Stephen was an attorney.

"Let's celebrate New Year's Eve at the villa," Russ said. "And then go over to Anegada on the first. Stephen has offered to take us by helicopter."

"I've always wanted to ride in a helicopter," I admitted. "Should we take Maia?"

He kissed my nose. "Next time," he said. "This trip is just for us."

Just for us; I liked the way that sounded. He would extract himself from Ascension with the help of coolheaded, legal-minded Stephen Johnson, and we would go to Anegada to stay in the pristine white clapboard cottage—where, maybe, oh please, a diamond ring would be waiting for me.

When I went home to pack, I heard Maia and Joanie giggling in Maia's room. I tapped on the door.

They were sprawled across Maia's bed, both on their phones, which I didn't love, but what I did love was the evidence of their bath-bomb business strewn about—the Epsom salts, the food coloring, the citric acid, the tropical fragrances.

I chatted with the girls for a minute—they were starting to have crushes on boys—and then I gave Maia a squeeze and a kiss and wished her a happy New Year.

"I love you, Mama," she said.

I left the room but then I peeked back in. I wanted very badly to tell Maia the truth: I was going to Anegada with Russ because he planned to propose! We were going to be a real family!

But instead, I simply caught her eye and mouthed, I love you.

And I closed the door.

IRENE

Irene watches Huck's back as he leaves. What is she doing? She's asking for more time because she's scared. She has never felt so drawn to a man in her life and it's terrifying; she doesn't like the sensation of losing control.

But what did Russ's accident teach her? What is the number-one thing?

She's alive.

She, Irene Hagen Steele, has today and God knows how many days after. Why not spend those days falling headlong in love with Captain Sam Powers?

"Hey, Huck?" she says.

But he has disappeared down the stairs.

She shakes her head. *Go to bed, Irene,* she thinks. *You can talk to Huck in the morning.*

Yes, that's a smart idea—but even as she decides this, she's walking toward the villa stairs, envisioning kissing Huck through the open window of his truck.

And then she sees a flash of light. Headlights, more than one pair, are coming up the hill.

"Huck?" she calls out.

The headlights get closer, and before Irene can process what's happening, four black SUVs pull into the driveway.

What must be ten people climb out of the cars and start up the steps. Irene's instinct is to back up all the way to the far railing of the deck.

The first person to arrive at the top is a woman, red-haired, attractive. She flashes her badge and a piece of paper that could be a shopping list for all Irene can tell; she'd need her glasses to read it.

"Hello?" Irene says. "Can I help you?"

"I'm Agent Vasco, and as of right now, this villa, one Lovers Lane, is the property of the United States government." She looks at Irene, not unkindly. "Mrs. Steele?"

Irene nods.

"Your husband, Russell Steele, bought this property as well as the property at thirty Church Street, Iowa City, Iowa, with illegally acquired funds. We've arrested Todd Croft and charged him with one hundred and seventeen counts of fraud, money-laundering, and tax evasion for a total of over three point five billion dollars. He named your husband, Russell Steele, as a co-conspirator, and he has documentation to prove it. I'm afraid we have to seize both properties."

"Wait," Irene says. "You're taking this house?"

"This house, yes," Agent Vasco says. "And there are federal agents at your home in Iowa City right now."

"But that's my *home,*" Irene says. "I invested six years restoring it. I *live* there."

"You may pack one suitcase of personal effects," Agent Vasco says. "But I'm afraid you have to vacate the property."

"But my boys," Irene says. "My grandson." Irene can't think. Baker and Floyd are in Houston, but they're on their way back. Cash is asleep upstairs.

"I'm sorry," Agent Vasco says. "I'm afraid I'll have to oversee your packing."

"But I've done nothing wrong," Irene says. "I met with Agent Beckett in Iowa City. I was very forthcoming. I told him everything I knew. I *helped* him."

"I wish it were different," Agent Vasco says. "But it's not. This is no longer your property, I'm afraid."

For one suspended moment, Irene mentally leaves the scene. She's back on the unnamed beach, naked. She hears Russ say, *The storm is coming. It will be a bad storm. Destructive.*

This is the storm. It's here. The villa. Her home in Iowa City. What is she going to do? Where is she going to go?

"Huck?" she cries out.

She sees him running up the villa stairs toward her.

"I'm here, AC," he says. "I'm here."

ACKNOWLEDGMENTS

Every year for the past eight years, I have been lucky enough to spend five weeks on the island of St. John in the U.S. Virgin Islands. While I consider it a home away from home, it is not my main residence, nor do I own property there. It is for this reason that I am so grateful to and humbled by the people of St. John, all of whom have been so kind, welcoming, helpful, and supportive.

I have to start by thanking my St. John family: Julie and Matt Lasota and their wonderful children. I'd also like to thank Beth and Jim Heskett for giving me "a room of my own" at the St. John Guest Suites for four idyllic years.

Shout-outs to those people who assisted with my research by either talking to me or providing me with valuable experiences. In no particular order: Karen Oscar Coffelt and head of school Liz Morrison from the Antilles School; Captain Stephen and Kelly Quinn of Singing Dog Sailing; Bridgett and Jimmy Key of Palm Tree Charters; Heather and the whole staff on Pizza Pi (the pizza boat!); Matt Atkinson, who was literally my first friend on St. John in 2012; Peter Bettinger; Chester of Chester's Getaway; Colleen from Pizzabar in Paradise; John Dickson from the Pink Papaya; Jorie Roberts; Sarah Swan; Richard from Lime Inn—thank you for saving Maxx's life (story for another day); Jerry and Tish O'Connell from the Soggy Dollar (and you too, Leon!); and huge, enormous thanks to Alex Ewald for the wonder that is La Tapa.

Last and most important, thank you to my partner in crime, Timothy Field. Here's to many, many more days of being the last people left on Oppy.

ABOUT THE AUTHOR

Elin Hilderbrand is the mother of three 3-sport athletes, an aspiring fashionista, a dedicated jogger, a world explorer, an enthusiastic foodie, and a grateful seven-year breast cancer survivor. She spends part of every winter writing on St. John. *What Happens in Paradise* is her twenty-fourth novel.

Troubles in Paradise

ALSO BY ELIN HILDERBRAND

The Beach Club

Nantucket Nights

Summer People

The Blue Bistro

The Love Season

Barefoot

A Summer Affair

The Castaways

The Island

Silver Girl

Summerland

Beautiful Day

The Matchmaker

Winter Street

The Rumor

Winter Stroll

Here's to Us

Winter Storms

The Identicals

Winter Solstice

The Perfect Couple

Winter in Paradise

Summer of '69

What Happens in Paradise

28 Summers

Golden Girl

Troubles in Paradise

A Novel

Elin Hilderbrand

BACK BAY BOOKS
Little, Brown and Company
New York Boston London

The characters and events in this book are fictitious. Any similarity to real persons, living or dead, is coincidental and not intended by the author.

Back Bay Books / Little, Brown and Company
Hachette Book Group
1290 Avenue of the Americas, New York, NY 10104
littlebrown.com

Originally published in hardcover by Little, Brown and Company, October 2020
First Back Bay trade paperback edition, October 2021
Boxed-set edition, October 2021

Back Bay Books is an imprint of Little, Brown and Company, a division of Hachette Book Group, Inc. The Back Bay Books name and logo are trademarks of Hachette Book Group, Inc.

ISBN 978-0-316-43558-1 (hardcover) / 978-0-316-54174-9 (large print) / 978-0-316-59312-0 (Canadian) / 978-0-316-70647-6 (signed) / 978-0-316-70645-2 (Barnes & Noble signed) / 978-0-316-70646-9 (Barnes & Noble signed Black Friday) / 978-0-316-43562-8 (paperback) / 978-0-316-37156-8 (boxed-set edition)
LCCN 2020938382

Printing 2, 2023

LSC-C

Printed in the United States of America

For TGF

AUTHOR'S NOTE

The Paradise series has come to an end. (And oh, how I hope all of you who are about to read this book are not only now realizing that it is the third one in a trilogy. If so, first go and read book 1, *Winter in Paradise,* and book 2, *What Happens in Paradise,* and then this one will make more sense!) I will dearly miss Irene, Huck, and the gang, and I hope you will too.

As many of you may realize, the hurricane described in this novel is fictional, though it is based on the all-too-real events of the fall of 2017, when Hurricane Irma and then Hurricane Maria—both category 5 storms—hit the Virgin Islands. This is a case where real life is far stranger than fiction. I could never have ended this series with not one but two life-threatening storms rolling through the islands; no one would have believed it. As with the other books, the St. John portrayed in these pages is one that lives only in my imagination. The hurricanes hit a few months before I started writing this series, and, having nothing to draw on but my memories, I created an island that is half before-the-storms St. John and half after-the-storms St. John. The most important thing to know now is that the Virgin Islands have recovered; America's Paradise is once again open for business, and it's even better than it was because of what it has survived.

We're just a sinner's choir, singing a song for the saints.

—*Kenny Chesney, "Song for the Saints"*

Troubles in Paradise

ST. JOHN

The gossip recently has been as juicy as a papaya, one that gives just slightly under our fingertips and is fragrant on the inhale, the inside a brilliant coral color, bursting with seeds like so many ebony beads. If you don't fancy papaya, think of a mango as we crosshatch the ripe flesh of the cheeks with a sharp knife or a freshly picked pineapple from the fertile fields of St. Croix, deep gold, its chunks sweeter than candy. Like these island fruits, the talk around here is irresistible.

The drama began on New Year's Day with tragedy: a helicopter crash a few miles away, in British waters. One of our own was killed, Rosie Small, whom some of us remember back when she was in LeeAnn's belly. Because LeeAnn's first husband, Levi Small, left the island when Rosie was a toddler, we'd all had a hand in raising her. We sympathized with LeeAnn when the cute Rosie girl we doted on turned into the precocious Rosie teenager LeeAnn couldn't quite control. At the tender age of fifteen, Rosie dated a fella named Oscar Cobb from St. Thomas who drove the Ducati that nearly ran our friend Rupert off Route 107 right into Coral Bay. We were all overjoyed when Oscar went to jail for stabbing his best friend. *Good riddance!* we said. *Throw away the key!* A group of us took LeeAnn out for celebratory drinks at Miss Lucy's. We thought we'd dodged a bullet; Rosie would not waste her life on a good-for-nothing man with shady business dealings like Oscar Cobb.

The man Rosie ended up with was far more dangerous.

After LeeAnn died, five years ago now, Rosie took a secret lover. We called him the "Invisible Man" because none of us had ever caught more than a glimpse of him. But while Paulette Vickers was under the dryer at Dearie's Beauty Shoppe, she let something slip about "Rosie Small's gentleman." Then Paulette clammed up and it was the clamming up that made us suspicious. Paulette was a little uppity because her parents had started the successful real estate agency Welcome to Paradise. She liked to talk. When she stopped talking, we started listening.

The Invisible Man's name was Russell Steele. He was killed in the helicopter crash along with Rosie and the pilot, an attorney from the Caymans named Stephen Thompson. They were on their way to Anegada. The callous among us commented that they should have taken a boat like normal folk, especially since there were thunderstorms. The perceptive among us noted that, while there were thunderstorms on New Year's morning, they were south and west of St. John, not northeast, which was the direction the helicopter would have been flying to get to Anegada.

Both Virgin Islands Search and Rescue and the FBI had reason to believe that the helicopter exploded. Maybe an accident—an electrical malfunction—or maybe something else.

If you think this is intriguing, imagine hearing of the arrival of the Invisible Man's family. For, yes indeed, Russell Steele was married, with two grown sons and one grandchild. And did his wife and sons stroll right down the St. John ferry dock on January 3 and climb into the car belonging to Paulette Vickers, who then whisked them off to whatever grand, secluded villa Russell Steele owned?

Yes; yes, they did.

Would the family of Russell Steele find out about Rosie?

Yes; yes, they would.

It was one of the taxi drivers, Chauncey, who witnessed a determined-looking woman marching down the National Park Service dock calling for Captain Sam Powers (we all know him as Huck), LeeAnn's devoted second husband and Rosie's stepfather, and then talking herself right onto Huck's boat, the *Mississippi.* Chauncey remembers whistling under his breath because he had seen women on a rampage like that before and they always got what they were after.

The two sons appeared out and about in Cruz Bay, going to the usual places tourists go—La Tapa to enjoy the mussels, High Tide for happy hour. We saw these young men (one tall and clean-cut with a dimple, one stocky with bushy blond hair) in the company of two young women we were all very fond of (charming and lovely Ayers Wilson, who had been Rosie's best friend, and Tilda Payne, whose parents owned a villa in exclusive Peter Bay), and that set us speculating, even though we knew that beautiful young people find one another no matter what the circumstances.

When we learned that one of the sons, Baker Steele, took his child on a tour of the Gifft Hill School and that the other son, Cash Steele, had joined the crew of *Treasure Island,* we began to wonder: Were they *staying?*

When we discovered that the Invisible Man's wife, Irene Steele, was working as the first mate on Huck's fishing boat, we thought: *What exactly is going on?*

We couldn't run into one another at Pine Peace Market or

in line at the post office without asking in a whisper: *You heard anything new?*

Sadie, out in Coral Bay, was the one who learned that the FBI had come looking for Paulette and Douglas Vickers, but Paulette and Douglas had taken their six-year-old son, Windsor, and fled by the time the FBI arrived. They went to St. Croix to hide out with Douglas's sister in Frederiksted. Did one of *us* tell the FBI where they were? No one knew for sure, but Paulette and Douglas were arrested the very next day.

We'd barely had time to recover from this shocking news when the FBI sent agents in four black cars along the North Shore Road to whatever secluded villa Russell Steele owned to inform Irene Steele that the villa and the entire hundred-and-forty-acre parcel we called Little Cinnamon was now the property of the U.S. government, since it had been purchased with dirty money.

Whew! We woke up the next morning feeling like we had gorged ourselves. We were plump with gossip. It was, almost, too much.

We feel compelled to mention that this kind of scandal isn't typical of life here in the Virgin Islands.

What is typical?

"Good morning," "Good afternoon," or "Good evening" at the start of every conversation.

Sunshine, sometimes alternating with a soaking rain.

Wild donkeys on the Centerline Road.

Sunburned tourists spilling out of Woody's during happy hour.

Silver hook bracelets.

Hills.

Swaying palm trees and sunsets.

Hikers in floppy hats.

Rental Jeeps.

Turtles in Salt Pond Bay.

Full-moon parties at Miss Lucy's.

Mosquitoes in Maho Bay.

Iguanas.

Long lines at the Starfish Market (bring your own bags).

Cruise-ship crowds on the beach at Trunk Bay.

Steel-drum music and Chester's johnnycakes.

Snorkelers, whom we fondly call "one-horned buttfish."

Driving on the left.

Nutmeg sprinkled on painkillers (the drink).

Captain Stephen playing the guitar on the *Singing Dog*.

Eight Tuff Miles, ending at Skinny Legs.

A smile from Slim Man, who owns the parking lot downtown.

Nude sunbathers on Salomon Bay.

Rum punches and Kenny Chesney.

Afternoon trade winds.

Chickens everywhere.

St. John has no traffic lights, no chain stores, no fast-food restaurants, and no nightclubs, unless you count the Beach Bar, where you can dance to Miss Fairchild and the Wheeland Brothers in the sand. St. John is quiet, authentic, unspoiled.

Some people go so far as to call our island "paradise."

But, we quickly remind them, even paradise has its troubles.

IRENE

Cigarette smoke. Bacon grease. Something that smells like three-day-old fish.

Irene opens her eyes. Where is she?

There's a blue windowpane-print bedsheet covering her. She's on a couch. Her neck complains as she turns her head. There's a kitchen, and on the counter, a bottle of eighteen-year-old Flor de Caña.

Huck's house.

Irene sits up, brings her bare feet to the wood floor. A suitcase with everything she owns in the world is open on the coffee table.

She hears heavy footsteps and then: "Good morning, Angler Cupcake, how about some coffee?"

She drops her face into her hands. How can Huck be thinking about coffee? Irene's life is...over. This time yesterday she'd been steady and stable, which was *no small feat* considering only a little over a month has passed since her husband, Russell Steele, was killed in a helicopter crash and Irene, who'd believed Russ was in Florida playing *golf* and schmoozing with *clients,* discovered that Russ had a secret life down here in the Virgin Islands complete with mistress, love child, and a fifteen-million-dollar villa. Irene handled that news *pretty damn well,* if she does say so herself. Another woman might have had a nervous breakdown. Another woman might have set the villa on fire or taken out a full-page ad in the local paper (in Irene's case, the *Iowa City Press-Citizen*) announcing her husband's treachery. But Irene adapted to the shocking circumstances. She found that she liked the Virgin Islands so much that she's returned here to live—maybe not forever, but for a little while, so she can catch her breath and regroup. Just yesterday she was looking around Russ's villa, thinking how she would redecorate it, how she might turn it into an inn for women like herself who had survived cataclysmic life changes.

Just last night, Irene felt like a teenager falling in love for the first time because, in a plot twist that happens only in novels and romantic comedies, Irene has developed feelings for Huck Powers, the stepfather of Russ's mistress. The universe did Irene "a solid" (as Cash and Baker would say) when she met Huck. He's an irresistible mix of gruff fisherman, devoted grandpa, and teddy bear. What would Irene's situation look like if she hadn't become friends with Huck? She can't imagine.

But entertaining notions of a love life is a luxury she can no longer afford. Last night, FBI agents seized Russ's villa. It's now the property of the U.S. government.

If Irene was painfully honest with herself, she would admit that, once she got down here, she'd realized there was no way the business Russ had been involved in was aboveboard. From the minute Irene set eyes on it, the villa had a bit of a magic-carpet feel: Was it real? Would it fly?

It was a tropical...palace. Nine bedrooms, each with its own en suite bath. The outdoor space featured an upper pool and a lower pool connected by a curvy slide, a hot tub dropped into a lush gardenscape, an outdoor kitchen, a shuffleboard court (which Irene had never used), and, eighty steps down, a small, private sugar-sand beach (which she had). The view across the water to Tortola and Jost Van Dyke was dramatic, soaring. The villa was so over-the-top *luxurious* that Irene was able to get past the fact that it had been the home of Russ and his mistress, Rosie, and their daughter, Maia. She had been looking forward to putting her own stamp on the place—choosing lighter, brighter fabrics, redoing a bathroom in an under-the-sea theme for her four-year-old grandson, Floyd, creating a custom window seat where she or Maia could read or nap.

The far bigger, more devastating development is that, as Agent Colette Vasco of the FBI informed Irene, the authorities were, at that very moment, also seizing her home on Church Street in Iowa City, an 1892 Queen Anne–style Victorian that Irene had spent six years renovating. The Church Street house is Irene's *home.* It's where her photo albums, her cookbooks with the sauce-splattered pages and handwritten notes, her clothes, her teapot, and her Christmas ornaments are. She has the idea that maybe, with luck, some of these items might be returned to her, but how is she to accept the loss of, say, the third-floor landing, paneled in dark walnut with the east-facing stained-glass window, or the mural of Door County on the dining-room walls? Those "moments" in her house are priceless and irreplaceable. Irene thinks longingly of her amethyst parlor, the velvet fainting couch, the absurdly expensive Persian rugs, the Eastlake bed in the Excelsior suite, the washstand, the sepia-toned photograph of Russ's mother, Milly, as a child in 1928.

Thinking about that photograph brings Irene to her feet.

Huck, it turns out, has been watching her every move. "Coffee?"

She casts her eyes around the room and finds her phone plugged into the far wall. That's right; Irene remembers being methodical about packing her suitcase and double-checking for essentials like her phone charger. Agent Vasco had looked on suspiciously, as though she thought Irene might try to slip in a stash of cocaine or blocks of hundred-dollar bills.

When Irene got to Huck's house, they each did a shot—or two? three?—of the Flor de Caña, and Irene only barely recalls plugging her phone in before sleep. She remembers so little about the end of the night that she supposes she should be grateful she woke up on the sofa and not in Huck's bed.

He's a gentleman.

"I need to make a phone call," she says. "Do you have any…aspirin?" She points to her head. "Good morning," she adds, because she has learned the number-one rule of the Virgin Islands: "Good morning," "Good afternoon," or "Good evening" begins every conversation.

"Two aspirin coming right up," Huck says.

"Three," Irene says. *Four,* she thinks. "Please."

"The best reception is out on the deck," Huck says.

Irene slips through the sliding glass door, going from the pleasant air-conditioning of Huck's house (though she gathered last night that he turned it on only because she was there) to the mounting heat of the day. Her phone says seven o'clock, which means it's five o'clock in Iowa City.

Five a.m. Will Lydia be awake at five a.m.? She is going through menopause and complains that now she never sleeps, so maybe. Even if she is asleep, Irene needs to wake her up. Dr. Lydia Christensen is her best friend; she claims she is there for Irene no matter what. The bonds of best-friendship get tested infrequently, especially as Irene prides herself on being self-sufficient.

Today is a different story.

"Hello?" Lydia says. She's laughing. Irene hears the whisper of bedsheets and, in the next instant, a deep male voice. This would be Brandon the barista, Lydia's new boyfriend. Irene doesn't want to imagine what the two of them are doing up so early.

"Lydia, it's Irene." She stops herself. "Good morning."

"Irene?" Lydia says. "Is everything *okay?* Did something happen? Something *else?*"

"Yes," Irene says.

Lydia is there for Irene no matter what. No matter that it's five a.m., no matter that it's negative ten degrees with the wind chill in Iowa City, no matter that Irene interrupted pillow talk. Lydia and Brandon are going to put on their parkas and drive directly over to Church Street to see what's what. She'll call Irene when she gets there.

Inside, Irene accepts the three aspirin and a glass of ice water. The Flor de Caña bottle has been tucked away and in its place is a cup of coffee that Irene understands is for her. There are eggs cooking on the stove.

"I don't want to seem ungrateful, but I just can't eat," Irene says.

"The eggs are for Maia," Huck says.

Right, Irene thinks. Maia has school. For everyone else, it's a normal day. It's Thursday.

"We have a charter," Irene says.

"That we do," Huck says. "I'm going to take it alone. I thought about passing it off to *What a Catch!* but it seems like now we could probably use the money. You stay home and figure out what you need to figure out and I'll be back this afternoon to help you in any way that I can." He gives her a tentative smile. "Maybe with fresh mahi."

Irene bows her head. She notices his use of the pronoun *we,* which she finds both sweet and confusing. What he doesn't understand is that there is no *we*. Irene has lost her house here and her home in Iowa City. She feels like Wile E. Coyote in the old cartoons: suspended over a canyon, running on air, and then looking down and realizing there's nothing beneath him. Irene's problem can't be fixed. It can't be made better by fresh grilled mahi for dinner. Irene's problem is that her husband of thirty-five years, in addition to keeping a mistress and fathering a child and lying about his whereabouts, had been evading tax laws and laundering money.

"Did I ever tell you that Russ sent me flowers on New Year's Day?" Irene asks. "Calla lilies, a beautiful bouquet. He must have arranged it with the florist ahead of time and paid extra because of the holiday. And do you know what I thought when I got them? I thought, *What a lovely man Russell Steele is. I am so lucky to have him.*"

"AC," Huck says. He turns off the heat under the eggs and takes a step toward her, but she holds up her palm to warn him away.

"He was dead by the time the flowers arrived."

"Irene," Huck says. "You're allowed to be upset."

Apparently, Irene hasn't avoided the nervous-breakdown stage after all because what she wants to do is scream, *You're damn right I'm allowed to be upset! It's a good thing the man is dead because if he were alive, I'd kill him!*

But Irene holds her tongue and a second later, Maia walks into the kitchen. She's wearing pink shorts, a gray T-shirt with a hand-painted iguana on the front, and a pair of black Converse.

When she sees Irene, she does an almost comical double take. "Um…hi? Miss Irene?"

"Good morning, Maia," Irene says. She turns the corners of her lips up, which physically hurts. Then, as a demonstration that everything's okay, everything's fine, she takes a sip of her coffee. It's strong. One small mercy.

Maia looks from Irene to Huck and back with raised eyebrows. "Did you…stay here last night?"

Irene nearly laughs. She has no idea what to say. Part of her wants to claim she's here just to pick up Huck for their charter, but in another second, Maia is going to notice Irene's suitcase open on the coffee table.

"I did," Irene says. "Huck was kind enough to let me sleep on the sofa."

"Okay…" Maia says.

Huck spoons some eggs onto a plate and pushes the button on the toaster. "Irene and the boys lost the villa, Nut," he says. "There's some…tax trouble."

Tax trouble is a useful phrase, Irene thinks. It'll put everyone to sleep.

Maia takes a seat at the table. "So you guys can't stay there anymore?"

The toaster dings. Huck pulls butter and jam out of the fridge and sets them on the table along with the plate of eggs and toast. "I have to get ready," he says, and he disappears down the hall, leaving Irene to explain the unexplainable.

"We can't," Irene says. Cash called his friend Tilda and spent the night at her house. Irene asked Cash to call Baker and let him know what had happened. Baker was planning on moving down to the island from Houston with his son, Floyd—though these plans will certainly have to change. Hopefully, Baker hasn't done anything that can't be undone. "The villa belongs to the government now. Because Russ…your dad…he owed the government money for taxes, and since he's not here to pay them, the FBI took the house instead." This isn't quite true, but it's close enough.

"So none of us can stay there?"

"No," Irene says. "They let me leave with only one suitcase. Just my clothes. So the stuff in your room...might be difficult to get back."

Maia's fork hovers over her breakfast. She looks so much like Russ's mother, Milly, in that moment that Irene wants to hug her. Those eyes. Milly's eyes.

"Are you guys leaving, then?" Maia asks in a wavering voice.

"Oh, Maia," Irene says, and her eyes fill with tears. "No? I don't know? The FBI also took my house in Iowa City."

"They did?"

"They did," Irene says. She can no longer stand, she's shaking too badly, so she takes the seat next to Maia. "That house is what's called a Victorian, and it had been a dream of mine since I was a young girl to restore and live in a real Victorian house. When Russ and I were first married, I kept clippings in a file folder of paint colors I liked, sofas, wallpaper, old sinks, light fixtures, doorknobs."

"Like Pinterest?" Maia says.

"Yes, like Pinterest," Irene says. "And once Russ...your dad...took the job down here, I had the money to buy a real Victorian house in a style called Queen Anne, which has elaborate gingerbread fretwork trim..." She looks at Maia. "Do you know what that is?"

Maia shakes her head.

"It looks like a house in a fairy tale, with a deep front porch and a turret and some stained-glass windows."

"Cool," Maia says. Irene thinks maybe Maia is indulging her, but it *is* cool.

"It was as if my entire Pinterest board came to life," Irene says. "The house is filled with antiques and hand-knotted silk rugs. There are built-in cabinets and salvaged fixtures and stained-glass windows and murals on the walls and chandeliers, and I have a doorbell that used to ring in a convent in Italy." She needs to stop. What is she doing, unloading all this on a twelve-year-old? "I would have loved for you to see it." This is true, Irene realizes. She wanted both Huck and Maia to see the Church Street house someday. It was her life's work. In a way, it was an incarnation of Irene herself. "But they're taking it. I'm losing my swimming pool and my rose garden with all my heirloom varietals and my two cars. It'll all be gone. They're taking it because of Russ. And now I have nothing left."

Maia stares at Irene and Irene is just sane enough to feel ashamed.

"You have Cash and Baker and Floyd," Maia says. "You have Huck. He really likes you... he was in a terrible mood when you went back to the States, you know. And you have me." She picks up her toast, butters and jams it, and holds it out to Irene. "And you have this papaya jam from Jake's, which is one of the best things I've ever eaten. Try it."

Irene accepts the toast—how can she not?—and takes a small bite. The jam is... well, it's delicious.

"Good, right?" Maia says.

Irene nods and takes another small bite.

"You can start a new Pinterest board," Maia says. "And the first thing on it can be the papaya jam from Jake's."

If only it were that easy, Irene thinks. She knows Maia is right; Irene still has what matters. Her family. Her friends. Her health. Her good sense, sort of.

"We aren't going to leave," Irene says. She doesn't add

Because we have nowhere to go. This isn't strictly true, anyway. Baker still owns a house in Houston that is untouched by Russ's tainted money. And Irene's elderly aunt Ruth has their family summer home in Door County. But the thought of moving to Houston or living with her eighty-something-year-old aunt isn't at all appealing. "We'll figure something out."

"You can stay here," Maia says. "And you don't have to sleep on the couch—we have an extra room. My mom's room." She takes a bite of eggs and seems to realize what she has just offered.

"The couch is fine for now," Irene says quickly. "And I'll find something. I'm not completely penniless."

Maia swallows. "Gramps told me I could move into my mom's room. That means you can have my room."

"Oh, Maia..."

"It's a mess, I know," Maia says. "But I'll clean it after school. I'm grounded anyway."

That's right; Maia is grounded. She'd pulled a disappearing act last night after lying to Cash to get him to drop her off in town. That drama now seems extremely minor, like running out of dinner rolls on the *Titanic.*

"You don't have to move on my account," Irene says, though there is obviously no way she's going to sleep in Rosie's room. "The couch is fine."

"I want to move," Maia says. "You being here is a good impetus." She scrunches up her eyes. "Did I use that word correctly?"

Irene can't help herself; she halfway smiles. "You did."

"So you'll stay?"

It's not in Irene's nature to accept help from anyone, but she can't turn down such a sweet offer—besides which, she is the definition of *desperate.* "I'll stay until I get back on my feet."

Suddenly, Huck is before them, dressed in his sky-blue fishing shirt and his visor, a yellow bandanna tied around his neck. "I'm glad that's settled," he says.

As Irene is standing at the window watching Huck's truck wind its way down Jacob's Ladder, her phone rings. It's Lydia. Irene hovers her finger over the screen. She would like to stay here, in a space where there's still a filament of hope. Maybe Agent Kenneth Beckett, who came to search the Church Street house a few weeks earlier, has intervened on Irene's behalf. There's always a good FBI agent in the movies, right? One who sees past the letter of the law to what's authentically right and wrong? Irene didn't do anything wrong. She doesn't deserve to lose her home.

"Lydia?" Irene says.

"It's been seized," Lydia says. "They have a sign on the door and a team has just arrived to remove the contents. I asked to see the warrant, and what do I know, but it looked official. The guy called the house the 'fruit of crime.'"

Irene's stomach lurches and she fears she's going to vomit. *Remove the contents. The "fruit of crime."*

"What about the things that are mine?" Irene asks. "What about the things I bought with my salary from the magazine? What about the things we owned before Russ took the job at Ascension?"

"I don't know," Lydia says. "We're sitting across the street in my car. Should I go ask?"

Irene tries to imagine Lydia asking these complicated questions. But the agents must get asked about this sort of thing constantly, every time they dismantle someone's life.

"Please ask if you can get one thing," Irene says. "A

photograph of Milly. It's in the navy-blue guest suite, hanging above the washstand."

"Photograph of Milly, navy guest room, above the washstand," Lydia repeats. "I'll ask right now. You stay on the phone. Here, talk to Brandon."

No! Irene thinks. She is in no mood to make small talk.

"Hey, Irene," Brandon says.

"Good morning, Brandon."

There's the predictable awkward pause. Brandon clears his throat. "So, this is a bummer, huh?"

A bummer is when Iowa loses to Iowa State. It can maybe be stretched to include a flat tire, a loose filling that results in having to get a root canal, and flunking your driver's test. What's happening to Irene is not a bummer. It's a...well, frankly, she lacks the right word.

"Yes," she says. "Yes, Brandon, it is."

Her tone must discourage further conversation because Brandon says, "Hang in there."

A few moments later, Lydia takes the phone. "Here's exactly what happened. First, he asked if I was your lawyer. I should have said yes, but I didn't think fast enough. I told him I was your friend and that all I wanted was one family photograph. I told him I knew where it was and that he could come with me while I retrieved it."

"What did he say?"

"He said no."

Irene needs to hang up. She needs to call Ed Sorley, her attorney, although Ed will be in way over his head with this. She needs to find another attorney. But first, Irene wants that photograph. Out of all the items in her home, that's the one she can't bear to think of being ignominiously tossed onto a pile in some storage unit. "Thank you, Lydia. I appreciate you getting out of bed to check on this for me."

"I wish there were more we could do," Lydia says. "I can't believe how *awful* this is...your beautiful house. You worked so *hard*...remember when they sent the wrong-size pool cover and we thought *that* was a catastrophe?"

"I have to go, Lydia," Irene says. "I'll call you later. Thank you for...I appreciate it." Irene hangs up, hoping she didn't sound rude or, if she did sound rude, that Lydia forgives her. Lydia is too nice to handle the FBI agents in Irene's driveway—but Irene knows someone who isn't too nice.

She scrolls through her contacts until she finds the number of her former colleague Mavis Key.

Irene barely has to explain; Mavis gets it. The FBI has seized Irene's property. Mavis doesn't ask why; she knows about Russ's second life in the Caribbean, so she can surely guess why. Irene tells Mavis that all she wants from the house is the photograph of Milly, Russ's mother, taken in 1928 in Erie, Pennsylvania.

"I'm on my way over right now," Mavis says. "And make no mistake, I *will* get that photograph."

For the first time all morning, Irene feels her shoulders relax. Mavis will get the photograph. Mavis is a thirty-one-year-old dynamo who moved to Iowa City from Manhattan, stole Irene's editor-in-chief job at *Heartland Home and Style,* and is turning the magazine into a midwestern version of *Domino* or *Architectural Digest,* complete with a snappy "social media presence." The magazine's publisher, Joseph Feeney, was correct in hiring and immediately promoting Mavis Key, Irene sees now. The woman is effective.

"Thank you," Irene says.

"Text me your mailing address," Mavis says. "I'll have it packaged properly and shipped with insurance."

"That's above and beyond—"

"And Irene," Mavis says, "I want you to call my twin sister. She's a corporate attorney in New York City, and she deals with white-collar criminals who make Russ look like Mister Rogers."

Irene very much doubts that. "I didn't know you had a twin," she says. Then she realizes she knows next to nothing about Mavis's personal life.

"Well, I'm warning you, she's very tough. I find her a bit intimidating, to be honest."

This gets Irene's attention. Mavis, with her extreme self-confidence, her stylish clothes, her cutting-edge vision, finds her sister intimidating? What must the woman be like?

"I'm not sure what I need," Irene says.

"You need Nat," Mavis says. "Natalie Key. Call her, Irene."

BAKER

Thursday, four in the morning, Houston, Texas. Baker sits straight up in bed. This is it. This is happening. Their flight to St. Thomas is in a few short hours.

His phone shows two missed calls from Cash the night before plus a text that says, Pick up, bro. It's urgent.

Baker still has last-minute packing and organizing to do before Ellen comes to take them to the airport. He doesn't have one spare second to talk to his brother, though he figures Cash must have heard the news: Maia saw Mick kissing Brigid on the beach, Maia told Ayers, and Ayers is going to break off the engagement.

Well, Baker already knows. Ayers texted him right after it happened.

It's a sign from above; this new chapter in his life is going to work. A tropical island, a nontraditional lifestyle, and, most important, Baker's relationship with Ayers Wilson. He's going to win Ayers over or die trying.

"We're going to miss you like crazy," Ellen says. They're curbside at the airport, which is congested with Ubers and taxis and people wheeling their roller bags while talking on their phones, but Ellen insists on getting out so she can give Baker a proper hug goodbye. "Becky is in charge of finding us a new school husband."

"What?" Baker's friendship with his school wives is rare and, he thought, special. He never dreamed he'd be *replaced.*

Ellen shrugs. "She's the one in HR."

"Just as long as it's not Tony," Baker says.

Ellen grins but her eyes are shining with tears. "I'm only kidding, Bake," she says. "You know what? We're already planning a trip to visit you this summer."

"You are?"

"I'm terrible with surprises," Ellen says. "Sorry about that. Yes, we'll see you in a few months."

"You can stay at the villa, you know," Baker says. "It has nine bedrooms."

"You're sweet to offer, but we wouldn't do that to your mom and brother," Ellen says. "I'm going to book rooms at Caneel."

Baker finds himself getting choked up as he shepherds Floyd into the terminal. His school wives are the only people in Houston he's going to miss, and he's touched that they feel the same way, so much so that they're already planning a trip down. Once they see St. John and Irene's villa and meet Ayers, they'll understand why he's making the move. He'd be a fool not to.

When Baker and Floyd check in with all their luggage, Floyd is carrying his copy of *The Dirty Cowboy* under one arm, and the woman at the United desk is so taken with him that she bumps them up to first class. "You're the only child I've seen in years who isn't mesmerized by a screen," she tells Floyd.

Baker wills his son not to mention the iPad that's tucked in Baker's carry-on or the fact that Floyd has watched *Despicable Me 3* ten times in the past week.

"Thank you," Baker says. First class! He's already dreaming of a Bloody Mary and a decent nap.

Turns out, Baker's and Floyd's seats are across the aisle from each other. Is this going to be okay? Sitting next to Floyd is a West Indian woman who is already situated, watching a movie with headphones on. The seat next to Baker is empty. Maybe Baker will ask about switching.

Baker stows his carry-on and Floyd's backpack but tells Floyd not to buckle up just yet. "I'm going to see if we can switch seats. That way you can sit next to me and have a window."

"I want a window!" Floyd says.

There's a guy in a knit cap with a hipster beard getting ready to take the seat next to Baker. He's wearing a T-shirt that reads WASPS OF GOOD FORTUNE—a band, maybe?—and jeans and a Gucci belt and a pair of black Sambas exactly like the ones Baker used to wear to soccer practice when he was nine years old, and on his wrist is a forty-thousand-dollar Rolex Daytona with a light blue pearlescent face. He has AirPods in.

The guy—he looks to be somewhere in his mid-twenties—nods at Baker and goes to lift his duffel into the overhead space.

Baker says, "Hey, man, any chance you would mind switching spots with my son so we can sit together? He's only four."

The guy blinks at Baker and says in a broad Australian accent, "Sorry, mate, I prefer the window."

"No problem, mate," Baker says. He slides out of the way so that Mr. Samba, Mr. Wasps of Good Fortune, Mr. Young Crocodile Dundee can take his seat. Baker tries not to feel put out. It's the guy's seat, Baker has no right to it, but still—who says no when asked to help out a four-year-old child? Baker glances at the woman next to Floyd, but she has fallen asleep.

"Looks like we're staying put, buddy," Baker says, and he fastens Floyd's seat belt.

"Daddy?" Floyd says. "May I please have the iPad?"

Baker doesn't speak to Young Croc during the flight, though he does keep tabs on him out of the corner of his eye. Young Croc orders Maker's Mark straight up (two) to Baker's Bloody Mary (one). Young Croc watches *Deadpool 2* (no surprise there); Baker chooses old episodes of *The Office.* Young Croc declines breakfast; Baker inhales the kale and sausage omelet, the soggy home fries, and even the sad, wrinkled cherry tomatoes. Young Croc does the sudoku puzzle in the in-flight magazine astonishingly quickly, which actually makes Baker like him a little better. He doesn't get up for the bathroom at all, whereas Baker gets up once for himself and twice for Floyd.

As the plane descends, Young Croc finally turns his attention to the window, tapping on the glass with his forefinger in apparent anticipation. And isn't that an emotion he and Baker share?

When the plane's wheels hit the runway, people sitting in coach clap and cheer. Baker checks on Floyd, who is fast asleep, then turns to Young Croc. "You going to St. Thomas?" he asks. "Or St. John?"

"St. John."

"Us too," Baker says. "We're moving down for good."

"Oh yeah?" Young Croc says. "You running a business down here? Doing the EDC deal?"

"EDC?" Baker says.

"Yeah, that's the tax-incentive plan for businesses that relocate to the USVI."

"Legal?" Baker asks, because this sounds like something his father might have been involved in. Anyway, it would explain why the hedge fund was run down here instead of in, say, New York or Chicago.

Young Croc laughs. "Yes, legal. Lots of people do it. I moved my company here from Houston in the fall. I'm saving tons of cash."

"From Houston?" Baker says. "Are you American?"

"Naturalized," Young Croc says. "Originally from Perth."

Perth is in…Australia? New Zealand? Baker should know but he hasn't got a clue and he's embarrassed to ask. "What's the name of your company?"

"Huntley International?" he says, like maybe Baker has heard of it. "Real estate development."

Baker is rendered temporarily speechless. The dude looks twenty-five. But that would explain the watch. It's probably his father's company. Or—he hears his ex-wife's voice in his head asking him to think and act in a way that promotes gender equality—his mother's company. "Baker Steele," Baker says, offering his hand.

"Dunk," the kid says and they firmly—aggressively?—shake. "Duncan Huntley. Nice to meet you, Baker. What do you do?"

Baker isn't eager to admit that he's a stay-at-home dad supported by his superstar-surgeon almost-ex-wife. He could say that he day-trades and has accepted a coaching job at the Gifft Hill School, but does that sound any more impressive? "Investments," Baker says.

"Oh yeah? For whom?"

"I have my own shop," Baker says. "Coincidentally, I've been thinking about getting into real estate myself." By this, Baker means he's considered getting his real estate license because he isn't sure what else he can do that will make a sustainable living on St. John.

"Take my card," Dunk says. "I'm always looking for investment partners."

Baker accepts the card even though he knows he has severely misrepresented himself. Baker has money in the bank—both a healthy brokerage account and a fund that he day-trades with—but he immediately realizes that he's not in a position to be anyone's "investment partner" unless Dunk Huntley is looking for an investment of five hundred dollars.

Still, it can't hurt to know people. DUNCAN HUNTLEY, CEO AND FOUNDER, HUNTLEY INTERNATIONAL LLC.

Founder? Baker thinks.

He's distracted by the business of getting off the plane. He pulls down his carry-on and Floyd's Toy Story knapsack, then he bends at the knees—protect the back—to pick Floyd up without waking him.

Baker gravitates toward Dunk while they're standing at the baggage carousel waiting for their luggage. Baker is sweating despite the air-conditioning. Floyd is as hot as a glowing coal.

Dunk smiles. "Seeing you with him makes me miss my girl."

"Your..." Baker isn't sure if Dunk means his daughter or his girlfriend. He doesn't seem like the paternal type.

"My girl, Olive. She's a harlequin Great Dane."

"Oh," Baker says. "Your dog."

"Yep," Dunk says. "Olive stays here and I fly back and forth to Houston. She weighs a hundred and fifty pounds, so she's too big to crate. I had to fly down private with her when we came initially."j

"Right," Baker says, nodding, although, honestly, every new sentence out of this guy's mouth is crazier than the last. "If you don't mind my saying so, you seem pretty young to be a CEO."

"I'm twenty-eight," Dunk says. "I look older without my hat." He shrugs. "Losing my hair."

"Still, that's really young to have your own company. How'd you do it?"

"I went to Baylor, majored in business...I've always sort of had a nose for what's hot. For my senior project, I developed a simple sex app. The user checked in every time she or he did the deed and joined a community of others who were reporting their sexual activity. People could add what positions they'd tried and a few other details." He glances at Floyd. "And then there was a rating system, points they could accrue, status they could gain. I did it as a riff on the swipe-left culture but it took *off.* Especially among the marrieds. Like my sister, Andi. She lives in Bellaire—you know it?"

Yes, Baker knows it. Wealthy Houston.

"Everyone in her neighborhood was on my app. She claims they were all lying about how much action they were getting."

"Well," Baker says. "Yeah." If Baker was ever on a sex app, he would have no choice but to lie. He and Anna got it on approximately twice a year.

"I sold the app for fifteen million and I got into the weed business in Colorado, making artisanal edibles."

"Ah," Baker says. "Now you're talking."

"We made gummies, lollipops, high-quality chocolate bars in nine flavors, cookie dough...we even had pot pasta sauce."

Pot pasta sauce? Who thinks of this stuff? "I can see where that would be popular," Baker says.

"As more states legalized marijuana, the business grew and I sold that company last year for ten times what I'd made with the app."

A hundred and fifty million? Baker thinks. Surely this is hyperbole.

"So I've given up the sex and the drugs," Dunk says. "And now I'm into the rock and roll." He points to his T-shirt. "Wasps of Good Fortune is my band."

"Oh yeah?" Baker says. "What do you do?"

"I sing," Dunk says. "I have kind of a Colin Hay sound, you know, early-period Men at Work?"

Baker blinks. He'd thought there was only one period of Men at Work, the "Land Down Under" period.

He's saved from commenting when the alarm sounds and the conveyor belt starts rolling. "Hey, do you guys want to ride over to St. John with me?" Dunk asks. "I have my driver coming, then we'll hop on my boat."

"Aw, man, that's kind of you, but we have so much stuff, it's just not practical. I'm going to need one of those big taxis all to myself."

"Just come with me," Dunk says. "It'll be way easier. My boat has plenty of room."

"Okay..." Baker says. "If you're sure."

Dunk helps Baker get all the luggage out to the curb, and seconds later, a forest-green G-wagon pulls up. It's unclear to Baker whether the G-wagon belongs to Dunk or a service he hires, but no matter—it's cool and comfortable, and Baker is finally able to set Floyd down. The driver delivers them to the dock at Havensight, where they climb aboard a sixty-five-foot Sea Ray Sundancer called the *Olive Branch*.

"Wow," Baker says. The boat is brand-new and beautifully outfitted; the salon is all leather and gleaming wood. There's a bouquet of fresh flowers, a bowl of tropical fruit. Dunk opens the fridge; one side is lined with bottles of Veuve Clicquot, the other with beer. Dunk grabs two Heinekens, hands one to Baker, and says, "Let's go sit in the cockpit. Charlie will have us to Cruz Bay in fifteen minutes."

Baker kicks back and relaxes in the sun while Floyd sits in the shade of the bimini, still sluggish from his nap. The captain, Charlie, starts the engines and away they go, zipping around the towering cruise ships to open water. They pick up speed and cut a neat seam through the turquoise water to St. John. Baker takes a sip of his beer and thinks: *This is my life now.* He said goodbye to Ellen outside of IAH just this morning, but it seems like eons ago. If he were back in Houston, he would be getting ready to pick up Floyd from the Children's Cottage. The two of them would go home, Baker would fix a snack, and then they'd head to the park or playground, or Baker would bribe Floyd with his iPad so that he could continue to trade until the markets closed, and by then it would be too late to go to the park and Floyd would have conked out anyway and Baker would think maybe he'd take a nap too, why not? And when the two of them woke up, the sun would be setting and Baker would start on one of his gourmet dinner menus as they waited for Anna to come home, and when Anna came home, she would say she had already eaten (pizza) at the hospital, and Baker would either throw half the dinner away or carefully pack it into a Tupperware container for Anna to take for lunch the next day, which she would inevitably forget to do and Baker would throw it away out of anger and disgust because his efforts around the house went unappreciated.

He's so glad he's not in Houston! He's so glad he's no longer with Anna!

Life in the Virgin Islands will be different. After school, Baker and Floyd will go on tropical adventures—to Salt Pond to snorkel with the turtles, to Scoops for ice cream, to the Reef Bay Trail to hike and see the petroglyphs. Even when they simply go home to the villa, they can swim in the dual-level pool or at their private beach. They can play shuffleboard. Baker will invest in field glasses and they'll bird-watch on the hillside. Irene and Cash are both finished with work in the midafternoon, so one or the other can take care of Floyd while Baker coaches at the school. One or the other will be home at night when Baker wants to take Ayers to Dé Coal Pot or visit her at La Tapa or when they just hang out in Ayers's studio apartment.

Here in St. John, he has a support system. Here in St. John, he has everything he needs.

* * *

The *Olive Branch* pulls up to the National Park Service dock in fifteen minutes flat. While they tie up, Baker texts his mother and Cash to see if either of them can come get him and Floyd; if they can't, he'll have to take a cab to the villa.

"Where do you live?" Baker asks. "We own a villa in Little Cinnamon."

"I have a villa in the East End," Dunk says. "I like the quiet."

Baker nods, though he hasn't been to the East End. Has he heard of the East End? He's not sure. It must be special if Dunk lives there.

Dunk points at an island behind them. "That's Lovango Cay," he says. "My next project. I bought the island, and now I'm looking for partners to fund a resort, a beach club, and some world-class dining. In case you're interested?"

Baker laughs. He's drawn to Dunk, no doubt, but he can't wait to get away from him. He shakes Dunk's hand. "Thanks for the ride, man. It was a real treat to meet you. Right, Floyd?"

Floyd shrugs. "You talk funny."

"Floyd!" Baker says, but Dunk just laughs.

"No worries, mate. You have my card, call anytime, we'll shoot over to Foxy's and have a painkiller."

"All right," Baker says. "I'll take you up on that!" He picks up the biggest suitcase and tries to roll it down the dock while holding Floyd's hand. He needs to check his phone to see if his mother or Cash responded.

"You gonna be okay here?" Dunk asks. "Someone is coming to get you?"

"Yep, all set, all set," Baker says. It won't be a G-wagon with a driver but someone will come, he hopes, or if everyone is busy, he'll schlep every gosh-darn thing they own to the dock in the scorching heat and flag down one of the open-air taxis, the driver of which will probably balk when Baker tells him he lives on a hilltop in Little Cinnamon.

He should have returned Cash's call from the Houston airport. Not setting up a ride was very shortsighted.

Floyd starts to cry. "It's hot," he says. "I want a snack and a juice. Where's Grammy?"

Baker pulls Floyd along like a toy on a string. "You were asleep when they served the meal on the plane, honey, but I'll get you something the second we get home. And you can swim in the pool for as long as you want. There are still three whole days until you start school, so we can do some exploring in the Jeep. We'll take the top off and make it a convertible."

Instead of placating Floyd, this agitates him further and a minitantrum follows. *I want the pool now, I want a snack now*... Baker swivels his head to check that Dunk Huntley has left and isn't watching Baker. Dunk Huntley has no idea how difficult dealing with a four-year-old can be.

Sex app, artisanal weed edibles, real estate development. Wasps of Good Fortune. Baker wonders if it's supposed to be *WASPs*, as in "white Anglo-Saxon Protestants." That's an obnoxious name for a band, and they probably stink despite the early–Men at Work sound, yet Baker can't deny he finds Young Croc Dunk Samba WASPy Wunderkind Huntley fascinating.

Baker checks his phone. Nothing from his mother or Cash.

He calls Cash. Straight to voicemail.

He calls Irene. She answers on the fifth ring. Her "Hello" is little more than a whisper.

"Mom?" he says.

"Oh, Baker," she says. Her voice is broken; something is wrong. Baker will ask once he's off this dock and in one of the air-conditioned Jeeps.

"Is there any way you can pick us up?" Baker says. "We got a ride over from St. Thomas with this guy on his boat and so we're on the National Park Service dock instead of the regular ferry dock."

"What?" Irene says. "*Where* are you?"

"The National Park Service dock."

"Here?" she says. "On St. John?"

"Yes, here on St. John," he says. "It's Thursday, Mom." He tries not to sound so exasperated because if he's learned one thing about the Virgin Islands, it's that every day feels like Saturday.

"Didn't Cash call you?"

"Yes, he called me—"

"Didn't he tell you?"

"Tell me what?" Baker says.

HUCK

He doesn't understand women—and how is that possible after so many years of loving them?

Huck grew up with a sister, Caroline, who was a scant two years younger than him and who learned to fish from their father right alongside Huck. But whereas Huck was all about sport-fishing—the hunt, the fight, the elation that came from landing a big one—Caroline liked the quiet elegance of fly-fishing. She showed an uncanny talent for it early on, which was unusual for a child that young. She preferred dancing her line over the flats of Islamorada to a trip out to blue water, and to his credit, their father, the original Captain Powers, nurtured her gift. By the time Caroline was thirteen, she had won every youth fly-fishing competition in the state of Florida, competitions in which she was always the only girl.

All through high school, instead of dating or hanging out at the Green Turtle with her friends, Caroline would sit at her desk and tie flies. Caroline Powers became famous for her flies; grown men paid good money for them—*good* money, the price jacked up to an almost absurd level because Caroline didn't want to sell them. Her flies were works of art; she had the patience, the attention to detail, the slender, nimble fingers. She had the love and devotion.

While Huck was in Vietnam at the tail end of the war, 1974 to 1975, Caroline went to college in Gainesville, met a boy from the Florida Panhandle, followed that boy when he went to law school in Tallahassee, married him, and gave up fishing altogether. That, Huck didn't understand. Whenever Caroline and her new husband, Beau, came back to Islamorada to visit, they would go sport-fishing with their father on the big boat, and although Caroline was impressive the way she cast and reeled in the big fish, Huck yearned to see her with her fly rod again. He even suggested it once, the two of them out together on the flats at dawn in the pontoon. She shut him down immediately in a hushed voice: "No, Huck, I can't." As though fly-fishing were something embarrassing she used to do as a kid, like going roller-skating in just a bikini and a pair of red knee socks.

Caroline was diagnosed with a brain tumor the week after her fortieth birthday and was dead by forty-one. Soon after, her husband, Beau, gave Huck a flat tackle box. When Huck opened it, he saw Caroline's flies, one in each sectioned compartment like so many jewels. He has them still.

Before she met Huck, Kimberly Cassel was a bartender at Sloppy Joe's in Key West. In those days, Huck was not yet Huck—he was just Sam Powers—and he was not yet a captain; he was first mate for a guy everyone called Captain Coke. Every Sunday, Coke would invite Sam to go out on the water "just for fun," and nearly every Sunday, Sam said no because Sunday was his only day off and he had to do things like laundry and grocery shopping, and sometimes he hitchhiked up to Islamorada, where his mother would cook him dinner. But one Sunday in March of 1978, Sam said sure and Coke said, "Finally! I've been wanting to introduce you to my sister."

Huck remembers that he'd bristled—he did just fine in the women department on his own and he'd been looking forward to a day of real fishing (instead of baiting clients' hooks and turning back early if someone got seasick), and he wasn't sure he'd enjoy the presence of anyone's sister, aside from his own, on a fishing trip.

But then Kimberly came striding down the dock wearing cut-off army-surplus fatigues, a red bandanna around her neck, and a white visor; her sandy-blond hair was up in a ponytail. Huck recognized her as the bartender from Sloppy Joe's, the famous Key West watering hole where Hemingway used to hang out and where Huck liked to fish for women from time to time. Somehow he'd never realized that the most popular bartender in Key West was his crusty, hard-living boss's sister.

Well, okay, Huck thought. She was nice to look at, but could she fish?

Oh, yes. Like Huck, Kimberly was born and raised in the Keys, on and around boats. During that first trip together, Huck watched her land a one-hundred-fifty-pound sailfish, sitting in the fighting chair, screaming like she was having a baby.

He vowed then that he would marry her.

But first he had to beat out scores of other men—the salty locals and rich, sunburned tourists alike, all calling her name, throwing down money, telling her she was as beautiful as one of Charlie's Angels. It took endurance to get the first date. Huck had to stay at the bar drinking but not getting drunk until Sloppy Joe's closed at four a.m. This was no small feat when his wake-up for the morning charter was only two hours later.

Looking back, Huck realizes that he'd been so dazzled by Kimberly's obvious charms and—he'll just say it—so invigorated by the chase that he ignored the warning signs of a deeply troubled person. Kimberly routinely did shots with customers, sometimes as many as five or six. She never appeared visibly drunk at work, but after her shift ended, there was always a margarita or three or five. Back at the beginning, Kimberly had been happy and pliably good-natured when she was drunk.

Shortly after they were married, things changed. In year three, Captain Coke's own substance abuse got the best of him. He was spending all his money on cocaine and, apparently, none on his business. He'd taken out a line of credit on the equity he had left in his boat and then failed to pay. Just as the bank was ready to claim the boat, Huck stepped in and bought not only the boat but the whole charter business. Kimberly called Huck a savior, though she wanted Huck to keep Coke on as captain. No, sorry—that wasn't going to happen. Huck didn't want Coke anywhere near the boat or the business, though he was happy to pay for rehab. This went over poorly with both brother and sister, but

Huck stood his ground. He took over the charter business, hired a new young mate, and made so much money the first year that he was able to buy a second boat.

Huck wanted to start a family and Kimberly claimed she did too, but she refused to quit her job at Sloppy Joe's. It brought in too much money, plus it was her identity. Huck didn't say that if she had a baby, she would have a new identity.

He wouldn't dare.

Kimberly did go off her birth control but she continued with the shots and the after-shift drinking.

"For God's sake, Kimmy," Huck finally said, "any baby we have will be born pickled."

Kimberly didn't like this one bit, though it did make her slow down a little—and sure enough, she got pregnant. Huck remembers the mixture of giddiness and terror at the news; it was as though someone had told him he could travel to the moon with the astronauts or star in a movie with Clint Eastwood. Did he want to? Hell yes! Did he *really* want to? He wasn't sure. What did Huck know about having a child, about being a father? He was also afraid that Kimberly wouldn't be able to stay on the wagon for nine full months—it seemed impossible—plus both of them smoked like fiends, and that would have to stop.

Kimberly bought prenatal vitamins and went to see an ob-gyn in Miami and she changed her post-shift drink to one white-wine spritzer. She cut down to four cigarettes a day—breakfast, lunch, dinner, and late at night—and Huck thought, *Okay, maybe this will work*. He couldn't expect her to quit everything cold turkey; that was how people failed.

Then, late on the night of December 1, 1983—Huck still remembers the date and probably always will—Kimberly came home stinking drunk, waking Huck up when she slammed into their bungalow on Catherine Street singing "Piece of My Heart" at the top of her lungs and crying.

Huck jumped out of bed. He would never lay a hand on a woman but he wanted to throttle her. He took her gently by the shoulders, pulled her in close, and whispered, "It's not just you anymore, Kimmy. You have to think about our baby."

Kimberly said, "Baby's gone, Sam. I started bleeding at work."

Huck was crushed; Kimberly was worse than crushed. She was riding a pendulum of emotions. When she swung one way, she was fine—it happened to a lot of people; they could try again. When she swung the other way, she was a mess—it was her fault, she was damaged and broken and unfit to be a mother.

Kimberly went back on the pill.

Huck felt like he was on a bike without brakes careening down a mountainside. He was afraid to jump off even though he knew he would crash when he got to the bottom. What followed was three years of Huck fishing and Kimberly drinking, drinking, drinking. This ended only once a beefy, tattooed loudmouth on one of Huck's charters bragged to his buddy that he'd gotten to third base with the bartender of Sloppy Joe's the night before.

"Oh yeah?" Huck said, blood pulsing in his ears. "Blond gal?"

"Ass like a valentine," the loudmouth said, and it took every ounce of Huck's willpower not to stab the guy in the forehead with the gaff.

When Huck confronted Kimberly, she admitted to it right away but said it was more like second base, maybe not even. She couldn't remember and wouldn't have been able to pick the guy out of a lineup. "The men are an occupational hazard, Sammy. They don't mean anything."

"Men?" he said, and he realized then that Kimberly hooked up with her customers all the time, maybe even every night. Was

the baby she lost even his? She had made him a laughingstock, an absolute fool for love.

He told her it was rehab or he was leaving. She agreed to rehab, and once she was safely inside the facility, Huck served her with divorce papers, which broke her heart but broke his heart even worse.

Once Huck left the Keys for St. John, it was only a few weeks before he met and fell in love with LeeAnn Small, who was Kimberly's opposite in every way. Maia liked to throw around the word *queen—Beyoncé is a queen, J. Lo is a queen*—but in Huck's life there had been only one queen and that was LeeAnn. She was statuesque, bronze-skinned, dark-eyed. She had a rich laugh and a slow smile that she shared with Huck like a secret.

On their first real date, at Chateau Bordeaux, Huck told LeeAnn about Kimberly. LeeAnn tsked him—because who couldn't have predicted how *that* story was going to end—and then said, "If you're looking for more crazy, you're in the wrong place."

LeeAnn didn't fish but she checked the wind, watched the sky, passed along fish sightings from their West Indian neighbors that Huck would never have heard about otherwise. She introduced Huck to the people at restaurants who would buy his catch. She never gave him a hard time about how long he spent on the water or tinkering on the boat. And, man, could she cook—conch ceviche, Creole fish stew, fresh tuna steaks with lime and toasted coconut.

LeeAnn was tough, stubborn, uncompromising, but unlike Kimberly, she stuck to a moral code and was utterly beyond reproach. Huck was a little scared of her at times. She was a nurse practitioner and the most competent person up at the Myrah

Keating Smith Community Health Center, where she treated everything from ankles sprained on the Reef Bay Trail to jellyfish stings to STDs. LeeAnn was strict with Rosie, but despite this—or because of it—Rosie broke the rules again and again and again, eventually getting pregnant by one of the rich men she waited on at Caneel Bay.

There were six golden years when Huck lived in the house on Jacob's Ladder with LeeAnn, Rosie, and Maia. He can remember sitting down to dinner in the evenings and seeing their bright faces and hearing their chatter or their squabbling and thinking how blessed he was to be among them.

He missed that sweet spot in his life now that it was over.

LeeAnn died of congestive heart failure.

Rosie died in the helicopter crash with Russell Steele.

Now here's Huck, five years after LeeAnn's passing and one month after Rosie's passing, in danger of falling in love with Irene Steele, the wife of Rosie's lover.

As his friend Rupert would say, *You can't make this shit up!*

It comes as no surprise to Huck that the Invisible Man, Russell Steele, was just another Caribbean pirate. Evading taxes and laundering money were nearly as common down here as snorkeling and drinking rum. Irene has now lost the villa in Little Cinnamon as well as her home in Iowa City, and the latter, Huck understands, is the greater loss by far. Most people down here are from somewhere else. They have another place they call home. It must feel pretty rotten to have that taken away, to be left with little more than the clothes on your back, the shoes on your feet.

Irene isn't bankrupt. She has twenty thousand dollars in an account down here, money from her magazine job.

"Twenty thousand isn't nothing," Huck says. They're standing out on the deck of Huck's house, elbow to elbow on the railing but not touching, gazing out at the water and the faint outline of St. Croix in the distance. A lot of people would call them lucky—people in Iowa City whose cars were buried under three feet of snow, for example.

"It's not enough to live on for very long," Irene says. "Both you and I know that. I need to find a decent place to live with reasonable rent and I'll need to buy a car."

Huck is relieved that she seems to be talking about staying on St. John, even though they both know that her money would last a lot longer if she lived almost anywhere else. "You can stay here as long as you want," Huck says. This turn of events doesn't seem all that bad to him. He *likes* having her here. He *likes* being the person who can put a roof over her head and food on her plate, though he would never, ever reveal this to Irene.

One trait all the women in his life have shared: They were "born on the Fourth of July." Independent.

Irene bows her head. Her hair is out of its braid; it's wavy and long as it falls around her face, a chestnut curtain shot through with strands of silver. When she looks up, she says, "I'm grateful for your friendship and the job on the boat—"

"You're an asset on the boat, AC," he says. "I *need* you on the boat. Today alone was hell on me." That morning, Huck had a Master of the Universe type on board—guy in his early forties, world by the balls, gung ho, let's go—and his four sons. The older three were complete hellions from the second they stepped onto the boat still in their basketball sneakers.

"Take your shoes off," Huck told them.

The oldest kid, maybe fifteen, said, "These are Cactus Jacks."

"Doesn't matter. Please take them off."

"It's Travis Scott's shoe," the kid said.

"This isn't Travis Scott's boat," Huck said. He didn't admit that he had no idea who Travis Scott was. He hadn't paid attention to basketball since Jordan retired. "It's *my* boat and you are to remove your shoes, please."

The youngest of the kids couldn't have been more than five; he was too little to be out on the boat without a dedicated caretaker, which his father—whose sole focus was catching mahi—most certainly was not. The father mentioned that the mother was having a spa day at Caneel, and he admitted that he wasn't used to having the kids by himself. The father took the first fish (Huck *hated* when grown men did this, ahead of their own kids, in the name of "Let me show you how it's done"), and he also took the fourth fish, forgetting about son number three, who was rightfully pissed off. Kid number three retaliated by grabbing his father's phone out of his pocket and dangling it over the side of the boat. This wasn't the first time Huck had seen this—it happened at least once a month, usually when Huck had a bachelor party on the boat; guys got drunk and bent out of shape or were screwing around—but Huck had never seen anyone flip out the way the father flipped out. He roared so loudly that even Huck flinched, and when the father went to grab the phone from his son, it fell in the water.

You deserved that, buddy, Huck thought.

Chaos ensued. They had to stop the boat, get the diving mask and the bait net, and go fishing for the phone, which was most certainly resting on the seafloor twenty feet below. The littlest kid fell when no one was looking and got a bloody nose but the father was only concerned about his phone. He couldn't live without it. Was there a store on this "stupid little island" where he could get it replaced that afternoon?

"St. Thomas," Huck said, his fists itching.

It had been a terrible charter and Huck was convinced that if Irene had been there, she would have established an order for the fish so that no one got overlooked, no one got angry, no one got hurt, and Huck didn't have to hear his home of the past twenty years insulted by a man-child.

He wants to tell Irene this story and let her know what a joy it is to have a woman in his life who understands the particular texture of his days, but she's in no state to hear it. He'll save it for later, after all this has been resolved and they're back to normal.

Will this be resolved?

Will they be back to normal?

"I appreciate your generosity but I can't impose on you forever," Irene says. "Unfortunately, I have nowhere else to turn right now. I feel like such a burden."

"You're not a burden," Huck says. "Maia wants you here and so do I." He moves an inch closer so that their elbows are kissing, and she doesn't move away. Huck wonders if he should hug her. He places an oh so tentative hand between her shoulder blades and she snaps to attention, ramrod straight. Huck lets his hand drop.

Okay, he gets it. No touching.

"This isn't a fairy tale where I'm a damsel in distress and you're the hero swooping in to save me."

"I know it's not, AC," he says.

"Please," she says. "Stop calling me that."

"Okay," Huck says, and now he's hurt. *AC* stands for "Angler Cupcake," which, she'd told Huck, was what her father used to call her. Huck likes the nickname. It doesn't exactly suit her—Irene is too sensible and straightforward to be any kind of cupcake—but he likes that he has a nickname for her. It suggests intimacy, friendship, something special between the two of them. But fine; she wants him to stop, he'll stop.

"I can't do this," Irene says. "I told you last night that I need more time."

But that was before ten FBI agents showed up to seize the villa, Huck thinks. That was before she learned her Iowa home was gone as well. Huck thought maybe that had changed things. But apparently not.

"I promised I'd give you as much time as you need," he says. "And I meant it."

"Except now I'm living in your house!" Irene says. "Mooching off you, taking advantage of your kindness! Don't you understand how…*confusing* that is?"

"No," Huck says. "I don't. We're friends, Irene. Okay? And coworkers. If you want to keep it just friends and coworkers, I'm good with that. I'm not exactly inviting you to share my bedroom, am I?"

"But you want to, don't you?" she asks.

"Want to what?"

"Invite me to share your bedroom!"

Huck can't figure out if his answer should be yes or no. The truth is yes. Should he be truthful? "I want you to sleep where you're comfortable. You know my feelings for you, AC. Sorry—Irene. But I'm not interested in forcing this along." He's so agitated that he lights a cigarette. This is the kind of conversation he likes the least—murky, ambiguous. They're middle-aged. Why can't they just say what they mean? "If it moves forward, it will be when you're ready. I'm a patient man, Irene. I'm a fisherman."

This gets a smile, though one so fleeting that Huck wonders if he imagined it. "I don't want to be a charity case. And I don't want to feel like I owe you something in exchange for…"

Huck exhales a stream of smoke. Now he's offended. "Please, Irene. Give me some credit."

"I do, but..."

"But you were married to a fella for thirty-five years who turned out to be a cheat and a liar and a criminal," Huck says. "So I understand how maybe you're hesitant to trust the very next man you meet. But I promise—Irene, I promise you on my precious granddaughter's life that I am pure in my intentions and my feelings. I've been hurt before too. Hurt badly." Huck pauses. At some point, he'll tell her the story about Kimberly, and she'll understand they're more alike than she knows. "I'm not going to use kindness to leverage something from you. Do you understand me?"

"Yes."

Are we okay, then? he wants to ask. Irene steps toward him and puts her hands on his shoulders, then moves closer and clasps her hands behind his neck. She rests her head on his chest.

Two things are apparent in that moment. One, they *are* okay. And two, Huck doesn't understand women.

Irene's phone rings, snapping them back to reality. Happiness is a butterfly that lands and then just as quickly flies away.

Irene answers the phone. "Hello?" There's a pause. "Oh, Baker." Another pause. "What? *Where* are you? Here? On St. John?" She turns to Huck, her eyes wide with alarm, and mouths: *He's here.*

Huck stubs out his cigarette. He imagines his buddy Rupert doing his best Chief Brody imitation: *Huck, my friend, you're going to need a bigger boat.*

AYERS

Treasure Island has a blown powerhead. It needs to go all the way to Puerto Rico to be worked on and won't be back in commission for a week.

Ayers is relieved. As usual, she wakes up facedown on her bed at the crack of dawn when her coffeemaker starts gurgling, but Ayers can barely even lift her head. She has to go to the bathroom but it's ten feet away, which might as well be a country mile.

Depression is setting in. Because of Mick.

Fool me once, shame on you.

Fool me twice, shame on me.

After Maia called to tell Ayers that she saw Mick and Brigid kissing on the beach—*They were all over each other, I saw it with my own two eyes*—Ayers nearly smashed her phone against the tile floor of her apartment. But she was stopped by her pragmatism (it would take seven hundred and fifty dollars and a trip to St. Thomas to replace it) and her skepticism. Maia must be mistaken. She'd thought it was Mick and Brigid, but it had to be another couple.

Mick had proposed only *two days before.* He'd planned the whole thing, luring Ayers out onto his boss's boat, *Funday,* rafting up in Christmas Cove near Pizza Pi among all their friends in the St. John service industry, asking Captain Stephen from the *Singing Dog* to play "Southern Cross," which was Ayers's favorite song. *My love is an anchor tied to you, tied with a silver chain.* He'd proposed in front of everyone, but aside from that, Ayers couldn't have executed it better herself. And maybe part of her *did* appreciate the public nature of the proposal. All of their friends knew that Mick had cheated on Ayers with Brigid and had then dated Brigid for two months, one week, and three days. (Yes, it was painful enough that Ayers kept track.) So it was *validating* to have everyone bear witness to Mick's ultimate choice.

It was Ayers. Ayers, not Brigid.

Or so she'd thought.

She wanted to dismiss what Maia had told her. Maia was only twelve. Could she really be trusted?

But Ayers trusted Maia more than anyone else she knew. Maia wouldn't have said it was Mick and Brigid unless it was Mick and Brigid. Ayers had to admit that Mick kissing Brigid on the beach wasn't out of the realm of possibility. She could only too easily imagine how it had unfolded. Brigid wanted "closure," she needed to have "a talk," she "deserved at least that." And then she gazed at him a certain way or she nudged her knee between his legs or she stroked his earlobe—and Mick broke. Mick might have thought that since he'd proposed and would be with Ayers the rest of his life, he had one last pass.

He did not have one last pass.

Ayers had decided to verify Maia's sighting with a second source. She'd texted Lindsay, another server at the Beach Bar, someone she considered a friend, to ask if she'd noticed Mick and Brigid slip away during service.

The response: TBH, yes, B. stranded me tonight with all her tables for...half an hour? She's been crying since Monday, and I assumed Mick was going to talk with her about it because it's been distracting for all of us. But they were gone an unusually long time and when they came back, B. looked much happier.

Ayers pulled the ring off her finger and nestled it back into its little velvet box. She wondered about the happy bride-to-be who would eventually wear it.

She sent Mick a text: I know you kissed Brigid. I'm leaving the ring in the box under the big rock at the end of my driveway.

Mick texted back: K.

K? Ayers thought. What kind of response was *that?* Didn't he want to know how Ayers had found out? Didn't he want to try and *deny* it? Wasn't he going to *fight* for her?

Apparently not.

The engagement was over; it had lasted slightly more than forty-eight hours. Ayers should never have taken Mick back. Brigid was some kind of narcotic for him.

She sent a second text: Best of luck to you two.

She wanted to say something else, but *You deserve each other* was too cliché and *Just remember—once a slut, always a slut* seemed too mean. In the end, Ayers wrote, Poor Gordon. Because Ayers felt sorry for Mick's dog. She'd miss him.

And then Ayers had texted Baker to let him know what was up. Maia saw Mick kissing Brigid on the beach tonight. I'm giving the ring back.

Baker responded: Can't wait to celebrate your newfound freedom!

Ayers is so tired. She's flattened. She lies in bed until three thirty, which is the last possible moment she can get up and make it to La Tapa on time, but she still can't muster the energy to move. She picks up her phone—there's no word from Mick, or from Baker either, for that matter—and calls La Tapa.

Tilda answers.

"Til," Ayers says. "I can't make it in tonight. I know it's trash of me to bag on you so late but honestly..." Honestly, the mere idea of lifting trays, opening wine, remembering orders—nope, it's beyond her today.

"Don't worry about it," Tilda says. "We have only thirty on the books. Besides"—here, Tilda lowers her voice—"we all know what happened with Mick."

"You do?" Ayers says. She's not sure why she's surprised; it's a tiny island, the coconut telegraph and all that. Brigid is probably crowing about her triumph all around town. Ayers wonders if Mick came by to get the ring. Maybe he gave her ring to Brigid; he is just enough of a cheeseball to do exactly that.

"Yeah, he's staging a sit-in at Cruz Bay Landing. Him and Gordon."

"A what?"

"He's been at the bar at CBL since it opened this morning. He has the ring in front of him. He's stinking drunk and he claims he's not moving until you take him back. Gordon is tied to his bar stool."

"You're kidding me," Ayers says.

"Not kidding, saw it myself," Tilda says. "I think AK is going to cut him off soon, but he might have to call the police to get Mick out of there."

Ayers is slightly revived by the news that Mick is staging a sit-in at Cruz Bay Landing, crying into his beer. So he *is* upset after all.

"He gave me this whole song and dance about how Brigid was taking a new job at Island Abodes, something *he* arranged to get her away from him. And not two days later, they're making out on the beach. I don't care if he sits at CBL for the rest of his life, I don't care if he turns into petrified wood and moss grows on him and a bird builds a nest in his hair, I'm not taking him back."

"Good girl," Tilda says. "You're on the schedule Saturday night. I'll see you then?"

"Yes," Ayers says. "Thanks, Til."

Thursday passes in a blur. Friday comes and Ayers doesn't feel any better. She feels worse—dull, leaden, sluggish, and dizzy. Her coffee tastes sour; food holds no appeal. She doesn't have to work at La Tapa but she's supposed to hang out with Maia in the afternoon.

She can't imagine getting in her truck and driving to Gifft Hill, much less doing some kind of fun, enriching activity. Waterlemon—they were supposed to snorkel at Waterlemon. If Ayers tried to snorkel, she would end up sleeping on the sandy floor of the Caribbean.

She sends Maia a text even though Maia is at school and (technically) not allowed to check her phone: I can't pick you up, Nut. I'm sick.

Two seconds later (so much for the rules), there's a response: It's okay, I'm grounded anyway, plus there's been drama at home.

Drama? Ayers texts. *At home* meaning with Huck? This is unusual.

Too much to text, Maia says. Call me later.

Later is Saturday at noon. It takes everything Ayers has to get out of bed, take a shower (her hair is in the first stages of dreadlocks), and make herself eat a piece of toast at her tiny kitchen table. She fights to keep the toast down. Something is up with her; this isn't just emotional distress. After all, Ayers hiked the Reef Bay Trail only two days after Rosie died.

Ayers checks her arms and legs, praying that she has overlooked some kind of weird bite or sting that would explain this. She'd gone backpacking all over the world with her parents when she was growing up, and she'd witnessed travelers in the throes of all kinds of exotic ailments. There was a pretty, blond college student doing a gap year in Nepal who nearly died of giardia, a couple of Israeli kids in India who had leishmaniasis that they thought they'd gotten from sand flies on Goa, and in Thailand, they'd met a family who had been infested with sea lice.

Leptospirosis? A guy Ayers knows down here contracted that from cleaning palm rats out of traps.

Ayers is making herself sicker just thinking about this. *Stop thinking about it!* She texts Maia. You busy?

A second later, Ayers's phone rings; her screen says Nut and lights up with a picture of Maia at Carnival a few years ago, her face painted royal blue and crimson.

"Hi," Ayers says. "Whatcha doin'?"

"Decorating my new room," Maia says. "Or, as Gramps calls it, 'moving the mess.'"

"New room? Are you..."

"Taking Mama's room," Maia says. "I've slept in here the past two nights." She pauses. "The sheets still smell like her. How long do you think that will last?"

Ayers's heart feels like a dying rose shedding its petals. "Oh, Nut," she says.

"I worry I'm gonna make the smell disappear faster by sleeping in the bed and that one night it won't smell like her, it will smell like me. But I don't have a choice because Irene is sleeping in my room."

"Irene?"

"Yeah," Maia says. "Have you not heard? Baker didn't call you?"

Baker has *not* called her, which she finds strange, since he's supposedly so keen on celebrating her "newfound freedom," but she figures he's been busy getting settled in, and, frankly, she's relieved that he hasn't asked to see her. "No," Ayers says. "Heard what?"

Maia sighs like an adult. "Well, they lost the villa in Little Cinnamon."

This news propels Ayers out of her chair and over to the front window. It's another beautiful day in paradise; things are happening out there while Ayers convalesces. "Lost the...lost the villa? What are you talking about?"

"Gramps said it was tax trouble. But I heard him and Irene talking about the FBI. I think my dad was into something illegal."

Ayers's stomach lurches. She collapses onto the sofa. Hidden underneath it are all of Rosie's journals. Ayers had discovered the journals buried in Rosie's dresser and she'd...absconded with them, taking them from Huck's house. They were Ayers's own private archaeological find, no less precious or revelatory to Ayers than the Dead Sea Scrolls or dinosaur bones. These journals *told Rosie's story,* one Ayers didn't know, and Ayers was Rosie's best friend. Ayers found herself compelled to binge on them but she'd made herself read slowly and carefully. She'd made herself *savor* them.

In the final two volumes are passages in which Rosie described Russ telling her outright back in 2016 that his company, Ascension, sold the lots in Little Cinnamon to fictional entities—shell companies. He admitted to Rosie that Ascension was in the business of hiding money, laundering money. And then, in the very last pages of the journal, Rosie wrote about how Russ had informed his boss, Todd Croft, that he was leaving the company and how Todd Croft had shown up at La Tapa and threatened Rosie.

Six weeks later, both Russ and Rosie were dead.

Now the FBI knows and the villa is gone? Ayers's thoughts are all over the place. Do the FBI agents think Todd Croft killed Russ and Rosie, or do they think it was, in fact, a lightning strike? Ayers remembered hearing thunder that morning. So it was a lightning strike—simple, impossible bad luck. But the scene Rosie described with Todd Croft was…alarming.

The villa is gone.

Ayers can't help but wonder what this means for Baker. Obviously, if there's no place for him to live, then he's going back to Houston.

Ayers feels a deep, crushing disappointment, worse even than her pain about the broken engagement. Baker will leave—if he even arrived in the first place. And what about Cash? Will he leave too?

Ayers brings her mind back to the present. "So Irene is living with you guys?" she says. "For how long?"

"Until she gets back on her feet," Maia says. She lowers her voice. "I think Gramps is happy. He cut my grounding down to a week."

"Won't Irene go back to Iowa?"

"She can't," Maia says. "The FBI took that house too."

"You're kidding."

"I told you, there's been drama."

"What about Cash?" Ayers says. Because *Treasure Island* is out of commission, Ayers hasn't spoken to Cash since Tuesday night. "Is he staying with you guys?"

"He's living with Tilda," Maia says.

Living with Tilda? Ayers knew they were kind of seeing each other; they'd been together the afternoon that Mick proposed at Christmas Cove. That was five days ago. Now they're living together? "Wow," Ayers says. The toast won't settle in her stomach; she feels like it's on a seesaw. Is it coming up or staying down? "Where's Baker?"

"He and Floyd are at the Westin," Maia says. "I'm actually headed there in a little while to watch Floyd while Baker looks at some rentals."

"You are?" Ayers says. She feels a tiny arrow of optimism shoot through her, though she's too lethargic to even smile. "So they're staying?"

"Yes, they're staying. Floyd starts at Gifft Hill on Monday," Maia says. "Wait until I tell everyone he's my nephew."

Oh, boy, Ayers thinks. *The Gifft Hill mothers will have a field day with that.* "Have fun," Ayers says. "I love you; you're my number-one girl. Let's hang out next week."

"We can..." Maia says. "But I might be busy with my friends or babysitting for Floyd."

"Right," Ayers says. "Only if you can fit me in."

"I'll have my people call your people," Maia says, and she hangs up.

Baker is staying! For a second, Ayers's happiness is greater than the dread that she feels about the rest of the story—the lost villa, the FBI, Russ's illegal business dealings.

She should tell someone about the journals; it feels like they're smoldering beneath her. But...they're personal, private. Rosie wouldn't want anyone to see them, of that Ayers is certain. Ayers plans to give them to Maia when she gets older.

The FBI knows Russ was laundering money, so the journals

wouldn't offer anything new. But what about the mentions of Todd Croft? *Was* there foul play with the helicopter?

Argh! Ayers doesn't want to hand the journals over. It's her own private line of communication with Rosie. And if Huck read them, or, worse, *Irene* read them—well, that wouldn't be good. And yet to *hide* them... no, Ayers has to show someone.

She'll show Huck. Or Baker? No, Huck.

I'm sorry, Rosie, Ayers thinks—and then she races to the bathroom to throw up.

CASH

I'm sure you understand my concerns," Granger Payne says.

Before Cash can respond, Granger dives into the T-shaped pool and powers out six laps. Then he lifts himself out of the pool, triceps flexing, and dries his face with one of the fluffy white Turkish towels. Over the past week, Cash has become very familiar with all the luxuries on offer here at Tilda's parents' house in Peter Bay.

Which is precisely Granger's point.

"I do indeed, sir," Cash says. He's relieved that the *Treasure Island* is back up and running and that he's dressed for work. Every day for the past few days, while the boat was being repaired, Cash woke up late with Tilda, and over banana pancakes and mango smoothies, they picked a beach or a trail or both to hike. On Tilda's day off, the two of them climbed into Tilda's Range Rover and drove out to Hansen Bay in the East End. They rented a kayak and spent the entire afternoon drinking grapefruit margaritas and eating the sublime tacos—rum rib with chipotle slaw, green chicken curry—at the floating-barge restaurant Lime Out. Lime Out had bar seats attached to the barge, which Cash and Tilda sat in before claiming a floating table. They reclined on inflatable chaises, faces to the sun, drinks in hand, toasting the good life, which they were undeniably enjoying. Cash had to actively fight off encroaching guilt. His family had just undergone a huge financial crisis and what was Cash doing? Drinking cocktails that his brand-new girlfriend was paying for with her black American Express card.

Granger wraps the towel around his waist. He's about Cash's size, five nine or so, and is in extremely good physical shape, possibly even better shape than Cash, and he's fifty-six years old. The villa has a full gym with two Peloton bikes; Granger and Tilda's mother, Lauren, get up at five thirty every morning to ride together, then Granger does his weight regimen, then he swims.

"Want some green juice?" Granger asks Cash. On the counter of the outdoor kitchen is a carafe of liquid the color of shamrocks. It was most likely put there by Virgie, the housekeeper, who moves around the villa with the stealth of a ninja and who, this past week, has refused to let Cash do so much as take his own dishes to the sink.

Guilt—his mother; Baker; Floyd. If they knew how Cash was living, what would they think? "Sure," Cash says. He accepts a glass of green juice, takes a sip, and immediately wants to spit it out. It's liquefied kale, he suspects, with maybe a thin slice of apple or one green grape thrown in.

"Lauren and I are very protective where Tilda is concerned," Granger says. "She tends to show all her cards. She doesn't have much of a poker face, I'm afraid." Granger gulps down the entire glass of juice and Cash shivers just watching; he's unsure he can manage even one more sip. "It's clear how much she likes you. She says you have other places you can go, so it's not like you're using her to avoid being homeless."

"Right," Cash says quickly. "That's right, sir."

"Please, call me Granger."

"Granger, sir," Cash says. He can't help it; the *sir* comes automatically. Granger Payne is a *sir* as surely as Johnny Cash or Muhammad Ali would be a *sir*. "I could move in with my mother or my brother. And I'll do that if it makes you more comfortable." Here, Cash holds Granger's gaze, willing the older man not to call his bluff. Irene is presently living in Maia's bedroom at Huck's house, and Baker is still at the Westin hemorrhaging five hundred dollars a night while he looks for an affordable year-round rental. Cash told Baker that if he found something big enough, Cash would happily move in, share the rent, provide child care for Floyd.

"Okay," Baker said. "But you'd better have a backup plan."

Cash had initially considered asking Ayers if he could take over her lease, since she had gotten engaged to Mick and would likely move in with him. He wasn't sure how much she paid but if she could afford it, then he could, right? They worked at the same place. But Ayers had a second, very lucrative job waiting tables at La Tapa. Cash would likely need to get a second job as well. He should be looking now instead of goofing off every day with Tilda.

The plan of taking over Ayers's place vanished when Tilda came home from La Tapa with the news that Ayers was no longer engaged. She had given the ring back to Mick.

"Stay here for the time being, please," Granger says. "I have to admit, I like the idea of having another man around. Tilda and her mother tend to gang up on me. I could use some support."

"Thank you, sir," Cash says. He needs to excuse himself so Tilda can drive him to work. He's dependent on her for everything, and she has been a total rock star, accommodating him and never making him feel bad. *I have more than enough privilege for both of us.*

"Tilda tells me you used to be in the outdoor-supply business in Colorado," Granger says. "What happened?"

"Ah," Cash says. He has any number of responses ready: *I got tired of the cold, the lack of oxygen, the stoner teenagers who worked for me stealing from the register.* But he suspects that Granger Payne has run a background check on him and maybe also investigated his credit. "I blew it. My father bought me the stores and expected me to know how to run them. But I didn't learn how to manage them properly until it was too late. I got behind with the bank and they went under. It was quite a learning experience."

"I'm happy to hear you learned something," Granger says. "Because I have an exciting business proposition on the horizon, and Tilda is dead set on having you be a part of it. Sweat equity, boots-on-the-ground type of stuff. You're good with people, I can see that, and you seem to have personal integrity. Another man might have lied to me about the stores or tried to blame the failure on someone else."

Cash nods. Integrity he has. It's everything else he's lacking.

"How well do you handle unexpected setbacks?" Granger asks.

"Um..." Cash says. "Pretty well. I mean, yeah, my life has been one unexpected setback after another recently, but I'm still standing. So I'd say I can deal with just about whatever life throws at me."

"Good," Granger says. "Because although Lauren and I are happy to welcome you with open arms, your dog has to go."

Cash feels like Granger has just taken him into a headlock and is squeezing his windpipe. "Winnie?" he squeaks.

"Winnie," Granger says. "Lauren and I are far too peripatetic to have pets, and the way she decorated the house—"

"In white," Cash says. "Right, I get it." He swallows. "We've kept Winnie mostly outside..."

"'Mostly outside' won't cut it with my wife," Granger says. "And it's not fair to the dog. So best to find another place for her to wait out this time of transition you're in."

"Yes, sir," Cash says. He's saved from breaking down in tears in front of Granger when Tilda honks the horn of the Range Rover. "Steele, let's go!" she calls out.

"Exactly like her mother," Granger says. He claps Cash on the arm. "All right, Cashman, glad we understand each other."

On the steep, twisting drive from Peter Bay to town, Tilda says, "How was the inquisition?"

"Most of it was okay. But—"

"But it was a complete ambush," Tilda says. "I know. I'm sorry. They normally text or call to let me know they're coming so I can go to Starfish and get their soy milk or whatever. This is highly unusual. I think after I told them you were staying here, they wanted to catch us unawares."

They succeeded, Cash thinks. The night before, Tilda got home from La Tapa bearing goodies from the kitchen in to-go boxes—a gorgonzola Caesar, pork belly, and wood-grilled sirloin. They lit the candles on the patio table; Tilda opened a good bottle of cabernet from Granger's wine collection—the Lail 2016 Blueprint—and after she tasted it, she winked at Cash and said, "Notes of fire coral, DEET, and the Tide Pod challenge."

"Good one!" Cash said. Nonsensical wine descriptions had become a verbal tic of Tilda's ex, Skip, the bartender at La Tapa, and Tilda and Cash couldn't stop themselves from riffing on it.

They had just picked up their forks to dig in when they heard voices, and Cash, for one panicked moment, feared another FBI raid—were they coming for *him?*—but then Tilda scooted back her chair and said, "Well, hello, parents!"

"Don't you two look cozy," Lauren Payne said. She was tall with a slender yoga physique like Tilda, but while Tilda sported a pixie cut, Lauren had long golden-brown hair that she'd pulled up in a ponytail. She wore a white linen dress and a pair of leopard-print wedge sandals. She was...pretty. And looked way younger than Cash had expected.

Granger followed close on Lauren's heels. He wore a tan suit, white shirt, and no tie; he had his hair slicked back, and reading glasses were perched on top of his head. His handshake was brutal, but somehow Cash had anticipated this and gave his firmest effort, complete with eye contact and smile. On the inside, however, Cash felt his confidence evaporate. Her parents were here. What would they think about Cash moving in? Did they know what had happened to his father? His mother? The optics weren't great; Cash realized this. His father, now dead, had been revealed to have a second family hidden down here, and his sketchy—indeed *illegal*—business practices had been uncovered. His mother was newly destitute and worked on a fishing boat.

It wasn't exactly the platinum pedigree that the elder Paynes no doubt wanted for the romantic partner of their only child.

However, the only thing Tilda's parents had objected to in that moment was her opening the 2016 Blueprint. Granger fetched two balloon goblets from the crystal cabinet (Tilda and Cash were drinking the wine out of regular tumblers) and poured wine for himself and Lauren, then they retreated to the master wing, which was so far from Tilda's wing that it was like a separate house.

When Cash asked how much Tilda's parents knew about his situation, she said, "I tell my mother everything and she tells my dad."

"And do they…care?"

"Granger will probably have questions in the morning," Tilda said.

But neither Tilda nor Cash had thought about the dog.

"So *most* of it was okay," Tilda says now. "But not all of it?"

Cash thinks back to the first time Tilda brought him to the Peter Bay villa. Tilda and Cash were caring for Tilda's very drunk friend Max, and Cash had noticed the villa's terrifyingly white furnishings because he was afraid Max might vomit on them. And then later, at dinner, Tilda told Cash she volunteered to walk dogs at the shelter because *her parents wouldn't let her get a dog of her own.*

But Tilda hadn't balked for even one second about Cash bringing Winnie with him, though she did suggest Winnie stay only in Tilda's wing of the house. (The line about Winnie living mostly outside was a lie.) And Virgie, the housekeeper, had seemed not only unbothered by Winnie but downright delighted by her. She had even brought Winnie treats!

"Your dad told me Winnie has to go," Cash says.

They have reached the parking lot across from Mongoose Junction. Tilda pulls in. "I was afraid of that."

"I'm not sure what to do," Cash says.

"Your mom?" Tilda says. "Baker?"

"Maybe?" Cash says. Baker is at a hotel, so the answer is no, or not yet. His mother…argh. She loves Winnie, but she's a guest herself, just like Cash. He manufactures a smile. "I'll figure something out. Can you come pick me up at four? If not, I'll hitch."

"If you think I'm going to let someone else pick you up, you're crazy," she says, and she leans over for a kiss.

"Thank you," Cash says.

"You're not allowed to thank me."

"I know, but…I want you to know that I'm grateful. The timing on all of this was so…bad. Our relationship is still so new and you've done so much."

"All I've really done is save you from pining after Ayers," Tilda says. "I told my mother you used to have a crush on her."

"You did not," Cash says. "Why did you do that? It wasn't even a thing."

"It *was* a thing," Tilda says. "But it's over now."

"Over before it began," Cash says. "Please don't tell me you're worried about Ayers."

"She's newly single," Tilda says, shrugging. "And you're with her every day."

Cash takes Tilda's face in his hands. He did have quite an intense crush on Ayers when he first got down here—he and Baker both did—but she ended up with Mick, and Cash's feelings for her vanished as quickly as they'd appeared. He can still see she's attractive, but all he feels for her is a brotherly fondness.

"I like *you,*" Cash says. He looks into Tilda's hazel eyes. She's so young, and yet so self-possessed and clearheaded and *unspoiled* despite her parents' wealth.

"You'd better."

"I do."

"I feel bad about Winnie," Tilda says. "But my parents will not be moved on the topic of a dog. I'm so sorry." She kisses him again. "See you at four."

* * *

What is he going to do about Winnie? What is he going to *do?* He feels unreasonably angry at Tilda's parents. Winnie is such a good dog—the best of dogs. She's more human than dog. They would realize that if they took the time to get to know her.

My parents will not be moved on the topic of a dog.

It's their villa, they make the rules, and they aren't bad people just because they aren't dog people. What Cash is angry about is that he has no power. He's at the mercy of others.

Peripatetic. Cash Googles it: "Of or relating to traveling or moving frequently; in particular, working or based in various places for short periods. Synonyms: *nomadic, itinerant.*"

Fortunately or unfortunately, there's no time to ruminate on the situation with Winnie. *Treasure Island* has a completely full charter today since the boat has been out of commission for over a week, and the first person Cash sees is the captain, James, who does not look happy.

James is six foot six, West Indian, and though he's only a little older than Cash, Cash thinks of him as a *sir.*

It's seven thirty on the dot, so being late isn't the issue, though there's already a line of passengers waiting to check in, including a group of forty-something women who, Cash can tell, are ready for a good time. He thinks back to the charter when he babysat Tilda's drunk friend Max and decides then and there that he's not opening the bar until the snorkeling part of their trip is over.

"Hey, bruh," James says and he shakes Cash's hand. "Ayers isn't coming. She called in sick."

"Called in sick?"

"Yeah, bruh, so you're on your own today." James glances over at the group of women, who are making no secret of checking out James and Cash. "Good luck."

Cash can't believe Ayers called in sick on their first day back. She had all of last week to be sick. He wonders if maybe "sick" has something to do with her broken engagement. Maybe she's depressed? Should Cash be worried? He'll text her later. Right now, he has to check in twenty-seven people, record their passport information (since they're heading to the British Virgin Islands), and collect their money. Mr. and Mrs. Bellhorn from Coral Gables would like to talk to Cash about getting a partial refund since the boat's mechanical issues pushed this trip back five days, which was quite an inconvenience.

The phrase *partial refund* spreads like a virus. Everyone in line starts to repeat it because every single person—except for the group of women, who are from Wichita, Kansas—was originally scheduled to come on a different day.

Cash nearly makes a stern announcement that he isn't the person who handles refunds and if they want to explore that possibility, they need to call the office, but then he realizes that without Ayers, he has an opportunity to shine—and by *shine* he means "make some serious tip money." In an instant, his attitude changes. He's not going to be grouchy Cash who has been left to do the paperwork and make the breakfast and wash the snorkel equipment and check the lines and make sure no one goes overboard and give the historical and ecological details of the Virgin Islands by himself. He is going to be warm, funny, solicitous, helpful Cash. He is going to go out of his way to ensure this is the best charter these twenty-seven people have ever been on.

"This is the number for the main office," Cash says, sliding Mr. and Mrs. Bellhorn a card. "You want to ask for Whitney. I certainly hope she offers you a partial refund, though of course I can't guarantee it. I'm very sorry about the inconvenience. I'm a planner myself and I do appreciate your patience."

Cash smiles. The Bellhorns smile back.

Okay, then. Next!

Somehow, Cash gets it done—everyone present, documented, paid up, and on board enjoying the fruit platter and the coconut-banana bread. People are applying sunscreen. Cash puts on Kenny Chesney's "Get Along." The ladies from Wichita belt out, *"We ain't perfect but we try!"* That's Cash's motto today as well. No matter that he's flying solo, no matter that he's been on this job only a few weeks, no matter that his father is dead and his mother broke and his dog homeless. He's in the Caribbean; the turquoise water is smooth, and the emerald-green islands create an artistic landscape. He doesn't want to leave St. John, ever. He needs to find someone to take Winnie, at least for a while. He needs to find a way to make his life work.

Granger has a business proposition "on the horizon" that Tilda wants Cash involved in. Yes, Tilda has been talking ambitiously about opening a business—adventure ecotourism, which would be right in Cash's wheelhouse. Boots on the ground, sweat equity. He doesn't have to front any money; he just has to show up. Cash wishes that *on the horizon* meant next week or even tomorrow.

Cash is the only crew member and James thinks the planned itinerary—a trip to the Baths, snorkeling at the Indians, and then two hours of merrymaking on Jost Van Dyke—will be too much for Cash to handle alone. Instead, James says, they're going to Smuggler's Cove, on the western tip of Tortola, followed by stops at Sandy Spit and Willy T's.

"Oh, man," Cash says. "Are you sure about that? I've never been to any of those places."

"They'll snorkel first thing in Smuggler's Cove," James says. "There's a beautiful beach and they can have lunch at Nigel's. Then back on the boat to Sandy Spit. Then Willy T's for an hour, then home." James starts the engine. "Trust me."

What choice does Cash have?

He's afraid the passengers will rise up in protest. Not only have many of them had this trip rescheduled, but now they're not even going where they were supposed to go. They aren't going to the Baths on Virgin Gorda, which is an experience like no other, and they aren't going to the world-famous Soggy Dollar.

He expects a mutiny.

But then he gets an idea.

He heads up to the top deck where the nine women from Wichita are sitting. Midwesterners are *nice,* they're *helpful*—Cash knows this because he is one. When Cash checked the women in—Christine, Stephanie, Kelly, Amy, Jennifer P., Jennifer A., Michelle, Tracy, and Donna—he learned that it was Donna's fiftieth birthday. Over their bathing suits, the women all wore navy T-shirts that read DONNA, DO YOU WANNA?, which Christine told him was a private joke.

"Ladies," Cash says. "I need a favor."

He tells them what the favor is and they fall all over themselves assuring him that they've got his back. He's so cute, he's so hot, they say, and all they want in return are some pictures with him for their Instagrams and a promise that he'll hold Donna's hand as she jumps off the Willy T. (Michelle read on Tripadvisor that jumping off the Willy T is a bucket-list item, which is news to Cash.)

"Yes, I will, I got you," Cash says. "Thank you, ladies."

Cash gets ready to announce the change of itinerary over the microphone; it's his first time wearing the headset, and he has to admit, he kind of likes the authority. "The captain is allowing us a rare and exciting opportunity today, ladies and gentlemen," Cash says. "We're heading over to Smuggler's Cove on Tortola, where we will snorkel in the crystal-clear water and then you'll have ample time to enjoy the secluded white sand beach. If you'd like lunch and cocktails, you can visit Nigel's Boom Boom for a taste of the authentic Caribbean. When we leave Smuggler's Cove, we'll swing by Sandy Spit for a terrific photo op. We'll end our day at the world-famous Willy T's, a decommissioned freighter that has been reimagined as a beach-bar mecca. How does that sound to everyone?"

From the top deck comes the sound of ecstatic screaming and everyone looks up to see Donna, Christine, and company jumping up and down as though they've just been picked as contestants on *The Price Is Right.* The other passengers do high fives and cheer like they can't believe their good fortune.

Cash relaxes. He's good at this.

James is right; this itinerary is extremely easy for Cash to manage, even alone. They arrive in Smuggler's Cove in just half an hour. The beach is a crescent of white sand fringed by palms, and it's deserted, as though it has been ordered up and is waiting just for them. James asks Cash to drop the anchor and then he runs through the snorkel spiel. *Defog your mask with this simple solution of dish soap and water; stay away from fire coral and the spiny black sea urchins, nothing else in these waters will hurt you.*

"And after you finish your snorkel," Cash says, "we'll open the bar."

Cheers. Zac Brown sings "Chicken Fried." *There's no dollar sign on a peace of mind, this I've come to know.*

The day unfolds without a hitch. Cash joins his new lady friends from Wichita at Nigel's Boom Boom, where Nigel himself makes the best hot dog with griddled onions Cash has ever tasted. The ladies ask him questions that he avoids answering in detail, but they're into Nigel's rum punch, so they don't really notice. *My first winter in St. John, I came down here to be with my mother after my father died* (the ladies *love* this; he's so sensitive, such a devoted son). *I used to be a ski instructor in Breckenridge, then I lived in Denver for a while, but I've traded in my ski boots for flip-flops, my poles and goggles for a mask and snorkel, and I'm staying here. Yes, I have a girlfriend, Tilda, the relationship is pretty much brand-new.*

"Well," Amy says, "I hope she knows how lucky she is!"

They leave Smuggler's Cove and head to Sandy Spit, which is half an acre of pure white sand with light foliage, including a couple of palms, making it look like a Corona ad. Everyone jumps off the boat to swim ashore, and Cash takes pictures with his ladies for their Instagrams.

Then it's off to the Willy T, properly the William Thornton, the floating bar named for an infamous nineteenth-century pirate. They tie up, and the nine ladies head directly upstairs to the bar and order the shot ski, something Cash is only too familiar with from the bars in Breckenridge. The "ski" has four holes for four shot glasses and on the count of three, four of the ladies lift the ski to their mouths and do the shots in unison. Because there are only four shots per ski, this has to be repeated a number of times so the other passengers from the *Treasure Island*—

including the inconvenienced Mr. and Mrs. Bellhorn—can take turns as well.

The ladies want Cash to do the shot ski—it's a bar trick that never gets old—but no, sorry, he says, he's on the clock. He can, however, fulfill his promise to step out onto the jumping platform, twelve feet above the water's surface, and jump off while holding Donna's hand. Cash won't lie; he's a little nervous, even though he'd think nothing of a ski jump this steep.

He checks in with the birthday girl when they're standing on the platform. "Donna, do you wanna?" he asks, thinking he's the epitome of wit, but she doesn't answer, just flings herself forward, and Cash has no choice but to follow.

Shot skis, jumping from high ledges—what could go wrong? Nothing, as it turns out. It's exhilarating. Everyone loves it, everyone's happy. The day is a resounding success.

It's only after Cash has mixed up the last batch of painkillers and the charter is on the way home that he thinks to text Ayers.

Missed you today, he says. This is true. Today went well but it would have been easier and more fun with Ayers. You okay?

A couple of seconds later, she sends the thumbs-up emoji, which tells him nothing but the bare minimum: she's alive. Cash is debating whether or not to ask a follow-up question—emoji answers sort of discourage longer text exchanges—when she texts again.

I'm taking a leave of absence from the boat.

What? he writes. Why?

I heard about your mom, she says. How're you doing?

Cash feels like sending back a thumbs-up emoji as a little *Screw you,* because what does she mean, she's taking a leave of absence from the boat? But what he says is I'm living up at Tilda's but today her parents said Winnie has to go so I'm scrambling.

There's a pause. Then three dots. Then: I'll take Winnie if you want?

Cash quickly checks on everyone. They're happy, the sun has mellowed, Jimmy Buffett is singing "Nautical Wheelers."

If you wouldn't mind for a few weeks? I would be so grateful.

Happy to, Ayers says. I'll pick you up at the boat and we can go get her.

Ahh! Cash feels an overwhelming sense of relief. Ayers will take Winnie; Winnie is crazy about Ayers, she's going to think she's died and gone to heaven. This is a good solution, much better than asking the housekeeper, Virgie, to take the dog home, which was Cash's only other idea.

Cash texts Tilda: I don't need a ride, Ayers will bring me to Peter Bay, she's going to take Winnie.

Tilda texts back: Kk. There is no heart-eyes emoji, her signature signoff, which is odd.

Cash texts, Are you okay? He thinks about what Tilda said about Ayers that morning: *She's newly single*. But come on, Tilda can't be *that* sensitive. And the bald fact remains that Cash needs someone to take Winnie.

Tilda texts, I'm fine. I have a meeting anyway. I was going to tell you to hitch.

Okay...should Cash be offended? Because he's feeling a little offended. A meeting with whom?

No time to wonder because the boat is pulling in. And yes indeedy, the tip jar is filling up.

* * *

Cash is standing in front of Mongoose Junction three hundred and ten dollars richer when Ayers arrives in her little green pickup.

"Hop in," she says. She really does look sick—pale, washed out, heavy-lidded. She's wearing cotton sleep shorts and a St. John Concrete T-shirt (STAY LEFT, POUR RIGHT), and her curly blond hair is a mess. Not a sexy mess, just a mess.

"I hope whatever you have isn't contagious," Cash says, getting in.

She hits the gas.

"So . . . you broke things off with Mick?" Ayers nods but doesn't offer anything else. Fine, she doesn't owe him an explanation. "How did you know about my mom?"

"Maia told me."

"Oh, right," Cash says. He hates to be a talker but he feels like there's something going on. "Have you seen Baker?"

"He called once but I didn't pick up," Ayers says. "I'm not feeling great and I need some time."

"Right, right," Cash says. He will stop talking even though he wants to brag about how smoothly the charter went.

They swoop and dive around and over the hills—past Caneel, past Oppenheimer and Jumbie, past everyone packing up from a day spent at Trunk Bay—and then begin the climb up to Peter Bay. Cash speaks only to direct Ayers to the correct house. They careen down Tilda's driveway, and when Ayers stops, Cash hops out. "I'll go get Winnie, her food, her bowl, her leashes. Be right back."

He returns with Winnie in tow and there's a bit of a long goodbye because although Winnie is going to the best possible home, Cash is still going to miss her like crazy. "I'll come see her tomorrow after work," he says. "I can't thank you enough."

"You don't have to thank me," Ayers says. She sighs, and if

Cash isn't mistaken, her eyes glaze over like she might cry. "The more the merrier."

The more the merrier? Cash thinks. He wonders if maybe Mick has left Ayers with his dog—that would be weird—and then he wonders if maybe Ayers plans on letting Baker and Floyd move in with her.

"Are you... do you have company?" Cash asks.

"Kind of," Ayers says. "I'm pregnant."

MAIA

Her grounding lasts six days instead of two weeks, but even so, Maia misses the first meeting at the new clubhouse. She arrives at the second meeting early, by herself; everyone else is getting a ride but because Huck and Irene have tripled up on their charters, Maia has to take the bus and then hike. The new clubhouse is *very* inconveniently located in the middle of nowhere—but that's the point. It's Par Force, the great house of the Reef Bay plantation, and it can be accessed only by a spur of the Reef Bay Trail. Maia hikes down the trail, and when the three tourists ahead of her veer to the right to see the petroglyphs, Maia goes left up a steep hill that switchbacks up an even steeper hill. Par Force is engulfed in vines and coral creeper; the brick walls and stone columns are barely visible. There's a low hum surrounding the house that sounds like some kind of electrical force field. It's bees, Maia realizes, feasting on the pretty pink flowers of the creeper. Maia heads up the staircase to the main entryway. Unlike most of the ruins of houses on the island, this one still looks like a house. It has arches and columns and window openings, and the walls and roof are still mostly there.

But—Maia's not gonna lie—it's spooky, even during the daytime, and she wishes someone else were here. They all agreed they would meet at two thirty on Saturday; earlier today, Bright had basketball practice, Colton guitar lessons, and Shane an orthodontist appointment over on St. Thomas. Joanie is getting a ride from her mom, who's happy Joanie and her friends are "finally taking an interest in hiking."

Maia tries to text Joanie to ask if she's OTW, but she has no signal. In her backpack, she has three bottles of water, a peanut butter and jelly sandwich, and a banana, so she won't die, but the idea of hanging out here alone much longer doesn't appeal. Maia's mother, Rosie, had brought her to Par Force only the year before. *I can't believe I've never shown you this place,* she said. Then, once they were inside: *I probably avoided it because it's haunted.*

Now that Rosie is dead, ghosts aren't as scary as they used to be. Maia would welcome a visit from Rosie right now, in any form. Because where is everyone? She worries that this is some kind of prank, that while she was grounded, the rest of the group decided to trick her into going alone. Or maybe at the first meeting, they picked a different clubhouse location—Annaberg or Catherineberg, somewhere easier to get to—and forgot to tell Maia. Maia scrolls back through her texts with Joanie. Meet you at the place. Leaving for the place now.

Snap, Maia thinks. What if *the place* Joanie is talking about isn't *this* place?

But then Maia hears voices. She pokes her head through one of the crumbling stone window openings to see Joanie, Colton, and some girl Maia doesn't recognize all climbing up the hill together.

"Hey," Maia says. She's relieved to see her friends but she wishes it were Shane. Shane is a year older than Maia and he goes to the Antilles School; he's her crush, and recently he's become more than just a crush. They have held hands on three separate occasions. Joanie has a crush on Colton, but Colton likes Joanie only as a friend. For now. Both Maia and Joanie are hoping the clubhouse—where they're going to hang out without any adults watching them—will change this.

"Maia!" Joanie cries out. She runs up the stairs and gives Maia a hug, which seems a little strange since they just saw each other at school the day before, then gives Maia's hand an extra-hard squeeze. It's a message of some sort about this unknown girl. Friend or foe?

Colton and the girl follow.

Maia says, "Hey, I'm Maia." The girl has milky-white skin, long red hair, and a pointy nose. She's wearing white shorts and a regular pair of beach flip-flops that show off her green-polished toenails and silver toe rings. How did she hike all the way here in flip-flops?

"I'm Lillibet," she says, shrugging. She peers around the dank inside of Par Force. "I'm in seventh; I go to Antilles. Is Shane here?"

"Not yet," Maia says. "He had the ortho—"

"Yeah, I know, but he said he'd be here waiting."

"You know who Lillibet's sister is, right, Maia?" Colton says. "Dusty. Dusty Beck."

Maia tries to hide her surprise. Dusty Beck is a bona fide St. Thomas celebrity. Maia—along with twelve million other people—follows Dusty on Instagram. Dusty was on the cover of last year's *Sports Illustrated* swimsuit issue, and Shane has a copy that she signed; he'd said he got it from "a kid in my class." Which must have been the sister, Lillibet. What is she doing here?

"Cool," Maia says. Joanie, behind Lillibet, has her arms locked across her chest and is rolling her eyes. Not cool with Joanie. Okay, then, not cool with Maia either. "Shane invited you?" Maia asks.

"Hey!"

They all turn to see Shane and Bright Whittaker racing up the hill. Maia tries to harden her facial expression, form it into some kind of shell. They created this club the night they met on the beach in Frank Bay because Colton was upset about his parents' divorce. Colton is staying on St. John with his mom, but his dad is moving back to the States—to North Carolina, the Outer Banks—and Colton will see him only half the summer and at Christmas. As they were talking to Colton that night, trying to make him feel better, it came out that they all had stuff to deal with at home and no one to talk to about it. (That was really true for Maia—her mother had died and a new family had appeared out of nowhere!) So they'd decided to form a club and have meetings in person, not online, which felt old-fashioned in a cool way. They weren't allowed to discuss club business on their phones. They weren't allowed to take any pictures or post about the club. It would be a secret society, like the kind they had at Harvard and Yale.

Maia didn't realize they were allowed to invite outsiders to join. She'd thought it was supposed to be just them—Maia, Shane, Joanie, Colton, and Bright. But five is an odd number, so Maia supposes adding another girl makes sense. She had sort of figured they would discuss it first and vote. But this isn't Congress or Parliament; it's a bunch of middle-school kids in the Virgin Islands.

Maia decides to give Lillibet the benefit of the doubt. Maybe Shane invited her for a reason—maybe her sister the model is addicted to drugs, or maybe Lillibet is being bullied at school, or maybe Lillibet's parents ignore her because Dusty is so pretty and famous.

"Shane!" Lillibet screams. She goes flying down the steps in her stupid flip-flops, and forget the benefit of the doubt—Maia wishes for her to fall flat on her face. But she doesn't. She goes up to Shane and says, "Let me see."

Shane smiles. His braces are off.

Whaaaa? Maia thinks. She knew Shane had the orthodontist but she didn't know he was getting his braces off. Unfair! He looks hotter now than he did before by, like, a *lot*.

Lillibet squeals and gives Shane a side hug and Shane leans into her.

They all head deeper into Par Force and wander through different rooms until they come to what must have been the kitchen—there's a giant fireplace opening. There are a bunch of piles of bricks that they can sit on.

Shane turns to Maia. "Are you surprised the braces are off? What do you think?"

She shrugs. She isn't going to fawn all over him like Lillibet.

Lillibet is touching the columns, poking her head through the window openings. "This place is sublime," she says. "What's it doing here?"

"This was the main living quarters of the family who owned the sugarcane plantation," Maia says. She gives an ironic laugh. "So two hundred years ago, someone who looked like me would have been working in this kitchen as a slave."

Everyone is quiet. Maia has made her friends uncomfortable, but oh, well—the history of the Virgin Islands is uncomfortable.

Lillibet says, "Maybe we should meet somewhere else? Do you want to pick a different place, Maia?" Her voice is concerned without being patronizing, and the benefit of the doubt resurfaces. Is Lillibet *nice?*

"It doesn't bother me," Maia says. "My mom brought me here." She hopes that mentioning Rosie will lead them into the kind of soulful conversation that they had on Frank Bay, but nobody is paying attention to Maia except Lillibet.

"Shane told me that your mother was killed in that helicopter crash on New Year's," Lillibet says. "I felt so bad for you. And honestly, you're kind of famous at Antilles now. I knew Shane was your friend, so I asked to meet you."

Lillibet is here because of Maia? This *sounds* like a compliment, but it also makes Maia feel like a circus sideshow. *Famous* at Antilles? Because she tragically lost her mother?

"It's too bad we can't meet at the villa in Little Cinnamon," Shane says. He turns to Lillibet. "Maia's dad...it *was* your dad, right? Your real dad that nobody knew about? Yeah, he was really rich and owned this huge villa with a two-story pool. Maia gets to hang out there whenever she wants."

"A two-story pool?" Lillibet says.

Maia feels like her heart is being stung by a swarm of bees. She has confided a lot to Shane, but the things she told him were private, and here he is, telling everyone.

Maia shrugs. She isn't about to admit that the villa has been seized by the FBI. She can't afford to be any more "famous" at Antilles than she already is.

Colton and Bright are watching a YouTube video of surfing in Portugal on Bright's phone, and Joanie joins them. Maia nearly says, *I thought we said no phones,* but she doesn't want to sound like a teacher or a parent.

"I have no service," Maia says—to no one, because Shane is now telling Lillibet the gory details of getting his braces off. Maia could join in and say, *That sounds like medieval torture,* but she knows three's a crowd. She takes a minute to study Shane and Lillibet together. They're just two kids talking, right? Or does Shane *like* Lillibet? They move on to the topic of their math teacher, then to something that happened at morning meeting the day before, and then Shane relates all the near-death experiences he's had taking the shuttle to Antilles from the Red Hook ferry. Maia smiles to herself, pretending to be deep in thought. If Lillibet is here because she wanted to meet Maia, then why is she talking only to Shane? Maia doesn't go to Antilles. She wants to, but her mother said not until ninth grade.

Maia wonders if there will be enough money to pay for Antilles, or college—Irene had said she'd handle it, since Russ was gone, but now Irene has no money. What if Huck hasn't saved enough and Maia can't go to college in the States like she wants to?

She feels like demanding everyone's attention so she can bring up this monumental issue—her entire future hangs in the balance—but looking around, she realizes no one will care. Colton and Bright are engrossed in the video; Joanie is shamelessly hanging over Colton's shoulder (later, Maia will suggest Joanie stop being so obvious). Lillibet and Shane are talking, and maybe they've inched closer together, maybe Lillibet is flipping her hair for Shane's benefit.

Here is the group the five of them created because they had no one to talk to about the important stuff, and Maia still has no one to talk to about the important stuff.

She sits unnoticed for five minutes, ten—then the boys' interest in the video ends and Colton says, "This clubhouse sucks. There's nothing to do."

Maia can't help herself. "We were supposed to *talk,*" she says. "Remember?" *Remember crying on the beach about your parents and remember who was there to listen?*

Lillibet checks her phone. "I've got to go," she says. "My dad's coming to get me in our boat in twenty minutes and I have to get down to the beach." She looks at Shane. "Do you want a ride back to Chocolate Hole? It's on our way."

Shane raises his eyebrows. He seems like a different person without his braces. Older. Out of Maia's league.

"Can you take..." he starts, casting his eyes around.

"I live in Coral Bay," Joanie says. "Wrong direction."

"It should probably be just you," Lillibet says. "My dad knows you."

Say no, Maia thinks. She and Shane can hike back up to the Centerline together. She'll share her sandwich with him, her banana. They can help each other up the steep parts. It's frightening how bad she wants this.

"Okay," Shane says. He stands up and gives the rest of them a wave. His eyes linger on Maia and she looks down into her lap. She knows it's unreasonable to expect Shane to turn down a boat ride home. It's a ten-minute walk downhill to the beach—Lillibet will be fine in her flip-flops after all—and then he'll be back in Chocolate Hole ten minutes after that. But still, it feels like Shane is choosing Lillibet over Maia.

There are goodbyes but they don't pick another day and time to meet. Shane and Lillibet race each other down the trail, with Lillibet, predictably, shrieking. Maia's insides have become crumbling ruins. Ahhh—but just like Par Force, she has a sturdy foundation. It's a nice thought that doesn't make her feel any better.

"I'm leaving too," Maia announces.

"Well, wait for us," Joanie says.

"Yeah," Bright says, and he tugs on Maia's ponytail. "Wait for us."

Maia backhands Bright against the chest. She dislikes anyone touching her hair. Bright grabs her arm and pokes her in the ribs, then tries to tickle her. She shoos him away.

"My mom can probably give you a ride home," Bright says to Maia. "It's not that far."

Bright lives on Gifft Hill, across from the school. It's not that far but it's not close either. Bright probably has a crush on her. He used to like Posie Alvarez, but that's over. Maia thinks about how easy it would be if she could just transfer the feelings she has for Shane to Bright. Bright is in her grade and he goes to Gifft Hill. He's tall and he's good at sports and his parents own a rental-car company, which is cool because he gets driven around in all these brand-new Jeeps in juicy colors. But Maia likes Bright only as a friend. Probably because she knows him too well; she remembers when he threw up during library time in second grade.

Colton and Bright run up ahead, leaving Maia and Joanie to eat their dust.

"Hey, wait up!" Joanie says. "Cole!"

Her mother was right, Maia thinks. Love is messy and complicated. And, most of all, unfair.

IRENE

Because she no longer has a vehicle of her own, Irene joins Huck on his errands after their fishing charter. This means going to a few places:

1. Starfish Market for (most) groceries. It's BYOB—bring your own bag. Huck keeps a stash of reusable shopping bags behind the driver's seat of his truck, which Irene finds charming. Russ rarely (if ever) shopped for groceries, and the idea of him remembering reusable shopping bags is laughable.
2. Papaya Café and Bookstore for a Vietnamese coffee and a browse through the stacks of used books. Huck is a particular fan of the coffee (he has turned Irene on to it as well) and of Michael Connelly. He's patiently waiting for some tourist to turn in a copy of *Dark Sacred Night*. In the meantime, he buys a James Patterson novel, one of the Women's Murder Club series, which he says aren't half bad.

"I'll take your word for it," Irene says.

"Why don't you pick out a book?" Huck says. "My treat."

It's kindnesses like this that make Irene emotional. She thinks back to New Year's Day, her dinner at the Pullman Bar and Diner with Lydia followed by a trip to Prairie Lights, where Irene thought nothing of buying whatever books struck her fancy. Now it feels like an unreasonable luxury to spend ten or twelve dollars on a used book. Irene shops carefully. What will help her escape? She finds a well-loved copy of *The Vacationers* by Emma Straub for six bucks. She hands it to Huck. She wishes they were merely vacationers.

"Thank you," she says.

Huck studies the cover. "Maybe I'll read it when you're done. Do you want a coffee too, AC?"

She has stopped trying to get him not to use the nickname. She likes it more than she cares to admit. "Please," she says.

3. Pine Peace Market for beer, wine, and a fresh bottle of Flor de Caña. Best prices.
4. St. John Market for anything they didn't have at Starfish. St. John Market is right across from the Westin resort and time-shares, so it's heavily populated by fish-belly-pale tourists buying groceries. (It's to be avoided at all costs on Saturdays, when families arrive for the week; Irene learned this the hard way.)

A few days earlier, Irene bumped into her own son at St. John Market. Baker was buying a jar of peanut butter and a loaf of white bread, for Floyd's school lunches, Irene assumed. He had been too busy considering the ingredients on the peanut butter jar to register any surprise at seeing Irene. (Maybe he wasn't surprised, Irene thought. It was a small island.)

"This isn't organic," he said. "And it has a lot of sugar." He held up the bread. "This isn't sprouted whole-grain spelt or whatever. If my school wives from Houston saw this, they'd stage an intervention."

"They'll never know," Irene said, and she and Baker shared a smile for the first time in what felt like forever.

Irene and Huck had also bumped into Ayers Wilson at St. John Market. They were walking in while Ayers was untying Winnie from the railing outside.

"There's my granddog!" Irene said, crouching down to rub Winnie's silky butterscotch head. Winnie's tail was going nuts. Winnie was happy to see Irene—but Ayers seemed to be another story.

"Hey," Ayers said flatly. She didn't look good. Her hair was unbrushed, her eyes puffy, her skin sallow. Cash had told Irene that Ayers had taken a leave of absence from the boat and also that her engagement had ended, leaving her free to care for Winnie.

"I owe you a huge thank-you for helping Cash out," Irene said. "I'm not sure what would have happened otherwise."

"It's no big deal," Ayers said. "I like having her around...good distraction and all that. It gets me outside a couple of times a day, anyway."

"Are you okay, honey?" Huck asked. "If you don't mind my saying so, you look like death on a stick."

"Huck!" Irene said.

"It's okay," Ayers said. "I'm just...going through some stuff right now." She frowned at Huck. "And I've been meaning...there's something I need to talk to you about. Later. I'll call you later."

"Anytime," Huck said.

Irene wanted to ask Ayers if she knew that Baker was staying at the Westin or if she knew Baker was moving to the island permanently if he could find a suitable rental, but she couldn't get into everything that had happened while they were all there at the store, so Irene said, "We're on the hunt for mangoes for Maia," and Ayers led Winnie back to her little green truck.

Huck said, "Did she seem off to you?"

"Yes," Irene said. "But you should never tell a woman she looks anything less than radiant."

"Oops," Huck said.

5. St. John Business Center. This is where Huck picks up his mail. There's always a long line of people who need to scan or make copies or ship something back to the States. Last time, Irene went inside with Huck. Candice, the woman in charge, asked Huck if Irene was his new lady friend, and Huck said, "Irene is my business partner," and Candice said, "Okay, if that's what you want to call it."

This time, Irene stays in the truck. She has now been living with Huck for nearly two weeks, and everyone on the island must think they're a couple. Irene has far bigger worries than what other people think, but she has decided it's best to maintain a bit of distance by letting Huck get his own mail. There are still condolence letters about Rosie that arrive, and there are bills for the house. Irene has tried to contribute to the household but Huck says, *Absolutely not.*

And, frankly, Irene is relieved.

Huck emerges from the business center holding a square, flat package and grinning. He's got his sunglasses on and his visor; he wears a navy bandanna around his neck. *He's handsome when he smiles,* Irene thinks. *He's handsome all the time. He's strong, he's kind, he's trustworthy, he's honest.*

But she's not ready.

He comes to her window and hands her the package. "For you."

"Me?" She studies the package. It's from M. Key in Iowa City.

Mavis Key has sent Irene…what?

Milly's picture! Irene opens the box, slides out the bubble-wrapped bundle inside, untapes it, unfolds it, and yes—there's Milly's portrait. Irene's eyes fill with tears. Mavis got it back. Amazing. Simply amazing.

"Look," Irene says, showing the picture to Huck. "This is Russ's mother, Milly, back in 1928 in Erie, Pennsylvania. Who does she remind you of?"

Huck takes the picture. "God*damn,*" he says. "Maia is her spitting image."

Irene leans back against the seat and closes her eyes. "I'm going to give that picture to Maia. Thank God Mavis got it back."

"There's a note here," Huck says.

Irene opens her eyes and Huck pulls a card from a corner of the frame.

Call Nat! the note says. There's a number.

Irene already has Natalie Key's number—Mavis texted it to her back on day one of the Destitution—but Irene hasn't called her yet because…well, because she can't afford a lawyer, especially not a big fancy lawyer in New York City. And yet Irene knows she has to do something. She has been so busy trying to make it through each day—working on the boat, helping out around Huck's house where she can, checking in with Cash and Baker and Floyd—that she has been able to avoid thinking of all her worldly possessions in the custody of the FBI. If she ever wants to see them again or figure out what the hell is going on, she needs to do exactly what this card says and call Natalie Key.

"I think we should celebrate," Huck says. "What do you say we go to Candi's for some barbecue?"

Irene places the photograph in her lap. It does feel like a victory, having Milly back. Maybe Milly will be good luck. Maybe Milly will help them.

"Yes, please, and thank you," Irene says. She'll call Natalie tomorrow, she decides. Tonight, she's going to eat some ribs, pasta salad with peas, and coleslaw with raisins and pretend she's a vacationer.

"Before we get started," Natalie says, "I want you to know that a guardian angel of yours has already sent me a retainer for ten thousand dollars."

"What?" Irene says. "Who did that? Was it Mavis?"

"I'm not supposed to tell you, but I don't play games," Natalie says. "It was your former boss, Joseph Feeney."

Joseph Feeney, Irene thinks. The big boss at *Heartland Home and Style.* "Mavis must have told him what happened," Irene says.

"No doubt—and she probably strong-armed him," Natalie says. "Mavis is tough, as I'm sure you know."

"Mavis told me that *you* were tough," Irene says.

"Ha!" Natalie says. "I guess we're both tough. We had three older brothers who were state champion wrestlers, so we learned how to get out of a headlock and a half nelson at a very young age. Now, normally I charge nine hundred dollars an hour, but for you, I'm dropping my fee to three hundred—again, that's at Mavis's request, and I always honor her requests when I can—so

I'm really hoping, Irene, that we can get this done without any out-of-pocket expenses on your end."

Irene is so relieved, she feels dizzy. *Thank you, Joseph Feeney,* she thinks. *You underpaid me for twelve years and essentially demoted me when you hired Mavis, and I called you all kinds of ugly names in my head. But when I needed you, you came through.*

Thanking him should be done by phone but she can't risk the follow-up questions. She'll e-mail. "Wonderful," Irene says.

"Now that that's out of the way," Natalie says, "I need you to tell me everything."

Irene expects that, because Natalie is charging only a third of her usual fee, Irene will receive a third of Natalie's usual attention. But in only a matter of days, Natalie calls and gives her some answers.

1. The helicopter that Russ and Rosie took to Anegada was privately owned by Stephen Thompson, the third principal in Ascension. This particular helicopter had no black box, so there's no voice recording of the ride or the moments before the crash. Irene is relieved. There's a limit to what she can handle.
2. The people from VISAR—Virgin Island Search and Rescue—told the FBI that they had reason to believe the helicopter was *not* struck by lightning but rather exploded due to an electrical issue or, possibly, foul play. They are still investigating. The helicopter presently belongs to the British authorities because it went down in British waters.

"In theory," Natalie says, "the Americans and the Brits work together, but after talking to both sides, my guess is that there's an intentional withholding of information by the Brits, which always has to do with money. The Brits will hold the copter hostage until they get some kind of recompense." Natalie pauses. "Hard to know if this is all aboveboard or if there's bribery going on." She chuckles. "Actually, there's definitely bribery going on. Just so you know, even the good guys aren't good all the time."

3. Todd Croft had been arrested north of Trinidad and Tobago the same day that Irene lost the villa. There are a lot of charges against him, but the only one that they're presently holding him on is resisting arrest. Apparently, he gave the Feds quite a chase. The other charges, Natalie says, might not stick. Most of the paper trail that ties Ascension to money laundering and tax evasion has Russ's signature only; a few documents also include Stephen Thompson's name. Although Todd is the founder of the company and the last remaining principal, without any concrete evidence tying him to the illegal activity, he might soon go free, and, if his lawyer is good, he'll avoid jail time.

"He's telling the FBI that it was your husband and Mr. Thompson who ran the illegal business dealings, that he was involved only in the legitimate side of things—the soccer stars and casino owners who used Ascension to avoid taxes by residing in legal gray areas. He claims he didn't learn that Mr. Thompson and your husband had 'ventured to the dark side' until September. Ascension is, technically, Mr. Croft's company and he says those two threatened to take it down if Mr. Croft contacted the authorities. He cited the fact that Russ and Mr. Thompson were scooting off to Anegada without him as proof. And yet the FBI found him heading for Venezuela, where there are no extradition laws. Among Ascension's clients are entities that are into, among other things, narcotics trafficking, human trafficking, explosives, cybercrime, underground gambling, organ trafficking, and good old-fashioned counterfeiting. According to the paper trail, these entities gave their money to Russ, and Russ created shell companies at offshore banks in the Cayman Islands. He then invested that money in legitimate businesses on St. John and in the BVIs, where regulations are looser than they are in the U.S. They bought and sold a lot of land over on Anegada. They used SGMT, an offshore bank with a reputation for secrecy. That's the bank your personal finances were drawn on. Stephen Thompson joined the company only a year before Russ. Now, I did a little poking around on him. He was a British citizen, worked for Barclays out of law school, then disappeared for a few years, only to resurface down in the Caymans. But Mr. Thompson also held a passport from Suriname."

"Where's that?" Irene says.

"It's a country in South America," Natalie says. "They have a pay-for-citizenship policy. Invest two hundred thousand in the country's economy and receive a passport. That would have allowed Mr. Thompson to move around more freely, without the oversight of the British government."

"I'm sorry," Irene says. It's nearly seven o'clock; Natalie called just as Irene and Huck were driving home from a double-charter day. They are both exhausted and irritable. "I'm sorry, Natalie, but there is no way Russ was the mastermind behind all this." Irene laughs. "He—I swear to you—didn't have it in him. Let's start with...we lived in Iowa. Russ was a member of the Rotary.

He was on the school board. He liked puns, for Pete's sake." *Underground gambling?* Irene thinks. *Human trafficking?* Russ's definition of *underground gambling* was the office football pool, and he would have thought *human trafficking* was something a crossing guard took care of. "He was a decent man. I do still believe that. He must have been bribed by Todd Croft and that was why he was the one who got his hands dirty." Irene turns and looks out the open window. They're climbing Jacob's Ladder. It's one steep switchback after another and the engine of Huck's truck wheezes like an out-of-shape geezer on the StairMaster. But they make it, they always make it, and they're treated to a magnificent sunset—brilliant orange, like a wildfire across the sky. The beauty of these islands is completely at odds with the news Irene is now hearing. Or maybe it's not at odds. Maybe this beauty was what seduced Russ. Irene knows better than anyone that once you experience life in this paradise, you'll do anything to keep it. "Todd Croft offered Russ more money than he could possibly imagine," Irene says. "Russ made fifty-seven thousand dollars a year selling corn syrup. We were *always* struggling before he took this job. All I can think is that Todd offered him millions, and in exchange, he agreed to be the fall guy if they ever got caught." Irene swallows. "He was that desperate, that eager to please me. I was hard on him."

"Maybe it was bribing at first," Natalie says. "But I'm going to guess that, as things progressed, it became blackmail."

"Blackmail."

Natalie lowers her voice. "If Todd Croft knew about Rosie…and about Maia…well, he could have gotten Russ to do anything."

Huck pulls into the driveway. Irene sees Baker and Floyd out on the deck with Maia. She can't continue a conversation that involves organ trafficking—and not the church kind of organ—while she's looking at her grandchild. She has to end this call. "Right," Irene says.

"But we have no way to prove Todd did that," Natalie says. "Yet."

AYERS

Baker must have had a sixth sense that something was going on because he'd called Ayers while she was in the bathroom holding the pregnancy test with a shaky hand.

Positive.

Ayers had stared at the screen of her ringing phone. Baker was listed in her contacts as "the Tourist" with a photo of a leatherback sea turtle.

She'd declined the call.

She was pregnant? Well, yeah. Obviously. Of course.

Ayers wasn't a complete idiot; *pregnancy* had been her first thought, but she'd dismissed it immediately because it was too awful and Ayers had had so much *awful* piled on her recently that there wasn't room for any more. Rosie dying, a broken engagement, and now…

When Ayers got back together with Mick, she'd insisted he use a condom because of Brigid. He'd been good about this. Not happy, but conscientious. Even the night of their engagement, he'd used a condom.

The only time Ayers had had unprotected sex was with Baker

on their single night together. It was just that one night. A couple of times, but still.

Still, that was all it took. One egg and one sperm—baby.

Well, she couldn't have a baby. She could barely take care of *herself*. She lived in a studio—cute, but unsuitable. Her houseplants were dying. Where would she put a crib? A high chair? A Pack 'n Play or a bouncy chair or a swing or any of the other large, noisy paraphernalia that babies required?

She could, maybe, have had Mick's baby, because Mick was a known quantity to Ayers. But to have a baby with Baker, a person she had been on exactly one date with and slept with twice?

She wasn't prepared for any kind of conversation with Baker. She sent him a text: I've come down with something. It's bad and I wouldn't want you or Floyd to catch it. I'll call you when I'm better.

Rosie had been in this exact same predicament. No, Rosie had had it worse. Rosie found herself pregnant by a man she thought she'd never see again. She'd kept the baby—and who was that baby now? It was Maia, the most wonderful human Ayers knew. Didn't Ayers want a Maia of her own? A child who was wise and sweet and smart and funny? A child who would love her the way that Maia loved Rosie?

Theoretically, yes; Ayers wanted children. She had always pictured herself with children, and she even knew what kind of mother she wanted to be—the kind of mother who dressed up with her kids for Halloween, the kind of mother who let the kids have hot fudge sundaes for dinner on their last day of summer vacation. She wanted to be a Scout leader. She wanted to be fun and involved and reliable, a buoy during the unpredictable currents and undertow of growing up.

Just like everyone else, she wanted to be exactly like and completely different from her own parents.

Oh, jeez, Ayers thought. She had to tell her parents the news. But first, she would need to find them.

Treasure Island was fixed, but Ayers couldn't handle an all-day boat charter either physically or mentally. She called Whitney in the office and told her that she needed some time off—a couple of weeks, she thought, but maybe longer.

"But you're not quitting on us, right?" Whitney said. "No pressure, girlfriend, but you're the heart and soul of this operation. Cash is good but he's brand-new."

"I'm coming back?" Ayers said. "I mean, I'm coming back. Of course I'm coming back."

At La Tapa, Ayers was shaky and sweaty and distracted. Tilda covered for Ayers's lethargy and her mistakes. Tilda thought the problem was Mick, both the broken engagement and his week-long sit-in at Cruz Bay Landing. It had become a *thing.* Mick had been going to work, but directly afterward, he sat at the bar at CBL with the ring in front of him and Gordon tied to his bar stool, and he drank. He was there on his days off as well, from open to close. Tourists had started posting pictures of #heartsick-mick with the beer and the ring box in front of him and Gordon snoozing dutifully at his feet.

Mick had managed to make the breakup all about himself; he'd cast himself as the victim, and he'd gotten his own hashtag in the process. Meanwhile, Brigid was still working at the Beach Bar and *not* at Island Abodes like Mick had promised, so frankly Ayers didn't care if *60 Minutes* came to do a segment about his broken heart—Ayers wasn't going back.

"I feel bad for the guy," Skip, the La Tapa bartender, said at the end of service. "I'm going over to have a drink with him."

"Birds of a feather," Tilda murmured.

Ayers needed to confide in someone—and that someone should have been Baker. However, on Wednesday afternoon, Ayers got a text from Cash, and the next thing she knew, she had offered to adopt Winnie for a while because Tilda's fancy, type A parents didn't "do dogs."

This, at least, felt right. It was the least she could do after abandoning Cash on *Treasure Island.* It would also be nice to have a warm body around, one who wasn't going to ask her any questions.

Ayers had picked Cash up from the boat and driven to Peter Bay to collect Winnie. Ayers had never been to Tilda's fancy, type A parents' villa before—she had never been to any of the homes in Peter Bay; it was exclusive, private, gajillionaire territory—and when she drove down the steep chute of Tilda's driveway, she got vertigo. It felt like they were driving off a cliff into the sea.

Whooooooo! When Ayers parked, her heart was slamming against her chest.

She watched Cash as he strode into the house.

Uncle Cash, she thought. *My baby's uncle.*

She was about to leave—she had Winnie's leash in one hand and her bowl in the other—but then...*then* she blurted it out. Without intention, without planning, without warning.

I'm pregnant.

"Whoa!" Cash said.

"It's Baker's," Ayers whispered.

Cash's eyes bugged. "It is?"

Ayers nodded.

"You're sure?"

"I'm sure."

"You haven't told my brother yet, have you?"

Ayers shook her head. The mere thought made her want to hurl. She'd inhaled the scent of the frangipani bushes that surrounded Tilda's fancy, type A parents' villa. She needed to get out of there. The last thing she wanted was for Tilda to come home and ask what was wrong.

"I haven't told anyone," Ayers said. "Not even my parents."

"That explains your leave of absence."

"Just for a couple weeks," Ayers said. "Until I get a better grip on things."

"I'm sure it seems scary," Cash said. "But I'll help. We'll all help. Baker has his flaws, but he's an excellent father."

Ayers wasn't ready to hear this; she wasn't even sure she was going to go through with it. "Don't tell a soul," she said. "Not Tilda, not your mom, not Baker."

"Are you kidding?" Cash said. He bent down to rub Winnie's head. "I'm giving you my best friend. The last thing I'm going to do is cross you."

"Thank you."

"I'm here," Cash said. "And you know what? I'm psyched."

To track down her mother and father, Ayers clicks on the Wandering Wilsons Facebook page. Her parents share a cell phone and they call her when they're in a place with reliable service, which isn't often. Ayers's parents—Phil Wilson and Sunny Ray—have never married, though they've been together for thirty-five years. Each refers to the other as "my partner," and they call each other "my love." Their relationship is nontraditional—and enviable. They have a shared vision of seeing the world on its own terms, abiding by the old adage "Take nothing but photographs, leave nothing but footprints." Phil and Sunny met during a semester abroad in the Canary Islands in 1984; Phil was at Berkeley, Sunny at the University of Wisconsin. After that semester, they both dropped out and hopped on a freighter headed for Portugal, starting a life of wanderlust that has continued to this very day. Ayers's earliest memories are of walking between her parents down the dusty streets of one foreign country or another, the smell of diesel fuel, the sound of unfamiliar languages. Phil was the navigator; he had the map. Sunny was the ambassador; she did the talking, learning the words for *Hello* and *Thank you* in the language of every place they visited. They stayed in hostels or cheap hotels, Ayers and her parents sometimes all sharing a bed. They cooked in communal kitchens, showered in communal bathrooms. They slept on trains. They hiked and camped, snorkeled, tubed, ziplined, canoed, rafted, spelunked. They shopped at local markets, napped in botanical gardens, hopped on and off the goat-and-chicken bus, lit candles in churches, swam with dolphins and whale sharks, ate from street carts, bathed in hot springs, climbed to the scenic lookout at the crack of dawn, rode the elephant or donkey or camel, awoke to the call of the muezzin from the local mosque, swapped paperbacks, hand-washed their laundry and hung it to dry stiff as cardboard in the baking sun. As soon as they stayed somewhere long enough to feel comfortable, they packed up and moved on. Ayers had seen it all: the Pyramids, the Taj Mahal, Torres del Paine, the Galápagos, the northern lights, the Monteverde Cloud Forest, the Amazon River, the fjords, the glaciers, the mountain ranges, the deserts, the lakes, all of the oceans.

That must have been so cool, people say when Ayers describes her upbringing. *You're so lucky.*

We all want what we can't have. Ayers wanted a house. She wanted a subscription to *Seventeen* magazine that would arrive reliably on the first of the month. She wanted parents like Coach and Tami Taylor. She wanted siblings.

Every week or two someone aboard *Treasure Island* asks Ayers, "What do your parents think about you living on a tropical island?"

The true answer: *They think it's boring.* "Oh," she responds. "They're proud of me."

Ayers's parents have money now—inherited from Ayers's paternal grandmother—and so their travel has become far more comfortable. They stayed at the Shangri-La in Paris, which must have been interesting. Phil and Sunny still travel with large backpacks instead of proper luggage. Sunny wears pants and dresses made from khaki cotton; both of Ayers's parents wear Birkenstocks. While in Paris, they had dinner at La Tour d'Argent—because, as Sunny said, it was a classic Parisian experience they'd yet to have in their half a dozen visits to the city. Had Sunny worn her Birkenstocks to La Tour d'Argent? Ayers was afraid to ask.

The last time Ayers spoke to her parents, they were in Morocco, staying with friends they'd met in Ibiza in the 1980s, before Ayers was born; these friends now own a home on the coast in Essaouira. All of Phil and Sunny's close friends are people they met on one adventure or another—hiking around the crater of Mount Batur in Bali or shopping for an authentic Panama hat in Montecristi, Ecuador. That conversation with her parents was on the morning of Rosie's funeral, and a *lot* has happened since then. It feels like nearly everything important in Ayers's life has happened since then.

A Facebook post from yesterday puts Phil and Sunny at Fairmont the Norfolk in Nairobi. A scroll back through their pictures shows they've been on safari in the Maasai Mara.

Bah! Ayers thinks. They never took *her* on safari! They always said it was too expensive. There are the requisite pictures of giraffes, zebras, lions, elephants. And some of a hot-air balloon ride they took at sunrise. Cheetahs, leopards, rhinos, baboons, hippos. A Maasai warrior posing with Phil and Sunny in their Birkenstocks.

Ayers sighs. Her parents are in Africa. They couldn't *be* any farther away. Still, she tries their cell phone. What's the time difference? She doesn't care. She calls.

Her mother answers on the first ring. "Freddy!" Sunny says. "Your timing is perfect! The front desk just sent us a bottle of champagne. They think we're travel bloggers." She laughs. "I may have misled them a bit—"

Suddenly, Ayers's father is on the phone. "She misled them a *lot,*" he says. "Though it works. We've gotten free stuff every place we've checked in since your mother started referring to her 'blog.'"

"Great," Ayers says weakly. Her parents are in high spirits; they're about to open a bottle of champagne at a five-star hotel after having been on safari. In other circumstances, Ayers might have made a sarcastic comment about the "good old days" when they drank river water that they'd purified with iodine tablets and stayed at a hotel in Borneo where the sheets were crawling with tiny golden ants.

"We've been expecting your call for over a week." Her mother again. In the background, Ayers hears the cork pop—the mere sound makes her stomach lurch—and the Tubes singing "Talk to Ya Later," Phil and Sunny's favorite song, straight out of the early eighties. Ayers's eyes water. Despite the fact that she can't remember the last time she saw her parents, Ayers knows them well. They're her family.

But why were they expecting her call? She never calls them; it's always the other way around. "You have?"

"There's something you want to tell us, isn't there, Freddy?" It's her father again. Freddy is their nickname for Ayers; it's short for "Ready, Freddy," which was apparently what Ayers said nonstop when she was little.

"I do…" Ayers says.

"You're engaged!" Her mother blurts it out; the champagne must have gone to her head already. "Mick sent us a Facebook message asking for our blessing."

"He *did?*" Ayers says. She's taken aback by this news. Mick has met Phil and Sunny three times—the two times they swung through St. John to visit and then at Ayers's cousin's destination wedding in San Juan. Phil and Sunny like Mick. Phil and Mick are both craft-beer fanatics and they have a friendly rivalry in the sunset-picture-taking department (#sunset; Ayers doesn't miss this habit of Mick's one bit). Mick won Sunny over by dancing with her at Brinley's wedding and by agreeing to tour Castillo San Cristóbal at seven o'clock the next morning. But even so, asking for her parents' blessing isn't something Ayers ever thought Mick would do. It seems too formal and old-fashioned.

It also seems unfair. If Mick was so invested in the engagement, why did he blow it less than two days later? Who *does* that?

"When we did an overnight in the Maasai village," Sunny

says, "we told the elder that our daughter was getting married, and he insisted on roasting a goat, which is a very big honor."

Ayers falls facedown across her bed. Mick asked for her parents' blessing without her knowledge. Her parents celebrated her engagement with Maasai villagers without even hearing if she'd said yes, which feels vaguely dishonest of them, just like intimating they wrote a travel blog. And yet this is typical of her parents. When they travel, living is done in the moment. The strangers they're with become friends. The particulars of their lives can be stretched and even distorted without any consequence because tomorrow, they'll be gone.

Ayers lifts her head from the bed. "Why didn't you call *me?*" she asks. "You had goat with the Maasai but you didn't call to say congratulations?"

"It was your news to share," Phil says. "We've been waiting for this call. Frankly, it took so long that we began to wonder if something had happened."

Ayers hesitates. She feels bad about ruining her parents' happy champagne drinking. "Something did happen. Maia saw Mick kissing Brigid a couple days after he proposed. I gave the ring back."

On the other end, there's silence. Who has the phone now? Did they drop it? Ayers can ever so faintly hear Fee Waybill sing, *I'll just see you around!*

"Mom?" Ayers says. "Dad?"

"Sorry, Fred, it's just we're..." Phil says. He clears his throat. "The Maasai assured us killing the goat would mean a long and happy union."

The goat lies, Ayers thinks.

"Darn it," Sunny says. "I liked Michael."

"I liked him too, Mom," Ayers says. "But I'm not going to stay with someone who cheats on me; sorry." She pauses. "Anyway, I have more news, and I'm sure it will come as an even bigger shock, so sit down."

"Go ahead, Freddy," Phil says. "Your mother says she needs her drink."

Yes, Ayers thinks. *Yes, she does.* "I'm pregnant."

"She's pregnant!" Phil shouts.

In the background, Sunny shrieks.

"But wait," Ayers says and she silently curses Mick for being thoughtful enough to contact her parents and despicable enough to cheat on Ayers two days later. "It's not Mick's baby."

"It's *not?*" Her mother. "What do you mean? Whose baby is it?"

"Mom, stay on the phone, please." They always do this, pass the phone back and forth like they're playing a game of hot potato. "I'll explain it to you and you can explain it to Dad." Ayers rolls onto her back. The spinning ceiling fan above makes her nauseated, so she closes her eyes. "While Mick and I were broken up, I met a man named Baker Steele."

"Baker Steele?" Sunny says. "That sounds like a name from a soap opera. *Baker Steele.*"

"I liked him a lot but he lived in Houston—"

"And you don't date tourists."

"That's right. But he has...family ties here, so he came back and I slept with him and now I'm pregnant."

"Oh, Freddy," Sunny says.

"I haven't talked to Baker about it yet, but I...I think I'm going to have the baby, Mom."

Phil gets on the phone. "Your mother is crying," he says. "Happy tears? Yes, happy tears, happy champagne tears. We're going to be grandparents."

Ayers sighs. "The baby isn't Mick's, Dad, it's this other guy's—Mom will explain. Anyway, I called because I was feeling overwhelmed and alone and I wanted to hear your voices."

"We love you," Phil says. "And guess what, Freddy—you weren't exactly planned either."

"I know, Dad," Ayers says. Her parents were living on Wineglass Bay in Tasmania when Sunny realized she was pregnant. They figured out the baby had been conceived a few weeks earlier at Ayers Rock, and they decided that would be the official name, boy or girl.

"But out of all the good things we've experienced in our lives," Phil says, "becoming your parents is on the top of the list."

"We'll be there as soon as we can," Sunny says. "Remember what we taught you to do when you get to the end of your rope?"

"Make a knot and hang on," Ayers says.

The next day, Ayers steps out of St. John Market—she bought lemons, a knob of ginger root, a two-liter bottle of ginger ale, and white bread, hoping one or all of these would cure her nausea—and bumps into Huck and Irene.

Irene comes right over to hug Winnie. "My granddog," she says.

Grandmother, Ayers thinks. *My baby's grandmother. Or one of them. The other one is probably flying over the Congo right now on her way here.*

Ayers thinks about how surreal it is that she's pregnant with Irene's grandchild and Irene has no idea, but when Ayers sees Huck, she starts thinking about Rosie's journals and what they say. This makes her even queasier.

When Ayers gets home, she pulls the journals out from under

her sofa, and Winnie sniffs them, tail wagging. Ayers moves them to the center of her kitchen table to be safe. She should photocopy every page in case the FBI confiscates them as some kind of evidence and they vanish into the black hole of bureaucracy. But to copy them requires a trip to the St. John Business Center, and Ayers lacks the energy for that, plus she's bound to see people there she knows, people who will peer over her shoulder and ask what she's doing.

The journals contain relevant information about Russ. Ayers will give them to Huck and let him deal with contacting the FBI.

But...she needs to do this when Irene isn't around. And now Irene works with Huck on the fishing boat *and* she *lives* with him. She drives everywhere with him. They're joined at the hip.

Ayers sends Huck a text: That thing I need to talk to you about is sensitive and confidential. Any chance you can swing by La Tapa after service tomorrow?

Past my bedtime, Huck says. But yes, I'll see you tomorrow night.

Huck shows up at La Tapa at nine thirty and Ayers still has three tables lingering, so he takes a seat at the bar and orders a beer from Skip.

Ayers goes over and tells Skip, "That's on the house. You remember Captain Huck, Rosie's father?"

"Captain!" Skip says, reaching a hand across the bar. "It's an honor to have you in. We all miss Rosie very much. We have customers asking about her every day."

"Well," Huck says. He clears his throat. "Thank you. She was...yeah."

"I'll get your beer," Skip says.

* * *

Ayers lavishes her last tables with extra love and attention—*Can I get you a box for that? Would you like another decaf latte?*—because suddenly, she questions what she's about to do. The journals are private. They're intimate. And no one except Ayers knows they exist. What if she holds on to them for ten years and gives them to Maia when she's in her twenties, long after this whole mess has blown over?

Her tables pay their bills and wander out to the street. Skip cashes Ayers out.

"You look better today," he says. "Peppier."

Huck throws back what's left of his beer. "Skip was telling me what a fixture Mick has become over at Cruz Bay Landing. I hear they're planning on having him bronzed."

Ayers gives Huck a weary smile. "Walk me to my truck? I have something for you."

When they're out on the street, Huck says, "I must admit, my interest is piqued."

They walk past the Tap and Still, up by the baseball diamond of the Sprauve School, and around the traffic circle to Ayers's truck. Ayers says, "Back when we cleaned Rosie's room and you asked me if I found anything, I lied to you."

"Money?" Huck asks. He sounds hopeful. "More money?"

"Not money," Ayers says. "Rosie's journals about her relationship with Russ." She forages under the passenger seat of her truck, then hesitates ever so slightly before she hands the journals over. Is this the right thing to do? "I intended to save them for when Maia's older. But this whole thing with the FBI has me spooked." Ayers pushes out a breath. "They're pretty detailed, Huck, about how the whole relationship unfolded. There's stuff in there about Irene, and Russ's boss, Todd Croft..."

"Oh, jeez," Huck says.

"Yeah, exactly. It's sensitive." Ayers pauses. "Which is why I wanted to talk to you alone. Irene...she probably shouldn't see these. But the FBI might be interested."

"Agent Vasco said she'd hoped there were diaries," Huck says. "I'll probably just call her and hand them over. I'm sure Rosie wouldn't want me reading them."

"I should have told you sooner, though. I'm sorry."

"You did the right thing in telling me now," Huck says. "And I'll make sure we get them back."

Ayers nods. She feels as flat and insubstantial as a paper doll. Giving away the journals is like having an arm ripped off.

Huck leans over and kisses Ayers on the cheek. "You handled this just right, honey. I'll take it from here."

"Thank you for not being angry," Ayers says.

"It's no wonder you look so worn down," Huck says. "You have your crazy ex over at Cruz Bay Landing making a public spectacle of himself and you've been carrying the burden of these journals. Plus you miss Rosie. We all miss Rosie."

Plus I'm pregnant, she thinks.

"Have you seen Baker yet?" Huck asks. "Apparently, he has a good lead on a rental."

"So he's definitely staying, then?"

"They're all staying," Huck says. "Is that crazy or what?" Huck stretches out his arms in a gesture that takes in the hibiscus bushes lining the sidewalk, the sound of steel drums wafting over from Tamarind Court, the velvet sky filled with stars above them. "Then again, who ever wants to leave paradise?"

CASH

He and Tilda are eight minutes late to meet Granger and Lauren at Extra Virgin Bistro for dinner, which makes Cash crazy. Tilda has changed her top three times and spent half an hour putting on makeup, including some kind of sparkly silver stardust around her eyes. Cash can't fully appreciate the effect of the makeup because Tilda is beautiful even without makeup and because he hates being late for anything but especially for a work meeting, which this dinner technically is. Tonight, Granger and Lauren want to discuss the "exciting business opportunity" with Tilda and Cash.

Extra Virgin is a sexy restaurant. Outside, there's a spacious deck surrounded by tropical vegetation; in the dining room, there's a horseshoe-shaped bar backed by a glowing wall of bottles. There are leather banquettes, huge open windows, and low lighting. The buzz is high; stepping inside feels like arriving somewhere important. Cash has eaten in plenty of fine establishments in his life, though he consciously avoids any restaurant that can be called "a scene"—he prefers a taco and a beer, to be honest. Also, he doesn't like to eat in places he can't afford.

Granger and Lauren are already sitting, and a bottle of red has been decanted. (This is a phenomenon Cash has learned about in detail in the past week, how certain fine vintages of cabernet and Syrah and pinot noir need to be "aired out"—poured from the bottle into a glass carafe—so that the wine can breathe and become even more complex and sublime than it was when it was just wine in the bottle.) Granger is wearing one of his limited-edition Robert Graham shirts, another fancy thing Cash has recently been schooled on. Robert Graham designs, among other things, colorful, whimsically patterned sport shirts with dazzling contrasting cuffs. Granger collects Robert Graham shirts, registering each one like it's a Thoroughbred horse. After he bought his one hundredth shirt, the creative geniuses at Robert Graham designed a shirt specifically for Granger, called—unsurprisingly—"the Granger." Granger showed it to Cash the other evening at the house. It's vivid green and embroidered on the back with a psychedelic palm tree, only instead of a cluster of coconuts at the top, there are skulls, skulls being a popular Robert Graham motif.

The thing Cash likes about the Robert Graham shirts is that you can look dressed up without wearing a coat or tie. Cash could probably use one in his wardrobe, but again, he can't afford it; he can't even afford a knockoff of one. To this dinner, Cash is wearing a red polo shirt, a pair of Dockers, and flip-flops because his only other shoe options are sneakers and hiking boots. He's worried he's underdressed; he looks like he's been hired to park cars.

Oh, well—it's the Virgin Islands.

Granger and Lauren stand up; they're all smiles as they greet Cash and Tilda, though Lauren says, "We were wondering what became of you two!" The elder Paynes run a tight ship; one needs to watch them for only five minutes to see why they're successful. They do things impeccably—they get the best table at the most sought-after restaurant and then they welcome you into the place like it's their home. Cash's parents had money for years, but they never quite acquired the easy confidence that the Paynes exude.

Tilda instructs Cash to scoot over so he's across from Lauren. Maybe Tilda is trying to save Cash from an evening of tough face-to-face interaction with Granger, or maybe she would like to be her father's focus in this discussion. Granger pours them each a glass of wine. It's the Archery Summit pinot noir, "just to get everyone started." Cash sees from a quick check of the menu that the Archery Summit costs a hundred and twenty-five dollars a bottle, or roughly twenty-five bucks a glass. He tries to sit up straighter.

Granger says, "We'll wait until Duncan arrives to order."

Duncan? Cash thinks. *Who's Duncan?* Then he notices a fifth seat at the end of the table, between Granger and Tilda. He feels better about being eight minutes late because this Duncan is even later.

In a moment, Granger and Lauren are back up on their feet again, beaming, and Tilda stands, and Cash, a beat later than he probably should have, also stands to shake hands with a guy—maybe Cash's age, maybe younger—who's wearing jeans, a Gucci belt, a Revivalists T-shirt, and a forty-thousand-dollar watch.

"Hey, I'm Cash," he says.

"Hey, how you doin', mate, I'm Duncan Huntley, call me Dunk, nice to meet you." Dunk has an Australian accent, which puts Cash at ease a bit. Cash has never met an Aussie he didn't like. It seems to be a country filled with friendly, outgoing, well-adjusted people.

They all sit and pick up their menus. Granger says, "We ordered a bottle of the Archery Summit to start." He checks the bottle; there's less than a full glass left. "But we are definitely ready to move on."

"Let's go with a couple bottles of the Penfolds Shiraz," Dunk says. "I love a good Shiraz and Penfolds is the best in the Barossa—the best in the world, if you ask me."

"The Lewis reserve cab is pretty good too," Granger says. "Lauren and I visited the estate in Napa in January."

"Don't brag," Tilda says.

"You were invited," Granger says.

"I have a *job,*" she says.

"You can't compare the two—sorry, mate," Dunk says. "Penfolds is head and shoulders above." He waves over their server, a pretty young woman with long dark hair. "Jena, would you please bring us a couple bottles of the Penfolds Shiraz? We'll need to decant it."

"The Lewis will be drinkable right out of the bottle," Granger says. He turns to Jena. "One bottle of the Lewis reserve as well, please." He looks across the table. "What about you, Cash? Are you more a cabernet guy or a Shiraz guy?"

Cash would very much like to admit that he's an Island Hoppin' IPA guy. He has the wine list open in front of him. The Lewis cab is $240 a bottle, and the Penfolds Grange Shiraz is...Cash blinks. Is he seeing things? No; it's $700 a bottle. Which is, what, $140 a glass? Cash has a list of things as long as his arm that he would do with $140 before he blew it all on one glass of wine.

Dunk draws a circle with his finger. "So, Cash, how do you fit in with these bludgers?"

Cash would like to ask Duncan Huntley the same thing. "I'm a friend of Tilda's," he says. He doesn't use the word *boyfriend* because he is already having some manhood issues.

"Well, then," Duncan says. "That makes two of us."

The wine arrives, there's an enormous amount of theater involved in the tasting and decanting, and then Jena runs through the specials. She asks if it's anyone's first time eating at Extra Virgin, and Cash admits that he's an Extra Virgin virgin—only Jena laughs—and she tells them that they have a rooftop garden where the herbs and vegetables are grown, that they use local farms for eggs, and that they get their seafood from local fishermen.

"The mahi for the special tonight was caught just this afternoon by Captain Huck of the *Mississippi.*"

"Hey," Cash says. That's cool, right? Huck caught tonight's fish? But nobody is paying attention and Jena is off describing how the pasta, the stracciatella cheese, and the sausages are all made in-house.

"Would you ask Chef to do the tuna preparation I like?" Granger asks. "I don't see it on the menu tonight."

Cash expects Tilda to give her father a hard time—ordering off the menu is a gratuitous flex—but Tilda seems unbothered. She orders the lamb, Cash the mahi, Lauren the gnocchi. Dunk has a bunch of questions about the short rib preparation and Cash wonders if Dunk will be the first Aussie he'll ever hate.

He wants to go home—and by *home* he means...he's not sure where. He now lives under Granger's roof.

He throws back several mouthfuls of the cabernet, which is the most incredible wine he's ever tasted. All other wine hasn't been wine; it's been Kool-Aid, lacking the layers of this complex liquid. No, Cash is kidding. The wine is fine, nothing special. The best thing about it is it's getting him buzzed.

And once he's buzzed, he notices that Tilda is sitting with her chair pivoted toward Dunk; Cash has a fine view of the back of her shoulder. Is she into him? he wonders. Or just mesmerized by his accent, like a typical American? Tilda and Dunk are discussing *something* in depth, though it's hard to tell what exactly because Lauren, gracious, wonderful Lauren, is thoughtfully asking Cash about his years skiing in Breckenridge. How does it compare to Aspen? she wants to know. Deer Valley? Jackson Hole? Cash has answers for her because if there's one thing he knows about, it's the ski resorts of the Rocky Mountains. Cash is probably saying too much; he's had a large, seemingly bottomless glass of wine, and although Tilda and her mother ordered salads and Granger the hand-pulled stracciatella, Cash didn't order an appetizer. He lifts his empty glass and says, "I'll try some of the Penfolds. See what all the fuss is about."

Dunk eyes his glass, and for one instant, Cash thinks he's going to say no, that Cash isn't worthy of a $140 glass of wine. Dunk is going to call him out for what he is—a wine hack.

"Let's get you a clean goblet, mate," Dunk says in the most patronizing way possible.

The Penfolds Shiraz is heavier on the tongue, thicker; it's the consistency of ink. Everyone is watching Cash as he tastes. Even Tilda has swiveled toward him.

"Notes of goose fat," Cash says. "And the rain in Spain. And Russian interference in our elections."

"Now, now," Granger says. "No politics at the table."

"It's a joke, Dad," Tilda says. She rolls her eyes. "An old, tired joke."

Is it old and tired? Cash wonders. Because he thought it was *their* joke.

As soon as their entrées arrive and they all toast "to the next step," Granger says, "I guess it's time to talk particulars about what that next step is. Cash, you need some background about the meetings that Tilda and Lauren and I have been holding with Dunk."

Dunk has the short rib in all its gorgeous, umami glory in front of him but he makes no move to eat. "I bought Lovango Cay, the island just across the way from Cruz Bay, and I'm partnering with Granger, Lauren, and sweet Tilda here to build an eco-resort. We're thinking of selling off a number of lots for private homes, and then we'll build both hotel units and glamping tents. We'll have a world-class restaurant and a beach club with an oceanfront pool."

"That's ambitious," Cash says.

Tilda bubbles over like a glass of champagne. "It's exactly what I've always wanted. And Lovango is the perfect location. We'll run ferries to Red Hook and Cruz Bay, but because it's a separate island, it'll have built-in exclusivity."

"A boaters' paradise," Granger says.

"We've needed a destination like Lovango for a long time in the USVIs," Lauren says. "Just think about all the people who spend their money at the Baths and Jost and the Willy T."

"Yeah—I mean, you're right," Cash says. Tour stops in the USVIs versus the BVIs is another topic he knows something about. "I had a woman the other day who booked a trip on *Treasure Island* with her husband and their kids but she forgot her passport and couldn't go." Cash drinks some wine; he wonders if he has blue teeth like everyone else at the table. "We offer our USVI itinerary only once a week, and it's never as popular because there aren't as many destination stops."

"You work on *Treasure Island*?" Dunk says. "I guess I should apologize. I make a bit of a habit out of bouncing you blokes around in my wake."

"What's the name of your boat?" Cash asks, though he fears he already knows: the *Olive Branch*.

"Olive Branch," Dunk says.

Yep, it's the sixty-five-foot Sundancer that not only routinely buzzes by at top speed but also cuts *Treasure Island* off. James, the captain, *hates* the *Olive Branch*.

"The boat is named for Dunk's dog," Tilda says. "He has a harlequin Great Dane."

"We love Olive," Lauren says.

Cash turns to face Lauren. She loves Olive? Is this the woman who doesn't do dogs? "Harlequin Great Danes are…quite a breed," Cash says.

"It's not a dog," Granger says. "It's a horse!"

"She's so sweet," Tilda says.

"That face," Lauren says.

They have obviously all met Olive and fallen in love with her—after casting Winnie out onto the street. Cash stares at his mahi. It's a beautiful piece of fish, and the pan sauce is probably heaven, but Cash can't eat. He's furious with Tilda for not telling him that Duncan was coming to dinner. This is why she was being so extra with her outfit and sparkly makeup—it's all for Duncan. She has already met with him, maybe with her parents or maybe alone, but when Cash asked about her meeting last week, she claimed it was top secret.

Dunk says, "I guess my question for Cash is, what position are you qualified for? Do you have any management experience? What do you do on *Treasure Island*?"

"I'm the mate," Cash says. He holds Duncan's gaze, just daring him to smirk. Cash wishes he'd chosen a different shirt, one that makes him look less like Gilligan. He's tempted to throw his napkin on his plate and leave. He doesn't belong here. But he likes the idea of an eco-resort on Lovango. *Treasure Island* passes Lovango Cay every day, coming and going. It's just sitting there, beautiful, lush, undeveloped, filled with potential. What a great opportunity to build something from the ground up.

"I'm a Colorado guy, actually," Cash says. He nods at Dunk's T-shirt. "I saw the Revivalists at the Mission Ballroom before they hit it big."

"Cool, cool," Dunk says. "I saw them in Austin. Great show, probably best show I've seen in a while."

"Duncan, *eat* something," Lauren says. "You haven't touched your food."

Tilda glares at her mother and mouths, *Mom, stop!*

"I'm a people person," Cash says. "I enjoy the interface on *Treasure Island,* and I'm good at it. Before I moved down here, I taught skiing in Breckenridge."

"Love Breck," Dunk says. "We'll have to talk about *that* after we get into the whiskey."

Cash relaxes enough to take a bite of mahi. His mother might have caught this fish.

"We'll find a place for Cash," Granger says. "I'm already conferring with engineers about the desalinization plant. We greased the palms we needed to grease for the permitting." Granger leans forward. "How much time can you take off work, Til? Will the restaurant shut down if you're away for a week?"

"Ayers owes me a bunch of shifts, so, yeah, I can probably take a week. Why, are you flying me to Napa?"

"I'd like to send you on a reconnaissance mission," Granger says. "Island hopping. Three high-end resorts. I want a report on everything from the kind of ice they serve in their cocktails to the brand of toiletries in the bathrooms to the temperature they keep their fitness centers."

"Oh my God," Tilda says. "Can Cash come?"

"Obviously your mother and I would feel more comfortable if you weren't alone," Granger says. "And we have to be in LA next week for work." He pours Cash the last of the Shiraz. "What do you say, Cash? Can you swing it?"

A week away? Cash thinks. He would be a fool to turn the opportunity down, but he's the only crew member on *Treasure*

Island right now. Whitney in the office and the boat's owners, who live on St. Croix, are desperately looking for someone else. Any warm body will do; all they need is someone without a criminal record who can pass the required drug test. But even if they do miraculously find someone, Cash won't be able to leave for a week. Ayers is too sick and exhausted to come back, and she has seniority; she shouldn't *have* to come back because Cash wants to skip like a stone across the Caribbean.

"I can't," he says.

"But—" Tilda says.

"I just can't leave them in the lurch, Til. You know that."

"Dedication," Granger says. "Personal integrity. Frankly, if you'd said you could go, I would have wondered if you were the right person for our project."

Cash drinks what's left of the precious wine. He's passed a test.

"I can go," Dunk says. "I have zero personal integrity." He laughs. "Kidding, of course. But I am free and I would love to put my eyes on a few places, gather some intel."

Cash opens his mouth to protest. Does Dunk understand that Cash and Tilda are dating?

"Great idea," Granger says. "Til, is that okay with you?"

Say no! Cash thinks.

"Sure," Tilda says.

The drive home is tense. Cash isn't sure what to say. He and Tilda have been together a couple of weeks. They haven't said *I love you;* they aren't even close to that. They're still in the gaga-infatuation stage, which was, admittedly, rushed along a bit by Cash's circumstances. But he likes Tilda. A lot. They're exclusive. They're *living together.* So what will happen while Tilda's gone?

Is Cash going to just stay in her villa as she's gallivanting around the Caribbean with another guy?

"Thank you for being so cool about this," Tilda says, which is rather ingenious of her because Cash is not feeling cool at all. "If it puts your mind at ease, I'm not attracted to Dunk—like, not even a little bit. He's too intense."

Intense. She's making this sound like a flaw, but is it?

"Who *is* he?" Cash asks. "How does he have the money to buy an *island?* He's my age. Do his parents have jack?"

"He hasn't mentioned parents," Tilda says. "He was born in Australia, moved to the States when he was twelve..."

"Twelve?" Cash says. "Wow, he really milks that accent."

"I believe accents develop when you learn to talk," Tilda says. "Why are you being ungenerous?"

"I'm not," Cash says, though he is.

"Dunk is self-made, he's built and sold a couple of companies, and now he does real estate down here. He has a palatial home out in the East End. It's bigger than my parents' place—six buildings, including a pool house, two guesthouses, a gym, a theater, the whole enchilada. But as far as I know, it's just him and Olive."

"So he's single?" Cash says. "No girlfriend? Aren't guys like him required to run around with the supermodels from Fyre Festival?"

Tilda doesn't laugh.

"Is he...gay?" Cash asks. If Dunk is gay, Cash can relax. Somewhat.

"No idea," Tilda says. "It doesn't matter. I'm not interested in him. I'm interested in you."

Cash finds little comfort in these words. It sounds like Tilda has been to the villa in the East End. When did that happen and why didn't she tell him? And how to explain the makeup and sexy outfit? She didn't get all dolled up for her parents.

"Did you notice he didn't eat his dinner?" Cash says. "Not one bite. He asked Jena all those questions and then he didn't even touch it. He told me he was taking it home for his dog. That short rib cost forty-five bucks. Who does that?" Out of all the uncomfortable moments at dinner, the worst was when Jena dropped off the check and Dunk and Granger fought over it. It felt like a test of manhood, one that Cash couldn't even pretend to compete in. He'd just looked on with Tilda and Lauren while Dunk and Granger threw down their credit cards, which were radioactively glowing with money.

"He fasts," Tilda says. "I mean, he drinks, obviously, but he goes for days at a time without solid food."

"What?" Cash says. He thinks about living in the East End, which is within shouting distance of Lime Out, and denying himself the pleasure of a rum rib taco.

"It's a willpower thing."

"He sounds like a sociopath," Cash says. "Be careful while you're away, please."

"I'll text and call and we'll FaceTime every morning and every night, and when I get back, we'll skinny-dip at Hawksnest and go to the pig roast at Miss Lucy's and get drunk one night at Skinny Legs and do all the things we haven't done as a couple yet."

"I'll miss you," Cash says. Tilda is a beacon for him, and a buoy. They have gotten so close so fast, he can't imagine a week without her.

"Awww," she says. "You're sweet."

Cash perks up a little. "The project sounds amazing. I'm honored your parents are including me."

"They would do anything to make me happy," Tilda says.

Cash doesn't love the implication of this statement—that Cash's involvement on Lovango is due solely to his relationship with Tilda. If Tilda comes home from St. Lisa or St. Roger and announces that she's fallen in love with Dunk, Cash will be heartbroken, but will he be out of luck on the project as well?

Yes. If the whole mess with Cash's father has done nothing else, it has prepared him for the worst.

BAKER

Every now and then, when Baker is sitting by the pool at the Westin watching Floyd play with Aidan/Nicholas/Parker/Dylan/Maddie/Eli—it's a revolving cast of best friends for the day when you live at a hotel—he wonders if things are really as bad as they seem. The room—garden-facing with two queen beds and a balcony that is off-limits to Floyd—is five hundred bucks plus tax plus resort fee plus service charge, which is obviously a lot. But if Baker can ignore his mounting bill, he's able to appreciate the fine weather and all the amenities on offer—the pool, an excellent gym, daily housekeeping, the playground, kayaks and paddleboards, a private beach featuring a water trampoline, and a plethora of organized kid-centric activities, like movie nights and ice cream socials. Temporarily, anyway, Baker and Floyd are living the life.

The villa is gone. Russ was laundering money using offshore accounts and shell companies to hide profits for some of the most evil human beings on earth. According to Irene's lawyer, Russ's is the name that shows up most often on the incriminating paper trail, and his boss, Todd Croft, is claiming Russ and the third principal, Stephen Thompson, masterminded the illegal underbelly of his legitimate business without Croft's knowledge. This assertion is outrageous. And yet, what does Russ have to recommend him in the way of personal character? Zero, zip, and zilch. He had a second family—a mistress, a love child. Plus, he's dead and not able to defend himself.

Baker's determination faltered for a moment when he and Floyd arrived and he heard the news. He checked into the Westin thinking he would have to turn tail and run back to Houston. He couldn't make a life here without a place to live and without a car. Anna had agreed to let him bring Floyd down only because she had seen the villa—and even then, she had expressed reservations.

The second Floyd fell asleep their first night at the Westin, Baker had taken a cold beer (thirteen dollars for a six-pack of Island Hoppin' IPA at St. John Market, which was nearly the same price as a single beer from room service) out to their balcony and called Anna. She was, technically, still his wife, and she would forever be Floyd's mother, and Baker couldn't hide their reduced circumstances from her. He figured Anna would insist they return to Houston or else make a plea for Baker and Floyd to move to Cleveland, where she and Louisa would be living.

But Anna surprised him. "First of all, you need to know it wasn't me who sent you that text," she said.

Louisa and I have some concerns about you uprooting Floyd.

"Louisa stole my phone," she added.

"Sounds like you're finally in a healthy relationship," Baker said.

"Please stop," Anna said. "Weez was concerned. Once I tell her the villa is gone, she'll go ballistic."

"You do realize that Louisa isn't Floyd's parent," Baker said.

"I do realize that," Anna said. "Which is why I'm not going to tell her."

Baker took a nice long pull off his beer. For the first time in a long time, he felt like he was talking to his wife. "Thank you."

"I never expected you to move to Cleveland with us," Anna said. "But the job offer was too good to turn down. It's the top job in my field in the whole country."

"Anna, I get it. I'm proud of you. Floyd is proud of you."

"Since I'm chasing my dream, you should too," Anna said. "Give it a try down there. You have a lot of potential, Bake, and it's gone untapped for a while now. Put Floyd in school, then follow your passion."

"I'm supposed to be coaching," Baker said. "Which pays approximately five dollars an hour. So I'll need to find something else."

"I believe in you," Anna said. "You're a hands-on, involved father, an eleven out of ten. Maybe I didn't tell you that as much as I should have."

You didn't, Baker thought.

"You're incredibly smart and you're wonderful with people."

"Not as wonderful as Cash..."

"Every bit as wonderful," Anna said. "The two of you always claim to be polar opposites, but you do share similar strengths—and shining in social situations is one of them. You both have a magnetism. People gravitate toward you. All those mothers at Floyd's school, for example. They *love* you."

"Well, thanks," Baker said. He was surprised at how this little bit of validation boosted his spirits. He'd assumed Anna left him because she thought he was a slacker, weak and useless, good for nothing except taking care of their child, a job that she felt was beneath her.

"Just remember that this isn't the end of the world," she said. "Ischemic heart disease—now, *that's* the end of the world."

"You're right," Baker said. Anna saved lives every single day. Losing a villa that wasn't his to begin with fell into the no-big-deal category.

"I'm getting an absurd signing bonus at this new job," Anna said. "I'll wire you half in the morning. Buy a Jeep. And rent a place, something comfortable."

"Oh, Anna, I can't—"

"Sure you can," she said. "You helped me get where I am. You were the wind beneath my wings." She cracked up in a way that was very unlike her. "And, yes, I have just had a glass of wine." She sighed. "Kiss Floyd for me."

The next morning, there is a hundred and twenty-five thousand dollars in Baker's bank account.

The wind beneath her wings, he thinks. *Hot diggity dog.*

His first order of business is to buy a Jeep. Why not ask right there at the Westin? They have a rental-car concern that must have turnover. And yes, sir—he scores a 2017 four-door soft-top bluebird-colored Jeep Wrangler with 1,200 miles on the odometer for half its original price.

Next up is getting Floyd settled in school. Floyd had loved the Gifft Hill School when they'd visited and Maia was there to show him around, but this, of course, is different. This is for real. Floyd is now the new kid; he doesn't know a soul, and it's the middle of the school year.

Floyd takes getting ready in stride. He protests about the shower but submits and then eats four bites of Cheerios. (They have been eating like paupers. Baker bought Cheerios and milk, a carton of OJ, a loaf of white bread, a jar of peanut butter, a package of hot dogs, and a twenty-four-pack of ramen noodles at St. John Market, and even those low-end groceries had cost him thirty-five dollars. It has been a week in his life that he's not anxious to repeat.)

When Baker pulls the Jeep into the parking lot of Gifft Hill with the other parents, *he* feels nervous. "It's going to be fine, buddy," Baker says. "You've already met your teacher. She knows you're smart, and you're going to meet new kids."

"I know," Floyd says. He has his lunch box with the peanut butter sandwich that Baker made that morning in their hotel room.

A rental, he needs to find a rental—and a real job.

Being with Ayers was Baker's primary motivation in moving down to St. John, but he has to push thoughts of her away for now. Food, clothing, shelter—then love. He called her; she didn't answer, but she sent a text: I've come down with something. It's bad and I wouldn't want you or Floyd to catch it. I'll call you when I'm better. Frankly, this was a relief; it bought him some time. He assumes she knows what happened from talking to Cash or Maia. As soon as Baker gets settled, he's going to swing by La Tapa and see her. He'll ask her out to dinner. They'll start fresh, as though the whole fraught way they met (at Rosie's memorial reception, where Baker lied about who he was) and their bizarre first date (they had sex in a beach chair that ended when the chair collapsed) and their one night together (which took place only hours after Ayers had broken up with Mick and two days before she became engaged to Mick) never happened.

They need a clean slate. They'll get to know each other gradually, without any heavy emotional baggage weighing them down. Everything will be aboveboard, out in the open, uncomplicated.

"Hey there!"

Baker and Floyd have just climbed out of their new Jeep when Baker sees a tall, rail-thin blond woman in expensive yoga clothes (Baker's eyes land on the woman's nipples completely by accident) walking toward them and smiling.

"You must be the new dad," she says. "I'm Swan Seeley. My older son, Colton, is friends with Maia, and my little boy, Ryder, is in kindergarten just like Floyd." Swan bends over, hands on knees, and looks at Floyd. "Everyone has been waiting for you to get here, Floyd. There's already a cubby with your name on it and a chair right next to my son Ryder at the blue table, which is where the cool kids sit."

Baker tries to imagine his school wives' reaction to the term *cool kids.* One of them would point-blank tell this woman not to project her own insecurities about social status onto children. Which one would say it? Debbie, he thinks. Unless Ellen beat her to it.

"Blue is my third favorite color," Floyd announces. "Green first, then red, then blue." He glances up at Baker. "Can we go in, Dad?"

"Yes, of course," Baker says. He holds out his hand to Swan and is careful about looking her in the eye. "Thank you for the words of encouragement. I'm Baker Steele."

She grasps his hand and lays her other hand on top. "Oh, I know who you are. We've all been waiting for you to arrive too."

Floyd has a good first day, then a good second day. All the kids are cool kids. Floyd is happy. Baker is getting there. He has a new Jeep and money in the bank. He checks in with his mother and his brother. Irene is living with Huck, working on the fishing boat, driving around with Huck in his truck like a local. She seems fine...better than fine. Her former boss at the magazine is paying for a real lawyer, a woman who is unraveling the tangle of Russ's deceits. Cash, meanwhile, is living high on the hog with Tilda from La Tapa, but that hardly seems like a sustainable arrangement.

Maybe, just maybe, Baker will be able to find a place that's big enough for all of them.

Welcome to Paradise Real Estate, which was owned by Paulette and Douglas Vickers, is now out of business, so Baker decides to try an agency called the Love City Villa Experience, which sounds sort of like an adult film from the 1970s—but maybe that's a good sign?

Baker walks into the agency and approaches the desk of a middle-aged West Indian woman wearing a cantaloupe-colored blouse and glasses on a chain. The nameplate in front of her says FRANCES.

"I'm looking for a villa rental," Baker says.

"Good afternoon," Frances says, sounding like a teacher correcting a student's grammar.

"Good afternoon," Baker says quickly. He chastises himself; the most important thing when speaking to anyone in the Virgin Islands is a proper greeting. Frances has probably already pegged Baker as a tourist from a busy place like New York—or Houston—where civility and manners don't exist. "How are you today? My name is Baker Steele."

Frances blinks. "Oh," she says. "Hello."

Does Frances know who he is? Does she know who his father was? Something about the way she said those two words conveys a *yes* on both counts. Will she work with him anyway?

He tells her his budget and says he'd like a villa with four bedrooms. She gives him the death stare. He says three. She shakes her head, tsks him. He says, "Two?" She picks up her keys and says, "Come along, son. Let's find you a home."

Baker has spent enough time lounging on the couch watching HGTV to know that the places you love are always too expensive and the places that are within your budget are always underwhelming for one reason or another. Frances takes him to look at an apartment on the first switchback of the Centerline Road. It's fine but the traffic noise is a problem, plus the place looks run-down and the communal pool is green with algae. No. They look at a tiny cottage all the way out past Salt Pond in Coral Bay. It's a forty-five-minute drive from town, which means ninety minutes spent commuting each day. No. There's a place near the Cinnamon Bay campground that smells like rot and is swarming with mosquitoes and doesn't have air-conditioning. No.

Well, Rome wasn't built in a day. Frances says she'll make a comprehensive list; they'll look again on Saturday. In the meantime, Baker will continue to hemorrhage cash at the Westin. It's starting to feel like home. There's a young woman at the front desk named Emily who flirts with Baker, and he flirts back. It's harmless! The morning after Baker's fruitless house search, he's getting his coffee in the lobby when Emily says, "I heard my aunt Fran is helping you find a place to live. And here I thought you were planning on staying with us forever."

"I'm moving here," he says. He wonders how his name came up in conversation with her aunt. He wonders if the entire island is whispering about him behind his back. "And I need to find a job."

"Got a minute?" Emily says. She leads him outside and

then across the Westin property to the building where they sell time-shares.

"Oh, I can't afford to buy a time-share," Baker says. "Though, don't get me wrong, I'd love to live at the Westin permanently. It'd be a dream come true."

"I didn't bring you here to buy," Emily says. "I brought you here to sell."

What is she talking about? She's talking about an opening they have for a sales associate in the time-share office. Emily leaves Baker with a woman named Jacqui who plops him down for an informal interview. There's no experience required for the job, though Jacqui loves that Baker has a degree from Northwestern and an MBA. He's personable. And he now knows the Westin property very well and can extol its many virtues. Baker wanted to get into real estate anyway, didn't he? This is one way in. There's a built-in clientele, Jacqui tells him. People show up at the hotel and fall so in love with St. John that they buy time-shares so they can keep coming back. The commission scale is generous—it's real money—and the hours are flexible. He can work seven thirty to two thirty and then pick Floyd up from school. The job comes with full benefits, and he'll be good at it. He knows he'll be good at it.

"I'm a team player," Baker says. "Sign me up!"

And the hits keep coming! On Baker's next outing with Frances, they look at a villa called the Happy Hibiscus. It's a beautiful stone home with cathedral ceilings, two bedrooms, two baths, a modern kitchen, a laundry room, and a small jewel of a pool out back in the garden. It has a gas grill, cable TV, and a yard planted with bismarckia trees. It's a bit beyond Baker's budget but he likes it so much, he bends. The house is on the flat part of Fish Bay and has no view; frankly, looking at it, you wouldn't even know you were on an island. Is Baker going to let this bother him? He's not. The house is *directly* across the street from Ayers's place; he can see her little green truck in the driveway when he stands at his front door. This is more of a downside than the price or the lack of a view; Baker doesn't want to crowd Ayers or have her think he's stalking her. How will he ever explain that he's now renting the house across the street? She's going to think he's psycho. It's a small island, but not that small. If he rented any other house, it would give her more breathing room.

Frances must sense his momentary hesitation because she chimes in, "You'd be a fool not to take it, son."

"I'm no fool," Baker says, though he suspects he'll feel like one when he tells Ayers they're neighbors. "I'll take it."

Baker and Floyd go out to dinner to celebrate. Baker stays away from La Tapa. It's too fancy for Floyd, plus Ayers works there, plus Swan Seeley was lurking in the school parking lot that afternoon (waiting for him?), and she told Baker that she would be having dinner at the bar at La Tapa that evening around seven and why didn't he join her? The invitation had unmistakable romantic intent, so now Baker has to avoid Swan at all costs.

They try the Banana Deck, but from the bottom of the stone steps, Baker can see Cash sitting at the bar by himself. It's surreal, bumping into his family around the island (Baker saw his mother at the market). Under other circumstances, Baker might say, *What the heck, let's eat with Uncle Cash and catch up.* But the truth is, he's not quite ready to fill his brother in on everything that's been happening, meaning that he doesn't want to break the news to Cash that he's renting a two-bedroom place that doesn't have space for him (except a sofa to crash on in case of emergency) and that is directly across the street from Ayers's house. Ayers might not call him a stalker to his face, but Cash most certainly will.

"Let's go, buddy," Baker says, wheeling Floyd around. They check at Lime Inn, but there's a forty-five-minute wait, and that won't work—Floyd is four years old; Baker has to get him fed. The Longboard has a line, and High Tide is still filled with happy-hour revelers.

What about Cruz Bay Landing? Someone at the Westin pool this past week was raving about the shrimp appetizer, which sounds good to Baker, and he can get Floyd a burger. They go over, and there are a couple of seats at the bar and a guitar player singing "Waiting on a Friend."

"Ooh, making love and breaking hearts, it is a game for youth," Baker sings quietly. He orders a beer for himself and a ginger ale for Floyd and checks out the menu. He's so happy to not be eating ramen noodles with hot dogs again tonight that it takes him a minute to realize that he knows the guy sitting a few stools away with a rum punch and a Corona and a velvet ring box in front of him, a bucket-headed American Staffordshire terrier leashed to his bar stool.

It's Mick.

Baker is halfway off his bar stool, ready to leave—they can just go to Ronnie's for pizza—when Mick sees him.

"Hey," Mick says. "Banker! It's Banker, right?" Mick sounds like the town drunk, his voice overly loud and his speech slurred. The guitar player ends the song; the bartender says, "Easy, Mick," as though he's expecting a scene. But there's not going to be a scene. Floyd is there. Does Mick see Floyd, Baker's little boy?

"Baker," Baker says, extending a hand. "How've you been, man?" Baker asks the question in earnest, though anyone can see Mick has not been well. What's with the velvet box? (Baker can guess.) And the poor dog. Floyd clambers down off his bar stool and stands a respectful distance away, regarding the dog.

"Can I pet him?" Floyd asks Mick.

"Sure!" Mick says. "His name is Gordon. Old Gordie-Gordo. You can take him for a walk around the park if you want. He could use the exercise."

"Is it okay, Dad?" Floyd asks.

No! Baker thinks. It's getting dark and Powell Park is cast in shadows. But the park is only a couple steps away from the restaurant patio and what kind of father tells his son he can't walk a dog? "Why not?" Baker says. "Once around only, okay? Stay on the path. Don't let him go."

"Gordie won't run off," Mick says. "He's a good dog. Likes to sniff things."

Floyd takes Gordon's leash and, looking self-important and three inches taller, leads him a few steps away. Baker puts in an order with the bartender for the shrimp appetizer, a grilled mahi sandwich, and a kid's burger.

Then Baker drains his beer and pretends to watch the basketball game on TV, Duke against North Carolina. Mick is here, and Floyd is walking Mick's dog, so there are no hard feelings. Everything is fine. Is everything fine?

"Word on the street?" Mick says.

"Excuse me?" Baker says.

"Word on the street is that Ayers is pregnant," Mick says.

Baker flags down the bartender for another beer, then puts his eyes on Floyd. Floyd has stopped to let Gordon sniff. Ayers is pregnant.

"Really," Baker says. He thinks of the text she sent him. I've come down with something. It's bad and I wouldn't want you or Floyd to catch it. I'll call you when I'm better. She's pregnant?

"That's what I heard," Mick says. He raises his Corona to Baker. "So I guess congratulations are in order."

Baker feels like he's suffered a grave injury—lost a limb, maybe—but has yet to feel the pain. "Yeah, man, congratulations." He would like the congratulations to be accompanied by giving Mick a sock in the mouth or pouring Mick's drinks over his head. Mick doesn't deserve Ayers. He sure as hell doesn't deserve to have a baby with Ayers. But that's the way the world always works, isn't it? The jerks win.

"Congratulations to *you,*" Mick says. "The baby's not mine."

"What?" Baker says.

"It's not mine," Mick says. He drains his rum punch in one long swallow and bangs the empty glass on the bar. "It's yours."

HUCK

He sees the Jeep with the tinted windows idling at the base of Jacob's Ladder in the morning when he and Irene take Maia to school, then he sees it again in the National Park Service lot when he and Irene are letting off their charter clients. The clients were a couple, the husband reeking of weed and high as a kite and the wife spending the entire six-hour offshore trip glowering at him from under her wide-brimmed sun hat. Irene had tried to draw the woman out, tried to put her on a mahi, but the wife was having none of it. That was fine; Irene cut bait and left her alone. It wasn't her job to make friends or play marriage counselor.

"Some people like being miserable," Irene murmurs to Huck as the couple head off the dock like two of the Seven Dwarves—Dopey and Grumpy. "It's what brings them joy."

I love you, Huck thinks, and that's when he notices the Jeep again. Black Jeep, tinted windows. He checks the license plate and repeats it in his head—*TP 6756*—but two seconds after the Jeep drives away, he's forgotten it.

Could be just a coincidence, a tourist driving around. Tinted windows are legal, though you don't find them on rental vehicles.

He shakes his head. He's thinking of Oscar Cobb, Rosie's old boyfriend, the one with the Ducati motorcycle who, after he was released from prison, drove a Jeep with tinted windows. Oscar's Jeep called attention to itself; it was jacked up, sitting on top of thirty-five-inch BFG mudders.

Huck is thinking of Oscar Cobb again because even though he promised himself he wouldn't, he has been reading steadily through Rosie's journals. It was as simple and irrevocable as Eve taking the first bite of the apple; one taste and Huck was damned.

The journals were a trip back in time. Rosie was single, working at Caneel Bay, living with Huck and LeeAnn. Oscar Cobb came sniffing around, and Rosie resisted. (LeeAnn, Huck thought, would have been so proud of how Rosie resisted!) Russell Steele had stepped between Rosie and Oscar one night. He put Oscar into some kind of death grip, and despite himself, Huck cheered for the guy. That was the beginning of the relationship; it was damn near accidental. Russ hadn't been on the prowl looking to hook up with anyone. He'd seen a person in trouble and he'd helped out. The affair lasted the weekend, and that, Huck supposed, would have been that—were it not for Maia.

There are two places in the journals where Huck choked up. The first was the description of the morning Rosie announced she was pregnant. If Huck had had to remember this on his own, he would have come up blank. But reading the scene in Rosie's handwriting carried him back to the exact moment—his own kitchen, a typical morning. LeeAnn was wearing her raspberry scrubs, her nails painted to match. She was drinking the cup of coffee that Huck always made for her, awaiting her egg and toast. Huck had been dressed for a charter. He wonders now who he'd taken out on the boat that day and what they'd caught and if he'd seemed distracted because of the news his stepdaughter had dropped at breakfast. What Huck does remember is his fear about LeeAnn's reaction. LeeAnn's number-one priority since the day Huck met her had been keeping Rosie from messing up her life in exactly this way. She had gotten Rosie through high school and through college without her becoming pregnant with Oscar's baby.

That day, Rosie swore the baby wasn't Oscar's. She said it was a white fella's, a businessman who'd stayed at the hotel. A pirate. Huck was skeptical. LeeAnn was more than skeptical.

"We'll know the truth when this baby is born," she said.

The second place Huck tears up is at Rosie's description of Maia losing her first tooth. Again, the breakfast table, again toast, because at some point, Huck began making an egg and toast for Maia as well as for LeeAnn. The tooth popped out and skittered across the kitchen floor. Huck found it after a few minutes of hunting—Maia had been worried, the Tooth Fairy and all that—and when he held it up, she'd wrapped her arms around his legs. That was right before LeeAnn got sick and died. The end of the golden days, though of course, none of them had any idea it was the end.

And that, Huck supposes, is why it makes him emotional. His life was blessed and he hadn't appreciated it like he should have.

Rosie got back together with Russ after LeeAnn died; she was vulnerable—and she was free.

The journals mention Irene, the wife at home in Iowa City, a woman Rosie saw as a rival. Was Russ planning on leaving Irene and moving down to the islands permanently? It's anyone's guess. Starting in 2015, there are mentions of Russ's business dealings—the villa and land in Little Cinnamon, the business trips to Anegada, to Grand Cayman. There's mention of Russ wanting to get out of his business dealings and Todd Croft not allowing it; Todd Croft showed up at La Tapa to threaten Rosie.

He killed them, Huck thinks. They were headed to Anegada on New Year's Day and Todd Croft blew them up.

What did Irene say? That the charges might not stick; Croft might be released.

The journals have to go to the FBI. Huck has Colette Vasco's number programmed into his phone. He should call her; she needs to see these.

But... maybe not yet.

Huck believes in honesty. In this situation, does that mean that he should tell Irene he has these journals and that he's planning on handing them over to the FBI? Should he ask Irene if she wants to see them? Or, out of regard for her emotional well-being, should he spare her? Should he give the journals to Vasco and when Irene finds out say he didn't read them and didn't think she should read them either? Is this reasonable? This sounds reasonable, but it's not honest. Is it better? Will it save Irene's heart from breaking again?

Irene is adjusting to their new circumstances better than Huck expected. She's now sleeping in Maia's room. They have developed a routine. Irene worries about money, he knows, but guess what—so does everyone else in the world.

Irene's attorney in Iowa City calls and leaves a message while they're out on a charter. Her mother-in-law's estate is through probate and Milly Steele has left behind "assets," though in the message, the attorney doesn't say what kind.

"Do you think it's money?" Irene asks Huck. "Do you think it's a lot of money? Do you think Russ used Milly's account as a place to hide cash? Do you think Milly knew what Russ was doing? Was she in on it?"

Most of these questions sound rhetorical, so Huck just answers the first. "*Assets* could mean money," Huck says. "Or it could mean a pile of crocheted afghans and used bingo cards."

"You're making an old-lady joke," Irene says. "By definition, *assets* are worth something. Maybe Milly owned real estate I don't know about?" Her voice is hopeful, then, sounding defeated, she says, "I'm actually hoping that Russ hid money with his ninety-seven-year-old mother and that now it will be mine and somehow the FBI won't find out."

"And you won't tell them?"

"I'm not sure," Irene says. She fiddles with the end of her chestnut braid, worrying the band that keeps it together, which is something Huck has noticed her doing a lot recently. This gives Huck hope that Irene Steele is just a regular gal after all and not some kind of superhuman who elegantly copes with whatever life throws at her. "I hate to say it, but I might be tempted to keep it." She honks out a laugh. "But you're right. It's probably afghans. Or her cane. Or a fifty-percent-off coupon for an order of wings at the Wig and Pen."

* * *

Two days later, Huck sees the Jeep with the tinted windows parked outside the minimart in front of Rhumb Lines just as someone is climbing into the front seat. The "someone" appears to be a white female, small in stature. Huck chuckles. Probably just some local concerned about the sun. Although...if it were a local, he would have seen the Jeep before. Maybe she just bought it. It's not impossible.

Irene gets hold of her Iowa City attorney, Ed Sorley. The assets are a collection of blue-chip stocks that Milly has apparently had for decades; converted to cash, they will net Irene one hundred and seventeen thousand dollars.

Irene is jubilant. "The assets are clean!" she says. "They were investments Russ's father made years and years ago that Milly never touched."

"And she left it all to you?" Huck says. "You're rich!"

"It's breathing room," Irene says. "I'm going to split it four ways—me, Cash, Baker, and Maia."

"Maia?"

"For her education."

"AC..."

"Just let me do it, please," Irene says. "She's Russ's daughter, Milly's granddaughter. I'm not arguing with you about it."

"Okay," Huck says. "Should we celebrate? Maia is with Ayers tonight, so it's just the two of us."

"Shambles?" Irene says.

Huck chuckles. Shambles is Irene's new obsession. It's a brightly painted local bar at mile marker two on the Centerline Road that overlooks the Paradise Lumberyard and a mechanic's car-strewn lot. The place puts the *loca* in *local,* which is maybe what Irene likes about it, along with the drinks. The first time they went, the bartender, Nathan, made Irene a rum punch that she claimed was "magic" (or maybe just strong). The food is better than it needs to be; it's downright delicious.

Huck and Irene grab two bar stools, then order a couple of rum punches and pulled pork sandwiches with fries and slaw. They chat with the mechanic and his wife and a couple visiting from Toronto. Nathan slips Irene a second rum punch and, Huck suspects, maybe even a third, because by the time they're ready to leave, Irene has talked the couple from Toronto into booking a fishing charter.

"Ha!" Irene says as they climb into the truck. "That was fun. And I made it rain! We have a full-day charter on Friday."

"Good job, AC," Huck says. When he pulls into the driveway at home, he turns off the ignition but he stays in the truck, and Irene stays in the truck, and it feels for all the world like he's taking her home after a date. Should he kiss her? He promised to let her make the first move.

She places her hand on his thigh. She takes off her seat belt and scoots closer to him. She raises her face to his cheek; he can smell the rum and fruit on her breath. How magic were those rum punches? he wonders.

"AC," he says. "There's something I have to tell you."

He warns her they'll be difficult to read.

"It's the story of their relationship," he says. "Start to finish. I can give you the CliffsNotes version, if you'd rather?"

Irene shakes her head, clutching the journals to her chest. Instantly, he wants to snatch them back. Rosie never intended those journals for Huck's eyes and she *definitely* never intended them for Irene's eyes.

"When I found out about Rosie and Russ, I told myself that I would find a way to forgive them," Irene says. "Maybe understanding how it all unfolded will make that easier."

No, Huck thinks. *It won't.* "Maybe," he says.

She's standing in front of her bedroom door. The air between them is charged—yes? Maia is away overnight for the first time since Irene moved in.

"I appreciate you giving these to me," Irene says. "I'm sure it was a hard decision."

"Torturous," Huck says. He needs a cigarette, badly. "Well, good night, AC."

"Wait," Irene says. She opens the bedroom door, sets the journals on the nightstand, and reemerges to give him a kiss. It's a real kiss, long and delicious, that leaves Huck breathless and aching. She pulls away for a second, then comes back in for more. Huck is very careful with his hands. One is on her shoulder, one on the side of her face. Her fingers are linked through his belt loops. He forgets about the cigarette, about the journals, about the FBI, about the Jeep with the tinted windows, about Rosie, Russ, LeeAnn. He's here with Irene in this moment. It's all he wants in the world.

She reels him in; she lets him go; she reels him in a little closer. He's hooked. She is the Angler Cupcake.

She lets him go. Pulls away. Smiles at him. "That's all for tonight," she says.

Huck raises his palms. He can't speak.

She disappears into her room. Huck grabs the Flor de Caña from the shelf in the kitchen and his pack of Camels and goes out to the deck.

* * *

The next day, Irene is fine, she's normal. She tells the boys about the money from Milly. Baker says he doesn't need his share; he got a windfall from Anna. He tells Irene to split his portion three ways.

And Cash is…

"He seemed more relieved than anything," Irene says. "Thirty-nine grand is a big boost for him, so I thought he'd be more excited. He sounds preoccupied. Tilda has just left on a work trip with an investor in this project her parents have cooking and he's bothered by that."

"Women," Huck says. "They'll get you every time."

Irene's expression is inscrutable. Has she read the diaries? Huck is afraid to ask, but his gut tells him the answer is no.

The next day, they have the charter with the couple from Toronto whose names, Huck sees when he checks the confirmation text from Destiny, are Jack and Diane Boyle. *Little ditty,* Huck thinks, *'bout Jack and Diane…* He wonders how many times those poor folks have heard people sing that to them. Huck makes coffee for himself and Irene, makes an egg and toast with papaya jam from Jake's for Maia. Irene has yet to come out of her room, which is unlike her.

"Is Irene okay?" Maia asks. "I thought I heard her crying late last night."

Crying? Huck's heart sinks. "Hurry it up, Nut. I'm going to run you to school a little early, then come back and scoop up Irene."

Maia shovels in her egg, takes her toast to go.

Huck calls out, "Be right back, AC!"

The black Jeep with the tinted windows is waiting in the elbow joint of Jacob's Ladder, a step closer than it was the last time. Huck stares at the place where the driver would be. If the Jeep is still there when he comes back, he's going to knock on the window.

As soon as Huck and Maia pass, the Jeep follows them. In his rearview, Huck can see the woman—brown hair pulled back, round face. He doesn't recognize her. When he turns left, the Jeep turns right, toward Cruz Bay.

Okay, Huck thinks. The driver doesn't seem particularly villainous, but there's no denying she's watching them. Who is she?

When Huck gets back to the house, Irene is out front. Her hair is braided, she has her sunglasses on, her face is grim. She climbs in the truck and slams the door a little harder than necessary.

"I take it you read the journals."

"I don't want to talk about it until after this charter," Irene says. "But you should know, today will be my last day working for you."

"What?" Huck says. "Irene..."

"I don't want to talk about it," Irene says, "until after this charter. This charter was my doing and although I would rather be anywhere else today, I'm honoring my commitment. But after today, Huck, no, I'm sorry."

She's angry, Huck thinks. *She's hurt.* He's an idiot. He should have handed the journals over to Agent Vasco, honesty be damned.

What makes matters worse is that the charter with Jack and Diane is magnificent from start to finish. Diane is a nurturer—she's the mother of six, she tells them—and she has brought treats for the entire day, starting with a thermos of coffee and sausage-and-egg sandwiches from Provisions, which Huck knows Irene loves, though since losing the villa, she can't spare the money for them. Jack is a terrific guy, a regional manager for a Canadian bookstore chain called Indigo. (Huck has never heard of it but Irene has. Apparently, it's like the Barnes and Noble of Canada.)

Jack and Diane are hearty; they're excited to go offshore and try their luck with the fish. "We're here, aren't we?" Jack says. "Let's go for it."

Huck cranks the music. He starts with John Cougar just for fun and they love it, singing along, arms raised in the air and then wrapped around each other. In his mind, Huck changes "Jack and Diane" to "Huck and Irene." *Hold on to sixteen as long as you can.*

Amen, Huck thinks.

The water is smooth, and the boat skates along with barely a bump. Right before they reach Tambo, they get a hit on the outrigger line. Huck stops the boat. Irene is already handing the rod to Diane, who, after a short fight, brings in a respectable-size wahoo, bright as a bar of sterling silver. Irene handles the gaff like a pro now. As Huck watches her he thinks there's no way she's leaving; she loves this boat too much, this job, him—that kissing the other night was real stuff. Nothing that's in the journals—things that happened years ago—can dismantle that.

They move on to Tambo. The birds are out; there are fish around. They get another bite and Jack takes it. Mahi, a beauty. Then they get another hit, and another. Diane takes one rod, Irene the other, while Huck helps Jack with his fish. Diane brings in a barracuda, Irene another wahoo.

Then there's a lull, the best kind of lull, Huck thinks. Jack cracks open a beer and Diane and Irene settle down to talk about books. Irene says she just finished *The Vacationers*. Diane says she loves Louise Penny.

"I'm probably biased because she's a woman and she's Canadian, but I think she's the best mystery writer alive."

"Huck likes mysteries," Irene says at exactly the same time that Huck says, "I read mysteries."

"How long have you two been together?" Diane asks. She smiles from under the brim of a Blue Jays cap. "Jack and I have been dating since eighth grade."

"My one and only," Jack says.

Huck waits for Irene to answer Diane. They've been asked this before, of course, and Irene normally handles it by saying they're not together, that she is just the mate, and everyone is always surprised because they seem like a couple. They finish each other's sentences.

"I'm just a hired hand," Irene says. "And today is my last day. I'm moving on. You guys will be my last clients on the *Mississippi*."

"Saved the best for last," Jack says, raising his beer.

Huck has a lump in his throat. She said it out loud to strangers—she's leaving. Today is her last day. This doesn't mean it's carved in stone, he tells himself. She'll calm down. She'll reconsider. She has to. Please, God. He can't believe he's being punished for telling the truth.

"Will you leave the island?" Diane asks. "Go back to..."

"Iowa," Irene says.

Huck lights a cigarette in the stern. His nerves are splintering.

"No," Irene says. "I'm going to go for my captain's license and get my own boat."

What? Huck thinks. *What?*

"Good for you," Diane says. "Girl power!"

The line whizzes. "Fish on," Huck says, though he couldn't care less.

Wahoo, mahi, barracuda, mahi, then lunch (sandwiches from Sam and Jack's) and a bottle of champagne that Diane brought.

"It's the forty-fifth anniversary of our first date," Diane says. "Way back in 1974." She pours the champagne into four paper cups and passes them around. "But we had no idea you had something to celebrate as well, Irene. Captaining your own boat!" Diane raises her cup. "Hear, hear!"

Somehow, Huck makes himself sip the champagne. He sees Diane grinning at him.

"You must be an excellent teacher."

"She's a natural," Huck says. He's directing his words at Irene, willing her to look at him. "She's the Angler Cupcake."

When Jack and Diane disembark at the National Park Service dock, there are hugs and handshakes all around. Great day, perfect weather, tons of fish, highlight of their vacation; they'll post their pictures on Facebook and write a five-star review on Tripadvisor.

Huck's heart is broken.

Irene is silent in the truck and Huck knows not to make any stops on the way home. When he pulls up Jacob's Ladder, he looks for the Jeep with the tinted windows, but it's not there.

He says, "There's a strange Jeep that's been lurking around here. Black, with tinted windows. Female driver."

Irene says nothing.

Maia is at Joanie's, which is good, Huck thinks, because they can talk freely. Irene hops out of the truck and goes around to grab the smaller cooler out of the back like she always does, leaving Huck to handle the bigger cooler. Jack and Diane took four pounds of the mahi, but there's a lot of fish left. Huck needs to call the restaurants—La Tapa, Morgan's Mango, Extra Virgin, Lime Inn.

But first.

"Irene," he says.

She disappears inside and when Huck comes in, she's standing in the hallway with the journals in her hands. She reads aloud. "'I'm sex and lobster and champagne-drinking under a blanket of stars. Irene is home and hearth, mother of the boys, keeper of the traditions that make a family.'"

"Irene," Huck says. "Please stop. I tried to warn you—"

"'Can I lure Russ away from her? Can I make him feel his family is here? I can try. In the new year, I decided, I'm going to introduce him to Maia.'"

"I know, Irene. I read them."

"You don't know," Irene says. Her voice wavers. "He was my *husband.* I *trusted* him. Rosie knew I existed, Huck. She knew about me, she knew about the boys from day one, minute one. She knew about the house I was building, she knew how I was decorating it. She thought I was some kind of...*shrew* who didn't appreciate Russ, didn't respect him or honor his sacrifices, didn't love or worship him the way he deserved." In a move so uncharacteristic that Huck can't believe it's happening, Irene throws the journals down the hall. They land at his feet, splayed open, like birds shot out of the sky. "She wanted him to leave me. She wanted him to propose."

"For the record," Huck says, "at the time, I had no idea any of this was going on."

"Your wife did," Irene says. "LeeAnn!"

"Watch it," Huck says. "Please."

"LeeAnn knew I existed. She knew my *name!*"

"Yes, and if you read carefully, LeeAnn said that if Rosie didn't stop seeing Russ, she would call you." Huck clears his throat. "LeeAnn didn't condone the relationship for one second, Irene. She never would have. She wasn't like that."

"What about *you,* Huck? You expect me to believe that LeeAnn didn't tell you what was going on? You weren't informed that Rosie was seeing a married man?"

"LeeAnn kept her business with Rosie between herself and Rosie."

"But you were her husband."

Huck gives Irene a hard stare. "I'm not sure I owe you an explanation." He sighs. "LeeAnn and Rosie's relationship was tumultuous, Irene. It had deep fault lines that weren't visible to the casual observer. Although most of the time things were fine between them, there would be tremors. And some of those tremors turned into earthquakes. I didn't get in the middle. So, no, I didn't know Rosie was seeing a married man."

"And when she started seeing Russ after LeeAnn died? The Invisible Man, Huck? You didn't ask questions?"

"After LeeAnn died...I was lost for a long time. I was self-absorbed. I knew Rosie was dating someone; I asked to meet him, and Rosie was dead set against it. I didn't push. Maybe I should have, but she was a grown woman."

"She was living under your roof! She was your—"

"Daughter," Huck says. "Yes, yes, she was. But you have two

grown children of your own, Irene. Are you accountable for their actions?"

"My sons are good people," Irene says. "I raised them right."

"Fine, I agree, you did. That's not my point. My point is you can't control how they act. Cash lost the stores in Colorado. Was that *your* fault? Both Baker and Cash lied to Ayers about who they were when they first got here. Was *that* your fault?"

"No," Irene says.

"Rosie made a mistake, Irene, but as the saying goes, it takes two to tango. That affair was fifty percent her fault." Huck feels his blood pressure rising. "I could just as easily be furious that Russ led Rosie on for so many years. That Russ's business dealings *got her killed.* Leaving my granddaughter *without a mother!*" He's losing control—and it feels good! Irene isn't the only one allowed to feel angry and hurt. The affair was 50 percent Russ's fault, but the illegal business was 100 percent his fault.

Irene stares at Huck for a long second, her eyes narrowed. " 'Love is messy and complicated and unfair,' " she says. "Quote, unquote, from Rosie herself, and I agree. It's not fair that I have feelings for the man who should be my enemy. Your words just now crystallized our problem. You *should* be furious with Russ. He *was* to blame for their deaths, at least indirectly. We're on different sides of this, Huck. And because of that, I can't work for you and I can't live here. I'm sorry."

"So—what?" Huck says. "You're quitting and you're moving out? Where will you go?"

"To Baker's for the time being, then I'll figure something out," Irene says. "It's none of your concern."

None of your concern. How can she *say* that? "What you told Jack and Diane is true?" Huck asks. "You're striking out on your own? Getting your captain's license? Starting your own charter?

Any idea how difficult that's going to be? You don't know anyone on this island except for me." This comes out all wrong; he sounds like a complete bastard when what he really wants to say is *Please don't leave me.*

"I'm going to pack my things," Irene says. "Which shouldn't take long, but I'd appreciate it if you weren't here when I left."

"Oh, that's rich," Huck says. "You're ordering me out of my own house. After I took you in and gave you a *home* and gave you a *job* and..." He wants to say *Gave you my love*—but no, he won't let her have the satisfaction. She wants to leave? Fine, she can leave. She wants to throw away the relationship? Great. Maybe she's right, maybe they are on different sides of this goddamned situation, maybe the stupidest thing he ever did was let her on his boat that first day.

But even as Huck is thinking this, he knows it's not true. They are on the same side because they're alive. They're the survivors. "I'll leave," Huck says. "But just remember what you told me yesterday, Irene."

She cocks an eyebrow. Her expression now is more sassy than angry; she looks like a rebellious teenager.

"You said you would find a way to forgive them."

Irene retreats to the bedroom and slams the door behind her.

When Huck gets out to his truck, he lights a cigarette and flies down Jacob's Ladder faster than he should. He checks the spot where the black Jeep with the tinted windows was waiting that morning, but it's not there. Too bad, because he's in the mood for a confrontation. He wonders if the woman is a reporter. Or someone sent by the FBI to watch them. Or...someone sent by Croft to watch them. Maybe it's good that Irene is leaving. He doesn't need strangers lurking around him and his granddaughter.

When Huck reaches the bottom of the hill, he has to decide

where he's going. He could pick up some barbecue from Candi's but he won't be able to eat a thing and Maia would be just as happy with peanut butter and jelly.

Her own charter boat. Ha!

He should have passed the journals on to Vasco. People think they want the truth but they can't handle the truth! Huck supposes it's possible that Irene would have reacted like this if he'd given the journals to the FBI without telling her about them. He was damned either way.

He toys with the idea of going to a bar for a beer and a shot, something to calm him down, but that's not the answer tonight. He could only too easily end up like Mick, chained to a bar stool at CBL making a spectacle of himself.

Huck drives through town, past Mongoose Junction, and up the wide, sweeping hill to the sunset-view spot over Cruz Bay. He pulls over and parks. There are a dozen or so people, several couples and one family, waiting for the sun to drop into the ocean. They have their cameras out—of course. These days, a picture of a thing is more important than the thing itself. But Huck is old enough to remember otherwise. He's old enough to watch the sun go down and the fiery pink brush-stroking the clouds and do nothing but think.

At first he's melancholy. The sun is setting on the last day he will ever spend with the Angler Cupcake, Irene Steele.

But then he thinks, *No, that won't do.*

He's a pretty smart guy, resourceful. He's going to find a way to get her back.

AYERS

The phone rings at midnight but Ayers doesn't wake up until she feels Winnie's cold nose pushing against the back of her hand. The dog has proven to be eerily in touch with the human world. *Your phone is ringing!* Yes, Ayers hears the muffled tone; she digs it out from under the rumpled covers of her bed.

The screen tells her it's Mick.

Ayers huffs and hits Decline. She was so tired after her shift at La Tapa that she face-planted on her bed still in her uniform, still in her *clogs,* and when Winnie jumped onto the bed with her, she didn't protest. The phone goes dark for a second, then lights up again, and again Winnie nudges Ayers.

"Argh," Ayers says, but she answers. "What? What, Mick, what?"

Mick is crying.

"What's wrong?" Ayers asks, then remembers that she no longer cares what's wrong.

"Can I come over?" he asks.

"No," Ayers says.

"Please?"

Ayers summons her resolve. It would be only too easy to relent. *Okay, fine, you can come, but you're not staying long.* Mick would step inside, bringing their nine-year history with him. It's not that Mick is even that attractive, but he's attractive to her. He has that something. Ayers loves his hands, and the tattoo of Gordon's paw print under his left rib, and the way he squints when he looks at her like he's looking at the sun. They have good memories, years of them—snorkeling and hiking and partying on the water and on land. How many times had Mick anchored a boat off Water Island so they could swim ashore and get bushwackers from Dinghy's? How many times had they played the brass-ring game at the Soggy Dollar or rolled the dice at Cruz Bay Landing? How many times did they stand in line together at the post office or at the bank to deposit their paychecks, pinkie fingers entwined? How many brunches up at the Banana Deck, how many hikes to Ram Head, how many times had Mick dropped Ayers off at Driftwood Dave's on their way home from the beach so she could run in for two rum punches to go while he drove around the block? How many times had Mick saved Ayers the corner seat at the Beach Bar while he was working so she could have a front-row view of the band? He used to sneak up behind her and kiss her shoulder, take a surreptitious sip of her drink.

"I'm asleep," Ayers says. "Go home to bed, Mick. Or call Brigid."

"I don't want to call Brigid. I don't care about Brigid. That night at the beach, she trapped me."

"You kissed her, Mick," Ayers says. "Right?" They haven't had a conversation since Ayers broke their engagement, so she hasn't heard Mick admit his guilt.

"Yes," Mick says. "I kissed her. We kissed."

Something inside Ayers zips shut, a tiny compartment where she held out hope that maybe it wasn't true. "Thank you for telling me. We're done. I gave you a second chance, and you blew it. I have self-worth and self-respect and you, my friend, have a problem with commitment, fidelity, and honesty." Ayers runs her hand down Winnie's back for comfort. "This theater production you've been starring in at Cruz Bay Landing is a pathetic plea for attention but it's also a subtle way to make everyone we know think that this is my fault. You're playing the injured party when *you're* the one who screwed it up." Ayers's anger energizes her; she sits up, kicks off her clogs. "You're making an ass of yourself. You've become the village idiot."

"I kissed Brigid," Mick says. "I own that. But even if I hadn't kissed Brigid, the engagement would be over. And why? Why, Ayers? Because you're pregnant with Banker's baby, that's why."

Ayers falls back. Winnie gets to her feet and stands over her. "Who told you that?"

"It's all over town," Mick says.

"No," Ayers says. Did Cash tell Tilda, who then told Skip, who then told Mick? "I haven't told anyone."

"You didn't have to," Mick says. "You took a leave of absence from the boat, you missed shifts at La Tapa, Skip said he heard you retching in the ladies' room before service. It doesn't take Sherlock Holmes to figure it out. Skip actually congratulated *me,* thinking I was the father. But I'm not. Both you and I know that I'm not."

"No," Ayers says.

"And now Banker knows too."

Ayers feels dizzy, like she's on some kind of crazed rocking horse. "What?"

"He and his little boy sat next to me at CBL earlier tonight," Mick says. "I told him."

Ayers is so addled that she's certain there's no way she'll be able to fall back to sleep.

But she does, immediately.

When she wakes up in the morning, there's a text from Baker. Good morning! You feeling any better?

He knows.

Does she tell him that she knows he knows? Or should she just pretend the phone call with Mick never happened and tell him herself?

The latter. Mick is irrelevant.

She thinks about sending a text back, something along the lines of *Not sick, pregnant. It's yours!*

Whoa! The room is spinning. Ayers races for the bathroom and throws up. When she emerges, Winnie is stationed outside the door.

"Do you need to go out?" Ayers asks. Winnie trots over to the front door and waits. "I can't walk you this second, I'm sorry. Just do your thing and come right back, okay?" Ayers opens the door and Winnie obeys, taking care of business efficiently and then slipping back inside past Ayers's legs. She's such a good dog; much better than Gordon, if Ayers is being honest. Gordon would have sniffed around for twenty minutes and couldn't be trusted if a car or another dog came past. Of course, Winnie is female, so that alone explains it.

Ayers takes a four-seven-eight breath and pours herself half a glass of warm ginger ale. She calls Baker, who answers on the first ring.

"Good morning!"

"Good morning?" Ayers says. He sounds awfully chipper. It occurs to Ayers that maybe Mick lied about telling Baker that Ayers is pregnant. "Listen, Baker, there's something I need to talk to you about."

"If you want to talk in person, I can be there in two seconds," Baker says.

What she wants is to hang up and go back to bed. She sighs. She can't put this conversation off much longer. "Okay."

One Mississippi, two Mississippi, three—there's a knock at the door. Winnie shoots over and starts barking.

"Just a minute!" Ayers says. Is that *him?* Had he been standing outside when she called him? Ayers hurries to the bathroom, takes in her pasty complexion, her bed-mussed hair, her rumpled uniform shirt. Does she stink? Probably. She tries to rub deodorant on without taking off her shirt. She piles her hair on top of her head. Better? Worse? Worse, she decides. She lets it go. Oh, well.

When she swings the door open, there's Baker, looking tan and relaxed. He's gorgeous—tall, broad, smiling in that gee-whiz midwestern way. Ayers is struck by something she has willfully ignored until now. She *likes* Baker. A lot.

Winnie barks. She wants to jump on him, Ayers can tell; her slender golden body is shimmying with energy, her tail is going nuts. It's not her daddy, but close—his brother.

"Hey, I recognize you," Baker says to Winnie. And then, to Ayers, "Hello, beautiful."

If Ayers weren't pregnant, this moment would be so sexy. She would be wearing a bikini or a sundress or hiking shorts and they would be heading out into the sunshine to start their relationship.

"I'm pregnant," she says.

"I know," he says. "Can I come in?"

Ayers figures she's about six weeks along. A check of the internet reveals that her baby is likely the size of a pea.

Will there come a day twenty-five or thirty years from now

when Ayers tells Sweet Pea about the morning she invited Baker Steele inside her tiny, disheveled home to discuss Sweet Pea's very existence? What will Ayers remember? Baker's handsome face may be forgotten, but what will stick with Ayers is her own sense of bewilderment. She's attracted to Baker, but she doesn't know the first thing about him. He might as well be a stranger at the airport who asks her to travel with a mysterious piece of luggage.

They settle on the sofa. Winnie is at Baker's side now—fickle girl.

"It's your baby," Ayers says.

"I heard."

"I want to make that clear. It's yours, not Mick's. Also, I'm finished with Mick."

"You're sure? Because you said that last time and it didn't end up being true. I was gone for two days and you got engaged to the guy."

When he says it that way, it sounds awful. It *was* awful. In agreeing to marry Mick, Ayers was unfair to all parties involved—Baker, Mick, and, most of all, herself. "I thought it was what I'd been waiting for," Ayers says. "It was validating after what happened with Brigid to feel like he was choosing me, to feel like I'd won."

"You told me that story about your parents in Kathmandu. The hiccup, your mother with another man." Baker's gaze wanders over to the travel photographs Ayers has on her wall. "In telling me that story, you made me feel like the hiccup."

Ayers can't believe she told Baker the story about her parents in Kathmandu. Her mother had had a brief affair with a British expat bar owner...or she hadn't; Ayers isn't sure to this day. Ayers pulled that story out, she supposes, because she wanted to justify forgiving Mick. She was making excuses for him. But she was finished with that now.

"This doesn't have to look any certain way," Baker says. "First question: Do you want to keep the baby?"

"Oh. Yes. Yes, I do."

"Great. Second question: Do you want to have the baby and still be with Mick, Ayers? If the answer is yes, I will understand."

"You will?"

"Yes. Is that what you want?"

"No," Ayers says. "I told you, I'm finished with Mick. That's my final answer, in the name of self-respect."

Palpable relief emanates from Baker.

"But," Ayers says.

"But?"

"I don't know that I can be with you either, not right away. I think I need to be alone for a while."

"Alone."

"Romantically alone, yes. I need some time and I need some space." This is something Ayers has given a lot of thought to. If she weren't pregnant, she might have climbed right into bed with Baker, forging ahead without any introspection. On to the next guy! She would have used Baker like a bandage, plastering his love and devotion over the wounds that Mick left. But being pregnant changes things. Ayers needs to be alone. She needs to worry less about falling in love with someone else and instead fall in love with herself. It's the best gift she can bestow on this child: a mother who is happy and capable and whole.

Ayers puts a hand on Baker's arm. "But we can be friends."

"Friends."

"Until I feel like I'm ready to start something new. I don't want this baby to dictate my love life. I want my heart to dictate that."

"We're not exactly starting from ground zero," Baker says. "We have something to work with. I fell in love with you the second I saw you—"

"Don't say *love.*" Ayers collapses back into the cushions. "Before I found out I was pregnant, I figured we could just start over, go on some dates, take things slow, do it properly."

"That's what I thought too."

"Nothing says *taking it slow* like instant family."

They laugh. It's funny for a few seconds.

"You heard we lost the villa?" Baker says.

"Maia told me. She said you were looking for a rental?"

"Yep, yep. I stayed at the Westin for so long that they offered me a job selling time-shares, which I accepted."

"Seriously?"

"I start Monday," Baker says. "And I got Floyd settled at Gifft Hill with the cool kids."

"All the kids at Gifft Hill are cool," Ayers says.

"My feelings exactly," Baker says. He gives her an uncomfortable smile. "And I found a villa."

"You did?" Ayers says. "Where?"

"Across the street," Baker says. "The Happy Hibiscus."

At this, Winnie barks in a way that sounds like a laugh.

"The Happy Hibiscus? *Right* across the street?"

"Yes," Baker says. "Floyd and I are moving in . . . today."

"Today?"

"I was just over there dropping off groceries."

"Ah," Ayers says. She rubs Winnie behind the ears. *So much for space,* she thinks. She and the Steeles are becoming one big extremely nontraditional family. She casts her eyes skyward. Rosie is either laughing or crying up there. Or both.

CASH

The night before Tilda leaves on her weeklong research trip with Dunk, she and Cash drink a bottle of Granger's Cristal while skinny-dipping in the pool (Granger and Lauren are gone, off to LA) and then Cash makes love to Tilda on the round sun bed under a crescent moon. Later, when they're wrapped in the luscious Turkish towels, gazing at the twinkling lights of Tortola, Tilda cries a little. She doesn't *want* to go away without him, she says. She's going to *miss* him.

"It's only a week," Cash says. His casual attitude is an act. He can't believe this is happening. Tilda is going to Anguilla, St. Lucia, and a tiny private island called Eden, home to a resort so exclusive that you have to be invited to stay there; management curates its guests as though it's selecting art for a museum. (How did Tilda and Dunk make the cut? Cash wonders. He hopes it was through Granger's prodigious network and not Dunk's influence.)

Tilda and Dunk have separate rooms at Midi et Minuit, the resort on Anguilla, and at Emerald Hill on St. Lucia. But of the dozen freestanding villas at Eden, only one is available during Tilda and Dunk's stay. So they'll be sharing.

"You'd better behave yourself," Tilda says, resting her head on Cash's chest. "No picking up women at the Soggy Dollar."

"What about you?" Cash asks. "Are you going to behave yourself?"

"Oh, please," Tilda says. "You never have a thing to worry about with me. But especially not with Dunk."

The next day, as Cash is aboard *Treasure Island* heading for Virgin Gorda, a boat cuts in front of them going at least sixty knots—it's coming from the direction of the East End and heading for St. Thomas. It's the *Olive Branch,* of course. Tilda and Dunk are sitting in the stern, laughing. Cash hears the captain yell out and Cash wonders if this will finally be the time James calls the Coast Guard to complain. Or maybe Cash will call the Coast Guard himself. Dunk did this on purpose; is he trying to make a point to Cash? *I'm taking off with your girl.* Tilda is wearing a black sundress Cash has never seen before; it's sleek and sophisticated, possibly borrowed from her mother's closet. She's also wearing a pair of dark cat's-eye sunglasses, Tom Ford, that Cash knows she lifted from Lauren.

When Tilda sees Cash, she waves and blows a kiss. She seems older and more glamorous, as though she outgrew him overnight.

"Hold on!" Cash calls to his passengers as the boat slams into the *Olive Branch*'s wake.

With Tilda away, Cash has the villa in Peter Bay to himself; Virgie, the housekeeper, has been given the week off. Another guy might revel in the freedom, might make a list of all the ways to push the envelope. Cash can borrow liberally from Granger's wine fridge and make a trip to Starfish Market for thick, marbled steaks and charge them to the house account. He can snoop through the master wing—Granger and Lauren's bedroom, sitting room, closets, offices, and bathroom—and see what secrets he can dig up. Money? Pills? He can bring Winnie back; he can let Winnie swim in the pool. Of all these ideas, only the last one holds any appeal—although Cash suspects that the villa has cameras placed so strategically that he can't even find them and block them.

The first night alone, Cash cracks a beer and checks his phone frequently to see if Tilda has texted or called. She and Dunk were taking his boat all the way to San Juan and flying to Anguilla from there. Tilda sent the full itinerary to Cash's phone and when he looks at it, he sees that she was supposed to land in Anguilla at three o'clock. At seven, he still hasn't heard from her and so what is he to think but that she has forgotten all about him? She and Dunk landed on the tiny airstrip and were whisked away by a private car—Cash pictures a vintage Peugeot—to the lush tropical entrance of Midi et Minuit. Midi et Minuit, built in the 1920s, was the private beachfront estate of French perfume heiress Helene Simone until the early 1980s, when it was transformed into a resort. In those days, it attracted guests like John and Cristina DeLorean and Burt Reynolds and Loni Anderson, and it was famous for its midnight disco parties. The owners went bankrupt in the crash of 1987, and Midi et Minuit closed until the year 2000, when it was bought by a businessman from Monte Carlo who poured fifty-five million dollars into the property and turned it into the epitome of "low-key luxury" and "barefoot chic."

Cash wonders if Tilda and Dunk were greeted with welcome cocktails and chilled towels while the hotel's most famous resident, Bijou, a Yorkshire terrier, yipped around Tilda's ankles until she scooped him up and gave him kisses. Were Dunk and Tilda mistaken for a couple? Undoubtedly yes, despite the reservation for separate rooms. Or maybe during their day of travel, Tilda and Dunk had bonded over their excitement about this new venture; maybe they'd had drinks on the plane, and maybe Tilda fell asleep with her head accidentally leaning on Dunk's shoulder. Maybe by the time they reached the resort, they asked to share a room. But no, not yet, not the first night. Cash has enough faith in Tilda to know that nothing has happened between them yet.

Why hasn't she called? Or at least texted to let him know she arrived safely?

Cash's fingers hover over his phone. Should he text her?

No, he won't. And he's not going to sit around the villa pining away either. He doesn't have money to waste on going out to dinner, but, oh, well, he's doing it anyway. He drives Tilda's Range Rover into Cruz Bay and sits at the bar at the Banana Deck. He orders the shrimp curry and chats with the bartender, Kim, who immediately says, "You hang out with Tilda Payne, right? I saw you two at Christmas Cove a few weeks ago. Is she working tonight?"

"She's…away," Cash says. Kim seems friendly enough for Cash to spill his guts to. He could tell her that Tilda is away for a week with some millennial millionaire who lives out in the East End, but how pathetic would that sound? Instead, Cash raises his beer glass. "I'll have another one, please."

He stops at two beers, eats his curry, and chats a little more with Kim, telling her that he works on the *Treasure Island.*

She says, "Oh yeah?" and studies him for a second. "You know, rumor has it that Ayers is pregnant."

Whoa! This is unexpected. Cash's face must register genuine shock because Kim leans across the bar. "I shouldn't have said that, it's probably not true, please don't tell anyone."

"Oh, I won't," Cash says. Kim moves down the bar to help another customer and Cash realizes their conversation is over. He scans the place to see if anyone looks familiar or even promising to talk to; he needs some *friends.* He thinks about stopping by La Tapa on his way home to give Ayers a heads-up that her secret is out, but that will only upset her, and swinging by Tilda's place of work while Tilda is away feels weird and desperate. Besides which, Skip will be working, and he hates Cash's guts.

Cash pays the bill, waves to Kim, and tries to look like a man who has important people to meet. He could check out Beach Bar, see if a band is playing tonight, or he could try his luck at the Parrot Club, though he definitely does *not* have money to gamble away. Another drink sounds appealing—maybe at the Dog House Pub, where he can watch basketball on TV? But he's driving Tilda's Range Rover, it's a seventy-thousand-dollar vehicle, and two drinks is a wise limit.

He checks his phone, which he miraculously avoided doing all through dinner (there is nothing more pathetic than a dude alone at dinner looking at his phone) and finds nothing from Tilda. For an instant, he wonders if she's okay. Did her plane crash? Was she kidnapped? Or, a more likely possibility, did something happen to her phone? Did she leave it in the airport restroom? Did it fall into her personal plunge pool? If anything dire had happened, Cash assumes he would have heard from Granger or Lauren. If something happened to her phone, she would have simply texted from Dunk's phone.

Tomorrow, maybe he'll see if James the boat captain wants to grab a drink. James will say no; he has a wife and a baby girl out in Coral Bay, and he likely gets his fill of Cash while they're on the boat.

Well, it's not like Cash doesn't know anyone else on the island. He calls his mother—gets her voicemail. Then he calls his brother—gets his voicemail.

Cash tosses his phone onto the seat beside him and yells as loud as he can. The sound, desperate even to his own ears, is absorbed by the expensive leather.

Cash wakes up in the morning to a new day—chirping geckos, singing birds, blue sky, pearlescent sunlight. There's a text from Tilda. Finally. Cash opens it.

It says: Arrived! Followed by a single kissy-face emoji. Sent at... 12:47 a.m.

Cash stares at the text, willing it to say something else, something more. She was supposed to land yesterday at three in the afternoon. Why is she only texting him at a quarter to one the following morning? He checks to see if there's a missed call from her. Nope. So this is it. Technically, it checks the box—she's let him know she made it safely—but it feels perfunctory, like an afterthought. *Oops, forgot to text Cash.* Does she miss him? If the answer is yes, why doesn't she say so? She used to text that she missed him if the *Treasure Island* was a few minutes late pulling into Cruz Bay or if he got held up in the customhouse coming back from the BVIs. This feels like a blow-off. Why did she wait so long to text and what was she doing up so late?

Cash texts back: Glad you made it safely. I miss you!

He waits to see if she responds, but there's nothing. She must still be sleeping.

While Cash is driving to work, his phone rings and his whole body relaxes. There she is.

He's on the dicey curve above Hawksnest so he answers without checking the display. "Hello?" He has the radio up, 104.3 the

Buzz out of San Juan, which is playing Michael Franti, and he makes no move to turn it down. He wants to sound happy, busy, unconcerned.

"Cash?"

It's not Tilda. It's his mother.

Cash is so crushed, he nearly hangs up.

"Hey," he says, and he does turn down the music. He's no longer in a "Sound of Sunshine" mood.

"Cash? It's Mom. Listen, I have some good news."

Good news at this point would be Tilda calling to say that Dunk's picture should be next to *douchebag* in the dictionary and that she can't stand him another second and is on her way home, hotel research be damned. He can't believe how strongly he feels about Tilda. He knew the relationship was promising but his feelings have ratcheted up to the next level now that she's gone. Gone with Dunk. "Oh, really?" Cash says. He wonders briefly if Irene's attorney somehow managed to get the villa back. What a major relief *that* would be! He could leave Peter Bay and regain at least a little of his self-respect.

"Milly's estate is through probate," Irene says. "She had stocks that your grandfather bought back in the late 1970s that were sold for us. To the tune of a hundred and seventeen thousand dollars. Now, I wanted to split that four ways—you, your brother, Maia, and myself."

"Good call including Maia," Cash says. "That's really decent of you, Mom."

"Well, just listen. It turns out Baker doesn't need the money. He got money from Anna. So Milly's money will be split three ways. By next week, you'll be thirty-nine thousand dollars richer."

Thirty-nine thousand dollars. Cash knows he should be grateful but all he can think is that Dunk has enough money to buy an island. Buy! An! Island! This little jaunt Tilda is on must be costing nearly thirty-nine thousand dollars, if not more.

"Thanks, Mom," he says. "That is good news. I can buy a truck." *Used,* he thinks.

"Your brother bought a Jeep," Irene says. "And he found a rental."

"He did?" Cash says, perking up. "How big?"

"Two bedrooms," Irene says. "In Fish Bay."

Cash's mood darkens. "I thought he was looking for something bigger. I can't stay at Tilda's forever, Mom. And what about Winnie? She's living with Ayers."

"The villa Baker rented is across the street from Ayers," Irene says. "I forgot to ask Baker if he's allowed to have pets. He might be."

Which means that Winnie might have a home—but Cash does not. "Thanks for the call, Mom. I'll get you my bank information but I'm at work now, so I should go."

"Honey?" Irene says. "Is everything okay?"

Cash sighs. His mother knows him; his mother loves him. They have always been allies, and if anyone on this earth can relate to feeling abandoned, it's his mother. Except she seems pretty happy with Huck. "Tilda went away for a week with another guy," Cash says. "Some super-wealthy investor who's funding this eco-resort that Tilda and her parents want to build on Lovango Cay."

"They went away together? Like, *together*-together?"

"Supposedly all business," Cash says. "Tilda said he turns her stomach." *Had* Tilda said this? No; this is how Cash feels. Dunk turns *his* stomach. "Whatever. I guess we'll see."

"If it makes you feel any better," Irene says, "she'd be a fool to leave you."

Cash shakes his head. "Thanks, Mom."

* * *

On the second day, Tilda texts Cash a selfie. It's just her face. She has her mother's sunglasses on; she's lying back on a chaise in the sun.

Cash responds by texting her a selfie he takes on the bow of *Treasure Island,* his sunglasses and headset on, wind blowing his hair. He feels like a jackass.

The third day, Tilda sends a text that says, Off to St. Luscious! With a kissy-face emoji.

Cash texts back: Have fun. He can't believe the minimalist nature of her communication. One text a day? No calls at all? Of course, Cash hasn't called her either. Should he? No, he thinks. But an instant later, he does call her. The phone rings six times, he hears the funny tone that means she's in another country, then her voicemail picks up. She texted only two minutes earlier; is she so busy that she can't say a quick hello? Maybe she's on the plane, or maybe she's frantically packing, trying to get out of the hotel room to meet her car to the airport. There could be lots of reasons she can't talk. Cash hangs up.

Cash realizes he hates being trapped in the villa in Peter Bay and—hidden cameras be damned—he starts flagrantly breaking the rules. Okay, maybe not *flagrantly,* Cash doesn't have a rule-breaking bone in his body. He *cautiously* breaks the rules. He drinks six of Granger's Island Hoppin' IPAs and samples the whiskey in the crystal decanter that he finds in Granger's study. Granger's study is dark and serious—there's a portrait of Abraham Lincoln on the wall. Then again, the Payne family *is* from Illinois, so maybe this makes sense. The desk is backed by a wall of books, nothing leather-bound, though they're all hardcovers; fiction, it looks like—Tilda mentioned that Granger is a prodigious and serious reader. Cash sees they're alphabetized by author, like in a bookstore—Nabokov, Nesbo, Ng. The surface of Granger's desk is clear, and the drawers are all locked (Cash checks; he's looking, of course, for notes, some record of Granger's impressions of Duncan Huntley or possibly even their financial arrangement), so Cash takes only the whiskey, but even that feels like getting away with something.

Before going to sleep on the third night, Cash moves out of Tilda's wing and into the guest wing, which is where Cash brought Tilda's friend Max after Max got drunk and sick on *Treasure Island.* Tilda's wing of the house is cluttered with Tilda's clothes, books, magazines, sunglasses, bikinis, hair products, a bunch of half-burned Nest scented candles, corkscrews, the cheap vinyl drawstring backpacks she likes to carry, and pairs of hiking boots, water shoes, and work clogs as well as receipts and piles of cash, her tips from various nights that she doesn't ever bother to count or deposit, but the guest wing is immaculate. The wing is two stories connected by a floating staircase that appears to be magically suspended in air. Upstairs is a comfy sitting room with a huge television and a perfect little palm-green-and-white-tiled kitchenette that has a petal-pink minifridge filled with soft drinks and beer. How did Cash not know about this? He takes an Island Hoppin' IPA, thank you very much. The bedroom is downstairs. There's a four-poster mahogany bed draped with white sheers that looks like what a bed in heaven must look like. Out a sliding glass door is a private garden and a deep, circular plunge pool.

Home for the night, Cash thinks. He doesn't have to go into the main house at all.

He's getting thirty-nine thousand dollars free and clear. After he finishes his beer, he feels happy about this. He can buy a truck and stop driving Tilda's Rover around like he's the errand boy.

Cash has a difficult time falling asleep in the guest wing. The bed is too soft and it doesn't smell like Tilda. It's quarter to eleven; he could still go out. Cruz Bay isn't exactly a late-night town but Cash knows the Parrot Club will be open. He can take what's left in his bank account and gamble, now that he knows there's more money coming.

Cash gets all the way out to the driveway before he comes to his senses. He's been drinking; he should not get behind the wheel of the Rover and he should *not* piss all his hard-earned money away at the Parrot Club. He has a full charter tomorrow. He should go to bed.

He does go to bed—back in Tilda's wing, his face buried in her pillow.

Working on *Treasure Island* has been a good distraction. There's nothing like being responsible for thirty people as they swim, snorkel (often for the first time), and drink copious amounts of alcohol to keep one in the present moment. But on day four of not talking to Tilda—honestly, what's going on? Has she not thought to call Cash even once?—Cash finds himself short on patience. It doesn't help that he has a guest on the boat who reminds him of Duncan. This guy, Bradley, is an aggressive, in-your-face hipster. He's exactly Dunk's height and build, and he's wearing jeans—jeans, on a trip to the BVIs!—and a plain white T-shirt that looks like it came out of a three-pack of Hanes but probably was made by Rick Owens and cost four hundred dollars. And he's wearing a flashy gold Omega. Cash notices the jeans and the watch when Bradley checks in but not his Versace slip-on loafers, which he refuses to be separated from when it's time to board the boat.

Cash says calmly, "Take your shoes off and put them in the basket or I will leave you here."

"Oh yeah?" Bradley says, squaring his shoulders.

Cash lifts the rope from the bollard. Everyone is aboard except for Bradley, who remains in his shoes on the dock.

"Yeah," Cash says.

Reluctantly, Bradley removes his precious shoes and hands them over to his girlfriend, who, Cash remembers from check-in, is named Gretchen Gingerman. She puts them in her oversize Fendi bag.

Bradley stays in the shade of the wheelhouse while Gretchen fetches him drinks. Gretchen has golden hair, is three inches taller than Bradley, and has the face and body of a supermodel; Cash tries not to look too closely but Gretchen Gingerman seems pretty damn perfect. And unlike Bradley, she's cool. She leans across the bar and apologizes about the shoes, then says, "Bradley has a thing about people seeing his feet," which is a statement so bizarre that all Cash can do is laugh, and Gretchen Gingerman laughs right along with him. Then Gretchen's phone rings and she checks the display and says, "That's him. He must be wondering where his drink is."

"He called you?" Cash says. He takes his time making two painkillers. Let Bradley wonder.

Bradley stays on the boat during their trip to the Baths, since it can't be done in jeans. Gretchen goes (she's wearing a gold-lamé string bikini; Ayers would have had a field day, but Cash is inclined to cut Gretchen some slack, and besides, she looks amazing in it) and has a wonderful time. Gretchen also goes snorkeling at the Indians. Cash shows her his favorite staghorn coral formation, where they see a school of parrotfish and a baby barracuda, and when they get back to the boat, Bradley is glowering.

He says to Cash, "You trying to make time with my girl?"

Cash holds up his palms. "Just showing her the fish, man."

They go to Pirates Bight on Norman Island for lunch; it has a dock, so Bradley can finally disembark. Cash always sits at the bar and orders the mahi sandwich (he isn't required to socialize during lunch), but he can't keep from seeking out the two-top in the corner where Gretchen and Bradley are sitting by themselves. This seems a little sad. By this point in the trip, most people have bonded with other guests and all sit at nearby or connecting tables so they can chat. Cash knows he shouldn't...but he heads over to Gretchen and Bradley's table. Gretchen is eating the fish and chips like it's her last meal on earth, swiping her fries liberally through the tartar sauce, but Bradley has only a painkiller in front of him.

"Not hungry?" Cash asks. He's poking the bear, he knows this, but he can't help himself. "Did being on the boat make you nauseated?"

"He's fasting," Gretchen says. "He's like Jack from Twitter. It's a control thing."

"A *productivity* thing," Bradley says. He shoots his watch to the end of his wrist; it actually looks a little big, like it's his father's watch. "Not that it's any of this squid's business whether I eat or don't eat."

Squid? Cash thinks. Did *Bradley,* who came on an all-day swim-and-snorkel charter in a pair of skinny Calvin Kleins like he's Brooke Shields, just call *Cash* a squid?

Gretchen is giving Cash big apologetic eyes, probably

imploring him not to engage, an expression that doesn't escape Bradley's notice. "Don't ogle him," Bradley says. He drains the painkiller top to bottom in one long gulp like it's some kind of party trick. *Guess what, Bradley,* Cash wants to say. *I see it all day, every day. Chugging a painkiller does not make you a badass.* "Don't you have to go swab the decks?" Bradley asks.

He's small, Cash tells himself. *And he's insecure, even though he probably makes millions and has a smoke-show girlfriend.* "Yes," Cash says. He grins because Bradley is so mired in his own pointless misery that this seems like the response that would irk him the most. "See you on the boat at one thirty sharp."

Their last stop is White Bay on Jost Van Dyke. On the way over to Jost, Cash mans the bar and Gretchen comes in for two painkillers.

"I'm sorry about Bradley," she says. "I made him come on this trip when he didn't want to. He agreed just to make me happy."

So is it making you happy? Cash wants to ask. He believes that if you agree to do something you'd rather not do for someone else's sake, then you should do it *graciously,* with some *enthusiasm,* like a *good sport.*

"I told him I'd stay on the boat with him when we get to Jost," Gretchen says. "He can't get onto the beach without getting wet?"

"No," Cash says. "We anchor about ten yards out and people wade ashore." He laughs. "There's a reason the bar is called the Soggy Dollar."

"We'll stay on the boat, then. I just wanted to tell you in advance."

"You do you," Cash says. "But I would be a terrible first mate if I didn't warn you that you're making a mistake. Leave your boyfriend on the boat and come ashore, just for a little while. White Bay is the most joyous place on earth. You have to experience it. I can't let you be a bystander."

"Aww," Gretchen says. "You're sweet to look out for me like that, but I'd better stay with Bradley."

"Okay..." Cash says.

Gretchen comes over to Cash's side of the bar, snakes an arm around his shoulders, and holds her phone up for a selfie. "Smile," she says. "I'm going to make you famous."

Late that night, Cash's phone rings. He grapples around in the dark until he finds it on the nightstand. He is, once again, in Tilda's wing.

The screen says NO CALLER ID.

Great, he thinks. Just what he needs, an anonymous call in the middle of the night. "Hello?"

"Cash?"

It's Tilda. Now, on night four, she decides to call. At—he checks the bedside clock—2:17 a.m. Man, he would love to just hang up, but he's been waiting a long time for this, and besides, he *is* living in her house. "Hey," Cash says. "What's up?"

"What's *up?*" She sounds...angry for some reason. *She* sounds angry. That's rich, Cash thinks. She was supposed to call him days earlier, was supposed to call and text and FaceTime, and she said she'd send pictures of every cool detail so he would feel like he was right there with her. Has any of that happened? No, it has not.

"How's your trip?" Cash asks. "You having fun?"

"My trip *was* great. My trip *was* the best four days of my life until just now, when I logged on to Instagram and saw a picture of you cozied up with Gretchen Gingerman!"

"Who?" Cash says, though he obviously knows who Gretchen Gingerman is. What he doesn't know is how or why Tilda knows who Gretchen Gingerman is. Are they *friends?*

"Gretchen Gingerman, Cash, don't play dumb. She was on *Treasure Island* today and she posted a selfie with you for her sixteen million followers."

"What?" Cash says. Sixteen million followers? "Who is she?"

"An influencer," Tilda says. "One of the biggest in the country. Literally every single person I know follows her, and hence, *everyone* saw you drooling over her in her Lisa Marie Fernandez bikini."

"I wasn't drooling," Cash says. He can't believe Gretchen Gingerman is an influencer with sixteen million followers. That's...insane. He can't quite wrap his mind around that. "She was just a guest on the boat, Til. Her boyfriend was a world-class jackass and I was nice to her. Not extra-nice, just regular nice."

"Her boyfriend, Bradley?" Tilda says. "The one whose father invented Bitcoin?"

"Yeah, that was him." Cash doesn't care about Gretchen, and he cares about Bitcoin Bradley even less, though he's unsurprised to hear Bradley is a spoiled rich kid without any identifiable talent or skills of his own. "So I've been wondering why you haven't called," Cash says. "I guess you were just waiting for me to turn up on some famous chick's Instagram." He tries to keep his voice light, but actually, he's furious.

"This is a work trip," Tilda says. "My parents laid out a lot of money for this and I'm trying to be mindful of that and do a good job here. You know how distracting the phone can be. It's black magic that sucks you right out of the present moment."

"All right." Cash closes his eyes and tries to be mindful about enjoying the sound of Tilda's voice. "How's it going? Tell me everything."

"Our first stop was Midi et Minuit on Anguilla. It was very chic, very French. Edith Piaf was playing over the speakers in the lobby; we were greeted with glasses of Taittinger—that's their house champagne, hello—and these tiny, airy gougères. The place was so elegant and gracious, it was like we were visiting a fantastically wealthy French aunt with impeccable taste. The rooms were minimalist in the best way. The linens . . . don't get me started on how divine the linens were. I sourced everything with their GM. And the lighting in the bathroom was so flattering—I will never look as beautiful as I did in the Midi et Minuit bathroom. The pool was huge and had different areas. It was the perfect temperature, twenty-six degrees—that's Celsius, I have to convert that. It was cool enough to be refreshing but not chilly. But . . . the service . . . well, I thought it was fine, excellent even, but Dunk found it obsequious."

Dunk found it. Cash gets out of bed and goes out onto Tilda's deck. At the mention of Dunk's name, Cash wants to throw his phone into the pool. "Nothing worse than obsequious service."

"Yes, there is, Cash. Slow, careless service is worse. Island time is worse."

"I was kidding, Til. I don't even know what *obsequious* means."

"It means there's a person fawning over you, trying to anticipate your needs every time you turn around. Like I said, it doesn't bother me; these people are simply doing what they're paid to do. Dunk got bent out of shape when he was helping me with the headrest of my chaise and the pool guy nearly took him out."

Cash now has to picture Dunk helping Tilda with her chaise,

which necessarily puts Dunk and Tilda side by side in chaises, Tilda in one of her skimpy bikinis.

"How was the second place?" Cash asks.

"I'm getting there, hold on. So, our two days on Anguilla are sublime, we feel pampered, the place is elegant as hell, and I'm thinking nothing can possibly top it. Then..."

Then? Cash thinks.

"We get to Emerald Hill on St. Lucia. Now, Anguilla is a flat white sandbar, no topography to speak of. But St. Lucia is volcanic, like St. John only...much prettier."

Cash feels offended by this statement, which is funny, seeing as how he has lived here only a couple of months. "I don't believe it."

"Believe it. St. Lucia has these tapered volcanic spires called the Pitons, and Emerald Hill is positioned to display their fifty shades of green to maximum advantage. Now, you want to talk about an eco-resort? You won't believe how committed to minimizing ecological impact this place is, but in the most aesthetically jaw-dropping way. Listen to this..."

Cash drifts in and out of Tilda's monologue. *Twenty species of tropical hardwood harvested in environmentally sustainable ways...bloodwood, locust, purpleheart, cabbage wood...walls of crushed coral plaster quarried in Barbados...and the food...mahi banh mi, conch tacos, guava pulled pork...*

"It was so delicious, even Dunk ate."

Cash snaps to attention. "He did?" Cash is dismayed to hear that Dunk loosened up enough to let food pass his lips and that he exhibited the behavior of a normal human being.

"He's been eating three squares. I mean, I had to work on him for a few days but nobody could resist the breakfast buffet that Emerald Hill lays out. The fruit alone! They have a secret chilled drawer filled with champagne mangoes, but you have to know about it to request them."

"I take it our resort will have a secret chilled-mango drawer?" Cash says. *Our resort* sounds a little too presumptuous, so he quickly says, "The Lovango resort."

"You bet," Tilda says. "But the best part of Emerald Hill is the spa. Dunk and I went for massages and before you enter the treatment room, they ask you to sit in this round shallow pool that's inlaid with iridescent rainbow tiles. It's like sitting inside a kaleidoscope."

"Wait a minute," Cash says. "Go back. You and Dunk had massages…together?"

Tilda pauses. "We each had a massage, yes."

"Together? Were you naked under a sheet side by side while you got massages?"

"Technically, it *was* a couples massage, but that's not what I requested. I requested two massages at the same time so that our schedules were aligned and I wasn't sitting around waiting for him to go to dinner. But the woman in the spa misunderstood and booked it as a couples massage and once I figured that out, I'm sorry, it was too awkward to fix, so I rolled with it." Tilda pauses. "I kept my bikini on."

"Did Dunk keep his shorts on?"

"I have no idea, Cash. I didn't check to see what Dunk was doing. I promise you, the massage wasn't a big deal."

"But me in a selfie with Gretchen Gingerman was?" Cash says. "Why don't you explain what the dynamic between you and Dunk has been?"

"It's been…better than I expected, I guess. At first, he was a little over the top with his hokey Australian shtick—*Crikey! Good on ya! Bob's your uncle!*—but he's toned that down and I have to admit, I'm impressed by how informed he is. He did his research on these islands before we got down here—the history, the culture, the industry, the hidden treasures. So, for example, today we had the resort pack us a picnic and we hiked into the rain forest to see this fifty-foot waterfall in the middle of a natural garden. It was like something out of a fairy tale."

Cash clears his throat. Does she realize what she sounds like? She "worked on" Dunk and got him eating the chilled champagne mangoes and the conch tacos; he adjusted Tilda's chaise; they had a couples massage (no big deal!); they hiked with a picnic to the fairy-tale waterfall. Cash can, maybe, accept all that (no, not the massages, sorry), but what about the things Tilda *isn't* telling him? Has Dunk touched her? Reached for her hand? Kissed her good night? Rubbed sunscreen into her back? Held her in the water? Played footsie under the table? Has Dunk told Tilda he had a dream about her? Have they had heart-to-heart conversations? Has Tilda talked about Cash, and, if so, what has she said?

"They have live music at all meals," Tilda says. "A classical piano player at breakfast, a jazz combo at lunch, a guitar player who sounds exactly like Zac Brown at dinner. The Zac Brown guy is named Ezra, we sort of befriended him and he took us to this local bar in Gros Islet tonight where they had real reggae music, not just warmed-over Bob Marley, and we danced. That's why I'm home so late. I told Dunk I wanted our resort to have live music at every meal but I didn't think we could afford it and Dunk said we have carte blanche and everything is possible." She sighs. "Tomorrow we go to Eden by private seaplane."

"Private seaplane?" Cash says. "I thought it was commercial to St. Vincent and then a prop plane."

"Dunk arranged for a private seaplane," Tilda says. "We save half a day that way."

Cash has heard enough. The signs are all right in front of him: Tilda and Dunk are a "we" now. If they haven't slept together yet, they will on Eden when they're sharing a villa. This thought—that it hasn't happened yet but will imminently—is gut-wrenching.

"You haven't asked about me or things here, but you should know that I won't be living at your parents' when you get back."

"Wait," she says. "How come? Did you find a place, or—"

"No."

"Did...oh, jeez, did Granger say something about you going into his study?"

Cash feels a hot flush creep up his neck. Granger knows Cash was in his study? He told Tilda? Cash is being monitored, his every move watched and questioned, while Tilda is free to do as she damn well pleases! Couples massage! It was a misunderstanding! Too awkward to fix!

"Listen, Tilda," Cash says. "Staying here isn't working out for me. Enjoy the rest of your trip. I'll see you around."

He hangs up and feels extremely proud of himself—for approximately sixty seconds.

His phone pings with a text from Tilda: Are you breaking up with me, then?

No! he thinks. *I want you to come home. I want to wake up tomorrow and have things back to the way they were before Duncan Huntley walked into Extra Virgin and ordered his pretentious Australian wine.*

Yes, Cash types. Sorry. His finger hovers over the Send button.

Picnic at a waterfall, like something out of a fairy tale?

He squeezes his eyes shut and presses Send, and the swoosh sound marks the end of his relationship with Tilda Payne.

Tilda called to accuse him of drooling over a social media influencer? That wasn't jealousy, he sees now. That was a manifestation of her own guilty conscience! Cash was the one who did the right thing; he stayed on St. John to work so that he didn't leave *Treasure Island* in the lurch. Why is he getting kicked in the balls?

Dunk arranged for a seaplane? Bah! What Tilda means is that Dunk is rich and ordered a seaplane as a flex, whereas Cash swabs the deck and doesn't know the meaning of the word *obsequious*.

First thing in the morning, Cash calls Baker.

"Does your new place have a sofa?" Cash asks. "Because I need to crash with you for a while. This thing with Tilda blew up."

"It has two sofas," Baker says. "Which is a good thing, because one sofa is already taken."

"What?" Cash says. "By whom?"

"Our mother," Baker says.

ST. JOHN

The Gifft Hill mothers among us are the first to notice the black Jeep with the tinted windows. It drives slowly past the school at drop-off one morning, then the next. None of us have ever seen it before, but for a second we think maybe it belongs to Janine Whittaker. She and her husband own the Beach Bum Car Rental company and it feels like she gets a new Jeep every week.

The Gifft Hill School mothers who are romantically available—

Swan Seeley (divorcing), Bonny Kizer (divorced for years), and Paula Morrow (open marriage)—have taken to loitering in the school parking lot, pretending to share parenting woes while they wait for Baker Steele to drop off his son, Floyd. Swan is a natural flirt so she always finds a way to engage Baker in conversation, and Paula Morrow is a pleaser, a flatterer, and touchy-feely—on those occasions when Baker climbs out of his Jeep to chat, she squeezes his biceps and compliments his legs. We can all agree: Baker Steele has very fine legs. Bonny Kizer inevitably mentions that she is the only one of the three who is technically free. Swan and her husband, Brent, are in the throes of a nasty custodial and financial battle (Swan has family money and Brent has a gambling problem), and Paula Morrow *has a husband who lives with her on Pocket Money Road* (although he travels to the States for work and they have an "arrangement").

Swan, Bonny, and Paula are all standing in the school parking lot on the day that the bluebird Jeep pulls in and it's *not* Baker driving but rather some other man—cute, with blond surfer hair.

When Floyd gets out of the car he fist-bumps this man and says, "See ya later, Uncle Cash."

"That must be Baker's brother," Paula says.

"Maybe he has two brothers," Bonny says.

"I've seen that guy before," Swan says, and Bonny and Paula mentally roll their eyes. Swan has an acute case of Been There, Done That. "He goes out with Tilda Payne from La Tapa."

"I don't think so," Paula says. "Mark and I were out to dinner at the Terrace over the weekend and we saw Tilda there eating with someone else. Mark said it was that Australian guy, Duncan Huntley, who just bought Lovango Cay."

"Is that guy *single?*" Swan says. "I could use a boyfriend with money."

The three of them watch Floyd's uncle Cash back out of the parking lot. He notices them and waves—he's friendly!—but then Julie Judge pulls into the lot in her falling-apart RAV4 with the duct-taped soft top to let Joanie out, and the three women disperse. "Judgy Julie" is a marine biologist and a vegan and a stick-in-the-mud. She wouldn't approve of them checking out Baker Steele or his cute brother.

But who cares what Judgy Julie thinks?

A few days later, the three women are once again gathered, drinking chai lattes from Provisions, when the bluebird Jeep pulls in and a woman is driving. She's too old to be Baker's love interest, they think (though look at Emmanuel Macron!).

Floyd says, "Bye, Grammy!"

"It's Baker's mother?" Bonny says.

Grammy Steele is just about to pull away, when Captain Huck's truck swings in and lets Maia out. Maia notices the bluebird Jeep and waves to Floyd's grammy. Captain Huck calls out, "Irene!" Grammy Steele throws the car into reverse and hightails it out of there.

"That only makes sense," Swan whispers. "Because you know, girls, that Baker is the Invisible Man's son, which means Irene was the Invisible Man's wife..."

"And Rosie was the Invisible Man's lover," Bonny says. "No wonder Grammy doesn't want to talk to Huck."

"For some reason, I thought they were friends," Paula says. "I thought they worked together?"

"Take off the rose-colored glasses, Paula," Bonny says. "Would you work with the father of your husband's lover?" Then Bonny realizes she's talking to Paula Morrow. Who knows what kind of rules are bent in that household? "Never mind. Don't answer that."

None of those mothers are in the parking lot when the little green truck named Edie pulls in to pick up Maia from school—but Julie Judge is there and she goes over to say hello to Ayers. The poor woman has been through so much—losing Rosie, taking over mom duties with Maia, breaking up with Mick from the Beach Bar, and enduring his antics at Cruz Bay Landing.

"Ayers," Julie says. "How're you doing?"

Ayers places a hand on her abdomen. "I'm pregnant," she says. "Due in September."

Ayers Wilson is pregnant? No wonder Mick is so despondent! He's losing not only a fiancée but also a child.

No, no, no, Brigid tells first her coworker Lindsay, then Skip from La Tapa, then anyone who will listen—Mick isn't the father of Ayers's baby. Baker Steele is.

"What?" Swan Seeley yells when she hears this. "Are you kidding me?"

"There's always his brother," Paula says dreamily. "Uncle Cash."

With all this drama and excitement going on, it's a wonder they notice the black Jeep with the tinted windows. But they do, and then there it is again a day or two later, rolling by the school—at pickup this time.

"Creeper," Swan Seeley says. She cups her hands around her mouth. "Take a picture, it lasts longer!"

"It looked like a woman," Bonny says.

MAIA

The group has fallen apart; nobody wants to meet anymore. Maia and Joanie can occasionally talk Huck into dropping them off in town, and they get ice cream from Scoops, then hang out in Powell Park until the Antilles kids get off the four o'clock ferry. Maia sees Shane climb into his dad's truck but she's never brave enough to call out to him. One awful day, both Shane and Lillibet get off the ferry and hop into his dad's truck. Maia still Snapchats with Shane at night and he hasn't said anything about Lillibet being his girlfriend, but he also hasn't asked to hang out with Maia after school.

Things between Joanie and Colton aren't much more promising. All Colton wants to do is play Fortnite at Bright's house.

Boring.

They need to arrange another meeting, but where? Par Force is too hard to get to, and although it's private, it's just an old abandoned house where there's nothing to do but think about the people who lived there who are now dead and maybe ghosts.

Maia has an idea for a meeting spot but she's not sure she's brave enough to go through with it.

She has more freedom than ever. Irene has moved in with Baker and Floyd at the Happy Hibiscus in Fish Bay. Huck said that Irene wants to be with her family—yes, this makes sense—but what he hasn't explained is why Irene is no longer working on the *Mississippi*. Huck is in such a foul mood all the time that

Maia's afraid to ask. He says he doesn't want to find another mate; he'll just do all the work himself. He's almost never around to give Maia a ride home from school, but Joanie's mom and Ayers pick up the slack.

The good news is that Huck isn't paying much attention to Maia. He still makes her eggs and toast in the mornings but the eggs have been dry, which is *no bueno*. He doesn't bother checking one Saturday when Maia says she's going to Cinnamon Bay to swim with Joanie and a few other friends. They all meet in the parking lot—Maia, Joanie, Colton, Bright, and Shane (but happily, happily, not Lillibet; she's been grounded for talking back to her parents)—but instead of heading to the beach to swim or watch the volleyball game that is always happening on the eastern end, they walk down the Centerline single file to the turnoff up the hill to Little Cinnamon.

This is how Maia persuaded the boys to show up: they're going to hang out at her father's villa, the one with the two-story pool.

The one that has been seized by the FBI.

Shane says he can't believe Maia is letting them do this. She's too clever to show her hand; if she wants to get Shane back, she needs to come up with something irresistible. Which in this case is also something illegal.

Maia feels anxious on the Centerline Road. It's a short walk, but at any moment, one of their parents or teachers could drive by and see the five of them. Once they turn onto Lovers Lane, Maia's nerves fray with anxiety. The FBI have seized the house. There's no way Maia should be going anywhere near the place.

They climb up the hill past the dummy driveways, and Shane grabs Maia's hand.

This makes the whole plan worth it. Maia doesn't care if she goes to federal prison!

At the top of the hill is the villa. The gate is wide open. Maia had assumed it would be closed but she knows the code—her mother's birthday—and if that didn't work, she knows a way around the gate through the dense landscaping, which isn't great but would work as a last resort.

They walk up the empty driveway. A piece of yellow police tape hangs limply across the stairs up to the deck. Maia ducks under it and the others follow suit. Colton and Bright, who usually never shut up, are silent.

Maia climbs the stairs. The deck looks…the same. The furniture is all there. The pool is full but the water down the slide has been shut off. Maia goes over to the control panel and flips the switch, and water starts flowing down the slide.

She's going to get arrested for sure.

"Can we go in?" Bright whispers.

Maia holds up a finger. "Let me check out the house first." The outdoor kitchen is the same; there are fancy Italian sparkling waters in the fridge—and they're ice-cold! "Help yourself," Maia says.

There's a sign on the sliding glass door into the kitchen: PROPERTY OF THE UNITED STATES GOVERNMENT. NO TRESPASSING. VIOLATORS WILL BE PROSECUTED. The door is locked. Maia cups her hands around her eyes and peers inside.

It looks…the same. The kitchen counters, the sink, the cabinets, the fridge, the living-room furniture, the television. Everything is exactly where it was. But what about her room?

"Do you know where there's a key?" Joanie asks.

Maia says, "Follow me." They go across the deck, past the hot tub, and down the stairs to the shuffleboard court. The cues are hanging on the rack and the black and red disks are stacked in a milk crate. Maia reaches around to the back of the crate and feels the key taped just under the lip. *Ha!* She pulls the key loose. This is the key her mother used when she and Maia arrived before Russ got here (sometimes Rosie brought home-cooked meals—her jerk chicken with beans and rice—or pints of coconut ice cream from Scoops, which was Russ's favorite), and this was where they put the key when they stayed after Russ left (which was sometimes very, very early in the morning). This means the last person to touch this key was Rosie. Maia brings the key to her lips.

She leads Joanie to the door that the key fits. It pulls right open, and seconds later, they're up in the kitchen, opening the slider.

"Hey, guys," she says to Shane, Colton, and Bright. "Who's hungry?"

There's still food in the fridge, though all of the fresh stuff has grown mold or gone bad. The cabinets and pantry, however, are a treasure trove. The boys dive on the bags of chips while Joanie unearths a package of hot dogs from the freezer (Joanie's parents are vegan; for her, a hot dog is the ultimate forbidden treat). Maia opens three cans of SpaghettiOs and dumps them in a pot.

Ten minutes later, they have a feast: bowls of SpaghettiOs, hot dogs with yellow mustard and relish, Cheetos and dill-flavored potato chips—all washed down with Italian sparkling water.

Maia thinks maybe now is the time to start a conversation. "Does anybody have anything they want to talk about?" She looks at Colton; it was his parents' divorce that brought the group together. But Colton and Bright are tussling on the banquette; Colton bumps up against Joanie, who must love it.

"Let's go back in the pool," Bright says.

"Should I turn on the hot tub?" Maia asks.

"Yeah!" they all say. The afternoon is sunny and very hot but there's still something alluring about the bubbles and all of them close together.

"I'll do it after I clean up," Maia says.

Colton, Bright, and Joanie head outside. Shane stays to help Maia bring the plates and the bowls to the sink. He throws the empty bags and cans away.

"The FBI owns this house now?" he says.

Maia shrugs. "I guess so."

"It doesn't look like anyone's living here." He gazes upward. "Do you think they installed cameras?"

"I think..." Maia tries to remember if she overheard Huck and Irene saying anything about the fate of the villa. *Gone* was all they said. *It's gone.* "I think maybe the government will sell it? And take the money and put it into their budget?"

"Yeah," Shane says. "You're probably right. When do you think the new owners will move in?"

"Probably not for a while," Maia says. "Everything looks the same. It's almost like the FBI locked it up and then forgot it was here."

"So maybe we can use it again?" Shane says. "Because this is an awesome hangout. What's upstairs?"

"There are nine bedrooms," Maia says. She knows this is an outrageous number because she heard her mother say so. "Want to see my room?"

Shane's eyebrows shoot up. "Sure."

Sure, sure, sure, Maia thinks. Is this happening? She should *not* be doing this, she's twelve and a half, too young to have a boy in her bedroom. If you listen to Huck, twenty-five is too young. But this is an opportunity she may never get again. What if the new people move in next week, or tomorrow?

The upstairs is unpleasantly hot and stuffy; the air-conditioning is off. Maia leads Shane down the long hallway past the other bedrooms, all of them the same as Maia remembers, with their camel cashmere blankets and fluffy white duvets folded at the bottom of each bed and the arrangement of six pillows plus bolster at the head. She wonders briefly about the people who will end up buying this villa. Will they be older with a lot of children and grandchildren? Will they be young with a lot of friends they invite for weekend house parties? Will they ever learn anything about Maia—or Russ and Rosie?

Maia reaches the end of the hallway and opens the door to her room. It's a swirl of turquoise and purple tie-dye; pillows that spell out her name hang on the far wall.

"Wow," Shane says. "This is way cooler than my room."

"It's way cooler than my room at home." Maia feels disloyal to Huck in saying this, but it's undeniable. Here, she has bean-bag chairs and a dressing table with a lit mirror. She remembers her mother handing her the Pottery Barn Teen catalog and telling her to "go crazy." Maia had pointed to her favorite picture in the catalog, and the next time Russ came back to the island, her room looked like this. He had thought of the name pillows himself, he said. Maia picks up her copy of *The Hate U Give.* "I forgot I left this here. I'm taking this home." She sits on the bed and Shane sits next to her. He kicks at her foot and then their two legs are intertwined. She's afraid he's going to kiss her. But isn't that what she wants? The door is halfway open. She's safe here, safe with Shane.

She falls backward on the bed and he does the same. When she looks at him, he smiles. He's so cute without his braces. He inches his face closer and she thinks, *This is it.* She closes her eyes. His lips touch hers and they kiss. He lingers and she thinks, *Is this where we open our mouths? Yes; yes, it is.* They are, suddenly, tongue-kissing, which makes Maia feel like she's flying down the pool slide upside down and backward.

"Maia!" Joanie shouts from somewhere.

No, Joanie, please, Maia thinks. *Go away! Don't ruin this!*

"Maia, where are you?" Joanie calls. "Someone's here!"

Shane jumps to his feet. "Someone's here?" he says. "Should we hide?"

Should they hide? Maia opens her bedroom door wide and sees Joanie's stricken face; Colton and Bright are right on her heels, trailing pool water down the hall.

"There's a woman here," Joanie says. "She pulled up in a black Jeep."

"With tinted windows," Bright says. "It's a four-door Sahara Limited, plate TP six-seven-five-six."

"She asked to talk to you," Joanie says. "By name. She said, 'Is Maia here?' "

"What?" Maia says. She can't hide if they know her name. "Did she show a badge? Is she with the FBI?" Maia can't even fathom the massive amount of trouble she's in. And maybe not only her, maybe Huck as well. She feels her SpaghettiOs repeat on her; she's going to hurl.

Shane comes up behind her and squeezes her hand. "I'll go down with you."

"We'll all go down with you," Joanie says.

"We're just kids," Colton says. "We can say we didn't know we weren't allowed to be here."

Maia is trembling when she gets down to the bottom of the stairs. "You guys stay here," she says. She steps out to the deck.

The woman is gazing at the view across the water to Tortola and Jost Van Dyke. She's short and has brown hair that's pulled back in a ponytail; she's wearing white capri pants and a beige linen shell and sandals, and when she turns around, Maia sees she has a round, pale face with wide brown eyes. She doesn't look like the FBI, but maybe this is how they trick you. They send someone who looks like the person who cleans teeth at the dentist's office.

"Hello, Maia," she says.

"Hello?" Maia says. Who is this woman? "Am I in trouble?"

"Oh," the woman says. "Not with me, but I'm sure you kids realize you're not supposed to be here."

"We're leaving," Maia says. "We were just...I left some personal things behind that I wanted back." She wishes she'd thought to bring the Angie Thomas book out. "I mean, it's okay to take personal items? That have no value?"

"I'm not going to report you," the woman says, but it sounds like there's something else coming. "I just have one question. Something I need help with."

"Okay..." Maia says.

"I'm a friend of Irene Steele's," the woman says. "An acquaintance. And I know she was living with you and your grandpa, correct? Up on Jacob's Ladder? Has she moved? Left island, maybe?"

"Irene?" Maia says. "She lives in Fish Bay now with my brother Baker." Maia absolutely loves using the phrase *my brother*. "And my nephew, Floyd. They live in a house called the Happy Hibiscus."

Irene's friend nods and brings her hands palm to palm up to her heart like a yoga person. "Thank you. That's all I needed to know."

"Do you...want her phone number?" Maia says. She wonders if it's okay to give out Irene's number, but this woman does not look threatening. She looks like someone from Iowa.

"No, thank you," the woman says. "I'd like to speak to her in person." She moves toward the stairs. "You kids should probably skedaddle. And don't forget to lock up."

* * *

Maia goes into the kitchen, where everyone is huddled in the far corner by the trash.

"Let's go," Maia says. "She wasn't the FBI."

The boys and Joanie shoot out the door and Maia does a check—lights out, stove off, everything put away. She locks the sliding glass door and turns off the water on the slide.

Goodbye, villa, she thinks. *Site of my first kiss.*

Together, they run down Lovers Lane shrieking with heady joy. Maia can't believe they got away with it.

BAKER

He feels like he's starring in a sitcom about a single dad who moves from the big city to a tropical island to woo the girl he fell in love with on vacation. In episode 2, he finds out this girl is pregnant. Twist: It's his child. Twist: She is just out of a long-term relationship and needs time alone. Twist: He moves in across the street.

In episode 3, his mother moves in. There's no room for her but she's adamant and says she has nowhere else to go.

"What about Huck's?" Baker said when Irene showed up on his doorstep with her suitcase. "That was working out. You had your own bedroom. You drove to work together."

"I quit the boat," Irene said. "I need to be with family. Huck isn't family."

"You quit the *boat?*" Baker said. "You like the boat."

Irene stared at him. She was impossible to read but he couldn't just let her stand outside so he held the door open. She set her suitcase behind one of the sofas in the living room.

"So you're here for a while?" Baker said. "Why don't you take the second bedroom. Floyd can sleep with me."

"I'll be fine on the sofa," Irene said. "I'll use Floyd's bathroom. I hope he won't mind."

"Mom," Baker said. "I insist. Floyd will sleep with me. Are you kidding? He'll be thrilled."

"I'm not putting either one of you out," Irene said. "I feel horrible about this as it is. The sofa is fine."

He decided that after she spent a few nights on the sofa, he would offer again. "What are you going to do for work now? Do you have a plan?"

"I'm going to get my captain's license," Irene said. "I have that money coming from your grandmother. I'm going to buy my own boat and start my own charter."

"Your own charter?" Baker said. "Here?"

Irene nodded. Wow, she did not look happy.

"You're going into direct competition with Huck?" he said.

"Oh, yes," she said.

Something had happened, but what? She would tell him when she was ready. Or she wouldn't. It would be nice to have his mother around, but he needed to catch her up. "That house across the street is where Ayers lives," he said. He considered asking Irene to sit down—but if anyone could handle the news standing up, it was his mother. "She's pregnant."

"You're kidding."

"With my baby."

"*Your* baby?"

"Yes." Baker paused. "We aren't together. I mean, we *were* together, I suppose that's obvious, but then she got engaged to Mick, then she broke the engagement with Mick because he was unfaithful, then she found out she was pregnant."

"But the baby's not Mick's?" Irene looked dubious. Baker's private fears were written all over his mother's face. "You're sure? She might just be telling you that because... well, because you're you, by which I mean a wonderful father."

"She insists the baby is mine," Baker said. "Don't women have a sixth sense about things like that?"

Irene frowned. "I'm not sure. I never had any doubts about the paternity of my children."

The last thing Baker wanted was for Irene to take issue with Ayers. "Here's the thing. I want to be with Ayers eventually. The cart came a little before the horse—"

"You think?"

"And she needs space right now and I'm giving it to her."

"She's across the street."

"Emotional space. We're building a friendship first." What Baker didn't tell Irene was that Ayers resisted every attempt at friendship that Baker made. On Saturday morning, he and Floyd had gone to Provisions for coffee and scones. When they knocked on Ayers's door with the offerings, she hadn't answered, even though her green truck was in the driveway.

Baker had said, "She's probably still asleep, bud."

"But we waited until ten," Floyd said. He was eager to open the door because he wanted to play with Winnie.

They wandered back across the street and although Baker told Floyd they'd try again later, he ate Ayers's scone and drank her coffee. The second coffee made him feel so unhinged that he became convinced she hadn't answered the door because she had Mick over. Or maybe she wasn't home. Maybe she was with Mick at his new villa, Pure Joy. (Baker had scoped out the villa once—okay, twice—on his way to work at the Westin. It wasn't as big as the Happy Hibiscus but it had an unbeatable view and an outdoor shower.)

Speaking of the Westin, Baker had asked Ayers if she wanted to join him and Floyd at Greengos after Baker's first day of work and she said no, thank you, she had the night off from La Tapa and was looking forward to getting takeout from Dé Coal Pot and streaming *The Marvelous Mrs. Maisel.*

She had waved to Baker from her driveway once. They passed each other at the steep, tight curve by Ditleff Point and the hoods of their cars almost kissed, but that was as close to physical contact as Baker had gotten.

So now he's at episode 4: His brother moves in. Baker has to go pick Cash up at Tilda's villa in Peter Bay. The place is like something plucked off the cover of *Architectural Digest.* During his downtime in the Westin time-share office, Baker has been researching the St. John real estate market. Peter Bay fetches top dollar. It's a private community on the north shore with a prime location between Trunk Bay and Cinnamon Bay. While Tilda's villa doesn't have as many bedrooms as their villa in Little Cinnamon did, it has nearly exactly the same amount of square footage. Cash gives Baker a tour of the place. The three wings are connected by covered walkways bordered on either side by lush landscaping—hibiscus, frangipani, birds-of-paradise. The T-shaped pool is unique. The kitchen has a curved island topped with white marble and three light blue suede bar stools that look like egg cups. Baker sits in one and swivels. Cash will be getting a serious downgrade at the Happy Hibiscus.

* * *

"Explain to me again why you're leaving," Baker says as they pull out of the extremely steep driveway. The views are ridiculous! From the top of the driveway, Baker can see the entirety of Tortola and beyond. Beyond!

"Tilda went on a work trip with someone else," Cash says. "Her parents are building an eco-resort over on Lovango Cay so they sent her on a three-stop tour of the fanciest, most expensive resorts in the Caribbean." He stares out the window. "Today, for example, she's on an island resort called Eden where management decides what guests are allowed to stay there."

"Who'd she go with?" Baker asks. "A guy?"

"This dude named Duncan Huntley," Cash says. "He bought Lovango Cay. Bought the entire island. And this guy is, like, our age."

Duncan Huntley? Baker opens his mouth to say, *I know that guy. He gave Floyd and me a ride on his boat from the airport.* But for some reason, Baker stops himself. "So he and Tilda are a thing, then? Or they just went on this trip as business partners?"

"They went as business partners," Cash says. "But Tilda didn't call me at all for the first four days, which I found fishy because she cried when she left and promised to be true, blah-blah-blah. When I asked her what she thought about Dunk, she said, 'He's too intense.'"

Intense is a good choice of word, Baker thinks.

"He fasts," Cash says. "Which is apparently a lifestyle we've been missing out on. Starving yourself brings better focus and productivity."

"I'll never know," Baker says, thinking about the scones from

Provisions and the container of Red Velvet Cake ice cream he has hidden in the freezer.

"So, anyway, after four full days away, she hits me up at two thirty in the morning and all she can talk about is Dunk this and Dunk that. Dunk adjusted her chaise by the pool, she and Dunk took a picnic to a waterfall, Dunk arranged for a private seaplane, and—get this—she and Dunk had a couples massage at the spa."

"Couples massage?" Baker says. "I'm sorry, bro. You were right to leave."

Episode 5: Baker, his brother, his mother, and Floyd all cohabitate in Baker's villa, which, although blessed with cathedral ceilings, a spacious laundry room, and a picturesque backyard with sapphire pool, has only two bedrooms. Irene and Cash each take a sofa; every morning, Irene folds up their bedding and hides it away in the closet. Irene shares a bathroom with Floyd, and reluctantly, oh so reluctantly, Baker lets Cash share his bathroom, which makes them both feel like they're teenagers again. Cash spends sixteen thousand dollars of his inheritance from Milly on a silver Dodge pickup with only eight thousand island miles on it. Irene borrows Cash's truck or Baker's Jeep, alternating between the two, which would be annoying, except she occasionally drives Floyd to school and picks him up, and she takes over all the grocery shopping. Baker does the cooking; he finally has an appreciative audience—or sort of. Cash gets home from *Treasure Island* each night so spent and hungry that he ravenously shovels in whatever Baker puts in front of him without even seeming to taste it, and Irene helps herself to doll-size portions, then eats half. She's losing weight again, just like she did when they first got here, right after they'd received the news of Russ's death.

Baker shows Irene his secret stash of Red Velvet Cake ice cream—he was hiding it from himself, and now he's hiding it from Cash—but Irene just shakes her head. "I'm not hungry."

Something happened between Irene and Huck—but what?

One afternoon while Baker is in the Gifft Hill School parking lot waiting for Floyd, he sees Maia and her little friend Joanie emerge. Maia zips right over and offers Baker a fist bump. "Hey, bro."

"Hey, sis," Baker says. Joanie is now hanging back, talking to a boy, so Baker seizes the moment. "Do you know what happened between Huck and my mom? Did they have a fight?"

Maia shrugs. "He told me she just wanted to live with you guys. She thought she was imposing."

"Fair enough," Baker says. "But why did she quit the boat?"

"Gramps won't talk about it," Maia says. "But he refuses to hire another mate. So he's doing two jobs by himself and he's never home." A beat-up RAV4 pulls up. "That's Joanie's mom. I have to go, bro."

That night over dinner, Baker says, "I saw Maia at school. She said Huck refuses to hire another mate."

Irene freezes with her fork suspended over her plate. They're having pineapple fried rice with grilled shrimp, and Irene has helped herself to one spoonful of rice and one shrimp. "Well," she says finally. "That's his prerogative, I guess."

"Why don't you go back, Mom?" Cash says.

"I want to do my own thing," Irene says. "I bought the study materials for the captain's license, and I've been working my way through. I'll go to St. Thomas to take my test, and while I'm over there, I'm looking at a boat. I just need a marketing plan, advertising, some way to get my new venture out there."

"What's the name going to be?" Cash asks. "Of the boat?"

"Angler Cupcake," Irene says. Her lips hint at a smile. "That was what your grandfather used to call me."

Why shouldn't Irene have her own fishing boat? Baker wonders. Why shouldn't *Angler Cupcake* be every bit as successful as the *Mississippi*? Well, he suspects his mother will have a challenging time attracting male clients with a boat called *Angler Cupcake.* Which means she'll be going after a female clientele. Are there enough women who fish for her to sustain a fishing-charter business?

Baker decides to ask his Gifft Hill School–mom friends. They're not school wives, not yet, but Baker, Swan, Bonny, and Paula are bonding. Whenever Baker drops Floyd off or picks him up, those three are reliably waiting for him.

He broaches the fishing-boat question one afternoon while Floyd plays for a few extra minutes on the jungle gym with Swan's son Ryder.

"I think she could be very successful," Paula says. Baker has learned that Paula is a bit of a Suzie Sunshine; she says whatever she thinks will make someone happy, regardless of whether or not she believes it's true.

"I don't," Bonny says. Bonny balances Paula out; she's a naysayer. "Women don't fish."

"Some women fish," Swan says. "Your mother could start a trend, Baker. Lots of women with money are planning girls' trips, and your mom's fishing boat would be perfect. Plus, she could market to families with young children. And…bachelorettes?"

"Families, maybe, but bachelorettes do *not* want to fish," Bonny says. "Do you even watch the show? The girls on *The Bachelor* will fish or bungee jump or go to the machine-gun range, but only to seem cool and beat out the other girls. It's never their choice."

"I majored in marketing at Florida State," Swan says. "Have your mom reach out. I'm happy to help her, free of charge."

"You are such a kiss-ass," Bonny says.

"Maybe we could all help?" Paula says, and Swan gives her a withering look. These women make Baker miss Ellen, Debbie, Becky, and Wendy because they were relaxed, stable…and not after him.

"I'll run it past my mom," Baker says. He needs to get out of there before they come to blows. "Thanks, ladies."

Episode 6: Baker is *killing it* at work! He feels like the host of a new HGTV show called *Do You Want to Buy a Time-Share?* He's aware that most people take the tour only because they want the free breakfast (with bottomless mimosas) or the free appetizers (with free-flowing rum punch), plus the hundred-dollar resort credit. But Baker finds that the clients he interacts with at least consider the *possibility* of buying.

One day, he puts two units under contract, a one-bedroom and a three-bedroom! He experiences a surge of pure, unadulterated confidence that feels like mainlining a drug. Nothing is going to happen with Ayers until he makes it happen. It's ludicrous that she's right across the street and they almost never see each other. *Cash* sees Ayers more than Baker does because he goes over every day to visit Winnie. Floyd sees more of Ayers than Baker does because he tags along with Cash. Baker told Cash that the property manager of the Happy Hibiscus explicitly stated there were no pets allowed—but this was a lie. Pets are fine. Baker just wants Ayers to keep Cash's dog so there is still one filament connecting Ayers to Baker. And anyway, the household is crowded enough as it is. (Sorry, Winnie.)

Baker swings by Our Market to get Ayers a pineapple-mango smoothie, then he stops at Sam and Jack's for a bag of their homemade potato chips. This is the perfect afternoon snack. He still has an hour and a half before school pickup. He can bring Ayers these goodies and stay for a visit—catch up, see how she's feeling, ask if she wants him to go with her to her prenatal appointment at Schneider Hospital. This will show he's thinking of her. He's never *not* thinking of her, but it won't be overbearing.

Her green truck is in the driveway—wonderful. He strides up to the door and knocks. The pineapple-mango smoothie is sweating in his hand, and while he waits, he worries that her favorite type is pineapple-banana, not pineapple-mango. He should have written it down the second she mentioned it. This is the kind of thing that Mick knows by heart and Baker doesn't.

He hears voices. A man's voice. Is Mick there? The voice is very deep. Not Mick's. Mick has a reedy voice that reminds Baker of some pimply adolescent playing the oboe. So someone else is here. Another man. Someone who took advantage of the broken engagement to make a move?

Baker turns to leave. He doesn't want to know who it is. Naturally, as Baker is retreating, the door swings open.

"Hello there, young man, can we help you?" The deep male voice is attached to a very tall, very thin older gentleman with a high forehead and curly silver hair sticking out in tufts on either side, like an aging Bozo the Clown, although Bozo might be an ungenerous comparison. Baker immediately knows that it's Ayers's father.

"Hello," Baker says, retracing his steps back to the front door. "I brought some things for Ayers. A smoothie. And chips."

"Wonderful!" the man bellows. He holds the screen door open. "I'm Phil Wilson and my sweetheart, Sunny—Ayers's mom—is here as well. You must be the infamous..." Phil turns and calls to someone who is out of Baker's field of vision. "What's the soap opera guy's name again, Sunny?"

"Baker Steele," a woman's voice says.

"Baker Steele!" Phil says.

This isn't exactly the way Baker was hoping the afternoon would go, but he steps inside because he sees no other choice. "Yes, sir," he says. "Nice to meet you."

Ayers and her mother are sitting cross-legged on the sofa. Sunny is beautiful; she looks just like Ayers, only older. She's slender with curly blond-silver hair; she's wearing a beige jersey dress and lots of silver jewelry. Ayers doesn't look unhappy to see Baker, which he supposes he should take as a win. "Mom, Dad, this is Baker," she says. Her expression is neutral, as though she's introducing her parents to the pizza-delivery guy.

"You're the one who impregnated my daughter?" Phil says.

"Um..." Baker looks to Ayers to see if she confirms this.

"Dad, please," Ayers says. "Yes. Baker and I were together. This is his baby."

"We're over the moon," Sunny says. "We flew all the way from Nairobi to be here."

"Nairobi, wow." Baker looks at the photographs hanging on Ayers's living-room wall—her at the Great Pyramids and the Taj Mahal—and he picks out younger versions of Phil and Sunny. "You're world travelers."

"Nomads," Phil says. "The earth is our home."

"Where are you staying?" Baker asks. He looks around Ayers's studio; Winnie is asleep on Ayers's bed. "Not here?"

"We have a room at Caneel Bay for now," Phil says. "We're planning on staying a few weeks, then maybe spending some time in Jamaica, the DR, Antigua and Barbuda, St. Vincent and the Grenadines..."

"Bequia is supposed to be relatively unspoiled," Sunny says. "We've avoided the Caribbean for the most part because it's so tacky."

"Gee, thanks, guys," Ayers says.

"St. John is different," Phil says. "It still has that rugged-nature-lover vibe."

"With spots of luxury," Sunny says. "Like Caneel."

"There aren't any all-inclusives," Phil says. "Just the term *all-inclusive* makes me shudder."

"They're travel snobs," Ayers says.

"Anyway, once we complete our little jaunt, we'll come back here and wait for the baby to be born," Sunny says.

"That wait could be weeks or months," Phil says. "So I was going to look into buying a time-share at the Westin."

"We'll need a home base here if we ever want to see our grandchild," Sunny says.

Baker hates to be opportunistic, but... "If you decide you do want a Westin time-share, I can help you," he says. "I'm working at their sales office right now."

"Great!" Phil says. "We'll take one."

"Dad," Ayers says. "Don't tease."

"Who's teasing?" Phil says. "I'll be by to see you in the morning."

"Free breakfast with mimosas," Baker says. "And a hundred-dollar resort credit."

"Hear that, gorgeous?" Phil says to Sunny. "She loves free stuff. We got a discount on our room at Caneel because she told them she's a travel blogger."

"We should ask Baker some questions," Sunny says. "We know nothing about you. Freddy told us the two of you are just casual acquaintances."

"Mom!" Ayers says.

"Freddy?" Baker says.

"That's my daughter's nickname," Phil says. "Short for 'Ready, Freddy,' which was something she used to say often as a child. I can't believe you don't even know her nickname."

"Nobody knows my nickname," Ayers says. "No. Body."

Baker is still holding the chips and the smoothie, which is turning his hand numb. He's afraid to make himself any more comfortable until he's invited to do so. "Well, I grew up in Iowa City, went to Northwestern, graduated with a business degree, worked on the commodities exchange in Chicago for a few years, and then my soon-to-be-ex-wife, Anna Schaffer, got a job offer in Houston. She's a cardiothoracic surgeon."

"A cardiothoracic surgeon?" Sunny says. "That's impressive!"

Yes, yes, story of Baker's life—the most impressive thing about him is his wife's career. "We're in the process of getting a divorce," Baker says. "She fell in love with a coworker of hers, a doctor named Louisa Rodriguez"—Baker glances at Ayers's parents; they seem unfazed by this—"and I have custody of our son, Floyd, who's four."

"We'd like to meet Floyd!" Phil says.

"Another time," Ayers says. She checks her phone, which is sitting in front of her on the coffee table, and what can Baker think but that he's overstaying his welcome.

"My brother, Cash, and my mother, Irene, are also living with me right now," Baker says. He takes a breath. He *has* to put down the smoothie. "Here." He sets it down in front of Ayers. "I brought you this. It's pineapple-mango. Your favorite."

"My favorite after pineapple-banana," she says. Baker deflates and hands over the chips without adding that he made a special trip to Sam and Jack's for them.

"You don't know her nickname or her favorite smoothie?" Phil says. "I can see we still have some work to do."

"Please stop, Dad," Ayers says.

"It was very thoughtful of you to bring these," Sunny says, opening the chips and helping herself to one. "How interesting that you live with your family of origin."

"Yes, well..." Baker says. He glances at Ayers. Has she not explained *any* of his situation to her parents? "My father died in a helicopter crash on the first of the year..."

"So did Rosie," Phil says.

"We adored Rosie," Sunny says.

"Was the fella she was with...your father?" Phil asks.

"Yes," Baker says. Ayers is staring at her own crossed legs. Why didn't she give her parents the thorny background? "And so my mother and brother and I all flew down here to figure out what was going on."

"What *was* going on?" Phil asks.

"Well, we learned about his relationship with Rosie..."

"Had your mother suspected anything?" Sunny asks.

Baker can't believe he's being put on the spot like this. But it's refreshing, in a way, to answer questions that everyone must be asking in his or her head. "She had no idea," Baker says. "It came as a complete shock. Jaw-dropping. For days I think we all believed there'd been a mistake, that it was a different Russell Steele. But then, yeah, we accepted it was my dad. He owned a giant hilltop villa that we knew nothing about. He had a whole life. A second life."

"You'll forgive me for saying so," Phil says, "but it seems unusual that you stayed on the island where your father had a second family."

"Dad!" Ayers says.

"It wasn't our *plan* to stay," Baker says. "Each of us ended up back here for his or her own reasons. I can only speak for myself. I was living in Houston, my marriage fell apart, my almost-ex-wife took a job at the Cleveland Clinic—"

"Impressive!" Sunny says.

"—and I met Ayers. I decided I wanted to try to make our relationship work." He can see the warning in Ayers's eyes but he ignores it. "I came down here without knowing about the baby. But I'm excited—no, thrilled about the news, and I plan to be a hands-on father, just like I am with Floyd."

"Well," Sunny says, "I'm overcome. What a beautiful thing to say."

"We ended up losing my father's villa a few weeks ago," Baker says. He clears his throat. "There was tax trouble. Legal trouble. And that was a hurdle for all of us—my mother, brother, and me—because we had all planned on living there. It was... spacious."

"Um, yeah," Ayers says.

"It's almost better that we aren't at the villa anymore." Baker realizes these words are true only as he's saying them. "It was... tainted. Don't get me wrong, it was luxurious, the wow factor was high, but I think that masked the truth, which was that we didn't belong there. I've rented the place right across the street from here, and although it's a tight fit right now, I'm confident my mom and brother will find their own spaces in time."

"Across the street from *here!*" Sunny says. "How convenient."

Phil leads Baker to the door. "You've made a very fine first impression, Baker Steele."

Baker raises his eyebrows at Ayers. *Your parents like me!* Ayers whistles, and Winnie lifts her head, jumps off the bed, and joins Ayers on the couch.

"We must arrange a dinner with your mom and brother," Sunny says. "A family affair! But we can't do it tonight because we're taking Freddy and Michael out."

"To the beach bar at Caneel," Phil says. "Supposedly, they have decent sushi."

"We spent nine months traveling through Japan in the early aughts," Sunny says. "And do you want to know where we found the best sushi?"

"Gate thirty-five at Narita Airport," Phil says. "The tuna special. I dream about it."

Baker is still trying to figure out who "Freddy and Michael" are. Friends of theirs? A gay couple? Then he remembers that Ayers is Freddy. But who's Michael? "Who's Michael?" he asks.

"Mick," Phil says. "We're taking out Ayers and Mick."

"'Mick' makes him sound like an Irish hoodlum or a horny rock star," Sunny says. "I prefer to call him by his given name."

Ayers rubs Winnie's head. Is she even listening to this conversation?

"You're taking out Ayers and Mick?" Baker says.

"It's been so long since we've seen him," Sunny says.

Somehow, Baker makes it through the door, saying graciously, *Enjoy the sushi, hope it's decent, come see me in the morning, we'll look at one-bedrooms and two-bedrooms, nice to meet you, all righty, will do, yep, yep, yep, bye-bye.* And then, mercifully, Phil closes the door.

Taking out Ayers and Mick?

Baker heads across the street, limping like he has an old sports injury—Mick is the old sports injury, the one Baker can't seem to recover from—until he's at his front door and can safely disappear into what should now be known as the Heartbroken Hibiscus.

HUCK

He calls Agent Vasco to tell her about the diaries.

"Have you read them?" she asks.

"Yes," he says.

"Are they going to give me what I need?"

They better, Huck thinks. *Because I sacrificed my relationship with Irene for them.* "Only you would know," Huck says. He's on his deck, smoking. He's been going through half a pack a day since Irene moved out. "Should I mail them to you or are you on the island?"

"We're on the island today," Vasco says. "Can I swing by around eleven?"

"I have a charter," Huck says. "I'll leave them on the mail table just inside my front door. You remember where I live? Up Jacob's Ladder?"

"You don't lock up?"

"I have nothing to steal," Huck says.

"Fine, we'll be by," Vasco says. She pauses. "Thank you for calling me."

"I want to cooperate," Huck says. "Can you tell me what's up with Douglas and Paulette Vickers?"

"In the vault?" Vasco says.

"Of course."

"We offered them a deal if they gave us something tangible on Croft, but they refused, insisted he was no part of it, that it was only Steele and Thompson."

"Wow," Huck says.

"So the Vickerses will serve time for fraud and money laundering. They allowed Ascension to buy and sell land from one fictional entity to another using their real estate concern. Welcome to Paradise Real Estate was as dirty as they come."

"They'll both serve time?" Huck says. "What about their son?"

"Staying with Douglas's sister on St. Croix." Vasco sighs. "Those diaries are my last shot. Croft is a slippery bastard. I'd love to nail him."

Vasco is tough; Huck likes that about her.

Huck is distracted on his charter. He has three lawyers from Philadelphia on board who are going out on the boat only so they can escape their wives, smoke the Cuban cigars they scored in the BVIs, and enjoy a day on the water. They don't care if they catch any fish. All good; less concentration required from Huck. He hates to phone it in but he can't get his mind off the question of whether or not to call Irene when they get back to the dock. Would she want to know about Paulette and Douglas Vickers? He normally would say yes but now all bets are off; she has been radio-silent since she left. He thought she'd come to her senses and that one of these mornings, he would find her waiting by the *Mississippi* with two sausage biscuits and two cups of strong black coffee. But no such luck.

He won't call her, he thinks. She made it clear she didn't want to talk about those diaries ever again.

He misses her at work. He misses her at home. He tries to maintain for Maia's sake. He continues to grill mahi or he stops at Candi's for barbecue, but more often than not, he feeds Maia and drinks his own dinner, smokes his dessert. He doesn't make any move to hire a new mate because he can't handle the idea of breaking someone in—and, too, he thinks Irene will return if he waits her out.

Without a mate, he often can't pick Maia up from school so he leans on Julie Judge more than he should. He feels like he's losing his grip on where Maia goes, how she spends her days. Well, she needs food on the table. And she likes to be able to order new clothes from Amazon. Her bath-bomb business seems to have stalled; something new has her attention. Boys, probably.

One night over dinner—it's not even Candi's, it's *leftover* Candi's, that's how sorry a state Huck is in—he says, "Maybe you could make some extra money babysitting for Floyd."

"Floyd has plenty of babysitters now," Maia says. "Irene is there. And Cash moved in too."

"Cash moved in?" Huck says. "I thought he was living over in Peter Bay with what's her name."

"Tilda," Maia says. "They broke up. Tilda is dating some super-rich guy who bought Lovango Cay. Tilda's parents are building an eco-resort there."

Yes, Huck has heard whisperings about this around town. A resort on Lovango will bring in some high-end clientele, which everyone is excited about. It means more potential fishing clients.

Huck would be excited too if he could only summon the energy. "How do you know all this?" Huck asks.

"Ayers," Maia says. She finishes her coleslaw and eyes Huck as she sets down her fork. "If I tell you something, can you keep it a secret?"

All he can think is that she's going to tell him something about Irene—she bought a boat, she signed on with rival fishing boat *What a Catch!,* she's moving back to the States. "I can, yes," he says.

"Ayers is pregnant!" Maia says. "With Baker's baby!"

Huck would have said he was too old and jaded for anything to bowl him over, but Maia just proved him wrong. He thinks back to the last time he saw Ayers—when she gave him the diaries. She looked...peaked. To say the least. "You're kidding."

"Nope. She told me the other day."

"And Baker is the father? Baker, not Mick?"

"Isn't that crazy?" Maia says. She lifts a rib off Huck's plate that he didn't have any appetite for. "Their baby will be my niece or nephew. And if Ayers and Baker get married..." Maia's eyes light up. "Ayers will be my sister-in-law! We'll all be related!"

Huck wonders if Irene knows. She must. What the hell does she think about that? Well, there is one silver lining: Irene Steele isn't going anywhere with a new grandbaby on the way.

The next morning, Huck sees Irene pull into the Gifft Hill School parking lot to drop off Floyd. Even the sight of her—chestnut braid, white scoop-neck T-shirt, the blocky sunglasses that look like what an elderly person with cataracts wears—addles Huck.

"Irene!" he calls out through his open window. He wants to talk to her about Ayers and Baker, a baby coming, her new grandchild. Forget the FBI and Russ and the diaries—the pregnancy is good news, beautiful news.

He catches Irene by surprise. She glances over, sees it's him, and, without missing a beat, throws Baker's Jeep in reverse, backs out of the lot, and goes screaming down Gifft Hill, which is in the opposite direction of her house. She must really want to get away from him.

After dinner that evening, Huck smokes two cigarettes in rapid succession on the deck. He passes through the kitchen, then hits reverse, pulls the Flor de Caña off the shelf, does a shot, then a second shot. He checks on Maia. She's at her desk studying, not on her phone, a small miracle.

"I'm going to read for a bit, Nut," he says. "Good night."

He goes into his bedroom and sits at his desk, which is where he keeps his laptop and a paper calendar listing all his charters as well as files for bills and boat maintenance. He pulls a piece of paper from the tray of his printer, finds a pen that works, and thinks, *Here goes nothing.*

He writes a letter to Irene. He doesn't worry about his spelling or word choice; he doesn't start over when he wants to change his phrasing, just crosses things out. It doesn't have to be perfect; it just has to be true.

When he's finished, he reads it through, folds it in thirds, sticks it in an envelope. He's probably the only fool on earth who's still handwriting letters, but what he had to say shouldn't be texted and she won't talk to him. A letter is outdated, but it will also be difficult to resist reading. He hopes.

He just has to figure out how to get it to her.

* * *

A few days later, Maia stays overnight with Ayers. It's the first time Huck has been alone since Irene left. He could easily go out and spend a few hours tinkering on the boat, then grab a burger from the Tap and Still on the way home. Or he could buy some good beer, grill some tuna, lie down in his hammock, and finally crack open the Patterson book. But when he pulls up to the National Park Service dock and lets out his charter guests—a perfectly nice couple from he can't remember where and their three boys, who were all in boarding school; they obviously didn't see one another very often because they were so happy to be together—he hears steel-drum music coming from Mongoose Junction blending with strains of Kenny Chesney over at Joe's Rum Hut: *Save it for a rainy day!* And he decides he doesn't want to be alone. He calls Rupert. "You out?"

"Yes, sir."

"Skinny?"

"Aqua."

Good, Huck thinks. He's been craving the Aqua Bistro's onion rings for a while now. "I'll be there in an hour," he says.

"I'll be waiting," Rupert says. "But I gotta meet Sadie at Skinny at nine and Dora at Miss Lucy's at ten thirty."

Typical Rupert; he has a woman at every watering hole. No doubt Josephine will be singing tonight at the Aqua Bistro. Huck will hurry and shower. He loves Josephine's voice.

Forty-five minutes later, Huck is seated at the round open-air bar of Aqua Bistro next to Rupert. Josephine is playing the guitar, lulling everyone into a sense of well-being with her sultry rendition of "Come Away with Me." Rupert orders tequila shots with beer backs.

"Don't forget, I have to drive home," Huck says.

"Ha! That's no excuse on this island. Stay left, go slow, tell the donkeys to get out of your way. You and I both know you could do it blindfolded."

They click shot glasses and throw the tequila back. Huck feels okay. He slaps down five bucks and asks for the roll. The bartender hands him a leather cup filled with dice. He shakes it and lets them spill—nothing.

Rupert laughs. "Might as well have taken out your lighter and set your money on fire."

It's something to do. Only locals can roll. Irene can't roll. The Invisible Man couldn't roll. Huck's luck has been so damn awful this week that it'll surely take a turn soon. Why not now?

He throws the dice. Three threes, five, six.

"The pot is over a thousand bucks," the bartender says. "Nobody's won since before Christmas."

Josephine sings "Do You Know the Way to San Jose," only she changes "San Jose" to "Coral Bay."

"I love that woman," Rupert says.

"You love a lot of women," Huck says. Part of him wishes he were built this way, but he isn't. He loves Irene. *I love you, Irene,* he thinks and he throws the dice one last time. Two fours, two ones, and a six.

The bartender sweeps up his money. Rupert says nothing but Huck can sense him wanting to blurt out *I told you so.*

"Heard you and the Invisible Man's wife are shacking up," Rupert says.

"You're behind on your gossip. She moved out."

"Any fool off the street could have told you that wasn't

going to work," Rupert says. "There's too much tangled up between you."

Huck wants to tell Rupert he knows nothing about it but he doesn't like to bicker with Rupert, and also the phrase *tangled up* feels like a bull's-eye. Huck and Irene have always communicated on the level. But beneath all that was a mess both of them had willfully ignored—because neither of them had created it. Those diaries must have been salt in a wide-open wound. Huck should never, ever have showed them to her. It must have seemed like he *wanted* to hurt her, when the truth was, he assumed she was so strong and resilient that Rosie's words wouldn't matter.

Why would they matter when she has me? Huck had thought. He was there for her day in, day out, waiting, adoring, offering whatever support and encouragement she needed. Wasn't that enough? Why did the events of thirteen years or six years or two years earlier matter?

Huck spins his finger at the bartender. Another round—more shots, more beers. He found a way to get Irene the letter, ingeniously, or so he thought. He hasn't heard from her. Yet.

"You're right," Huck says to Rupert. "It was never going to work."

Josephine takes a break and comes to sit between them. Onion rings arrive, compliments of the kitchen. Huck admires them—fat, golden, glistening with oil, stacked on a dowel like so many rings in a game of quoits. (Did he eat any? He couldn't say. He might have waited for them to cool and then forgotten about them.)

Another beer.

Rupert says, "Jojo, you have any lady friends you could introduce to Huck here?"

"I hear Huck's taken," Josephine says, but Huck is saved from explaining that he's not, because it's time for her second set.

"Let's get out of here," Rupert says. "I'm late for Sadie."

Huck follows Rupert around the road in Coral Bay over to Skinny Legs. The place is crowded but there are two bar stools empty in the corner—how is this possible? Rupert must have called in on the way.

They take the seats; Huck orders a margarita with salt. Rupert says, "Who are you, Jimmy Buffett?" He asks for Cruzan Gold over ice. Heidi is bartending. She's in the weeds but she takes one glance at Huck and Rupert and says, "How 'bout a couple of burgers, fellas?"

Burgers, yes, sure. There's a band playing songs that Huck doesn't recognize and a bunch of kids in their twenties dancing. Tourists, spring-breakers. Huck and Rupert are geezers in this crowd but it doesn't matter, they're having fun, Heidi is taking good care of them. Huck feels a hand on his back and he turns to see Sadie. She pulls Rupert up out of his chair, and he claps a hand on Huck's shoulder, which is his way of saying he won't be back, please cover the check, Rupert will get him next time.

Fine, fine, Huck thinks. Good for Rupert. Sadie is Huck's favorite of the women anyway.

He should leave—but it's been so long since he's been out like this and it's working like a tonic against the ache in his heart. He orders a beer in an attempt to sober up.

He sees a familiar-looking blonde across the bar. She's one of the mothers from the Gifft Hill School, he figures out that much, though he couldn't in a million years come up with her name.

She's waving at him like crazy, and he raises his beer in a way he hopes says, *Yes, I see you, please don't come over here.*

The band plays one last song, and when it's finished, the bar empties out somewhat. Finally, Huck can hear himself think.

Heidi comes over and says, "Woman over there wants to buy you another drink. Beer?"

"Please," Huck says. "Which woman?" He assumes it's the Gifft Hill mother whose name he can't remember or never knew in the first place.

"Behind you," Heidi says.

Huck turns to see a redhead in a pale green dress sipping what looks like a painkiller over at the side bar. She's by herself, gazing out at the people drinking on the back deck. Is that who Heidi means? Well, yeah. She's the only woman behind him.

The beer arrives. Huck takes a swallow, then checks behind him again. The woman is gone.

Huh, he thinks. *Strange.*

A second later, someone takes Rupert's stool. It's the redhead in the green dress. "Good evening, Captain," she says.

Huck has had one—or a few—too many, perhaps. He has to back up a few inches to get a look at this woman. The mother on the boat today had red hair but no, no, no…this is…

The woman smiles.

Holy shit, he thinks. "Agent Vasco?"

"Colette, please."

Colette. Tonight, she looks like a Colette. Her hair is sleek and shiny. The green dress has buttons down the front; the top button has been undone to reveal a modest bit of her cleavage. She's wearing lipstick.

"Thank you for the beer," he says.

"I'm happy I bumped into you."

He wonders for a second if she followed him here. She's an FBI agent; is any contact accidental? "Are we breaking the law?" he asks.

"I'm off duty," she says. "And you're not under investigation." She orders another painkiller from Heidi. "I will break protocol to tell you a few things, though. First of all, those diaries didn't give us enough to lock up Croft."

Huck spins his beer by the neck. All that for nothing? "What about the stuff Russ told Rosie about the dummy driveways? About the illegal business dealings?"

"Hearsay."

"What about the end, where Croft shows up at La Tapa to threaten Rosie?"

"It isn't enough," Colette says. "The person who's implicated is Steele. And even Rosie. You turned over the cash you found in the dresser drawer, but I had to persuade my superiors not to go after the money in Rosie's accounts. I made the argument that the amounts were consistent with what she might have saved from her job." Colette takes a healthy pull of her drink. "But we could easily have called those tainted assets."

She did him a favor, and he's not ungrateful. He has that money to send Maia to college. "Thank you," Huck says.

She dips her head and gazes up at him. "I don't want you to think of me as the bad guy."

"You're just doing your job," Huck says. "I get it."

"Secondly, I got a call from the police in Charlotte Amalie. Apparently Oscar Cobb's girlfriend reported him missing. We watched Oscar a few years back because we knew he was selling drugs aboard the cruise ships—though ultimately he was too small a fish for us to pursue. I was surprised, though, to see his name show up in Rosie's diaries."

"Oscar Cobb," Huck says. "Not one of my favorite people. My wife, LeeAnn, wanted to disappear Oscar herself. He was terrible for Rosie—although I guess 'terrible' is all relative."

Colette says, "The police were wondering if we had any leads, which we didn't, but here's the thing: the girlfriend admitted that Oscar actually went missing on January first. She said they were at a New Year's Eve celebration and that Oscar left the party between two and three a.m., saying he had 'work' over on St. John."

This gets Huck's attention. He thinks about the black Jeep with the tinted windows—but no, it wasn't Oscar driving, and that woman didn't seem like a girlfriend of Oscar's. She was old enough to be his mother and, as Huck had learned, Oscar preferred his women much younger. "Did she say what kind of work?"

"She wasn't sure what he did exactly, but in the police report, she used the word 'investments.'"

"So Oscar Cobb disappears the same day that Rosie and Russ die in the crash. Could be a coincidence. Rosie doesn't mention Oscar again in the diaries and I haven't seen him around here. Believe me, I would have noticed."

"I don't believe in coincidences," Colette says. "But I also don't have anything that ties Cobb to Croft. I'll follow up with the girlfriend—she said she didn't report it earlier because she was scared, and I guess Oscar had a habit of disappearing for weeks at a time..."

Of course, he did, Huck thinks. He flashes back to the first time he laid eyes upon Oscar Cobb—at the Rolex Regatta in the late nineties. Rosie had been so young, only fifteen, and infatuated, completely blind to the fact that Oscar Cobb was bad news.

Though "bad news" is all relative.

"If I don't get anywhere with the girlfriend, I do have one last hope," Colette says. "Someone left a message at the field office saying she wants to talk to me about Croft. It was all very mysterious; she didn't leave a name, only a number. She might be a crackpot. Or she thinks there's money in it for her. The only thing is, she asked for me specifically. So she might be for real."

"You'll follow up?" Huck asks.

"I'll follow up," Colette says. "That's enough talk about work."

Huck has another beer and buys Colette Vasco another painkiller, and then he can't wait another second. He has to have a cigarette. He says, "I'm going out to smoke. I'll be right back."

"We share a vice," Colette says. "I'll come with you."

Huck tells Heidi they're coming right back and the two of them go stand in the grass past the back patio. There are a few crooked palm trees, then the lip of Coral Bay. Huck lights Colette's cigarette. It feels a little weird; the last woman he smoked with was his first wife, Kimberly.

She points to his left hand. "What happened to your finger?"

"Barracuda," he says.

"I love a man with scars," Colette says.

Huck lets that comment slide, though it's starting to feel like she's flirting with him, maybe more than flirting, which he can't deny is good for his battered ego. How old is she? Maybe closer to forty than he'd thought. "How did you end up in the Caribbean?" he asks.

She tells him she's originally from New Jersey, around Manasquan, Brielle, Belmar. Springsteen territory, she adds, because he's never heard of any of those places. Colette's father was a policeman; she went to Rutgers. The FBI recruited her. She spent years working the ports, fell in love with her boss, got married, and when he was transferred to the field office in Puerto Rico, she went with him. She got promoted, they split (it's unclear to Huck if these two things are related), he went back to New Jersey, she stayed in Puerto Rico. The FBI acknowledged the need for a bigger white-collar crime investigative team in the territories.

They're dangerously close to their original topic. Huck is still trying to process the news about Oscar Cobb. *Investments*? By "investments" the girlfriend must have meant "dealing drugs," because what kind of investments needed to be tended to at three o'clock in the morning on St. John?

"Time for me to call it a night," Huck says. They wander back inside and Huck flags Heidi for the check. "I have a charter bright and early."

"I should go too," Colette says.

They end up walking out to the parking lot together. It's dark and unpaved so Huck does the gentlemanly thing and offers Colette his arm.

"You didn't drive the Suburban out here, did you?"

"I'm staying out here," she says. "Company digs. I can't disclose the exact location but it's close enough to walk."

Huck is relieved. He's spared having to offer her a ride home. "Well, this is me," he says, nodding at his truck. He lifts his arm in an attempt to reclaim it from her and Colette grabs his hand, then winds her arms around his midsection and hip-locks him.

Whoa! Huck isn't sure what to do but he has to make a decision right now. Colette Vasco is pretty and there can be no mistaking her body language. She's ready to go—all the way.

Kiss her! Huck thinks. *Take her home. What's stopping you? She's divorced, you're single, you're both lonely, and admit it, there's been something between you from the beginning.*

He places his hands on Colette's shoulders, then cups her face and bends down. He kisses her once, gently, and is overcome by a strong wave of the worst emotion that exists in the world: guilt. He pulls away.

She presses farther into him. "Huck."

"Agent Vasco," he says. He reaches behind his back and unclasps her hands, holds them in both of his. "You're a very attractive woman. But I'm…involved with someone else." He stops. Is he doing the right thing? Is he? "And although it is quite tempting to take you home and let things unfold as they may, that wouldn't be fair to her. Nor would it be fair to you. So I'm going to say good night. Please get home safely."

Colette Vasco stares at him with half a smile—incredulous? embarrassed? drunk?—and then disappears into the dark.

Huck climbs into his truck, lights another cigarette, and blows the smoke out the window. *I hope you're happy, Irene Steele,* he thinks. *You've ruined me.*

He starts the engine, thinking, *Go slow, stay left. Donkeys, get out of my way.*

AYERS

During the first week of their stay on St. John, Ayers's parents cover a lot of ground. On the very first day, they meet Baker and then take Mick and Ayers out to dinner. On their second day, they buy a two-bedroom time-share at the Westin from Baker, and Ayers experiences predictably mixed feelings. On the one hand, she's comforted by this. On the other hand, she feels suffocated.

In the following days, Phil and Sunny hike the Reef Bay Trail, charter the *Singing Dog* with Captains Stephen and Kelly to the BVIs (no *Treasure Island* for them; they want to sail), experience happy hour at both Woody's and High Tide, snorkel with turtles at Salt Pond, dance to Miss Fairchild at the Beach Bar, buy matching hook bracelets at Bamboo, and kayak to Lime Out for tacos.

And yet somehow, they're still underfoot. They wake Ayers up with chai lattes from Provisions, they swing by with containers of sesame noodles and spinach-artichoke dip from the North Shore Deli, they appear at La Tapa while Ayers is working and introduce themselves to the guests at Ayers's tables until she has to ask them to either sit at the bar or leave. They choose the bar and end up getting into a deep conversation with Skip about his trust issues with women.

How is she ever going to survive them? When will they leave for Barbuda, Bequia?

The dinner with Mick was...illuminating. Ayers wonders if, in her parents' minds, Mick is still her boyfriend. Maybe they haven't yet fully absorbed the news of the breakup or the idea that Ayers is pregnant by someone else. At dinner at the Longboard—which unfortunately evoked the evening of their engagement—Mick was his most charming self, sucking up to Phil and Sunny in every possible way, asking about their travels, begging to see their pictures, giving Sunny too much encouragement about her prospective blog. Ayers bit her tongue and thought, *Fake it to make it,* all the while hoping the staff at the Longboard weren't getting out their phones in the back to broadcast the news that Mick and Ayers were together again.

What Ayers realized while being smushed up in a booth next to Mick was that her feelings for him had changed.

She'd broken the engagement because she was smart—Mick would never stop cheating—but it hadn't changed the fact that she loved him. Being pregnant with Baker's baby hadn't canceled out her feelings for Mick either. It was amazing the things that love could endure; nothing demonstrated this more than her ups and downs with Mick had. But at dinner with her parents, Ayers had been pleasantly surprised to find that she felt nothing for Mick other than a mixture of mild annoyance and nostalgic fondness. After Phil and Sunny headed back to Caneel, Mick walked Ayers to her truck and tried to kiss her. She ducked out of the way; she felt no attraction to him. *Finally,* she thought. The vine Mick had wrapped around her heart was withering. She had spent much of the previous six months hating Mick for what had happened with Brigid—but hate was not the opposite of love. Indifference was the opposite of love, and for the first time, Ayers felt like she could take Mick or leave him. Tonight, she would leave him.

"Good night," she said.

Later, when Ayers was home in bed with Winnie snoring softly at her feet, she'd texted Baker. Survived dinner with Mick. Sorry about that; my parents wanted to see him.

There was no response, which was unusual. Ayers wondered if maybe she'd blown it. At noon the next day, Baker still hadn't responded, and she nearly sent a second text asking if he wanted to grab lunch—but she decided this would be confusing. She was the one who had asked for space; he was giving it to her.

When their visit enters its second week, Phil and Sunny decide it's time to introduce themselves to Irene Steele. Ayers tries to dissuade them; Irene is reserved. She may not appreciate being ambushed without warning. But Sunny waves Ayers's concerns away like incense smoke. They see Baker and Floyd get back from school, and the instant Irene arrives home with Cash, they gather up Winnie, a bottle of champagne, and a charcuterie platter from Island Cork.

"Come over after you shower, Fred," Sunny says, which bugs Ayers. She doesn't want to shower and she doesn't want to socialize.

She says, "I'm tired, Mama. I'm going to lie down for a little while."

Sunny immediately changes her tune. Yes, Ayers should sleep, the first trimester is so taxing on the body. Sunny starts talking about being in western Australia on an ostrich farm that was owned by a woman who was also a potter, she made the most beautiful bowls...

"Mama, please," Ayers says. She lies down on her bed and pulls the comforter over her head. The last thing she hears is Sunny saying to Phil, "Leave her be, honey."

When Ayers awakens, it's dark outside and her parents are back, laughing, whispering, bumping into things, shushing each other. Ayers checks her phone—ten thirty. They went across the street at five. "Mom?" she says. "Dad?"

They erupt in giggles. Ayers feels like she's the parent right now. "Have you been across the street this whole *time?*"

"Oh, Freddy," Sunny says. "It's going to be so great!"

"What is?"

"Irene took a while to warm up," Phil says. "But by the fourth bottle of wine..."

"Fourth?"

"Plus the champagne," Sunny says. "So, technically, five."

"Irene likes her chardonnay," Phil says.

"*What* is going to be so great?" Ayers asks.

"Our family!" Sunny says. "The family we're creating with the Steeles. And that Cash—what a cutie!"

"Your mother has a crush on him," Phil says. "She made that much obvious."

"He's single," Sunny says. "I'm surprised you didn't end up with him, Freddy. He's much more your type. Outdoorsy."

"Cash and I are friends, Mom. We work together." Ayers sits up in bed and pats the comforter. Winnie leaps up. "So you all had a great time and you drank the night away..."

"Baker made fish tacos," Phil says. "That guy can really cook."

"Floyd let me read to him before bed," Sunny says. "I feel like a real grandma already."

"We discussed our grandparent names," Phil says. "Irene is Grammy, so Mom will be Mimi. I'm torn between Pop-Pop and Granddaddy." He clears his throat. "It's a big responsibility, being this child's only grandfather."

"We heard the whole story about Russ," Sunny says. "Very interesting."

"If by *interesting,* you mean 'tragic,' then yeah," Ayers says.

"I think what's interesting is the way Irene has come to terms with the situation. She blames Russ, but she also blames herself for taking Russ for granted, for not paying attention to the marriage, for all kinds of things."

"Wow, you guys really got into it," Ayers says. "Did you talk about me?"

"When we first got there, we told them you were tired," Sunny says. "And we talked about the baby."

"But other than that, your name didn't come up," Phil says.

Ayers is both relieved and bothered by this. Her parents and the Steeles are out forging a new family together but somehow the most important person—the person carrying the baby that will unite them—doesn't matter.

Her parents gather their things to return to their room at Caneel—in two short days they're off on their Caribbean adventure, thank goodness—and as soon as the front door closes, Ayers sends Baker a text. Thank you for entertaining my parents; I'm sure they overstayed their welcome. Baker doesn't respond. Well, maybe he's asleep. But when Ayers gets up to check, she sees a light on in what she knows is Baker's bedroom.

She has a strong impulse to tiptoe over and knock on his window. Maybe even encourage him to come over. Maybe even...

She climbs back into bed. *Space,* she thinks.

Two nights later, Ayers is working at La Tapa. Her parents left that morning on the ten o'clock ferry; they'll be gone for six to eight weeks. Ayers is relieved; happy, even. They'll be back, but she doesn't have to deal with them right now.

Tilda approaches Ayers at the back service station. "I assume you've heard?"

God alone knows what Tilda is going to drop on her. *Heard you left Cash for some wealthy guy who doesn't eat?* Yes, Ayers has heard about that, in gory detail, from Cash. Ayers won't lie—it has colored her opinion of Tilda. Tilda is entitled to see whomever she pleases but going away with a rich boy and leaving Cash in the dust seems crueler than your average breakup.

"Heard what?" Ayers asks.

"Mick quit the Beach Bar," Tilda says. "He's leaving island."

"That must be a mistake," Ayers says. "He told me at dinner last week that he signed a one-year lease at his new place, Pure Joy."

"He's trying to find someone to take over his lease."

"Really," Ayers says. "Where's he going?"

"You should probably ask him that," Tilda says.

Tilda is back to being very annoying, even more annoying than when she had a crush on Skip.

On her way home, Ayers calls Mick. "Word on the street is that you quit the Beach Bar? You're leaving island?"

"Yes," Mick says. "And yes."

"Wow," Ayers says, though she still doesn't believe him. He's been at the Beach Bar a Caribbean eternity—eleven years.

"I can't live on this island and not be with you," he says.

Ayers knew it. This is all a ploy to get her back. He *planned* this with Tilda; they're in *cahoots!* "Well, I'm never coming back to you. I'm not in love with you anymore. So I guess you'd better go."

"Yeah." He clears his throat. "Any chance you want to take over the lease on Pure Joy?"

"Damn straight I do," she says. He may be bluffing but she's dead serious. Pure Joy is a one-bedroom with incredible views across Great Cruz Bay over to St. Thomas, views that are best enjoyed sitting at the cute bar counter on the front porch. Ayers is sure her parents will help her with the rent.

"I thought you might move in with Banker and his kid. Play house, happy family, and all that."

"No plans to," Ayers says. "I definitely want your place."

"Cool," Mick says. "I want to leave as soon as I can. I've been offered a position as food and beverage director at Tucker's Point in Bermuda."

Ayers hoots. "Will you wear knee socks?"

"I think I might have to," Mick says. "The resort is five-star, so the job has more responsibility. The only downside is the shorts-and-knee-socks look. My legs are so stubby."

"So you're doing this?"

"Yes," he says.

Things move fast, so fast! The next day, Ayers meets Mick at the real estate office to sign paperwork for the lease. Mick is leaving this weekend; Ayers can move in as soon as he's out.

"What are you doing with your place?" Mick asks.

"Cash is taking it," Ayers says. This whole thing is almost too easy; Cash can move off his brother's couch right into Ayers's studio apartment across the street. He and Winnie will be reunited. Ayers isn't sure how Baker feels about her leaving Fish Bay, but it's not like she's leaving for St. Thomas or even Coral Bay. She'll be on Great Cruz Bay Road, halfway between the Happy Hibiscus and the Westin time-share office. And it's only for a year.

It will be a big, scary year, but Ayers isn't going to let that stop her. She loved the cottage when Mick showed it to her. Now it's hers!

On Saturday when Mick is scheduled to leave, Ayers drives down to the car barge to say goodbye. She can't quite figure out why she wants to do this. She supposes that part of it is to witness the milestone—the moment her boyfriend of nine years moves on. Part of it is to make sure he actually goes. And part of it is to kiss Gordon one last time.

The car barge is, as always, a whirl of activity with a snaking line of cars and Jeeps and pickups and huge Mack trucks waiting to board and a notoriously unflappable West Indian woman named Sheila overseeing who goes where. More than once, Ayers has witnessed Sheila letting her friends and sweethearts jump the line, which isn't fair—but nobody ever questions Sheila.

Sheila is a cousin of Rosie's on her father's side and because of this, Sheila likes Ayers. "You getting on, doll?" she asks.

"Saying goodbye to someone," Ayers says.

"And good riddance?" Sheila asks.

"Kind of, yeah," Ayers says and Sheila chuckles.

Ayers almost doesn't recognize Mick's blue Jeep because it has the top on. Has she ever seen his Jeep with the top on? She doesn't think so. She and Mick got caught in rain showers in that thing probably a hundred times. The seats held a damp smell and Mick eventually pulled up the rugs so that water emptied through the holes in the floorboards. Ayers parks her truck over by Sheila's guardhouse. As she strides toward Mick's Jeep, she hears Gordon barking. Automatically, she tears up. She promised herself she wouldn't become emotional, but that dog was like her first child and she's going to miss him.

They're loading the boat; she has to hurry. She runs up behind the Jeep and goes to the driver's side, where Gordon is hanging his head out the window.

"Who's a good boy?" she says.

"Hey!" Mick says. "What are you doing here?"

"Came to say goodbye to my pup—" Ayers is at the window, her hands cradling Gordon's bucket head, when she realizes there's someone in the passenger seat of the Jeep.

It's Brigid.

"Hey, Ayers," Brigid says. "Thanks for seeing us off. Good luck with your *baby*." She says the word like it's something imaginary and she holds up two fingers in a peace sign.

Ayers is...she's...she looks at Mick. "Brigid's going with you to Bermuda?"

He nods. "Yeah."

Ayers kisses Gordon between the eyes, then leans in past Mick. "Goodbye, Brigid," she says. She returns the peace sign—ironically, but Brigid will never know this.

Sheila whistles, windmilling her arm; it's time for Mick to go.

Ayers watches the blue Jeep drive up the ramp of the barge.

"And good riddance," Ayers says.

The very next day, Ayers wakes up feeling like a new woman. She got a long luxurious night's sleep, and for the first time in weeks, she feels hungry. She makes not only buttered rye toast but also cheesy scrambled eggs. She takes her prenatal vitamin, drinks a glass of juice, eats a banana.

She figures she needs two days to pack her things and one day to move them. Then she'll be back in action.

She calls Whitney at the *Treasure Island* office. "I can work again, starting on Wednesday," she says.

It's as though Ayers has crossed an invisible boundary. Her body was her enemy, but now it's a friend. She has energy; she has vitality. The tiny life inside her might as well be a supercharged battery. Ayers moves into Pure Joy. While Ayers's studio was funky and bohemian but gloomy, with a view only of the Happy Hibiscus, Pure Joy is bright and airy, filled with sunlight. She has actual rooms—a living/dining/kitchen area, a brand-new bath with gleaming white subway tile, a bedroom with a king-size bed, and a bona fide walk-in closet. The cottage has a gas grill and an enclosed outdoor shower and Ayers will spend every spare minute on one of the stools at the bar counter gazing at the dreamscape across her new front yard—the striated blue and green shades of the Caribbean.

Ayers sets her mugs and plates and wineglasses on the fresh white shelves in the kitchen; she puts new sheets on the bed; she hangs her photographs; she sets her houseplants in the sun. During her last check of her old studio, she discovers the hidden pack of cigarettes on top of the refrigerator and throws them away.

Her first night in the new place, she gets barbecue from Candi's—ribs and chicken and pasta salad and coleslaw and plantains—and she sits at the bar counter on her front porch to watch the sun sink into the Caribbean. *Hashtag sunset,* she thinks. Mick is gone, she's pregnant, and she has a new place to live—it all feels like a fresh start. She picks up her phone and nearly sends a text to Baker saying, *Want to see my new place?* But it's only her first night. There's plenty of time.

A leave of absence from *Treasure Island* was exactly what she needed because she comes back rejuvenated. Virgin Gorda Baths, snorkeling at the Indians, White Bay on Jost Van Dyke, where Leon, the bartender at the Soggy Dollar, makes her a virgin painkiller.

"Congratulations, love," Leon says. "When will I meet this child's daddy?"

"Soon?" Ayers says. She wonders if she should invite Baker and Floyd out on the boat so they can experience the BVIs and see her in action. Yes, they would like it. When they get back to Cruz Bay, Ayers checks the schedule and sees there are plenty of spots on Saturday's charter. She texts Baker. BVI trip Saturday, you and Floyd, my treat?

The response comes: Nice offer, thank you. Floyd doesn't have a passport.

Ah, bummer, Ayers thinks. He's only four, but yeah, he still needs a passport. How about just you, then? Leave Floyd with your mom?

I shouldn't, he says. Weekends are my time with Floyd. Sorry about that.

He's a good dad, she thinks. *He's a really good dad.*

A few nights later, Ayers leaves La Tapa after service and she's so tired that she drives to Fish Bay without thinking. It's only when she pulls into her former driveway and sees Cash's new-used truck that she realizes she's on autopilot.

Ugh! She might need Tilda to close from now on so she can get out of the restaurant earlier. Tilda won't like this. She has been the one slipping out early, rushing her tables, neglecting to offer dessert, coffee, or aperitifs, snapping at Skip for change—all because her new beau, Dunk, likes to linger across the street outside the Tap and Still, vaping and waiting for Tilda to emerge. Ayers has studied him. He's always in jeans and a T-shirt and a baseball cap and Sambas, looking more like a guy with an online-poker habit than a multimillionaire with an estate out in the East End, but Ayers supposes that's part of the appeal. Dunk looks shady, which Tilda has mistaken for mysterious; she finds his fasting intriguing rather than ridiculous. She's young. She'll learn.

As Ayers is backing out of her former driveway she sees, in her rearview mirror, two people coming out of the Happy Hibiscus. It's Baker and... a woman. Tall, blond.

Wait a minute. Ayers pulls back into her former driveway, turns off her lights, cuts her engine. She squints into the mirror. Do they see her? No. Baker and the woman are standing by an ivory Land Cruiser that Ayers recognizes as belonging to Swan Seeley.

Baker is walking Swan Seeley out to her car at ten thirty at night. Are they *seeing* each other? Is this why he hasn't responded to her texts?

No, Ayers thinks. *No!* She can't let this happen. And yet this is all her fault. She told Baker she needed space; she told Baker she wanted to be friends. Friends! After he moved his entire life down here, after he handled the news of the pregnancy like a hero. Has he complained? No. Has he been even a little bit of a jerk like literally any other guy in America would have been? No. He stopped by with a smoothie and chips. She had seen him another time, with Floyd in tow, bearing coffee and a bakery bag, and she'd burrowed into her bed, not even answering the door. She'd skipped the impromptu visit by her parents. She had been so certain that Baker would be there when she was ready that she had never considered another woman might step in, a woman such as Swan Seeley, a Gifft Hill mother who is going through a divorce and who *told* Ayers the afternoon that Mick proposed that she thought Baker was hot. And now here they are, Baker and Swan, standing by the driver's side of Swan's car, about to have a moment.

They're talking, but not touching. Swan tosses her hair, leans her head back, raises her face to his. She lays her palm on Baker's strong chest, and Ayers feels a pang of longing. The first time she saw Baker was at Chester's Getaway, when he crashed Rosie's funeral reception. He had seemed such a stunning, fresh presence in that sea of all-too-familiar faces, some of which were also all too unpleasant (Mick had had the gall to bring Brigid).

At first, Ayers thought Baker was a tourist. Learning he was the Invisible Man's son had been shocking, but on later reflection, she'd known there was *something about him.* She sensed that meeting him wasn't random luck. Rosie, in a way, had sent him to her.

Then he went back to Houston.

Then he returned. They'd slept together. It had felt... right. They clicked. There was light, heat, chemistry.

Then he left again. For only a few days—but a few days was a few days too many. Mick proposed.

Then Baker came back. He's here now. He has a job, a Jeep, a villa. Floyd is in school. Baker is a tourist no longer.

Swan takes hold of Baker's arms and stands on her tiptoes.

No, Ayers thinks. She gets out of the truck, slams the door. Both Baker and Swan turn toward the noise. Swan's heels hit the ground.

"Hey," Ayers calls out. She crosses the street and strides up the driveway to the two of them. They're standing farther apart now.

Swan looks... miffed. "Ayers?"

Baker says, "Ayers, hey!" He takes a step away from Swan.

"Sorry I didn't text or anything," Ayers says to Baker. "But I just got out of work and I was wondering if you wanted to come see my new place?"

Swan emits an audible breath and Ayers thinks, *I know. This is brazen. You will rewind and replay this moment for your school-mom friends dozens of times until they're all sick of hearing it, and maybe none of you will ever speak to me again. Maybe you'll boycott La Tapa and post anonymous nasty comments on the* Treasure Island *Tripadvisor page, but I don't care. Baker is the father of my baby and although I've treated him carelessly, I'm not giving him up without a fight.*

Then she thinks, *The good news is, Skip is still available.*

"Yeah," Baker says. "My mom can watch Floyd, and Swan was just leaving." He takes Ayers's hand and squeezes it. "I'd love to come with you."

IRENE

Baker sees Maia at school while he's picking up Floyd and invites her over for dinner.

"I hope that's okay?" he says when he tells Irene. "I'll go get her and drive her home."

"Of course," Irene says. She still isn't ready for a détente with Huck—nope, not at all. Rosie's relationship with Russ happened while Rosie was *living under Huck's roof.* He said he'd never met Russ—Irene believes this—but could he not guess the man Rosie was involved with was married? Obviously, the Invisible Man was married. That was why he was invisible!

Huck should have asked more questions. He should have followed Rosie to the villa. He should have *put an end to it.*

Are these unreasonable expectations? Maybe. But the bald fact remains: Huck stood by and did nothing. For years.

He's the only one left for Irene to blame. She can't summon the same ire or resentment toward Maia. Maia is a child. Russ's daughter. The boys' sister.

"Maia is always welcome," Irene says, and she sees relief cross Baker's face.

Maia arrives bearing two large square packages—one light, which she carries, and one heavy, which Baker carries.

"These came for you," Maia explains. "To Gramps's post box."

While Maia and Floyd take a predinner swim in the pool, Irene slices the packages open. One of them holds her Christmas ornaments, still carefully wrapped up in tissue. Irene sighs, recalling her *industriousness* on New Year's Day before her dinner with Lydia at the Pullman Diner, before the phone call when she learned Russ was dead.

On New Year's Day, she had been a different person—irritated and hurt that her husband was traveling for work over the holiday but determined to make the best of it and be productive. She'd wanted to wake up on January 2 and have all traces of Christmas gone. Back then, nothing had annoyed Irene more than lazy neighbors who left their outside lights up until Martin Luther King Jr. weekend, their wreaths up until Valentine's Day. She had carefully removed and wrapped all the ornaments because she was a methodical person who believed God was in the details. She would be grateful for the effort the following Christmas when she opened the box and everything was just so.

She'd never imagined she'd be opening the box that spring in the Virgin Islands.

The most precious ornaments aren't her collection of intricate and clever Christopher Radkos or the vintage ornaments she picked up at estate sales across the country but rather the ornaments the boys made in elementary school. A cardboard disk covered in green foil decorated with beads and dried macaroni, CASH written in glitter on one side. A puffy painted Santa face with cotton glued on for a beard. Irene is happy to have these back, even though they belonged to that other lifetime.

The other box holds photo albums and the framed family photographs that Irene had had on display around the house on Church Street. The photo that greets Irene is the last picture taken of her and Russ together. They're side by side on the front porch swing at her aunt's house in Door County, Wisconsin. They're smiling at Cash, who took the picture. Russ's arm runs along the back of the swing behind Irene, and Irene's hand rests on Russ's thigh, lightly but proprietarily. Why wouldn't it? He was her husband of thirty-five years. She would characterize Russ's expression as content. Irene then flashes back to the photograph she found of him and Rosie lying in the hammock. He had looked ecstatic, as though he had no idea how he'd gotten so lucky. A girlfriend whose beauty was as rarefied as the Mona Lisa's.

Irene had wanted to smash the photograph of Russ and Rosie but she feels an even greater violence toward this picture of her and Russ. The audacity of him to smile at the camera as though nothing is amiss. As though he doesn't have a mistress and a child waiting for him down in the Caribbean!

Irene steadies her breathing and checks out the window. Baker is drinking a beer, his legs dangling in the water. Maia is carrying Floyd around the pool on her shoulders. He's shrieking with joy. He adores her.

Irene digs a little deeper in the box and finds the navy leather photo album and the red vinyl photo album. These hold pictures of the boys growing up. She can see the snapshots without looking at them: Baker on the pitcher's mound in his green and yellow uniform, all spindly arms and legs; Cash on the ski slopes, goggles resting on top of his helmet, braces glinting in the glare off the snow; both boys in khakis and navy blazers escorting Milly out of church on Easter.

Beneath these is a photograph of Baker and Anna on their wedding day. Anna is stunning in her sleek ivory silk, but she's not smiling.

Irene closes up the box and puts it in the closet. When she's had a chance to properly go through it, she'll show some of the pictures of Baker and Cash to Maia. But for now, it's important that Maia not see any of the photos. What would she think if she saw the picture of Russ and Irene on the swing? Irene shudders. She would never put a child through what she has just experienced—being starkly confronted with evidence that she was being lied to.

At dinner, Maia says, "So what was in the boxes?"

"Christmas ornaments," Irene says. "And other knickknacks from my house in Iowa."

Maia takes a knife to her fried chicken. "I had to give up being a vegan," she says. "It was too hard."

"How's the bath-bomb business?" Irene asks.

"I kind of gave that up too," Maia says. "I'm busy with other things."

"What kinds of things?" Baker asks. "Not sports? I was supposed to coach the upper-school baseball team but only four kids signed up—three girls and a boy."

"Not sports," Maia says. "I hang out with my friends mostly. Joanie, Colton, Bright, and...Shane. Shane is sort of a special friend." Maia's face shines and for a moment, her beauty takes Irene's breath away. She's Milly, she's Russ, and she's someone else—Rosie, Irene supposes.

Maia makes it through the entire meal talking about her life without mentioning Huck even once. This must be on purpose; maybe Maia thinks Huck is a forbidden topic.

Irene clears her throat. "How's your grandfather?" As soon as the words are out, she feels like she's lost a test of wills.

"Oh," Maia says, shrugging. "He's good." This seems to be all Irene is going to get. *He's good. He's good?* Then Maia locks eyes with Irene and says, "He misses you."

Irene is startled by the simple frankness of this statement.

I miss him too, she thinks—and it's the first time she's allowed herself to admit it.

"He gave me this to deliver," Maia says. She pulls an envelope that has been folded in half out of the back pocket of her shorts.

"Oh," Irene says. Her name is on the front in Huck's handwriting. Maybe it's an accounting of what she owes him for rent and utilities—but she knows Huck wouldn't ask for money even if he were angry. "Thank you." She takes the envelope. "Who wants dessert?"

She would like to throw the envelope away unopened, but she isn't strong enough. She waits until Baker returns from running Maia home and starts giving Floyd a bath, then she takes the envelope to the back deck and opens it.

It's a letter.

Dear AC,

Maybe you'll read this, maybe you won't. In the event you are reading this, I want to start by saying that this is not an apology because I didn't do anything wrong.

When LeeAnn died and Rosie got back together with Russ, she was nearly thirty years old. She described Russ as "this man I'm seeing, Russell Steele"—she said his name to me only that once—and I had no idea that this was the same man as "the Pirate," the one who had gotten her pregnant. She very deliberately led me to believe it was someone new.

I asked the usual questions: Where was he from, what did

he do, when could I meet him? Rosie provided no answers. She wanted to keep the relationship private; she was concerned that the island would poke its nose into her business. After the way that LeeAnn rallied every single one of her friends and relations against Oscar Cobb, I couldn't blame Rosie for feeling this way. Rosie told me that, just like certain plants, some relationships do best with a lot of sunlight, and some thrive hidden in the shade, and her new relationship was the latter. It concerned me, I made that clear, but I also want to explain that I was lonely without LeeAnn and my greatest fear was that Rosie would take Maia and move out. I wanted to avoid that at all costs.

If you read the diaries closely then you know that Rosie didn't start taking Maia with her to see Russ until 2016. Once this happened, my questions grew more insistent. I didn't like the idea of Maia spending time with any adult I hadn't met.

Again, I was shut down.

There were whispers around town about the "Invisible Man," and some of it reached my ears. I learned he was white, he was wealthy, he had a villa somewhere on the north shore. Did I think he was married? It crossed my mind, but again, Rosie was in her thirties, old enough to know what she was doing.

To be honest, AC, I was worried about Rosie—and Maia—getting hurt. I didn't give a thought to any woman Russell Steele might have been betraying. When I think of it this way, I understand what you mean about us being on "opposite sides" of this thing.

Although this isn't a letter of apology, I do want to say that I'm sorry. I'm sorry this happened to you. I'm sorry you were betrayed and I'm sorry you were hurt. I also want to tell you something about my past that you might not know.

Before I moved to St. John and met LeeAnn Small, I was married to someone else, a woman named Kimberly Cassel, whom I met when I lived in Key West. Kimberly was a hot ticket—a star bartender and one hell of a fisherwoman. She was also a serial philanderer and an alcoholic. Before our marriage ended, Kimberly revealed that she had fooled around with hundreds, maybe even thousands, of the men who came into the bar where she worked. Kimberly got pregnant and miscarried at fourteen weeks, which was devastating to me at the time and felt even worse when I discovered the child might not even have been mine.

I put Kimberly in rehab and divorced her, which might sound like a door that shut clean and firm, but I assure you, the hurt lasted for a very long time after.

I tell you this only because I want you to feel less alone and to know that I do have some idea of what you're battling.

If you made it this far in the letter, AC, then I'm grateful—and not only grateful but hopeful that, at some point in the future, we can have a conversation and mend things between us. I miss you for many reasons, but mostly I miss our friendship. As unlikely as it might be, the friendship is genuine.

With love,
Huck

Irene clears the emotion from her throat and reads the letter again. Then she folds it up and returns it to the envelope. She heads back into the kitchen to unload the dishes from the drying rack and she holds the letter over the kitchen trash. It feels like

Huck is, once again, rushing her. If he'd learned anything from watching and listening to her the past couple of months, he would have known that what she needs is time.

She can't bring herself to throw the letter away. She tucks it into the front pocket of her suitcase.

As she's falling asleep, she thinks, *Huck wrote me a letter.* And she smiles.

The next day, Irene e-mails Natalie Key to thank her for the boxes. She doesn't call because she knows Natalie is handling a new, highly sensitive, high-profile embezzlement case and is very busy. She's surprised when the phone rings.

"I'm sorry I couldn't get you more," Natalie says. "Your books and clothes will be returned eventually, once they've been documented and it's been determined that they have minimal resale value. Certain other personal items as well—your teakettle, kitchen utensils. But no antiques, and not the rugs. Not your cars. I'm sorry."

"It's okay," Irene says—and the strange thing is, she means it. She owned a house filled with *things,* some of them very expensive. But none of it matters. She's doing just fine without *things.* Why had she put so much time and energy into them in the first place?

"Also..." Natalie says. Her voice takes on a sober tone and Irene assumes she's about to say that Irene's retainer has run out. "I heard from the Feds. There were personal journals of Rosie Small's that were discovered—but unfortunately, these didn't contain enough hard facts to incriminate Todd Croft."

Irene closes her eyes. All of that pain...for nothing? Huck

should have buried the diaries in a drawer and given them to Maia ten or fifteen years from now. In ten or fifteen years, the love affair between Russell Steele and his Mona Lisa wouldn't hurt Irene the way it does now.

"That guy Croft," Natalie says. "He's the mastermind. There's no other way."

"He's such a mastermind, he managed to walk away unscathed," Irene says.

"Fined," Natalie says. "Heavily fined. But make no mistake, that guy has money hidden."

"He killed Russ," Irene says. "And Rosie. And Stephen Thompson. And he's getting off scot-free."

"I thought for sure we were going to help send him to jail," Natalie says. "I'm sorry, Irene."

She received the study materials for her captain's test, but when she starts reading the introduction, she sees that, in addition to passing the test, she has to have at least three hundred and sixty days logged on the water as a mate or crew member.

Three hundred and sixty days!

She has, maybe, thirty.

Irene sags at this news. She chastises herself for not realizing this would be the case. If it were just a little studying and a test, then every clown out there would have a captain's license. She feels so naive. Here she announced her grandiose plan—her own charter, *Angler Cupcake,* direct competition for Huck. She had cinematic fantasies of standing proud at the helm of her own boat with a full charter, puttering past the empty *Mississippi.* In some versions, she waves to Huck. In others, she ignores him.

He must have known she didn't have enough hours on the

water when she mentioned her plans to Jack and Diane. How embarrassing.

How will she get three hundred and thirty more days on the water? Who would hire a fifty-seven-year-old woman as a mate?

Treasure Island? she wonders. Maybe. Cash and Ayers could definitely use a third crew member to cover their respective days off, and once the baby is born…Cash says all they're looking for is a warm body, and Irene is much more than that. She's good with the clients. It's a little babysitting, a little psychology. Irene has the touch.

How would Cash feel about working all day with his *mother?* Not great, she predicts. Living together is taxing enough.

She could approach a different fishing boat, like *What a Catch!* But those guys are young, single, wild. They don't want Irene on their boat.

Could she work on Pizza Pi as a delivery person, zipping the pizzas to yachts on a little Zodiac? Would that count? What about asking at Palm Tree Charters or the *Singing Dog*? There's a new charter Irene heard about, a Midnight Express called *New Moon* owned by a very cool couple named Brian and Michelle Zehring—*that* boat might be too sexy for Irene, but she could always ask.

Even if she can cobble something together, it's still going to take an entire year for Irene to realize her dream. She has an appointment to see a 2006 forty-five-foot Hatteras on St. Thomas next week. The asking price is fifty thousand, but on the phone the guy said he's willing to work with her and she can hopefully take out a loan at FirstBank.

Baker's new friend Swan Seeley is scheduled to come over tomorrow after dinner to talk to her about a marketing strategy. Irene considers canceling but this woman Swan might be well connected and could have leads on where Irene might look for work. Irene confirms with Swan, then texts Lydia to see if Brandon the barista is willing to part with his recipe for lemongrass sugar cookies. Irene needs to have something to offer the woman. Other than wine, of course.

Swan arrives right on time. She's tall, blond, and stunning; Irene puts her at thirty-five or thirty-six. She's wearing white pants, a formfitting white T-shirt, a slender gold watch, and gold hoop earrings. Irene peeks behind her in the driveway and sees an ivory Land Cruiser.

"Hello, Mrs. Steele, I'm Swan Seeley." Nice handshake, smile; she's wearing makeup and she smells divine, some kind of expensive perfume. Maybe Swan thought tonight was going to be more formal than it is?

They sit at the dining-room table. Swan pulls a Moleskine notebook out of her supple leather hobo bag. This woman is smooth, polished. Wealthy. She's the Mavis Key of St. John.

Irene offers Swan wine—"Yes, please"—and sets out a plate of the lemongrass sugar cookies, which turned out splendidly. (Brandon's suggestion to undercook them by two minutes was spot on; they're pale golden and have alluringly crinkly tops.) Irene offers the plate and Swan takes not one but two—oh, Irene likes this woman already.

Irene says, "I'm not sure what Baker told you..."

Swan's head swivels around. "Is Baker *here?*" she asks. "I saw his Jeep out front."

"He's reading to Floyd," Irene says. "He'll be out in a minute."

"He's *such* a good father," Swan says. "Not just a good father but a good *parent.* My ex...well, this time of night you could usually find him in front of the slots at the Parrot Club."

Irene suddenly understands that Swan's presence here has little to do with Irene and much to do with Baker. Does Swan know that Ayers is pregnant with Baker's baby? Maybe that doesn't matter. Baker and Ayers have hardly seen each other at all. The week before, Ayers's parents came over and Ayers stayed home. Irene figures she'd better state her case before Baker comes downstairs and distracts Swan.

"I want to start my own fishing charter," she says. "Here's what I've found out..."

Swan agrees the three-hundred-and-sixty-day requirement is a bummer and means it'll be another year before Irene's charter is up and running.

"I would hire you as a mate on my boat," Swan says. "But it looks like I have to sell it to pay off my ex."

"Divorces are tricky," Irene says. She's had a glass and a half of wine, so she nearly adds, *But better than staying married and finding out your husband has a secret family!*

"I'm confused about why you're not working for Huck anymore," Swan says. "He's *such* a great guy. *Such* a wonderful grandfather. Completely devoted to Maia."

"That he is," Irene says.

"You know, I saw him on Friday night out at Skinny Legs." Swan sips her wine. "He was with a woman, a very pretty redhead. I saw them leave together, so I think maybe Huck got lucky!" She leans in conspiratorially and bumps Irene's shoulder.

Irene nearly falls over in her chair. "A redhead?" she says. "Was she his age?"

"Younger," Swan says. "Closer to my age, I'd guess. Go, Huck!"

The wine and cookies churn in Irene's stomach. Her neck flushes. She has to get out of there.

"Hey, ladies." Baker saunters into the kitchen. "I don't mean to interrupt—"

"Baker!" Swan says. She jumps up from the table to give him a hug. Here is Irene's way out.

"Thank you for all your help, Swan. I'll let you two kids chat. I need to hit the hay."

"Hit the hay," Baker says. "Can you tell we're from the Midwest?"

"Are you sure, Irene?" Swan says. "We didn't get to talk about my marketing ideas. I have a bunch."

"We've got plenty of time," Irene says. "I hope you'll come back once I buy a boat and get closer to my hours..."

"You don't have to run off, Mom," Baker says. His expression seems to be asking Irene *not* to run off.

Sorry, Baker, she thinks. *You're an adult. You deal with your romantic entanglements and I'll deal with mine.* "Enjoy the cookies," Irene says.

Very pretty redhead. I think maybe Huck got lucky! Go, Huck!

The living room, where Irene is sleeping, is too close to the kitchen to be private. Irene slips through Floyd's room to the bathroom and sits on the edge of the tub in the dark.

Huck was out with Agent Vasco. She's a redhead, about Swan's age, very pretty. Well, Irene thinks, *very pretty* might be overstating things, but yes, she's attractive. She's also the person who took away Irene's house. *She took my house, Huck, and you two are out canoodling at Skinny Legs!*

Just as Irene was starting to soften a little and wonder if she should let him know she read his letter.

Vasco!

I think maybe Huck got lucky!

Did he take her home? Did he *sleep* with her? Irene can't let herself imagine this. The night she and Huck went to Shambles, he kissed her. It could have gone further but Irene stopped him. She was right to stop him, because when she read the diaries, she realized how wrong it was that she had become friends with Rosie's father!

Irene's face is wet. She's crying. She quit the boat and moved out of Huck's house because she was hurt by *Russ,* angry at *Russ.* And now Huck is with someone else. He's had the hots for Vasco this whole time; he'd admitted as much, this could hardly come as a shock. The letter said he missed their friendship. Apparently, he's getting his "friendship" somewhere else now!

She'll never speak to him again, she decides.

Should she call him right now? It's nine thirty. He's asleep.

Irene cracks the door of Floyd's room; she hears Baker and Swan talking. She lies down on the other half of Floyd's king bed and falls asleep.

When she wakes up in the middle of the night, she has no idea where she is. Then she hears the steady purr of Floyd's breathing and remembers.

Her mouth is cottony; she's still in her clothes. She brushes her teeth in the bathroom and applies her nighttime moisturizer. Her reflection in the mirror is unforgiving. *You messed up.*

The house is now dark and quiet. Irene grabs her pillow and blanket from the closet and heads to the sofa.

She needs to see Huck tomorrow, she thinks. She isn't going to lose him to Vasco. Nope, sorry. She has lost too much already.

She wants to be waiting for Huck by the *Mississippi* in the morning but there are the logistics of cars. Baker needs his Jeep to drop Floyd off at school and then get to work. Cash has to be at *Treasure Island* by seven. If Irene had let Cash know the night before, he would have dropped her at the National Park Service dock first, but she can't spring it on him now.

She says to Baker, "Is it okay if I borrow your Jeep after you pick up Floyd from school? I have errands."

"No problem!" Baker says. He's unusually chipper. He has made Floyd banana pancakes for breakfast. "Would you mind watching Floyd tonight? I have plans with Ayers."

"Ayers?" Irene says. "What about Swan?"

"Swan?" Baker says as though he isn't sure who Irene is talking about. "Oh, we're just friends."

Just friends. Maybe Huck and Vasco are just friends as well. Maybe Swan misunderstood the situation at Skinny Legs. *Oh, please. Oh, please!* Irene isn't sure how she's going to make it until three o'clock. She would text Huck right away but she knows he's out on the boat. She'll be waiting when he pulls back in. If, God forbid, Agent Vasco is also waiting for Huck on the dock, Irene will...push Vasco in.

I'm crazy, Irene thinks. *Crazy about him and just plain crazy.*

She sits by the pool with her captain's-license study materials but she can't concentrate on characteristics of weather systems or lifesaving equipment. She heads to the kitchen.

She isn't hungry, but what about a drink? The bottle of wine she opened with Swan is gone, but Irene has plenty of other bottles. What if she starts drinking now, at eleven o'clock in the morning, and shows up at the dock completely blotto?

This is so out of character, she's tempted to try it.

She still has a few Ativan left. Should she take an Ativan?

I think maybe Huck got lucky! Go, Huck!

She hears a car in the driveway. Yes? No. Yes—a car door slams. Did Baker come home for lunch? Irene goes to the front door and sees a black Jeep with tinted windows in the driveway and a small woman with a limp brown ponytail approaching. Probably she's lost. Hikers come out this way looking for the start of the Reef Bay Trail coastal walk, but that's up the hill.

"Can I help you?" Irene says.

"Irene Steele?" the woman says.

Irene blinks, looks again at the Jeep. Didn't Huck say something about a black Jeep with tinted windows? Yes. He saw one loitering on Jacob's Ladder.

"I'm sorry," Irene says. "Do I know you?" The woman is wearing a plain white short-sleeved blouse and khaki capris. She has a pale, round face and brown eyes. FBI? Irene wonders. They've taken everything she has. If they ask for anything more, she'll give them the Christmas ornaments.

"Irene." The woman checks their surroundings as though she thinks they're being watched. "May I come in? I need to speak to you confidentially."

"About?"

"Your husband," the woman says. "And Todd Croft."

"Are you with the FBI?" Irene asks. "I'd like to see some ID."

"I'm not with the FBI," the woman says. She takes a step

closer to the screen door and lowers her voice. "Irene, we've spoken on the phone. I'm Marilyn Monroe."

Irene's hand flies to her mouth. Marilyn Monroe was the person who called Irene on New Year's Day to tell her Russ was dead. She was Todd Croft's secretary, but it seemed like she'd dropped off the face of the earth.

She looks *nothing* like the famous Marilyn Monroe. Under other circumstances, Irene might find this amusing.

Irene holds the door open, then locks both the screen and the solid wood door behind Marilyn. Turns the dead bolt.

"Yes," Marilyn says, as though this is a necessary measure.

"Can I offer you anything—"

"We just need a quiet place to talk," Marilyn says. She looks around the Happy Hibiscus. "He hasn't gotten in here, so it's safe."

"Who?"

"My husband," Marilyn says. "Todd."

"Todd Croft is your *husband?*" Irene doesn't mean to sound incredulous but she'd thought Todd Croft, with all his money and power, would have a trophy wife. Someone like...Swan Seeley. Polished, put together, a woman who wears five-hundred-dollar-an-ounce perfume and carries a two-thousand-dollar bag, someone who owns a cigarette boat so she can zip over to Virgin Gorda for a facial at Little Dix. This woman looks like she drives in a carpool, then heads home to scrapbook. She's neither fat nor thin, neither pretty nor ugly. How would Irene describe her to the police? Round face, clear skin, a nice straight part in her brown hair. She wears a gold wedding band next to a diamond engagement ring; her nails are filed into pretty ovals, though they're unpolished. She has leather thong sandals on her feet and a gold anklet so thin it's almost imperceptible. Irene can't recall the last time she saw anyone wearing an anklet. Her sorority sister Sandra, maybe, back in 1985. She must be Irene's age, maybe a few years younger. Fifty-two or fifty-three, Irene would guess.

"Yes," Marilyn says. "We've been married for twenty-five years."

"So before all this started."

"Todd started Ascension the year after we got married," Marilyn says. "My family owns marinas and boat-building concerns in Florida. My father got Todd set up in business." She nods at the sofa. "Okay if we sit down?"

Yes, yes. Irene leads Marilyn into the living room but the midwesterner in her will not be quieted. "Are you sure I can't get you any coffee, tea, or...will we be needing wine?"

Marilyn doesn't smile at that, and Irene starts to worry. "I've been trying to talk to you alone for a while now. But you were always with the captain."

"Huck," Irene says. "Yes."

"And then, suddenly, you weren't. I thought I'd lost you. I thought you left the Virgin Islands."

"No, I moved in here with my son. You found that out somehow?"

Marilyn nods. "I asked someone close to you."

"That narrows it down," Irene says. "I know only five people."

"I have things to tell you, things I wanted you to hear directly from me. When I leave here, I'm meeting the FBI to turn state's evidence against Todd."

Irene lowers herself down to the sofa inch by inch, as though Marilyn has a gun trained on her. Where is Irene's cell phone? She wants to record this conversation but she doesn't want to frighten Marilyn away. "You are?"

"After I do that, I'll go into protective custody—assuming he doesn't find a way to kill me first. But it's been eating at me since I spoke to you on the phone in January, the wrongs that have been done to you. And your sons. And the captain. And the girl."

"Maia."

"I feel like I've been carrying all of you around on my back," Marilyn says. "But I don't want to get ahead of myself."

"No, by all means," Irene says, "start at the beginning." *Where is the beginning?* she wonders.

Marilyn takes a deep breath like she's about to jump into cold water. "Back when my father gave Todd the seed money, ten million, Todd's investing business was legit. Todd is…good-looking and quite charismatic, so his main strategy in building a client base was to court new widows, especially the gold diggers who'd hit it big, and there are an endless supply of those women in Florida. Todd was a savvy investor, and it was the heady first days of the internet bubble. Cisco, Oracle—everyone was printing money. Todd brought me to the Virgin Islands on vacation, we stayed at Caneel, and while he was chatting with someone at the bar there, he heard about the EDC, the Economic Development Commission, which offered tax incentives to lure businesses down to the territories. Todd immediately applied. He could work from virtually anywhere, and he wanted the tax break because it freed up that much more capital for him to invest. And, too, he loved the Virgin Islands."

She pauses, checks that Irene is still with her. Irene bobs her head: *Yes, yes.* She can't believe Marilyn Monroe is sitting here. She can't believe she is hearing all of this in what would look to an observer like a regular social visit.

"I was ambivalent about the EDC. I thought it sounded shady, though now I know it's perfectly legal, but also, I wanted to start a family, and I wanted to do that at home, in Miami, where the schools were good and my parents were nearby. No problem; Todd had to spend only a hundred and eighty-three days per year in the islands, according to the EDC guidelines, so he bought a simple villa on Water Island, which is undeveloped, deserted, overlooked. That's the way Todd wanted it, and he traveled to and from Florida by himself.

"Well, I didn't get pregnant, probably because we rarely slept together. I quickly realized Todd was using his time down here for more than just business. I also became aware that Todd had one client who, among his legitimate business interests, owned marijuana farms. This gentleman had a high net worth, and Todd didn't want to lose him as a client, so he found a way to shuffle the dirty money deep into the deck. That, as far as I know, was the first time he hid a client's money."

"Marijuana farms seem nearly quaint," Irene says.

"They call marijuana the gateway drug, which was true in this case," Marilyn says. "In 2005, Todd hired Stephen Thompson, an attorney from the Cayman Islands who had a lot of experience with offshore accounts. Stephen brought along clients who were big dirty-money guys—the human traffickers, the exotic-animal dealers, the gem smugglers—but both Todd and Stephen were looking for a third partner." Marilyn clears her throat. "A fall guy."

Russ, Irene thinks.

"Todd bumped into you and your husband at the Drake Hotel in Chicago. He remembered Russ from college and the arrangement they had where Todd sold alcohol to the underclassmen while Russ looked the other way in exchange for a part of the profits. He ran a background search on Russ. He found out Russ's salary with the Corn Refiners Association, learned about his membership in the Rotary Club and his position on the school board. He got information about your house, your cars, what they were worth, what you owed, and even the ages of your sons, who he assumed would be heading to college in a few short years. Todd decided Russell Steele would be the perfect front man. He was both respected in your community and strapped for cash—overextended beyond what you probably even knew. And he had that history with Todd. Todd knew Russ would be willing to look the other way while someone else broke the rules.

"Todd called Russ, brought him down to the Virgin Islands, wined and dined him on his new yacht, *Bluebeard,* and at Caneel." Marilyn stops. "Todd had a local man working for him named Oscar Cobb."

Irene's breath catches. *Oscar Cobb!* Oscar Cobb worked for Todd Croft?

"I know of him," Irene says. "He was Rosie's former boyfriend."

"Well." Marilyn shakes her head. "Is it okay if I continue candidly?"

Irene nods. It can't be worse than what she read in Rosie's diaries. She hopes.

"When Todd and Stephen brought Russ down to the Virgin Islands, they didn't mention any of their sensitive clients. They let Russ believe that Ascension's dealings were on the up-and-up—which they were, for the most part—and that Russ's job would be to capitalize on his natural charm as a salesman and his trustworthy persona as a midwestern husband, father, and citizen. Ascension's clients were investing tens and sometimes hundreds of millions of dollars. They wanted a friendly face who would answer when they called, who would lose to them at golf, who would make them feel safe and comforted."

"Yes," Irene says. "This is exactly the way Russ explained the job to me."

"They planned to ease into the black money so gradually

that Russ would become acclimated to it bit by bit." Marilyn shakes her head. "Like the old frog-in-a-pot-of-water myth where supposedly if you raise the temperature a few degrees at a time, the frog won't realize it's boiling."

Irene understands the simile—it's apt—but she hates thinking about Russ that way.

"The marijuana farmer was already on the books, and next might be someone who moved cocaine, heroin, oxycodone. So... on that first trip down here, they set Russ up."

"Set him up?"

"Oscar Cobb was in the restaurant at Caneel on their first night. He'd told Todd that his former girlfriend, Rosie Small, would be working as a cocktail waitress. He also told Todd that Rosie was single, vulnerable, and extremely beautiful. Oscar staged a situation where he followed Rosie out to her car and harassed her, allowing Russ to step in and save the day."

Irene gasps. "You mean the part...I'm sorry, I read about this in Rosie's diaries...Russ put Oscar in some kind of headlock. That was *staged?*"

"Yes," Marilyn says. "Rosie left the restaurant, Oscar followed, and he knew Russ would be heading back to his room along the same path. He let Russ get the better of him. If you knew Oscar, you'd understand that a headlock from someone like Russ wasn't going to stop him. Once Oscar told Todd that he'd been successful, Todd and Stephen took *Bluebeard* over to the BVIs, leaving Russ alone for the weekend. That was all by design."

Russ had been set up. Irene felt almost embarrassed for him.

"But Rosie had no idea?"

"None."

"Russ still could have acted like an upstanding and faithful husband," Irene says. "But he didn't."

"That's right," Marilyn says. "Todd and Stephen saw Rosie in Russ's hotel room and they knew he could be blackmailed. He certainly wouldn't want the news getting back to you in Iowa City. And then Rosie reached out to Russ using Todd's e-mail, and Todd suspected she was pregnant. Todd flew down to confirm this and saw with his own eyes that it was true. He told Russ, and Russ confirmed with Rosie that it was his baby. She said she didn't want to see him again and he honored that, but he started sending money."

Marilyn leans forward; her pretty nails gently scratch at the knees of her khaki capris. "Does this come as a surprise?"

"I'm aware he sent her money."

Marilyn purses her lips, sighs, shakes her head. "Because both Todd and Stephen knew about Rosie and the baby, there was nothing they couldn't ask Russ to do. They put all of the 'sensitive' business deals under Russ's supervision, in a whole separate subdivision of the company. They made it seem like this offshoot was independent of Ascension. Russ's name alone was on the paperwork as the principal for all of the money laundering, all of the tax fraud, even things that weren't so bad, like hiding money for a European soccer star who owed alimony. He couldn't object, and Todd paid Russ handsomely to keep him happy. You had plenty of money at home? For the renovation of the Victorian?"

"Yes," Irene whispers.

"In 2014, Rosie's mother died, and Russ and Rosie reunited. Because there had been no oversight on any of the company's deals, Russ grew bolder. He wanted property down here, a villa. He couldn't very well keep bringing Rosie to Caneel; someone would find out about them. Through a tip from Oscar Cobb, Todd approached a failing real estate concern, Welcome to Paradise, owned by Douglas and Paulette Vickers. They'd bought a hundred and forty acres in Little Cinnamon with the intention of developing the hillside, but they ran out of money. They were about to lose the whole thing to the bank when Todd paid a visit." Marilyn shakes her head. "You want to talk about two people who are completely under my husband's sway? It's the Vickerses. Todd saved them from ruin just after their son was born. They allowed dozens of phony real estate deals to be run through their office. But officially, Paulette and Douglas worked for Russ and Russ alone."

Marilyn pauses. "They could have turned Todd in. I wish they had. But they were too afraid."

"Afraid of what?"

"Being killed," Marilyn says.

Killed, Irene thinks. For turning in Todd, which is what Marilyn is going to do. Irene has no idea how Marilyn is remaining so composed, though Irene admits that she's comforted by it. Marilyn reminds Irene a little of herself. She might not always have been strong, but she's strong now.

"They're both serving time instead," Marilyn says.

Irene recalls her initial meeting with Paulette Vickers, which was during her very first hour on this island. Paulette had seemed flighty and completely insensitive to Irene's emotional state, which was numb shock. She had prattled on about the hiking trails, about the landscapers. She had displayed nothing but calm acceptance that her employer was dead.

What else had Paulette told her?

"The villa was in Russ's name," Irene says.

"Everything is in Russ's name," Marilyn says. "That's what I'm telling you."

"Because of me," Irene says. "He allowed himself to be blackmailed *because of me.* Because he didn't want me to find out about Rosie and Maia."

"I can't speak for Russ," Marilyn says, "but I think some men get a thrill out of leading a double life. I'm sure Russ was sick with guilt most of the time. But there was also probably a rush or a high from... pulling it off. I think it made him feel superhuman."

Irene presses her fingers into her temples. "This is what I can't reconcile," she says. "At home, he was... the same. We had more money, yes, and we both changed because of that. We bought the Church Street house, we bought new cars, we ate out all the time, we donated to local causes, we set the boys up to succeed. But as people, we stayed the same. I worked at a magazine and oversaw the house renovation. Russ... he was *exactly* the same. Corny. Goofy. He could be insufferable with his earnest enthusiasm. The money didn't make him sophisticated... or smug... or self-congratulatory. But neither did he seem like a man who was racked with guilt. He did make the occasional grandiose gesture—he hired a plane to fly a happy-birthday banner when I turned fifty; he would send me lavish bouquets. But I thought he was doing these things because he could. Because he loved me. He felt bad about being away so much, and he apologized about this the normal amount, but he never overplayed his hand. He never seemed *tortured*. So what can I think but that he was a complete *sociopath?*"

Marilyn says, "I met Russ a handful of times in my capacity as office manager. He was always so... guileless, so genuine. Every time I talked to him, I felt sorry for him. He didn't belong in business with my husband. He was a sheep running with wolves."

"You'll forgive me for saying this, but Russ was neither guileless nor genuine. You knew he had a second family. There was no reason to feel sorry for him."

Marilyn stares at Irene. "Of course you're right. I just wanted you to know that he was... different from the other two. He was a nice person."

"Nice," Irene says. "But a wolf just the same."

"Maybe deep down I knew he wouldn't survive this," Marilyn says. "Todd is ruthless. He's greedy, and I'm not talking about money. He wants control, he wants power, he wants...*domination*. That's what led us here. Russ, I think, was more than happy to let Todd pull the puppet strings. But Stephen wasn't. Stephen realized that Todd was taking more than his share of the profits, and Stephen feared he wasn't as protected as he needed to be. The danger in any entity with three principals is that when one side of the triangle weakens, another is reinforced. Stephen did the predictable thing and cozied up to Russ. Russ was already having a crisis of conscience about the despicable people whose money they were laundering. They were working with a Russian company who moved assault rifles—big, big money—but there was that rash of school shootings in the States, as I'm sure you'll remember, and in several cases, the illegal guns could be traced back to our client. It was a tense time, and there were some uncomfortable inquiries into that client. Nothing came of it, but Russ and Stephen took advantage of the scare to say they wanted out. Before they talked to Todd, they both came to see me. Russ was first. He visited my office in Miami in early September."

September, Irene thinks. End of summer, beginning of fall, students returning to the university, football games on Saturdays, *Go, Hawks!*

"He told me he was ready to retire; he wanted to go home to Iowa and be with you. The house you'd been renovating for years was finally finished and he wanted to enjoy it—throw parties, host holidays. He wanted to spend time with his mother, who was quite elderly. He wanted to travel to Denver to help his younger son manage the outdoor-supply stores. He wanted to fly to Houston to see his grandson. He'd had a wonderful run in the

Virgin Islands, he said, and he was grateful for all Ascension had given him, but it was time for him to return home."

Irene can't believe it but her immediate thoughts are *What about Rosie? What about Maia? Was he just going to leave them behind?*

"I told him that wasn't possible. I told him he was too deeply vested in the company to just walk away. I told him the smartest thing to do was not to breathe a word of what he'd shared with me to Todd. I told him to protect his assets and protect you."

September was when Russ made his new will, changing the executor from Todd Croft to Irene. *Irene is the only person I trust to do the right thing,* he'd said.

"Russ listened to my advice but Stephen did not. He went to Todd and turned it into a test of wills. He said both he and Russ wanted out. He said there was nothing Todd could do to stop them. Todd was...furious. He pointed out that both Russ's and Stephen's fingerprints were all over incriminating deals, and if they left, Todd would go to the authorities. To his credit, Stephen called Todd's bluff. He didn't think Todd would sacrifice the company. He wrote up sophisticated NDAs and presented them to Todd, and, at that point, Todd changed his tack and said, 'Fine, you sign the NDAs, you can walk away.'"

Irene's breathing is shallow. She knows what's coming. She knows this is the end. She should stop Marilyn now; she doesn't need to hear any more. Marilyn can tell it all to the FBI, that's fine, but Irene doesn't want to hear the truth spoken. "Marilyn."

"Do you want me to stop?" Marilyn says. "Now?"

"Is there any way...I'm just afraid..." She's thinking of Baker and Cash. And Floyd. Ayers and the baby. She can't put them in danger just because she wants to hear how the story ends. Furthermore, she already knows how it ends.

However, to stop Marilyn now is to destroy, in some sense, the integrity of her intentions. "If you continue," Irene says, "will my family or I be in any danger?"

"When I leave here," Marilyn says, "I'm going directly to the FBI. Todd is still in custody. His boat captain was released and, I heard, fled the country. Todd's business was so sensitive that we weren't able to hire a lot of support staff. It was Russ, Stephen, the Vickerses...and Oscar. You're safe. Or you will be, I promise."

Irene takes a deep breath. Half of her wants to ask Marilyn to leave—but that might be even more dangerous. "Go ahead."

"Todd used Paulette Vickers to bug the villa and compromise Stephen's phone, Russ's phone, and even Rosie's phone. Todd discovered that Stephen and Russ planned to meet with British authorities on January second on Tortola. They were traveling in Stephen's private helicopter—he was an accomplished pilot. To make it seem like a holiday trip, Russ invited Rosie to Anegada. Stephen would fly them over, they would stay at the beachfront cottage owned by one of their shell companies, and then, the following morning, Russ would claim he had a work emergency. The three of them would fly to Tortola, Russ would put Rosie on the ferry back to St. John, and Russ and Stephen would go to their meeting. Todd knew all this. He asked Oscar Cobb to put explosives on Stephen's helicopter."

"Oscar?" Irene whispers.

"Oscar refused to do it. He knew what Todd was up to, knew that he was planning on killing Stephen, Russ, and Rosie. Oscar had been drinking, it was late on New Year's Eve, they had a fight, Oscar told Todd to find some other fool to do his dirty work because Oscar was out and Oscar was going to put a bounty on Todd's head with his friends over in St. Thomas. Todd told Oscar that he understood Oscar was angry, it had probably come time for them to split ways, new year and all that. He told Oscar he should come see me in the office the next morning, that I would give him his severance pay."

Finally, Marilyn shows some emotion. Her eyes glass over. "Oscar and I had a nice relationship. He did a lot of bad things, I knew this, but I could see glimmers of goodness in him, and I think I might have been the only one. He trusted me, he called me 'Mama.' He got to my villa on Water Island before Todd, woke me up with his pounding on the door. He told me what Todd was planning to do and begged me to stop it. He said..." Here Marilyn's voice cracks. "He said he'd called Rosie—he still had her number after so many years—to warn her not to go, but the call had gone straight to her voicemail. He begged me to call Russ." Tears are fully rolling down Marilyn's cheeks. Irene wants to offer the woman a tissue, but she's afraid to move. "So, if I were a better person, this would be where I would tell you that yes, I did call Russ and that through my connections, I saved them, and that they are still alive on an island so remote it doesn't even have a name."

Still alive, Irene thinks. Despite everything, her heart yearns for this—not only Russ, but Rosie, too. Still. Alive. Baker and Cash would have their dad back, Floyd his grandpa. Huck would have his daughter back. And Maia. What Irene wishes for *most of all* is for Maia to have her mother back.

Now that Irene knows what she knows, might it even be possible that she and Rosie could have been friends? Or was that just a hopeless fantasy?

"I've had dreams," Irene says, "vivid dreams, where Russ is alive."

"I was not a better person," Marilyn says. "I was the same pathetic, dutiful coward I've been since the day I married Todd.

I kept Oscar in the office, comforting him, when I should have been telling him to run for his life. Todd showed up with a gun and took Oscar to *Bluebeard.* I knew I would never see Oscar again, and I had an idea that I would never see my husband again. There was no way he could stay in the Virgin Islands after he killed Oscar. Oscar knew too many dangerous people." Marilyn wipes a finger under each eye. "Todd filled *Bluebeard* with documents incriminating Russ and Stephen. Then, with the captain's help, he tied Oscar up, shot him, and tossed him overboard as soon as they were on the open sea, and he took off for Venezuela." Marilyn takes a breath. "Todd has a girlfriend in Venezuela, girlfriends everywhere, but the most important thing is that Venezuela has no extradition laws. I think he dreamed of a life on Margarita Island with Gloriana—and he almost made it. I think part of him *enjoyed* the chase, to be honest. But it was the chase that got him arrested. Todd called me to let me know he'd been taken into custody and that I was to destroy all the incriminating documents in the safe on Water Island—Todd's offshore account information, payouts from the sensitive deals, correspondence from Todd to these clients. That had been our contingency plan for years."

"But you didn't do it?"

"I did the opposite," Marilyn says. "I made copies of everything."

"Why?" Irene says.

Finally, Marilyn looks like someone describing an epiphany. "I guess I realized I could go down with Todd or I could watch him go down alone." She shakes her head. "Wasn't that hard of a choice. He killed four people."

"And he has no idea what you've done?"

"None," Marilyn says. She gives Irene a rueful smile. "You

might think he would be more wary of the only person who knows everything."

"Yes."

"But Todd doesn't even see me," Marilyn says. "He stopped seeing me the second my father handed over the seed money. To Todd, I'm invisible."

Irene makes a noise of recognition. What had Lydia said during their New Year's Day dinner at the Pullman Diner? *The CIA should hire women in their fifties. We're invisible.*

"Of course, tomorrow that will change." She places her hands on her thighs and pushes herself to standing. "I should go. I need to get ready to meet Agent Vasco."

Agent Vasco, Irene thinks. She has completely forgotten about Agent Vasco.

Irene leads Marilyn Monroe to the front door; she wants to hug the woman. "You are... so brave. How can I thank you?"

"No thanks necessary," Marilyn says. "I was a coward for a long time, Irene. I had a chance every single day to come clean and I didn't, and now four people are dead. Their blood is on my hands."

Irene says, "Do you still love him? Todd?"

Marilyn's eyebrows shoot up; the question has clearly surprised her. "Do you still love Russ?" she asks, but she slips out the door without waiting for an answer.

Because, Irene realizes, there is no answer. Irene watches Marilyn climb into her Jeep. In the movies, this would be where Marilyn's car explodes into a ball of fire. Irene releases a breath as Marilyn backs out of the driveway and pulls away.

Irene lingers in the parking lot across from Mongoose Junction until she sees the *Mississippi* pulling up to the National Park

Service dock. Huck does the complicated choreography of pulling in and, at the same time, tying up.

He needs a mate, Irene thinks.

The family aboard hop off, a couple and two little kids, one of whom is screaming bloody murder. There are no fish to be filleted, so they must have struck out, even inshore. Irene watches the father tip Huck as the mother carries the kids off.

Irene smiles at her as she passes, but the mother doesn't see her.

Huck doesn't see her either. He's checking around the boat, making sure the family hasn't forgotten anything. He goes to lift the rope off the bollard, but Irene beats him to it.

He looks up. He's wearing his wraparound sunglasses so it's impossible to tell how her surprise is being received.

"Permission to board?" Irene says.

Any given moment can hold an infinite number of thoughts, Irene realizes. She wonders if he'll tell her to buzz off, that he's found someone new, Agent Vasco, that Irene has been replaced, sorry. She wonders if she'll have to cajole her way onto the boat by telling Huck she has finally learned the whole story from none other than Marilyn Monroe. Marilyn Monroe was the woman in the black Jeep with the tinted windows. How will he feel hearing it confirmed that Todd murdered Rosie and Russ? How will it feel to know that Oscar Cobb, of all people, *had tried to save Rosie's life?*

Irene travels back in her mind to the first time she ever saw Huck, which was nearly in this exact same spot. She didn't know him, he didn't know her, but somehow, *somehow,* she'd broken down his defenses or piqued his curiosity, and they became friends. More than friends. *It was a long shot,* Irene thinks, *maybe even a miracle.* Out of this whole ugly tale of deceit and betrayal, something pure and true was born.

As unlikely as it might be, the friendship is genuine.

Slowly, maybe even hesitantly, Huck spreads his arms. "Permission granted, AC."

The rope; her shoes. When one boards a boat, there is a protocol. But in the moment, Irene doesn't care. She jumps—and Captain Sam "Huck" Powers catches her.

ST. JOHN

April turns to May, and our high season officially ends. Rates at the hotels and villas drop, restaurants close one night a week to give their staff a much-needed rest, there are finally parking spots at both Trunk Bay *and* Oppenheimer—and it's hot, hot, hot.

We also get to see one another more frequently. Did you *hear?*

Douglas and Paulette Vickers are going to prison for money laundering and fraud. Douglas will serve three years; Paulette, five. Their son, Windsor, is living with Douglas's sister, Wilma, on St. Croix. He cried every night for a month, Wilma tells her friend Sadie on St. John, and then one day the crying stopped and now he's the same sunny child he was before. He's doing well in school, making new friends, asking for second helpings of dessert (which Wilma always gives him, poor, sweet child).

Ayers Wilson is showing a subtle baby bump. She has been to two prenatal appointments at Schneider Hospital and has had all the testing. She and Baker have decided not to find out the gender of the baby; all they care about is that the baby is healthy. Ayers is due September 23. She has opted to stay in her cottage,

Pure Joy, until the baby is born. She and Baker are now dating, but they haven't quite reached "boyfriend and girlfriend" status. Maybe soon, Ayers thinks.

Ayers's parents, Phil Wilson and Sunny Ray, are the proud owners of a two-bedroom time-share at the Westin; they're banking their weeks for when the baby comes. They arrive back from a seven-stop jaunt through the Caribbean—Bequia was their favorite, no surprise there—and immediately start planning a summer trip to Croatia. (Everyone raves about the city of Split.) Sunny decides that, instead of pretending to write a travel blog, she *will* write a travel blog. She calls it *Love, Mimi.* The blog takes an epistolary form; the entries are descriptive, evocative travel letters from grandmother to grandchild. As soon as Sunny's Caribbean letters are posted, she receives sponsorship from the AARP and Road Scholar.

Things are happening over on Lovango Cay (which was named for a region of Africa, *not* because a brothel there in the days of piracy had been so popular that the island was dubbed "Love and Go"). The cay has been approved for fifty bungalows, fifteen glamping tents, fourteen private homes, a restaurant, and a beach club with a swimming pool that will offer daily, weekly, and season passes.

Swan Seeley has been hired to handle the resort's marketing strategy, but when she saw the architect's plans, she feared she'd be fired. They don't need Swan to sell this place; it will sell itself. The design is ingenious—the eco-friendly resort will be the hottest spot in the Caribbean! Swan feels incredibly blessed to be part of it. She'd thought her life was over with the divorce, but she was wrong. The curtain is rising on her second act.

Swan is collaborating closely with both Tilda Payne, who works at La Tapa, and the guy who bought the island, Duncan

Huntley. Duncan and Tilda are a couple; they walk around all googly-eyed, holding hands. He calls her mate (he calls everyone mate); she calls him Stallion, which is almost more than Swan can handle. They treat Duncan's dog, Olive, a harlequin Great Dane that is the size of a show pony, like their child. They speak to Olive in baby talk; they constantly fret over whether Olive is hungry, thirsty, or tired, even though Olive is as chill as an ice sculpture.

One morning, Swan and Duncan are alone in the air-conditioned work trailer at the slanted drafting table reviewing Swan's marketing plan. Swan worked hard on the plan; she included ideas for Lovango resort merchandise that they could sell at the gift shop. She went so far as to sketch cute logos for the T-shirts—every woman Swan knows would pay good money for a flattering T-shirt or tank to wear over her Lululemons—and she created a list of local artisans whose work they can feature. She's hoping to impress Duncan. When she Googled him, she found out that he'd started two companies—a sex app and an edible marijuana concern—that he'd then sold, the first for eight figures, the second for nine. In addition to a whole bunch of money, he has a very appealing Australian accent.

Duncan glances at the T-shirt designs and then shuffles them aside.

Swan says, "Merch might be more important than you think because it serves as a source of revenue *and* a form of advertising. Have you ever heard of the Black Dog on Martha's Vineyard?"

Dunk blinks at her and brings his vape pen to his mouth. His eyelids seem a little heavy and she wonders if he has marijuana pods in his vape pen.

"No," he says.

"It's a restaurant," Swan says. "They have clam chowder and other New England specialties, but their T-shirts are what's making them millions. Millions! It's just a silk screen of a black dog, but that's part of the mystique. If you know, you know." She lifts her favorite design, a logo with the words LOVE AND GO. REPEAT. "This has potential, I think? I mean, if you don't mind propagating the myth of how Lovango got its name?"

"Propagating?" Duncan says. A smile oozes across his face. He's definitely high. Or maybe just creepy; Swan can't tell. Either way, he's one of her bosses. He owns the island. "Are you *smart,* Swan?"

Swan flinches. He's joking, right? And if she acts offended, he'll think she's rigid and humorless. "I am," she says pleasantly. "Which is why you hired me."

Duncan leans in so that the side of his body presses into the side of Swan's body. "I hired you because you're a hot little bird," he says. "A dime." His hand snakes up her back. He's touching her back. Swan holds her breath and thinks, *What do I do?* He hired her because she's *hot?* She isn't an underwear model!

She straightens up so that Dunk's hand slides off her back. "Smart *and* hot," she says. She points to the next page of her plan. "I made a list of influencers that we should invite to the property. Market research shows that influencers are worth more bang for our buck than regular print advertising—"

"Bang for our buck," Dunk says. "Now you're talking." He stands behind Swan and starts to massage her shoulders. His groin grazes her backside.

Nope, sorry, this is *not* okay. Swan twists away, gathers up her papers, and storms out of the trailer, stumbling into the searing-hot sunshine. There's a picnic table in the shade of the rocky path where the workers eat their lunch. Swan sits on the table with her feet on the bench seat and tries to steady her breathing. Did she overreact? Is she being too sensitive? No, she decides. That was classic #MeToo stuff back there. Swan shouldn't have agreed to meet with Duncan alone. But why is she blaming herself? She should be able to meet with whomever she wants under whatever circumstances without being touched inappropriately and told that she was hired because she was hot.

Her eyes sting with tears. She had been *so* happy to land this job, but she knows she can't stay on. She has a degree from Florida State, a business degree.

She doesn't want to cry. She put a lot of effort into her makeup today, not to lure Duncan or anyone else but because she wanted to look professional.

"Hey," a voice says. "You okay?"

It's Tilda, walking off the dock with Olive at her side.

Before Swan can think it through, she says, "I was just in the trailer showing Duncan my marketing ideas. He told me he hired me because I was hot, a dime, and then he touched me inappropriately."

Tilda's eyebrows shoot up above her sunglasses. She places a hand on Olive's back, and Olive stands still as a statue. When Tilda opens her mouth, no sound comes out.

Swan drops her head into her hands. On top of everything else, she has to be the one to let Tilda know that her boyfriend is a predator.

"Oh, Swan," Tilda says. "Do you think maybe you misunderstood? Dunk can be a little familiar, that's his personality, that's how he was raised back in Australia, I think, but I'm sure he didn't mean anything by it."

This is so *textbook!* Nobody *ever* believes the woman! "Listen to me, Tilda. He leaned against me in a suggestive way and put his hand on my back, and when I moved away, he started to massage my shoulders. He...grazed my behind."

"Swan," Tilda says. She's shaking her head when she should be either hugging Swan or storming into the trailer to kick Dunk in the nuts.

"Tilda," Swan says. She understands denial. Swan willfully ignored her husband's gambling problem for fourteen years. But how about some *solidarity* here?

"I'll ask Keith to run you back to Cruz Bay," Tilda says. "Thanks for coming over."

Irene Steele and Captain Huck Powers are living together, and Irene is back working as the first mate on the *Mississippi.* Irene is logging her days on the water, and as soon as she has three hundred and sixty, she'll take her captain's test. Huck thinks it's a great idea. He even goes to St. Thomas to look at the boat Irene inquired about.

The boat is in good condition and the seller is motivated; he's leaving the Virgin Islands altogether at the beginning of June. Huck advises Irene to make an offer of forty thousand.

"I don't have forty to spend," she says.

"How about we split it?" Huck says. "Add it to the fleet. It needs work, which I can do myself. And then once you get your captain's license, we can run two boats, the *Mississippi* and the *Angler Cupcake.* God knows we have enough business."

More than enough, Irene thinks, with a growing number of women-only charters. All it took was a few complimentary trips. The first of these was for Baker's school-mom friends Swan, Bonny, and Paula. The three of them took pictures with the fish they caught and posted them on Facebook and Instagram. Next, Huck and Irene invited Joanie's mom, Julie Judge, and her three sisters out on the boat, and *they* all posted pictures. And finally, they had a paying charter for a young woman named Gretchen Gingerman who came with her mother. It turned out that Gretchen had met Cash on her previous visit to St. John, a trip that had gone badly, and it was only because of Cash that Gretchen gave the island another try, with a different travel partner.

Gretchen's post brought in a flurry of business, including a bachelorette party. Six beautiful young women, five in matching pink T-shirts and one in a white T-shirt and a short white veil, all in great spirits thanks to a thermos filled with cosmo punch and a playlist of Lizzo and Billie Eilish. They caught a couple of small wahoo, which elicited high-pitched shrieks, and they took fifty million pictures, including one with Irene. All of the girls loved Irene, she was "such a beast," and when they were older they were going to do something "sick" like move to the Virgin Islands to work on a fishing boat.

The bachelorette party tipped extremely well but when the women got off the boat, Huck turned to Irene and said, "I can't wait for you to get your captain's license so I never have to do that again."

It all sounds rosy on the Huck-and-Irene front—until the story that united them rears its ugly head. Todd Croft is brought up on four charges of first-degree murder thanks to the evidence that Marilyn Monroe presented. (In addition to the three murders we all suspected he was behind, we learned Todd had also killed Oscar Cobb. Sure enough, once Marilyn Monroe had voiced her suspicions, traces of Oscar's blood were found all over the stern of *Bluebeard.*) Somehow Todd's lawyer cuts a deal. Todd pleads guilty to one charge of second-degree murder and three charges of manslaughter and pays fines of nearly four hundred million dollars. He's sentenced to twenty-two years in federal prison. With good behavior, he could be out in eighteen.

Both Huck and Irene are aghast. Four lives violently snatched away, and the guy gets only twenty-two years? It's the money, Irene thinks. The territory wanted Todd's money. Either that or he agreed to talk to the Feds about some of his clients—which may end up getting him killed.

"I'll tell you who will be waiting for him the day he gets out," Huck says. "Me."

Irene squeezes Huck's hand. The estates can sue for reparations in a civil case. Natalie Key is asking for two million dollars on behalf of Russ and ten million on behalf of Rosie. Stephen Thompson has a brother who lives in London, but the brother won't sue because he wants "nothing to do with the whole sordid mess."

Huck and Irene have decided not to even think about the possibility of that money. Instead, they focus on their daily blessings. Irene receives boxes filled with her clothes—most of which she'd forgotten she owned—as well as her books and kitchen implements. When she pulls her food processor out of the box, she says, "The cooking in this house is about to improve."

"How can you improve on perfectly grilled fish?" Huck asks. "How can you improve on Candi's barbecue?"

Another blessing: Agent Vasco's job on St. John is finished. She goes back to Puerto Rico.

Adios, Irene thinks.

Swan Seeley tells Baker what happened between her and Duncan Huntley, and Baker nearly drives out to the East End to give the guy the thrashing he deserves. When Baker tells Ayers the story, she mentions that Dunk routinely waits for Tilda across the street from La Tapa after service. Baker can jump out of the shadows and scare him to death.

But then fate intervenes and Baker bumps into Dunk at Pine Peace Market. Duncan is buying vape pods and Baker is buying pizza-flavored Pringles for Floyd and Ben and Jerry's Red Velvet Cake ice cream for himself. When Dunk sees Baker, he gives him a little bro-nod but it's clear he can't really place him. He's not important enough for Duncan to remember, Baker supposes. He stands behind Dunk in line, glaring at the back of his neck. Duncan seems shorter than he did when Baker met him on the plane, and he's downright scrawny. What does Tilda see in this guy? Is it just the money?

Dunk leaves the store and Baker sets his chips and ice cream down and says to Nestor, the cashier, "I'll be right back." He follows Dunk out and catches him as he pulls open the driver's-side door of a forest-green G-wagon.

"Hey," Baker says. "Duncan? Dunk?"

Dunk turns. "G'day."

"It's Baker. Baker Steele? My little boy and I met you on the flight from Houston. You gave me a ride over here on your boat?"

"Ah, yeah?" Dunk says, though it's not clear he remembers who Baker is. "How ya doin', mate?"

Baker reaches out his hand, and when Dunk takes it, Baker squeezes as hard as he can and holds on a little longer than he should. "I'm good. Real good. Except for a couple of things."

"Sorry, mate, wish I could shoot the shit but I'm in kind of a hurry."

Dunk makes a move to get into his car but Baker reaches over Dunk's head and slams the driver's-side door shut, then leans against the car, arms folded across his chest. He has six inches and at least sixty pounds on Dunk. Baker hasn't been in a fight since high school, and even then, he mostly scrapped with Cash.

He's thirty-one years old, the father of one with another one on the way. He never thought he'd find himself trying to physically intimidate someone. But that's exactly what he's going to do right now.

"First off," Baker says, "you moved in on Tilda when she was dating my brother, Cash."

"Cash is your *brother?*" Dunk says. He laughs nervously. "I didn't make the connection, mate, I'm sorry."

"But you did know Cash and Tilda were together," Baker says. "When you and Tilda went away, you knew she had a boyfriend. You had *dinner* with him."

"Right, but I wasn't sure how serious it was," Dunk says. "She told me they'd known each other only a few weeks. And she said that Cash moved in with her because he had nowhere else to go." Dunk fiddles with the packet of vape pods in his hands. He's trying to pop one out. "Your father was part of that whole Ascension thing? That's some nefarious shit, mate."

Baker snatches the pods out of Dunk's hands and tosses them beyond the truck. He whips the vape pen out of Duncan's shirt pocket and tosses that too.

"Nefarious?" Baker says. "Are you *smart,* Dunk? No, not terribly. Because the next thing you did that pissed me off was you insulted my friend Swan Seeley, told her you hired her only because she was hot—"

"It was a *compliment,*" Dunk says. "Show me a bird who doesn't like hearing she's hot, come on."

"It was *inappropriate,*" Baker says. "And then you touched her. You leaned into her, you put your hand on her back, you gave her a massage, and you rubbed up against her from behind."

"Her word against mine, mate," Dunk says.

Baker grabs the front of Dunk's shirt and pulls him in.

Will Baker hit him? He wants to. He would love to pop Duncan Huntley in the face and watch him bleed. "I'm *not* your mate."

Nestor pokes his head out of the market. "You okay?" he asks Baker. "Need any help?"

"*I* need help!" Dunk says. "He's attacking me!"

Nestor goes back inside.

"Here's what you're going to do," Baker says. "You're going to apologize to Swan in an e-mail. You're going to offer her her job back. Do you understand me?"

"Yes," Dunk says. His eyes keep sweeping to the other side of the truck. He's worried about his vape pen, Baker realizes. Baker is never going to let Floyd start vaping.

Baker lets Dunk go, and in a few quick strides, Duncan retrieves the pen and pods from the ground.

Baker leans back against the driver's-side door. "One more thing," Baker says. "There's nothing I can do for Cash—all's fair in love and war, and Tilda chose you, a decision I'm sure she'll come to regret. It was dirty pool. I know it; you know it. I now work with Jacqui at the Westin time-share office, and what you might not know about Jacqui is that she is *very* well connected. We wouldn't want her spreading any rumors about you. People on this island already think you're sketchy—the sex app, the weed-edibles company, the jeans-and-Sambas thing, the fasting—but what if they hear that you're an untrustworthy snake, a two-timer, a Me Too menace?"

"What do you want?" Dunk says.

"I'd like full use of your villa for one week this summer," Baker says. "I donated a week at my father's villa at an auction to benefit my son's school, but now my father's villa is gone so I'm left in a bit of a pickle. The high bidders paid fifty thousand dollars, so in addition to the villa, I'll need at least one vehicle and staff, if you have any."

"A housekeeper," Dunk says. "And a landscaper. Any week in July works. I spend the month skiing in Tazzie."

"Great, thank you," Baker says. "I have your card. I'll call you to confirm. Don't forget the e-mail to Swan."

"Granger will call her," Dunk says. "He wanted to hire her back anyway."

"*You* reach out to her," Baker says. "With a sincere apology." He moves toward Dunk and Dunk stutter-steps back.

"Okay, mate, I will."

"You'd better," Baker says. "Jacqui's a talker..."

"I will," Dunk says.

"Good," Baker says. "Now, if you'll excuse me, my ice cream is melting."

Everyone knows that Huck tries to stay away from Jake's at the Lumberyard because he had a brief fling with Teresa, the breakfast waitress, after LeeAnn died.

It's therefore unfortunate that when Huck asks Irene what she wants to do to celebrate her fifty-eighth birthday, which is in the middle of July, she says, "I want the whole gang to go to breakfast at Jake's."

"Jake's?" Huck says. He has to head this off at the pass. It's not that things between him and Teresa ended badly, but they do their best to steer clear of each other. Huck doesn't ever go up Margaret Hill Road, where she lives; he doesn't drink at the Quiet Mon Pub, where she likes to hang out; and he no longer goes for breakfast at Jake's, where she (famously) works seven mornings a week. "Why don't you pick another place? How about a nice dinner for everyone at Morgan's Mango? Or the Terrace?"

"I don't want anything fancy or over the top," Irene says. She gives him a stern look and he recalls that her husband hired an airplane to pull a banner on her fiftieth birthday. "And I want the kids to come. What I'd like is a long, leisurely breakfast with mimosas and Bloody Marys at Jake's."

"Or," Huck says, "we could all go to the Concordia in Coral Bay. They do a terrific breakfast and it overlooks Ram Head."

"Listen to me, Huck," Irene says. "The morning after my first night at your house, Maia offered me a piece of toast slathered with papaya jam from Jake's. It was the first thing on my new mental Pinterest board."

"Your new mental what?" Huck says.

Irene shakes her head. "I want to celebrate my birthday at Jake's. Besides, it's an island institution and I've never been."

"It's always crowded," Huck says. "And it gets hot up there."

"It's open-air," Irene says. "And we'll have nine people."

"Nine?"

"I want Ayers to come, obviously," Irene says. "And her parents, Phil and Sunny. Let's make it ten people—I'll see if Cash wants to bring a friend." She puts her hands on the sides of Huck's face and brings him in for a kiss. "They take reservations for parties over six. Do I have to call to arrange my own birthday party, or will you do it?"

"I'll do it," Huck says.

The day of Irene's birthday, July 21, is hot but not beastly hot—a stroke of luck—and the sky is a deep blue. The members of the Steele party (Huck made the reservation under Irene's name) climb the stairs to the legendary open-air breakfast-and-lunch spot, Jake's, which is decorated with fun tropical kitsch. The faux vintage sign that greets them says DRINK COFFEE: DO STUPID THINGS FASTER, WITH MORE ENERGY! The place is packed, as Huck predicted. Brian and Michelle Zehring, who own the sleek new Midnight Express charter boat *New Moon,* are there with their daughters. Candi from Candi's Delights is there with her husband, who some of us jokingly call Mr. Candi. Bridgett and Jimmy from Palm Tree Charters are having cocktails with their favorite clients, DeeDee and Michael Napp. A trio of National Park rangers are drinking coffee at the bar; James, the captain of *Treasure Island,* is having pancakes with his wife and daughter; Slim Man, who owns the parking lot in town, is there with his new bride. Skip, the bartender from La Tapa, is sitting next to Jacqui from the Westin time-share office at the bar counter in the front of the restaurant, which has magnificent views over Cruz Bay. (Skip and Jacqui were seated next to each other randomly, and Jacqui is worried people are going to think this is a morning-after date.)

Off to the left side is a table set for ten (though Cash did *not* end up bringing a friend). The Steele party has so much crossover with people already in the restaurant that when they walk in, the decibel level rises considerably. Cash and Ayers talk to James; Maia talks to Candi and Mr. Candi; Baker talks to Jacqui; and Phil and Sunny talk to Skip. Huck stops to talk to the Napps, who own a racetrack in New Jersey. As he's hearing about life in the fast lane, he scans the restaurant for Teresa but sees only Diane, the other waitress. Is it possible that Huck has hit the jackpot and Teresa isn't working today? Did she maybe take a summer vacation to visit her sons in...Idaho?

Eventually the members of the Steele party settle; Irene sits between Huck and Floyd.

Huck feels a hand land on his shoulder, a subtle squeeze.

"How are we all doing?" Teresa says. "I hear we have a birthday!"

Mimosas: Irene and Sunny.

Bloody Marys: Phil, Baker, Cash.

Fresh pineapple juice: Ayers and Maia.

Fresh OJ: Floyd.

Coffee and a Bloody Mary and a michelada while you're at it: Huck.

"Looks like someone's *celebrating.*" Another hand lands on Huck's shoulder. It's Rupert.

Rupert? In Cruz Bay? What's happening here? Well, it turns out that Josephine is providing the live entertainment at Jake's this morning. Rupert takes the tenth seat at their table, and when the drinks arrive, they all raise their glasses and toast Irene.

"To Mom," Cash says. "May this year be better than last year."

"I'll second that," Baker says.

"To Irene," Sunny says. "My sister-grandmother."

"To Grammy," Floyd says, holding up his juice glass. "My . . . grammy."

"To the Angler Cupcake," Huck begins. He waits a beat; he has to swallow the lump in his throat. "The most remarkable woman I know. Happy, happy birthday."

Josephine sings "Ain't No Sunshine." Cash checks his phone and answers a text under the table. Teresa asks Diane to help her run the food—biscuits and gravy, south-of-the-border omelets, a breakfast burrito with extra home fries, banana-walnut pancakes, sweet bread French toast, a "regular" (eggs, bacon, home fries, toast) with a side of chocolate pancakes (this is for Ayers, who is eating for two), and...an order of gingerbread pancakes with a side of sausage for the birthday girl, with two jars of papaya jam to go. Teresa sticks a candle in the pancakes. She cues Josephine and the whole restaurant sings "Happy Birthday."

More mimosas. More Bloody Marys. Coffee for Baker, who is falling asleep at the table. Ayers elbows him in the ribs. "You think you're tired now, wait until the baby comes."

Josephine sings Leonard Cohen's "Hallelujah," which has long been one of Teresa's favorite songs. It's a hymn, an anthem, and it only adds to the cinematic quality of the scene, the restaurant perched high above the streets of Cruz Bay on a summer Sunday morning.

I've heard there was a secret chord...

Churches across the island will be letting out about now, so the restaurant will get a little busier, but not much. Teresa always jokes that, for Jake's clientele, pancakes are their religion. (As is strong coffee. And vodka.)

Teresa takes a minute to gaze out at the water—the ferry coming in from Red Hook, the *Singing Dog* heading out for a sail, maybe with a stop at Carval Rock for a snorkel. When Teresa gets in the weeds at the restaurant, she always imagines herself afloat, her mask submerged in the clear turquoise water, taking in the teeming life of the coral reef. Other people like the fish, the rays, the turtles, but Teresa is fascinated by the coral itself: the intricacies of the brain coral, the grooves of which look like a maze; the staghorn; the boulder star; the elkhorn (Teresa's favorite); the layers of lettuce coral; the ivory bush; the clubbed finger. It's a city down there, a world, a universe that manages to be productive but very, very quiet.

That David played, and it pleased the Lord.

Teresa doesn't remember every detail of the night she first hooked up with Captain Huck Powers, but certain things stand out. She'd met her coworker Diane at High Tide, then they'd cruised down to the Beach Bar with a stop at Joe's Rum Hut. There was a band at the Beach Bar, and Teresa danced with a charter captain named Pat; he was a full head shorter than Teresa and a little handsy. She escaped to the bar, and that's where she found Huck.

"Why the long face?" Teresa asked. As soon as the words were out, she realized her mistake. She had heard that LeeAnn Powers, Huck's wife, had died a couple of months earlier. She didn't know Huck well, though he would, on occasion, come into Jake's for a cup of coffee and the breakfast sandwich to go, or he'd bring his granddaughter in for the chocolate pancakes. (That was back when the girl was small, five or six years old; Teresa can't believe how grown-up she looks now, and how much like her mother.)

To cheer Huck up, Teresa asked Mick to hand over the dice to roll, but the dice did nothing but take Teresa's fiver, so then she asked for the Connect Four. It was a kids' game but everyone at the Beach Bar was so far gone that it was just about all they could handle.

Huck and Teresa split the first two games and then Huck won the third, which cheered him a bit. They headed over to Drink for a shot—a prairie fire, which was whiskey with tabasco—and then, feeling no pain, they went to 420 to Center. Pat was there. He bummed a cigarette off Teresa and tried to engage her in conversation, and Huck took over then, wheeling Teresa out of the bar, saying, "Let's get you home."

He spent that night with her and was up and out at five thirty, which was when she left for work. He didn't ask for her number and she didn't offer it—but the next week, she was drinking up at the Quiet Mon and Huck took the stool next to hers. That was how he found her the third time as well, only the third time he suggested stopping by the side door at Castaways to get a couple of orders of the blackened mahi tacos and, why not, the disco fries. They ate on Teresa's tiny deck and they talked. Teresa told him about her kids, Jasper and Graeden, both working as bartenders in Sun Valley, Idaho, and their dad, Teresa's ex, a former member of the U.S. ski team who'd become a sales rep for Salomon and who lived it up, bouncing from one ski resort to the next, good for him. Huck didn't talk about LeeAnn but he did talk about Rosie and Maia and how he knew Rosie probably wanted to move out and get her own place now that her mother was gone but that he hoped to God she didn't.

Although I'd like her to meet someone, he said. *A good man.*

After that third time, Teresa thought maybe their relationship would continue; maybe she would be a rebound for a while or maybe it would become something more. She wanted that, naturally, because Captain Huck Powers was—excuse the pun—a catch in anyone's book.

But Huck must have gotten scared about sharing as much as he had, by their talking and breaking bread (stuffing cheese-and-bacon fries into their mouths) in addition to sleeping together. Teresa never heard from him again. There were a couple of times she felt someone take the seat next to her at the Quiet Mon and thought it was him, but it was just Pat—at which point, she got up and made the lonely walk home.

She didn't think much about Huck after that—not until Rosie was killed on New Year's Day. Teresa was serving up breakfast to a very hungover clientele when Clover, the hostess at La Tapa, came in with the news, and even though it was eighty degrees, a polar-cap wind blew through Jake's. Teresa remembered what Huck had said about wanting Rosie to find a good man, and she damn near cried.

How does it feel for Teresa to see Huck with his granddaughter and Ayers and the Invisible Man's widow and two sons? (Because we all know who they are by now; they aren't quite locals—that will take *years*—but neither are they strictly tourists.) Well, Teresa isn't hurt or jealous. What passed between Huck and Teresa was half a dozen years ago. If Teresa had to pick a word, she would say that she's *surprised*—not just by Huck and Irene cozied up together but by the whole situation. The people at the table are talking and laughing and singing along to Josephine and sucking down drinks and debating whether or not to start ordering food from the lunch menu now that they've finished breakfast.

They look happy, Teresa thinks. *They look like a real live happy family.*

ELLEN

Has anyone out there tried to plan a weeklong vacation for four women who are all single mothers of young children? That's what Ellen, the ringleader of Baker's Houston school wives, is trying to do. Simply finding a mutually agreeable week requires both a flowchart and a deep reserve of patience. Becky has full custody of her girls all summer while her ex-husband fishes for salmon in Alaska. She calls on her mother to stay with the girls, but her mother decides she wants to go to Branson during the week they've tentatively picked. Three of Debbie's four kids are with her ex all summer, but her son Teddy is with her because he has sports camps in Houston, though he can maybe stay with his buddy Campbell for the week. (Ellen knows Campbell's mother, Tish—stick up her ass. Poor Teddy.) Wendy's ex-husband, Ian, will take the kids "as a favor" (can parenting your own children ever be called a "favor"?), but he has to work such long hours and travel so often that she has to find a sitter anyway. Ellen has recently hired a full-time au pair from Thailand named Za; she is still learning English and still learning to drive, so this week will give new meaning to the phrase *trial by fire.* But Ellen's bar is low—"Just keep him alive" is her parenting motto. She promised herself when she became a single mother by choice at the age of forty that she would not act like a typical older parent. She would neither coddle Walter nor shield him, and she wouldn't insist on organic milk and produce. Ellen grew up on frozen waffles, Cheetos, and ice cream sandwiches—Walter can too.

Ellen has known her school-mom friends for over five years, ever since she had Walter, but in planning the trip, she discovers new things about them. Becky prefers to roll without a set plan while she's on vacation because her usual life is so regimented. (Ellen gets this, in principle, but she must have a plan at all times. If she went on vacation without a plan, she might miss something!) Debbie is a tough negotiator and enjoys herself more when she thinks she's getting a bargain. (Ellen just pays the asking price for things, like an idiot.) Wendy is very concerned about exercise. (Ellen is concerned with breakfast, lunch, happy hour—preferably with snacks—and dinner.)

Ellen learns something new about herself as well: she loves to take credit for everything.

They end up picking August 29 to September 5, Thursday to Thursday, because the one thing they all agree on is that there's no experience more soul-destroying than traveling on the weekend.

They fly United. Ellen would like to upgrade to first class but Debbie feels the best value is in premium economy. Then Wendy announces that her ex, Ian, has donated his miles so they can all fly first class. They immediately forgive Ian for his "as a favor" comment.

Ellen has booked two beachfront suites at Caneel Bay—one room for herself and Debbie, one for Becky and Wendy. She rents a four-door Jeep Wrangler hardtop, though Baker has warned her against ever taking the top off. It rains every day for fifteen minutes in the summer.

Baker! They will finally be reunited with their school husband, Baker. They will get to experience St. John, the island he now calls home.

"More important," Debbie says, "we'll get to meet the girl."

"She has no idea what she's in for with us," Becky says.

"We have to be nice," Wendy says. "She's pregnant."

Ellen obviously wants to meet the mysterious Ayers Wilson but she also wants them to have at least one night with Baker alone so they can find out what's really going on.

Not to toot her own horn, but Ellen's planning pays off. The trip down is smooth, their luggage is the first off the carousel, they get into a shared taxi that delivers them to Red Hook with just enough time for one rum punch before the ferry. When they disembark in Cruz Bay, they can't stop talking about the color of the water. It's pure Crayola turquoise, clear to the white sandy bottom. It's the most beautiful water any of them have ever seen. (They're used to the chocolate-milk-hued water of Galveston, and Debbie, the only East Coast transplant, grew up going to the Jersey Shore, which looked nothing like this.)

Caneel Bay is the epitome of old-school gracious hospitality. It's elegant. It smells like coconut lotion, frangipani, and money.

Their rooms are side by side in a one-story row that sits on a pure white crescent of sand. Each room has two mahogany queen beds sheathed in crisp white linens, marble bathrooms with soaking tubs, ice waiting in a silver bucket, rattan ceiling fans. The rooms have deep front porches with wicker furniture for lounging around with coffee or a cocktail. Beckoning out front are four chaises wrapped in rose-and-white-striped terry cloth. A server stands in the shade of the nearest palm, ready with cocktail and lunch menus.

Next door, Ellen can hear Wendy gushing: "I love it here. I need this. So badly."

They *all* need it so badly. Time away—from the swampy heat and humidity of Houston, from the Astros frenzy, from the Texans hype, from the incessant demands of small children. Ellen feels light and free, like she's lost forty-nine pounds, which is what Walter weighs. No one is asking her for juice, a snack, the bathroom, one more time down the slide, one more time watching *Wreck-It Ralph,* another story before bed, "Just sit here while I fall asleep, please, Mommy." *Mommy, Mommy, Mommy.*

They're free for an entire week!

"Does it feel like we're the only people here?" Debbie asks as she settles into a chaise.

The beach is deserted.

When Woodrow, their server, brings the menus, Ellen says, "Where is everyone else?"

"You're the only guests on this stretch," Woodrow says. "We're at low occupancy because of hurricane season."

Hurricane season, Ellen thinks. Yes, that's why these beachfront suites were so affordable. The hotel is due to close for two months the Sunday after they leave. They made it in just under the wire. Ellen lounges in her chaise, and not to toot her own horn again, but she feels like a wizard. They'll reap the benefits of hurricane season—low prices, the place to themselves—but there isn't a cloud in the sky.

Because of Ellen's impeccable planning, their first three days are packed with highlights: Trunk Bay, smoked brisket and live country music at the Barefoot Cowboy, happy hours at High Tide and Woody's, hiking to Ram Head and taking a mud bath in Salt Pond, dancing at the Beach Bar, a Kenny Chesney sighting inside the Parrot Club (although when Wendy runs in to check, she sees it's just a guy who *looks* like Kenny).

And then, finally, the day they've been waiting for—their charter to the BVIs aboard *Treasure Island.* This trip has all four ladies dialed up for a couple of reasons. One is that Baker is coming with them. (They've seen Baker only once in their first three days; he stopped by the afternoon they arrived to make sure they'd made it safely, but he had Floyd with him, so no actual news was exchanged. Their second evening, he sent two chilled bottles of Veuve Clicquot to their rooms, probably because he felt guilty about not spending more time with them. But they get it: They're on vacation; he's not.) The other is that Ayers Wilson, Baker's girlfriend, the mother of his child, is a crew member aboard *Treasure Island,* and so is Baker's brother, Cash. They're just as excited to meet Cash as they are to meet Ayers. They've seen Cash's picture, but he's never once visited Houston.

They're supposed to be at the dock across from Mongoose Junction at seven a.m., but Wendy is late getting back from her run, Becky is on the phone with her girls, and Debbie is taking forever to get ready even though all she needs is a bathing suit, a cover-up, and sunscreen.

"Let's go, ladies!" Ellen yells from the path behind their suites. Woodrow is waiting in the golf cart.

One by one, her friends appear. Not to toot her own horn yet again, Ellen thinks, but if it weren't for her keeping them to a schedule, they would miss their chance to meet Ayers, which—as far as Ellen is concerned—is one of the main reasons for coming.

Ayers Wilson is a goddess. She's one of those annoying women who glow during pregnancy and who don't gain weight anywhere except their baby bumps.

"Look at those legs," Debbie says. "I hate her. We all hate her, right?"

Except they can't hate her because she is as lovely as she is beautiful. She greets them all with warm hugs—not a trace of snark or jealousy. "Such an honor to meet you, Baker talks all the time about how much he misses his Houston school wives." Ayers lowers her voice. "He likes you better than his St. John school wives."

"You have St. John school wives?" Ellen says to Baker.

"I'll explain later," Baker says.

Not only is Ayers lovely, she's a badass. She's the one who explains how the trip will unfold—Virgin Gorda Baths, snorkeling,

Jost Van Dyke—and provides the safety regulations and a brief history of the island. There are only ten people on the boat—their party of five and a single father and his four teenagers. The father, Gary Dane, is cute in a rugged-ranch-hand kind of way; it turns out he's in real estate in Tulsa, which means he's best suited for Ellen, but Ellen passes him on to Debbie because she has too much urgent business to attend to at the moment. Debbie engages Gary Dane in conversation while Becky and Wendy chat up Cash. Cash is adorable, though he looks nothing like Baker; he's a whole different species. He's shorter than Baker, very blond, muscular. Does he work out? He's perfect for Wendy!

Ellen busies herself watching Baker watch Ayers. He's enchanted, that much is apparent; his eyes follow Ayers wherever she goes. She's wearing little white shorts and a green polo that is probably a men's medium to accommodate her belly. When they get to the Baths, Ayers explains that they're all going to swim from the boat to the shore.

"It's a little rough today," Ayers says. "The weather in early September is always unsettled." Ayers slips off her shorts and shirt to reveal a green tank suit that hugs her curves. She's a movie star, a superhero. Although she's eight months pregnant, she lowers herself down the ladder (thank goodness; Ellen worried for a second that she might dive in) and executes an elegant freestyle all the way to the beach. She takes the front as they tour the Baths—a series of granite boulders that have formed tunnels and chambers holding shallow baths. Some of the passageways are tight squeezes and there are steep stairs, but Ayers just glides along as though she's carved from butter.

Ellen brings up the rear with Baker. "She's remarkable. When I was pregnant with Walter, I gained fifty-two pounds and sat in my house eating cherry pie filling from the can."

"She's been craving steamed artichokes," Baker says. "Thank goodness her mother knows how to prepare them because I don't have a clue."

Steamed artichokes? Ellen decides not to comment. "How are things between the two of you? Is she still living alone in Mick's old place?"

"She is," Baker says. "Things are good. I see her almost every night. I've helped her fix the place up so that it's ready for when the baby comes. She's due in three weeks."

"She's going to stay in her own place after the baby is born? I thought she was moving in with you."

"She wants to wait until we organically reach the moving-in stage of our relationship," Baker says. "She's keeping our relationship on a different timeline from the pregnancy."

"What stage are you in?" Ellen asks. Up ahead, Wendy jumps down from a rock ledge, and Cash catches her. Becky is taking pictures with her phone, which Ellen hopes is waterproof. Debbie is asking the oldest of Gary Dane's kids what colleges she's looking at.

"Boyfriend and girlfriend," Baker says. "I'm madly in love with her. I tell her this all the time, and in response, she laughs and kisses me."

"She doesn't say it back?"

"Not yet. But she will."

He sounds pretty confident, Ellen thinks. "She better."

The bar on the boat doesn't open until after they finish snorkeling. "That's by design," Cash says as he pours painkillers for everyone. "To keep you alive."

* * *

When they anchor in White Bay on Jost Van Dyke, Ellen feels let down. The sand is like powdered sugar, the water a spectral blue, there's reggae music, and the smell of grilled meat wafts over from the Soggy Dollar, but there are only two other boats anchored there. Ellen had been anticipating something like an MTV beach party; this is decidedly more civilized.

The silver lining is that Ellen finds herself taking a seat next to Ayers in one of the Adirondack chairs placed in the shade of a small grove of coconut trees. The others are all up at the bar—Debbie is with Gary Dane, Wendy is with Cash, and Becky is talking to the bartender, who, Ellen can see, is falling in love with Becky (all men fall in love with Becky). Gary Dane's daughters are lying out on the chaises, and the boys are playing catch in the shallows. If Gary Dane and Debbie get married, Ellen thinks, they'll have eight kids—four girls and four boys. The Brady Bunch plus two.

"I don't know how you do it," Ellen says to Ayers. "Aren't you tired? Don't you want to sit in front of *Real Housewives* and eat Doritos?"

"My first trimester was like that," Ayers says. "But every week since then, I've felt healthier and stronger."

"Baker says you're staying in your place after the baby is born."

"I am," Ayers says. "Baker will be nearby. My parents too. But yeah, I want to live on my own for a while longer." She leans in. "You had a baby by yourself, didn't you?"

"*All* by myself," Ellen says. "Sperm donor."

"It wasn't Baker, was it?" Ayers asks.

Ellen hoots. "No! Ahhh, that would have made this a very awkward conversation."

"He's a good father," Ayers says.

"He's a good person," Ellen says. As she squints at the surreal view of the water and the green islands beyond, her vision blurs. Sunscreen in her eyes, maybe. "That's why we all came down here. I mean, yeah, we wanted a Caribbean vacation away from our kids"—she laughs—"but we came to see Baker. He was our best friend at home. He was always helping us out, and not in a douchey, mansplaining way; in a genuine, caring way. He would clean our gutters, change the oil in our cars, bring us homemade lasagnas when we were having a tough week. He went with us to the Houston Ballet every year to see *The Nutcracker.* He took our kids to the park when the four of us wanted to go to yoga together; he gave us solid investment advice; he came to pick us up when we were out on a bad blind date; he gossiped with us, sent us songs he thought we would like, asked us for advice when he was having trouble in his own marriage. He listened. He was there. All together, the four of us have dated—and married—a lot of guys, and we've all agreed that each of us is looking for her own Baker Steele. He's the gold standard." She swallows. "Diamond. Platinum. What I'm trying to get at is, you have a treasure. And what I'm also trying to say is, please don't hurt him." Ellen closes her mouth before she can add, *Or we'll come back down here and haunt you.*

Ayers puts her hand on top of Ellen's. "I won't," she says. "And thank you for telling me all that, but I assure you, I know what I have. I know how lucky I am."

Ellen studies Ayers for a second. *Do I believe her?*

Yes.

"Good," Ellen says. "Now, please dish on the St. John school wives."

* * *

When *Treasure Island* pulls into Cruz Bay at the end of the day, Ellen is happy, satisfied, and drunk. She's so drunk that when they get back to Caneel Bay, it takes her a minute to make sense of the paper that has been slipped under her door. The words are blurry. Maybe it's not the rum; maybe she needs reading glasses.

"What does this say?" Ellen asks, handing the paper to Debbie.

"They're evacuating the hotel tomorrow," Debbie says. "There's a hurricane coming."

TILDA

La Tapa closes at the end of August, which seems like a natural time for Tilda to give her notice. Her future is on Lovango.

She thinks maybe the staff will plan a party or an outing for drinks on her last night—this is what normally happens when someone moves on—but when Tilda finishes her last shift, no celebration is mentioned, so she hands in her uniform, hugs Chef, and leaves.

It's not that the staff members don't like *her;* it's that they don't like Dunk. He's developed the (admittedly, obnoxious) habit of waiting for Tilda across the street by the Tap and Still, vaping and glaring at the restaurant in a menacing way. Clover, the hostess, said she felt threatened; Skip wanted to punch his lights out. Ayers seemed indifferent, though Tilda knows that Ayers dislikes Dunk on principle because of Cash. Chef invited Dunk in for dinner but Dunk turned her down because Dunk doesn't eat. He has espresso in the morning, fruit juice at lunch, and either vegetable juice or broth at dinner. He drinks wine and Maker's Mark. Tilda isn't sure how he's still alive. There isn't an ounce of fat on his body; he's as lean and supple as a lizard.

If Tilda were being honest with herself, she would admit that Dunk's fasting bothers her. First of all, it's embarrassing that he can't socialize over meals the way other people do. No wonder he's essentially without friends and living like a hermit in the East End. Second, he makes Tilda feel bad when she eats. He stares at her with thinly veiled disgust when she bites into the Uncle Peep turkey sandwich from Sam and Jack's or when she asks him to stop at Scoops so she can get a cup of their salted peanut butter ice cream. Tilda is naturally slender, so she can eat whatever she wants and not gain an ounce, but Dunk makes her feel gluttonous and weak.

Tilda thinks back on her brief time with Cash, remembering how excellent it was to have someone to eat with. She and Cash planned every meal like it was their last whether they were cooking at home or eating out. It was sensual, Tilda thinks. Sexy.

Dunk's fasting isn't the only thing that's chafing at Tilda. There are also the accusations from Swan Seeley. Swan claims Dunk insulted her and touched her inappropriately during their marketing meeting, a meeting Tilda was supposed to attend until Dunk announced that he'd forgotten Olive's lunch at home, which was all the way back in Hansen Bay. Unlike Dunk, Olive ate like royalty—prime rib, lamb chops, chicken Kiev. It was twisted. Dunk asked Tilda if she would take the skiff back to Cruz Bay and buy two pounds of ground beef at Starfish Market for Olive. Tilda agreed even though by all rights it should have been Tilda meeting with Swan while Dunk ran the stupid errand. This was Tilda's resort—well, okay, her parents' resort. Dunk owned the land, and he and Granger and Lauren had come to some kind of agreement about a partnership, but Tilda didn't think that meant Dunk's presence was more important than her own at a marketing meeting. Still, she went to the market because she had a difficult time saying no to Dunk. And that's when the thing with Swan either happened or didn't. According to Swan, Dunk had said he'd hired her because she was "hot," "a dime" (Tilda abhors both of these terms), and then he'd touched Swan's back, massaged her shoulders, and brushed up against her behind.

Tilda had shocked herself by coming to Dunk's defense even though she knew that massaging a woman's shoulders and brushing up against her behind were two of Dunk's signature moves. He'd used both of these moves on Tilda! Tilda is a firm believer in the #MeToo movement; she always, *always* believes the woman—except, apparently, when the perpetrator is her own boyfriend. She was stunned by Swan's accusations—and hurt, too, of course. Why would Dunk go after Swan when he had Tilda? After Swan was safely on the skiff heading back to Cruz Bay, Tilda marched into the trailer and said, "What just happened with Swan, Dunk?"

Dunk had been poring over the designs for the T-shirts. He didn't even look up. "I was giving her a pat on the back, a good-on-ya, and she spit the dummy."

"Spit the dummy" was something Dunk said all the time; it had something to do with a baby losing his pacifier. "So you weren't inappropriate?" Tilda said.

Dunk inhaled on his vape pen—that thing drove Tilda crazy—and on the exhale said, "I was trying to give the woman a bloody *compliment.*" Then he held his arms open. "Come here, mate." And like a fool, she went.

Swan e-mailed Granger and Lauren to tell them she didn't

feel comfortable working with Duncan or Tilda. She wanted to be paid for the time she'd spent on it so far, and thanks for the opportunity, but she was leaving the project. Tilda's parents had called from their business trip in Cape Town to ask for a full explanation, and when Tilda told them what had purportedly happened, they were livid. Especially Lauren. She said, "I'm calling Swan now to get her back. Your father will have a chat with Dunk. Is he trying to get us hit with a lawsuit?"

Lauren did persuade Swan to come back, but Swan said she would report to Lauren only. Not Dunk. And not Tilda.

Where do things stand with the Lovango resort? Well, that's the good news: Everything is moving swiftly and smoothly along with an anticipated opening date of April 1, right before Easter. The desalinization plant is nearly finished; the pool has been dug; the foundations of the cottages are in; the beach has been cleared. All the permitting is in place, and Granger and Lauren are in the process of buying boats that will transport guests from both Red Hook in St. Thomas and Cruz Bay in St. John to the resort. The restaurant is framed out, and only the week before, the granite was delivered for the bar. Lauren and Tilda FaceTime every day to discuss the design details—light fixtures, fabrics, paint colors. They both loved Swan's ideas for merchandise.

The Lovango Resort and Beach Club. It's going to be real. Tilda almost can't believe it.

After Tilda quits her job at La Tapa, she's on Lovango all the time. There's a tiny cottage perched just above the beach that came with the sale of the island. It's bare bones but livable, and Tilda spends a couple nights a week there so she doesn't waste precious time in the mornings commuting from Peter Bay.

She stays alone. Dunk prefers to sleep in his own bed, and so does Olive—fine, whatever. Tilda's feelings toward Dunk have cooled considerably; she's beginning to suspect that, behind the sexy accent and all the money, there's just a little man, like the Wizard of Oz. For dinner, Tilda runs the skiff over to the Pizza Pi boat or grabs sushi from the bar at Caneel, and then she sits in the cottage with the air-conditioning cranked and stuffs her face without anyone judging her.

One day, she sees *Treasure Island* heading out of the harbor in the wrong direction—toward St. Thomas—and realizes the boat is probably going for its yearly maintenance. They don't run charters in the autumn. Tilda wonders what Cash is doing over the break. She'd love to invite him to work on the resort. That had been the plan. Everyone is keen to have a robust water-sports program and a series of hikes across the island both as workouts and nature walks, and this was supposed to be Cash's department—but Tilda blew that chance. She hasn't even told her parents the truth. They know that Cash broke up with Tilda but they don't know that Tilda and Dunk hooked up on St. Lucia right after their couples massage, which was *before* she talked to Cash, so, technically, she cheated. And Cash could tell, she knew he could, so the breakup was her fault. Tilda generally discusses everything with her mother, but her behavior was so shameful and so unlike her that she can't share it with Lauren.

Tilda has just woken up in the Lovango cottage when her phone rings. Granger, calling from Dubai, where her parents are attending a conference this week.

"Inga is going to be a problem," Granger says.

Tilda must still be asleep because she has no idea who Inga

is. Maybe it's the woman at the Health Department over in St. Thomas? "Why?" Tilda says.

"She's picking up speed and strength, and right now she's on a direct course toward St. Thomas, St. John, Tortola, Jost, Virgin Gorda, and, although they didn't mention it by name, Lovango."

"Dad," Tilda says. "What are you talking about?"

"Inga," Granger says. "The hurricane."

Like a newborn with indecisive parents, a hurricane first forms without a name, as a collection of thunderstorms—so says Tilda's favorite weatherman, Dougie Clarence of the *CBS Evening News*. Tilda is watching Dougie on her phone in bed—the cottage has no TV, and even if it did, there's no cable—as he explains that Hurricane Inga started a few days earlier, August 27, as a Cape Verde hurricane, forming off the African continent and organizing near the Cape Verde Islands with a big push from the westerly trade winds, a term originating from the beneficial wind direction for early colonial traders. (Dougie always throws interesting factoids into his forecasts, which Tilda loves.) Inga has had a thousand miles of warm tropical waters to nourish her. In the past forty-eight hours, Dougie says, Inga's maximum winds have increased from forty miles per hour to one hundred and fifteen.

"It will bear down on Barbuda, the sister island to Antigua, in the next twenty-four hours," Dougie says. "It might disassemble a bit with landfall, but if it doesn't, it will hit the Virgin Islands with its full strength."

"Um...okay?" Tilda says.

She calls Dunk, gets his voicemail. She checks the time; he must be meditating. He'll meditate until eight thirty, then he'll drink four espressos while he prepares Olive's daily meals. Then they'll drive to town and he'll call Tilda to pick them up in the skiff right around nine thirty. Can she just wait until then?

The chyron on the screen beneath Dougie says HURRICANE INGA ON DIRECT PATH FOR VIRGIN ISLANDS.

She calls Dunk again. Voicemail.

Texts him: Call me! Urgent!

Calls him again, even though she realizes it's pointless. He's unreachable while he's meditating.

She calls him at 8:31 sharp.

"What?" He sounds pissed for some reason, maybe because she called during his sacred time. She doesn't care.

"There's a hurricane, category four, Inga, bearing down on Barbuda. And then, maybe, us."

"I've been tracking it all night," Dunk says.

Good, Tilda thinks. She doesn't want Dunk to accuse her of manufacturing drama, hurricane as monster under the bed. "Is it something we need to worry about?"

"Hell yes," Dunk says. "I have blokes coming to shutter this place up and I talked to Topher. He's coming to scoop up Olive and me tomorrow morning."

Wait... what? "You and Olive? Scoop you up to go where?"

"Back to Houston first, then probably on to Vegas. You know Topher."

Tilda does *not* know Topher; she only knows *of* Topher. He's Dunk's friend and bandmate in Wasps of Good Fortune (he's the bass player), and he's even wealthier than Dunk. He has his own plane, a G5.

"So you're leaving the island?" Tilda says. "You're just... leaving?"

"There's a hurricane coming, mate. A ballbuster. Maybe a cat five."

"What about...this place? Lovango? The construction, the work trailer, my cottage, the de-sal plant, the pool? We can't just leave it."

"If I were you," Dunk says, "I'd have Keith and the crew secure what they can over there and then you and your parents should have the caretaker shutter up Peter Bay and hunker down on the bottom floor."

"My parents," Tilda says, "are in Dubai."

"You must have the caretaker's number? Call him yourself. Be an adult."

"I *am* being an adult," Tilda says. "I'm not worried about my parents' house. It's made of stone."

"Even so, mate. It needs to be shuttered."

"I'm worried about here. Lovango. The resort we're building." She laughs. "I can't believe you're leaving with Topher. For Vegas. Do you not care about the resort?"

"I own the land," Dunk says. "Nothing is going to happen to the land."

"So now you care only about the *land?*" Tilda says. "What about the hundreds of thousands of dollars my parents have poured into building this place? That doesn't interest you, I guess. Unless it gives you a chance to meet one-on-one with a hot woman, then you're front and center." She understands in that moment that Dunk "forgot" Olive's lunch that day on purpose so he could meet alone with Swan.

"You're acting like a possessive child. If you're so worried about what you and your parents are building, then protect it, mate. I'm protecting what's mine, then I'm getting out of Dodge."

"I'm not going with you, Dunk. I'm staying on Lovango."

"I didn't invite you," Dunk says. "Did I?"

Did he? No, he didn't. Tilda can't believe how much she *hates* him in this moment. She isn't sure how to respond but she wants to pour gasoline on his heart and set it on fire with her words.

But she isn't quick enough. Dunk hangs up.

"I'm *not* your mate!" she says.

Tilda calls her parents and the three of them make a plan. Granger will get their caretaker to shutter the Peter Bay house. Tilda will meet with Keith and they'll secure Lovango the best they can. There are tens of thousands of dollars of building materials to protect. Tilda will shutter the cottage herself. There are three generators on the island; Tilda will get gas for all of them and stock up on provisions. She needs to go soon; the markets on St. John will be complete pandemonium. Or maybe not. Maybe she's overreacting.

"You'll stay at Peter Bay," Granger says.

"No," Tilda says. "I'm staying over here."

"Tilda," Lauren says.

"The cottage is sturdy, Mom," Tilda says. "It faces northwest and the storm is coming from the east-southeast. I'll be fine."

"I don't want you staying by yourself," Lauren says. "Call a friend. Or ask Keith to stay with you."

"Keith has a family, Mom. Little kids."

"Where's Dunk?" Granger asks. "Will he be there with you?"

"He's going to Vegas," Tilda says.

"Vegas!" Lauren cries.

"I don't know why you started seeing him," Granger says. "That had disaster written all over it."

You were the one who sent us away together, Tilda thinks. *What did you expect would happen?* Though there she goes again, acting like a child, not taking responsibility for her own decisions.

She entered the relationship with Dunk of her own free will—and yes, it was a disaster.

"What about Cash?" Lauren says. "Cash is so sweet."

Cash *is* sweet. And cool. And superior to Dunk in every way, starting with the fact that Cash would never abandon Tilda on Lovango with a hurricane coming and go to Vegas with his filthy-rich degenerate buddy. But Cash is also very, very angry with Tilda. And can she blame him? A couple months earlier, Tilda reached out to him via text just to see how he was doing, and he'd shut her down, saying, Fine, thanks for asking. Tilda deserved no more than this; she'd been awful to him, so awful that, frankly, she doesn't like to think about it. She ditched him for Duncan Huntley because...why? Dunk is rich, Dunk has a beautiful boat and an enormous villa with staff and a G-wagon and a lovely dog. Dunk has built and sold companies. Listening to Dunk's accent gave her a buzz. When they were on vacation together, he wowed her with how generously he tipped and how much he knew about the islands; he seemed like an evolved person who cared about the actual *place* and the actual *people,* and he made Tilda want to be more than just a resort tourist. All of Dunk's weird rituals made Tilda think he was *enlightened* and *interesting.* He knew a lot about old punk rock, which wasn't too surprising because he was in a band, but then one morning at breakfast on St. Lucia, he had identified Brahms, then Mozart, then Schubert coming from the piano player, and Tilda had been gobsmacked by his *range.*

Fine, he has range, but he's a jerk—and by *jerk,* Tilda means a lot of other things she's too polite to say.

She closes her eyes and does her own meditating. It was a mistake to date Dunk. Everyone could see that but her. But she's young, and Tilda is at least self-aware enough to admit failure, pick herself up, and dust herself off. She needs to apologize, big-time, to Swan Seeley. She will do that—but right now, there's a hurricane bearing down.

There's another person to whom she owes an apology, and this one can't wait.

She calls Cash.

HUCK

A hurricane watch is issued for the U.S. Virgin Islands. The clock starts ticking; they have forty-eight hours.

Cash calls Huck. "I need a favor."

Huck closes his eyes and summons every bit of patience he has as Cash talks. Cash would like a ride over to Lovango Cay because he's going to wait out the hurricane in a cottage on a cliff overlooking Congo Cay and Jost Van Dyke with... Tilda Payne, the girl who left him for the guy who bought Lovango.

"I have no other way to get over there," Cash says.

Huck and Irene swing down to the Happy Hibiscus so Huck can pick up Cash and drop off Irene. They find Cash and Baker talking in Baker's driveway. Cash throws his duffel in the back of Huck's truck.

"Are you sure about this?" Huck says. "I can take you there, but once I do, that's it. I won't be able to get you until after the storm passes."

"It's a terrible idea, bro," Baker says. "We should all stay here at the Hibiscus. Together. Besides, Tilda screwed you over, and the second she crooks her finger, you run back to her? Seems a little weak."

Huck's glad Baker is the one who said this.

"She's all by herself," Cash says. "Dunk left her. He's flying to Vegas with one of the guys in his so-called band."

What a douche-canoe, Huck thinks.

"She made her bed," Baker says. "You should *not* get back together with her. And besides, I thought you liked Wendy."

"She lives in Houston," Cash says.

"What about Bonny, then?"

Huck can see Cash's neck growing flushed. "Bonny's fine. I went on one date with her, she's nice, but it wasn't a love connection. Tilda means something to me."

"She let you stay with her for weeks," Irene says. "Do you feel like you have to repay the favor?"

"I want to be there for her," Cash says. "She can't stay over there alone." He appeals again to Huck. "Can we go?"

"We can go," Huck says.

First they stop at St. John Market, which has both registers open and ten people in each line, including—Huck gathers from eavesdropping—two couples who have only just arrived for a week's vacation at the Westin and who are provisioning with things like Doritos and mango-flavored Cruzan rum. Huck wants to tell these people that their time would be better spent trying to book a flight back to where they came from. For years, there've been false alarms—cat 1 or 2 hurricanes that fell apart and made landfall as nothing more than forty-mile-per-hour winds and two inches of rain—but this storm is picking up power like a snowball rolling down a mountain. This isn't going to be a "Let's get drunk, play gin rummy, and listen to that Scorpion song on repeat" kind of hurricane.

Cash buys two cases of water, two loaves of bread, peanut butter, jelly, crackers, Cheez Whiz, pickles, a bag of apples, a carton of pineapple juice, and two bottles of Cruzan aged rum. He wants beer as well but Huck steers him toward toilet paper, candles, batteries, bug spray.

From their spot way back in line, Huck texts Irene. Fill the gas cans first, then get to the store. This place is packed already.

Huck drops Cash off at the Lovango dock; Tilda is waiting at the end in a John Deere Gator. The construction site seems to have been secured but there's a trailer sitting on concrete blocks and all Huck can imagine is this bitch Inga picking it up like a toddler with a toy and tossing it into the sea.

"That's not where you're staying, is it?" Huck asks Tilda.

"No," Tilda says. "There's a cottage on the other side." She and Cash load the provisions into the Gator. "Thank you for bringing him."

"You two be smart," Huck says. "Charge your phones. Do you have a generator?"

"Yes," Tilda says. "And plenty of gas."

"Your place is shuttered?"

"It is," Tilda says.

Huck doesn't like leaving Cash and Tilda all alone on an island, not one bit, but he realizes he doesn't have any say in the situation and he needs to get out of there.

"Be safe," Huck says.

* * *

Huck is taking his boat to Hurricane Hole, where he will secure it with three anchors, strip it of all valuable electronics, then hope for the best. When he pulls into the Hole, he sees Captains Stephen and Kelly of the *Singing Dog* heading out.

Where are they going? he wonders.

He sees a few boats prepping in the Hole but not nearly as many as he thought he would. He putters over to *What a Catch!* "Where is everyone?" he asks Captain Chris.

"Hurricane watch just turned to warning," Chris says. "And they're advising everyone to pull their boats. This storm is going to be a monster, worse than anything we've seen. Sustained winds of one fifty or higher."

Huck swears under his breath. The *Mississippi* can't handle winds like that. "Where's the *Singing Dog* going?"

"They said the boat will be a goner on land or on sea," Chris says. "So they're going to try to outrun it."

"For the love of Pete," Huck says. "What are you doing, staying here or trailering up?"

"I was tempted to chance it here," Chris says. "But now I'm having second thoughts."

Yes, so is Huck—and the decision needs to be made immediately. He waves to Chris, spins his boat around, and heads back to Cruz Bay.

He calls Irene. "I need to trailer the boat," he says. "Then I have to shutter my house." Or should he shutter first, then deal with the boat? No, he can shutter in the dark if need be.

"What can I do to help?" Irene says.

"You and Baker are shuttering Hibiscus?"

"Yes," Irene says. "I'm making clam chowder, white chicken chili, a Mississippi roast, and your favorite cookies. Ayers is here, and so is Floyd. Phil and Sunny are on their way. Maia is at the school."

That's right; Maia begged to be allowed to go to the Gifft Hill gymnasium to assemble and distribute hurricane survival kits, which include gallon jugs of water, flashlights, extra batteries, granola bars, and fudge that some of the mothers made (because who doesn't need fudge in a hurricane?). All of Maia's friends are doing it, she said. Plus, she wants to *help*.

"Can you pick up Maia?" Huck asks.

"Already planning on it," Irene says. "Curfew is at eight. I figure I'll get her around seven thirty."

Huck breathes out a "Thank you" and marvels at how much better his life is with Irene Steele in it.

Huck hitches up his trailer and drives down to Chocolate Hole, where the boat is waiting. Getting the boat onto the trailer by himself isn't something he would do under any but the most dire of circumstances. He should have called Rupert for help but Rupert is all the way out in Coral Bay and Huck doesn't have time to waste. He has other friends but they all have their own boats to worry about. He considers driving back to Fish Bay to enlist Baker's help, but again, there's the issue of time.

There isn't a dinghy for Huck to borrow so he wades into the water up to his chest in order to climb aboard. The air is as hot and heavy as a blanket; the water feels wonderful. The sky glows an ominous green color. It seems to portend danger. Destruction.

Or maybe that's all in Huck's head.

* * *

He gets the boat trailered. That ends up being the easy part. The hard part is driving the trailer up Jacob's Ladder. He has to take it slowly, begging the chipmunks in his truck engine not to die on him yet. Right before he faces the final hill, the steepest, his neighbor Helen comes out of her house holding a covered plate. Helen was LeeAnn's best friend, a friend since childhood, though Huck has noticed she's kept her distance since Irene moved in.

"Chicken, beans, rice," she says. "Make sure you eat."

"Thank you," Huck says. "I will."

But there's no time just then. He gets the boat to the house, unhitches the trailer, secures the boat, and hopes like hell it doesn't go flying and end up through the roof of his house. It's getting dark. He's shuttering the house when his phone rings. Irene.

"I ate," he says. "Helen fed me." This is a lie—the plate is on the counter, untouched—but he assumes Irene is calling to check on him.

"Huck," she says. Her voice is an urgent whisper.

"What is it?" He *cannot* go back to Lovango to pick up Cash. Cash is stuck over there, sorry, unless he wants to swim.

Irene says something in such a low voice, Huck can't hear it. "I'm sorry, AC, what?" He realizes he sounds a little impatient. It's all fine for her to be making her white chicken chili and Mississippi roast, whatever the hell *that* is, but Huck has serious tasks to complete and he's racing against the clock.

There's a pause, then a noise—a door closing—and she says, "Ayers is in labor."

Well, she's going to have to wait, he thinks. "What kind of labor are we talking about?"

"Her water broke," Irene says. "The contractions are coming

every three to four minutes. It's pretty clear she's not going to make it over to Schneider. We called up to Myrah Keating, which is in full-on hurricane mode and has only emergency doctors on staff for the next twenty-four to forty-eight hours."

"The emergency docs can deliver a baby," Huck says. "Go now." It's almost seven thirty and there's an island-wide curfew that starts at eight. "Wait, where's Maia?"

"She's still at the school," Irene says. "I was about to go pick her up."

"I'll get Maia," Huck says. Goddamn it, he doesn't have *time* for this! He still has all the kitchen windows to shutter. "Why don't you take Cash's truck and get Maia, and Baker can take Ayers in his Jeep. Or Phil and Sunny can take her in their Jeep, it's bigger. Are Phil and Sunny there?"

"Oh yes, they're here," Irene says. "That's the issue. Sunny doesn't think Ayers should go to the health center."

"For crying out loud, why not?"

"I should rephrase that. Ayers claims she's in too much pain to move, and Phil and Sunny have assured her she doesn't have to go anywhere. They're telling her she can just have the baby *here in the house.*"

"Is anyone there a *doctor?*" Huck says. "If the answer is no, then get that girl to the health center. Have Baker step in if you need to. That baby is his as well."

"I've told them all that," Irene says. "What if there are complications? But Ayers said she had a checkup at the beginning of the week, and the baby is in place, apparently. Sunny keeps saying that women all across the globe have babies at home and there's no reason Ayers can't as well. She says it might actually be safer."

Huck can't believe this. "I can't believe this," he says.

"Apparently it's the low pressure that brings the babies," Irene says. "I should go get Maia now. Everyone else is with Ayers. Can you please come home?"

And do what? Huck thinks. He's not a doctor, and although he has sixty-plus years of wide and varied life experience, he has never delivered a baby. Then he gets an idea.

"I'm going to make a call," he says. "Long shot, but it's all we've got. You bring Maia home safely, please, and I'll be there as soon as I can." Huck hangs up and calls Rupert.

"This best be an emergency," Rupert says when he answers. "Not sure if you heard, but there's a storm coming."

Rupert's lady friend Sadie lives in Coral Bay on Upper Carolina. She's waiting at the bottom of her steep driveway, thank God, wearing blue scrubs and a silk scarf over her hair and holding a small duffel. Sadie is a nurse practitioner up at Myrah Keating; her mother, Blythe, was a midwife, the best in the Virgin Islands. When Huck called and told her about Ayers, she said, "If you come get me, I'll help out. I have my bag of tricks right here ready to go."

As soon as Sadie climbs in, Huck swings the car around and heads back down the Centerline Road like a bat out of hell.

"It's one thing asking you to deliver a baby at home and another thing asking you to deliver a baby at home with a category five hurricane on the way."

"Low pressure brings the babies," Sadie says. "I remember my mama delivering two or three babies during Marilyn in '95."

"I'm not sure how I'll ever thank you," Huck says.

"I'll tell you how you can thank me," Sadie says. "Convince your old friend Rupert to stop seeing Josephine."

Oh, boy, Huck thinks.

"And Dora."

It's a small island, Rupert, Huck thinks. He takes the curve above the Reef Bay Trail at breakneck speed. The wind is picking up; trees aren't swaying, they're *bending.*

"And anyone else he's got on a string," Sadie says. She slaps Huck's arm. "You hear me?"

"I hear you," Huck says.

MAIA

That was sick," Maia tells Irene as she climbs into Cash's truck. She puts down the window. "Bye, Shane! Stay safe! Text me!"

"Buckle up, please," Irene says. "And put up your window. It's starting to blow."

"We gave out six hundred and twenty-two emergency kits," Maia says. "Each one with two jugs of water, flashlights with batteries, bug spray, energy bars, and matches. The volunteers got to take home the extra fudge." Maia pulls a piece of fudge wrapped in wax paper out of her pocket. "Do you want some? It's fudge with Oreos."

"No, thank you, honey," Irene says. "Seat belt?"

"It's on," Maia says. "Is everyone at the house?" Maia knows this hurricane is going to be very destructive, but she can't help feeling something like excitement anyway. Shane and Bright and Colton and Joanie were all at the volunteer effort, and Bright said that every news station in the States is focused on the Virgin Islands. They keep calling it "America's paradise." Maia is happy people are paying attention; normally, the USVI are overlooked because they're a territory and not a proper state.

"Cash is on Lovango with Tilda," Irene says.

"Ahh," Maia says. She has been waiting for those two to get back together. Maia had caught Cash texting Tilda under the table during Irene's birthday breakfast at Jake's, and when Maia asked if they were starting back up, Cash said, *She's dating someone else.* And when Maia kept staring at him, he said, *It's one text, Maia, relax.*

"Your grandfather will hopefully be back by the time we get home," Irene says. "And Maia..."

Maia has just popped fudge in her mouth. "Mmm-hmm?"

"Ayers is in labor."

"What does that mean?"

"She's having the baby."

"Tonight?"

"Tonight most likely, yes. Or first thing tomorrow. Her water broke." Irene sighs. "Her contractions were close when I left the house to get you. And she doesn't want to go to the health center..."

Maia asks, "Why not?"

"She thinks that because of the storm, it will be better to have the baby at home."

"Like in the olden days, when there were no hospitals?" Maia says.

"Yes," Irene says, shaking her head. She hits the gas.

When they get to the Happy Hibiscus, it's chaos. The front door is the only thing left unshuttered for now because people are still going in and out. Phil is on the front lawn on the phone with a doctor friend from Reykjavík, who is giving him advice. Sunny is guarding the bedroom where Ayers is. Nobody's allowed in, not even Baker.

"Is Huck here?" Irene asks.

"Not yet," Baker says. "Floyd fell asleep, thank God, *The Dirty Cowboy* does it every time. Someday I'm going to learn how that book ends. We filled both bathtubs and every pot we could find with water." He looks at Irene. "You made a lot of food."

"We have a lot of mouths to feed," Irene says. "How's she doing?"

"She's working through the contractions on her own for now," Baker says. "That's what she wants, and who am I to argue?"

"Huck told me help is on the way," Irene says.

Maia hears Ayers groaning in the bedroom.

Sunny says, "Make a knot and hang on, Freddy!"

"What should I do?" Maia asks.

"There's nothing any of us can do but wait," Irene says.

Phil comes inside as he finishes his call. "Anders says she needs to work with each contraction until it's time to bear down."

"That's not helpful!" Ayers shouts.

"Does she want some fudge?" Maia says.

"No, sweetie, thank you," Sunny says. "She already lost her dinner."

"Is that Maia?" Ayers says.

"Yes," Maia and Sunny say.

"Send her in," Ayers says.

The room is dark but there's an outline of light around the bathroom door. Ayers is sitting on the bed crying.

"Nut," she says. "It hurts. They tell you it's going to hurt but that doesn't prepare you for how white-hot, teeth-crushingly painful it is." She stand up, paces the room, then sits down again. "Here it comes, Nut. Hold my hand."

Okay, okay. Maia sits next to Ayers on the bed and Ayers grips Maia's hand so hard that Maia wants to cry out. Ayers is making a wheezing sound that turns to a whimper that turns to rapid breathing.

Finally, she relaxes. "Oh God," she says. She turns to Maia. "Hi."

"Hi. Is it over?"

"For now," Ayers says. "I can't recommend this. Promise me you'll never have children."

"Are you sure you don't want to go to the health center?"

"No," Ayers says. "No way. There's a storm coming, Nut."

"There is?" Maia says, and they both laugh.

"I don't want to be in a hospital filled with strangers when the power goes out. There are going to be emergencies that need to be addressed. And it sits up on that hill...I just don't think it's safe. Plus I can't ask all of you to come up there with me. I just...don't want to go."

"But what about the good drugs?" Maia says. Any time the topic of Ayers's delivery has come up in the past few weeks, all Ayers talked about were the good drugs. "Don't you want the good drugs?"

"I do," Ayers says. "I really do. Here comes another one, give me your hand."

Reluctantly, Maia surrenders her hand, and Ayers squeezes even harder than before, with nails, and Maia squeals but Ayers doesn't notice, thank goodness. Maia doesn't want to be asked to leave. She's honored that Ayers wants Maia—and apparently only Maia—in the room.

"You know who I miss right now?" Ayers says. "More than anyone else, do you know who I need here?"

"Mama?" Maia says.

"Rosie," Ayers says, and she starts crying again. "I need Rosie Small right here, right now! You know what she would be doing?"

The door to the bedroom swings open and a West Indian woman in scrubs walks in and says, "Rosie Small would be pouring two shots of tequila, one for you and one for her, we both know that." The woman puts her hand on Ayers's head. "How we doing, Mama? I'm Sadie. I'm here to deliver your baby." She glances at Maia. "You're the spitting image of your mother, sweetheart. If we hit a lull in here, I'm going to tell you some stories about your ancestors. Can you help me with a couple things?"

"Okay," Maia says. She will do literally anything to avoid holding Ayers's hand through another contraction.

"Clean towels," Sadie says. "Ice chips. And see if anyone has a Coca-Cola for me." She eases Ayers back onto the bed, spreads her knees, and says, "Let me check and see where we're at, doll. Whoa! Whoa, whoa, whoa! We got a baby crowning."

Ayers screams through the next contraction. Maia grabs a stack of towels from the bathroom and puts them on the bed.

"Ice chips," Sadie says. "And send the father in here, please. This baby is on its way."

When Maia leaves the room, she nearly collides with Phil and Sunny, who are stationed outside the door. "It's time to send the father in, she said."

"That would be me," Phil says.

"Why Phil and not me?" Sunny says. "That makes no sense."

"I think she means the baby's father," Maia says. "Baker, bro, it's time."

Baker leaps off the sofa and slides between Phil and Sunny and into the bedroom.

Maia fetches a bowl of ice chips and a Coke but she can't get back into the room because Phil and Sunny are blocking the way. Ayers is screaming. Maia gets tears in her eyes and thinks, *I am never, ever having a baby.* It's incredible that each and every person in this world had a mother who'd endured some version of this.

Rosie went through it with Maia; LeeAnn and Huck were there. Maia hands Sunny the ice chips and the Coke to pass into the room and then she goes out to the front yard and stands with Huck while he has a cigarette. Maia isn't supposed to hang around Huck while he smokes but there's a new life entering the world and a hurricane coming, so the usual rules don't apply.

"Do you remember when I was born?" Maia asks.

Huck exhales, then gives a dry laugh. "Do I *remember?* Maia Rosalie Small, that was the happiest day of my life."

Ayers screams again. They hear her, even outside.

"Must be getting close," Huck says.

Close but not yet, not yet. When Maia goes back inside, she hears Sadie saying, "Push, doll, push for me," and Ayers screaming, "I can't!" And Sunny calling out, "Push, Freddy, push!" Phil gently leads Sunny away from the bedroom door and back to the living room. He says, "I think I'm going to try some of that chili. Do you want some, my love?"

Sunny says, "How can you think about eating when our grandson is about to arrive?"

"Or granddaughter," Irene says, and Maia smiles. She knows that Sunny visited a medium on her trip to Croatia and the medium told Sunny the baby was going to be a boy. Sunny fully believes this and she has bought ten outfits for the baby in blue.

Ayers screams.

"There we go," Sadie says. "One more push, doll!"

Maia puts her hands over her ears so she doesn't have to listen to Ayers. A second later, Irene jumps off the sofa. Maia drops her hands.

"It's a girl!" Sadie calls out. "A beautiful baby girl."

A split second later, there's a noise unlike anything Maia has ever heard—it's a cry. A baby's first cry. Maia shivers. It's a girl. Her niece.

Maia stays up late because sleeping arrangements in the Hibiscus are a little crazy. Baker, Ayers, and the baby will sleep in one bedroom; Irene will sleep with Floyd; Huck and Maia are taking the sofas; and Phil and Sunny are sleeping in the laundry room on an air mattress. The wind has picked up but there's no rain yet; the storm is due to make landfall the following day between noon and two.

Once Sadie has finished checking Ayers and the baby—Ayers and Baker haven't given her a name yet because they want to get it just right—and helped Ayers latch the baby onto her breast and taught Ayers and Baker all about newborn care, Huck says that despite the curfew, he's going to run Sadie back to Coral Bay.

Maia approaches Sadie as she's scrubbing her hands and her equipment at the kitchen sink. "We didn't have a lull," Maia says, "so I didn't get to hear the stories about my ancestors. Did you...*know* my ancestors?"

"Well," Sadie says, "my mother, Blythe, was a midwife here on the island, and believe it or not, she delivered your mother."

"She did?" Maia says.

"When I was fourteen, my mother started bringing me with her to the births," Sadie says. "I'm fifty now. So…thirty-six years ago, the very first baby I saw being born was your mom."

For a second, Maia is left breathless. Here's someone who wants to talk not about Rosie dying but about Rosie being born. "What…" Maia isn't sure what to ask. "What do you remember?"

"Your grandmother was the most elegant woman ever to grace this island," Sadie says. "She was a model for a while, you know, in Paris and Milan."

"I know."

"She left all that and came back to St. John to marry Levi Small."

"Did you know my grandfather?" Maia asks. She checks around the house. Their voices are low, but this topic—Rosie's father, Levi Small—is so forbidden that Maia doesn't want anyone overhearing. It also feels wrong to refer to anyone but Huck as her grandfather.

"Course I did," Sadie says. She dries her hands finger by finger on a paper towel and lowers her voice to a whisper. "He was singing to LeeAnn the whole time she was in labor, mostly old Motown tunes—'My Girl' and 'You Can't Hurry Love.' Your grandfather had a magnificent voice."

"He did?" Maia says. She has never heard anyone say one kind thing about Levi Small.

"He used to sing in the church choir," Sadie says. "He was a soloist. I remember that from when I was younger than you are now."

"Do you know what happened to him?" Maia asks.

Sadie shrugs. "He left when your mama was little. Two or three years old. Some people say he ran off with another woman;

some say your grandmother kicked him out and told him never to come back. Nobody knows for sure what happened and nobody knows where he went."

"So he might still be alive?" Maia says.

"Man I dated before Rupert told me he saw Levi Small playing the piano at a fancy restaurant in Miami, Florida. But don't get your hopes up, honey. The man I dated is *very* untrustworthy."

Still, it's exciting for Maia to think that she might have one relative on her mother's side left. She imagines being older, in college or in her twenties, walking into a fancy restaurant in Miami, and coming face to face with her grandfather.

Sadie bends down and gives Maia a hug goodbye. "I bet you didn't know your family had so many secrets, did you?"

Huck calls from the living room, "Sadie, you ready?"

Sadie disappears with a blown kiss and a wave, leaving Maia in the empty kitchen.

Secrets? Maia thinks. *My family? Never!*

MARGARET QUINN

In the four years since Margaret Quinn retired as the anchor of the *CBS Evening News,* she hasn't felt a single pang of regret or experienced one moment of FOMO. She has been quite content to get her news like everyone else—online. Gracing her inbox every morning are the *New York Times,* the *Wall Street Journal,* the Skimm, the BBC, the *Hollywood Reporter,* and Refinery 29. She follows *New York* magazine and *People* on Instagram. She still has *Time* and *Vogue* delivered to the house. She watches the six o'clock news on CBS, but not every night—because she's busy!

Her daughter, Ava, and Ava's husband, Potter, and their twins, Maggie and Homer, live in the city, but Ava keeps threatening to move to New Canaan (the lawns! the schools!), so Margaret wants to spend as much time as she can with them while they're still just across the park. Margaret and her husband, Dr. Drake Carroll, travel to Boston to see Margaret's son Patrick, his wife, Jennifer, and their three teenage boys, and then often they take the ferry over to Nantucket to visit Margaret's son Kevin, his wife, Isabelle, and their children, Genevieve, Kelley, and baby Arnaud.

Just this past year, Drake has cut back his surgery schedule at the hospital in anticipation of full-on retirement, so he and Margaret have been able to travel. They took a Viking River cruise down the Rhine and the Rhône; they trekked Milford Sound in New Zealand. It's been a long time since Margaret has been able to travel for pleasure. While she was working, the network sent her places like Kosovo, Tel Aviv, Fallujah, Medellín, Lagos, Haiti, and, once—a happy lark—to London to cover William and Kate's wedding.

Margaret sits on the boards of three charities—one hospital, one museum, one homeless shelter. She emcees each of these organization's major benefits; she plays in celebrity softball games; she has been approached by *Dancing with the Stars* (she said no); and she's been toying with teaching at the Columbia School of Journalism.

She's been asked to write her memoirs but she's nowhere near ready for that—too much living yet to do.

She'd like to write a book describing the magic of being a grandmother, but Leslie Stahl beat her to it.

* * *

When Margaret's phone rings on the third of September and she sees it's her former boss Lee Kramer, head of the studio, she thinks he's calling to make an elaborate excuse for why he and his wife, Ginny (editor in chief of *Vogue*), can't attend the hospital benefit three weeks hence. *That's fine,* Margaret thinks. There are so many worthy causes in this city and you can't go to everything, though Margaret plans to hit Lee up for fifty thousand at least.

"Don't say no."

This isn't the greeting Margaret was expecting. "Good morning, Lee. How are you?"

"Please just hear me out."

"How are Ginny and the kids? How does Evie like Cornell?"

"I'd like you to come back for one assignment."

"Thanks for calling," Margaret says. "Bye."

"You don't even know what it is."

"No, but I know how this works. I say yes to one assignment, then another assignment comes along, then *Sixty Minutes* offers me a ten-segment deal, then you offer me my own half-hour show aimed at baby boomers, and the next thing you know, my grandchildren are seeing me more on TV than they are in person."

"This is one assignment and it's your favorite kind of story..."

Margaret's favorite kind of story is military moms and dads who come back and surprise their children at school. Margaret cries every time. But she knows Lee wouldn't ask her back for that reason. "What is it, Lee?"

"The weather."

Ahhh, right. Margaret does love a good weather story.

"Hurricane Inga, down in the Caribbean, is shaping up to be an event. It's aimed at Antigua and Barbuda right now and will likely hit the Virgin Islands after that. St. Thomas, St. John, Tortola, Virgin Gorda. This is a hundred-year storm, Margaret."

"Like Katrina?"

"Like Katrina, yes."

Margaret experiences a surge of excitement so powerful, it's almost sexual. "What about Dougie? He already fancies himself the next Jim Cantore, and I don't want to steal his thunder…so to speak. Send Dougie."

"Dougie won't go," Lee says. "His wife is due to have their first baby *tomorrow.* So he's going to man the anchor desk on this coverage, and when I asked him who he thought I should send down in his place…"

"He said me?"

"He said you."

"Even though I retired four years ago."

"He said you."

Margaret inhales, exhales, looks at herself in the mirror. They're sending her into a war zone, essentially, so there won't be any hair or makeup, which means the entire country will become acutely aware that Margaret is rapidly closing in on sixty-five. It's flattering; hell, it's an *honor*—not only for Margaret but for every woman of a certain age—to be chosen to cover this. Just being asked makes Margaret realize she does miss it.

"When do I leave?" she asks.

"When can you be ready?"

Margaret calls Drake at the hospital from her car service to Teterboro. CBS is sparing no expense—she has her driver, Raoul, back, and she's flying down on the CBS jet because commercial flights have been canceled.

Drake isn't happy. "I thought this part of our lives was over."

"So did I," Margaret says. She realizes she sounds giddy.

"Please be safe, Margaret," Drake says. "I need you."

Four hours later, Margaret lands at the Cyril E. King Airport in St. Thomas. The weather is surprisingly clear and sunny, and the island pops with all the bright colors that one expects from the tropics—emerald green, turquoise, coral, and near-blinding white. Margaret didn't tell Lee or Drake this but she has been to the Virgin Islands before. She and her first husband, Kelley Quinn, came for a week's vacation back when Patrick was three years old and Kevin just a baby. They stayed at the Maho Bay campground in a "cabin" with a canvas roof. Kelley filled a dark rubber bladder with water from the pump and left it in the sun to warm up for a "sun shower." It had been rustic, funky, unbearably hot, even more unbearably buggy—Kevin's pale, chubby baby body had been an all-you-can-eat buffet for the mosquitoes—but Margaret had loved every minute of it. Even when they found a scorpion in Kelley's shoe. Even when they got lost on a hike to Ram Head in the scorching heat with Kevin strapped to Margaret's chest. They spent luxurious afternoons lying under a cluster of palm trees on Trunk Bay, where Kelley rented one mask and snorkel and the two of them took turns marveling at the manta rays and the schools of brilliant fish.

When Margaret's marriage to Kelley hit the skids, she'd suggested a getaway to revive the romance. She went so far as to book a week at Caneel Bay—but they never made it.

Margaret has always wanted to come back. Now, here she is.

* * *

The crew from the CBS affiliate picks Margaret up, and although they've reserved her a room at the Ritz-Carlton on St. Thomas, the storm is predicted to be so fierce that the Ritz is no longer deemed safe. Plan B is an emergency shelter in the basement of the CBS studio building. It has cinder-block walls, a buffet "catering spread" that includes Kind bars and packages of ramen noodles. They have a generator. There's a men's room and a ladies' room on the first floor but no shower. Margaret is shown a cot. She thinks longingly of the Ritz-Carlton. She thinks even more longingly of the king bed in her apartment on the Upper West Side overlooking Central Park, where the leaves are just hinting at fall.

"We should get our outdoor shots now," the producer, Rhonda, says. "We'll take footage on Sapphire Beach first—"

"And then we'll go over to St. John?" Margaret asks.

"Yes, we'll shoot from the dock in Cruz Bay," Rhonda says. "Then we'll come back here and hunker down."

Good afternoon, Dougie. I'm reporting from the Sapphire Beach Resort in St. Thomas, where, right now, the water looks pretty inviting. However, by this time tomorrow, the scene will be quite different...

Good evening, Dougie. I'm reporting from Cruz Bay on the island of St. John, where both locals and visitors are preparing for what will very likely be a direct hit from Hurricane Inga...

* * *

Rhonda hurries Margaret into the boat. The waves are much choppier on the way back to St. Thomas; the wind has picked up and there's a line of gray clouds on the horizon. Is that the hurricane? No, not yet, Rhonda says. Tomorrow afternoon. If the weather is clement tomorrow morning, they might do one more live report from St. Thomas.

"Let's get you a proper dinner," Rhonda says. "How do you feel about goat?"

Maybe she's kidding. Maybe she's trying to see how tough Margaret is. Well, Margaret drank cow's blood in Nigeria; she ate rattlesnake in China. She's tough.

"Love it!" Margaret says.

That night from her cot, Margaret tracks the storm. It's now 215 miles to the east and has sustained winds of 155 knots. This is going to be devastating. Maybe Margaret isn't so tough after all. She's sixty-four years old and the grandmother of eight. What is she *doing* here? Has she lost her mind?

Both Rhonda and the camerawoman, Linda, are sleeping in the studio basement with her. Margaret bids them good night, and from her little corner, she calls Drake, then she calls her kids in order of age. Patrick is spending the weekend taking his oldest, Barrett, up to look at Colgate, Hamilton, and Skidmore; he doesn't seem to know there's a hurricane coming and Margaret decides not to mention where she is. He's bringing Barrett to the city the following weekend to look at NYU and Columbia. Margaret says, "Can't wait to see you!" then hangs up, hoping she makes it home in one piece—hoping she makes it home, period. Kevin is consumed with the closing weekend of Quinn's Surfside Beach Shack. He sounds harried; Arnaud is teething and Genevieve is starting kindergarten. *I can't believe she's going to school already,* Kevin says. *It feels like she was just born.* Yes, Margaret knows the feeling only too well. Kevin was once that chubby baby who was such a delicacy for the island's mosquitoes. The years—where do they go?

Finally, Margaret calls Ava, who says, "I stopped by your apartment today, and Drake told me you're in the Virgin Islands covering that monster hurricane. What were you *thinking,* Mom?"

The next day dawns calm and still. Rhonda makes a big pot of coffee and produces a beautiful tropical-fruit platter and a bakery box filled with muffins and bagels.

"The café down the street saw you on TV last night," Rhonda says, "and insisted on sending these."

They head out to do one more live spot for Dougie back in New York. The wind is picking up. The outer wall of the hurricane will be arriving in a matter of hours.

"Stay safe," Dougie says. "We'll see you on the other side."

Margaret, Rhonda, and Linda go back down to the studio basement.

Margaret traces the storm on her laptop. It's coming. She hears the wind screaming like a woman in labor (it must be the situation with Dougie's wife that puts this image in her mind). Then the lights flicker, and the power goes out; the studio's generator comes on, but the lights in the basement are low and there's no longer any air-conditioning. Things outside the studio crash, smash, shatter. Margaret can't see what's making the noise because the windows are shuttered. *Dear Lord,* she thinks, *please don't let the windows break. Don't let the roof blow off. Don't let the place flood. Please don't let anyone die.* But as the minutes pass and then the hours, as the wind gets so loud that Margaret can't hear her own voice praying, as her cell signal cuts out, as she lies on her back unable to even read the book she brought, she marvels at how profound the weather is, how mighty, how inexplicable and unpredictable.

Life on these islands is changing right now, right this second, she thinks. Maybe forever.

ST. JOHN

After Inga left us—as definitively as someone leaving a room and slamming the door behind her—we picked up our heads and looked around.

Let's start with Cruz Bay, our "downtown." It was... *ruined.* Wharfside Village lost its roof; the Beach Bar's dance floor was buried under two-foot drifts of sand; the palm trees along Frank Bay were snapped in half, reminding us of gruesomely broken bones. Someone's boat, *Nell,* landed upside down on the deck of High Tide, where so many of us had enjoyed rum punches during happy hour. The Lumberyard building—home to the Barefoot Cowboy, Driftwood Dave's, the barbershop, and Jake's—looked like the proverbial cake that someone had left out in the rain; the building simply caved in on itself. Homes were violently torn apart, their contents thrown out into the yard, the street. Who could tell what had been a ceiling or a wall or a bathroom door? There was plaster, glass, metal in heaps and piles everywhere. It looked like a bomb had detonated; the damage was…atomic, nuclear.

Word started rolling in from the North Shore Road, Chocolate Hole, Gifft Hill. One family of six survived by hiding in their laundry room. One man crouched behind a table on its side for three hours as the sliding glass door across the room bowed in and out as though it were breathing. Multiple witnesses saw telephone poles flying through the air like missiles. Cars were flipped. A couch ended up in the neighbor's front yard; a refrigerator ended up in the bedroom; a hot-tub cover was caught in the high branches of a tree.

What about beyond the stone gates at Caneel Bay? This was, perhaps, what most took us by surprise. The genteel, elegant resort had been ravaged—roofs ripped off, trees uprooted, buildings flooded and filled with sand, the entire place simply annihilated.

The Centerline Road was impassable due to downed trees. The hillside between Maho and Leicester Bays looked like a winter landscape; all of the trees were stripped bare, broken, left a burned-looking brown.

Eventually, we heard from our friends on the "other side of the world," in Coral Bay. Shipwreck Landing, one of our favorite places to order coconut shrimp and listen to live music, had been decimated. Concordia, which had such delicious breakfasts, was blown away. Boats were dashed against the rocks, or they capsized and sank. The carnage in Hurricane Hole turned our stomachs.

Few of us realized that tornadoes are a common phenomenon when a hurricane hits land. The friction between open ocean and hills can cause spin, especially when the feeder bands roll through. The spot on St. John that saw the most tornado activity was the East End because it has elevation and because it's so exposed. There were thirteen tornadoes recorded on the East End alone. Unlike a hurricane, a tornado's path is unpredictable. One villa remains untouched while the villa next door is turned into kindling.

The compound belonging to Duncan Huntley was pulverized. When his closest neighbor saw the damage, he said, "It seemed like Inga had a personal vendetta against the place." A cast-iron planter that must have weighed seventy pounds had smashed through the roof of Dunk's garage and crushed Dunk's G-wagon. Every building lost its roof; the 140-inch screen from the home theater ended up in the swimming pool. Nothing was salvageable. The neighbor said that even if Dunk lost his shirt in Vegas, he was still a lucky man. "If he'd stayed in the villa," the neighbor said, "he'd surely be dead."

Imagine our relief when, the morning after the hurricane ended, the *Singing Dog* came sailing into the harbor. Captains Stephen and Kelly had successfully outrun the storm—and not only that, they had a working satellite radio that allowed many of us to contact our relatives back in the States to let them know we were still alive.

At first, that's all we could claim: We were upright and breathing.

The satellite radio also brought news that help was coming; the National Guard and the U.S. Navy were on their way.

There was no power, no water. Never mind rebuilding it; just cleaning it all up would require a Herculean effort.

Someone discovered that if you stood on the third-floor balcony of the Dolphin Market building downtown, you could get a very weak cell signal. Hey, it was better than nothing, and before we knew it, that balcony was as crowded as the bar at Skinny Legs after the Eight Tuff Miles race. A line started to form because someone wisely pointed out that the balcony would hold only so much weight and the last thing we wanted was for someone who'd survived the hurricane to plunge to his or her death trying to call Cousin Randy in Baltimore.

The balcony and the line to get to the balcony became the place where we connected not only with the outside world but also with each other. Nestor from Pine Peace Market let everyone know that he would open the store. The owners of the Longboard would cook a community dinner, everyone welcome. There would be stir-fry and Chinese noodles over at 420 to Center.

Someone declared that what he really wanted was Candi's barbecue—but, alas, Candi's didn't survive.

Those who had generators and gas offered assistance to those who didn't. Other items we needed included chain saws, bottled water, shovels, and insect repellent—because the heavy, still, hot weather that arrived in Inga's wake brought all the familiar bugs as well as larger, flashier, meaner bugs that looked like they'd escaped from some exotic tropical zoo. Because money had no immediate value, people bartered. Overall, there was a spirit of gratitude and compassion for our fellow islanders, even those we had previously disliked. The hurricane had happened to all of us—West Indian, white, Latinx, Catholic, Episcopalian, evangelical, Cruz Bay, Coral Bay.

Had anyone seen the wild donkeys? Where, oh where, did the donkeys take cover in the storm?

* * *

No sooner does the storm clear than someone sees Margaret Quinn herself in a pair of Hunter rain boots and a bright green anorak broadcasting from the Cruz Bay ferry dock. Margaret Quinn! Candice from the St. John Business Center and several others saw Margaret's broadcast from the night before Inga hit, but the rest of us, of course, were too busy preparing for the storm to casually watch TV. After Margaret Quinn finishes her spiel on the dock—what can she say but that St. John sustained monumental damage that will take a long time to recover from?—she insists on walking over to the Dolphin Market building so she can talk to real people. We see her producer and even the camerawoman trying to dissuade her but Margaret Quinn strides ahead. That's why we love her, after all; she's a strong, independent woman who will do what it takes to get to the beating heart of a story.

Margaret sees a couple about her age waiting at the end of the line. The woman—nice-looking with a neat chestnut braid—is handing out what appear to be cookies to the people ahead of her in line.

"Lemongrass sugar cookies," Margaret overhears her saying. "Homemade."

This will be her first interview, Margaret decides. A woman who brought homemade cookies to share while she stands in line to maybe get a cell phone signal is someone Margaret would like to meet. "Excuse me," Margaret says, touching the woman's elbow.

The couple turn and the woman's eyes widen. "Why!"

The man says, "Holy smokes. Margaret Quinn!"

The woman holds out the platter. "Would you like one? They're lemongrass sugar cookies. Homemade."

"I'd love one," Margaret says.

Their names are Captain Huck Powers and Irene Steele. Margaret had pegged them for a long-married couple but she's apparently mistaken. This must be one of these magic relationships—not unlike Margaret and Drake—where people of a certain age find love later in life.

Huck reveals that he's a charter fishing captain who has lived on St. John for over twenty years. His boat is called the *Mississippi.* Irene is from Iowa City; she moved to the island in February because she needed a life change.

Huck wraps his arm around Irene's shoulder and pulls her in close. "She sure changed *my* life."

Who are Huck and Irene waiting to call? Family back in Iowa?

"Most of my family is here," Irene says. "My son Baker and his girlfriend, Ayers, had a baby last night at home."

Margaret thinks she must have misunderstood. "They had a crying baby last night at home?"

"They *had* a baby last night," Irene says. "Ayers gave birth in the bedroom with a nurse practitioner who happens to be a friend of the family. So I have a brand-new granddaughter."

Margaret can't help herself. "Will she be named Inga?"

"Oh," Irene says. "I hope not."

"No," Huck says. "They haven't settled on a name yet, but rest assured, it will not be Inga."

Irene says, "And that's not all. My other son, Cash"—here, Irene pivots and casts a concerned glance behind them, at the water—"is over on Lovango Cay with his friend Tilda. Her family is building an eco-resort on Lovango, and, if I'm not mistaken, Cash and Tilda are the only two people on the entire island. I'm going to try to call Cash to make sure they made it through okay."

This is such a good local story that Margaret feels like she hit the jackpot on the first try. She asks Huck and Irene to repeat all of this—including the shtick about the name Inga—with the cameras rolling. She has Linda get a close-up of the cookies and then she asks Linda to pan across the water toward Lovango Cay.

When they finish filming, Irene says, "I'm not one to play the name game but I think you know my cousin."

Margaret smiles. She loves this woman, this couple; they're authentic and charming, and even if Margaret has no idea who Irene's cousin is, she might pretend she does. "Who's your cousin?"

"Mitzi Quinn," Irene says.

Ha! Margaret thinks. *Ha-ha-ha!* "Mitzi? Mitzi is your *cousin?*"

Irene nods shyly. Huck looks lost. "Who's Mitzi?"

"Mitzi was married to my ex-husband for many years," Margaret says. "Mitzi's son, Bart, is my children's half brother." She beams. "We're practically *related!*" She pulls out a business card and hands it to Irene. "Please, let's keep in touch. If you ever need anything..."

"Thank you," Irene says.

Margaret tilts her head. "Before I move on, I have to ask one more question. How did the two of you meet?"

Irene and Huck smile at each other and Margaret can see something pass between them that seems to indicate it's a story too complicated for a sound bite. *Of course,* Margaret thinks. *All the best stories are.*

"We could tell you," Huck says. "But you'd never believe it."

IRENE

Cash and Tilda are okay. The cell phone reception when she's talking to Cash goes in and out but the gist is that they're going to stay on Lovango for a few days to try to clean up before they take the skiff back over to St. John.

"It was scary," Cash admits. "The cottage shook so bad, we felt like dice in a cup. During the worst of it, I looped my belt through the handle of the front door and pulled, and Tilda sat behind me, bracing me. We knew if we lost the door, the roof would be next."

Irene gets a chill. *You should have stayed with us,* she almost says. The Happy Hibiscus didn't sustain any damage because it's made of stone, because it's sheltered from the water, because the yard has only bismarckia trees, no palms. The wind was loud, the windows rattled, they could hear the branches of the trees coming down, but that was the worst of it. The baby cried a little, which was a sound everyone loved, and Winnie whimpered, which was a sound nobody loved but everyone tolerated. "Isn't it lonely being the only two people on that whole island?" Irene asks.

"Actually," Cash says, "it's kind of romantic."

Well, Irene thinks, *looks like Tilda is back in the picture.* "We have a surprise for you when you get home," Irene says.

"A what?" Cash says.

"A surprise!" Irene says. There's no answer. "A surprise!" She turns to Huck. "I think I lost him."

Suddenly she hears Cash say, "Thanks, Mom. Hug Winnie for me."

When Huck and Irene leave town, Irene says, "Shall we go to your house?"

"Our house?" he says. He sighs. "Can't put it off forever, I guess."

They've avoided it until now because the most important thing was making sure everyone was safe, including Cash and Tilda. The fate of Huck's house and the boat is secondary.

Sort of.

If the house is destroyed, where will they live? If the boat is destroyed, *how* will they live?

Slowly, they begin the climb up Jacob's Ladder. Irene is surprised when her phone pings with a text.

It's from Lydia. We saw you on Channel 2 with Margaret Quinn! it says. Congrats on your new granddaughter! Brandon was so happy his cookies made it on TV!

There are branches down on the road up to Huck's house that Huck has to clear. One of their neighbors lost his entire roof; it's like someone pried the lid off a jar. Where is it? Somewhere down the hill? The destruction is everywhere and it is epic. There's a truck on its side with the doors ripped off. Entire homes have been reduced to rubble—insulation and beams and crumbling bricks. The Ladder looks far, far worse than Fish Bay.

When they're still fifty yards away, they can see the *Mississippi.*

Huck exhales. It's a little crooked on the trailer but otherwise fine. It must have been shielded by the house. Huck jumps out to look at the boat more closely while Irene heads up the front stairs.

They still have a roof, and the deck is intact, although the railings are all broken. She has to wait for Huck to retrieve his drill from the truck so he can take the shutter off the front door. Together, they step inside.

Something is wrong—the windows in the kitchen have blown out. There's glass everywhere and the living room looks like it's been ransacked; lamps have been knocked over, cushions from the sofa are all over the room, everything is wet. There's at least three inches of water in the kitchen, the chairs are all smashed; the sugar bowl, the toaster, Irene's food processor are all sitting broken in the shallow pond of their kitchen. There's a palm rat feasting on what looks to be an overturned plate of chicken and rice.

Irene gags. Huck comes up behind her. "I'll get him out in a second," he says. "Let's check the rest."

Huck and Irene head down the hall to the bedrooms, the bathrooms. They're hot, stuffy, unbearable—but fine. Except...

"Uh-oh," Huck says. He emerges from Maia's room with the portrait of Milly. The glass has one long crack down the front. "I think the actual photograph is okay, though."

Irene takes the frame from him. Yes, it looks like the picture is okay. What this picture has survived in the past year. "Why...the kitchen?" Irene says.

"I didn't shutter the windows," Huck says. "I was about to when you called and then I got on the phone with Rupert and I had to track down Sadie and then I thought I'd come back and do it later." He turns to Irene with tears in his eyes. "I got so caught up in the baby coming that I completely forgot about those three windows. I forgot until just this moment."

"It's nothing we can't clean up," Irene says. The rat has disappeared, though no doubt he's lurking around here somewhere. "I kind of wanted to remodel the kitchen anyway."

They remove the shutters from the slider and Huck checks to make sure the deck boards are secure before they step outside. All the railings are broken; one whole side has disappeared. Irene is sure Huck is craving a cigarette but he busies himself with stacking the broken pieces of the railing in a pile. The whole thing will have to be torn down and rebuilt.

Irene remembers when she used to wake up believing that Russ was still alive. One nightmare in particular returns to her now: Russ staggering down the beach, his shirt soaking wet, his pants ragged. He wanted to tell her something. *The storm is coming. It will be a bad storm. Destructive.*

When Huck turns around, his breathing is shallow. Irene takes his left hand, the one with only half a pinkie, and presses it between both of hers.

"Look at this place," he says, pointing down the hill at the wreckage, which extends all the way to the water. "St. John is destroyed."

"Damaged," Irene says. "Not destroyed." *Like me,* she thinks.

This island—and this man—have taught Irene some things about resilience, about patience, and, most of all, about hope. Bad things can happen, terrible things. You can lose the people you love the most; you can lose homes, cars, antiques, hand-knotted silk rugs that cost five figures; you can discover that the very life you're living is a terrific lie. And despite this, *despite all this,* the sun will continue to rise. Tomorrow morning, over the bruised and broken body of St. John USVI, the sun will rise again.

Irene Steele knows this better than anyone.

EPILOGUE

Millicent Maia Steele
September 6, 2019
6 pounds, 14 ounces, 21 inches

I can't believe you named her after me," Maia says.

"We did," Ayers says. "Because, you know what, Nut? I want Milly to grow up and be smart and strong and fun, just like you."

"And precocious?" Maia says.

Ayers laughs. "And precocious."

Maia leans over into the bassinet to look more closely at her niece. She's asleep, and her little bow of a mouth is making a sucking motion. Maia reaches out her pinkie, and baby Milly's impossibly tiny hand grasps it.

"Just watch me," Maia whispers. "I'll show you how it's done."

ACKNOWLEDGMENTS

I want to start by thanking my brother, Douglas Hilderbrand, who is a meteorologist with the National Weather Service and who provided all the weather details in the last section of this book based on his research of Hurricane Irma. He is also the inspiration for the character Dougie Clarence, the CBS weatherman who appears here and in my novel *Winter Storms.*

There is a real-life version of the Lovango Resort and Beach Club being built as I write this, and no one like Duncan Huntley has any part in it. The owners are my dear friends Mark and Gwenn Snider, who own the Nantucket Hotel and Resort and the Winnetu on Martha's Vineyard. I've held my bucket-list weekends at both of their properties and we all hope that at some point in the near future, we can host a St. John bucket-list weekend on Lovango!

I have taken ten trips to St. John. Eight of these were my usual five-week writing-retreat visits, one was at Christmas, and my most recent trip there, in March of 2020, coincided with the outbreak of COVID-19. I ended up staying on St. John for seven weeks and "sheltered in paradise." Over the course of these visits, I have made friends and acquaintances. I always say that the places we love are about people, and that is certainly true in the U.S. Virgin Islands.

Thank you to Julie, Matt, and Shane Lasota; Beth and Jim Heskett of St. John Guest Suites; Bridgett and Jimmy Key of Palm Tree Charters; Captains Stephen Sloan and Kelly Quinn (no relation to "our" Kelley Quinn!) of Singing Dog Sailing Charters; Brian and Michelle Zehring of New Moon; Alex Ewald of La Tapa; Ryan Costanzo of Extra Virgin Bistro and 1864; Allison Gould of Sam and Jack's; Hank and Karen Slodden; Sarah Swan; John Dickson from the Papaya Café and Bookstore; Dana Neil of Cruz Bay Watersports; Richard Baranowski of Lime Inn/Lime Out (who saved my son Maxx's life, but that's a story for another day); Karen Coffelt, head of school Liz Morrison, and all of the amazing teachers and staff at the Antilles School; Jorie Roberts; Meredith DeBusk from St. John Provisions; Sarah Bigelow, Peter Bettinger, Mattie Atkinson, Rhonda McCay, and Linda Beer (I told you I'd get you in!); and Heather Hearn Samelson of Pizza Pi VI. If I have forgotten any of you, it's because I'm old, not because I don't love and appreciate you.

A huge and special thank-you to Judy Clain, my new editor at Little, Brown, who took me in as an orphan and made me feel like her favorite child. She is brilliant, and this book owes her an enormous debt.

To my kids, Maxwell, Dawson, and Shelby: Everything, always, is for you.

For me, St. John is, above and beyond all else, about Timothy Field. The man has been setting up my towels, pouring my cocktails, and keeping the water from washing me (and my notebooks) away for years. I love you in Love City, HB. XOX

ABOUT THE AUTHOR

Elin Hilderbrand is the mother of three 3-sport athletes, an aspiring fashionista, a dedicated jogger, a world traveler, an enthusiastic foodie, and a grateful seven-year breast cancer survivor. She spends part of every winter writing on St. John. *Troubles in Paradise* is her twenty-sixth novel.

Keep reading for an excerpt from Hilderbrand's newest novel, *Golden Girl.*

MARTHA

She receives a message from the front office: a new soul is about to join them, and this soul has been assigned to Martha.

Martha puts on her reading glasses and finds her clipboard. The soul is arriving from...Nantucket Island.

Martha is both surprised and delighted. Surprised because Nantucket Harbor is where Martha met her own fateful end two summers ago and she'd thought the front office was intentionally keeping her away from coastal areas so she didn't become (as Gen Z said) "triggered."

And Martha is delighted because...well, who doesn't love Nantucket?

Martha swoops down from the northeast so that her first glimpse of the island is the lighthouse that stands sentry at the end of the slender golden arm of Great Point. Martha spies seals frolicking just off the coast (and sharks stalking them a little farther out). She continues over Polpis Harbor, where the twelve-year-old class of Nantucket Community Sailing are taking their lessons in Optimists. One boat keels *way* over and comes dangerously close to capsizing. Martha blows a little puff of air—and the boat rights itself.

Martha dips over the moors, dotted with ponds and crisscrossed with sandy roads. She sees deer hiding deep in the woods. A

Jeep is stuck in the soft sand by Jewel Pond; next to the Jeep, a young man lets a stream of swears fly (*My oh my,* Martha thinks) while his girlfriend tries to get a cell signal. She's sorry, she says, she just really wanted the early-morning light for her Instagram photos.

Martha chooses the scenic coastal route along the uninterrupted stretch of the south shore. Despite the early hour, there are plenty of people out and about. A woman-of-a-certain-age throws a tennis ball into the rolling waves for a chocolate-Lab-of-a-certain-age. (Martha misses dogs! She's far too busy to ever make it over to the Pet Division.) A white-haired gentleman charges into the water for his morning swim. There are a handful of fishermen out on Smith's Point, a cadre of young (and *very* attractive) surfers at Cisco, and a foursome teeing off—*thwack!*—from the first hole at the Miacomet Golf Course.

As Martha floats over Nobadeer Beach, she sees the town lifeguards gathering in the parking lot. Their conditioning session starts at a quarter past seven and it's nearly that time now. Martha has to hurry.

She has one more minute to appreciate the island on this clear, blue morning of Saturday, June 19—the sun glints off the gold cupola atop the Unitarian church; a line chef at Black-Eyed Susan's runs full speed down India Street, late for his shift. Across most of the island, irrigation systems switch on, sprinkling lawns and flower boxes, but not out in Sconset, where residents like to do things the old-fashioned way: they put on gardening clogs and grab watering cans. People are pouring their first cups of coffee, reading the front page of the *Nantucket Standard.* The thirty-five women who will be getting married today open their eyes and experience varying degrees of anticipation and anxiety. Contractors pull into Marine Home Center because they have punch lists that need to be completed *yesterday;* the summer people are arriving, they want their homes up and running. Charter fishing boats motor out of the harbor; the first batch of sugar doughnuts is pulled from the oven at the Downyflake—and oh, the scent!

Martha sighs. Nantucket isn't heaven, but it is heaven on Earth.

However, she isn't here to sightsee. She's here to collect a soul. The pinned location on Martha's map is Kingsley Road, almost at the intersection of Madaket but not quite.

Martha arrives with a full thirty seconds to spare, giving her a chance to inhale the heady fragrance of the lilacs that are in full bloom below. There's a dark-haired woman with fantastic legs jogging down the road, singing along to her music, but the rest of Kingsley is quite sleepy.

Fifteen seconds, ten seconds, five seconds. Martha double-checks her coordinates; it says she's in the right place…

In the time that Martha takes her gaze off the road, tragedy strikes. It happens quickly, the literal blink of an eye. Martha winces. *What a pity!*

All right, Martha thinks. *Time to get to work.*

VIVI

It's a beautiful June day, the kind that Vivi writes about. In fact, all thirteen of Vivian Howe's novels—beach reads set on Nantucket—start in June. Vivi has never considered changing this habit because June on Nantucket is when things *begin.* The summer is a newborn; it's still innocent, pristine, a blank page.

At a few minutes past seven, Vivi is ready for her run. She takes the same route she's taken ever since she moved into Money Pit ten years ago, after her divorce: down her dirt road, Kingsley, to the Madaket Road bike path. The path goes all the way to the beach, though Vivi hasn't made it that far in years. Her hips. Also, she doesn't have time.

Vivi is agitated despite the sunshine, the bluebird sky, and the luscious bloom of the peonies in her cutting garden. The night before, Vivi's daughter Willa called to say that she's pregnant again. This marks Willa's fourth pregnancy since last June, which was when she and Rip got married.

"Oh, Willie!" Vivi said. "Yay, hurray—good, good news! How far along are you?"

"Six weeks," Willa said.

Still very, very early, Vivi thinks. Willa basically *just* missed her period. "You took a test?"

"Yes, Mother."

"More than one?"

"Two," Willa said. "The first was inconclusive. The second had two lines."

What Vivi did *not* say was *Don't get your hopes up.* Willa had miscarried three times. The first pregnancy had progressed to fifteen weeks. Willa started bleeding while she was giving a tour of the Hadwen House to a group of VIPs from the governor's office. She ran out on the tour and drove herself to the hospital. It was a horrible day, the most physically painful and difficult of the three miscarriages, though after the third, Willa became convinced there was a problem.

A thorough examination at the Brigham and Women's fertility clinic in Boston, however, showed nothing wrong. Willa was a healthy twenty-four-year-old. She had no problem getting pregnant. If Rip even looked at her, she conceived.

Privately, Vivi suspected the miscarriages had something to do with Willa's type A personality, which Vivi and her ex-husband, JP, used to call her "type A-plus personality," because regular As were never good enough for Willa.

"If this doesn't work out, why don't you and Rip take a break?

You're so young. You have years and years, decades even, to conceive. What's the *rush?*"

Predictably, Willa had become defensive. "What makes you think this won't work out? Do you think I'm a failure?"

"You succeed at everything you do," Vivi said. "I just think your body might benefit from a reset—"

"I'm *pregnant,* Mama," Willa said. "I will give birth to a perfectly healthy baby." She sounded like she was trying to convince herself.

"You *will* give birth to a perfectly healthy baby, Willie. I can't wait to hold her." Though Vivi didn't feel quite old enough to be a grandmother. She was only fifty-one and in terrific shape, if she did say so herself. Her dark hair, which she wore in a pixie cut, didn't have one strand of gray (Vivi checked every morning). She might occasionally be mistaken for the child's mother. (Well, she could hope.)

The conversation had ended there but an unsettled feeling had lingered in Vivi through the night. Are children ever punished for the mistakes of their parents, she wondered, or was that just her novelist's mind at work?

Vivi had woken up at five thirty, not only because it was June and sunlight streamed in through the windows like it was high noon, but also because she heard a noise. When she crept out into the hallway, she saw her daughter Carson stumbling up the stairs, smelling distinctly of marijuana.

Vivi had last seen Carson the afternoon before, dressed for work in cutoff jeans and her marigold-yellow Oystercatcher T-shirt, her dark hair still a little damp, neat in two French braids. Carson was the most attractive of Vivi's three children, though of course Vivi wasn't supposed to think that. Carson alone favored JP—the dark hair, the clear, glass-green eyes, the fine pointed nose, and teeth that came in white, straight, and even. She was a Quinboro through and through, whereas both Willa and Leo favored the

Howes. They'd inherited Vivi's overbite and crowded lowers and spent years in braces.

Carson was still in her cutoffs, but she had downgraded her T-shirt to something that looked like a silver-mesh handkerchief that only just covered her breasts and left her midriff and back bare except for one slender chain. She had no shoes on; her hair was out of its braids but held kinky waves. When she saw her mother standing at the top of the stairs, her eyebrows shot up.

"Madre," she said. "What's good?"

"Are you just getting home?" Vivi asked, though the answer was obvious. Carson was walking in at five thirty in the morning when her shift had ended at eleven. She was twenty-one, fine, so she'd had a drink at work and she probably went to the Chicken Box to catch the band's last set, then she either went to the beach with friends or hooked up with a random stranger.

"Yes, ma'am." Carson sounded sober, but that only served to make Vivi angrier.

"The summer isn't going to be like this, Carson," Vivi said.

"I hope you're right," Carson said. "Work was slow, my tips were trash, the guys at the Box all looked like they were on the junior-high fencing team."

"You can't stay out all night then come home reeking of marijuana—"

"Reeking of marijuana," Carson mimicked.

Vivi searched for extra patience, which was like trying to find a lost shoe in the depths of her maternal closet. *This is Carson.* Ten years earlier, when Vivi learned that her husband, JP, had fallen in love with his employee Amy, Vivi had moved out. All three kids took it hard, but especially Carson. Carson had been almost eleven years old and unusually attached to Vivi. Vivian's novel that year, *Along the South Shore,* had been something of a breakout book, and Vivi, wanting to escape the inevitable divorce fallout—people asking what happened, people asking was she okay, people telling her she was brave—had gone on a twenty-nine-stop book tour that kept her away for seven weeks (she'd missed the first day of school and Carson's birthday). By the time Vivi got back, Carson had changed from the funny little spitfire of the family to a "troubled child" who threw tantrums, swore, picked fights with her siblings, and generally did everything in her power to get attention. Vivi blamed the transformation on JP's affair (which their therapist had insisted they not disclose to the children), and JP blamed it on what he called Vivi's "abandonment."

Ten years had passed. Carson was no longer a little girl but she still had her challenging moments.

"This is my house," Vivi said. "I pay the mortgage, the taxes, the insurance, the electric bill, the heating bill, the cable bill. I do the shopping and make the meals. While you're sleeping under this roof, I don't want you out all night drinking, smoking, and having sex with complete strangers. Do you know how that *looks?*" Vivi stopped just short of reminding Carson that she'd already had chlamydia once, the previous summer. "You're setting a rotten example for your brother."

"He doesn't need me to set an example," Carson said. "He has Willa. I'm the screwup. It's my job to be a hideous disappointment."

"No one said you were a hideous disappointment, sweetheart."

"I'm twenty-one," Carson said. "I can drink legally. I can smoke pot legally."

"Since you're so grown up," Vivi said, "you can move out on your own."

"That's the plan," Carson said. "I'm saving."

You're not *saving,* Vivi wanted to say. Carson made good tips at the Oystercatcher but she spent them—on drinks, on weed, on clothes from Erica Wilson, Milly and Grace, the Lovely. Carson had finally dropped out of UVM after struggling through five semesters—her cumulative GPA was a 1.6—and although Vivi was initially aghast (an education makes you good company for yourself!), she knew college wasn't for everyone.

"I'm not giving you a curfew," Vivi said. "But this behavior won't be tolerated."

"This behavior won't be tolerated," Carson mimicked. It was the response of a seven-year-old, and yet it brought the reaction Carson wanted. Vivi took a step toward her, arm tensed. "Are you going to spank me?" Carson asked.

"Of course not," Vivi said, though she kind of wanted to. "But you have to clean up your act, babe, or I'll ask you to leave."

"Fine," Carson said. "I'll go to Dad's."

"I'm sure Amy would take *very kindly* to you coming home like this."

"She's not as bad as you think," Carson said. "When you demonize her, you show how insecure you are."

Vivi stared at her child, but before she could come up with a response, she smelled something. "Did you . . . cook?" Vivi asked.

Carson stepped into the bedroom and slammed the door behind her.

Vivi flew down the stairs to the kitchen, which was filling with black smoke. The leftover sausage and basil pasta from last night's dinner was in Vivi's brand-new All-Clad three-quart sauté pan on a lit burner. The inside of the pan was charred black. Vivi turned the burner off, grabbed a towel, carried the smoldering pan outside, and set it on the flagstone path. It was so hot, it would have scorched the deck or the lawn.

Brand-new pan, ruined.

The sausage and basil pasta in a luscious mustard cream sauce, which Vivi had been thinking of taking over to Willa's as a peace offering, ruined.

And what if Vivi hadn't gotten out of bed? What if the kitchen had caught fire; what if flames had engulfed Money Pit while Vivi—and Leo—were sleeping? They would all be dead!

Back in the kitchen, Vivi caught sight of her bottle of Casa Dragones tequila on the side counter next to a shot glass. She felt a formidable strain of fury brewing inside her. That tequila was *hers;* she wouldn't even let her (almost-ex-) boyfriend, Dennis, make margaritas with it. Carson had come home, put the pasta on a burner, done two—or three?—shots of *Vivi's* tequila, which Carson knew was *not for public consumption,* and then left the pasta to burn on the stove.

Vivi marched back up the stairs and pounded on Carson's locked door.

"You left the pan on an open flame!" Vivi said. Leo would definitely be awake now, which Vivi felt bad about because it was Saturday morning, but oh, well. "What is *wrong* with you, Carson? Do you honestly not think about *anyone* but yourself? Do you not think, period?" There was no response. Vivi kicked the door.

"Please go away" came the response from inside. "I'm trying to sleep."

"And you drank my tequila!" Vivi said. "Which you know is off-limits."

"I didn't drink the tequila," Carson said. "I haven't had a drink since I left the Chicken Box and that was hours ago."

Vivi blinked. Carson sounded like she was telling the truth and she had seemed sober. "Who drank it, then?"

There was a pause before Carson said, "Well, who else lives here?"

Leo? Vivi thought. She looked at Leo's bedroom door, which was shut tight. Leo had been going to high-school parties since he was a sophomore, but a run-in with Jägermeister had propelled him away from the hard stuff. He drank Bud Light and the occasional White Claw.

Vivi turned back to Carson's door. "You are scrubbing that pot, young lady," she said. "Or buying me a new one."

* * *

After Vivi poured herself some coffee, opened all the windows, turned both sailcloth ceiling fans to high, washed the shot glass, and hid what remained of the Casa Dragones in the laundry room (her kids would never find it there), she calmed down a bit. She was the mother of three *very young adults* and parenting very young adults required just as much patience as parenting very young children. No one ever talked about this; it felt like a dirty little secret. Vivi had always imagined that by the time her kids were twenty-four, twenty-one, and eighteen, they'd all be drinking wine together around the outdoor table by the pool, and the kids would be cooking, clearing, and giving Vivi sage investment advice. Ha.

Vivi ties up her running shoes and stretches her hamstrings, using the bumper of her Jeep—then she clicks on her iTunes on her phone and takes off.